W9-CTB-119

BOOK TWO
of The
CRIMSON
HEIRLOOMS

THE PAINTED CROSS

HUNTER DENNIS

 A-R-B

 BOOKS

thousand oaks, ca

Europe, 1788
DENMARK
GREAT BRITAIN
NORTH SEA
CELTIC SEA
ENGLISH CHANNEL
United Netherlands
P.
G.B.
S.S.
Sax
A.
SMALLER STATES
Bavaria
FRANCE
Switzerland
Sardinia
Parma
Modena
Genoa
Lucca
N
0
100
Scale in Miles
BAY OF BISCAY
SPAIN
Portugal
BALEARIC SEA
France
Papal States
Sardinia
ALBORAN SEA
OTTOMANS
Morocco

BAY OF BOTHNIA
SWEDEN
RUSSIA
BALTIC SEA
RUSSIA
POLAND-LITHUANIA
AUSTRIA
OTTOMAN EMPIRE
BLACK SEA
ADRIATIC SEA
V.
Naples
IONIAN SEA
AEGEAN SEA
MEDITERRANEAN SEA

Books by
Hunter Dennis

THE CRIMSON HEIRLOOMS

Book One:
The Crimson Heirlooms

Book Two:
The Painted Cross

THE PAINTED CROSS

BOOK TWO
OF
THE CRIMSON HEIRLOOMS

BY
HUNTER DENNIS

thousand oaks, ca

Cover by Damonza.com

We invite you to join our mailing list at:
www.arb-books.com

Author photograph by Erick Bech

Complete illustration and photography credits are located at the end of the book. For additional information or disputes, contact publisher@arb-books.com.

ISBNs: 978-0-9994936-4-9 paperback,
978-0-9994936-5-6 hardcover, 978-0-9994936-3-2 e-book

Library of Congress Control Number: 2019902133

Dédié à Sandra Dennis et Sean Domachowski,
mes deux merveilleux rédacteurs.

Maps, Illustrations, and Photographs

Europe, 1788
ii, iii

Atlantic Naval Distances
Xvi

Nantes, 1788
4

Château de Vizille
14

Haiti, 1832
26

Le parc au sommet du mount Glonne, regardant au sud, 1788
34

Engraving of Nantes and the Loire
46

Paris, 1788
58, 59

Palais Royal Theater, 1788
60

Plan of Colonial Le Cap
80

Foyer
90

Playbill
96

Comédie-Française
110

Paris Environs, 1788
116

Château des ducs de Bretagne
126

Layout of the Grand-Danseurs/Ambigue-Comique
132

Ballroom
138

Currency during the time of Louis XVI
156

Stock Characters of the Commedia dell'Arte
162

Boston, 1788
180

Jardins de la cour du Palais-Royal, 1788
186

Le Véve du Loa Voodoo
198

Une cour du Palais-Royal, 1788
208

L'abbaye de Saint-Florent-le-Vieil, au sommet du mont Glonne, 1789
228

Revered French Saints in the Time of Louis XVI
236

Europe, 1832
242

Parlor
252

Plan of Colonial Port-au-Prince
270

Brittany
284

France, 1788 (Cities)
292

Oath of the Horatii (Le Serment des Horaces), Jacque-Louis David, 1784
300

1422 AD
310

The Empire of Charlemagne, Furthest Extent, circa 814 AD
318

Boston Environs
330

Nantes (Ramparts and Skyline)
338

Cordeliers, Paris
346

Wellesley Environs
354

Laveuses et un pêcheur de Paris
362

Palais des Tuileries, le dix-septième siècle
368

The Americas, 1832
378

April 28th, 1789
388

Cathédrale de Nantes
400

Elm Bank, Massachusetts
408

Flags of the Royal Provinces
414

Saint-Florent-le-Vieil (Countryside)
422

Lake Waban, Massachusetts, in Winter
432

Une rue de Paris
438

Les États Généraux, 1789
458

Table of Contents

Primary Characters .... *xiii*

Prologue *1*

One --- Estelle and Xavier --- July, 1788 .... *5*

Two --- Beau-Brave --- July, 1788 .... *15*

Three --- Jake --- Fall, 1832 .... *27*

Four --- Jonathan --- July, 1788 .... *35*

Five --- Estelle and Xavier --- July, 1788 .... *47*

Six --- Beau-Brave --- July, 1788 .... *61*

Seven --- Jake --- 1832 .... *81*

Eight --- Jeannine --- July, 1788 .... *91*

Nine --- Beau-Brave --- August, 1788 .... *97*

Ten --- Estelle and Xavier --- August, 1788 .... *111*

Eleven --- Beau-Brave --- September, 1788 .... *117*

Twelve --- Estelle and Xavier --- September, 1788 .... *127*

Thirteen --- Beau-Brave --- September, 1788 .... *133*

Fourteen --- Estelle and Xavier --- September, 1788 .... *139*

Fifteen --- A Letter to Guillaume --- November, 1788 .... *157*

Sixteen --- "Introduction to Lavoisier" *163*

Seventeen --- Xavier --- November, 1788 .... *181*

Eighteen --- Beau-Brave --- November, 1788 .... *187*

Nineteen --- Jake --- 1832 .... *199*

Twenty --- Talma --- December, 1788 .... *209*

Twenty-One --- Jonathan --- January, 1789 .... *229*

Twenty-Two --- Estelle, Xavier, and Jeannine --- February, 1789 ... 237
Twenty-Three --- Jake --- 1832 243
Twenty-Four --- Estelle, Jeannine, and Xavier --- February, 1789 . 253
Twenty-Five --- Jake --- 1832 271
Twenty-Six --- Estelle --- March, 1789 285
Twenty-Seven --- Féroce --- March, 1789 293
Twenty-Eight --- Beau-Brave --- March, 1789 301
Twenty-Nine --- Estelle --- March, 1789 311
Thirty --- Xavier --- March, 1789 319
Thirty-One --- Jake --- 1832 331
Thirty-Two --- Estelle --- March, 1789 339
Thirty-Three --- A Letter from Guillaume --- April, 1789 347
Thirty-Four --- Jake --- 1832 355
Thirty-Five --- Réveillon --- April 25th, 1789 363
Thirty-Six --- Beau-Brave – April 27th, 1789 369
Thirty-Seven --- Jake --- 1833 379
Thirty-Eight --- Beau-Brave --- April 28th, 1789 389
Thirty-Nine --- Estelle --- May, 1789 401
Forty --- Jake --- 1833 409
Forty-One --- Beau-Brave --- May, 1789 415
Forty-Two --- Jonathan --- May, 1789 423
Forty-Three --- Jake --- 1833 433
Forty-Four --- Four Letters --- 1789 439
Appendix --- Pronunciation and Definition Guide 459

Please supplement your read with the pronunciation and definition guide located on page 453.

Primary Characters

The Time of the Heirlooms

1788-1789

Xavier Traversier – the richest man in Nantes, a bourgeois Freemason.

Estelle Guerrier – a pious, young lady of mixed heritage from Saint-Domingue.

Philippine Traversier – Xavier's mother, Madame Traversier, imperious, and occasionally possessed of premonitions.

Jeannine Cœurfroid – the beautiful daughter of the wealthy Cœurfroids of Centre-Ville, Nantes.

Maurice Cœurfroid – Jeannine's father, a Freemason, and friend of Xavier.

Caroline Cœurfroid – Madame Cœurfroid, Jeannine's cold, unforgiving mother.

Jacque-Louis David – a Parisian painter possessed of a terrible speech impediment.

Beau-Brave – in actuality Guillaume Guerrier, the handsome twin brother of Estelle.

Father Jonathan Courgeon – the young, educated priest of the abbey of Saint-Florent-le-Vieil.

L'Oublié – the mysterious and terrifying henchman of Xavier Traversier.

Talma – an up-and-coming actor of the Comédie-Française.

The Time of The Detectives

1832-1833

Jacob Esau Loring – Jake to his friends, an American student in Paris who has been legally blackmailed to search for the Crimson Heirlooms.

Monsieur Tyran – a mysterious, wealthy, middle-aged man who manipulated the legal system of France to entrap Jake.

North America
CANADA
UNITED STATES
Boston
Boston to Cap-Haïtien 1564 miles
CUBA
Cap-Haïtien
HAITI
Caribbean Sea
VENEZUELA
South America
Atlantic Ocean
Nantes, France to Cap-Haïtien, Haiti 4324 miles
GREAT BRITAIN
London
Europe
Paris
Nantes
FRANCE
Nantes, France to Cape Verde 2434 miles
Africa
Cape Verde to Accra, Ghana 1760 miles

Prologue

Crimson Heirloom was a legal term coined in 1832 by the highest court of France, the *Cour d'Assises Spéciale*.

There were precisely two.

The first was a priceless crucifix. Named the *Cross of Nantes*, the necklace had a storied history closely tied to the fortunes of its creator - the Traversier family of Nantes. It was stolen in 1754, miraculously reappearing twenty years later, then was lost again in 1805… although *hidden* would be more accurate.

Soon after, a rumor abounded that if the Cross were found, a provision of will entitled the possessor to unconditional ownership of the Traversier Mercantile Trust. After journalists discovered this fantastic tale was actually true, a legend was born. The Cross of Nantes became part of the national folklore of France. It was a mysterious lost treasure, a pendant fit for a king – whose owner would be worthy of it, being christened merchant royalty upon bestowal of the trust.

Those who had actually seen the Cross wrote and spoke of it as if nothing - no story, no price, no fortune - could ever compete with the beauty of the thing itself. It was made of Olmec jadeite and diamonds of the rarest crimson hue. When light touched the necklace, Antares bowed its head to truer stars of scarlet.

Not a year went by without false headlines proclaiming the rediscovery of the Cross, or a group being formed to search for it based on some new clue or evidence. The mystery proved to be so intriguing that these stories never grew old; new rumors always made the front page of the newspapers.

As decades passed, the Cross entered the realm of myth - in spite of its existence, and the promise of the Traversier Trust, being very real.

The second Crimson Heirloom was less tangible, if not utterly mysterious - or even the product of madness. It was legally defined - by no less than the highest court of France - as, "*the words of the devil's song, as he danced across the blood-drenched hills of the Vendée Militaire*." This definition was not ironic or metaphorical – it was literal, and serious as a sword thrust.

It was the court's ruling that a specific individual, upon pain of death, search for the Crimson Heirlooms for a period of no less than five years or until their discovery. It seemed absurd that such a quest could be legally binding in the modern age, but stranger things have happened.

Such facts might be remembered only as trivia to amuse at dinner, except for one thing: The Cross of Nantes, and the words of the devil's song, were both found.

Ironically, but not at all coincidentally, the detective who searched for the Heirlooms found that he himself was part of their riddle. Even stranger, the motivations behind the men and women who created the mysteries of the Heirlooms could not be fully understood without comprehending that of the detective, who searched for them decades later.

Indeed, the search itself was part of the intrigue – from the very beginning.

Nantes, 1788
N
Saint-Clément
FAUBOURG SAINT-CLÉMENT
ERDRE
Université
de Bretagne
FAUBOURG DU
MARCHYS
FAUBOURG DE
RICHEBOURG
Saint-Pierre-et-
Saint-Paul
CENTRE-VILLE
Place de
Bretagne
Hôtel
Couerfroid
Château des ducs
de Bretagne
PRAIRIE DE LA
MADELAINE
LOIRE
Port au Vin
Manoir de
Jean V
Théâtre Graslin
FEYDEAU
0
600
1200
feet

Chapter One

The Time of the Heirlooms

July, 1788

Estelle and Xavier

She was a lit cannonball, coming to rest at the feet of the surviving members of the Traversier family. As when a bomb exploded, forever changing the nature of everything in its wake, so too would she change everyone inside the Château Meilleur, the ancestral hall of the ancient clan.

The recumbent girl under the sheets in the downstairs bedroom wore nothing but her shifts – and, of course, the priceless necklace. She had awakened only briefly. Madame was fetched and Xavier appeared soon after. The mystery girl was told that she had been struck by the lead right gelding of Xavier's coach, and taken here to be ministered by Doctor de Trémargat. Obviously distressed, she was gently admonished by the doctor to remain calm.

She would have none of it. "Please, you don't understand," she said, "I am not who you think I am."

Madame made to speak, but was interrupted.

"The clothing I wore, every tailor's stitch and bolt of cloth, was paid for by my employer. I am not noble-born, nor elite, or even from a family wealthy enough to afford a ribbon."

Madame spoke softly, "Yet you are welcome here none-the-less."

"My name is Mademoiselle Estelle Guerrier," said the girl, "I am a paid companion for Mademoiselle Jeannine Cœurfroid, of the Cœurfroids of Centre-Ville, Nantes. I am originally from Saint-Domingue. I am legally white. I am a poor but devoted servant of God. Please do not mistake me for someone who deserves to be in such splendor."

Young Estelle was pale as new milk, freckled, gap-toothed, busty, and possessed of thick, curly chestnut hair. She looked more British than black.

Madame spoke, her voice quivering, "Mademoiselle, are you not from Saint-Florent-le-Vieil?"

Xavier raised an eyebrow. His mother had one of her premonition spells regarding that town several years ago.

"No," replied Estelle.

Madame's shoulders deflated from relief.

"I only lived in Saint-Florent-le-Vieil for short years. But my memories are quite fond."

Madame's eyes widened, her breath quickened – but she spoke calmly. "Rest. You are welcome here. The Cœurfroid family we know well. We will send them word that you have been hurt in a coach accident but are recovering. I will hear no more protestations from you, young Estelle. You will accept our full hospitality with humility and grace, and I will hear no more of it. Do you understand?"

"*Oui*, Madame."

"Rest now. We will speak when you are further in your recovery."

"*Oui*, Madame. Thank you." And with that, Estelle fell back to her pillow, dead asleep from the exhaustion of her simple efforts.

That was yesterday.

The morning saw Xavier and Madame with their *café*, croissants, and unspoken thoughts. Sounds became magnified. Sipping from cups resonated like reverse waterfalls, the servants' heels sharply echoed, the clip-clop of horseshoes on stone.

It was a terrible accident, this collision. It was made even more unwholesome that the poor girl was in the employ of the Cœurfroids, with Monsieur being the best friend and business associate of Xavier for many years. Xavier had even met Jeannine once, although it seemed like a million years ago in a far-away place, when in actuality it was in Centre-Ville Nantes in 1776.

All of that was meaningless compared to the horrific augur presaged by other aligning stars.

It was the necklace around Estelle's neck, the famed necklace, the Cross of Nantes, that reflected doom from its polished cuts. If Madame had screamed with the perturbation that she actually felt, and it were possible, fifteen other painted Cross of Nantes would hear her wail, for its image graced canvasses across the Château Meilleur. One Traversier had paid for its creation long ago, and another had seen it lost, and those present never expected to see it again by accident or fate, much less in their own ancestral home. Whether this omen was a fair doom or a fell one, neither knew but both pondered, laying the silence thick on the room, like pitch and oil by deck brush.

Madame's face was expressionless and gave no hint to the nature of her churning cogitations.

Xavier had offered a mirthless joke, "It is good our young lady was not brought to a better furnished bedroom. She would have burst into flame upon waking." His heart was not in the jest. He cared nothing for class or opulence, and Estelle's words were humble and well-meant. It was a lame attempt to push his mother's thoughts off the road, for he knew they were of him, however tangentially.

Xavier decided to try to derail her thoughts once more. "The troops have finally arrived to quell the unrest caused by the May edicts. I'm sure order will be restored in the countryside forthwith. It is the petty nobility and loyal peasantry, the traditionalists. Dauphiné is still coming apart at the seams. Other places."

She said nothing.

He cleared his throat and continued, quieter so the servants would not hear, "In Grenoble, a lawyer named Barnave has come to the fore as the leader of what could only be called an uprising. He is part of no lodge, yet he is as radical as a Master Mason. It is astounding to me. Ideas that were once secret, spoken only behind closed doors, are not only announced, but acted upon."

Silence.

More silence.

"Don Quixote," she said blankly.

Xavier stared at her, but she said nothing more.

"What of it?" he replied evenly.

"It was a message, hidden in a fictional story."

The comment was apropos of nothing, but it did no good to doubt the logic of her universe; she would simply argue until he engaged with her inside of it. "Cervantes laughed chivalry and the knight errant out of existence. The book was a clarion call for the forced birth of the modern age."

She nodded, still deep in thought. "The words have two meanings. The first being the facts of the story, descriptions and speech and so on, the second a deeper meaning conveyed without words, perhaps seen *through* the words - in a language only understood through intuition or semiotics."

"Words on the page, with truer words somehow being spoken behind them." *Is she having an episode?*

"So too are our lives, I think. Yet we do not search actions or thoughts for the hidden meaning, through intuition or symbols."

"We do. It is called superstition. Literature is ennobled superstition. The modern Delphics deign to use ink and not entrails."

A bit cynical, Xavier, he thought.

"You lied to me," Madame said, her expression unchanged.

"Of which lie do you speak?" Xavier asked, although he knew.

"You swore that if the angels came down from heaven and spoke to you whilst on your trip to Saint-Florent-le Vieil, you would listen."

"However, they did not."

"Are you to say that you did not see that woman, or the Cross of Nantes?"

Xavier did not reply for a moment, for he did see her - and the Cross – and was loathe to admit it. "I saw her. I saw a red spark emanate from her neck in the driving rain. I thought it could not be, given the weather and lack of light."

"What else did you think it could have been after my words to you, Monsieur?"

Xavier resettled himself in his chair. "I thought it was the Cross of Nantes. I dismissed the thought as whimsy."

Xavier did not expect a polite reply from his mother – but her tone did not change. "Xavier, how would your life have been different had you spoken to her, and somehow she imparted a different purpose within you, one of a better destiny, devoid of the forced concerns of the world?"

The top of Xavier's head tensed. His cheeks were helmet straps, taut and pulled tight. He remembered a younger version of himself; sobbing, blowing spittle and mucus, screaming, swearing, beating a man chained to a beam with a wooden ax haft, breaking him into pieces. The nightmares. Every night, sweating, waking in the darkness. His will had forced him to an action his weaker conscience could not countenance.

Or perhaps his conscience was ultimately stronger than his will.

He sipped his coffee. He did not reply.

His mother saved him from his memories, "Both the doctor and the servants have noticed she is very religious, which fits her status as companion, especially for Jeannine Cœurfroid, who is said to be good-hearted but incorrigible."

"I see."

"Do you?"

Xavier did not answer, confident her intent would be exposed sooner if he remained silent.

She continued. "God has turned his mighty head and pierced us with the brightness of his stare. "

"You do not believe in God, and neither do I."

"We cannot say such a thing now, my son," she whispered, "For He has sent us a sign."

"We have certainly observed a remarkable coincidence, but there is nothing supernatural regarding any of it. It is only remarkable serendipity."

"You are the man of this house. I defer to you in all things."

Xavier snorted.

"But I am the woman of this house and in some small matters I have my say. I am the mistress of the interior space, Monsieur. That is the way it has been and will always be. The woman has her cage, and the man the world. But in my cage, I am queen. I am Hera of my hearth and home."

There was only one thing to say - if he did not want to fight a very bitter war, ending only when his forces were utterly spent, surrendered, then ground underfoot. "I am at your disposal, Madame."

She leaned back, deep in thought. "The Cross is possessed of something supernatural. Whether it is blessed by God, commanded by a spirit, or imbued with magic to become sentient, I do not know. I only know that its nature has changed, and the eyes of God are upon it. In any case, the Cross no longer belongs solely to Traversier. It has married into another family, the Guerriers of Saint-Domingue. Our fortunes are now tied together, for good or for ill."

"And what does this mean, Madame?"

"It means the Cross stays on her neck. Were someone to take it, we would bring our resources to bear for its recapture – but only to return it to her. If the Cross is restored to our family, it must be by honorable means, in accordance with God's will, whether you believe in Him or not."

"According to your will, it will be done, Madame."

"Thank you, Monsieur, for your indulgence." Madame sipped her coffee and looked away.

The rest of the meal was spent in silence.

***

Estelle's eyes opened.

She had only vague recollections of time already passed in this room. Her head did not hurt so terribly as it once did. A servant, a pleasant-looking, thick-boned girl, stood from her chair and crossed to her. She sat on Estelle's bed with a smile and stroked her hair. "How are you, Mademoiselle?"

Estelle sensed that this girl had ministered to her while she was unconscious. "I am feeling much better. What is your name?"

"Mercier, Mademoiselle. Paige Mercier."

"Please call me Estelle, Paige."

She giggled and tweaked her nose, "Only when no one is about."

There was then heard a knock. Paige bounded to the door and opened it a crack. She shared words with someone, then closed the door and turned, "A Monsieur David to see you, Estelle."

A stranger.

"Allow him in, by all means," she said as she adjusted her sheets.

The door was opened and a curious man entered. He was middle-aged, thin, and not particularly tall. One of his cheeks was larger than the other for some inexplicable reason, but otherwise he had good features, which moved with intense shifts of force, giving him an intelligent and perceptive mien.

The man bowed. Estelle tried her best to nod, as she held her covers to her neck.

He looked her over, but as a father would. "M'gutnissshile."

Estelle was momentarily taken aback, then understood. *My goodness, child* is what he meant to say. She smiled at him. Whoever this man was, he had no ill intentions toward her - as far as she could tell.

"Awholways wannid ta paininhr becasata lite. Butide never totid havrs 'ject beiku."

It took all her concentration to decipher it - *I always wanted to paint in here because of the light. But I never thought I'd have a subject like you.*

Dear goodness! The poor man!

"You are a painter, Monsieur?" she asked with a smile.

"Yesh."

"And what do you paint?"

She did not regret asking, but it took a while for her to understand. As far as Estelle could tell, the man's name was Jacque-Louis David, to be called David, and he was a Parisian painter. He was known for one particular style, for which he had attracted renown, but, truthfully, was attracted to all manner of different forms, and always wanted to try different techniques. His work was heavily critiqued, so he had to be careful what he showed to the public. Being in Nantes and amongst friends, he wished to paint something totally different, knowing it would not be seen by the public for years, if at all, even though he would have to finish the canvas in Paris. He admired the light of this particular room, and always had, and would be able to experiment with its effects, akin to Vermeer's passion for interesting luminosity. He prized Estelle for a quality of emanating character and wished to infuse her sleeping form with emotion and personality, akin to the evocative portraits of his contemporary, the talented Élisabeth Vigée Le Brun.

In his excitement, he sat down unceremoniously on the bed, perhaps inappropriate to *honnêteté*, the high manners, and showed her his drawings. Estelle realized he had sketched her as she laid unconscious - even as she noticed that his pictures were magnificent, even in their hurried simplicity. Some of them were simply color stains, to perhaps jog his memory of the tricks played by light at certain times as it came through the windows.

Under any other circumstance, Estelle would have been horrified, taken aback to have been drawn without permission as she slept in such a disheveled condition. She did not consider herself to be worthy of being the object of a drawing, and to be so smacked to her of vanity.

But, surprisingly, David made her look appealing to her own sensibility. He had recreated her in a truthful manner. There was no quality present in the rendered Estelle that she did not have in reality. He did not lie through his art, rather he saw her as God did, as the best version of herself. She felt as if a gentleman had paid her a compliment, in a perfect and subtle manner, that she could gracefully accept. She was, in fact, deeply touched.

"Thhlongnshorofitis, I would paint thu, ifulfme. Idackh pay you, izzidumymn models."

Please, no more! thought Estelle, although she willed the smile to stay on her face.

The meaning came slowly. *The long and the short of it is, I would paint you, if you'll have me. I would, of course, pay you, as I do my other models.*

"I would be honored, Monsieur David. But I will not take a sous from you. The kindness of our hosts is more than enough. I am actually grateful for the opportunity to repay them."

"Erryell," David smiled and stood, "Arrandistime tomorrow, arl require a-"

With a bang, the door swung wide open.

Jeannine burst in, braced by flustered servants of the Meilleur. "I have been worried sick, *mon chéri*." She kissed Estelle on both cheeks, her forehead, and then embraced her. "There is no one here but servants and they are ever so protective of you. Please tell them I am your dearest friend and we should never be separated."

Estelle rolled her eyes. Of course, the servants had been told to admit her, she was expected at some point. That meant that Jeannine did not tell them her name, and simply wanted to be admitted on sight, although they had never seen her.

Jeannine continued, "I have the very best and very worst of news. Papa is moving the date of the ball so that we can both attend together. But it will most likely be at the end of Summer. I cannot abide it."

Estelle was surprised to see David look uncomfortable. Without exaggeration, Jeannine was by far the most beautiful woman Estelle had ever seen. And yet David stood, the smile gone from his face, looking as if he wished to leave the room as quickly as possible.

"Monsieur David, this-," Estelle began, but before the thought was finished Jeannine had jumped from the bed and turned to him.

"Monsieur David, I am Jeannine Cœurfroid."

"Hrm, yes. Amitchur fadder sebral daibago."

"I must tell you how much I absolutely adore your work. I have seen prints of all of your paintings, Monsieur. *The Death of Socrates*, *The Oath of the Horatii*! You are a wonder! I would only say this, why do the Horatii women weep when the men are strong? Cannot women be strong as well?"

"Thedonot cry ferwikniss buther love. Theluvey havfer mener fam lethgo to fight."

What?

Jeannine, however, understood – or replied as if she did, "*Mon dieu*! I had forgotten the story! Of course!"

Jeannine's eyes were wide and expressive, dipping slightly closed to punctuate her ideas. Her lips were curling, smiling, a delight to watch in and of themselves. To Estelle, Jeannine was some kind of human machine. As when the lever is pulled in a mill to grind flour, so did Jeannine change her mannerisms – and create force like a grinding millstone.

David was her antithesis - expressionless. After several more rounds, he attempted to excuse himself from his zealous admirer. He did not succeed. He tried again and was finally able to extricate himself and he quickly left the room.

Estelle, ignored and invisible, suddenly became the center of the universe once more. "My poor girl! I came as soon as I could!"

It occurred to Estelle that she had been at the Meilleur for at least two days, and to Jeannine this was apparently soon - and just as quickly she silently admonished herself for having such a dark thought.

"I have brought your things," Jeannine continued, "for the doctor has said Madame Traversier does not deign to part with you until you are fully healed." Jeannine suddenly threw herself on Estelle and sobbed like a little girl. She calmed, then reached up and touched Estelle's necklace. "I love your cross."

"I know," Estelle said dryly.

"I desire nothing from you, Estelle. Except your company and your lovely jewelry. Why won't you give me both?" pouted Jeannine like a child.

"It belonged to my mother, it is my memory of her."

"Yes," half-cried Jeannine, "But I like such things, very much – and you don't. Should not pretty things belong to those who truly value them?"

Estelle laughed. "You are being silly."

An odd look came into Jeannine's eyes - odd because it was genuine – and she teared and looked concerned. "I am so heartened that you have survived this ordeal. I was worried. I am ever so fond of you, Estelle. I don't know what I would do without you."

Estelle ran her fingers over her hair. "Oh Jeannine, my queer sister. So winsome, and yet so strange."

Château de Vizille

Chapter Two

July, 1788

Beau-Brave

Claude Perier was a symbol of the new France.

Claude's father was a successful linen merchant in Grenoble. Smart, diligent and well-liked, he married the daughter of an even wealthier merchant.

Fleshy, broad-featured, capable Claude had his father's ambition… and the great fortune of starting life several rungs up the economic ladder. He began in manufacturing, created his own bank, and – by the age of thirty-six - was appointed secretary and advisor to the King in the Chamber of Accounts of Dauphiné. He eventually moved into textiles, specifically the printed cotton fabrics called *indiennes*. He bought the well-known castle Château de Vizille - for a little over one million livre - and stuffed it with workers and equipment to the very brim. Soon after, his father died, leaving him four-hundred-thousand livres. Claude promptly invested his inheritance in sugar cane and was well-rewarded for his foresight. Thereafter Claude traveled extensively throughout Europe, especially Great Britain, opening his eyes to the benefits of a free society - especially when it came to banking and finance, the two institutions that fired entrepreneurship and built national wealth. He was also involved in local politics – that of Grenoble and Dauphiné - and educated himself in the national dialog of Versailles, the rest of Europe, and Philadelphia, the temporary capital of the new United States.

Claude could not have been more of a model beneficiary of his society, yet he yearned for more progress and change, in his mind believing that objective common sense could provide a problem-free path to a brighter future. Mankind did not require spirituality or superstition, no indeed. Man was math, an intriguing equation with a utopian answer. It was bourgeois rationality that had brought Claude success - and it would bring success to France as well, once political change was achieved. It was these beliefs that made Claude Perier a symbol of the new France - perhaps even more so than his self-made success.

His home, the million-livre Château de Vizille, had a storied history that had just now - this very day - reached its apex.

It was an amazing place; eight stories of beige, ornamented, Mannerist stone, with clouds of graceful arcs, and curves of grey slate roofs. It was shaped as two sides of a square but looked winsomely irregular with its well-planned towers and spires. Inside the angle of the building were grand balustraded staircases leading up to the second story entry. Attached to the main building and stretching to the northeast in a perfect rectangle were the carriage garages and servants' quarters. Atop its roof was a landscaped garden, outdoor ballroom, or anything else quickly arranged when the weather was agreeable. This entrancing wonder was the epitome of fair and pleasing. To be special, it certainly did not need to be in Vizille - one of the most beautiful places on earth – but it was indeed, surrounded by green mountains, grey cliffs and waterfalls.

Claude and his château had found themselves at the epicenter of change. Grenoble, a little over ten miles away, had exploded as violently and assuredly as a magazine hit by lightning. Brienne's Edicts of May had caused widespread chaos across the country - but nothing like Grenoble.

Theories abounded.

Long ago, Dauphiné had been a separate nation. Perhaps some kind of vestigial, hibernating patriotism awakened to resist the distant King's efforts to put the local nobles in check. In any case, to keep the city from descending into permanent chaos, the Estates-General of Dauphiné had been allowed to convene.

To prevent trouble, it could not be held in Grenoble.

Claude stepped in.

The Estates-General would be held in Vizille, at his gorgeous, storied château. He would host, feed, and attend to over five-hundred of his fellow Dauphinois, composed of the Three Estates – those who prayed, those who defended with arms, and those who tilled the land – as they debated and legislated their demands for reform.

The concept of the Estates-General was symbolic, powerful... and hopelessly antiquated – Diderot's encyclopedia had defined it as an obsolete institution over thirty years ago.

The First Estate was composed of those who prayed – the church. The clergy was led, however, by the Second Estate - sons of nobles who, with few exceptions, did not pray at all. Those amongst the clergy who did pray and performed actual ecclesiastical work were mostly from peasant or town stock, who resented their bishops and cardinals ... who were Enlightened theists as often as deist Catholics.

The Second Estate was composed of the nobility, a class created to fight and defend France. Now, however, only the poorest or most traditional actually fulfilled this responsibility. Many now had legal or political employment, lived off the fruits of other's labor or, more recently, were active in trade and commerce, occupations that were not represented by the estates at all.

The Third Estate was supposedly composed of peasants, those who tilled the land. Somehow the bourgeoisie, the town dwellers, were excluded from definition and had no estate at all. Ironically, the peasants were barely represented at the Estates-General: rather, the delegates would be lawyers, tradesman, politicians, financiers, jurors, merchants, and manufacturers – bourgeois townspeople. The Third Estate was then the greatest lie of all, unless the definition of the Third Estate was now to include anyone who did not belong to the First or Second.

Importantly, in the minds of all, that redefinition had already taken place.

It was a false and devious redefinition. The Third Estate was now composed of many different types of people at cross-purposes. Claude, in his castle, was labeled the same, supposedly thought the same, as one of his workers, or one of the desperately poor farmers trying to work the mountain land outside his grounds.

No matter. In one sense, the most important sense, all were the same: The delegates of all three estates were nearly united in their radical and progressive politics.

Now it was almost over. Claude had outdone himself. The regional Dauphiné Estates-General had been a roaring success. The best lawyers were still working by candlelight, arguing over individual words and turns of phrase. Others who had contributed were asleep, exhausted, or drunk.

Which brought Claude to Beau-Brave, who was one of the more interesting and influential characters of the bunch, an elected member of the Third Estate who had come to prominence during the fighting in Grenoble.

The fading, silver twilight was quickly losing the battle against the orange flames of tall torchière braziers burning brightly across the grounds. Seen in the competing light, Beau-Brave sat on a chair south of the gardens. His red velvet bergère was tipped up, and his feet rested on the stone balustrade. He looked completely lost in thought, so much so that Claude wondered if he should be bothered at all.

Many things were said of Beau-Brave, but, in his presence, it was hard to see past his physicality. He was tall, handsome, long of limb - built of softly curving muscle and not much else. His hair was a mass of black waves, his olive-skinned face godlike, his green eyes shocking and bright. He was whip-smart, fearless, and usually found pensive, bored or angry. He was also dangerous – he could stir a crowd into a rioting mob before a rider could switch his pace to a gallop. It was said he had the soul of an artist, the temper of a Gascon baronet, and the patience of a bourgeoise princess.

It was interesting how the times had created a hero of this man.

In recent times, there had also been a rise of egotism - the practice of talking and thinking about oneself excessively, a widespread and undue sense of self-importance. Such ego desires worship, and sentimental personality cults developed around celebrities. Beau-Brave was a hero, suicidally courageous, an egotist, and beautiful. He was therefore worshiped in Grenoble like a living god.

Claude enjoyed his company, even though Beau-Brave did not give him any of the deferential courtesy or obeisance usually given to a generous host and man of stature – not to mention a fatherly elder. Rather, Beau-Brave was friendly, rambunctious, and informal.

"Good evening, Claude."

"Good evening. It has suddenly occurred to me that I do not know your true name."

"Do you wish to know it?"

"Certainly."

"Guerrier. Guillaume Guerrier. Are they quite done now?"

"Not yet. Do you wish to join them?"

"No."

"You do not love the variance of language," Claude offered.

"I do, most assuredly. I adore language. I hate *them*. I hate what they do to language. I hate the bickering over commas and the elimination of legal loopholes or, even worse, their purposeful formation. It bores me senseless when it does not anger me."

"What were the broad strokes?"

"A demand for the convoking of the national Estates-General, the refusal to pay any tax not voted by the aforementioned assembly, and a call for the abolition of arbitrary imprisonment on the King's order by *lettre de cachet*."

Claude narrowed his eyes, "The third seems apropos of nothing."

"It's brilliant actually. We are telling the King what to do - and taking away his ability to punish us for it."

Claud nodded. "It is cooler out here."

"It is. I am glad that you are here."

Claude did not know what that meant. "Thank you."

"I have a favor to ask of you."

Claude smiled, amused at his arrogance, "How may I help you?"

"I am walking to Paris."

"A grueling three or four-week journey, perhaps. With hills, if not mountains."

"I think I can do it in fifteen days."

Claude could have sent him to Paris on a carpet of lilies. He sensed that Guillaume had no concept of his wealth and what it could do. He thought it was best to play things safe and appear to be one of the comrades. "Do you not have the money for a coach? Perhaps we can all pass the hat."

Beau-Brave replied, "All I wish is to fill a blanket with salted meats and bread from the buffet. I'll soak the bread in fat and coat it in salt to keep it. After these pigs have been at the trough you might not even notice it gone."

Claude shrugged. "My home is your home. Fill your blanket."

"Thank you." After a moment, Beau-Brave spoke again, "I think you and this house might live forever."

"At least the indoor tennis court." That was where the Estates-General met.

"You created a special moment." Beau-Brave said wistfully.

"And you were part of it as well. Perhaps you will live forever too, along with my tennis court," said Claude as he leaned back against the balustrade, facing the man.

Beau-Brave shook his head. "This is not my cavalry charge, Monsieur. The Estates-General of Dauphiné belongs to Jean-Joseph Mounier and Antoine Barnave, as different from each other as vanilla and basil. Those men will become legends."

"Not your charge?"

"No. My destiny lies elsewhere."

"But you have distinguished yourself, Monsieur. I would say the same if you were only elected here, but you have done so much more."

"I did not even put myself on the ballot and I was elected here."

"Are you serious?"

"Quite."

Claude guffawed.

Beau-Brave continued, "I was so bored, in the beginning. I soon had no thought whatsoever for the proceedings or what we were doing, I simply wanted to be recognized, out of boredom or ego I do not know."

"Then what did you do? Shoot a hole in my ceiling?"

"Perhaps metaphorically. I simply… started to look for chinks in armor."

"What armor, which chinks?"

"If someone said, 'We should make sure there is enough bread,' I would point at him and say, 'Do you not care if we have enough meat and wine? Listen to this man! Listen to this *petit roi!* Should we hang him from the rafters?' And of course, such a man who inquires of bread surely wishes for meat and wine and vainly protests his innocence - yet is embarrassed and ashamed in spite of himself by the nature of my charge. He is shouted down, and promptly hung from the rafters, and then I give a rousing speech, and am applauded. And in the end, I have simply wasted everyone's time and created a chandelier that produces no light. But my goal has been achieved, my needs met, for all I wished for was acclaim, and perhaps to take authorship of some action or change, however ridiculous or counterproductive."

What an astounding statement, thought Claude. In Beau-Brave's words were found blatant ego, selfishness, destructiveness… and self-awareness.

What a damnably strange man!

Claude decided on a light tone. "No one was hung, *mon ami*. Not even discredited. Phenomenal work was accomplished. Friction is to be expected. This meeting was no more contentious than any other."

"Had it not been for Barnave, who took me to one side at lunch and admonished me, I would have shut down the entire proceedings."

"He is a bit oleaginous, that one. I am surprised he had the fortitude."

Beau-Brave shrugged. "We are friends. I respect his opinion. And he was right. If I really believe in progress and change, I cannot be motivated by boredom and the need for acclaim."

And now loyalty and self-restraint!

"So…?"

"So, I kept my mouth shut and attempted to stay awake. And realized that I have no interest in politics whatsoever."

"It is a shame. You could have had a bright future."

"I do not care. I do not like to be bored."

"So, you are walking to Paris with salt pork and bread."

"Yes."

"To what end?"

"To be a playwright."

"You are going to write plays?"

Beau-Brave shrugged.

Claude felt pity for the man. Beau-Brave was lost in cloud-cuckoo-land, as they say in Strasbourg. But Claude engaged in the conversation as best he could. "I would have thought you more suited to be *on* stage."

"I fear that if I was on stage and speaking another's words, I would eventually become resentful and angry."

"I see."

Beau-Brave suddenly looked off. "I feel as if I am on the edge of a great revelation regarding art. Specifically, the relationship that art possesses with our new beliefs."

"The Religion of Sensibility some call it." Claude had to give him credit; when Beau-Brave spoke, he was thoroughly magnetic. The man could convince a Puritan to bow before the Pope.

"Yes, the Religion of Sensibility. There is something preying on the back of my mind. I know where I belong. I know what I have to do. And someday soon, perhaps occurring to me on my walk, I will fully realize this idea that plagues me. I will give it order."

"Perhaps I can help. What specifically brought you to the genesis of this idea?"

"A painting? The Horatii. No. Most assuredly, a play. The Marriage of Figaro."

"Mozart?"

"No! Mozart? *Salope!* He plays his little pretty notes for Kings. *En enfer* with Mozart. A genius of the conventional - an oxymoron. *Bougre de vérolée!*" He calmed. "No, Monsieur. I speak of Beaumarchais."

Claude was a physically-imposing, confident man and felt no need to challenge Beau-Brave for his tone. Instead, he nodded sagely and the tension was past.

Beaumarchais wrote comedies that were frequently turned into operas. *Figaro* was one, *The Barber of Seville* was another, which was the first part of the *Figaro* trilogy. The last of the three was *The Guilty Mother*, which was not as popular. *Figaro* was hugely successful. It was said people were crushed to death trying to get into the theater on opening night. The play ridiculed and criticized the aristocracy... and had an unsurprisingly tumultuous relationship with the censors.

It was rumored that the Queen rather enjoyed it.

Claude took his shot at the target, "Perhaps you see art as a way of enabling political change by instigating reflection, a more subtle and invasive way of convincing hearts and minds."

"I would say yes, but no. Yours is a first thought, a surface thought. What I am seeking is fathoms beneath the surface. An entirely new definition of art. A new purpose, subsuming a present foundational cultural institution."

"It sounds as if you know your answer."

"No! I do not, Monsieur. I assure you. I am only describing vectors. I do not know the true coordinates of my point."

"You are hunting a revelation."

"Precisely! A revelation."

Claude felt pity. Beau-Brave's aspirations had nothing to do with family, love, community, success, or ease of life. Rather, he was motivated by some passion of artistic essence, desire for acclaim, the fear of boredom. How can someone be happy driven by such things? It wouldn't matter how handsome, charismatic and smart this man happened to be. He was doomed, his own worst enemy. Claude inwardly lamented that Beau-Brave had a deep misunderstanding of how to achieve happiness and fulfillment.

How does the earth produce such a confused person?

Claude smiled, "Well, I wish you luck."

"Thank you."

There was something completely unrelated that Claude wished to discuss – a rumor regarding Beau-Brave. Ordinarily, it would have to remain a mystery, but Claude thought, considering his company, a significant breach of manners would be overlooked. "I burn to ask you a question, of a personal nature. It would not be appropriate in any other circumstance than the two of us alone with drinks in hand."

Beau-Brave laughed. "Then, by all means, ask."

"It is said you... *fertilized...* the entire city of Grenoble."

The laughter stopped. "Yes, I suppose I did."

"Every man has an idle fantasy, but how did such a thing manifest in reality?"

Beau-Brave had no jocularity regarding the subject. "My first was confusing – emotionally confusing - but I didn't have any time to think upon it, for they came hard and fast on her heels. We are told that promises and commitments should pass between men and women before such things happen. I was uncomfortable, unsure of my footing or status, then I stopped thinking or feeling at all. It was then a parade of faces."

"A parade of a great many different things, I should imagine."

"Well, yes, I suppose." Beau-Brave chuckled, then sobered. "Some of them were married. A good many, actually.... most. I began to realize they all wanted something from me apart from pleasure. Whatever they happened to see in me, I began to sense other, poorer intentions from many of them. I became cynical. If it weren't for my saintly sister, I would have lost all respect for women entirely. I saw a side of the sex that no one discusses openly, but is very real indeed. There is a fouler side to women, Monsieur, talking strictly between us."

Claude had no such experience. Everyone in his family, everyone he knew and dealt with, appeared to be honorable, respectable and law-abiding. He had, of course, heard of such behavior. He replied, for the sake of being agreeable. "Yes, every man comes to that revelation, sooner or later, forced by whatever varied experience, prurient or benign. It is not a good revelation to discover. It is a hard truth."

"To be honest, Claude, it is good to be here and away from all of it. So far, I am free of the Italian diseases, but one's luck cannot hold forever."

"So... off to Paris."

"Indeed."

"No party, no send-off?"

"No. There is no need. I will never see anyone here again."

Claude tipped his head to one side. "The world is becoming smaller. Who knows?"

Beau-Brave shrugged.

"Are you going to have enough shoes for the journey?"

"For long journeys I never wear shoes. It is a waste of leather and wood."

"Would you waste your feet rather than your shoes?"

"Yes. The leather on my feet grows back. I need my shoes for Paris."

There was a moment of uncomfortable silence.

"Good luck then," said Claude as he bowed.

Beau-Brave stood and bowed in return. "Thank you. Thank you for everything you have done here and the use of your beautiful home."

"*De rien.* You are welcome here." Claude then walked away.

Halfway to the manor door, he turned and looked back. He saw Beau-Brave in silhouette with the light of the lamps flickering over him in the darkness: seemingly a human torch, a firebrand - a sword enveloped in flame. He hoped the fellow Men of Sensibility whom Beau-Brave encountered in Paris knew a way to keep the human torch safely in the scabbard – or hearth - for such a man would surely burn a house to the ground.

Was it the abuses of centralized power that had created such a man? If so, why had they not appeared before? A better case could be made that these men were a product of the Enlightenment, for such figures as Beau-Brave had not been seen before, and now they were not uncommon. Also, the radical firebrand had found himself part of a regional Estates-General - a political institution that had real power and impact, however flawed and antiquated.

Claude had a dark thought.

Are the flames of these human conflagrations extinguished when the objectives of the cause are achieved? And, if they are not, what do they then burn?

Beau-Brave's thoughts were elsewhere.

He was not contemplating art, as he told Claude, although the subject was near and dear to him. Curiously, he contemplated the inner quality of fearlessness.

Most thought he was fearless and even dangerous, but Beau-Brave had seen the real thing, and knew he was but a pale imitation of something far more formidable. Beau-Brave's father, Féroce, was truly fearless - and deadly.

Féroce had given himself over to *l'instinct de survie.* To his credit, he was also a contradiction, being an honorable man, even a lawful one who never deserted a compatriot. He was a bounty-hunter, a soldier, a policeman. It was a sad truth, but such honored men can sometimes be cast-iron *bâtards*, and Féroce certainly was one.

The key phrase was *given over.*

Féroce had surrendered himself to this course. He was keen for a fight every second of the day. The world was a series of challenges, threats - and little more. There had been moments of tenderness with his wife, who was now passed, and camaraderie with men, and that was all the softness and humanity his heart desired. Féroce embraced the way he was, and never questioned his own actions. He was a horrific father. He was cruel to his wife but never beat her. In contrast, he beat Beau-Brave like a drum.

Fearless Beau-Brave was terrified of the world, however hard that was to understand. He believed any energetic emotion from a man would lead to serious violence, any from a woman to unending cruelty. Usually the world did not deliver on these phantom threats. When it did, Beau-Brave was ready, even *relieved.* Other men walked through their day without fear and trembled at threats. Beau-Brave walked about terrified, and calmed in the face of actual danger.

Beau-Brave's normal state was anxiety. He did odd things to relieve it. Violent action seemed to help, so did drunkenness - sometimes. Women did, at one point. Now they did not. Now writing helped.

It was easy to be Féroce. Beau-Brave had seen the example play out throughout his life, effortlessly overcoming all obstacles… except for farming. Farming, it seemed, required more than ballistic self-confidence and violent action.

In form, art was more like farming than fighting.

Or was it?

Beau-Brave did not want to be his father. He did not want to be the one who was feared and respected from a distance. He desired love and intimacy, impossible for a true survivor. He wanted to create art and beauty, and partake of both. Did any warrior but Marcus Aurelius and the Samurai of Nippon do such things?

Beau-Brave had spent time with good, civilized people as a youth. He had enjoyed comforts and diversions that would have disgusted his father.

They were certainly unlike yet, ironically, Beau-Brave found himself totally unable to face the world without imitating him.

He did not even use his name anymore, which was telling.

The person named Guillaume was a frightened child. He was, however, able to be happy and be himself - and feel emotion. Guillaume was a hothouse flower, only capable of blooming when loved and nurtured. His parents had certainly not done such things, but others had. Those others were gone or far away now. Forever gone, either way.

All that was left was a cold, hard world.

Hence Beau-Brave, the shadow of Féroce; a pretender, possessed of fearlessness born of terror. The attribute was not difficult to achieve for Beau-Brave, rather it was an *addiction*, a problem, a serious threat to his true self, and how he wished to be. It could erase his happiness. If he let it, it could erase *him.*

But how did he stop? How could he face the world without it?

An even more chilling thought occurred to Beau-Brave.

What if my father and I were once the same?

Perhaps, in the face of savagery, Féroce, little by little, took bits and pieces of his humanity and placed them into an iron-bound trunk. The trunk was stored away in some inner bulkhead compartment, safe from the world - never to be seen again. Before the boy became a man, there was more human in the trunk than walking in the world. Perhaps Beau-Brave would do the same thing - and he too would be lost forever.

That is what Beau-Brave contemplated, sitting in his chair in the light of the torchières.

Haïti, 1832
N
miles
0
20
40
elevation in feet
10,500
6,500
4,500
2,150
1,300
550
350
0
Ile de Tortue
Jean-Rabel
Port-de-Paix
Cap-Haïtien
Monte Cristi
Puerto Plata
Massif du Nord-Oest
Pilate
Milot
Cibao Valley
Cordillera Septentrional
Santiago de los Caballeros
Moca
Gonaives
Saint-Michel-de-L'Atalaye
Massif du Nord
Nagua
Las Terrenas
Sierra Samana
Samana
La Vega
Saint-Marc
Montagnes Noires
La Española
Cordillera Central
Chaine des Matheux
Las Matas de Farfan
Constanza
Cordillera Oriental
Ile de la Gonave
San Juan de la Maguana
Abricots
Jeremie
Port-au-Prince
Sierra de Nieba
El Seibo
Punto Cana
Anse-a-Veau
Miragoane
Carrefour
Petion-Ville
Sierra de Yamasa
Massif de la Hotte
Neyba
Sierra Martin Garcia
Azua
Massif de la Selle
Sierra de Bahoruco
Bahoruco Oriental
Santo Domingo
San Pedro de Macoris
La Romana
Les Anglais
Saint-Louis-du-Sud
Jacmel
Bani
Les Cayes
Barajona
Pedemales
Isla Saona

Chapter Three

Forty-Four Years Later

The Time of the Detectives

Fall, 1832

Jake

The heat and humidity felt like slaps from palm fronds wrapped in a steaming, wet cloth. One could only imagine what it was like in August.

Haïti now loomed in the distance.

It had been a long journey, one spent mostly in reflection and study.

Jake had trailed sailors and officers alike. He learned a great deal about their craft and was especially interested in navigation and rope making, which was a wonder to him. Fibers of nearly any length could be twisted together and made into strong twine. Twine strung together made rope.

Not that there wasn't anything to do in his cabin. Amongst the books Jake was given was a treatise in Latin entitled *Plantarum Americanarum*, a collection of scientific findings by the renowned botanist monk Charles Plumier. Mostly composed of full-color illustrations regarding the flora and fauna of the Caribbean islands, Jake delighted in the book and was soon an expert regarding its contents.

Mostly, however, his cabin was full of primary source documents from the Meilleur.

Jake was astounded at the meticulous care taken with their safekeeping. The overhead of his cabin was altered in order to detach completely from the bulkheads. The records were stored in latching, waterproof chests, each bearing a bronze placard proclaiming – in five languages – that a sizable reward awaited anyone who returned the chest to Nantes. So, if the ship sank, the overhead would detach, and the chests would float to the surface, hopefully to be found and returned to the huge library of the Meilleur. To Jake, the scope and cost of these precautions was unprecedented.

Jake was legally compelled to seek out the Crimson Heirlooms. No one else was. Monsieur Roquer, the *maître d'hôtel* for the Château Meilleur, was now a trusted friend and technically in charge of the records – but he was only a servant. He did not have the budget to fund such efforts. The Trust would have had to provide the personnel and money.

There was no reason for it.

The Trust had no vested interest in Jake's quest and no reason to help him. Roquer did not have the influence to make such a request and would probably hurt his position if he did. The Trust existed for the purpose of every other corporate trust: to be a good steward of its accumulated resources.

It had to be Monsieur Tyran behind this pharaonic effort. Either Tyran had some kind of leverage with the Trust's board of directors or paid them to execute his orders.

In any case, Monsieur Tyran had left Nantes before Jake. Jake was grateful; Tyran made him uneasy. During this time, Jake did nothing for his quest, rather he took walks, and made plans for his true goal, which was to escape from Tyran's clutches and return to Boston.

But he was not only escaping Tyran.

Jake was a revolutionary, a section leader for *The Society*. He had been recruited while at school at Louis-le-Grand, and took his fellow students and other Parisians on a merry chase after death, many finding their quarry behind a barricade in Faubourg Saint-Antoine. Jake's subsequent capture had started this whole madness. *The Society* tried to help him, but had failed. Unbeknownst to all, Tyran had legally bribed the court to sentence Jake and place him on the quest for the heirlooms. Tyran had singled him out long before his capture. No one who pondered knew why, and all suspected madness.

The Society followed Jake's quest intently, at least the half of it regarding the Cross of Nantes.

Jake would just as soon be rid of them as well.

Alas, the work completed on his cabin, he found himself onboard the fat, ungainly merchantman *Temps Nouveaux*, destined for Charleston, to be loaded with cotton and then to make a spectacular detour to Cap Haïtien.

Which loomed now.

For weeks, Jake had buried himself in the documents and records. He had found out much about the lives and events surrounding the drama behind the Crimson Heirlooms.

Something began nagging at him. The second Crimson Heirloom was *the lyrics of the devil's song, as he danced across the blood-drenched hills of the*

Vendée Militaire. Jake had no idea whether Tyran was insane or fond of colorful metaphors, but the *Cour d'Assises Special* had legally defined the second Heirloom as such at Tyran's insistence. Therefore, Jake's ears and eyes perked at any mention of the Vendée, if only to unravel the enigma behind his absurdly defined quest.

The Vendée Militaire had rebelled against the revolutionary government, against Napoleon - indeed, even at the very moment against the current King. It was a place to scare children, a catchword for backward, violent reactionaries. It was a made-up name for a place with no real border. To the royals, it was part Anjou, Brittany, and Poitou. To the revolutionary, it was part of the Vendée *département*, but also part Loire-Inférieure, Maine-et-Loire, and Deux-Sèvres. There were no major cities. Minor cities? Cholet, Bressuire, Thouars? Large towns, more like. The Vendée was a place never arrived upon by accident and rarely on purpose. Jake really knew nothing about it, which was telling - which was the problem.

Ominously, through his investigations, Jake was beginning to smell something rotting in the dark, perhaps as primeval and wicked as the devil singing and dancing in his scarlet mud puddles, as his queerly-defined quest implied. It seemed more and more as if a particular unknown event had occurred in the Vendée during the Revolution, one that transcended the norms of historical discourse and record keeping.

It was a wide, deep chasm, a secret abyss of which no one spoke - its existence only ascertained from the path of those who skirted the hole. Records and letters only hinted at its existence, as if there was some kind of conspiracy to avoid its mention: an unspoken, subconscious plot of silence, as if the events were so traumatic that no one wished to think upon it, as if doing so would set something free, or start the apocalypse.

But that was absurd.

Humanity, *abattoir extraordinaire*, had produced abundant horrors throughout the ages, all told in gory detail in books, theater, music - everywhere. Jake believed that oppression caused such things and that people were naturally good. Christians thought sin stemmed from the fallen nature of man and evil ultimately served a higher purpose. Whatever the case, no one would argue the splendid quality of violent debauchery displayed across the ages. Mongols killed a million innocents at Merv, simply out of peeve. Vikings pulled the lungs of Christians from their backs and hung their bodies from the tips of them - for amusement, to make them look like angels. In a peasant revolt in northern France, just a few centuries ago, they had made… well, some things were better left unsaid – and this hole in the Vendée road laid in those waters, the depths of what was left unsaid.

Why was there this unspoken conspiracy of secrecy? What had happened? Was the horror so intense that the devil was summoned to dance?

He would not find answers here, in Haïti. He was looking to solve other riddles, those regarding the Cross of Nantes – and to escape. It was ironic that in spite of his ultimate plan to fake his own death and evade Tyran and *The Society*, he found himself obsessed with finding the Heirlooms. Oddly, he was more interested in the history of the necklace and the meaning of the devil's song than he was with locating the Cross.

As Jake approached and keenly observed, Cap Haïtien reminded him of Nantes in that it had a post-cataclysm feel, akin to a Roman ruin. The city ran north-south, parallel to a nearly straight harbor, and emerged from the port onto small hills. Profligately verdant, le Cap was framed to the southwest and far south by gorgeous, emerald mountains. There was a fort-like church of brilliant white thrusting up from smaller edifices near the top of the hill. The dilapidated buildings looked to all need paint, even from this distance, but Jake also noticed some were quite large and regal, and the streets were straight and wide. There were only two ships docked where there once would have been scores. Even so, the only quick and businesslike activity belonged in the harbor, where only a small section of the colossal dockyards was being worked at all. The docks were in terrible disrepair and timbers had even fallen into the water in certain places. It was a proud, beautiful, busy city once – but not now.

The ship would not dock: the captain had flatly refused. Years before, the Haitians had slaughtered all the whites on the island. It was rumored that it was only the French who were slaughtered, but since Jake was the only non-Frenchman onboard it made no difference. Jake protested that both ships in harbor flew French colors, but his arguments proved fruitless. Jake would be rowed by cutter to the dock. Needed provisions for the return journey would be ferried. None of the crew would step foot on the island.

Jake was not the only one who thought it odd that the ship didn't dock. A variety of expressionless black faces on the dock watched the cutter as it approached the boat stairs.

Jake decided to hoist his colors. He gave himself a moment, switching the gears of his mind to English, "Good morning, gentlemen!"

Smiles appeared on all the faces. They waved and greeted him – almost exclusively in American English. One of the men, a burly, well-dressed *couleur* in his twenties, stepped forward. "Good morning, sir." He was undeniably from the States - rural and southern. *Gut mohnen, suh!*

"I hear a fellow American. I myself am a Yankee New Englander from Wellesley, Massachusetts. Jake Loring is my name." Jake's words were true but well-chosen. A Massachusetts man would have liberal ideas on race, and be cautious, trustworthy, and clever. It would be advantageous to be thought of in such ways.

"Well, Mister Loring, you want I'll be your porter."

"Done and done, sir. I have two chests, though. We may need another."

"Nah, I'll be all right." The others near the stairs moved away to find other work.

"Where are you from, sir?" The cutter arrived. The man helped Jake to the landing as the rowers unloaded his chests.

"From Baltimore, Mister Loring. Brightly is the name."

"Brightly from Baltimore, easy to remember." Brightly put both of Jake's chests on his shoulders as if they were spare coats and led Jake up the stairs.

"You looking for some place to stay, Mister Loring?"

"Yes. Is there an inn?"

"Well, kinda. They call it a sailor's public house. It dirty, sir."

"Is it my only choice?"

"Afraid so. Ain't no good to find yourself too far from the docks."

Most cities were the opposite. "The public house is fine, Brightly, but before we go any further, I must ask you something."

"Yes, sir?"

"A nasty rumor abounds regarding the murder of all the whites on the island."

"I don't know nothing about that, Mister Loring. There was all kinds of craziness a long time ago, but that was before I was born."

Jake shook his head and chuckled. "My ship captain refused to dock."

"Don't get me wrong. This ain't no nice place. They don't care much whether you're white, brown, black or whatever, they'll kill you up. It none too safe here. Bad folk don't get you, the police will."

"You don't say."

"The harbor safe. Nobody gonna hurt a foreign sailor, lessen they in their own street and knows who looking. City needs for trade."

They walked quickly toward a two-story building wrapped in verandas. "So Brightly, you are an American. I'm curious what brought you to Haiti."

"It's a sorry tale to tell, and mostly my own choices made it that way. Baltimore ain't like New England, Mister Loring. Maryland a slave state and all. No one gets along. They call you names to your face. You black, they think you a slave. I was a free man, sir. Ain't no need for folk to be treating a Christian man like that. No, sir."

"So, you came here?"

"Well, in Baltimore, white folk came and talked to us. Said they would send us back to Africa for free, give us a little coin to boot. Returning the black man to his native land. They was all so nice. Sounded so wonderful. I thought all of my problems would be gone. When I first stepped foot in Africa, I thanked God I would never see a white face again. I would beg your pardon for saying such a thing, if I didn't curse my younger self already."

"Yet you are not in Africa now."

"Thank God above. I was though. In Liberia."

"Liberia?" Jake had never heard of such a place.

"Yep. They say it mean 'land of the freed.' See, all these nice white people figure we have a better chance in Africa with our freedom, things just too hard in America for us black folk. See, in Africa, ain't nobody own no land near the coast, ain't like the States. Folks mostly out in the jungle killing each other, 'ceptin a few fishermens. So, all kind of American black folk go out there and set up a whole city name Monrovia, after the president. Let me tell you, Mister Loring, Africa is hell on earth as God is my witness. Them Africans is devil-worshippers. They come in the night, raping, killing and stealing. We had our fill of them. Ain't no other way to say it. We done went to war back on them, freeing our folk, putting them evil Africans in chains and putting them to work. Things I saw would turn your blood to spit, Mister Loring."

"You left, obviously."

"No God-fearing man want nothing to do with all that. Whole passel of folk leaving Africa just as fast as they sail in. Ain't no good out there. The salvation of every man in Liberia is in jeopardy, Mister Loring. Ain't nothing worth missing out on heaven for."

"So, you decided to come here?"

"I wanted to go back to the states, but they wouldn't take me back. Well, not just yet anyway."

"Aren't you considered a citizen though?"

"Just paperwork and madness holding me up. All I know is half of Liberia here in Haiti, trying to get papers to get back to America. See, Haiti taking American black folk just like Liberia. White folk sending us here too cause it a black country, so it was easy to get here." Brightly went to a whisper. "I tell you, Haitians is lazy. Americans got all the jobs down here. I'm saving up. Just a matter of time before I get my papers and get myself back home."

"I understand there is a thriving colored community in Boston."

"Might be too cold up there, but ain't no beggars be choosers up here. No, sir."

As they walked up, Jake noticed there had once been an old sign above the door of the public house, now only chains hung in tribute to its memory. Instead there was another name painted above the door, now faded. *Fantom An Asasen*, it said.

Phantom Assassin? Ghost Killer? Whatever it said, it was not exactly French. Perhaps the owners were foreign. Jake hoped it wasn't some kind of bigoted racial reference.

"Brightly, please put the chests down for a moment, I'd like to talk to you further before we go in." Brightly put the chests down and nodded. "I have a business opportunity for you."

"Yes, sir."

"Do they accept French francs here."

"Lemme tell you, them *gourde Haïtien* ain't buy nothing. They got them same to the franc, but they ain't worth what they say."

"So, francs are better than, uh, *gourdes*?"

"French francs, yes sir. Much better."

"Excellent. Brightly, I will pay you five French francs a day to be my guide here. And also, when I get home, I will send a letter to my congressman in regard to your situation. I don't know if it will help you overly, but it certainly can't hurt."

"Five francs? Goodness! Where you need guiding at, Mister Loring?"

"Honestly, I don't know. For a certainty, further into the city. We might even need to travel to other ports or even inland. I am doing an investigation. I don't know where it will lead."

"Well, not to put no sass on it, but you white, Mister Loring."

"I am indeed."

"This country, not even people, just the dirt, will kill you sure as sunrise, you go outside the city. Maybe even if you *in* the city, come Summer."

"I have no choice, Mister Brightly. I understand your concern and certainly appreciate it. The die is cast with the bet on the table. I must do what I must do – and I would like you to help me."

"All right, Mister Loring."

Jake held out his hand. Brightly looked uncomfortable. Jake found himself annoyed. "Well, shake on it, man."

Brightly looked at his hand as it were the river Rubicon made flesh. Jake's annoyance quickly ebbed when it occurred to him that Brightly had probably never shaken hands with a white man. Jake sized Brightly as a strong character, so he simply left his hand in the air. Brightly soon took it, and they shook on the deal, solemnly and seriously, as Americans were wont to do. Jake handed Brightly ten francs.

"This ten."

"It is for expenses as well. We're going to pretend for now that I cannot speak French."

"Ceptin the rich people, they don't speak no French here neither."

"Really?"

"It kinda like French, kinda not. They call it *Kreyòl Ayisyen*."

"Dear Lord. All right then. So, I'm not pretending. First, you must secure lodging for me."

Brightly picked up the chests, "Then what?"

"We need to talk to someone very old. A gossip and a storyteller, someone who prides themselves on knowledge of local history."

"Well, I don't know about that, but I know who to ask."

"Good enough."

"Just one thing, Mister Loring."

"Yes?"

"This here island ain't what you used to up wherever you from. We gotta git, I can't wait for you. Something happens, Ima say *run*, but I'm only gonna say it one time. One time, then *I'm* running. You hear me say *run*, you *run*, Mister Loring. Cause you on your own until we safe and away."

"I understand."

"One time only, Mister Loring."

"I understand."

Le parc au sommet du mont Glonne,
regardant au sud.
1788

Chapter Four

The Time of the Heirlooms

France

July, 1788

Jonathan

Father Jonathan Courgeon was a busy man, being responsible for the sacramental life of the abbey of Saint-Florent-le-Vieil.

The abbey, atop the hill of Mount Glonne, was primarily a place of prayer and contemplation for the residing monks. It was also a center of sacramental worship for the immediate community and a magnet for pilgrims due to the abbey's placement atop the tomb of the saint himself.

Father Jonathan dealt with all priestly matters relating to both groups.

In all, there were seven sacraments, or holy ceremonies. Jonathan performed every Baptism, Confirmation, Anointing of the sick, and Marriage. He was helped with Reconciliation – or confession - and he aided bishops for the three different masses of Holy Orders when need arose. Funerals were sacraments because they included the Eucharistic mass, and therefore he performed all of them. Last Rites was a sacrament for the same reason, specifically because it included Reconciliation; the Eucharist, or Holy Communion; and the Anointing of the Sick - and Jonathan was out and about performing the entirety of those as well. There was another service Jonathan performed for the community which should have been a sacrament but was not. That particular service was hard to explain. It was simply being everywhere, all the time, for everyone - offering spiritual advice, promoting harmony, and reinforcing the presence and love of God wherever he went.

The last, unspoken sacrament was the secret behind every contented priest.

The extroverted priests became part of every family in their parish. They were called father, but the title was misleading. Their place was unique and deserved its own appellation. They knew every secret, told none, and spoke to all as loved ones - verily, they spoke to the God present in every man, and worked feverishly to bring about the best version of every human in their parish. A good priest was overwhelmed with love, attention, concern and duty, which led directly to a fulfilling sense of purpose, and a true sense of belonging.

Right now, Jonathan felt nothing of the sort. Indeed, if he was a water mill, his sense of purpose was the frozen creek in which it laid stuck.

Father Jonathan suffered from two main problems.

The first was being surrounded by fellow clergy who had no desire for change or progress – or conversation, for that matter. They were Benedictine monks in the main, or provincial priests from neighboring parishes who could not look past the issues of their small demesnes. Father Jonathan burned for change. He loved his church and mourned that it had been hopelessly corrupted by money and power.

If irony could be condensed into venom, it would manifest itself as the leadership of the modern French church purporting to represent Christ.

It was not always so.

During one long period, after the fall of Rome and perhaps culminating in 1200 AD, the church had been a positive moral and civilizing force in the world. Slowly, this power and influence perverted the institution into something altogether different by the time of the Renaissance, pressuring good men to change allegiances, forcing Protestantism into existence, even into open religious war by 1524. The church had moved mountains to reform itself since then, a constant backpedal over the course of centuries. The reforms, the Counterreformation, had utterly changed and even cleansed the church in many important ways. Some said it was too little too late. It wasn't either: it was a lot, and it was *far* too late.

One thing had not changed. The French church was still its own entity, with its own special problems. The kings of France plotted against the power of the church, and simultaneously that of the nobles, and had undermined both in one fell swoop in 1472. Kings asserted the authority to appoint high clerical positions themselves, completely undermining ecclesiastical leadership. Nowadays, compliant nobles could secure a paid position within the church in exchange for loyalty to the Throne. This supposedly insured a leaderless church and a docile nobility. The nobility was anything but docile these days. The church, unfortunately, was more or less headless, although the random *curé* or *abbé* would sometimes lash out in a speech or pamphlet. The dynamic had, however, created a hunger for reform in the majority of clergy, but certainly not amongst the powerful.

The cycles of the church had never been a straight line in one direction. A few centuries before the supposed apex, there was the nadir of 1054, the Great

Schism when Roman Catholicism and Eastern Orthodoxy parted ways. There were times of corruption and purity before that, and more before those. There would probably, unfortunately, be cycles aplenty in the future. Through the centuries, the reputation of the church was like the tide - sometimes high, sometimes low, occasionally stormy or placid... dirty with sewage, pristine. The ocean tides have been many things within the memory of man, stranding ports and flooding streets. So too the church.

The Mitre was dedicated to a perfect God, and suffered from being wholly an institution of man – broken, imperfect, and oftentimes corrupt.

Truthfully, not many knew how the cogs came together. The Vatican presented itself as a monolithic, absolute monarchy with the Pope as its head. Father Jonathan discovered that nothing could be further from the truth. Instead, the church was akin to the chaos of Medieval Spain. At one point in history, the peninsula was a patchwork of powerful lords who swore fealty to none. Each lord was king, emperor and pope of his lands. If the lord was Jewish, the land was Jewish. Were they Mohammedi, Catholic or nothing at all, so too was the land. If the lord was evil, the land suffered. If the lord was just and righteous, the land thrived and prospered.

This was, unbelievably, exactly how the church functioned. Once appointed, a bishop was subject to none.

The pope had only nominal control over national bishops – in France, none. The national bishops had little control over the diocesan bishops. If the diocesan bishops did not exert control – or did not care, as in France - the parish priests became despots of their flock, for good or for ill. If the church leader was ill-intentioned, greedy or perverse, their flock suffered mightily and there was little anyone could do, for the leader was the unassailable lord of his demesne. When it came to everything but theology, the church was as decentralized in its power structure as a system could get - and still claim to be an organization at all. There were no Montesquieuian checks and balances on power, nothing to thwart the baser desires of evil individuals. Once an ill-intentioned man took the reins of power, he could do as he wished and no one could stop him. No modern, well-thought political system would ever promulgate such an ill-thought structure. It was a system designed for the unscrupulous to invade and corrupt – and they certainly had done so, to the shame of all selfless priests who truly served the will of God.

Medieval Spain. And what an impressive comparison for a modern institution with such power and influence.

The current King was a fervent Catholic, a true believer and a good man by all accounts. He was also a forward thinker. There was hope he could be convinced of the need for reform and things could finally change.

Indeed, change was in the wind, everywhere, in regard to all things.

Jonathan was of two minds. Firstly, he was hungry to move the church's sails to catch these winds. He saw nothing but potential for the institution; it could be so much more than it was. Everything was in place for strategic changes to be made, for effort based in good intentions to propel the Altar into the modern age and create a better organization to more aptly serve man and God.

Then again, the church was supposedly to remain above the concerns of the world, a constant, northern star pointing to God. Was reform therefore beyond the reach of the modern age? Should it be? Were these concerns baseless? Perhaps the modern winds could blow through the doors and do some cleaning, hurting no one.

Father Jonathan, urged on by his protégé Estelle Guerrier, had begun writing letters to every priest he knew - and every priest those priests knew. He developed a network of communication to discuss reform. His duties at Saint-Florent-le-Vieil were legion, but he dedicated himself to the promulgation of his network as he could.

Which brought Father Jonathan to his second problem, which was, sadly, Estelle Guerrier. She had left months ago, but her departure had not brought respite.

Several months ago, after seeing her for the first time after a long absence, he found himself unable to sleep. He took a midnight amble – and met Estelle in the darkness, walking as quickly and aimlessly as he was. They exchanged brief and uncomfortable pleasantries, nothing more. Before the next high mass – and without explanation - she was gone. He found out much later, by accident, that she had made her way to Nantes with help from a nearby priest named Father Aurélien who, tellingly, did not speak of it.

He could not sleep for thinking of her. What if Estelle had found herself walking for exactly the same reason?

Those thoughts had led to others, and those to others.

Now, in his reveries, he imagined her as his wife, or occasionally as a chaste nun with whom he could converse, or other roles less wholesome. With her gone, he believed he could let down his guard. It seemed he was wrong. He had built something in his mind that had, all at once, come alive, some sort of internal homunculus. He realized every decision he had ever made in regard to her had been wrong: It had not been the first time she had slipped his guard.

He loved her dearly – her, the real girl, not the multitudes imagined in his head. He had allowed dangerous feelings to fester, glowing coals of last night's fire, carelessly left to smolder.

There were reasons.

Attending to hundreds of people, he had never felt alone - until she arrived. With her he found intellectual stimulation and true emotional intimacy, two things he had never experienced before. When he was with her, he felt Spring. When she left, he moved into Winter. She was amazing, witty, razor sharp, and wonderful. He missed her terribly.

He knew he needed to stop thinking of her. He knew what to do and what was right, but it was a difficult cliff to climb, nonetheless. A priest had to have a high wall between himself and impropriety. Unfortunately, if the wall was not manned, the barbarians of impropriety simply climbed over it, and sacked the soul within.

Jonathan felt sacked indeed – until a cryptic letter arrived and took his mind off his troubles. The message was from Father Aleaume Cachemarée of Tourcoing, near Lille.

Dear Father Jonathan,

Not only am I your ally in this, I advance a cause even more radical.

We must meet at once.

I enclose credentials as well as references. Please discover who I am and what I represent before contacting me again.

If you do contact me, it will be to discuss when we can meet. I will travel to you.

Father Aleaume

Father Jonathan checked Aleaume's references. His contacts described him as thoughtful, dedicated, and pious. No one offered to illuminate Jonathan as to what Aleaume represented, which was strange considering the man's bold assertion. Jonathan had thereafter set up a meeting, and was somewhat chastened by his acceptance of Aleaume's generous offer of meeting him in Saint-Florent-le-Vieil.

Aleaume arrived in the chapel amidst a reading from Exodus during the Bernard infant's Baptismal mass. As he entered, Jonathan observed Aleaume was possessed of quick movements, and had thin but strong limbs. He had a bit of a belly, a round face below a bald pate, and wore spectacles. His robes were of good quality but were not ostentatious. He looked, for all the world, as someone who had walked a quarter-mile to be there. He took his place in the pews and did not look up until he was seated.

After the Baptism, Aleaume introduced himself to Father Jonathan, who was still beholden to his duties. "If you would but give me a moment, Father Aleaume. I must tell the Bernards I will be late for their celebration."

"No, no, goodness no. We must attend, of course. Our duties as priests are far more important than conversations between us, are they not?"

"Thank you for your patience, especially after such a lengthy journey."

During the celebration, held in the park outside the abbey, Aleaume was at Jonathan's side. When he did conversate, his words were encouraging and energetic. The celebration eventually drew to a close, and Aleaume appeared to be well-liked by the celebrants.

Jonathan hesitantly wondered if he had he found a friend and co-conspirator. Was he no longer alone in his campaign? Over protestations, Aleaume and Jonathan helped clean up the remnants of the meal. Jonathan found himself talking, nearly non-stop, regarding his consuming thoughts and ideas. "Men such as ourselves are constantly aware of temptation."

"Indeed," added Aleaume, "And never place ourselves in danger."

"Exactly!" exclaimed Jonathan, "If aware of a situation that could tempt impropriety, we disavail ourselves of it. We are aware of a line we cannot cross as oath-sworn, godly men."

"We do not walk this line. We stay far from it. The further the better. Then, when life or the devil pushes us off course, we are in less danger of crossing it."

"Exactly, Father. But now I will use this same argument in regard to our community. Our church is not above corruption. We are not to say such things, but there it is. Our church might be dedicated to Christ, but it is staffed by the progeny of Adam, Cain, and Esau."

"Yes, it must be spoken. We must be bold."

"The church must be aware of its lines, Father – no less than we are. And why not? It must also stay as far as it can from the temptation of corruption."

"Wisdom," said Aleaume with a nod.

"Greed, vanity, lust for power. Are these not the same vices that tempt our church as a whole, since our church is composed of men?"

"And indeed, the church is wealthy, influential, and vain. And corrupt."

"We must cast off our wealth, power, and lofty station. Post-haste. We must rededicate our institution to Christ before it is too late."

"You speak my mind, Father Jonathan."

Jonathan was elated.

They spoke more in the refractory before Jonathan handed off the Father to the monks, who gave him a bed. In the morning, Aleaume and Jonathan talked over breakfast, mostly regarding their congregations. They good-naturedly joked about the demanding old matrons, their peers, and their temporal discomforts.

When conversation waned, the outdoors beckoned.

The top of Mount Glonne was wondrous, and the park surrounding the abbey was inviting. It was surrounded by tall châteaux, old trees and manicured gardens. They walked the grounds in quiet reflection.

"I think it is obvious that the relationship between man and God has evolved," said Father Aleaume.

"The Three Ages - the time of the Father, the Son and the Holy Spirit - do more than hint at such an idea."

"Yes, of course."

"Please go on."

"We are constantly evolving, changing, discovering who God is, and what he wants from us."

Jonathan's mental wheels stopped turning, as if someone had stuck a steel bar between the gears. "Well, for that, we have scripture and tradition."

"Yes. Indeed, we do." Aleaume paused, thinking. After a moment he continued, "What is more similar to the church Martin Luther envisioned? Catholicism or Reformed Protestantism? The British churches? The more-modern Methodism?"

"A strange question."

"Indulge it."

"The Lutheran church."

"Perhaps," Aleaume said, a bit frustrated, "and if not Lutheranism, let us say Catholicism. Nearly all of his reforms were instituted. The church and Martin Luther would still diverge on some very important points, but I think Luther would have nothing but scorn for the more-modern Protestant approaches. So, one must ask, if Catholicism is so similar to Martin Luther, who is responsible for modern Protestantism?"

He reaches and scrapes to a false conclusion. No one thinks this.

Jonathan answered in spite of the thought, "Perhaps Jean Calvin."

"Ahh, the Frenchman. I agree."

"I thought he was Swiss."

"He spent much time in Switzerland, but he was French, I assure you."

"You were saying?" Jonathan asked, somewhat annoyed.

"Modern Protestantism is French, not German. Certainly not English. The true author of the most modern Christian church was a Frenchman."

Most modern? What does that have to do with anything? Jonathan had no idea where Aleaume was going with his thoughts.

Aleaume continued, "The relationship has evolved once again. We must bring these new ideas into the church, for purposes of modernization and reform."

"Which new ideas?" asked Jonathan.

"Let us simply say, it is time for the entirety of Martin Luther's ideas to be incorporated into the true church and therefore modernize it."

Jonathan felt a rising panic.

Why this rotten feeling?

Ahh – it was my expectations of this man... and how he is now exploding all of them.

"What specifically?"

"Man is fallen. Man is incapable of saving himself. Man cannot save himself by works. The idea that Man can ask for grace, to make a choice of free will and come to God, is to deny Christ. We are all saved by Christ's sacrifice. We do not save ourselves by making a choice for grace, for that would be saving ourselves through an act that we ourselves made. Are we then saved by our own actions? Are we saved through works? No, no. We are saved by the sacrifice of Christ and nothing else. A man cannot save himself through action – or choice, Father, for making a choice is an action."

Jonathan felt as if he was going to vomit. He thought he found a friend. What he found was a heretic.

Without doubt, Aleaume was a Jansenist.

Father Jonathan should have known. One of the epicenters of Jansenist thought was the convent of Port-Royal-des-Champs Abbey in Ypres. Tourcoing was but a stone's throw away.

The movement attracted intellectuals, nobles, and artists – Blaise Pascal and Jean Racine, amongst others.

Jansenius, an old bishop of Ypres, redefined the doctrine of grace. Among other ideas, his followers denied that Christ died for all men, claiming that he died only for those who would finally be saved, the Elect, who were chosen by God and given the ability to repent and find grace. This and other Jansenist errors were officially condemned by Pope Innocent X in 1653.

Aleaume spoke, but Jonathan was barely listening. He felt demoralized, and condemned himself for having such expectations. "We believe the state serves the church," he said, "But this is nonsense, is it not? The church is actually the perfect instrument to serve a modern French state."

"W-what?"

"Think upon this, Father Jonathan. You are no fool. You have studied these new ideas. A powerful state is the best way to serve humanity, to eliminate poverty, shape culture, and promote virtue. The church should be an instrument of the state, in charge of education and the promulgation of morals and values."

Jonathan swallowed, then spoke with a croak, "How does that eliminate corruption?"

"The church becomes subject to the law. Any law regarding corruption is applicable to church officials."

"No. We are too closely tied to government as it stands. The church must be kept separate from the state."

"Why?" asked Aleaume cheerfully.

"I-I'm not sure."

"Well then!"

"No, no. Let me think."

"Very well."

It was difficult for Jonathan to gather his thoughts. He did not want to be here. He didn't want to talk to Aleaume anymore. He felt betrayed. "The church transcends politics."

"Of course, you do not believe that. You have said the opposite in our conversation. The church is wholly a product of man."

"Yes, and must therefore be astutely careful of its alliances and beliefs. Christ had nothing to do with politics. The institutions of man, whether malevolent or productive, are utterly ephemeral. We must ride those tides and remain constant. We cannot waver in our task, much less our ideology."

"And you think our task is different than eliminating poverty, shaping culture, and promoting virtue?" Now there was a slight edge to Aleaume's voice, as if he believed there could be no argument against his assertion.

Jonathan found his head was suddenly clear. "None of those tasks belong to us."

"Then what is our purpose?"

It was an insult to God that a priest asked such a question, but Jonathan felt tired more than angry. "God created everything in the universe, out of love, out of joy. He is beyond our understanding, yet is so caring and merciful that we are precious to Him. We are hopelessly imperfect, yet He has come down from heaven and sacrificed Himself in a gesture of grace, and has provided for the salvation of our souls. It is the ultimate destiny of all men, unique out of all creatures in that we are able to perceive God, to be grateful and glorify in creation, to see the universe through the eyes of our Creator as best we can, to accept the grace we have been provided with love and humility of spirit. The church facilitates this, and provides community and spiritual sustenance. Poverty or wealth has nothing to do with this process, and sometimes wealth can hinder it. We do not shape culture, for culture involves outward signs of belonging, and we concern ourselves not with appearances but with the changing of hearts. If a man does not pursue God willingly, it is meaningless that he appears to do so, therefore laws promulgating appearances or limiting behavior are equally meaningless. And virtue? Roman virtue? What of it? Why does the church care how a man serves his nation? Give to Caesar what is Caesars, that is the end of it. How many times have soldiers of Alsace marched under a different flag? What are nations but castles made of sand? Rome was the greatest and longest-lasting state mankind has ever seen, yet it is dust, and God remains – his church remains. And both will be here still when France is no more. God and the church will be here when every man now living, whether heretic, deist, or theist, is dust in the ground."

"You have ascertained who and what I am."

"Yes."

Aleaume spoke quietly and politely. "The followers of Jansen are powerful, Father Jonathan, and we are legion. Paris is a Jansenist city and where goes Paris goes France, despite the king's absence."

"I have never heard this."

"But believe it now. We were responsible for the complete ejection of the Jesuits from the country. In Paris, we shut down the superstitious Catholic displays and parades. We were the first to call the King a traitor. We demand humble and attentive service from our leaders, for all are humbled before God. Our membership includes a cross-section of the elite at every level of French society. We infiltrate every organization, every power structure in the country."

"Then I think perhaps you are the very personification of corruption, and the personification of the most compelling reason why the church must be beholden to Christ instead of Versailles."

Aleaume nodded without emotion, then sighed. "You are no politician, Father Jonathan."

"Nor do I have a desire to be unpleasant. Forgive me."

"No, no. That isn't what I meant at all. I take no offense. You believe what you believe. I am simply disappointed. You could have been great, a man of influence whose ideas rippled through the ages, as if a great boulder was thrown in the pool of human thought. But you will be none of those things, and it saddens me."

"I think you overestimate me."

"Not at all. You could have been elected to the Estates-General – think upon that. You could have had a national voice."

"I am not seeking election."

"Now you would not be elected, even if you did. We are in a time when change is possible. We need unanimity of voice. You will not be elected, we will make sure of that. You are… not one of us."

So Aleaume and his ilk would block me if I ran? Some sort of vast conspiracy against the non-heretical parish priests of western Anjou? What a ridiculous thought.

Jonathan spoke carefully, "Man has free will. Neither are we wholly evil, being the creation of God. Our salvation is attained through aligning our will with God's Will. Christ died for all. If there was such a thing as the Elect, he would not have needed to die at all. No, indeed. His sacrifice is meaningful. And through his sacrifice comes all the meaning and purpose of our existence. You are wrong, Father Aleaume."

Jonathan was surprised at the quiet strength of his own words. They were an angel's battlement.

Aleaume spoke again, "I will be leaving."

"Yes, you will," whispered Jonathan.

Aleaume left.

Jonathan's words had been strong, even defiant. Still, he felt broken.

He had been naïve. In his mind, he had believed in a very simple polarization. There were church leaders invested in the present system, who were opposed by ideologues who believed in making things better. In between them were those who were asleep, who needed to be woken and convinced of a better course.

His ideas did not factor in opposed ideologues of change who were as deeply committed as he was, who were passionately plotting to make things worse. How could the ideologues disagree? There was scripture, catechism, tradition, the teachings of church fathers. It was all so clear. How could a priest – a priest! – stumble into such dangerous waters? If the clergy could not agree on the tenets of their own religion, how could they work together toward any common goal?

How could the foundation of everything Jonathan worked for suddenly turn into river silt?

The problem with human betterment, Jonathan ruminated, *are the people standing in the way of it. Unfortunately, ironically, clearing the way completely defeats your purpose – for your purpose then lies broken in pieces to either side of your pristine path.*

Over the next few days, Jonathan lost all hope. It had only partially to do with Aleaume. Their conversation was simply the last blow.

An odd internal arrangement came upon him. He felt as if only a small part of him was aware, the rest was bludgeoned comatose, underwater, unable to influence or contribute. The only spot of light and warmth remaining in his heart was the memory of Estelle Guerrier.

He could visit Estelle in Nantes.

There was no realization of implication or consequence. There was not even intention, good or bad, of which he was conscious.

He went to his immediate superior, Brother David. He did not expect the conversation to be easy or comfortable. He interrupted Brother David as he stood reading at a lectern. "A priest needs to be assigned to perform my duties, Brother David. I am leaving for Nantes."

Brother David was middle-aged but looked younger. That was, until one looked him in the eyes, then he appeared much older. "I see."

Jonathan stood in place for a good ten seconds. Brother David did not look up from his reading and was as fully intent on the printed words as before the interruption.

"I am quite serious, Brother David."

Brother David looked up and did something Jonathan had never seen – he smiled. "I will attend to your duties personally, Father Jonathan. Is there anything else?"

"No."

Brother David nodded and went back to his reading. Father Jonathan made a quiet exit, taken aback by this exception to protocol.

Although everyone was kind to each other, the rule of the abbey was tyrannical. Obedience was mandatory. Duties were obligatory. Jonathan had just quit his duties, and received a smile and kind words for it.

It was unexpected.

He went to his room and did nothing until nightfall, and then fell asleep.

Nantes

Chapter Five

July, 1788
Estelle and Xavier

Estelle felt quite well by evening and was invited to dinner. Unfortunately, Monsieur David would not be attending, but she would see him for their morning appointment before he left for Paris.

In preparation for dinner, Paige combed Estelle's hair and helped her dress in a simple white chemise tied with a gold sash. At Estelle's insistence, Paige only escorted her most of the way, Estelle being confident of finding her destination with simple instructions. Even with such guidance, the Château Meilleur proved to be Estelle's match and she found herself lost. The night's darkness, coupled with the feeble candlelight, gave the soaring ceilings and vast spaces the impression of a mysterious underground cavern, filled with riches and art of every description. She was then a Baghdad thief, tip-toeing through a Syriac treasure cave of marble and limestone.

She found herself in a long, dimly lit hall. Soaring gothic windows were to her left, a high stone wall set with doors and openings to her right. There were hanging tapestries on the walls and long carpets on the floor. Evenly spaced, identical baroque tables held lit candelabra.

A pale, dark-haired man stood half-way down the hall, staring into the nothingness of the abyss beyond the windows, as if the options behind him were no match for the lure of darkness. He was well-dressed, tall but not overly so. He was without fat, or really thickness of any kind, but had rope-like muscles: a hard, hypermasculine body - a taut wild animal. He might have been an underfed tug rower for the docks, save for his fine clothes and grooming.

"Good evening," said Estelle with a smile.

The man turned and looked at her.

Estelle realized she had made a terrible mistake. This was not a man. It was an animated corpse. He had the eyes of a shark – cold, black, unfeeling – and pale, amphibian skin to match.

Estelle found she was no longer smiling.

She willed the expression upon her face once more, although she felt no mirth, and repeated her greeting, "Good evening."

There was a twitch in his eyes.

Finally, "Good evening," he said.

Estelle stared at him, and realized her fear was gone. Instead, Estelle was nearly crushed by a wave of pity and empathy.

Six words were spoken, but words were not the only way in which people understand each other. Deep in the back of Estelle's mind, where such communications are comprehended, there was a revelation.

Estelle was no indoor orchid, waited on hand and foot like a princess - rather she was a desperate weed from Saint-Domingue. Her nature was not due to a perfect life, as a good soul being treated with love and respect from the wet-nurse tends to be. She had seen things beyond her years: good, bad… nightmarish. Perhaps her perspective gave her a unique ability, for in an instant Estelle realized she knew the essence of this man. "May God bless you, my poor man," she managed to say.

There was another flicker across his eyes, like a soft, distant breath across a candle flame.

She offered a conciliatory smile, "I have no manners, Monsieur. I am forward and inappropriate, in the best of times. But I must tell you my heart. I sense where you have found yourself in your life's journey, where your heart lies, but I do not know what horrors placed it there. I will only say this: the world has locks. God has keys. I will pray for you. Every day. From now until the day I die."

He regarded her, "Don't bother."

Estelle was actually surprised to hear unpleasantness, knowing what she knew. She waited for a different reply.

It finally came. "These are odd words you speak to me, Mademoiselle. I do not know how I revealed myself to you, but your concern seems genuine and well-meant."

"It is, I assure you, Monsieur. I have no intentions toward you, except of Christian charity."

He did not speak or smile.

"My name is Estelle Guerrier. I would be honored if you called me Estelle."

The man swallowed, his eyes flickered once more. "My name is Jérémie d'Uts Bouvillon, but you must never call me such a thing, I beg of you. Nor would I have you tell anyone else."

"Of course. You will forever be Monsieur to me."

"No…" but the man trailed off. Estelle only waited. "You will hear others call me L'Oublié."

The Forgotten.

He continued, "But I would have you call me something else. Monsieur… *Souvenu*, if it pleases you."

Remembered.

Estelle curtseyed, "Monsieur Souvenu."

"Mademoiselle," he said with a bow, "Estelle."

"Thank you ever so much for your hospitality, Monsieur Souvenu."

The man blinked twice. "You have mistaken me for my master, Monsieur Traversier."

Estelle blanched, "I… t-this is the home of Monsieur Traversier?"

Who was, of course, the richest man in Nantes, and one of the wealthiest in all of France.

"Indeed."

"I think I took a trip on one of his barges, long ago."

"There is a fair chance you did so. He owns many."

"Monsieur Souvenu?"

"*Oui*, Estelle?"

"Is your master perhaps at dinner?"

"He is indeed. You are hungry, and you have lost your way."

"I am and I have, Monsieur Souvenu."

He held out his arm, "I will escort you."

***

For years, Xavier and Madame had eaten dinner in the servant's parlor off the kitchen. At one point, ages ago it seemed, they could only afford to heat certain parts of the house, and only in Winter. The kitchen was always warm, and so was this particular adjoining parlor. But even when the château's hearths were burning bright, they continued to eat dinner at the small table, having grown fond of it, even though it was not truly a dining table at all. It was easier to talk, in spite of being able to hear the servants. In all truthfulness, they both enjoyed hearing them. The King's Swiss Guard could have disappeared inside the expansive Château Meilleur without a trace, and it would have taken more than one bugler to call them all to supper. Being empty of all but two remaining Traversiers and their staff, their home felt like a tomb - empty of the living, filled with mementos of the dead. The noise of the help was like the sun shining into a crypt and allowing the flowers inside to bloom.

It was at this humble table that L'Oublié and Estelle found them. Both Xavier and Madame jumped from their chairs. It was not from manners - if so, only Xavier would have stood. Rather both of them bolted up from surprise and consternation, being accustomed to L'Oublié scaring brave men witless and terrifying women into feints. Yet here he was, placidly escorting Estelle Guerrier to dinner, as shocking as if she had ridden into the room on a wolf.

L'Oublié turned to her and bowed. She curtseyed in return and he left the chamber. A servant quickly pulled her chair and Estelle sat in unison with her table. "Good evening. I am ever so grateful to now have the opportunity to properly thank you for your hospitality and ministrations," she said as her first course was tabled.

"Mademoiselle," began Xavier, "You are thanking the owner of the carriage horse that struck you."

Xavier was a handsome man with hard, sharp, masculine features and large, deep-set eyes. His voice radiated strength and command. She could sense no ill-intentions in him, only curiosity, and a mild humor.

"You are unkind to yourself, Monsieur. Accidents happen. Our character is tested by our actions amidst their consequences, and I have found your actions to be exemplary."

"In that case, you are quite welcome." Xavier found her to be a curious mix of confidence and humility. She was well-mannered and quick-witted, so far.

"Doctor de Trémargat is very kind. He said that it would be beneficial to take slow walks starting tomorrow. In three days, I will be able to return to Nantes by carriage without concern."

Madame spoke, "If Monsieur is not busy, I'm sure he would be honored, if not honor-bound, to keep you company."

"Oh, I would not dream of inconv-"

"And if he is not available, I will surely accompany you."

"You are too kind, Madame."

"Forgive me for my forwardness," said Madame, leading.

"I am at your service, Madame."

"I could not help but notice your necklace."

Madame Traversier seemed sharp as a Venetian dagger, despite her manner. Estelle chose her words carefully, "It is a bit… much… to wear every day, but I do so because it reminds me of my mother. Usually I tuck it beneath my linen, so no one can see it. It is said to be valuable and I do not want to attract undue attention. Of course, one would think you have many such things here in this house. Compared to the grandest of them, I am sure my necklace is but a bauble. I do not wear it to hide it. I cherish the feeling of it against my skin. My mother gave it to me, you see. In all honesty, I think it is quite lovely as well."

"I assure you," Madame said, "We own nothing that would make your necklace a bauble in comparison."

"Why, you must, Madame. You are too humble."

"Mademoiselle, I am obscuring a different truth, and certainly not out of humility."

"I'm afraid I do not understand."

"Quite simply, your necklace is known to me."

"Yes, I suppose it would be. I gather it was made in France, and its design was once fashionable. I saw paintings with similar necklaces as I lost my way here."

"No, Mademoiselle, you did not."

Estelle stopped eating.

Madame continued, "The painted crosses were not similar to yours or to each other. Not *similar* - no - rather they are all precisely, exactly the same. They are all portrayals of one necklace in particular - unique, priceless, and named the Cross of Nantes. The one which happens to be around your neck."

Estelle did not register this as truth. "Forgive me. Why would you have paintings of my mother's necklace?"

Xavier interjected, "One of my ancestors commissioned it, almost a hundred years ago. It was lost to the British during the war, when I was a child."

"Yes, my mother said a British captain had…" Estelle trailed off. "Does my mother's necklace belong to you then?"

"Do not tempt me," said Madame quickly.

Estelle said nothing.

Madame leaned forward, "Do not feign ignorance. You know of what I speak."

"Mother," said Xavier, worried that her madness was showing through the cracks.

But Madame only held up her hand to him. She kept it in the air and turned back to face Estelle – and said nothing.

Estelle finally answered, her syntax slow and oddly spoken, "Yes… yes. My mother, father, long ago, they were going to sell it and move to France. A buyer was…"

Estelle said nothing more. Her eyes moved as if she was lost in images of memory.

"Then you do know, and you do see. The necklace belongs to you. I would no sooner take it than leap into Leviathan's maw."

Estelle looked to be sick, "I feel quite strange."

Madame regarded her, "Do you serve the will of God, Estelle?"

"Yes, in all things, as best I can."

"Then you have nothing to fear. The Cross serves the will of God, of that I have no doubt. It now behooves us to discover the course of action He wishes us to take."

"Mother," hissed Xavier.

She said nothing more.

The rest of the dinner, lasting to the extent of reduced appetites, was mostly spent in silence.

***

The grounds of the Meilleur were not in scale with the buildings, although they were quite large. If they had been in proportion, they would have taken up half the city. The estate rather comprised the top of a wide hill, properly a plateau, with its gentle southern slope descending to the Loire in the southern distance, and the long, thick walls of Nantes and her outlaying suburbs down the hill and up another to the east. Manors, abbeys and farms dotted the acres around them, but all were dwarfed by the Meilleur, even the neighboring manor of *Jean le Cinquième le Sage* encircled by the same well-crafted fence. The grounds, at least the part of which resided in the province of nature, were not overly impressive. In fact, they were dull: a few trees, mostly common oaks, grass, simple gardens, some underwhelming flowers, mostly neglected Camellias. It was as if the structures of man, grand as they were, could not abide competition from Dionysus and Hegemone, and would stand alone to be admired.

But Estelle did not care. After being bedridden, she thought it all quite grand and loved the cool wind on her face. At first, the presence of Monsieur Traversier was somewhat awkward, but, strangely and in no time at all, they became comfortable. Soon they were laughing and making witticisms as if they had known each other for years.

Estelle sensed that he was utterly in control of himself and wasted not a breath of action. He was intelligent, worldly, and knowledgeable. She feared boring him, then realized he was as interested in her as she was in him. They were as different as two people could be, yet there was something between them that neither could yet identify.

Their walk was a lazy rectangle, following the ornate wrought iron fence encircling both the Meilleur and the manor. Xavier looked down as he spoke, "I am quite curious as to something I witnessed last night."

"What did you witness, Monsieur?

"My… companion, L'Oublié. You seemed to be on good terms."

"I must admit that my first impression was quite different than the second."

Xavier nodded, "Your first impression is most likely no secret. I have seen the effect he has on others. I am curious as to your second impression, for no one else has had one."

Estelle gathered her thoughts, "I was overwhelmed by an image. It was so clear I could not doubt it."

"I would have you tell me of it."

"I will, but if you think I am mad after hearing it, please forgive me and know I will do you no harm."

Xavier laughed. "I promise."

"Do you abide metaphors, or do they annoy you?"

"I do well by them."

"This man you call L'Oublié was once, long ago, a grand, proud sailing ship. The ship itself and everyone upon it, was L'Oublié. Do you understand?"

"I do."

"This ship and her crew were altogether noble and good. But one day the ship was boarded by malefactors. The crew was forced below decks. The bilge traps were opened, and the poor sailors were forced into the ballast hold, laying against lead ingots and stones with their face pressed against the oak planks above them. The bilge traps were closed and barrels put on top of them, sealing the crew in total darkness, the air so close and heavy they could barely breath. The pirates left and the ship sailed on, as if the absence of the crew had made her very timbers come alive, stirring some deep motivation for movement, a will to sail, forcing it across the ocean without need of supplies, harbor, or wind. Standing on deck, one was disconcerted, thinking there was no one onboard at all. Yet the crew was still trapped within, screaming in the darkness. That is L'Oublié, and what a horrible thing to be."

Xavier had known L'Oublié for years, yet had never had such a distinct revelation. He knew instantly that it was true. "It is evident you have sailed."

"Ha! I sailed my bunk, for most of the journey."

Xavier's brow furrowed. "To this day, I do not know why…" He did not finish the thought.

"Why, Monsieur?"

"Why L'Oublié became my companion."

"Is he a paid companion, like myself?"

"No. Although he lacks for nothing. Truthfully, what we spend on ourselves is usually equal to the other - and is a smaller amount than what you might think." The walk continued for a long moment in silence, then he spoke again, "I was waylaid, and L'Oublié submitted my ambushers. I allowed myself to believe that I employed L'Oublié as some type of bodyguard. Perhaps he is. But it is not why he is with me. To be honest, even before I was attacked, I was drawn to him. He was quite decrepit. There was no aspect of his existence that should have attracted me in the slightest. Yet from the moment I laid eyes on him, I sensed… something. I don't know. I was pulled to him. Inexorably."

"Perhaps it is because you are so similar."

No one had ever thought such a thing, but Xavier immediately knew it to be true. He forced himself to reply in a neutral voice, "In what way?"

"You are nearly the same ship, Monsieur. Only your crew was imprisoned by different means."

"How then?"

"They were not imprisoned by force. In a desire to sail faster, they hid themselves in the ballast hold, to force the ship to come alive. They scream as well, but they lie in the dark by choice. You are two empty, willful ships, simply created by different means."

Xavier stopped walking.

Estelle was not the sort to give offense; she was simply too full of empathy. But she had keenly ascertained Xavier, having known him but little, and it had taken him aback, creating such thoughts in him that he could do nothing else but ponder them.

Estelle turned and blanched, "*Mon dieu*, please forgive me, Monsieur. I am a ridiculous person. I have no manners at all."

Xavier recovered. "It is quite all right."

"No, no. It's… I recently received a blow to the head, you see. I am not in my right mind."

"Yes, I am aware of this," Xavier chuckled.

"Could you ascribe my behavior to this misfortune, and forgive me completely?"

"There is nothing to forgive."

"I am honorable but I am not… typical, Monsieur, for this place and time. I am from somewhere far away. Perhaps in the trials of my prior environment, I had to think hard upon people and circumstances. It has created in me an arrogance of assumption. And in my arrogance and weakened state, an ability to express the most impolite ideas without shame."

"I admire your insight and honesty. You have already given me much intellectual fodder. I think I would rather hear your thoughts than have you hide them out of misplaced etiquette."

Estelle felt like hugging him. She had the sense to not do so. "I would assume there are hundreds of people wanting to take walks with you, being such a good and forgiving listener."

"There is no one."

"Then I will start a list and put myself upon it."

"Then my list springs into existence. Now I suppose we must talk about your list, Mademoiselle."

"Oh, I assure you, my list is contained in a tome far weightier than even the one possessed of Saint Peter at the gates."

"I see," Xavier said, amused.

"I know all of the names on my list by memory."

"I would hear them."

"All of them?"

"Why yes. Every single one."

"Well, there is Jeannine Cœurfroid, and she pays me for my walks, elevating her name to the top of the list, quite obviously. Then there is Father Jonathan from the abbey of Saint-Florent-le-Vieil. Perhaps a few others from the parish and its surroundings. A few priests and fisherman from le Cap." Estelle realized she had said Father Jonathan's name without even a shred of shame or longing.

Xavier brought her from her thoughts, "An international list."

"Yes, quite an extensive international list."

"Your sense of wit and humor is endearing."

"Do you imply, Monsieur, that my list may not be quite so ponderous? That I am exaggerating out of self-pity."

"Not at all. I simply wish my name to be placed upon it, and as soon as possible."

Estelle's heart suddenly sank.

She realized the truth of her situation. She had no family. Her father was neglectful and far away. The same could be said of her brother. She was an employed companion and her continued employment depended solely on her honor and character. And here she was, walking with a bachelor: a handsome and rich bachelor. If she continued talking with him in this manner – one that could only be considered flirtatious – she might imply that she was available for some other role in his life. If she were not beholden to God, Estelle would have rather liked to be anything to Monsieur Traversier. But young women depend on strength of character when they are young in order to preserve their honor. Estelle had to stop this at once and be firm.

She spoke, "But that is not possible, is it Monsieur?"

"What do you mean?"

"It would not be proper."

"My intentions are wholly honorable."

"That is impossible, Monsieur."

"How so?"

"I am very aware of my humble nature, in the eyes of man and God. But I do strive to be the best woman I can be, the best and most godly version of myself. I am an honorable woman."

"Again, I have no ill-intentions toward you whatsoever, Mademoiselle. Your honor is safe with me."

"We are thrown together by accident, Monsieur. Our walk has the blessing of Madame and has been ordered by a doctor. But if we associate outside of this context, it would be dishonorable in and of itself."

"Why, for Heaven's sake?"

"Because you are not courting me, and we are both unmarried."

"How do you define courting?"

"Do you jest with me, Monsieur?"

"The family of the woman I was arranged to marry broke off the engagement. I am ignorant of the formality of other options."

"Courting is when a man seeks the company of a woman in order to decide whether he wishes to give her an offer of marriage. It is the only honorable alternative to being promised to wed, and must be conducted in accordance with strict protocol in order to retain the honor and good character of both parties."

"Nantes cares little for such things, but I know you are from a different place. I found Saint-Florent-le-Vieil to be very traditional. I assume you hold similar values."

"Do you say your own behavior is more in accordance with Nantes than that of mine."

"No, not necessarily. And I assure you, Mademoiselle, that anyone who knows me, anywhere in the world, will tell you I am a man of my word."

Estelle sighed, "Monsieur, you misunderstand. I cannot continue this unless you are courting me – and that is an impossibility. My family is composed of my father, who is nearly feral, and my brother, who eschews all convention out of philosophical arrogance. I am an utterly lowly person, and my ancestry is highly suspect. I could no sooner be your partner in your social circles as fly with the angels. I would only embarrass you and be the subject of gossip for the rest of your life. No one would ever tell you I am a proper wife for you, much less myself, and therefore no courtship is possible between us. Therefore, we must be circumspect in our behavior, however much I enjoy your company. We must be mindful of impropriety, for the sake of our salvation, if nothing else. My goodness, I have the subtlety of an African rhino."

Xavier was amused, "So what are the first steps in courtship? Do we need a license of some sort, or a priest's blessing?"

"No, I don't… I'm not terribly sure. I don't think so."

"Then how does one go about such a thing?" There was still mirth in his voice. Estelle had no idea why. Perhaps as the grand and celebrated idiot of the world, her words were risible.

"I suppose a man would ask permission of the woman's father to court her. If such a thing were not possible, he would have to ask her. If granted, the honorable thing to do would be to publish the arrangement, so that if they were seen together there would be no impropriety. I… I'm afraid I made half of that up from whole cloth."

"Very well. I will ask your father."

"Oh, please no, please do not ever meet my father." Estelle shook her head, "I cannot believe I just said such a thing." Then she realized Monsieur Traversier had just asked to court her. Estelle stopped walking, "Forgive me for my bluntness. But upon this subject, there can be no ambiguity. Do you wish to court me, Monsieur, for the purpose of discovering my suitability for marriage?"

He looked at her with amusement, "I do, Mademoiselle."

Oh, Mon dieu, what now? she thought. "I have absolutely no dowry. None, Monsieur. And if Jeannine Cœurfroid would ever become wroth with me and demand the return of what I possess that she has paid for, I would have to find a burlap sack to wear in order to preserve my modesty."

Xavier chuckled and shook his head. She also had a cross around her neck that could have bought the Meilleur –several times over. Perhaps she did not think of it, perhaps the word *priceless* meant something different to her - simply precious and beautiful. Upon reflection, it was better this way. Estelle would most likely be overcome had she known the truth.

"I am quite serious, Monsieur."

"Then I will be serious as well. I was hoping to secure your fortunes. Now that I know you have nothing, I'm afraid our courtship is over."

It was now Estelle's turn to laugh, and tears came unbidden with the laughter.

"Shall we walk again?" he offered.

"Yes. Why me, Monsieur?"

"Could you call me Xavier?"

"Yes. And in return you must call me Estelle."

"There are things I must admit to you, Estelle."

"Such as?"

"I have sold my soul. I want it back," he said mirthlessly.

"Do not even joke about such things."

"If I were a Christian, I would say that I have performed deeds that have placed my salvation in mortal jeopardy, for a reason no more banal than to succeed in business. At least, I believed my goal was to become successful. But after I had done so, I realized that gold was not my true end. Rather I believed that gold would lead me to what I truly desire."

Dire words spoken. But he did not say them as an evil man would, nor as a man consumed with regret or self-pity. He was rather keenly self-aware, a captain describing a treacherous harbor. "You are not a Christian?" she asked.

"No, I am not. Do you still wish my company?"

Estelle knew she should say no. "Yes. Very much so."

They both could now hear the soft swish their steps made through the grass.

Estelle broke the silence, "What do you truly desire?"

"Warm, abiding, and unconditional love."

"Such a thing only comes from God, Xavier. And requires no gold at all."

"I would say 'Where were you back then?' but I know the answer. I saw you long ago, before I wrought such destruction. I saw you, and I saw the Cross of Nantes around your neck. Yet I did not speak to you."

"You have seen me before?"

"Yes, you were walking with a young priest."

"Where?"

"Saint-Florent-le-Vieil. I was visiting the Marquis de Bonchamps."

"From La Baronnière, in La Chapelle-Saint-Florent. I know him well."

"Now that I discuss it and remember, I believe Bonchamps may have mentioned you in passing, though your name meant nothing to me at the time. He said you had half his books in your possession."

"Our meeting seems extraordinarily serendipitous and filled with strange coincidences."

"It does indeed."

They continued the rest of their walk, scored by contented silence.

MONTMARTRE
SAINT-HONORÉ
SAINT-DENIS
Rue du Faubourg Saint-Honoré
Avenue de Neuilly
Champs Élysées
L'Étoile
Salle Favart
Opéra-Comique
Comédie-Italienne
Madeleine
Place Vendôme
Jacobins
Manège
Place Louis XV
Tuileries Garden
Palais-Royal
SEINE
Pont Louis XV
Palais Bourbon
Tuileries
LOUVRE
Saint-Honoré
Les Halles
Louvre
Châtelet
Pont Royal
Pont Neuf
Île du Palais
Palais de Justice
Conciergerie
Le Procope
L'Abbaye
Saint-Germain
SAINT-GERMAIN
Invalides
Champ de Mars
École Militaire
LATIN
Cordeliers
Saint-Sulpice
Comédie-Française
Incurables
Sorbonne
Louis-le-Grand
QUARTIER
Sainte-Geneviève
Luxembourg
Rue de Sèvres
Rue d'Enfer
Rue Saint-Jacques
Left
SAINT-MICHEL
SAINT-JACQUES
N
0
1/4
1/2
3/4
1
MILES

PARIS 1788
Right
Saint-Martin
Temple
Marais
Saint-Antoine
Saint-Victor
Quinze-Vingts
Hôpital Saint-Louis
Eldorado du Dimanche
Saint-Lazare
Boulevard du Crime
Saint-Martin
Temple
Ambigu-Comique
Rue du Temple
Grand Danseurs du Roi
Père Lachaise
Rue de la Roquette
Rue de Charonne
Hôtel de Ville
La Force
Place Royal
Pont Marie
Bastille
Île Saint-Louis
Arsenal
Rue du Faubourg Saint-Antoine
Folie Titon
Rue de Montreuil
Port de la Tournelle
Île Louviers
Hôpital des Quinze-Vingts
Place du Trône
To Vincennes
Rue de Charenton
Jardin Royal
Seine River
Picpus
Bièvre River
Salpêtrière Hôpital
Marcel

Palais-Royal Theater

1788

Chapter Six

July, 1788

Beau-Brave

By choice, Beau-Brave was now a Nightsoiler. He was slowly losing his mind, but his writing was progressing at a splendid pace.

On the way to Paris from Vizille, he had stopped two miles north of Évry to bathe in the Seine and wash his clothes. It was a tough journey; even with a bit of shrinkage, everything hung loose on his frame.

He came upon Paris from the eastern hills of Montparnasse at noon and looked out over the storied metropolis for the first time. He knew the city from lore and maps, but not like he knew it now.

Over six-hundred-and-fifty-thousand souls were crammed into a six-mile diameter circle - less than thirty square miles which also contained huge swathes of parks, fields and undeveloped land. The city center, anything near the river islands on either bank, was a maze of urban canyons laying in perpetual shadow. The whitewashed buildings were darkened with age and soot, mostly built centuries ago, hodge-podge, irregular and tall. Seven-story structures were separated by fifteen-foot-wide streets – still sometimes dirt and mud from wall to wall. The slime of the alleys was choked with vendors; everything was sold – bread, water, music, entertainment. All had to share the congested streets with coaches, carts and carriages – even young noblemen blasting through the streets on galloping horseback, unmindful of any in their path.

Nearly every block of the city had an identity and a name, and its own representatives and police, who relied on the townsfolk for help. Powerful benefactors, tax laws, and city ordinances shaped each sector and faubourg, clustering crafts and businesses.

Seen on the right bank, to the east of the city center, was the Marais. It was newer, wealthier and better planned. To the north of the right bank were the elevations of Montparnasse, even newer, even wealthier. On Beau-Brave's side of the river, the ancient Latin Quarter stretched below, rife with schools, dotted with landmarks and parks. To the east abutting the river was tony Saint-Germain. The two main islands in the Seine were densely populated and held Notre Dame and the Conciergerie. The bridges were choked to death with traffic; luckily only one still had buildings upon it. Thousands of small workshop apartments were crammed into blocks just south and east of the Marais in Saint-Antoine, filled with ambitious craftsmen eking out a meager living in the tax-friendly district. Packed along the Bièvre river, a brook leading to the Seine just below him and running east-west, were the brick dungeons of heavy industry – factories, tanneries, mills and butchers – along with tall apartments filled with unfortunates forced to live in the acidic mists.

On the Seine were barges aplenty, delivering, taking away, some permanently moored, where the city dwellers did everything from washing laundry to bathing. The river was filthy with garbage, excrement, and run-off from the dead – whether from cemeteries or abattoir. The modern age had also come to the river. Plumes of steam and coal smoke rose to the west where huge engines pumped water for the wells and fountains. The pollution had also changed texture, for now it hissed with by-products of chemical, enamel and dye factories, or anything else of toxic, chlorotic horror that could be synthesized into profit.

Yet, dotted across the city, were magnificent places – churches, academies, universities, public squares, palaces, amusements, museums – not to mention world centers of art, fashion, and music. A thousand writers had already described her as a city of extremes, a thousand more compared it to heaven next to hell, never juxtaposed, always separate - rarely segregated, however much it tried.

Beau-Brave had lived in Cap Français, which was wealthy, open, well-planned, and green. Nantes was all blade and no handle, a purpose-designed commercial powerhouse - but also remade in limestone and modernized to its core. He had been to Angers, which was old and quaint but still busy with trade and manufacture. Grenoble was winsome and surrounded by mountains.

Paris was something else: a foreign environment for humans, malevolent - an Indian goddess smeared with blood and draped in diamonds, smelling of perfume, sulfur and rot.

Beau-Brave had no idea how anyone could live here, in these blackened crevasses made of plaster and wood. Why were they here and why did they stay? Were they all here for greed and greatness? Did ego and vanity trump their sense?

Is that why I am here?

Despite his observations and reservations, Beau-Brave descended into Paris, wearing shoes and clean clothes, carrying his diploma from the University School of Grenoble and little else. He was thin, but still good-looking, although a shadow of his former self. The city was encircled by non-defensive walls into which huge, ornamented arches and gates were placed at intervals. Outside the gates and along the walls was a riot of wine taverns, mostly housed in tents. All of them, even at this early hour, were packed. Beau-Brave had no idea why people would walk so far just to drink.

Coming through the *barrière* gate of Saint-Jacques, he saw every cart and carriage was held up by taxmen of the Farmer-Generals. Beau-Brave then understood. These Farmer-Generals had the brass to build a wall around Paris for no other reason than to make sure everyone was properly taxed. The excise on liqueur was probably especially odious, considering the profusion of customers in the tents outside the city.

Rue Saint-Jacques was paved, being the ancient Roman north-south *cardo* through the city. To the right was seen the wonder of Sainte-Geneviève, meant not to rival but to eclipse the greatest churches on earth. To the left and down the rise, the sprawling gardens and palace of the Luxembourg impressed. Further north stood the noble, hoary school of Louis-le-Grand and the Sorbonne University, dominated by the beautiful and subtle spire of the Chapel of Sainte-Ursule. Scholars, students and booksellers swarmed the streets.

He continued past the Latin Quarter onto the Petit-Pont, the star-crossed, many-times-rebuilt bridge over the Seine leading to the Île de la Cité. Through the narrow streets to his right, Beau-Brave saw Notre Dame. He could not believe its size. It impressed even more than Sainte-Geneviève. With its flying buttresses, it was a gargantuan stone spider - almost too exotic, perhaps built by Atlanteans or Egyptians. The bridge itself was carpeted with traffic, all trying to maneuver past vendors and beggars packed on both sides.

The people were pitiable. Across the street from a normal hunchback, Beau-Brave saw a woman whose back curved forward from her hips and bend upwards like the hull of a ship, giving her a strange, rocking gate. There was a harelip, a clubfoot and a dimwit – all seen at once, crossing on the same bridge. Beau-Brave had never seen so many birth defects in his life. Even those hale and whole were underfed, short, and strange of color. Half the children looked to have measles. Only the Lord knew how many would survive.

On the corner of the street and bridge was a news stand. Beau-Brave caught the eye of the proprietor, "May I, *mon ami*?" he said as he held up clean hands. The man made a generous face and nodded. Beau-Brave stepped forward and perused his wares. There was printed sheet music aplenty, a variety of domestic and foreign newspapers, books, pamphlets and also a huge variety of thin magazines with blue covers. Curious, Beau-Brave looked through them. Inside the blue magazines were tales, sometimes short stories of romance, retellings of the classics, or funny stories. Regardless of thematic differences, the tales were short, simply-told, and meant for the masses - an indicator that Paris was a literate city, perhaps even more so than Grenoble.

Interesting.

It had been information, more than anything, that riled Grenoble – not the long Winter. Anyone who claimed famine changed a mind was an imbecile. There had been less than a handful of successful peasant revolts in all of human history, and yet the peasants had always starved, and perhaps always would. There had been famines aplenty throughout history, some causing considerable devastation. France barely survived the cold in 1709, yet it did not have the rebellious effect of Grenoble's lesser frost in '88.

The differences were many and varied, but to Beau-Brave it boiled down to one simple fact: In 1788, there was a *message*.

It was quite simple: all difficulties stemmed from the flaws of the present system. In order for things to improve, the system had to change. In the past, the question was *to what?* In the present, the answer was *to Socialism.*

Such a simple message. A simpleton's message, really.

The efficacy of the replacement system, the one with the all of the answers, was never examined. The message, for some reason, did not have to be proven.

Why?

It was simple.

Rousseau had brought utopian thinking to the masses. If people could imagine something better, utopia had not yet arrived, they were then oppressed, and things had to change.

Every individual's idea of perfection was the new standard.

The disciples of Rousseauian Socialism did not have to explain why the elevation of their creed would enable utopian perfection… *because Socialism was the creed and wellspring of utopian thinking.* If someone believed in utopia, they were already a Socialist. The message did not need proof because the message was already scripture to those who believed.

Socialists preached to the choir. The widespread change in philosophical thought throughout the country had done their work for them.

Perhaps also this new philosophy couched itself as being the pinnacle of intellectualism. Intelligence and education naturally brought man to this new thinking. Whether that was true or not was immaterial: it was believed.

That was the difference between bad Winter then and bad Winter now. Peasants and craftsmen were foot soldiers of the bourgeois Socialist priests.

Something hummed at the outside of his consciousness, but Beau-Brave was not able to concretize the thought. He overheard the vendor, speaking with one of the ubiquitous tourists - a Piedmontese gentleman, distinguished by his accent.

"I say, these streets are choked – choked – with people. They can't all possibly live here."

"Well, Monsieur, they do now."

"New arrivals, are they?"

"Yes, Monsieur. The hail destroyed all of the crops this year, for leagues and leagues around Paris. The poorest of them have come here, looking for food and relief."

"Relief? From whom?"

"Why, from the King, Monsieur!"

"He cannot possibly feed them all."

"Sixty percent of the city is on some kind of welfare, Monsieur. The King does feed them, as best he can, may God bless him. And that is why they are here."

"I suppose the streets are in poor condition because of them as well."

"The streets? Oh, the refuse and garbage? Well, to be honest, the streets have not yet recovered from the celebration."

"There was no holy day that I know of."

"No, Monsieur. They celebrated the news! Brienne resigned. He has been replaced by Jacques Necker!"

"Necker of old? Indeed!"

"It is a new day. The banks have already agreed to loan the King seventy-five million, on the condition that the Estates General will have full powers to reform the system. The Estates-General is now a reality, Monsieur! And Necker is back!"

The conversation continued, but Beau-Brave walked on.

What do I now know?

Paris was a literate city, even near the bottom of the economic scale. A well-written pamphlet could light a fire, just like in Grenoble.

To Beau-Brave, Paris was, probably even in the best of times, a hellhole for the majority. Even worse, Paris was now flooded with gullible peasants who had no employment and no prospects, who survived only on the King's welfare.

Importantly, there was an *alternative order* that had not been present in ages past, one that offered perfection as the standard by which all systems should be judged.

In Grenoble, this new order was propagated by powerful men who had a successful recipe for rebellion, exploiting people's desire for hope and betterment. These rebel-rousers were ideologically homogenous, organized by the new voice of Rousseau, through books, pamphlets and secret societies.

These people had already successfully collapsed Royal order in an entire region of France.

With my help.

The only way for Paris to *not* go the way of Grenoble was for the King to commission free-thinking, devious and intelligent men to develop strategies to win the upcoming war of information, waged in wine taverns and on the poster walls and newsstands of Paris.

Beau-Brave would bet gold on the fact that *no one*, anywhere near the King, had any idea of the monumental changes that had enabled the catastrophe of Grenoble – much less a plan to counteract the efficient Socialist agitators, were they to come here.

They are here already.

The peasants were, however, being fed by the King. Would they not support him? Perhaps not: by the looks of things, his attempts were woefully inadequate.

Ahh, I am an idiot. None of that matters at all.

A rebel agitator would only have to say, "You barely survive on what the King gives you. Do you not think a government of your peers would give you more?"

Or perhaps, "The King feeds you? You fool! He put you in this position in the first place! He made you destitute and now he barely keeps you alive? What kind of *imbécile* you are to take a plate of *merde* and say *merci*?"

That was all that needed to be said to a gullible peasant, who would be grateful for the opportunity to believe his problems were due to something or someone tangible rather than the vagaries of weather or, even worse, the incompetence of the peasant himself. All generosity would be forgotten, unless the King had some kind of counter argument, which he wouldn't, not having the perspective to fathom the machinations of experienced street agitators.

Quod erat demonstrandum, Paris was *fait niquer la gueule*.

Beau-Brave was not particularly bothered by the revelation of an upcoming apocalypse. He was an outsider. When things burn, something must be rebuilt in its place. When that happened, perhaps he would be in a better position to get what he wanted. The Grenoble upheaval had been good to Beau-Brave. He went from begging for bread to drowning in skirt and dining with the powerful. Perhaps it would be the same here.

He looked up to find that he was on the Pont Notre-Dame, the bridge leading from the island to the right bank. He soon made land and headed for the open space of the Place de Grève. The entire eastern border of the square was taken up by city hall, the Hôtel de Ville, elegant and stately, surrounded by walls of wrought iron bars and decorated with statues. He knew he was near where he wished to be. He spotted a well-dressed man engrossed in a newspaper.

Beau-Brave hailed him, "Monsieur, the theater, if you please?"

He looked up, annoyed, even more so when he saw Beau-Brave's unshaved appearance, "Over there!"

The direction was northwest, along the Rue de Rivoli, and Beau-Brave was on his way. This was the *très riche* part of the city center. He approached the Louvre, solid and elegant to the left, the gigantic palace complex topped to the west by the stately Tuileries palace. On his right, cosmopolitan townhomes, government buildings and hôtels excited Beau-Brave's eyes and ambition.

And then Rue de Rivoli emptied into a square – and there it was. An incredibly long, beautiful, elegant building was before him, distinguished by Greek columns on every floor. It was another, equally impressive Louvre, stretching back from its façade block after block – indeed, Beau-Brave could not see its end.

The north part of the façade was taller, different, and possessed even more columns. A distinct entity unto itself.

It was a theater.

Beau-Brave stood there, struck. He did not know for how long. It was good that he was near a wall, for if not he would have surely been hit by a carriage.

The carriages.

They all seemed to stop at the columned palace, not the theater. Beau-Brave noticed pedestrians were disappearing into the palace as well.

What kind of palace admits such traffic?

Beau-Brave crossed the street. He noticed entrances into the inner courtyard of the gigantic hôtel were not guarded. There were even a few vendors in the dark hallways leading to the bright, landscaped courtyard. The columns were decorated with posters, proclaiming all of the events of Paris that one could possibly attend that night. Beau-Brave entered the hall, sure that he was going to be stopped at any time – but he wasn't.

From the posters, he realized he was in a place aptly-named the Palais-Royal.

And then he found himself in a gigantic, sculpted outdoor area, larger than most parks and encircled by the palace on all sides. There were cafés, chess tables, lemonade stands and wine bars, the new *restaurants*, paved walkways, trees, flowers and grass – all arranged to divert and occupy. Well-dressed, elegant prostitutes plied their wares in the open, much to his astonishment.

The unusual wonders of this place did not end there.

To his left and right were boutiques under a sky of impossibly tall wooden arcades. All these storefronts boasted gigantic window-walls hinting at the delights within. Beau-Brave had no idea that glass could be manufactured to be so tall and wide. A paved walkway fronting the stores ran the entire length of the palace under the arcades, so not only could Beau-Brave see inside the stores but could walk around and look inside without getting wet or muddy. It was unheard of – and yet, as Beau-Brave looked around, it appeared as if half of respectable Paris was doing exactly that: ambling about, watching people, and marveling at goods and wares through the wall-sized windows.

There was even something called a wax museum, which proclaimed to have life-sized dioramas of historical figures and events. Beau-Brave thought that life-sized wax figures would quickly disfigure or melt. He did not believe a word of it. It was some kind of swindle, men and women in makeup standing stock-still until the entrants passed their display. *Something*. He didn't bother.

Beau-Brave stopped at a men's millinery. Through the windows, he saw the hats were arranged in little works of art complete with props and scenery. The dominant display was a scale replica of the sculpture *The Rape of The Sabine Women* by Giambolgna. A hat dangled from every outstretched arm and head. At the base was the detritus of battle: little toy shields, helmets, swords and broken pieces of toy carts. Prices were placed on all of the goods, which was another wonder. No one need haggle or fear being taken by an unscrupulous salesman. Posted prices were so civilized – and were also unique to Beau-Brave's experience. All of the wares were of highest quality. The cheapest hat was thirty-five livres, which was more than a month and a half of pay for an unskilled workman.

It must be nice to afford such a thing.

Beau-Brave kept walking. Equaling the nearly infinite types of offered goods was a profusion of food and drink. An elegant store selling only different types of honey was next to a lace boutique that looked to be stocked by Athena and Arachne. Well-dressed women packed hair salons. Bolts of men talked politics - radical politics - loudly and without fear.

He stopped at a bookstore. The walls held racks of the usual newspapers, blue magazines, sheet music and periodicals, but the floor was an assortment of handsome wooden displays holding gleaming, well-bound books. The owner was immaculately dressed, but had a maleficent air to him, as if his face could not hide his intentions. He was friendly enough to Beau-Brave, in spite of the latter's rough appearance. "Bonjour, Monsieur. Let me know if you need any help."

"Thank you, Monsieur." Beau-Brave looked over a particular section, not knowing what it was. His choice activated the proprietor, who crossed to Beau-Brave with an unwholesome smile - and a book.

"Here," he said with his dark grin as he handed the work to Beau-Brave.

Les Amours de Charlot et Toinette, it was titled. Beau-Brave flipped to a random page and was stupefied by what he saw.

There was a full color illustration of the Queen, sitting in a chair, her dress pulled down to reveal her breasts - and up to reveal everything else – in shocking and graphic detail. The King – the King! – stood by her with his flaccid, pale member hanging from his trousers. Beau-Brave read the next page.

The king's verge is no bigger than a straw,
Always limp and always curved.
He has no bitte, except in his pocket;
Instead of baise, he is baisée.

The rest of the book was no better. The text was graphic and the illustrations were worse: accurate depictions of every imaginable prurient act, all involving the Queen - with men, with women, with men and women, with celebrities and public figures of all kinds, from Lafayette to Cardinal Rohan.

Beau-Brave quickly handed the book back to the man and scanned the room. The book was treasonous, completely illegal. The proprietor was still grinning. Beau-Brave shook his head, "Are you mad?"

"Monsieur?"

"Are you trying to get me arrested?"

"We are in the Palais-Royal, Monsieur." The proprietor said it as if his statement explained all.

Beau-Brave held his temper and spoke evenly, "I am from Grenoble."

The man looked furtive and suspicious.

Beau-Brave rolled his eyes, "I am Beau-Brave of Grenoble."

The grin brightly reappeared. He had heard of him. "Of course, you are! Who else could you be?"

Beau-Brave impatiently waved him off. "Tell me why being in the Palais-Royal excuses us from treason."

The grin only widened, "This is Philippe's home."

"Who is Philippe?"

"Louis Philippe Joseph d'Orléans, the First Prince of the Blood."

"The King's brother?"

"The police are not even allowed to enter, much less arrest."

Beau-Brave would kill anyone who looked wrong at his sister. He could not imagine the brother of the King condoning treasonous pornography involving his brother and his sister-in-law. "And you gave me this because…?"

"Ahh. This title was sold out, except for this very copy. This entire section is Queen pornography."

Queen pornography?!

Beau-Brave kept an even face. "Does Philippe know?"

"Does he know? *Mon dieu,* he adores these little daggers in the heart of the monarchy, Monsieur! He is like you! He is a revolutionary! A Socialist! He is a hero to the people! I assure you, no one despises the King and Queen more than Philippe!"

"Are there many high-ranking nobles who share this sensibility, Monsieur?"

"In Paris? All of them! I guarantee you, they all have a copy of this book, for I sold it to most of them. Versailles was once a place of mystery, intrigue, romance and seduction. The King has turned it into a humdrum Catholic wasteland! It is a place of listless decorum and duty, all bound to the rules and regulations of the court! *Mon dieu,* everyone knows the etiquette of Versailles was meant to preserve power and order for the King. For the King to serve the rules and not the other way around…" The man shook his head. "It is a travesty. I have heard rumors he has never cheated on his wife. He truly must be impotent. There is no other explanation. I tell you, Paris is full of nobles who are now refugees in Paris - simply out of boredom, Monsieur! Imagine leaving Versailles because it is boring!"

Beau-Brave realized this man, and perhaps a great many others in this city, were utterly corrupt of spirit.

There is only one question then. Am I any different?

The man leaned forward and spoke in a whisper, "The King might have his police, Monsieur, but I assure you the agents of Philippe are every bit as assiduous, and they are everywhere, Monsieur. Everywhere!"

"Doing what?"

"Why… undermining the infernal King, Beau-Brave! Fomenting revolution and spreading the words of Rousseau! Just like you, Monsieur!"

"I see. *Merci*, Monsieur, I will consider the purchase."

"As you will. It was a pleasure to make your acquittance, Beau-Brave, hero of Grenoble." The man bowed respectfully and Beau-Brave returned it.

"Adieu," said Beau-Brave and he was out the door.

He felt better immediately.

He was preoccupied until he found himself in front of the other side of the theater, which he now saw was called the Variétés-Amusantes. Next to it was a smaller theater, the Beaujolais, which had puppet shows and child performers.

Beau-Brave spotted a strange man head toward the Variétés. He was dressed in pink and black, which seemed odd but was actually quite striking. He had enormous hoop earrings and wore no wig, rather a ponytail that began nearly on the top of his head, seen because his hat was worn at a rakish angle. He knocked on a nearly-invisible side door of the theater and was quietly admitted.

In that moment, Beau-Brave had a vision.

It was time to return to the left bank and attend to practical matters.

***

Beau-Brave never worried about his ability to find bread in Paris.

Ordinarily, such inattention to detail would lead straight to a miserable death. No one moved to Paris unless they had connections and contacts. Even the vagabonds hailed from the country directly around Paris. Beau-Brave, by all rights, should have been absolutely destitute, with no other thought than surviving day to day.

He did, however, have two things in his favor, both of which he learned at school in Grenoble.

The first.

Starting nearly two hundred years ago, and trickling off to a drip by the time Beau-Brave was born, the Irish had been coming to France. They were booted off their island by the English and came mostly as soldiers. The Irish Brigade was a storied unit composed of divisions that had distinguished themselves in battle, sometimes even fighting other Irish marching for nations such as Spain. The trick with the dynamic, the thing Beau-Brave counted on, was *trickling to a drip*. With less and less new blood, Beau-Brave imagined that the Irish in France were quickly losing their identity and becoming more French and less Irish year after year. Probably, considering everything, they mourned this. He counted on the fact that they did.

The second.

Beau-Brave's mother spoke a secret language. She had taught it to the twins, who had no idea what it was or how she had learned it. He knew she came from Tír Chonaill and spoke Gaeilge. That did not help. At school, he discovered the truth: they all spoke fluent Irish.

Who in France spoke fluent Irish? Who in Ireland, for that matter? It was a tongue of the dark woods - men of the city would know only a smattering. The Irish in France? None at all. Beau-Brave, in fact, was counting on it.

To be gainfully employed in Paris required contacts, maneuvering through local politics and bureaucracy, and the joining of a guild or corporation. Beau-Brave figured that being the one man in Paris who spoke Irish, he could avoid all of it. He went to the Paris liaison headquarters of the Irish Brigade and made inquiries.

He was wrong.

Currently, there was indeed a guild for tutors of Irish. It was composed of one man, Andrew McLagin, who was ninety if a day, pale and white-haired, like a redhead who had lost every strand of scarlet. Beau-Brave soon met Mister McLagin and inquired of employment.

"I don't like the looks of ye. And ye speak the mother tongue like a Donegal highwayman. But I'm eleven-dozen years old and not getting younger, so I suppose I'll have to take ye."

Papers were inked. Beau-Brave officially joined the Guild of Irish Tutors as an apprentice, member number two. He would follow the master tutor, Mister McLagin, as he serviced nineteen families who wished their children to know Gaeilge, and hopefully, someday, would become a master tutor himself.

He would be paid forty sous a day - two livres - twice the wage of an unskilled laborer, four times as much as an unskilled woman. He would not work on one-hundred fifty holidays; therefore, his salary was four-hundred-thirty livres per year.

After taxes, which he could not avoid, he would have less than three-hundred livres.

Presenting his papers of employment to an agency in Saint-Germain, he rented the cheapest available room: an attic coffin, a large closet really, seven stories off the ground… in a building raised in 1423, two years before Joan of Arc heard Jesus at the age of thirteen. The rent was forty livres a year.

He checked in with the local *commissionaire*, Monsieur Boniface, an underemployed print-setter, and assured him he was sane and law abiding but was busy and wouldn't be seen much by anyone in their little neighborhood - and that was that. He didn't bother checking in with the priests. There were too many people and not enough collars; he could easily slip through the cracks.

If Beau-Brave did not wish to waste away or develop diseases, he had to spend at least five sous on bread and at least five on meat, eggs or vegetables every day. It could be done. Street hawkers sold dinner leftovers from the plates of the wealthy, butchers sold cuts the wealthy did not eat: tripe, brains, tongues, tails, hooves and so on. Of course, fruit and vegetables were seasonal. Water would be an additional expense. Water vendors waited in long lines at the fountains and wells and filled huge containers, with what was optimistically called *tea water*, and brought shares to their clients. Drinking the water without first adding wine or boiling it resulted in a week or two of intense stomach pain and voiding at both ends with uncontrollable pressure. That would be in the best of cases. The worst scenario was death from typhus. Wine started at eight sous a bottle and, at that price, could pass for vinegar with a strong taste of barrel wood.

The temperature of the room would dip below freezing in the Fall, Winter and Spring, and heating would bring additional costs, if he did not wish to risk his life, fingers or toes.

Living at lowest budget that would still ensure survival, Beau-Brave had less than eighty livres per year that he could spend on something other than room and board.

Unfortunately, there were other mandatory expenses.

For his work, he had to be well-groomed. An annual shaving and wig-dressing contract with a barber was fifty livres. A suit of appropriate clothing, including a winter coat that would double as a blanket, cost one-hundred livres. Two buckets were also a mandatory purchase. One was for things he might eat. The other was for things he did not eat.

With those purchases, he was already twenty livres short for the year, with no candles, much less a lantern or lamp, no coal or charcoal or firewood of any kind, no furniture and no bed. There were no funds for diversion of any sort, and he would be constantly hungry.

Regardless of how he balanced the budget, he could not forgo the winter coat. If he did, his frozen corpse, stiff as a board, would be removed from the attic walk-up sometime in mid-December. The only choice was to reduce food costs. Keeping his meat, egg and vegetable allowance, he would have to get a four-pound loaf and have it last for a week and perhaps steal bites of food from his tutoring clients, although that would be difficult. The servants were probably secretly eating from their larders as well and their gaze would be hawk-like. Stealing anything more substantial than a bite here and there would be risky. The Paris police were empowered to do just about anything to preserve order, and everyone was hungry. Thieves could not be treated more harshly, whether they stole to eat or not. Sometimes a thief's neighborhood would protect him from the police, if they knew he stole to eat. Beau-Brave, however, had no friends here.

But Beau-Brave was not here to eat, but to write.

Searching for hours through ash piles, he found a handful of rusty nails.

He secured inedible connective tissue from his butcher's offal pile in the alley. No one was going to miss it.

From building walls, he carefully pulled down old posters that would have been torn off or posted over anyway, so as not to incur the ire of the poster guilds or police.

An intact pigeon feather was found by the third day and carefully split down the middle to use as a writing quill. No self-respecting clerk would ever use it but Beau-Brave was on a budget.

Mud was brought into his room with the bucket, the good bucket.

Voilà. He had everything he needed for success, with the exception of light at night.

Nails went into opposite walls at a good height. The butcher's connective tissue was wound into a string that soon hung like a clothesline between the nails. The mud was used to create a small, narrow trough on the wood floor and was filled with water. The posters were soaked in the water, one by one, until they were free of ink, then were hung on the line. The paper was allowed to dry as the water in the trough evaporated and thickened.

Three weeks after arriving in Paris, Beau-Brave took one of the dried posters from the drying line, laid it on the floor next to the trough, dipped his quill in the trough water – which was now watered-down ink – and began to write.

One dip of the poor quill executed one capital letter, perhaps two words in lower-case cursive. Beau-Brave did not even register the movement when he dipped it into the ink; it was like breathing; a quick, perfect and reactive movement. He had weeks and weeks to think upon what he would write. His ideas were organized in his mind, outlined, and ready for the quill.

There was just one problem.

He also had a job.

If Beau-Brave focused on his writing, he was mentally exhausted. Also, writing wound him up like a clock, he found it hard to sleep, and was therefore physically exhausted as well. If he did not prepare for work and was not full of energy, his pupils sensed it. They would become unruly and bored and sometimes confrontational. Beau-Brave, tired and irritable, would wish that someone would ride in and cut him down with a saber.

If Beau-Brave focused on his tutoring, everything went well in the parlors. The children were attentive and the time would pass quickly. He would enjoy his time spent with the boys, and sometimes Mister McLagin would be fatherly and full of advice.

But then, when Beau-Brave tried to write, limited to daylight hours, he would stare at the paper, finally realizing he hadn't written a word for several minutes. When he did manage to write, the words were uninspired, a waste of his precious paper and ink.

He could do one or the other. He could write or he could teach.

Quod erat demonstrandum.

Beau-Brave left his attic and took a walk in order to think. He kept to the main avenues, lit by hanging *réverbère* lanterns. The city was not quiet, even at this hour. In fact, the main streets leading to the bridges were choked with farmer's carts, all bursting with the produce of early Fall.

What to do.

He was barely surviving, even with a good job that kept his fingernails clean. He was not able to write well and consistently.

What to do.

He had been walking for a half-hour when he saw a commotion on the border between Saint-Germain and the older neighborhood of Quatre-Nations. He changed course to investigate.

There was a bolt of mounted French Guard police under a lantern post, speaking with the local *commissionaire*. Nearby, a sinewy, filthy workman sat upon an even filthier cart. Another man, even less fortunate, was hanged from his neck from the lantern post. He looked beaten as a clean rug with a sign hanging on his chest which read *PAEDERAST*. Despite his poor condition, the dead man looked peaceful, as if in the throes of undisturbed sleep. As Beau-

Brave looked upon the scene, the police briefly studied him. Their experienced eyes discerned a bystander and they paid him no mind.

Beau-Brave decided not to disturb them. He crossed to the filthy man upon his filthy cart. "*Bon soir, mon ami.*" The smell emanating from the man and his cart was indescribably foul, almost as if it were carefully engineered to be repulsive.

"*Bon soir*, Monsieur," he said. The man's eyes were alert, his speech sharp and quick.

"What goes?"

"What do you mean?"

"*Putain!* There's a man hanging from *la lanterne.*"

"You have not been in Paris long," he said evenly.

Beau-Brave calmed. "No."

"Paris takes out its own trash, Monsieur. *À la lanterne*. They don't have many lantern posts in Quatre-Nations so they hang them here, on the border with Saint-Germain."

"You have seen this before?"

"A few times, Monsieur. Mostly on the right bank."

"So, are you some kind of ghoul then? One who enjoys the spectacle."

"You are here for the spectacle, Monsieur. I'm here for the body."

"The body?"

"The police pay us to take the body to the mass graves at Clamart. It saves them a trip."

"Will not his family pull him down?"

"One never knows, it might have been his family who hung him up. You are full of questions."

"Well, I suppose I am a bit ghoulish then, for I find myself intensely interested in this spectacle, *mon ami.*" Beau-Brave could not believe the unbelievable stench coming from the cart. He braved a look in back, "What on earth do you have back there? More bodies?" But it was not more bodies, rather a cornucopia of excrement: human, horse, dog, cat, goat, sheep, poultry and cattle. "*Mon dieu*! What an impressive collection! If given catalog and order, this assortment is worthy of a museum."

"Perhaps - for those with no sense of smell."

"How did your cart come to be filled with sewage?"

"I put it there, Monsieur. I have the most important job in Paris: I am a Nightsoiler."

"Pray tell!"

"It is simple; I shovel *merde*. Without those like me, you would swim through the streets, in the only liquid on earth dirtier than the Seine."

"Where do you take it?"

"Only the farmers surrounding Paris are entitled to it, for they feed the city. To them, it is gold."

Beau-Brave was suddenly struck by a thought. "Do you work mostly at night?"

The man shrugged. "There are many factors. At one in the morning, those same three-thousand farmers are allowed in through the Farmer-General's barrier gates to bring their crops to the markets of Les Halles. I cannot leave the city any time after that for hours, for the carts are held up as they pay the *Octroi* tax. Then, as soon as they are through, I have only a short window of time. The meat and fish come in starting at five, you see. There is a rush at nine, when many in the city start their work, then another at ten and another at noon. There is another at two, as some stop working, then at five when the rest are finished. Everything is quiet until nine, when dinner starts. Supper is another rush, at ten or eleven. At eleven and midnight everyone begins to head home, then things are quiet until one."

"The crops and such do not come by boat?"

"They do. They would come on the backs of griffins if they could."

"There is probably a rhythm to when you are able to clean certain streets, not just when you can dump a full cart."

"Indeed. With time, you begin to know the pulse of the city, Monsieur. It is like all things. We are assigned a district by the corporation. We know our route well."

"Where is the corporation located?"

The Nightsoiler gave him good directions. It wasn't far.

"How long does it take to fill a cart?"

"Hours, sometimes less."

"Less, you say?"

"Mostly we exist in a world of abundance, Monsieur."

Beau-Brave laughed and heard the police, now directly behind him, laughing as well. He turned and saw they were listening attentively to the conversation. One of them shook his head. "Fascinating," he said in awe.

It was indeed. And, over the next few days, the conversation preyed on Beau-Brave's mind.

Securing any kind of employment involved contacts, bureaucracy and paperwork aplenty. But nightsoiling could be an easier occupation to enter than, say, barrelmaking. It was simply too foul. Even with Paris being full of the unemployed, he might be able to secure a job as a Nightsoiler.

If he was a Nightsoiler, he could work when it was too dark to write. He could easily eat his fill in the farmer's fields without anyone being the wiser. He might be able to sleep on barn straw instead of a wood floor, using his walk-up closet of an apartment only as a place to write. He didn't need fancy clothes or wigs or shaves.

It was the perfect job.

He visited the corporation and spoke to the clerks. They informed him that to become a Nightsoiler, one needed a cart. It could either be drawn by the Nightsoiler himself or with a draft animal. The corporation could lend him a shovel. He had to bring out at least four cartloads of *merde* every twenty-four hours, and would be allowed some holidays if he wished to take them. For the first week, he would be accompanied by an old-timer, who would train him. There were reasons for this, but Beau-Brave surmised the primary purpose was to take care of the old-timer.

Very well.

Beau-Brave gave no notice to Mister McLagin, who probably thought him murdered. The act was sanguine. It was Féroce charging a trench, not sparing a second for the fallen wounded to his left and right. With such an action, Beau-Brave had just placed a little bit of himself in a trunk, without realizing he had done so.

Beau-Brave turned in his professional clothes for coin and cancelled his barber contract. He walked straight out the same gate of Saint-Jacques from which he had entered.

He was looking for a cart.

In times of dearth, even garbage was valuable. Old, broken carts were good firewood, after all. He had traveled a good distance from the city, nearly to Montrouge, when he found himself down a minor road. After a few minutes, he spotted a cart rusting in high weeds on the other side of a wooden cattle fence. He jumped the fence and inspected it. He realized that with minor repairs and some grease, it might be serviceable. It was a good omen. He walked onwards, past acres and acres of rich land, until he found a walkway leading to a quaint country house. There was a barn within the grounds near a stream, another good sign. All varieties of onions, garlic, spinach, broad beans, peas and asparagus were being planted as well as the winter wheat. There were wide pens for cattle, oxen, sheep and goats. Huge mounds of compost lay covered by pecking chickens, bordered by a huge coop the size of a barn. He saw a few workers who did not seem concerned with his presence. They were unaccustomed to strangers and did not fear them. Beau-Brave had inadvertently come upon the right farm.

A young woman, perhaps in her late teens, exited the house. Her hair and skin seemed the same color, a very light brown. She stood stalk-still, staring at him, then suddenly turned and went inside. A moment later an older man came out the door, spry but bent, and carrying a shovel, bright and sharp on its leading edge. He crossed to Beau-Brave.

Most likely, a huge farm like this was owned by some jackass sitting in a parlor in Versailles. This man was the *chef*, the boss.

Beau-Brave spoke first, "*Bonjour*, Monsieur. Are you the overseer?"

The old man nodded his head, "Uh-huh, uh-huh."

"I am living in Paris, in Saint-Germain. I am currently a tutor."

"Uh-huh, I have no need of you."

"Not as a tutor. I wish to shovel *merde* for you."

"We have contracts with Nightsoilers already."

"I saw that you have an unused cart. Such a huge farm. Why waste such a resource?"

"A cart? Where?"

"In the weeds, in the southeast corner of your cattle pen. It's quite serviceable."

"It is quite not. That is why it is there."

"I can repair it, Monsieur."

"Why would a tutor wish to shovel *merde*?"

"I want to use the daylight hours for writing."

"Writing?"

"To be a playwright. I have spoken with several Nightsoilers and the craft dovetails quite perfectly with the path I wish to take with my life."

"That is… preposterous."

"It is… the truth."

"Uh-huh. Why should I hire you? I don't know you."

"You have an unused cart, Monsieur. We help each other. I'm not afraid of Paris at night and I'll shovel coal in hell if it helps me achieve my goals."

"You will repair the cart?"

"My endeavors will cost you nothing, except to pay me for my work."

"I see. What do you think this occupation will pay you, Monsieur?"

"I have been to the Nightsoiler Corporation already, Monsieur, and know my wage. But I need several things in addition to payment."

He coughed. "You think too much like a tutor, *mon ami*."

"After I am done for the night, I will wash myself and my clothes in your creek, and sleep in the straw of your barn. That requires lye soap."

"Uh-huh. That will be hard in the Winter, if not harmful to your health."

"Then in Winter I will need water in the barn in some kind of container. I also need food in addition to payment. Something. I am not discerning."

"You can have one meal of greens, but only when you work. We grow a variety all year long. You can have one egg per day as well. When we have other things in abundance, we are generous - but I will not promise anything more."

Perfect. "The payment is set at five sous per load."

The man scratched his beard. "Five sous then. A good, full, heaping load mind you. Less is less."

Beau-Brave calculated that if he was working as fast as he was able, and he could learn to effectively maneuver around traffic times, he could earn twenty sous per day, a good wage for the lowest level of unskilled labor. But he would also be eating much better and could sleep on straw. Beau-Brave nodded, "I don't want to pay any taxes."

"Good luck. You will be catalogued going in and out of the city and it must match my tally as well."

"Are things so organized the Nightsoilers cannot escape the *octroi*?"

The old man nodded. "You must make the cart serviceable on your own."

"*Oui*, Monsieur."

"If you do, I will loan you tack and a mule - but only when you work. I will charge you five sous per day, but that includes the cart as well. Whatever repairs you make to the cart, it still belongs to the farm and we owe you nothing for improvements."

"But it is mine to use as long as I work for the farm, yes?"

"Yes."

"*Merci*, Monsieur."

"If you steal my cart or my mule, the police will break you on the wheel."

"I am sure of it, Monsieur."

Torture was recently outlawed, that wasn't going to happen. Death and prison, however, were still very much in vogue.

"Stay away from my daughter."

"*Oui*, Monsieur."

"What is your name?"

"Guillaume Guerrier." If he had said Beau-Brave, he feared the farmer would have laughed in his face.

"I am Monsieur Gagneux. You may start tonight if you wish."

"I will."

He did not. The cart was much harder to repair than he thought and it took days to scrounge for spare lumber and parts. But it was done, and he soon reported to the Nightsoiler Corporation.

The entire building smelled of flowers.

He was ushered in to see the corporation president, Monsieur Gamelin, who was an old Nightsoiler himself. Gamelin dressed like an aristocrat but had the hands of a carpenter. He shrugged a lot, calmly angry. "Once, all Nightsoilers had to be good Catholics. Not now. Now you can be anything or nothing, and still be a part of any guild or corporation in Paris. I don't know why the King has done this. I don't know why he puts up with the Jansenists and the Anabaptists and the followers of Voltaire. He shouldn't trust these new zealots. They do him no good at all. This is a Catholic country with a Catholic monarch. We support him because he supports the church. The further he travels from that point, the less power he has. Why can he not realize this? The King is the cornerstone of order. Why would he stand by while others create a system where he is obsolete? Does he truly believe everyone is as selfless and understanding as he is? Do you see my point, Guerrier?"

"Yes. Yes, of course. *Vive le roi*!"

Mon dieu! Are the Anabaptists still running around?

The man continued his quiet rant. Beau-Brave listened, daydreamed.

"…the long and the short of it is this: if you have your cart and do the work, we welcome you if we have openings. And we do, by the head of Saint Denis, we do!"

There were papers aplenty to sign, fees and administrative costs to fork over, and then he was given his one-week old-timer.

The ancient he was saddled with, Baptiste Talbot, proved to be a good resource. They were assigned the Latin Quarter, and Baptiste knew a good, efficient route that completely avoided other Nightsoilers. He also gave Beau-

Brave a shovel. It had a sturdy, long shaft and a wide, rectangular wooden scoop. A thick, metal reinforcement ran the length of the blade, black and sharp. He eventually would have to get his own and give it back, but it was his for the nonce.

Four or five loads, say twenty-sous every day – no holidays – was three-hundred-sixty-five livre a year before taxes. It was more than he made as a tutor and he had no special expenses for clothing or grooming. Every sous could be used for progress, as long as he could grit his teeth and live on a meager budget.

He took the uncomplaining Monsieur Talbot home and brought in his fourth cart load at noon, a nearly sixteen-hour day. He was completely exhausted, and hoped that he would become more efficient with time. After rubbing down the mule, polishing and putting up the tack, and composting the last load, he walked into the creek and stripped naked to wash himself and his clothes. After wringing them out, he went inside the barn. He climbed to the second level and carefully laid out his clothes, which would take two days to dry. A second set waited for him.

He did not have the opportunity to dress, for dusky Mademoiselle Gagneux had climbed the stairs.

She would end up taking care of needs for which he did not budget or think about at all.

Her name was Ciel and she was seventeen.

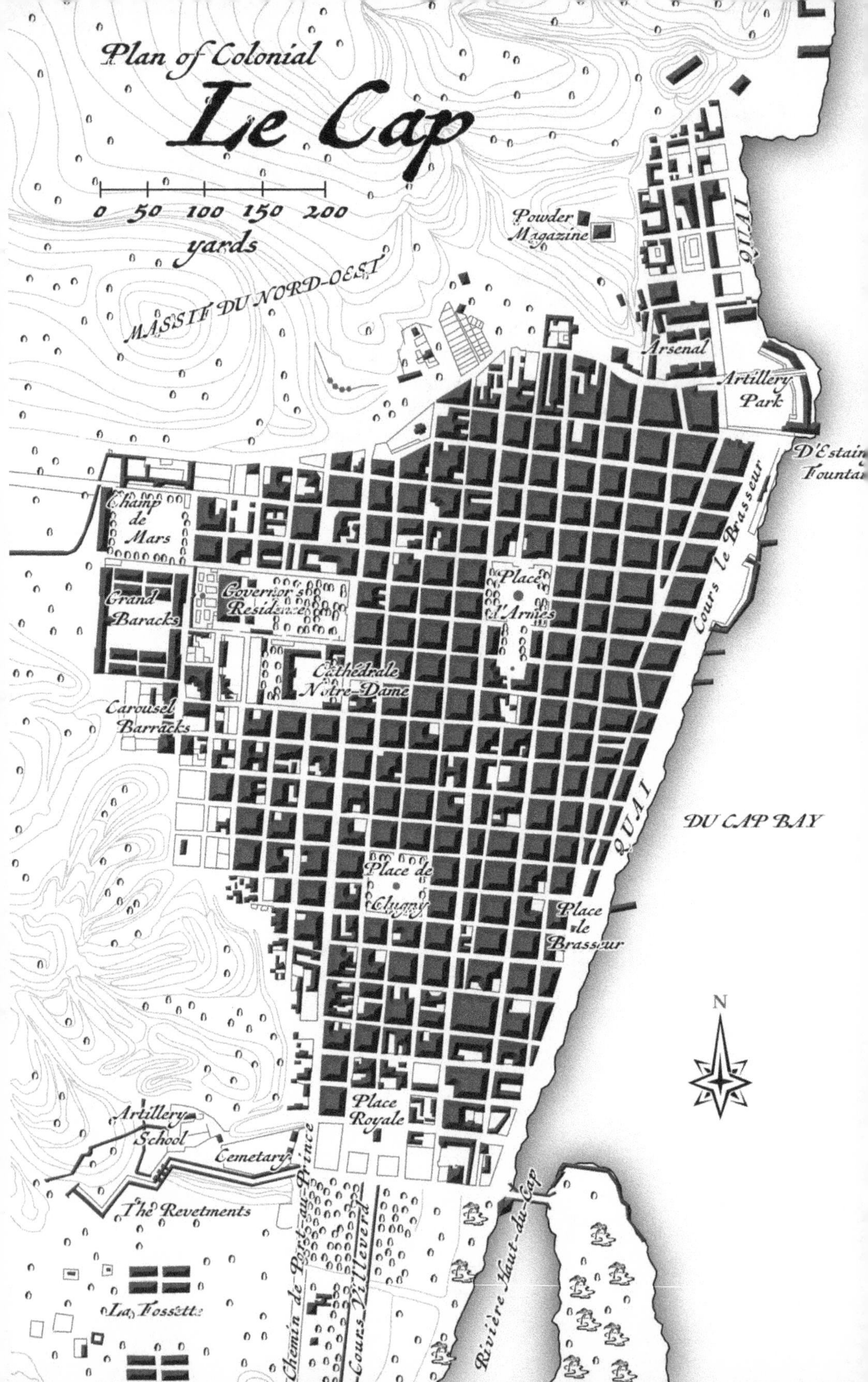
Plan of Colonial
Le Cap
0 50 100 150 200
yards
MASSIF DU NORD-OEST
Powder Magazine
QUAI
Arsenal
Artillery Park
D'Estain Fountai
Cours le Brasseur
Champ de Mars
Grand Baracks
Governor's Residence
Place d'Armes
Cathédrale Notre-Dame
Carousel Barracks
QUAI
DU CAP BAY
Place de Clugny
Place le Brasseur
N
Artillery School
Place Royale
Cemetary
The Revetments
Chemin de Port-au-Prince
Cours Villeverd
Rivière Haut-du-Cap
La Fossette

Chapter Seven

Haiti, 1832

Jake

The tavern keeper at *Fantom An Asasen* gave them an excellent lead. An ancient named Ou-La frequented a *crémas* at the intersection of Rue Ef and Rue Dizuit. Ou-La meant *You There* in *Kreyòl. Crémas* was a mixture of coconut, milk, spices and white rum, or a place that served it. Ou-La was a *bossale* ex-cane slave, the lowest caste in Haiti - African-born as opposed to *Caribe*, or American-born. Ou-La worked his way up to being an *Affranchis Commandeur*, a freeman overseer of slaves. He became a soldier but was retired by President-for-Life Jean-Pierre Boyer when he took over the entire island of Hispaniola and enforced a tyrannical peace.

Chests ditched in a foul, rented room at the inn, Jake was grateful he made the decision to keep nearly everything of value onboard the ship. He had his Haitian visa, some coin, and nothing more as they left for the city.

The uniforms of the police at the first street intersection were peacock proud but their muskets were rusted. Loud and kinetic, they studied Jake's paperwork upside down and sideways, and finally took a coin to let them pass.

It became quite crowded on the street. The wide avenues formed perfect squares of regular city blocks. The streets running north and south were lettered, east and west were numbered. As a matter of fact, *Ef* meant nothing more exotic than the letter *F* and *Dizuit* meant *Eighteen*. Half of the buildings were obviously new, perhaps even a higher ratio than that, and built around the same time. The older buildings were a testament to the French Colonial style: wide verandas encircled every floor - their ornate, wrought-iron railing wrapping the buildings like black ivy. Through brick archways were seen courtyards, arcades, and more cast-iron balconies. In the humid, hot air, one could still smell wealth, gentility and class.

The people of Haiti inherited this once-handsome place. It was built upon their own labors at a steep price of human suffering. Why then would it be so difficult to maintain what once was? In any case, all but memory was poverty. The people on the street were either furtive and wary or fatalistically stone-faced. Police were seen clustered in groups or not at all. Occasionally, a well-dressed, sharp-eyed man was seen amongst them.

"Don't look at that jack," whispered Brightly.

Jake turned away, "Why?"

"He *Tonton Macoute*."

"What's that?"

"Well, they ain't really named that. That's just what we call 'em. *Tonton Macoute* just mean like boogeyman or headless horseman or something. Man you scared of in the middle of the night."

"Very well. And what is he truly?"

"Whatchu call 'em?" Brightly thought about it. "He police who enforce the law without following no law hisself."

"Perhaps secret police, similar to those in Russia."

"I don't know about that. Let's just say more like the headless horseman."

Jake tried not to stare at them from that point onward but, truth be told, he couldn't help but peak when he could. They always seemed to be staring at him, even before he looked.

The tavern was near the Cathedral Plaza. The patrons sat outside enjoying the view, mostly under the veranda on old rickety café chairs circling small tables, smoking tobacco waste rolled in corn husks. As Jake and Brightly moved closer, a few of the men noticed and stood, smiles leaving their faces. The nearest, who was tall, young and strong, spoke with a tilt of his chin, "*Ki sa ou vle*?"

Brightly answered, "*Nou gade pou yon moun*."

"*Ki moun*?"

"Ou-La."

And with that, a short, older man wearing nothing but cut-off dungarees rose from a table in back and drew a long, thin machete.

Jake flipped a coin in his direction. Beautifully, it landed right on the man's table and drum-rolled to a stop.

Ou-La put away the machete, smiled and beckoned them over.

***

Crémas was sweet and tasty and spun heads like a top. Luckily, it was also cheap because Jake found himself paying for the entire bar. He didn't mind. It was the first time he relaxed since leaving the harbor. The customers were clustered around Ou-La's table, encircling Jake, Brightly, and the old timer. They listened intently and sometimes mumbled or nodded to each other. Whenever Jake's mug came anywhere close to empty, one of them filled it from a pitcher. Jake wasn't sure if the kind gesture was helping.

He hadn't found out much, except that in Haitian, people were called *negs* – which meant black. A white man was a *neg blan*, a black-white. That concept was only one grain of sand in a whole beach of words when it came to defining race. They had as many terms for different racial mixes as the French had for cooking techniques.

Ou-La could usually understand Jake in French, but Jake couldn't make heads or tails of Ou-La's reply in *Kreyòl*. Luckily, Brightly translated.

Jake leaned forward, "She would have been a young woman in '63. Quite young, indeed. She landed in mid-January. Irish-looking."

Ou-La spoke and Brightly turned to Jake, "He don't know no Irish from nothing."

"Black hair, pale or olive skin. Blue or green eyes. Perhaps freckles."

Brightly translated again, "He knew only few women who looked like that. He says some were *mambo asogwe*."

"What does that mean?"

"It devil-worshipping stuff. Like witches. *Asogwe*…like *powerful*. Powerful witches."

"She was introduced to a man named Féroce Guerrier by the captain."

Suddenly, the mood changed. There was a moment of silence, then a few talked back and forth with Ou-La. It was calm conversation, which didn't bode well - the Haitians were loudest when they were happy and friendly. "What is going on here, Brightly?"

"They know this jack. Everybody know him. He famous round here. He a legend."

"Tell them I'm no enemy of these people. If we met, they would help me."

Brightly spoke in *Kreyòl*, and the tension slowly eased from the air. Jake spoke again in French, "I was sent by the government of France to find out everything about them."

"Why them?" Brightly said for Ou-La.

"They had a necklace. A British captain stole it from a man named Priam-Paul Traversier. This girl, in turn, stole it back from the captain. It found its way to France and was lost again, or perhaps hidden. I have been sent to find it, or at least a clue to its whereabouts."

Now they all looked scared.

Ou-La, forlorn, threw up his hands and moaned something in *Kreyòl*. He stood and crossed to the wall and retrieved a carved and painted stick. All of the other men shook their heads and spoke amongst themselves. Ou-La sat down and spoke to the stick in a mournful tone. After a few minutes, he turned to Brightly.

Brightly translated, "He says you better be friends with Féroce Guerrier cause if that jack still alive, he kill you dead for a two-eyed stare. And yeah, your girl a *mambo asogwe*. Ou-La had to get his magic stick. He says there a *nummo* in that cane right there and now he's all right - he protected. Ou-La a little crazy, Mister Loring. Little crazy and a lot drunk. These old Haitians are devil-worshippers, all of them, just like in Africa. I mean, that's what they call it. *Sèvis lwa* – in service to the spirits. That's what they call it themselves, Mister Loring."

Jake's heart was pounding; Ou-La was turning into a gold mine of information.

Brightly translated again, "Guerrier one of the oldest families on this island. They all old *Boucanier*."

"What's a *Boucanier*?"

"He say *Boucanier* used to be all the folk on this island back in the day. They just big bands of folks out in the jungle, Arakowa injuns, blacks, French, Spanish. They just hunt swamp walrus and wild boar and anybody who mess with them. Eventually they joined the pirates and they all started sailing out and raiding everybody. When France took over this part of the island, some of the *Boucanier* helped out the *Grand Blancs*, being bosses and such. Folk descended from them old *Boucanier* don't get no sick out here, they immune to the island. Féroce, he magic, too."

"Magic?"

"From the day he born, everyone knew he had *mojo*."

"What's *mojo*?"

"It's like... you know how they put ball and powder in a musket and its ready to shoot?"

"Yes, of course."

"*Mojo* like ball and powder ready to shoot, but magic-style, like for a spell."

"So Féroce is a loaded magic pistol, ready to release a spell?"

"There you go. Ou-La say Féroce could turn into a wild boar in the jungle and track down any man. He used his powers during scuffles and he never lost a fight. His Mambo-wife made him move to the mountains, out there above Milot, because she was a *dlo sòsyè*, a water witch, and she could turn into an otter in cold water. She had a mountain lake that she put a spell on. But they came back to le Cap. Féroce went to war. Without his *mojo*, the Mambo die. She *blan-blan.* Her powers only work in the mountains."

"What does he know of the necklace, Brightly?"

Brightly asked in *Kreyòl*. Ou-La listened, then spoke, waving his hands and using exaggerated facial expressions. Brightly tried to translate as he went along, "He know. Everybody know. That necklace cursed, it's bad *mojo*. It alive, it can see and hear and have thoughts. He says it made the earth shake."

"Do they have earthquakes here? Is that what he's talking about?"

"Uh - he says they were trying to sell it, Féroce and the Mambo. It was for sure worth some money. The necklace got mad and killed Mambo first child who was *blan-blan* like she was. But they didn't listen. Féroce and Mambo-girl they went to Port-au-Prince try to get more coin. They gonna sell it and move to France. But the necklace punished them."

"When was this?"

"He say… like '70, thereabouts. They get to Port-Au-Prince and they going back and forth with this *Grand Blanc* name Louis Sabès."

"What's a *Grand Blanc*."

"Rich white man own lots of cane fields. The necklace done got mad again. It made the earth shake. It brought every building in Port-au-Prince to the ground, all the ones from Lake Miragoâne to Petit-Goâve. They knew it was magic because it even kick down the buildings that survived the quake in '54. He says a whole town near the coast done got sunk into the water. The necklace came down hard on Mambo and Féroce too. They had these *Mamelouk* twins-"

"What's a *Mamelouk*?"

"I dunno. Maybe someone who can pass. He say one twin killed by a falling building. The other killed by a huge wave that came outta the sea. They knew it was magic then too."

Jake's elation suddenly vanished. "They had more children, yes? Did they have any more children?"

Brightly listened and turned, "Yeah, they had other twins, boy and girl. Estelle and Guillaume. That's how they know it magic. Only *mambo asogwe* have two sets of twins."

"What did Estelle look like?"

Brightly listened, "*Blan-blan* skin, black hair wavy like sea weed, spots like a fawn on her face – ah, freckles. He means freckles."

Jake almost laughed. Estelle Guerrier had to be the girl in the painting, *The Mystery of Nantes*. Ou-La described her perfectly, and her looks were uncommon in France; she looked nothing like a Nantais.

Jake realized he knew that name. There was an odd blurb in an old newspaper. It was an announcement that Xavier was courting Estelle Guerrier. He remembered it because it was a strange thing to publish - a courtship was not binding, there was no need for an announcement.

He had found a real clue. No – two clues. When he went back to France, he had two more names to look for: Estelle and Guillaume Guerrier – if not three, Féroce.

Except he wasn't going back… was he?

"Mister Loring?"

Jake snapped out of it, "Yes, yes, Brightly."

"He wanna know if you got blood with the Mambo?"

Jake realized the crowd was staring at him intently. "Blood with the Mambo? Whatever does he mean?"

"Are you related?"

"No, no – of course not."

Ou-La spoke, quietly but strongly. Brightly turned, "He says before you find that necklace, you better find someone who got blood with the Mambo."

"I see."

Brightly listened, "There a *Bò madichon*, a big black magic curse on that necklace. Bad, bad *juju*. Only ones who can touch it gotta be blood of the Mambo or it punish you for a fool. He says that when Féroce left, off to find escaped slaves, off to war, it was just Mambo and the children in that house. When Mambo died, it was just the children. But ain't nobody even think about stealing that necklace. Even if Féroce wouldna track them down and kill them, the necklace would take its revenge first. No one woulda touched that necklace, even if they kids was starving."

Jake remembered words from another old drunk, far away in a jail cell in Londonderry. The mambo girl was properly Seonaidh Iníongael Ó Brollachain of the Ó Brollachain of Ards. For no fault of her own, she had been called a witch from the day she was born. The old Irishman said that if the Cross of Nantes was still known to man, it was in the possession of an Ó Brollachain of Ards and no other, by the prophesied will of God.

Just then, a cloud must have passed under the sun, for it was darker. Jake nodded at Ou-La, "I have heard your words before, months ago and far away."

Ou-La nodded and spoke. Brightly helped him, "He says you better get a *nummo* stick for protection - but you can't have his."

***

Brightly and Jake walked back to the harbor. It was getting toward late afternoon and the honest people of le Cap – and the police - were quickly finding their way to the safety of home and hearth. A different crowd was emerging, one more sinister. It was good they were headed back to the docks.

Brightly broke the silence first, "So you after that necklace."

"Yes, sir."

"Is all that stuff true?"

"Such as?"

"You know, the curse and all that."

"Well, I don't believe in curses. I'm not a superstitious man. I believe in rational explanations."

"So, you're not too smart. Or too smart for you own good."

Jake smiled, "To give you a better answer to your question, there have been some remarkable coincidences surrounding the necklace. It is actually well-known throughout France." *I should not have said that. I have told him too much already.*

"All France? Cause of all the coincidence?"

Not exactly. "Well, yes, I suppose."

"I think you crazy."

"Why?"

"Lemme ask you this – it in France, right? The necklace?"

"Yes, I believe so. It isn't here in Haiti, if that is what you are asking."

"All right. Good. Cause I don't want nothing to do with it. I'll help you, but I don't want to be within a hundred miles of that thing."

"You think its cursed?"

"It don't matter. Part of staying alive is not being in the wrong place at the wrong time. It ain't enough to not do nothing wrong. And if it cursed, it don't care if you're not superstitious. Bad *mojo* put the bad *juju* on you sure as sunrise."

"It's getting dark. Can we hire a cab?"

"Lordy, Mister Loring. Where you think you at?"

They turned down a seemingly empty avenue. They walked halfway down its length.

It wasn't empty. They were not alone.

Men were lounging against the walls, hidden by the pillars of the verandas. Jake and Brightly were too far down the block when they realized the men had peeled from the walls and were advancing on them from all directions. They were coordinated enough so that the men approaching them would force a stop at the exact moment the men from behind cut off their retreat.

Brightly turned and spoke one word, "Run."

With a swish of air and the patter of footsteps, he was suddenly gone.

Jake's eyes caught up with him. Brightly sprinted away at an incredible pace and soon disappeared from sight.

Jake had not moved. In spite of Brightly's prior words, it was not in Jake's character to simply flee. As the men surrounded him, he silently admonished himself. They were obviously villains of some sort. If he made it back to the docks wearing nothing but his undershirt, he would consider himself lucky. Jake didn't even have a pocketknife. How could he be so stupid? He vowed to never go about unarmed ever again.

The lead man - jet black, thin and muscular - drew a blade, "*Ki sa nou genyen isit la?*"

Jake shook his head. *Why didn't I run? What kind of fool am I?*

The man smiled. "*Lady Pè koupe lang ou?*" The other men laughed.

Jake heard a carriage. He hoped it was the police, but the men didn't look afraid, or even wary. It was probably their thief-boss. Jake would be placed in the carriage and abducted for ransom, or worse.

The man pointed at Jake with his knife, "*Wete tout rad ou yo.*"

Jake shook his head.

The man's face flashed with anger - soul deep and violent. The speed at which it appeared filled Jake with terrible fear. The man suddenly poked him with the knife. It was too fast to stop or avoid, but not strong enough to break the skin. "*Wete tout rad ou yo, neg blan!*"

The approaching carriage stopped next to them. To Jake's surprise, it was a large, elegant coach, the sort of model one would see in the tonier *arrondisements* of Paris. The windows were down but the interior was obscured by curtains of Chantilly lace. The driver and postillion were dressed in uniform, the riding footmen in livery stood on the backboards.

The driver spoke harshly to the man fronting Jake, who answered but was unimpressed. The conversation escalated into shouting. Soon the driver leveled a blunderbuss at the man. The postillion took out a huge dragoon's pistol and the footmen stepped to the ground brandishing Le Page pocket pistols.

The man in front of Jake rolled his eyes, spat, and walked away, purposely very slowly and leisurely. His mates followed in the same fashion.

The lace curtain of the coach window was moved to one side by an ebony cane. Jake saw the smiling face of a middle-aged *couleur* gentleman inside. "*Bon soir*, Monsieur," he said in perfect Parisian French.

Jake exhaled, "*Bon soir*, Monsieur. I'm afraid I was about to be in some distress. I am grateful and relieved that you arrived when you did."

"Of nothing, *mon ami*. But what finds a young Monsieur out and about at this hour?"

"Unfortunately, my prior errand ran late."

"Such things happen. It is not God's will that men be ambushed as penalty for late-running meetings, but such is the state of the world."

"Indeed, sir."

"But enough of this banter, Monsieur. Please." And with that, the footmen pulled out the stairs of the coach and opened the door. Jake stepped inside and found himself facing a couple: the man's presumed wife well-dressed and smelling pleasantly of lavender.

Jake bowed from a sit. "My name is Jake Loring. I am an American from Massachusetts but have been in Paris for my education."

"And where were you educated, Monsieur?"

"At Louis-le-Grand, Monsieur."

"Ah! I myself graduated from Lycée Saint-Clement!"

"I have walked past your school many a time, Monsieur."

"And I yours! What a treat to find myself in the company of a fellow Parisien! But where are my manners? I am Laurent Dubuclet and this is my wife, Ines."

Jake bowed again, "*Enchanté*, Madame."

Ines smiled, "Where are you staying, Monsieur?"

"At an inn by the harbor."

"I can think of no suitable inns by the harbor."

"I would agree, Madame."

"You will come to our home."

"I could not imagine imposing on you."

"You are not imposing in the slightest. We are already expecting a number of guests who are in from the country."

Monsieur gently tapped his knee with his cane, "I will hear no more protestations. We insist."

"Very well, Monsieur. I… I am actually very grateful."

Haiti, 1832

Chapter Eight

July, 1788

Jeannine

There were but few Helens in France who could force the sail of Greek triremes… and Jeannine Cœurfroid was surely one of them. The power of overwhelming sultriness cannot be overestimated. Beauty, the master smith, forged a blade of steel. It is a sword with a name – *Folly*, it is called; it has killed more men than plague.

Apart from her allure, a keen review of Jeannine's personality would produce only one adjective: *guarded*. She was hard to know, presenting such a formidable façade that she could appear superficial or even emotionless. But her walls did not protect a simpleton, nor even innocence, though according to the odd labels of man she could be considered pure. In reality, Jeannine was devilishly crafty and adventurous. She was highly competitive and found that she had boundless energy and perseverance for any kind of emotional or interpersonal conflict. She had secrets and told lies, and achieved hidden accomplishments of which she was quite proud.

She was a self-styled Freemason, although none of the Masonic brethren at the lodge knew it. She had found a hidden portal in her family chapel that led to a secret passage, ending at barred double-doors in the neighboring townhome. The doors led to the main lodge. She had long ago found a way to unbar the doors, sneak inside the lodge, then bar them again from outside so no one was the wiser. Doing this, she had rifled through the sanctuary and found a badge and, recently, a masonic apron. She felt she had a right to both – she had taken every oath of membership, at the same time as they were spoken to initiate others. Freemasons in other countries might meet once a month. She had listened in at every meeting, two every week, for years. French Freemasonry was different, in nearly all ways, especially philosophically. These were meetings of rebel minds; these men – and Jeannine – determined the future.

She attended tonight's meeting, sitting on the cold stones before the door, wearing her apron and badge, to hear Xavier Traversier speaking. His voice was deep and sonorous, and he was quite intelligent, although he spoke less and less at the meetings as time went on, and when he did speak, he was infinitely measured.

"My brothers, I have an announcement. I will not be attending meetings for some time."

Silence. "*Mon dieu*, Xavier. This is quite shocking."

"Still your hearts, my brothers. I am not leaving your fair company, *mes amis*. Rather, I am courting a young lady, and she is only available to me on the very days of our meetings. Indeed, the very hours."

The brothers wished him well and Godspeed. Soon the comments became ribald, then the subject was changed.

Jeannine pondered this. It was strange that his rendezvous schedule was exactly in accordance with the times of the mason meetings. Jeannine enjoyed mysteries, and she would solve this one as she had solved others.

In the Cœurfroid household, breakfast was little more than coffee and perhaps a croissant. Lunch was a languid two-hour affair. Dinner was nearly equal, but supper was light and was eaten quite late. Therefore, after her meeting, she was able to exit the family chapel – for her pretense was praying within it – and join her family and her companion for supper.

Estelle had been acting quite strange ever since she returned from her convalescence. Jeannine could not put her finger upon the cause of it. Tonight, the strangeness was upon her father as well. Jeannine and her mother usually despised each other and competed, but tonight they were one: both knew something was going on with Papa and Estelle, and it did not include them. Estelle's expression was especially bothersome. She possessed an aura of serene contentedness, an expression akin to a saint's statue or a queen pregnant with an heir.

Her father spoke softly to Estelle, "Congratulations, Mademoiselle."

She looked down and smiled, "Thank you, Monsieur."

Jeannine was almost unable to bear it.

Estelle spoke again, "Celebration is perhaps premature. We are not engaged, Monsieur."

Jeannine feigned her best and most excited smile, "Estelle, you must tell us what is going on right this instant!"

Madame's face twisted but she said nothing.

Papa looked at Estelle, then addressed the table, "This morning an announcement was published in *Les Annonces*. It seems there has begun an official courtship between Monsieur Traversier and one Mademoiselle Estelle Guerrier."

Jeannine found herself furious. She did not speak until she could hide her emotions completely, "You published a courtship announcement? Whatever for? There is no binding contract with a courtship."

Then another dark wave of thought washed over her.

Putain! She is courting Xavier Traversier.

Estelle looked embarrassed. "Being who I am, I thought it prudent to be as public as possible. I did not wish any misinterpretation of events if I was seen alone with Monsieur Traversier. I did not wish to jeopardize my employment nor the honor of this house."

Madame finally spoke, "If only others thought as you, Mademoiselle."

Estelle was shocked. Madame had never said anything positive in regard to her, or even *to* her, ever.

Jeannine, however, was not shocked. She knew the comment had nothing to do with Estelle, and everything to do with her. She decided to ignore her mother's veiled insult and did not turn from Estelle, "So… how did this happen? Did you have conversations with Monsieur while you were… you must have… what on earth happened?"

"Nothing, Jeannine. The doctor advised me to take walks at one point in my recovery. Madame was insistent that either Monsieur or herself accompany me. When people amble, they converse. It was utterly unplanned. There was no deceit in this, I assure you."

"It was most likely the dress," Jeannine thought out loud, "It was in the new fashion, exemplifying the Rousseauian ideal. He thought you were some kind of back-to-nature forest nymph, little knowing that I chose the outfit and you are actually Catholic as a mitre. I will take all the credit for your good fortune."

Jeannine had spoken in a light fashion, but what she felt was quite dark.

Estelle was fooled, "To be honest, I am uncomfortable with fashion. The Enlightenment styles are too fancy and the Rousseauian too simple. I am stuck in the middle, as I am with everything. However, I assure you, my sister, the first words out of my mouth regarded the truth of my station."

Jeannine was quiet for moment, "Oh, of course they were. I do not doubt you." In that moment, Jeannine had nothing but ferocious resentment. Estelle was her paid companion. Wondrous happenings were to be reserved for Jeannine, not her servant. She forced an innocent tone, "Are you then terminating your employment?"

"No, no, *mon chéri*. We are only meeting during your prayer times. You will never even see him or notice any change in our circumstance. And if we do not become engaged, things will go back to normal in their entirety."

Jeannine did not pray during her prayer times. She went inside the family chapel twice a week, but only to access the secret way to the mason lodge. Therefore, Estelle was only free during the meetings, hence Xavier's forced absence away from them.

Et voilà. My mystery is solved.

Jeannine pouted, "If you do not become engaged, you will go back to your walks and be struck by another carriage. With your luck, one belonging to Claude Villiaume."

"Claude Villiaume?" asked Estelle.

Monsieur answered, "A Parisian. He has a rather odd business. He uses posters to advertise the status of unmarried men and women, in an attempt to find suitable partners for them. For those who have no other recourse."

"So, a man or woman would come to Monsieur Villiaume, explain their status and situation, and he would… do what, exactly?" asked Estelle.

"Place them in advertisements."

"Advertisements?"

"Their image and bonafides on posters throughout the city."

"And if someone found them agreeable, act as matchmaker and chaperone?"

"Perhaps. Or simply a liaison."

"Liaison? How then is honor preserved? Or safety for that matter?"

"I do not know."

"How could a man make a living doing such a thing? Are there so many people without church, family and community?" Estelle wondered.

"In Paris, certainly. Circumstances change, in our time very rapidly. With our age has come a deluge of isolated individuals."

"I am perhaps the type of person who would benefit from Monsieur Villiaume's enterprise, but I believed myself to be quite different from most. Knowing what I do of alienation, it grieves me to know there are so many others in similar circumstance. I wonder, what has caused such a shift in the status of so many people?"

"Others share your questioning spirit – some even believe they have found dire answers. The peasants and nobles of Brittany are fighting against change, in the countryside all around us, as we speak. Well, let us not unduly criticize Brittany. There is unrest in Burgundy, Franche-Comté, Normandy, and in the south as well. But regardless of where the grumbling manifests in violence, it is folly. One cannot fight progress."

"Can we call it progress if it is something we desire to fight against?"

"Interesting point," Monsieur mused, "Let us simply call it change, if you will. One cannot fight change. It is inevitable. One must find new paths through unknown forests, sometimes several times in one life."

"Dark words, Monsieur."

"Not at all. Simply reality."

Jeannine barely heard the conversation she was so consumed in thought. In every way, she was Estelle's better. Yet Estelle's life progressed, and Jeannine was stuck. Papa tried to help her, but was thwarted by her controlling mother.

Still, Papa was hosting a ball – and the date charged ever closer. Jeannine believed the ball was actually for her, secretly in her honor since it was technically her debut. Madame would never allow such a celebrated event in her honor, never admit her child had become a woman, but her Papa had found a way around her. Jeannine resolved to be a captivating wonder at the ball, to change her fortunes forever - and steal back whatever fire had been taken from her. She could not possibly be outdone, especially by her own paid companion.

It was nothing against Estelle. Jeannine just didn't like to lose.

SPECTACLES.

ACADÉMIE ROYALE DE MUSIQUE. Dem. 30, la 16e repr de *Phèdre*, paroles de M. ***, musique de M. *le Moyne*; le Ballet de *la Chercheuse d'esprit*, par M. *Gardel* L.

THÉATRE FRANÇOIS. Auj. 29, *Andromaque*, Tragédie red mandée, dans laquelle l'Actrice nouvelle jouera le rôle d'*Andromaque*; & *le Mari retrouvé*, avec un Divertissement. Merc 31, la 1re représ. de *la fausse Inconstance*, Comédie en 5 acte en prose. En attendant la 3e des *deux Nieces*; la 21e d *Amours de Bayard*; & la 94e de *la folle Journée*.

THÉATRE ITALIEN. Auj. 29, *la Prévention vaincue*; & la représ. de *Richard Cœur-de-lion*. Dem. 30, *la Femme jalouse*; *Féodor & Lisinka*. En attendant la 2de représent. des *Deu* la 4e du *Mariage singulier*; la 10e de *l'Amitié à l'épreuve*; la 37e de *Nina*.

VARIÉTÉS, *au Palais royal*. Auj. 29, *le Dragon de Thionvill* *Esope à la Foire*; la 4e représ. de *la Loi de Jatab*, Comédie 1 acte; & *Gilles Ravisseur*. Dem. 30, la 39e représ. de *Gue ouverte*; & *le Revenant*. En attendant la 1re représ. de *la N aux aventures*, Comédie en 3 actes & en prose.

PETITS COMÉDIENS de S. A. S. Mgr le Comte *de Beaujolo* Auj 29, *l'Auteur à la mode*, Comédie en 2 actes, mêlée d'a riettes, la 3e représ. de *la Matinée du Jardin public*, Comédie e 1 acte; & *le Paysan à prétention*, Opéra bouffon en 1 acte.

GRANDS DANSEURS DU ROI. Auj. 29, la Danse de Corde *l'Enlevement d'Europe*, Pantomime en 5 actes, avec ses agrémens *le Paysan Seigneur*, Piece en 2 actes; *l'Oncle & le Neveu Ama teurs*, Comédie; *la Vigne d'Amour*, avec ses agrémens; & dan les entr'actes, différens Exercices par la Troupe royale de Londre & les autres Sauteurs.

AMBIGU-COMIQUE. Auj. 29, la 22e représ. des *Cornets d Dragées*; *Hurlubrelu*, Pieces en 1 acte; & *l'Héroïne Américaine* Pantomime en 3 actes.

L'Abonnement de ce Journal, *qui paroît tous les matins, est de* 30 liv *pour Paris &* 37 liv. 10 f. *pour la Prov. celui du* Journal général de France, *publié 3 fois la semaine*, 18 liv. *pour Paris &* 19 liv. 4 f. *pour la prov. & celui de la* Feuille du Marchand *une fois*, 7 liv. 4 f. *le tout port franc.* Le Bureau *est rue neuve S. Augustin.*

Chapter Nine

August, 1788

Beau-Brave

That morning, even Ciel's ministrations could not relax Beau-Brave. It had been a difficult night and today was important, a task for which he had planned and sacrificed.

Ciel's body moved against his under the straw. "You are the most interesting person I have ever known," she said.

Ciel herself was more compelling than her heritage would have hinted. Even so, at this moment, Beau-Brave didn't feel like talking to her. He rubbed her back instead and tried to think of nothing.

"You have been to so many different places. I have never even been to Paris - and I could walk there if I wished."

"You don't."

"I don't... I couldn't walk-?"

"You don't want to go to Paris. Especially on foot. And not in Autumn."

"Why?"

"The Autumn sickness."

"What is that?"

"Some call it malaria. It comes every year."

"Are you not afraid of it then?"

Beau-Brave snorted. "No. I am *Boucanier*."

She said nothing for a time. "I think I could be an interesting person too. If I was allowed to be."

Ahh, Rousseau. Even the peasant girls are individuals, capable of perfection, waiting for utopia.

She continued talking but Beau-Brave's mind had begun to wander.

Last night was a debacle.

First, he could barely focus on his work. Every day, more than ten different well-thought pamphlets were printed and distributed on the streets of Paris, coming from every point of view imaginable. Who knew who printed them? It could be agents of the King, agents of Philippe, Freemasons, Catholics, Protestants, Jansenists, followers of Rousseau and his Dionysian Nature God, ideologues of Monarchy or Socialism, or the not so ideologically driven who used advocacy to gain themselves coin or fame. He read them when he was too mentally exhausted to write, then soaked them for the papers and ink. The pamphlets were not only more numerous but were more strident and increasingly polarizing. It seemed half of Paris was ready to go to war to institute reforms regarding the Estates-General… and the other half ready to fight to prevent them.

Well, sixty-forty. Perhaps even eighty-twenty.

The current battlefield was over the composition of the Third Estate, which composed ninety-eight percent of the population. All three estates, however, would have equal power during the proceedings.

Not quite true.

The Third Estate would have *less* power, pound for pound.

Beau-Brave was angry nearly all the time. He couldn't understand how his ideological opponents could justify their political position. They had to be selfish, evil and power hungry, there really was no other explanation.

Needless to say, Beau-Brave and the rest of Paris were consumed with political passion. In addition, Beau-Brave was anxious regarding his plans and expenses. That was how he started his day: anxious and angry. It only got worse.

First was the pig. Illegally, swineherds in Paris sometimes let their livestock forage alone in the city at night, if the animals were big and mean enough to protect themselves… and smart enough to return. Beau-Brave had turned into an ally - and found he had inadvertently cut off a huge hog's escape route. The pig and mule became increasingly agitated as Beau-Brave tried to back the cart out of the ally. The pig could have won an easy victory over Beau-Brave and the mule, turned the cart into tinder, and left them both bleeding on the stones. Luckily, the mule cooperated and the pig trotted off to safety.

He was homicidally angry at the *bâtard* who had let his pigs forage through the streets, a sight that was becoming more and more common as people had difficulty feeding themselves, much less their animals. Fuming, he resumed his route through the Latin Quarter, minding his own business, working as fast as he could in an attempt to finish at a reasonable hour, when a group of well-dressed men his age passed by. One of them made a comment, something along the lines of Beau-Brave being a student who was kicked out of school who now had to shovel *merde*. Drunk, they all chimed in, laughing and hooting. Without thinking, Beau-Brave violently slung a shovelful of *merde* in a wide arc. He spattered most of them. There was a moment when they realized they were spattered, right before tempers flared and they all charged. Only one thing could stop the charge, and that was another shovelful of *merde* flung in their direction. They all jumped back, anger replaced by revulsion. Beau-Brave advanced on them, "I am not your mouse, little kittens! Come find trouble with me, I'll chop your head off with my shovel!"

"*Va te faire foutre*!" they yelled.

"*Va te faire enculer, fils de pute*!" Beau-Brave shouted back.

One of them charged forward and Beau-Brave swung with the shovel, the sharp, dirty edge missing his neck by a hair. The man stumbled back in fright. The rest shouted indignantly.

"Oh, so now you are civilized men? Mistreated by the *sans-culotte*, are we?"

A chorus of *you're just a this, you're just a that* came back.

Beau-Brave took a few quick steps to the nearest pile of *merde*, scooped and flung it with one action, scoring on many of them. They jumped back again, shouting, outraged. Beau-Brave screamed with blood lust, "Step forward into my shovel's blade! Let me see your pink insides, little girls!"

They walked away, yelling that he was a criminal and a madman, and they would get the police. Beau-Brave shouted back, taunting them, "Oh, first I was a failed student, then your victim, then your oppressor, and now I am a madman! When you talk to the Night Watch be sure to have your story straight. If not, you'll sound the drunken idiots you are!"

Beau-Brave seethed with rage, snarling as he shoveled, unable to calm himself. Then, of course, the Night Watch showed up, a fit man in a French Guard uniform on a white horse. "Monsieur," he said, "What exactly happened tonight?"

Beau-Brave humbly told him everything, but his anger returned. "I saw another pig roaming the streets. Had my mule not calmed, it could have killed me. It must have weighed six-hundred pounds."

"It is quite against the law to forage pigs in the city. I assure you, had I seen this, there would have been hell to pay. But that is neither here nor there. You swung at a young man with a shovel. You are lucky you didn't hurt anyone."

"I am a working man, Monsieur. They had no right to interfere with me."

"You are right, they were wrong. But when you started swinging the shovel…" The Officer shrugged his shoulders. "Had you gone to your corporation with the complaint, the Nightsoiler advocates would have scoured the Latin Quarter looking for these miscreants. Their school would have paid the advocates for their silence and disciplined the students themselves. You could have walked away with coin in your pocket and justice to boot."

"Yes, Monsieur, I see your point."

"That's why your corporation exists, to give you a voice, and equality before the law. Why not use it to benefit yourself, instead of this senseless behavior that will only get you into trouble?"

"You are right, Monsieur. I'm sorry. It won't happen again."

"Do not spill blood on my watch, *mon ami.* If you wonder what would happen to you, go to the Place de Grève during daylight hours. The sound of a neck snapping at the end of a rope will cure your desire for violence."

"I hear and obey, Monsieur. I will hurt no one."

The officer nodded and off he rode.

Beau-Brave felt very lucky. The outcome of such an encounter could have been much worse.

As Beau-Brave worked, his mind conjured up the taunting men and his blood would boil. His emotions seemed powerless over the incident.

Why?

Perhaps because they were who he should be – but wasn't. Beau-Brave had taken a left turn with his life, foregoing comfort, relationships and status in order to pursue a dream. In this moment he was a waste of all the resources and opportunities he had been given, utterly worthless, a wasted mind. The young men had simply driven the nail home on the point.

The young men… were right.

The drunks told him who he really was – right when he was on the verge of trying to become someone else.

Now Ciel wanted to talk.

Why did women always want to talk when he wished for silence? He supposed that was quite simple as well. He supposed it was unusual to wish for silence after intimacy, it would be more common to desire validation. Silence would imply a problem of temper or mood.

"Last night was wretched," he said.

"Tell me everything."

Salope!

"I almost found myself in a brawl."

"Why? What happened?"

More questions! "Nothing, really. There was a group of drunks who noticed I did not have the usual look of a Nightsoiler. They made witticisms and shouted insults. I lost my temper and swung my shovel at them."

"That is quite serious. You could have been arrested."

"I spoke with the police. Nothing will come of it."

She moved closer into him and rested her head on his chest. "I wish you would take me to Paris with you."

Merde! "Actually, it is a busy day for me. I must sleep, then go to the Palais-Royal."

"Is that where all the theaters are?"

"Several."

"I would love to see a play."

"I won't be seeing any plays."

"Then what will you be doing there?"

"I will only be learning of the world I wish to enter."

Silence.

She suddenly moved to a sit. "I will leave you to sleep." Ciel wordlessly put on her clothes, climbed down the ladder and was gone.

Was she angry?

Who knew? Who cared?

He had a long day ahead of him. He tried to sleep but it was difficult; He was exhausted, vexed, and excited at the same time.

When he woke, he dressed and walked into Paris.

***

The Palais-Royal was completely different at night. It was overrun by the corrupt, lowly and depraved. Suggestively-dressed prostitutes ditched all efforts at elegance, and came down to the courtyard en masse from their apartments on the second story. Besides the harlots, there were only men - drunken and rambunctious – soldiers, gamblers, thieves and debauchers.

Beau-Brave waited in the shadows near the Variétés-Amusantes. He was not bothered by anyone – indeed, most went out of their way to avoid him. It was chilly in the humid August air despite the season, which did not bode well for Winter.

The last show at the Variétés had finished quite a while ago. He could barely hear the host of carriages and conversation on the other side of the palace through the entrances into the courtyard.

Soon there was naught but silence.

The invisible door in the theater wall then opened. Men and women, actors, entourage, producers and technicians exited in a sudden cacophony of laughter and conversation. All were boisterous and excited, giddy from the performance and the company of wealthy or beautiful admirers. Beau-Brave did not stand a chance of monopolizing any of them. He waited like a leopard for the perfect opportunity to pounce.

Then he saw his prey.

He walked alone in the group. In the semi-darkness, he appeared a hard-looking man, pale with brown hair, serious and businesslike as he quickly walked away from the theater.

Beau-Brave moved from the shadows, "Monsieur, a moment of your time."

The man looked right and left, as if expecting an ambush. He turned to Beau-Brave but kept walking with the group, "Get away from me! I don't know you!"

"I am an aspiring playwright, Monsieur, yet I know nothing of the business of the theater. My pouch is full of coin this night, for no other purpose than to wine and dine a man of the stage and glean as much information as I can in the process."

The man gave Beau-Brave a hard stare. "Show me."

Beau-Brave held up his pouch so only the man could see it.

A hungry look came into his eyes. "They could all be copper."

"Some are, not all."

"Is there enough for me to eat and drink my fill at Le Grand Véfour?"

"I'm not familiar with the establishment, Monsieur."

The man looked annoyed, "Right behind you! By the Beaujolais. The sign still says Café de Chartres, but it's actually Le Grand Véfour."

"Yes, of course. Are you game then?"

"I will eat and drink my fill?"

"As you wish."

"Then lead on."

Beau-Brave turned and walked toward the Beaujolais. He had fifty livres in his pouch. The sum represented two-hundred cartloads of *merde*. The night might easily set him back the lot.

***

Le Grand Véfour was opulent, even by the standards of the Palais-Royal. The outside walls were set with gigantic windows. The interior was framed in equally titanic mirrors, and what did not reflect was then ornamented gilt, frescoes and paintings. Even the devious Philippe would not feel he was condescending had he found himself at a table, which he probably had.

The actor, one Monsieur Sitbon, had his back to a red velvet booth and Beau-Brave sat in a gilt chair across a brilliant white tablecloth. Sitbon had started the evening with a bottle of Champagne and, per the waiter, "Duck *foie gras* raviolis in a truffle emulsion cream sprinkled with caviar." It looked divine and the smell was even more enticing. Beau-Brave wasn't eating and was now so hungry he felt death would be a fitting release.

Sitbon was at ease, eating and drinking as he talked, as if this strange rendezvous was a common occurrence. "Have you seen the poster bills for the theater?"

"Yes."

"So, the poster tells the story. At the top are the three Royal monopolies: the Académie Royale de Musique, the Comédie-Française and the Théâtre-Italien. The Académie performs operas. They are also on the cutting edge of dance, especially ballet. Anyone who tells you the so-called Académie Royale de Danse has anything to do with the progress of art is a simpleton. They do *merde*."

"I see."

"The Française and the Italien are stages for any kind of tragedy or comedy in French, although the Italien used to be Italian-style comedy in Italian. That floated like hot lead shot. Really, the name doesn't matter – sometimes it even changes, usually with the moving of venue. It is the monopoly license, the company of players, dancers, musicians, tradesmen and administrators who go by those names who have shares in the profits. I am in the company of the Variétés. The theater burns down, we move somewhere else, change our name and move on."

What an unimportant, esoteric point. "I understand."

Interrupting, the staff of waiters surrounded Monsieur Sitbon, placing in front of him, "Deboned pigeon stuffed with *foie gras*, black truffles, and veal forcemeat," - along with another unannounced basket of assorted bread and another bottle of Champagne. Beau-Brave could stand it no longer. He casually reached out and took a chunk of bread and slathered it with butter. Sitbon didn't seem to mind.

Sitbon continued. "So, those three companies are the Royal Monopoly. All of us despise the Royal Companies - while secretly wishing to be part of them, of course."

"What does a monopoly mean in this context?"

"They are controlled directly by nobles of the court. They are the only theaters able to perform anything."

"Wait… how can that be? You yourself are part of another theater. Is it because you are in the Palais-Royal?"

"No. All amusements, of any kind, only perform with the permission and license of the Royal Theaters, which will sometimes give a monopoly for a specific type of entertainment, usually when they believe it is beneath them. The Royal Companies, of course, never give permission for a venue to compete with them. In fact, they can simply take competing material and perform it themselves and there is nothing anyone can do about it."

"Are you serious, Monsieur?"

"Quite."

"They can simply take anything they want?"

"Well, I mean, they pay for the material if they use it, but the original theater is certainly out of luck."

"So, the Royal theaters, the three, they are at the top and everyone else must pay them to do anything else – and they decide what you can and cannot do?"

"Exactly. The monopolies allow fifteen theaters in Paris, total, with most of them on the Boulevard. None of them are allowed to perform full-length operas, comedies, or tragedies. Mostly they are variety shows built around something resembling a full-length farce, melodrama, or Restif de Bretonne, or perhaps some shorter plays that resemble something the Royals would put on. Or a play that the Royals did put on that is surgically butchered. Non-Royals keep to material the monopoly will not steal."

"What is Restif de Bretonne?"

"Who and what, to be precise. He's a playwright. A Socialist and a moralist. He writes stories about the corruption of modern society. Stories about lads and lasses from the provinces coming to Paris and being destroyed by temptation, poverty, or the devious who take advantage of them. It is pornography under the guise of moralization, feeding some base desire to witness corruption and seediness. Whatever imitates his work is called by his name."

Beau-Brave snorted. "No lack of material there, I'm sure."

His mirth was interrupted by an army of waiters. Soon Sitbon faced, "Araguani milk chocolate mousse on a hazelnut pastry with caramel ice cream and a sprinkle of Guerande sea salt." Last came a generous glass of Sauterne.

Beau-Brave shook his head. "A frozen dish! In this season? How is such a thing possible?"

"I don't know. I don't care. So, on the poster, at the top, we have the three Royal Monopolies. There is a thick dividing line then, just below it, we see the program for the Palais Royal theaters, the Variétés-Amusantes and the Beaujolais. Neither are Royal monopoly theaters, obviously, but because of the popularity of the Palais Royal, they are billed second. After the theaters of the Palais Royal come the theaters of the Boulevard."

"Boulevard, boulevard. Which boulevard?"

"Boulevard du Temple. But no one calls it that. It is either the Boulevard or the Boulevard du Crime."

"Du Crime?"

"So named because of the duplicitous characters in the melodramas."

"I understand."

"The posters neglect most of the Boulevard. At most, they will list the programs of the Grand Danseurs du Roi and the Ambigu-Comique, two theaters almost guaranteed to still be there at show time."

"Du Roi?"

"Yes, a King – forget which - came and watched a show there. They promptly changed their name. They are not a Royal Theater, not in the slightest. They angle for respectability."

Beau-Brave snorted.

Sitbon raised his empty glass and it was promptly filled. He took a sip, raised a finger and began again, "The Danseurs have some of the best actors, rope dancers, acrobats and stage dancers in the world. They really put on a show. Even what you would consider their drama pieces aren't half-bad. Jean-Baptiste Nicolet runs the Danseurs. He's a real character. Grew up in the theater. Crazy as a sewer rat – but twice as clever. At least in business. All about the coin, a whore to his bones. The other theater, the Comique, mostly puts on pantomimes, spectacles, marionettes. Sometimes they use child-performers and acrobats, Vaudeville. Occasionally dramas, crime stories, exposés of sexual peccadilloes, whatever. In any case, a huge tax is levied on the theaters to fund the hospitals – and the police are always pressing the hospitals to expand to accommodate the poor, forcing the hospitals to raise their tax on the theater. For the successful, there are fortunes to be made, but it is a harrowing business, I assure you."

"Between the tax and the license, I can understand."

"Nicolet pays twenty-four-thousand to the Académie Royale for the Danseur license. It is rumored that his poor tax for the hospitals will be nearly seventy-thousand this year."

Ninety-thousand out the door before they make a livre!

"How much are tickets?"

"The cheapest are a few sous."

"How on earth do they make any money at all?"

"Those are not the only expenses. They must – must – have police on hand, in addition to their own guards and ushers. There are the performers and musicians, props, sets, upkeep on the theater, lighting, author payments. The total budget of the Danseurs is perhaps two-hundred-ninety-thousand."

Beau-Brave was stunned.

Sitbon shrugged. "Of course, they made nearly ten-thousand profit. Ten-thousand livre in Nicolet's pocket, after drawing a salary. I would take it. Who wouldn't?"

Beau-Brave was quiet for a moment. "You keep saying pantomime. I have an image in my mind of what it could be but, in reality, I have no idea. What's exactly is a pantomime?"

"A story told with everything but words. Crashing music, actors using grand expressions, dancers, whatever, all coming together to tell a story just as complex and cogent as a normal theater play."

"*Mon dieu*, it sounds as if whole new art forms have been created to simply dodge the monopoly."

"Precisely true."

"You said there were other theaters?"

"Fifteen. The Délassements-Comiques, Théâtre des Associés, Théâtre des Élèves. But in Paris, we are looking out a coach window at a changing landscape. Things are not so rosy for the theater as they once were. There has been an explosion in the variety of amusements, fueled by technology and innovation, and now there is plenty of competition. It seems the audience is hungry for something different."

"But all venues of any sort purchase license?"

"Yes."

"What sort of other licenses have been granted?"

"There are the fairs, a kind of public place usually centered around some kind of activity or amusement."

"Such as?"

"Astley's Anglais, which is a circus with performing animals, especially horses. There is the Wauxhall d'Hiver, a dedicated hall for dance – the Panthéon is another dancehall. There is the Redoute Chinois, a pleasure ground in Asian theme, with restaurants, cafés, games and spectacles. Other fairs specialize in dwarf shows, fireworks, physics and mechanical exhibitions, waterworks, optical shows, sports tournaments, marionettes, child actors. Technically, all of these are one of a kind, for they are all licensed by the monopoly. If two sound to the ear alike, a clever advocate came up with a good angle. On the boulevard, side by side with the theaters, there are all manner of cabarets and cafés as well. The street itself is choked with performers and street theater. They say twenty-thousand people a day go to the Boulevard."

"So, the monopoly has nothing to do with popularity?"

"I don't understand the question."

"As you said. The monopoly theaters do not seem as popular as everything else."

Sitbon shrugged. "It's difficult to say. The monopoly theaters have access to the best material and the best actors. Everyone else gets by with scraps and skits. Most actors, Royal or otherwise, are half-starved. But make no mistake, a lead actress for Nicolet is a rich woman, but the true stars are with the Royals. Although half cannot live within their means and die poor as peasants, if we are exposing hard truths to light."

"So how does one become a playwright?"

"One doesn't." The glass went up again and, moments later, came down full.

Foutre la merde! Could this end up being more than fifty livres? Is that possible? How on earth can anyone afford this?

"What do you mean?" asked Beau-Brave with gritted teeth.

"When you say playwright, I assume you are talking of high drama – tragedy, comedy, librettos for opera and so on."

"Let us say yes."

"All right then. So, we are speaking of the three Royals. They have at their disposal the library of the ages. Why would they put on a play written by some anonymous jack when they can perform Voltaire, Racine or Corneille? Molière alone has some thirty-six major works. Everyone has heard of Molière. No one has heard of you. Your name rents no seats."

"What if the play is well-written?"

"When have I ever spoken of well-written in this conversation?" Sitbon said evenly.

"But Molière became a legend because he was a good writer. If one keeps performing his plays exclusively, the next Molière will go unnoticed. There will be no artistic progress, no change."

Sitbon's face lost all expression. "No. The next Molière will kill, whore and starve to be the next Molière, and the world has yet to find the power to stop such a man. And if an artist is less than Molière, why then would the world care at all?"

"So, if you were to address this next Molière, this starving killer-whore, where would you tell him to start?"

"With Nicolet at the Grand Danseurs. They perform a million skits a day. They are absolutely desperate for content."

"For skits?"

"Yes."

"That is not being a playwright."

"Well, I am sorry to offend your dainty sensibilities. Be glad you are not an actress."

"Why?"

"Because their first purpose is to perform with their backs on satin. A distant second is to perform with feet on wood. Theaters are whorehouses, make no mistake. Metaphorically for some, literally for others."

"I suppose the trick is finding an actress who is good at both, so as not to embarrass the play or reduce profits."

"No one asks playwrights for horizontal crafts - usually. Be glad of it."

"This is a devil's business."

"Is that then news to you?"

"So, I become a skit writer for Nicolet?"

A coffee service with chocolate was placed before Sitbon – thankfully the last course. "In your wildest dreams. But, perchance, if you do, make friends and contacts in the world of the stage. Perhaps you will find someone rich who takes a liking to you, without seeing you as his mistress, if you are lucky."

"Are such perversions common in the theater?"

"The celebration of deviance and the need for coin frequently do battle in the world of the theater, occasioned by opposing forces of ego and greed."

Beau-Brave chortled. "I see."

"One of the greatest actresses of our generation, Mademoiselle Raucourt, walks around in men's clothing with her companion, the infamously perverse German, Madame Souck. They are both utterly depraved and their behavior in public shocks the city. Let me tell you: with this generation, that is not an easy feat. Cracks appear in the plaster of fame as the audience tires of their antics."

"Is it gossip that spreads the rumors?"

"Newspapers. Pamphlets. Whatever."

"One would think they had more pressing facts to impart."

"Not the case."

"Is there anyone of mundane tastes in this pursuit, I wonder?"

"There are only those who kill, whore and starve for celebrity and gold. Their tastes come with them."

"You are amongst this group, are you not?"

"Are you not?" Sitbon calmly shot back.

"So, I give samples of little, worthless skits to Nicolet and he hires me?"

"No, he buys the little worthless skits from you, at least the ones he wants. If he desires none, you starve."

"And then?"

"Learn. As you do here with me. As I am finishing my supper, I will tell you one thing more. Nicolet will know the quality of your work from a glance. Make sure you familiarize yourself with the form and style of writing utilized at the Danseurs. Ensure your work is of the absolute highest quality. You may get an opportunity to hand him something. If you manage to do this, you will have one shot at your target. He will not give you another. He has no time to train writers, no one does, no one really cares. You are a necessary evil and, if the play is not well-known, sometimes the actors will play their own tune with the writing anyway. Nicolet would rather spend time with his willing actresses or a bottle from his cellar, I assure you, or finding more of either to add to his collection. Or perhaps spending some rare time with his wife and children. Anything but execrable reading. Anything but talking to accursed writers."

"Grim words."

"When you look up at the night sky, you are dazzled by stars. But if you are wise, realize all of them are surrounded by darkness."

"Meaning?"

"Meaning it isn't enough to love the craft. One must realize the realities of the business of the craft. Milliners don't just ache to design hats, they have embraced the fact that something involved in their craft - evaporated mercury, glue, whatever – will eventually drive them insane, and they are sanguine regarding their future as mad hatters. Anyone involved in theater must be the same way. Embrace the shadow, for there is nothing else."

And, with that, Sitbon got up and left, never even knowing the name of his culinary benefactor. Beau-Brave never saw him again.

The supper came to forty-nine livres and eight-sous, more than his annual rent and a veritable mountain of *merde*.

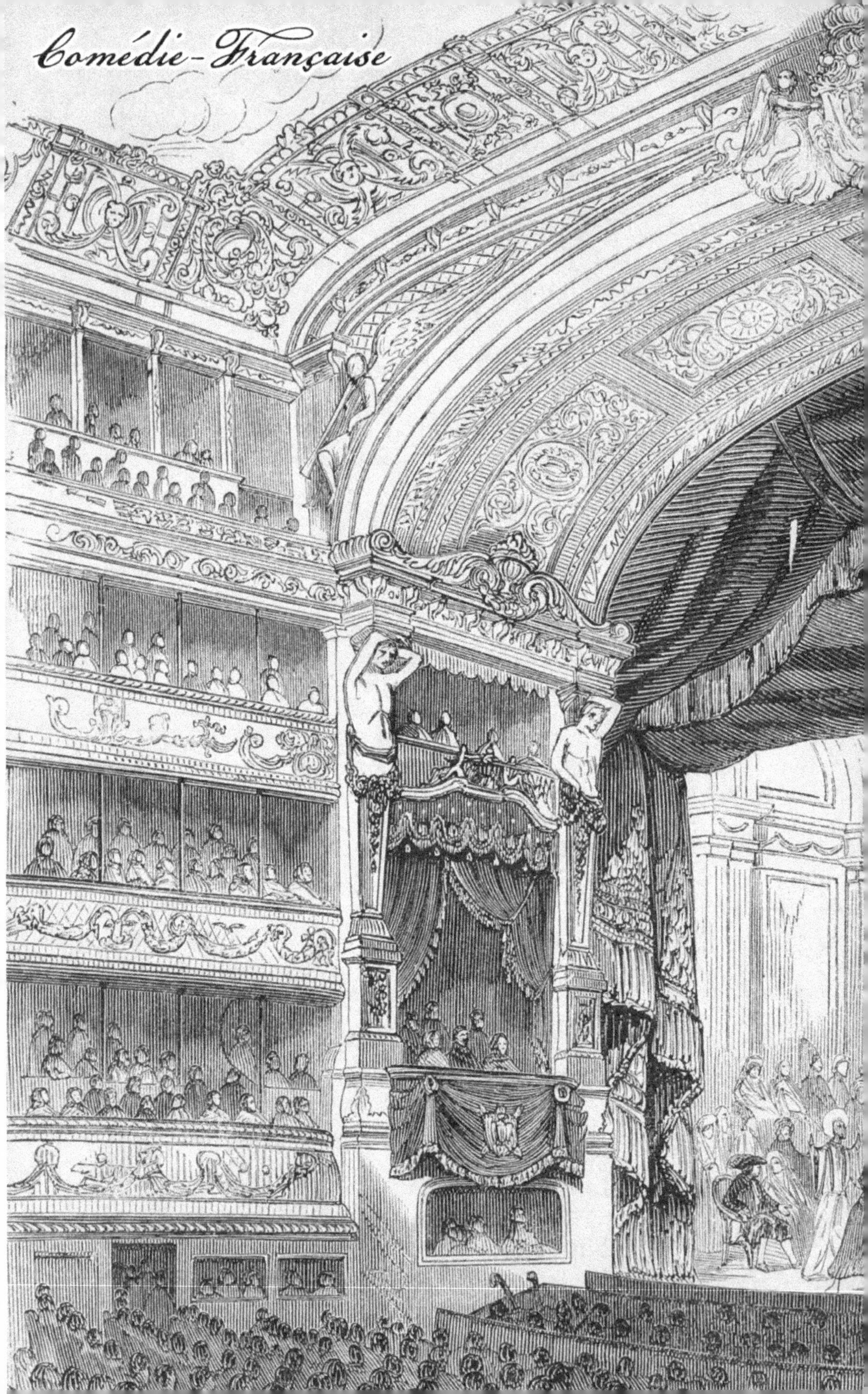
Comédie-Française

Chapter Ten

August, 1788

Estelle and Xavier

Estelle waited in the foyer.

She had never spent so much time dressing in her entire life. Darcy and Questa, the lady's maids, joyfully fussed and fretted over her for a full two hours. Now she stood before the front door, shifting weight from foot to foot to relieve her position and expend her built up energy.

Madame entered the foyer.

Downcast, Estelle bowed to her. Madame was the last person she wished to interact with in this moment. She was in a good mood and didn't want to be berated or insulted.

Unexpectedly, Madame smiled. "A woman should never wait for her escort in the foyer, Mademoiselle. Come with me to the salon. We will receive Monsieur Traversier there, as is custom."

Estelle was shocked. They were the first kind words that Madame had ever spoken to her. She nearly teared in thankfulness.

Madame took her to the salon, a large, high-ceilinged reception chamber, and played Brelan with her, wagering chess pieces instead of coins. The game required a great deal of bluff and bluster, and they played up their make-believe drama to drain the tension from the circumstance of waiting. As they laughed and joked, Estelle could not but think that Madame was entirely pleasant.

It made her sad in a way: If someone was entirely unpleasant but had the ability to be endearing, what then made them unpleasant? Were the circumstances of Madame's life so unbearable? Were there unseen problems or issues that weighed on her? Estelle resolved to forgive her of all slights and place her blessing upon her.

Before long there was a knock on the door and tall Thomas, the *valet de pied*, entered the room and bowed. "Monsieur Traversier has arrived, Mesdames."

"Show him in, Thomas."

Thomas bowed and exited the room.

Madame turned to Estelle and smiled, "Calm your nerves, Estelle. Self-respecting Frenchwomen must be sanguine within the realm of suitors and courtship. We are in command of this army, *n'est-ce pas*?"

Estelle took a deep breath. "As you will, Madame."

Xavier soon entered and bowed. His focus was on Estelle, and his gaze took her breath away.

Madame made a sound. Estelle turned and realized Madame was standing. Estelle quickly rose and they both curtsied. A strange look appeared on Xavier's face. "Forgive me. This home has many memories. I think perhaps this moment will become the image I will cherish above all others."

***

The coach traveled west from Centre-Ville and exited the Port au Vin.

Before it did, Xavier spoke, "I am honored by your presence. Thank you."

Estelle looked back at him and they locked eyes. As they continued in such a way, neither became bored or felt awkward. They did not need to speak to be content in each other's presence.

The theater itself was beautiful, new, and gleaming. It was part of the master plan of the powerful Farmer-General of Nantes, Jean-Joseph-Louis Graslin, to develop the area just outside the Port au Vin in the southwestern faubourgs of Nantes. The Théâtre Graslin was the centerpiece of development, aimed at selling the estates nearby. It was within walking distance of the Meilleur, just north and east of the Capuchin convent and its beautiful trees and gardens, and was a wonder of white and grey Tuffeau limestone, done in the Roman style with pillars, architrave, frieze, and pediments.

They descended from the coach to white cobblestones quarried from Gigant and continued up the stairs. Xavier was hailed every few steps by friends and associates before they entered the magnificent foyer, and ascended the stairs to the lounge, where was located the hallways leading to the balconies. The space was loud and packed with well-dressed patrons. There was something quite fantastic about the scene. Although fashion was changing, styles were still very much in the era of the Enlightenment; man displayed his hope for a utopian future with a stylized outward appearance, illustrating the height of civilization and human perfection. The women bathed in perfume and the men in cologne. It was a citrus forest, giving off scent from warm-blooded, silken branches.

Estelle was introduced to a hailstorm of luminaries, starting with the Mayor of Nantes, Pierre Richard, who looked unwell, and his wife. Monsieur Graslin himself was a slender, well-built man with a chiseled face, who spoke clearly and fast, as if his dialog was rehearsed. His few words with Xavier regarding high finance lost Estelle in moments. One Monsieur Bouteiller was old, corpulent and white-haired, and his wife looked quite bored. Monsieur exchanged pleasantries with Xavier before pulling him in close and whispering in his ear. Xavier replied with a smile, "I do not think so. I have no interest in politics. Versailles is a long coach ride from Paris, much less Nantes." There were others. Monsieur Olivier, a tall man the age of Monsieur Cœurfroid, who exclaimed Xavier's praises while compulsively touching him about the shoulders. He had the loud gracelessness of a confident and successful man who had not one iota of savoir-faire - and no self-awareness to ever gain a grain of it.

A bell sounded. With smiles, and amidst an air of expectation, everyone moved to their seats.

Estelle thought upon her night so far. She judged herself a fairly good imposter. She was dressed appropriately due to the generosity of her benefactors. She had been taught manners by her father, who rightly considered them to be necessary for advancement, and therefore she was able to speak in the manner of her fellow audience members. She was acquainted with Le Cap, and the accoutrements of wealth and class were not unknown to her. Here everyone was quite pleasant in the main, which made things much easier. Perhaps because of this she did not feel out of place. Behind satin, wigs and makeup, they were just people. It seemed they were more intelligent people on average than what she was used to, but that was not to say there were not intelligent bourgeois or even peasants. The theater-goers were well-mannered in the vast majority, and perhaps peasants, in the majority, held to simpler ways. The crowd was more cultured and worldlier, but that was only their perspective.

Estelle finally turned to Xavier, "What an interesting world."

"Indeed."

"I appreciate your escort. Everyone has been quite pleasant, but without your knowledge of theater etiquette, I think I would be quite lost. You have made this quite a pleasant experience for me."

"I have never been to the theater."

"Ever, or simply not to the Graslin?"

"Ever."

Estelle laughed, despite herself. "You appear for all the world to have attended the theater twice weekly for your entire life."

"As do you, Mademoiselle."

They smiled at each other, understanding.

Their box was closest to the stage and just above the floor seats. They sat on the plush cushions of their *fauteuil néoclassique*, and a moment later the curtain opened.

Estelle drew in a breath. The stage was huge and magnificently decorated – the actors dressed in even greater finery than their audience. Then it began - *Le Bourgeois Gentilhomme*, a *comédie-ballet*, a play with interludes of dance and music. The words were written by the master Molière, the music by famed Lully, and the choreography by Beauchamp.

Estelle was transfixed. She had never seen anything like this.

The play regarded one Monsieur Jourdain. Monsieur, the son of a cloth merchant, had dreams of becoming an aristocrat. A penniless nobleman named Durante flatters Jourdain, in an attempt to get him to pay his own creditors. As Jourdain unsuccessfully and comically attempts to refine himself through lessons and tutoring, his aspirations for himself and his family grow ever higher. Finally, convinced she could do better, he forbids his daughter Lucille to marry her bourgeois lover, Cléonte. By hilariously impersonating a Turkish sultan, Cléonte finally gets permission to marry Lucille. Nearly every character was skewered by eloquent wit and humor, all except the ones who truly loved each other.

And then it was over.

Estelle cheered the performers with abandon. Soon the stage was clear and the chairs below them began to empty. It was odd to see such a large space vacant and devoid of the high magic that, only moments ago, had filled it to capacity - overflowed it really, a sorcery of wondrous enlargement. But the power of such a spell did not dissipate as quickly. It permeated the air, the furniture, the building itself. No, the magic was not gone. Estelle guessed rightly that theaters were ever possessed of some special dwimmer deep in their bricks, enchanted by the plays performed there.

She turned to Xavier, "Thank you."

Xavier could not reply. He had never heard two words possessed of such sincere emotion.

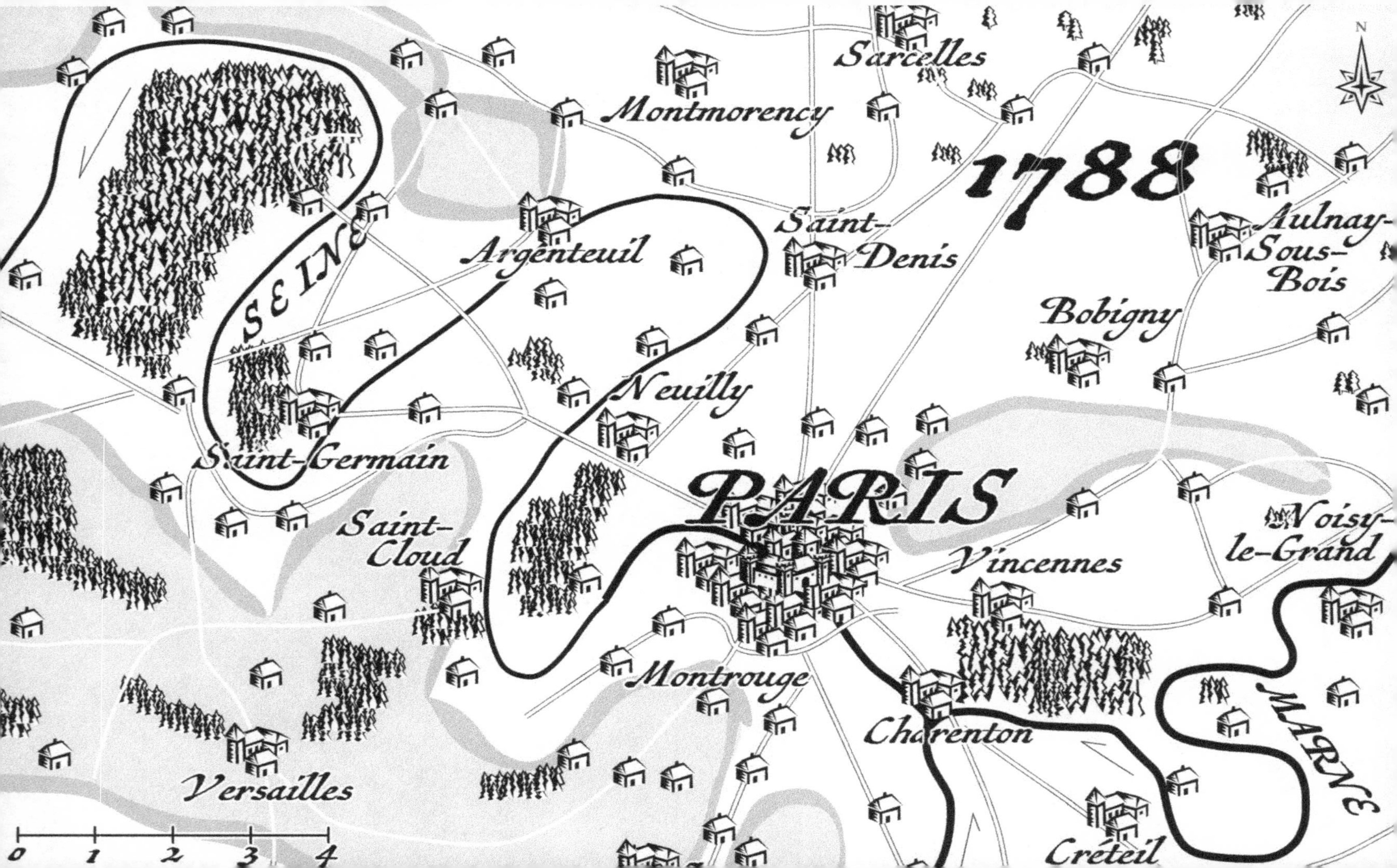

N
1788
Sarcelles
Montmorency
Saint-Denis
Aulnay-Sous-Bois
Bobigny
Argenteuil
SEINE
Neuilly
Saint-Germain
PARIS
Saint-Cloud
Voisy-le-Grand
Vincennes
Montrouge
Charenton
MARNE
Versailles
Créteil
0
1
2
3
4

Chapter Eleven

September, 1788

Beau-Brave

"I don't understand why you need to be so cruel to me," Ciel said softly, "What have I done to you that is so odious you find the need to punish me?"

She continued talking, but Beau-Brave could not bother to put the words together in his mind. It was sound, a brook babbling through stony shallows.

His mind was completely occupied.

After much rumination regarding his talk with Sitbon, Beau-Brave had decided that the best way to get his work to Nicolet was to mail it to him, with a polite letter thanking him for his time. He had done his research in regard to the form and custom of the writing at the Danseurs. His ally in this was the sinister Palais Royal book store owner of the unimaginatively-named *Palais Livre*, whose name was Monsieur Marmont. Beau-Brave explained his need and received his reply, "Of course, Beau-Brave of Grenoble. I can procure anything written – anything – regarding any subject. In fact, I have the complete works of the Marquis de Sade, smuggled from the Bastille and transcribed, if you are interested."

However perversely vectored, Marmont was as good as his word; Beau-Brave soon had a number of torn and discarded scripts of Danseur skits and pantomimes. The format was intuitive and simple. Beau-Brave wrote twenty skits and two pantomimes. In the end, he mailed only three short skits. Nicolet would only have to spend a few minutes perusing the contents to formulate an idea of his capabilities.

He sent the package nearly two months ago and had not received a reply of any sort.

Every second therefore passed as an eternity of suffering.

Physical symptoms started within days of sending the letter. Beau-Brave's blood hammered against his temples. His head felt lighter than the rest of his body and disconnected from his senses. Thoughts pounded in his head, far harder and faster than even his boiling blood. Every word he sent to Nicolet was analyzed over and over in his mind. He imagined the emotional journey that a reader would take as they read, what they thought, what their reaction would be. He cursed newfound mistakes he realized he had submitted and could not correct, became elated when he realized he had made the right decision, to be followed by shame, depression, and anxiety when he realized that perhaps his former instincts were right.

It was nearly impossible to create new material in such a state. He began to realize how much he relied on his writing to get him through each day. Without it, he was tortured further.

It did not help that the weather had changed. It was nowhere near Winter, yet it snowed nearly every night. It was a light snow, and never lasted past dawn, but it presaged an early and savage Winter. Suffering would be branded on the people with cold, blue flames. The rivers would freeze, preventing food transport and shutting down the mills for grinding flour. Animals would die. The harvest would be late and paltry. Prices would skyrocket. People would go mad. Agents would scramble for foreign crops, paying for what would arrive moldy and weevilled.

If the Winter was especially bad, the wheat planted in the Spring wouldn't grow at all. That had happened before. If it happened again, only God knew the scope of suffering.

The mood on the street was dismal. Everyone saw it coming. Everyone had seen it before. When it snowed in the early Fall, it wasn't snow at all, it was rather ashes dropped from the robe of the Angel of Death, who peered down on the nation awaiting a dark appointed time.

The appointed time was Summer.

Ironically, the humid heat of Summer was when the searing cold of Winter would be most acutely felt, for that was when the food would run out. There was a difference between high food prices and *famine,* which was the darkest fear. In 1709, people stared into their emaciated children's eyes, watching the life drain from them until they were naught but white leather over dead boney carcasses, not fit for a wolf to gnaw. Such sights changed people. The scent of blood traveled far, and a mother's keening wail over the death of a starving child perhaps even further.

Monsieur Gagneux, who Beau-Brave now called *Chef* Renaud, had already discussed additional summertime duties with the workers. With the dogs, they would all take turns watching the farm from all sides. Geese would be penned near animals and crops that were valuable or could be easily stolen, for they made the most alert and noisiest of sentries. The workers would have to familiarize themselves with any new animals to prevent false alarms.

It dipped below freezing every night. Sometimes the *merde* was frozen to the streets and it hurt his hands to hold the shovel. It hurt to bathe. It hurt to clean his clothes. If it weren't for Ciel, he would not be able to sleep for shivering. Even the mules he used were skittish, not wanting to stop or go.

All of that paled in comparison to the dire mental anguish of waiting.

In an attempt to further his defense, he tried to explain to Ciel how he felt, but she did not understand. She placed no importance on his dreams of becoming a playwright. The meaning of life was found in what they already had. Why would Beau-Brave destroy what really mattered for such fanciful nonsense?

The problem was that Ciel's treasures were of no importance whatsoever to Beau-Brave. Ciel was a mile marker on a long journey. He imagined himself with another woman entirely, someone perfect, the object of a herculean quest. She would make him whole – make him more. His life had not yet begun. Ciel was a character in a dream; soon he would wake up to a real woman, the one he imagined.

The irony escaped him entirely.

She finally left the barn.

Beau-Brave watched her before she departed. She shook her head, consumed with resignation, condemned to ignorance in the matters of her lover's heart. He had wished her gone – but not now, not when her warmth meant the difference between rest and cold torment under the straw.

He shivered into sleep, he woke, he walked to Paris.

He found the doorway to his building and up he trudged, up and up and up. He never saw his neighbors. They were working when he arrived and diverting themselves somewhere in the city when he left. He did not care in the slightest. They were temporary fixtures, like so many other things in his life.

His life!

This was not his life. This was some sort of phantom place, where nothing and no one mattered. He did not belong here. He should not be associating with these people; he was meant for other places, other faces. He was Beau-Brave once, and soon he would be someone equally as illustrious here in Paris.

There was a letter tucked in his doorframe.

Beau-Brave found himself shaking with anxiety and fear. He tore the letter from its crack and opened it. It was printed on Danseur stationery:

> *Dear Monsieur Guerrier,*
>
> *Please come to the Eldorado du Dimanche at eight o'clock in the evening on Wednesday, September 12, in order to discuss your manuscripts.*
>
> *You will be meeting with the writer Destival de Braban, the author of* The Abduction of Proserpine *performed here at the Danseurs.*

Sincerely,

Monsieur Minuscieu
Commis de Bureau
Grand Danseurs du Roi

***

The Eldorado du Dimanche was a seedy *guinguette*, a tented, outdoor cabaret placed outside the Paris walls to escape the liquor tax. They served a malicious local green wine called *ginguet*, hence the name. It was just outside the *Barrière Temple* and was the closest *guinguette* to the Boulevard.

It was a bloody cold walk but once inside the tent, warm bodies and outdoor hearths made it much more agreeable. It was an even mix between men and women with a scattering of children running about making ill-mannered pests of themselves.

Beau-Brave walked through the place, intent on finding his party. He bumped into a thick tradesman, "Watch yourself, imbecile," the man said.

It took every shred of restraint and control to prevent a fist from flying into the man's face. Beau-Brave now felt angry - and ashamed at having done nothing to redeem the slight. He took three deep breaths and approached the host.

"I am looking for Monsieur Braban. I have a meeting with him."

"He usually doesn't come until later."

"Can I stay inside? It is cold as a lord's heart out there."

"Are you drinking?"

Putain! "Yes, of course, give me a bottle of that horrid Seine water."

"Ginguet or actual Seine water?"

"Ginguet. Where can I sit?"

"Stand at the counter."

Beau-Brave moved to the counter and waited impatiently, watching the cask tender fill bottles of wine from the barrel taps. Soon one of the bottles was filled, corked and placed in front of Beau-Brave with a wooden cup. As Beau-Brave poured himself a drink, he found himself transfixed by the unhealthy green color of the liquid and the horrid, vinegar-sour smell.

The bottle, to him, represented nothing but hours of labor.

Soon it was eight-thirty.

Then nine.

The clientele had taken a turn for the worse: prostitutes, sinister-looking men who could only be criminals of some sort, starving artists of a thousand different types from the Boulevard, dreaming of stardom and wealth, washing down their lies with ginguet, coffee and snuff.

Beau-Brave saw himself as different from them. He was, in reality, exactly the same – except he performed for no one and had no community of like-minded with whom to commiserate. It didn't matter. Beau-Brave was not interested in community.

Nine-thirty.

Ten.

Ten-thirty.

Beau-Brave felt tricked – humiliated, disappointed. He was about to be a playwright in Paris. He was suddenly crushed by the realization that he was just a Nightsoiler, holding up a counter at a *guinguette.*

A fight broke out between two burly tradesmen. Their wives shrieked and grabbed them. Other tables tried to get out of the way. The fight crashed and broke things, shouts and screams hurt the ears. After long moments of bedlam, the crowd came to a non-verbal, communal decision to break apart the amateur pugilists. As they were separated, both shouted vile oaths at each other as the scene made its way outside at the insistence of the hosts.

"Well, that's our cue," said a sardonic voice from behind Beau-Brave.

He turned. A group of eight men had just entered. Their leader was dressed like a Versailles dandy. The others were motley, rakish, roguish; others were dressed strangely but with precision and purpose, or studied femininity. In any case, pompous intellectual superiority rolled from them like the stench of counterfeit cologne.

These jackanapeses were his party, sure as a whore sleeps at dawn. After they sat down at a table, he made his way over to them.

"Monsieur Braban?"

A host of replies. "It speaks to us!" "Is it harmful?" "It hurts our ears!" "Make it stop!"

The dandy spoke, "Who are you?"

Beau-Brave unfolded the letter. "I received a missive from Monsieur Minuscieu."

The dandy impatiently snapped the letter from his hands and perused it. "Ha! Eight o'clock!"

The rest of them laughed. "At eight, I was sleeping with the Queen."

"And woke to the walrus at nine."

"And where was its tusk then found sheathed, *mon chéri*?"

The dandy, evidently Braban, handed him back the letter. "You can *va te faire foutre* if you're not buying drinks for the table."

"I will."

"The minute you run out of coin, make yourself disappear."

"Very well."

The table shouted again. "It buys our drinks!" "Make room! Make room!"

Chairs were scooted to and fro. Without asking, Beau-Brave took a chair from a nearby table, moved it and sat down. He was promptly ignored by everyone except Braban.

"Who are you again?"

"Guillaume Guerrier. In Grenoble I was called Beau-Brave."

Beau-Brave could tell Braban had never heard of him. "Well, whatever you did in Grenoble doesn't mean anything here. But that's really not what I meant. I mean, what did you write that I read?"

"Three shorts. One about Caesar-"

"Oh, the cloak and the peasants. And those other two."

"Yes."

"They were smart but they weren't clever."

"I see."

"Smart is worthless, clever is king. Half the bastards in the audience can't hear a word of it anyway. But, even if they could, they wouldn't understand. The candle burns none too bright in the median reaches."

Beau-Brave was repulsed by this man and everyone around the table. He wished them murdered.

Braban continued, "It must be physical, it must be visual, and it must be clever."

"Perhaps an example?"

"Dorvigny!"

A ridiculous-looking fop looked up, "There is no Dorvigny here."

"Debtors begone!" shouted another.

Braban spoke, "We are about to discuss your work."

Dorvigny turned to Beau-Brave as if they were best friends. "I am like the Nightsoilers of Paris. Except I put *merde* upon the stage instead of the fields, where it truly belongs."

How ironic.

"Yes," said Braban, "And we frequently have to shovel *you* from the streets of Paris." He turned to Beau-Brave and suddenly began, "The curtain opens to a conversation between a coquette and her lover in her father's study. The lover exclaims, for there are puncture marks in the books upon the shelves. She says her father is a swordsman of note and practices his dueling maneuvers in his study. *Mon dieu*, we must be scared of this man, what a monster, whatever. And guess what happens next? He is home! The swordsman-father has returned. The coquette exclaims to her lover, 'We must hide you.' There is a secret space behind the bookcase where father drinks to escape mother's admonishment. We will hide you there. Where is it?"

"Why, it is behind the very bookcase that Monsieur uses for his practice."

"Exactly. So, we put the lover behind the bookcase. And, of course, Monsieur comes in. He says he believes he saw a young man hiding in their hedges this very morning. Of course, it is not the fault of his daughter, who is pure, but of these rapscallion young men who constantly pursue her. Oh, Monsieur is angry."

"He pulls out his sword."

"He pulls out his sword. Bang into the books. 'I wish I could find a brave, honorable man for my daughter.' Bang, the sword slides between the books and disappears. Soon, a stream of red liquid arcs from the bookcase like *pisse*. The daughter loses her mind. It must be her lover, dying from blood loss, yes? Bang into the bookcase, another red plume. Now the daughter truly loses her composure. The audience is dying of laughter. The father is talking but it doesn't matter what he is saying. Boom! Another red plume! Finally, the daughter can take no more. 'Father, my lover is behind the bookcase and I fear he must be dead. Please! No more!' The father throws open the secret door and lo! The young man stands with a very serious expression, holding a number of broken bottles of wine. 'Monsieur!' he says, 'I assure you, I did not drink your wine!' The father stands straight, 'Young man,' he says, 'Anyone this brave deserves the hand of my daughter!"

"Clever."

"Yes, clever. Not smart. Farcical, yes. Idiotic? Perhaps - but clever. Every situation and tension carefully set up, no surprises – only the building of expectation. Stock characters - we know the motivations of all, the placement, the tricks, the little ironies. Pretty daughter, her lover, her father – *voilà*. It is fun to see such an impossible amount of blood. It is satisfying to see the young man with the wine, for we knew drink had to be there - for it was where the father hid it - but we had forgotten, or paid the fact no mind, and did not expect the final image."

Dorvigny interjected, "I am a *putain* genius. Let it be known. To anyone who forgoes bathing, eating or riding in a coach, I am Descartes of the boards."

"You are Voltaire of the unwashed," said Braban sagely.

"I myself am unwashed. I smell gloriously of Dorvigny."

"Yes, a treat for us all," said Braban, then he turned back to Beau-Brave. "I remember sensing a bit of the artist in your work."

"Perhaps."

"We were named *playwrights* centuries before we were called anything else. A wright is a craftsman, not an artist. We use form, structure and stock characters. This is no place for artists. We are whores for money: beginning, middle and end – just like any *putain* cobbler in Saint-Antoine. The actors put on airs - but it is only because they are the grandest whores of all."

"Do you put on longform plays at the Danseurs?"

"Yes, of course – I've written them. Farces and melodramas - anything the three Royals won't touch. Don't you see the posters? Oh, you ask because you are interested in longform. Don't be. It would be a waste of your time – your name means nothing. Master these idiotic skits. Impress Nicolet with a pantomime or two. When it comes to longform he doesn't care about what's written on the page, he only cares how the Paris bees buzz your name. Enough buzz, suddenly you are a writer of repute - and your work must absolutely be on stage that very second. As of this particular moment, you are years and years from such a thing."

"I will get to work then. On short form."

"Don't be afraid to use stock characters from the *Commedia dell'arte*, especially the *zanni*. We all do, whether in longform or short. In pantomime, they are a necessity. In theater, they are amazing narrative short cuts. Tension and irony are already present the moment the character passes the wing. When Arlequin takes the stage, the audience knows who he is, what motivates him, and expectation builds immediately. They understand he lusts for Columbine, and so does the dour Pierrot. They know he wishes to undermine his master the Doctor, and so on. The characters are a machine, a mill. One only need supply the grain and one has flour. You cannot build a new mill with every skit. Also, don't be afraid to plagiarize. Have you seen the pulpy blue books at newsstands and such?"

"Yes."

"Everyone steals ideas from them. Massacre the story a little bit so no copyright advocate raises their ugly head from the swamp. Do the same with any other play, even the ones performed by the Royals."

"I see," said Beau-Brave lost in thought – and perhaps judgment.

"Are you always this boring?" asked Braban, quietly hostile.

"I almost found myself in a fight walking into this place. I've been waiting for over two hours, I'm paying for drinks, and all of you are a bunch of *chattes pourries*. How would you expect me to be?" said Beau-Brave calmly.

"I have formed an interesting impression of you. You seem fanatically confident, as if most-assuredly deserving of a career writing for the stage."

Beau-Brave said nothing.

"If ever I am on the receiving end of such arrogance and entitlement, spare yourself the trouble and pursue your natural inheritance at the Ambigu-Comique. Yes?"

"I understand, Monsieur."

He turned and looked directly at Beau-Brave. "Come to the Danseurs. I'll talk to the attendants. You won't have to pay but you'll have to stand backstage. Watch as many shows as you can, until your feet give out."

Beau-Brave nodded.

"Write something that will open Nicolet's purse." Braban fished in a pocket and came out with three business cards. "When you have new work, I'm in the offices upstairs from ten to two. Give this card to the attendant. If you run out of cards without selling anything, your time as a prospective writer has ended. You can return to Grenoble and be whomever you wish."

"Very well. Thank you. I will leave you to your libations."

"Out of coin, are we?"

"No. And that's the point."

Château des ducs de Bretagne

Chapter Twelve

September, 1788

Estelle and Xavier

As Estelle waxed, Jeannine waned.

They had gone shopping for silk fabric for their ball dresses. To Estelle's consternation, Jeannine lost energy half-way through their trek. By the end, it was Estelle who picked their colors: Estelle's dress was to be royal blue and Jeannine would wear emerald green. The best dress-maker in Nantes, Monsieur Vionnet, attended them. In Nantes, uncommon but not unknown, the tailor's guild incorporated the seamstresses as well - so capable Madame Audibet was able to come along.

As the tailors worked, Jeannine sat on the couch as much as she could, a far cry from her usual boundless energy when it came to such things. When she had to stand for measurements, she almost looked resentful, and repeatedly asked when they would be finished.

Estelle became concerned, "Jeannine, are you feeling well?"

"I'm tired."

"Why should you be tired, *ma jolie soeur*?

"I don't know, I just am," she said listlessly as she sat back down on the couch.

Monsieur Vionnet clicked his lips, "I was not finished, Mademoiselle."

Jeannine sighed audibly and labored to stand again.

Estelle was now a bit concerned, "Jeannine, what on earth is wrong with you?"

"I'm just tired, Estelle."

"Perhaps an espresso?" offered Vionnet.

"No," she answered, "It hurts when I swallow."

"Do you have other pains?"

"Yes," she sighed, but she did not elaborate.

Estelle placed a hand on her forehead. Jeannine was burning hot. "Jeannine, you are quite ill, I am sure of it."

"Well, we should at least allow Monsieur and Madame to finish."

Madame Audibet spoke as she measured, "It won't take long."

Estelle shook her head, "I will return shortly."

Estelle left the room and quickly headed downstairs, Thomas was in the foyer and he immediately stood from his chair, "Mademoiselle."

"Oh, Thomas! Mademoiselle is quite sick. Where is Monsieur?"

"Away on business, I'm not sure where. It is not his wont to give us his destination."

"And Madame?"

"In the green parlor, Mademoiselle."

Estelle spoke as she walked, "Have a doctor fetched immediately, if you please." Estelle realized she knew a doctor in Nantes, one that had healed a patient already. "Doctor de Trémargat, in the Place Saint-Denis."

"Yes, of course, Mademoiselle."

Madame was indeed in the green parlor, talking with two of her friends. Estelle entered and curtsied. All three looked at her with disdain, their lips curling in unison.

"Please forgive the intrusion, Madame."

"What is it?"

"It is Jeannine, Madame. I'm afraid she may be quite ill. She can barely stand for the tailors and she is burning with fever."

Estelle then saw something in Madame's eyes she had never seen before.

Fear.

***

Jeannine laid in bed, her arm outstretched over a porcelain bowl, the surgical cut in her wrist gently gushing blood, her upper arm tied to control the speed of the flow. Expertly, the doctor bandaged her wrist and removed the tourniquet. To Estelle, it did not seem as if the doctor's ministrations had helped Jeannine's condition, as they had helped her own after the accident. If anything, Jeannine looked paler than before. Madame and Estelle stood near the foot of the bed. All three lady's maids were at attention, if only to hand a full bowl of blood to the house maid waiting in the hall.

Jeannine spoke weakly, "With which ailment am I afflicted, good doctor?"

"With glandular fever, Mademoiselle."

Madame put her hands over her mouth.

"Is it quite serious?" asked Jeannine.

"It can be. It will be difficult to eat and drink, but you must force yourself to sip broth as much as you can. What can be dangerous is the swelling. If your throat closes, we may have to reopen your airway. That is, of course, only necessary in the worst of cases."

Jeannine closed her eyes, "How long will it take for the fever to run its course?"

"Two to four weeks, Mademoiselle."

Estelle stepped forward, "Jeannine, the ball is in two weeks. You must be well. You simply must!"

"I will try," she said weakly.

***

Dear Xavier,

I have the worst of news.

Mademoiselle is quite ill. She doesn't eat and is quickly becoming a shadow of her former self. It takes everything I have to even get her to drink. I am using a spoon to give her clear broth and she chokes upon it as if it were scotch bonnets from Saint-Domingue.

She is completely bedridden and I am by her side at all times. Jeannine insists that we will both be at the ball. In any case, to force me to go, she will most likely send me away from her the night of the party, with plenty of time for me to begrudgingly ready myself.

I suppose what I am trying to say is that I must suspend our happy twice weekly rendezvous with only the promise of seeing you at the ball. Our world is inscrutable to all but God. My responsibilities in regard to sickness and injury must supersede the wishes of our hearts.

It is my desire to spend as much time as I can with you. But our courtship must wait until poor Jeannine is better.

Please know my heart breaks for this and forgive me.

Truly Yours,

Estelle

***

Xavier read the note and sighed. Truthfully, he would have asked Estelle to marry him on their second outing. But he perceived her as an oak of spiritual strength, a good and honorable woman in every sense. He had one chance to win her permanent affection. In some respects, according to Estelle's deepest beliefs, he was actually a bad match for her. He feared what might happen if he misstepped. However strong and forceful Xavier happened to be, deep within he considered himself to be an utterly worthless person. It was difficult for him to believe someone would see him differently than he saw himself. As a result, he was always circumspect regarding his interactions; therefore, they were, in the great majority, successful, for he left nothing to chance. He would marry Estelle, and when he did, it would be wholly fortunate and timely.

Madame came into the room and Xavier stood. "Good morning, Madame."

"Good morning, Monsieur," she said as they both sat in unison. She noticed the stationery. "A personal missive?"

"From Estelle." Xavier leaned back and allowed the servants to place Madame's coffee service.

"How is she?"

"She cares for Jeannine, who is unwell. I will not see her until the ball. Have you picked your fabric for the dress?"

"The dress is almost done, Monsieur, but let us not speak of it."

In regard to the upcoming ball, Xavier's mother was surprisingly and remarkably calm, especially considering the fact that, for decades, she had completely removed herself from all social activity. He stole a look at her and saw only a pleasant look was returned in his direction.

He spoke without thinking, "What do you think of her, Maman?" He realized he had never called her by that title in his life.

The edges of her lips softly curled upwards.

His eyes were drawn to her hands as her thumb moved across the surface of the Godavari paragon diamond centered on her wedding ring. A scientist named Antoine-Laurent de Lavoisier had recently proven that diamonds were made of nothing more exotic than carbon. It was interesting how a substance could change from the type or manner of forces brought to bear in its creation. Perhaps people were the same way.

She slipped the ring from her finger and placed it on the table in front of Xavier.

"Do not give it to her until the *fiançailles*," she whispered.

Xavier was shocked. "She is not of the elite. She has no family. She is part of no *société*."

"Do those things concern you?"

"Not in the slightest. But I must ask, if she did not wear the Cross of Nantes around her neck, would your opinion be the same?"

Madame considered for a moment. "God knows I am proud. He also knows how scared I am, and my deepest fears. I am so humbled he has now communicated his wishes to me in such a plain manner. I am now in accord. I question nothing."

Xavier nodded. "It will not do to ask her at the ball, having not seen her for several weeks. I will ask her on our second outing after the event."

There was something Xavier did not tell Madame: he had a compulsive wish to tell Estelle that he was a murderer and the circumstances behind the act. He could not possibly withhold any secrets from her. She would be horrified, but any hope he had of erasing that moment from his soul would come with the airing of the act and not through hiding it – at least he believed so. She could dispel the curse, and he could marry her as a man reborn. It would be desperately unfair to dump this dark cartload of memory upon her at the ball. It would have to wait.

"If it is meant to be, you should not wait," said Madame, interrupting his thoughts.

"No, these things must be conducted properly. There can be no missteps."

"Marriage is sometimes little more than a business contract, Xavier - but not this one. This was meant to be. There is no reason for circumspection."

"It will be the most important contract of my life."

Madame sighed and nodded. "As you will, Monsieur, but… I believe you overthink this."

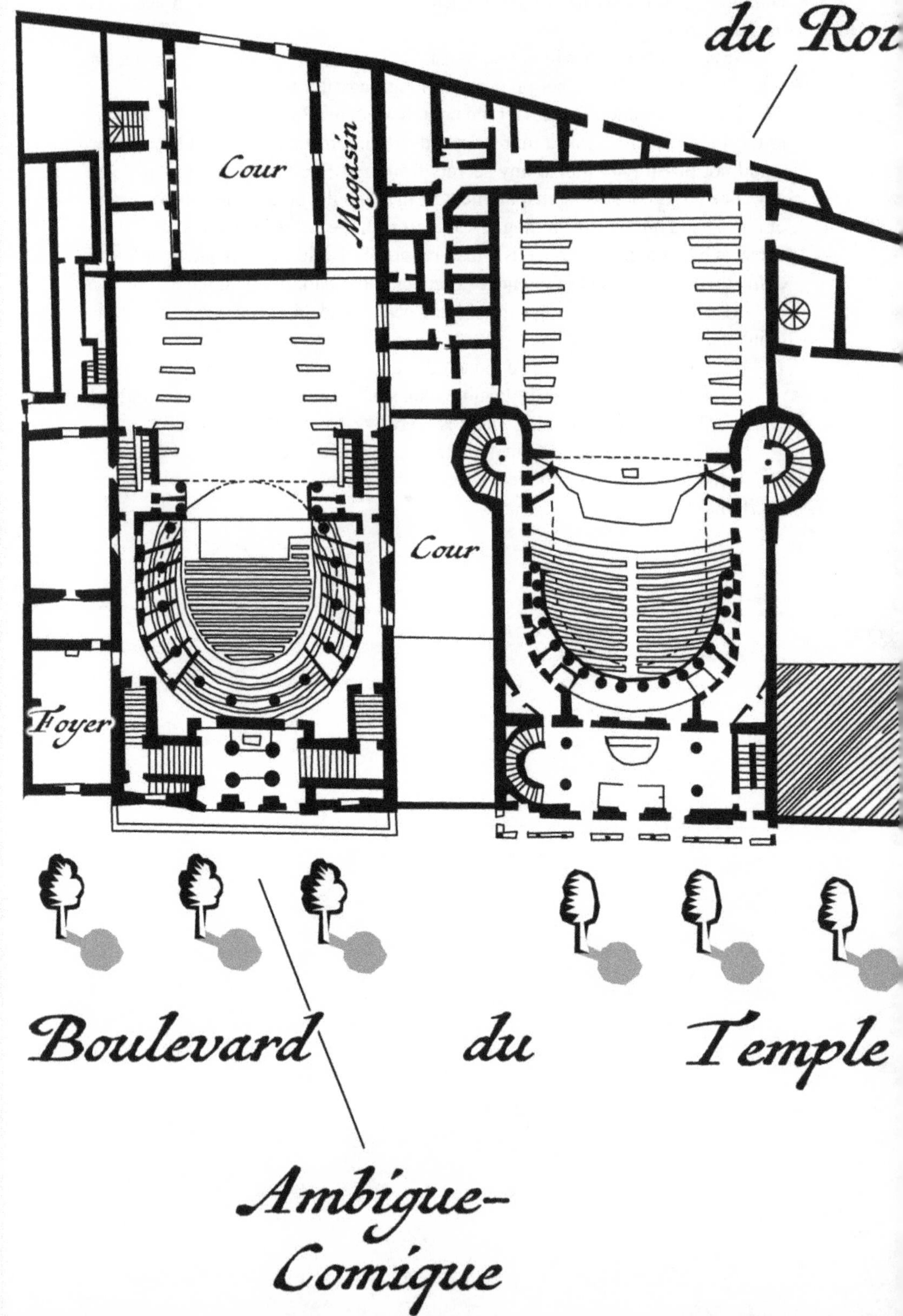
Grand-Danseurs
du Roi
Cour
Magasin
Cour
Foyer
Boulevard du Temple
Ambigue-
Comique

Chapter Thirteen

September, 1788

Beau-Brave

Beau-Brave decided not to watch his first show at the Danseurs from backstage. He would instead be a member of the paying audience to enjoy the spectacle from their perspective. He would watch future shows backstage, but for a different purpose - to learn the structure of theater and its logistical practicalities.

He walked to the Boulevard from the Hôtel de Ville. It was a wide avenue, four lanes of traffic separated by a divider of trees and grass. People were everywhere, walking in every direction. On his right passed a shoeless peasant, on his left a well-dressed noble couple. All were mixed together, whether wealthy, poor, noble, commoner, tradesman, trader, or financier. Square stages akin to raised fighting rings dotted the street, with actors fighting with swords, words, or wit in a parade of endless, short dramas. Little puppet shows kept the children occupied as adults sought steamier fair. Street performers, whether of man or animal kingdom, were seen at every intersection. The buildings down the Boulevard were tall and wide, some running an entire block. A theater usually occupied the lower floor, somehow carved out of a space originally built for something else.

Beau-Brave observed a near-by theater selling tickets for their next show. There was a rowdy group buying them - no organized line at all, only a fantastic, writhing knot of living human rope pushing at the door. Valets stood apart from the knot, waiting for a gentleman to secure their services – which was entering the fracas and securing tickets for gentlemen. A tradesman pushing at the door shouted, "My purse is gone! Who stole it! It's dyed blue, *mon amis*, and has my name on it!" The commotion attracted the police, as a French Guard rode up and looked around for offenders.

Who would want anything to do with such a place, save the goddess Entropy?

Beau-Brave finally noticed which theater he was fronting. This very place, this snake hole of chaos, was the Danseurs. It was offering a full-length play, a melodrama entitled *The Child of Nature* by Mayeur de Saint-Paul, who would play the lead.

Beau-Brave laughed at the irony.

He joined the fray and purchased a third loge ticket for twelve sous.

***

The interior was nearly pitch black after being outside. He could only smell - a heavy, humid scent of tallow, perfume, smoke, cologne, human effluvium of every kind, noxious and suggestive, male and female. He was braced by people on all sides as he maneuvered a narrow hallway parallel to the outside wall, turning abruptly at its end to the right. As his eyes adjusted, he noticed the candles puttering in wall sconces and set in iron chandeliers. Everything was filthy: walls, floor and ceiling - grimy with soot, oil and sweat.

Next to Beau-Brave were two courtesans of *haute société*, both quite lovely and well-dressed. In front of them, perhaps ten feet away, was another harlot, even more beautiful and well-dressed, who wore an old-style diamond necklace, the kind that looped long and ornately nearly to her navel.

Beau-Brave's two courtesans spoke amongst themselves.

"What a remarkably low-hanging necklace," said Mademoiselle Left.

"It is attempting to return to its source," said Mademoiselle Right, and both twittered and laughed as they moved down the hall.

When the long hall turned right, Beau-Brave found himself in a nexus of warrens leading to other parts of the theater. Ushers and even members of the French Guard divided the crowd. Here he left the courtesans behind – or, more accurately, they left him behind. Beau-Brave was quickly shunted up a narrow staircase to the very top of the forty-foot-high theater. He found himself in an open, balcony-like hall running the entire length of the horseshoe-shaped auditorium – with only a rail between him and the floor three stories below. In the enclosed space of the room, a thin layer of humidity floated like a cloud of swamp gas. Below him, on the floor and fronting the stage, were rows of close-set benches, where ushers forced patrons to sit as close as possible to each other, sometimes helping with an aggressive push. Tempers were short, manners were rude, insults were slung back and forth. People who would have never had anything to do with each other were pressed coat-to-coat like reluctant paramours.

Those particular seats were eighteen sous.

Right below Beau-Brave's standing-room-only hall, which was filling quickly – and, more ominously, *densely* - were true balconies, some covered with privacy screens of wood grills.

A balcony seat was two livres but one had to pay for all the seats in the balcony box, whether empty or not. Most of the seats in the balconies were empty but all balconies were rented.

An ornately-decorated curtain, complete with ruffles of lace and beautifully embroidered scenes from classic plays, hid the stage. Facing the curtain and coming up from the stage floor were mirrored sconces holding more candles designed to light the performers, who would sparkle bright in the otherwise dim light. Between the audience and the stage was the orchestra pit, filled with musicians tuning their instruments; the disorderly sound barely heard.

This place, the whole of the Danseurs, was perhaps thirty-six feet wide, a bit less deep and forty-feet high. Only counting the audience crammed on the benches, there must have been four-hundred people. All of them were talking, arguing, yelling. There were more patrons in the private balconies of course, then a *sans-culotte* army in the standing third loge with Beau-Brave. The din was indescribable.

Beau-Brave, despite the squalid conditions, had a feeling of expectation.

The chaotic orchestra suddenly went silent.

The cacophony of the audience died with it – most of it.

Then music.

Beautiful, melodious music, played by practiced masters. Beau-Brave shut his eyes and let it wash over him like a cool breeze. Music was the most primitive of arts. It seemingly carried no ideas, no thoughts, but most definitely emotions. In fact, music ran emotion on a lance, able to penetrate through a person's armor directly to the heart. Upon reflection, Beau-Brave believed it was a thoroughly Rousseauian art form.

The curtain opened on a set of the mountains and trees of a pristine island and a hut made from straw. Actors costumed as savages took the stage. The audience below hissed a hundred sibilant *shh*, a snake pit of irritated vipers quieting each other.

When the actors spoke, Beau-Brave was transfixed. The style was nothing akin to what he had seen or studied at Grenoble. The performers did not seem to be playing a part. Rather they appeared natural, just being themselves. It lent itself far better to an illusion of reality, rather than the normal goal of spectacle. The play itself was a study in simplicity of theme, a treatise on the nature of man. The savage, the natural man, lived an idyllic existence, completely free of the alienation and horror of modern society. His natural impulses were therefore innocent and good, however divergent they happened to be compared to society's mores. The audience was transfixed. Beau-Brave was surprised that the barbarians of the audience were so moved. They were actually quiet.

The urban modern thirsted for simplicity, nature and freedom – and here it was, at least for a soupçon of time, and it could not have been more beautifully performed.

To his right, on the balcony, perhaps five or six people away, a man was urinating – a happy rain to fall forty feet or so on the people sitting on the benches. The culprit did not have a malicious look on his face, nor some sort of indication of humorous intent. Perhaps he was a simpleton or was drunk – or did not want to find an appropriate place to relieve himself and therefore lose his spot at the rail. Who knew? Some others witnessed the uninhibition. Heads were shaking in disbelief, others chuckled. A voice was heard, "Now we rain on them, eh?"

The comment made no sense to Beau-Brave. The rich were in the balconies, protected from all. The poor sods on the benches below paid all of six sous difference from the third loge - all for the privilege of being soaked in another man's water.

No one said or did anything more. Beau-Brave turned back to the play. It was obviously written by a Socialist, the worldviews and assumptions starkly concretized, as if Rousseau's writings had become the dogma of a new religion. The characters were innocent, yet morally divergent from a Christian perspective. They were happy and their environment was serene - apart from conflicts that universally originated from without their happy world.

Then Beau-Brave understood.

He knew the answer to a question that had plagued him for some time.

He understood the new meaning of art, and what it was meant to replace. Beau-Brave now knew his purpose. He had his revelation - his forty days of wandering were over.

It was time to come in from the desert, but that would be a journey in and of itself.

After the play, he returned to shoveling *merde*, at least until he was able to buy a cured boar leg and a knife. He brought it into his room, ate nothing else, and began to feverishly write anew. He had no other thoughts. It didn't really matter at this point whether he lived or died - his only task was to walk into the offices of the Danseurs with material they would wish to buy. That was his first step out of the desert and it mattered more than anything else in the world.

Ciel must have thought him murdered, for Beau-Brave never showed up at the farm again.

Actually, she didn't.

She knew him better than that.

A little bit more of Guillaume had been carved off by Beau-Brave and put in the trunk.

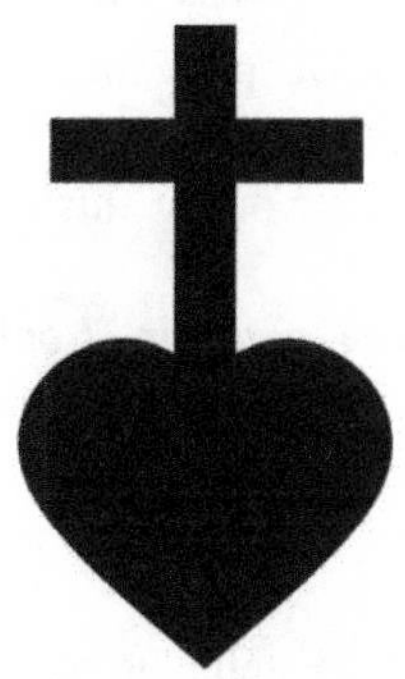

Chapter Fourteen

September, 1788

Estelle and Xavier

Estelle was called to Jeannine's room.

When she arrived, Questa, the lady's maid, stood before Jeannine, who was seated at the dressing table. Questa forced a towel down into the bodice of Jeannine's dress.

Jeannine looked frightful. Even with heavy makeup and powder, the dark circles under her eyes could be plainly seen. Her features were sunken or too sharp. She had lost more than a third of her weight and the dress hung like a blanket from her gaunt frame.

"Oh Jeannine, you should be in bed."

"I will get dressed, then I will nap at a sit so as not to dishevel my hair."

Estelle looked her over. "Jeannine, it may behoove us to wear another dress."

"They will all fit the same."

Estelle closed her eyes. She didn't want to say it. "Perhaps a dress from your youth. When you had your height but were still a girl. From four or five Summers ago, perhaps."

Jeannine leaned forward and placed an elbow on the dressing table. Her forehead rested into her palm. "This is so unfair. This was my ball, my debut. Why now?"

Estelle sighed. "There are cane slaves, who must work as fast as they can to bring in the harvest before the sugar turns to starch, who find themselves stricken with dysentery – and they must still work, from dawn to dusk. Whether we are fit or ill, one unknown day we pass into dust. We must have the proper perspective on our troubles, must we not?"

"I do wish to pull your hair out in this moment, sister Estelle. And then perhaps scratch out your eyes."

"I do not mean to vex you, poor girl. I only say we must have trust in the Lord. Not only at dawn, but when there is no light at all."

Jeannine nodded. "I love this dress. I am wearing it. The colors are perfect."

Questa and Estelle shared a look. It was no use. Jeannine was hard-headed when she wished to be.

Jeannine did not look up, "Estelle, go now and ready yourself. I will come later."

"As you wish."

Estelle walked out of the room and suddenly stopped. The blood drained from her face and her heart began to beat like a drum. Jeannine was to teach her the movements of the dances – for she had never been to a ball in her life. In all of the concern for Jeannine's condition, she had neglected to learn much of anything from anyone – or even to think of it until this very moment.

She could not dance.

She would embarrass Xavier. He would dance with others. He would find another girl, one with grace and manners - and dowry. Estelle's cloudless Summer was about to ignore Autumn to become the dead of Winter. She had no idea how she could survive such a change. She felt as if she was going to die.

And I lectured Jeannine!

In that very moment, Jeannine had an interesting thought as well.

The ball had been postponed because Estelle was struck by a carriage and needed time to recover from her injuries. Jeannine had contracted glandular fever, and the date of the ball had not changed.

***

Estelle, struck with anxiety as she sometimes was, waited until the Traversiers were announced to even come down.

She had never seen the ballroom so full of people. For so long, it had been an empty space to click-clack one's heels on the way to somewhere else. Now it was full of glittering people, dressed even more spectacularly than the upstairs crowd at the Graslin. But there was no air of expectant energy here. Rather, their attendance was the event itself. Their goal was to reaffirm their place in *société*. In Paris, the worldly people would spend nearly every day going from house to house, joining circle after circle, dining and talking and debating. In Nantes, things were not so. The uncommon events in the city were universally attended and the punishment for not attending could be banishment from what little *société* there was. On every face was therefore a haughty question, *"I belong here, as a ring belongs on a finger.*

"*Do you?*"

Estelle did not. At least she thought she didn't. But then something quite unusual happened.

Every glance that strayed her way stayed upon her – and was soon bereft of haughtiness. More and more, eyes found themselves fixed upon Estelle until nearly the entire room was spellbound. Estelle had no idea why. She thought of herself as barely noticeable in the best of times, yet here she was commanding the attention of a ballroom containing the silk-clad cream of Nantes.

As Estelle's perception sharpened, she noticed a galaxy of crimson stars projected across walls and ceiling, men and women – a galaxy that moved as she did.

It was her necklace.

They stared at her necklace.

The Cross of Nantes was not hidden under Estelle's shirt this night. It rested against her pale décolletage just above her bodice. In the candlelight, the gems exploded with color. Estelle's dress was blue, she herself was chestnut and alabaster. The Cross was gold, creamy stone, and scarlet diamonds. The combination effortlessly stole the light of every jewel present, whether real or figurative. The empress of finery had commandeered her court, and all subjects bowed.

The music stopped when the last dancer was shocked into a halt. The entire room stared, transfixed.

Madame Traversier crossed to her. She wore a dress, hat and accoutrement of black and white silk. No one had chosen such colors, and she stood out from all. It would have been disastrous, save for the exquisite effect she had managed with the design.

It was a message.

Yes, she was dressed differently – but no one had managed her sartorial splendor, much less her boldness. She was better, because she had taken a risk and won.

The Traversiers were back.

"Estelle," she said, and placed her hand upon her cheek.

It was a signal to the room. The ball resumed.

Estelle smiled, grateful, and remembered to curtsey. "Madame, you are absolutely resplendent."

"No, *mon chérie*, you have stolen the light from this room. Every candle burns for you."

"It is the Cross, I think. I have never worn it like this, so others could see."

"It reflects the goodness of your heart, Estelle. The Cross honors you."

In Madame's words, there was naught but sincerity. As if a spell was lifted, Estelle, for one heartbeat, finally saw herself as she was, as God saw her, and she was better for it. In that moment, Estelle was connected to Madame Traversier, every bit as strongly as any attachment of blood, then and forever more.

"*Merci*, Madame," Estelle said with another deep curtsey.

Madame touched her cheek again and moved away to a bolt of guests nearby. Estelle was so taken she didn't notice neither had excused the other; She was magicked.

From across the room, she saw Xavier and L'Oublié enter the ballroom from the hall under the balcony. Both wore plain outfits in the Protestant-inspired, dour, bourgeoise style, albeit of magnificent quality. A few glanced at them, but quickly turned away, as if intimidated or unworthy.

Soon he saw her and both smiled. He crossed to her alone and bowed, "Mademoiselle."

Every eye was upon them both. Perhaps they had read of Xavier's courtship of the mysterious Estelle Guerrier, a woman completely unknown to Nantes *société*. She curtsied, "Monsieur."

"May I have this dance?"

Estelle sighed and almost teared, "Oh, Xavier."

His eyes grew wide with concern.

"No! No!" she said quickly, "There is nothing wrong of import. It is all quite silly, actually. Jeannine was looking forward to teaching me how to dance. When she fell ill, I quite forgot this critical diligence until this very night."

He smiled, "So you do not know how to dance, but wish to learn?"

"Well… yes. Admittedly this problem is of little import, but in this moment, it seems quite Himalayan."

"Could you excuse me for one moment?" he said calmly.

"Of course, Monsieur."

Xavier bowed and quickly moved back to the hall and disappeared. Estelle's eyes turned to L'Oublié – Monsieur Souvenu - who had not moved since entering the room. He met her eyes and slowly bowed. Estelle found herself moved by his gesture, and curtsied in return.

Xavier reappeared from the hall. So too did Monsieur Cœurfroid, if only to smile and wave at her and disappear once again.

Xavier made a motion to L'Oublié, then to a valet named Charles. All three made their way toward her. Xavier bowed, "Mademoiselle, if you please," and offered his arm.

Charles unlocked a door and all of them entered a dark, expansive formal dining room. A half-dozen servants were in the room, mostly kitchen staff. They were listening to the music in the ballroom – and were now finding themselves caught in an inappropriate station.

Xavier turned to Charles, "Leave the door open and unlocked, if you please. Let no one assume we are about business separate from the occasion." As Charles propped open the door, Xavier turned to the guilty servants. "It is fortunate you have caught us. I need all of you. We are going to move the furniture in this room to the walls, then we are going to have a dance of our own, with kind permission already secured from Monsieur Cœurfroid. I realize this is in addition to your normal duties. I will give all of you a gracious *pourboire* for your trouble."

One of the scullery maids Estelle did not know spoke without thinking, "You are going to give us money to dance, Monsieur?"

"Indeed," Xavier said with a smile, "Now let us move the furniture."

And soon all of them were moving chairs and table sections. Laughter and whispers were not far behind. Estelle delighted in the moment. Xavier was light-hearted, and he laughed with the rest of them. It made her keenly happy to see him in such a mood.

"*Très bon*," he said, "We are ready. I must warn you all. My fencing teacher was nearly always my dance teacher. If I mix my lessons, this could turn quite gory." Everyone giggled. "In addition, unfortunately for all of you, I have no musical ability whatsoever." His head suddenly cocked, and he listened intently to the music in the ballroom, "Estelle, it is our friend Jean-Baptiste Lully."

"He composed the music of the play!"

"He did indeed. In addition, so all of you know, I am the world's worst dancer. Ah, it is a gavotte!"

Charles spoke humbly, perhaps encouraged by Xavier's casual manner, "Monsieur, is the song not a minuet?"

"They sound alike, do they not?"

"They do, Monsieur."

"The gavotte and the minuet are often paired with preceding triple-time. But the rhythm of the gavotte is steady, not interrupted by faster notes, and one's step is always lifted and never shuffled. And we begin! Everyone!"

And indeed everyone – the servants, L'Oublié and Estelle - faced Xavier in a line and danced as he did, following his moves. His instructions had to be quite loud to carry over the giggling of the servant girls.

"Three *demi coupé*… one two three, one two three… *mon dieu*, I sound like Monsieur Miroiter, my dancing instructor… now a full *coupé*!" All of them twirled their best, laughing, whispering. "Don't forget the arm movements! As Monsieur Miroiter says – 'Grace and form! Grace and form!"

Estelle laughed. Xavier was a terrible dancer but so enthusiastic and confident that his presence was utterly joyful. She wished she could cast a spell and have him be this mirthful forever. The world, much less Estelle, had never seen him like this.

She did not think that she herself was the spell, but she was.

He shouted and twirled, "Once forward and once back! Three *fouetté* in a circle to the right… now open *pas de bourrée*! Same to the left."

Even L'Oublié was dancing. He was obviously without knowledge of dance yet his movements were still exquisite; he had an intuitive understanding of where Xavier's move would end before he executed the maneuver. Others noticed as well.

Soon they all watched him.

Xavier nodded his head, "Somehow, I am not surprised."

L'Oublié finished and bowed. Everyone clapped. He did not smile, but something stirred behind his eyes.

***

They danced for hours in the big dark room. Afterwards, the furniture back into rightful places, they bowed their goodbyes, then Xavier took Estelle into the ballroom. It still looked intimidating, but no longer so foreign.

They looked at each other, both already sweating and disheveled. Xavier spoke, "May I have this dance?"

"May I check my *programme du bal*?"

"Certainly, Mademoiselle."

Estelle took a tiny pamphlet from her purse and flipped the blank pages from beginning to end. "I appear to be free, Monsieur. At least until the year 1850."

"Then let us proceed, Mademoiselle," he said in all seriousness.

They crossed to the middle of the floor and took their place with the other couples. They began to dance, and the very air changed. Estelle realized that this activity, the dancing itself, deserved to be the purpose of the night. Those on the dance floor were elevated, a transcending assimilation. It was a better world, the realm of those moving to music, Estelle thought.

Xavier was utterly graceless, Estelle completely inexperienced – and they did not care. Soon neither of them noticed anything else except for each other and the music. Time passed effortlessly, as if both were sleeping and dreaming. Exhaustion and pains in feet were not felt, even as more hours passed.

But then, one moment, Estelle looked up.

She saw Jeannine at the edge of the dance floor. She was not standing within the unmarked borders of onlookers, nor was she dancing. Instead, she seemed to take up a limbo space in between. On her face was a forlorn, broken look, made even more pathetic by her weakened, sickly state. She was a woman standing on a dock who could not swim, watching a loved one drown in the distance. Estelle couldn't bear to see her friend like this. "Xavier, could you dance with Jeannine?"

Xavier turned, "She does not look well."

"I doubt she could dance for longer than a song, but no one is going to ask her – at least, if you do not."

"Of course."

"I will be on the balcony."

"I will meet you there."

Xavier crossed to Jeannine and bowed, "Mademoiselle, we meet again."

She cleared her throat, "Will you not then kiss my hand."

Xavier did so and she smiled.

"Would you care to dance, Mademoiselle?" he said, raising his arm. She took it and they moved onto the dance floor. Xavier found her hard to look upon, for she seemed close to death. He forced himself to be polite. "I have not seen Madame."

"Madame is a Protestant and does not care for dances."

"It is said the Protestants and Jews are the most productive citizens of France. Perhaps the price for such an achievement is too high."

"But the Jews still manage to dance, do they not? As do the Protestants of England."

Xavier, unsure of a reply, changed the subject. "We met not twenty feet from this very spot."

"Yes, I remember. You were kind to me."

"You were quite precocious, as I recall."

"I was young."

Xavier nodded. She looked nearly the same, only taller. She was even thinner now, and the skin of her face looked as if pale vellum had been pulled over a skull.

"You have become the very essence of a gentleman in these intervening years." She spoke again before he could answer, "Congratulations on your courtship, Monsieur."

"Thank you." Xavier found it difficult to push his reactions into the lively expressions casual company required. She was absolutely ghastly.

Jeannine suddenly looked very tired and as if she were about to cry. "Please excuse me, Monsieur."

Xavier bowed. Jeannine turned and made her way through the crowd. She did so slowly, as if her destination did not matter in the slightest.

What a pity, thought Xavier.

He made his way to the balcony overlooking Haute Grand Rue. There was a flush of people cooling themselves in the cold night air. All were talking but sound was muted and quiet in the heavy air. Estelle stood by herself, leaning forward on the balcony. He joined her. She straightened, but he made a gesture and she took her former posture. They were silent for a moment.

Down below there was inchoate, panicked shouting. The other guests joined them at the edge to see what was happening. Soon a knot of men, shoeless and *sans-culotte*, ran down the street at a desperate sprint – the last man covered in blood but unwounded. Soon after, a good number of soldiers followed at the same pace. They all disappeared and the street was quiet once again.

The balcony exploded into conversation.

Estelle turned to Xavier, "My goodness. What on earth did we just witness?"

"Some vestige of the May troubles, perhaps?"

"The May troubles?"

"Brienne issued some rather unpopular edicts. There has been unrest throughout the country, if not outright revolt. The countryside of Brittany is still quite chaotic. Petty nobles lead backward peasants."

"Jeannine and Monsieur spoke of it, but I remember little."

"It is the ancient fight. The king attempts to disempower the nobles so he can tax them. The nobles see this as dire signs of tyranny. So, our nation is divided - some against the king, some against the nobles. But here we do not worry. There are enough troops in Nantes to quell the disturbances. Other places are not so lucky."

Estelle immediately thought of Guillaume. "My brother was in Dauphiné, in Grenoble. He wrote that the city has gone mad."

"It has indeed."

"Are you very involved with politics?"

"At one point in time, political events held a singular interest. But times have changed."

"What changed?"

"Since then? Everything. The power of the guilds has been lessened. The courts and prisons reformed, Protestants emancipated, torture abolished. There is a mandatory wait for the execution of death penalties. Education has been promulgated regarding everything from identifying toxic rye mold to the sanitary placement of slaughterhouses and cemeteries. We're moving toward a single tax. The major cities now have sewers. There are schools for the blind and the deaf. Academies teach everything from science and engineering to midwifery. The *diligence*, the coach lines, are moving faster and the roads are better. Even the Queen herself has stopped wearing the *robe à la Français* in favor of more Rousseauian garments that she designed and Europe emulates. Her corsage is made of potato flowers, to encourage the people to plant crops better suited to feeding themselves. Of course, the peasants hate her. The king is meant to be the benevolent nation-father and the Queen the idealized mother, both the picture of stability, honor and tradition. Her individualism unnerves them completely. But even the peasants must grudgingly see progress. Thirty percent of food is exported and sold somewhere else other than where it was grown. In 1776, there were thirty-four different duties and twenty-one checkpoint halts to move goods from Nantes to Paris. Now there are but a handful. Our overseas trade is robust, at least ten billion livres per year. French culture reigns supreme over the world. In many aspects of trade, science and industry, we are even beating Britain. Soon, we will beat them everywhere and in all things."

"What is the secret behind such success I wonder?"

"It is quite simple. In France, men have freedom. There is really no difference between the three estates. More and more, the barriers between classes are diminished. Most of the noble families of our time were commoner families less than two hundred years ago. In Britain, an ambitious man eventually hits his head upon an invisible ceiling, for no one is able to transcend their class. There are no limits in France, only difficulties. A man can be anything he wishes to be according to his ability. In 1765, even the nobles were constrained by law in their choice of endeavors. Now a peasant can become wealthy - with ability, hard work, and a little luck."

Estelle was not intimidated or bored by such lofty thoughts on a night of otherwise superficial diversion, not in the slightest. She was better educated than she had a right to be, and was stimulated by clever speech and thought. Men, however, sometimes talked in this way only to impress women. Estelle had a knack for rising to the occasion, challenging ideas, and presenting her own, despite her best interests. *I am too intellectually rambunctious despite myself. I must be careful here and let him show his feathers.*

"Everything seems very rosy for such chaos," Estelle said with a mischievous grin. A moment later, she closed her eyes. *Was that my version of careful? Oh, dear goodness!*

Xavier could only chuckle. "The King, the high nobility, the bourgeoise, everyone is quite besotted with progress – more so than the peasants or backward country nobles wish them to be. Chaos comes from change. France has flown men through the very air. When one of these brave pioneers came to rest in a field, he had to convince the peasants he was no supernatural creature - so they would not kill him with their pitchforks! It is a metaphor for our current state."

"But if everything is so exciting, why did you lose interest?"

"Perhaps I am so confident in the direction of our nation that my interest in politics has waned." *Perhaps I do not care at all... perhaps I care only for you.*

"Is your opinion widely shared?"

"These days, no opinion is widely shared. We are deeply divided, stuck in a political morass in spite of ourselves. I do believe there is only one problem, however."

"Which is what?"

"We are completely insolvent. Not only are we in debt, but the King's credit can no longer secure loans. The King must find a way to tax the nobles, or he must abdicate – and hope our next government has a place for him"

Estelle was shocked at such talk. For centuries upon centuries, the French monarchy had been bedrock, a completely solid, stable political entity that everyone could count on. It was a regime dedicated to God and godly principles. Radical change was unthinkable. "This doesn't sound very promising. A bit appalling, actually."

"It was just a run of bad luck. After Necker there was a series of incompetent ministers. They turned fixable problems into unsolvable tumors." Xavier shrugged, "It is no wonder. The tax laws are products of lunacy. For example, I purchased an office - I am the chamois leather inspector of Brittany. As such, I pay no tax. I can afford to hire an army to solve any chamois problems that may arise, but of course these problems are infrequent to nonexistent. Monsieur Cœurfroid is the tropical fruit inspector for Brittany, dropping his tax liability to zero. Of course, one can also purchase a title. Think of it: I am the richest man in Nantes. I went from being taxed to the very gills to not being taxed at all, based on the simple purchase of a meaningless commission requiring no effort and helping no one, much less the people of France."

"Perhaps you are right to worry about your nation in this moment. But I can hardly guess what the next step should be."

"At the Estates-General, we will trade our absolute monarchy for a constitutional one, in order to fund more debt. We go from our outdated system to the newer British way. It is inevitable. It is not a bad thing. Simply more progress. The nobles know this, that is why they do not cooperate with the king." He turned to face her again, "Things will change in Saint-Domingue, of that one can be certain."

"How?"

"I think slavery will be abolished."

Estelle shook her head, "I think that is naïve." Estelle immediately brought her hand to her forehead. *I just called Xavier Traversier naïve. I am the world's most foolish girl.* "Oh, please pardon me, Monsieur."

Xavier chuckled, "If only you knew how much I value your opinion – and how incompetent your ability to create offense."

"I am so poorly mannered, that is the heart of the problem."

"Not at all. I would ask quite humbly for your thoughts on the subject."

"On slavery?"

"Yes, if it pleases you."

Estelle looked at him, and realized his words were true. His ego was not pricked, only his intellectual curiosity. "I believe mankind is incapable of change. We are who we are. There are good people amongst us, and evil ones as well, and that will never change. I think we are no more capable of ending slavery than ending murder or theft."

"Perhaps. But we can certainly change the scale of slavery. When things are illegal, the scope narrows considerably."

Xavier was suddenly struck by an interesting thought.

He was a slaver, amongst other things.

Estelle spoke, "Yes, you are right. As laws against theft deter thievery, laws against slavery will deter the sale of slaves. But there will always be thieves and there will always be slavers, because we are who we are."

"You do not think man can evolve?"

"No! No, indeed!"

"Prussia was once full of murderous Goths. Now it is full of Protestants."

"The way the world is going, it might soon be filled with murderous Goths once again."

"I am not so sure. I have been to Prussia."

Her eyes twinkled, "I have another of my horrid analogies that doesn't quite fit."

"Please."

"It is said the Ottoman sultans have lions for pets. They lounge about like tabbies."

"I do not know about the Ottomans in particular, but have certainly heard of the practice of keeping great beasts as pets."

"Why would a lion lounge about like a house pet? Has it evolved?"

Xavier was about to launch into disagreement, but stopped.

Has it?

She continued, "Of course, the answer is no. The lion has not evolved. It has simply found itself in a position where it does not need to hunt or worry about competition - or really danger of any sort. If the lion's circumstances changed, if it were freed on the savannah, I think it would revert to behavior normally associated with lions – and quite quickly at that. Having faith that mankind as a whole has an evolving nature, rather than a constant nature interacting with an evolving environment, would be a mistake. If a sultan has a lion as a pet, his first and foremost concern is to regulate the lion's life to ensure it does not behave as a lion. If you are a human, your concern – first and foremost – is to regulate yourself, civilize your baser instincts so that you are then a child of God and not a savage. I think man would revert to barbarism every bit as fast as lions, given the right circumstances. It is the fear of God that civilizes man, nothing else."

Her words were gentle, warm Caribbean waves. When they got one wet, it was pleasant, not cold.

"You are not Rousseauian?" he ventured.

"No. I would even say, in my opinion, that he was direly misled in his conclusions." A heartbeat later, she spoke again, even faster and more forceful. "This world has a purpose, given to it by God. To say that we can change the purpose of the world is to imply that we can take the world from God and divert it to our own purpose. That is not only impossible, but harmful."

"An interesting perspective, Estelle."

Deep in thought, she continued, "We have free will. The most essential freedom is the choice to determine what is moral and ethical, and what one will do or not do, and the ability to accept the consequences. The highest moral choice is to serve God. If one serves God, one is driven to love man in the most ethical way, for then all men are your brothers. Individuals centering their lives on Christ, by choice of their own free will, leads to the best world, in spite of worldly concerns not being the first priority of a Christian. All in my opinion, of course. I would say, 'in my humble opinion,' but I am unworthy of calling myself humble, being the gauche chatterbox that I am."

He should have laughed to ease her mind, but Xavier, too, was pensive. He had a plethora of business interests. His most profitable, by far, was the transport of slaves to Saint-Domingue. He was, in fact, the most successful slaver in Nantes and, excepting corporations, the most successful individual slaver in France. His success had made him a person of prestige and note. He was now respected and an elite member of society. He had never felt a twinge of guilt or regret over his enterprises, only over specific, traumatizing incidents involved with the trade.

At least, not until this very moment.

Xavier realized that if he married Estelle, he could not hide his involvement, or even lie about it.

Ruminating, he realized he would rather end his involvement.

She put her hand atop his. "On a night such as this, brevity and levity should be our guide. There will be plenty of time for serious discussion between us."

Xavier smiled and held out his arm. "Indeed."

***

Walking to breakfast in the cold light of morning, Xavier heard Madame's laughter from several rooms away. He had never heard the like from her; it was a gay and mirthful sound, completely absent of darkness or schadenfreude. He entered the kitchen parlor with a smile and saw her sitting in front of a large pile of letters. She held a gold sword letter-opener with one hand and an opened letter with the other.

Xavier bowed and sat. "From?" he asked.

"The attendees of the ball. Invitations, in the main."

"The ball was last night and ended quite late."

"Indeed. But we are now assumed to be active in *société*. If we are to be given proper notice to place this event or that on our calendar, we must be caught early."

"We have been to one ball."

"Traversier has returned, Monsieur. It is as if the last thirty years never happened. Now there is only one thing we lack."

"And what is that, Madame?"

"Children, Monsieur. We need children."

Indeed, we do.

Xavier's coffee was placed on the table. He sipped, finding himself in good spirits. He fondly remembered the night before.

He changed his mind, right then, regarding his courtship of Estelle.

It was not her responsibility to give him absolution - everything within his soul was his own responsibility. He would ask Estelle to marry him the next time they met. He resolved to become the man she deserved to marry within the short days before their next rendezvous. He would cleanse his actions and the nature of his business and have nothing to hide, except for the past of a man who no longer existed – for true change in Xavier would erase an older version of himself from the earth. That, he realized, was the ultimate absolution.

If he exempted himself from the slave trade, his income would fall dramatically. Instead of Traversier being one of the twenty richest families in France, they would descend into the hoi polloi - one of the two or three hundred wealthiest families in the nation. Putting his sacrifice in such terms, the sarcasm was bitter. In essence, such a huge change would not affect him in the slightest.

Of course, the family would also inherit the Cross of Nantes, a tidy nest egg for a rainy day at three-and-a-half-million livres.

That fact begged a question.

Why was Xavier still leading his business like a Mongol khan? Why was he creating such suffering and pushing for growth at such a pace? He was intellectually engaged by some of it, but that did not answer the question. He enjoyed the status and reputation he had secured, but not overly. Was he afraid? Was he afraid of being an invisible person once again?

Yes.

If the business was not growing, it was shrinking – no, it was dying. If the business was dying, he was dying. If Nantes did not worship his family, they despised them. That indeed was the fear, the fear of returning to utter, abject humility. He was running away from death.

L'Oublié entered the room and bowed.

He had not done such a thing unannounced in years. Xavier jumped from his chair. L'Oublié turned and walked quickly from the room.

Xavier caught up. "What news?"

"Deschenes is here. With Perry and Bradford."

Perry and Bradford were from Boston, Rag's right-hand men. Perry looked more Dane than English. Bradford was half *gen de couleur* and half Christian Mashpee.

"Deschene has a letter."

"From Rag."

"*Oui*, Monsieur. From Rag to you."

"*Mon dieu*! What is going on?"

"He has disappeared."

"Who?"

"Boston Rag. He is gone."

And then their dark hallway became the daylit Carrara Room. Deschenes, Perry and Bradford stood not far from the main doors. The servants who had taken their coats and hats were only just leaving. Monsieur Fidèle, the *maître d'hôtel*, appeared quietly, sensing something important was happening.

Xavier spoke in English, "Gentlemen, I assume you have discussed how to report whatever news you have."

Deschenes bowed, "Indeed, Monsieur." He nodded at Perry, who stepped forward and handed Xavier a sealed letter. In Boston Rag's ridiculously poor handwriting was only one word upon it – *Xavier*. He tore open the seal.

> *I'm all right. I'll be back. Things will change when I do. You don't need to come here. Just trust me – Rag.*

"*Sang de merde*," said Xavier, perplexed. He handed the letter to Perry, who read it with Bradford. "*Que diable se passe-t-il*!"

"He left without warning. When I arrived in Boston from Saint-Domingue, he was already gone."

"The cargo?"

"We proceeded with everything according to custom."

Xavier turned to the Americans. "Tell me everything, Messieurs."

Perry spoke first, "As far as I can tell, he left mid-June."

"Who went with him?"

"No one that we know of."

"What did he say before he left?"

"That's the thing. Nothing. It took us until mid-morning on the fifteenth to realize he was nowhere to be found."

"How was his… *comportement*, his…. behavior?"

Bradford spoke, "Damnedly strange, sir."

"How? How strange?"

"I don't know how to…"

"When did it start?"

"Winter."

"Was he sick?"

"Yessir."

"How sick? Was he… *haluciner*?"

"Hallucinating? No, he wasn't that sick, I don't think."

"Did he have a high fever and become simple?"

"No, he was sharp as ever."

"*Bordel de merde! Tu me fatigues!*"

Bradford did not understand the words but Xavier's irritation was clear. "I'm sorry, sir. Let me start over. Boston Rag is always talking and everybody is always listening. He tells them what's up and down. He's the center, he's the big man."

This is much better. "Go on."

"Well, he just up and stopped being the center. He stopped talking. He stopped wanting everyone around him. He started taking walks. He was quiet."

"Quiet? Boston Rag? The first time I saw him I thought I was headed for a knife fight."

"That's him, sure enough. But it wasn't him after that Winter. No, sir. He just became someone else. It's hard to explain, sir."

Maybe not so hard. "Was there a woman?"

"We don't think so."

"So, he was sick, but not that sick. And he changed, disappeared and wrote a note addressed to me?"

Bradford and Perry nodded and spoke in unison, "Yes, sir."

"*Salope!* Who is running our business?"

Perry fidgeted, "Just… everyone."

"Everyone else?"

Perry looked Xavier in the eye, "We all know what to do. There's no man who'll take what isn't his, I'll tell you that. If Rag came back like old Rag, there'd be hell to pay, sir. Coin gets put in the bank. Things Rag was organizing don't happen, that's all. Only a matter of time before Boston harbor gets filled up with ships with nothing to do, but it hasn't happened yet."

Xavier turned to Deschenes, "What manner of ship brought you here?"

"A schooner, Monsieur. A fast one. The *Clarent*, she is called."

"Is it ours?"

"Rag's."

"Well, *putain*, let's turn it around. We are going to Boston. Find her crew before they start drinking. Put every man we have on her repair and resupply. Then hire the ones we do not have. She must be seaworthy in hours, not days."

"*Oui*, Monsieur."

Xavier turned. "Monsieur Fidèle."

The servant stepped forward, "*Oui*, Monsieur."

"A carriage for these gentlemen. A coach for myself. Post haste, if you please."

"*Oui*, Monsieur."

Xavier turned to L'Oublié, "Go with them."

"Where do you go, Monsieur?"

"To Centre-Ville."

L'Oublié understood.

***

Xavier ordered the driver to go as fast as the horses could pull.

Boston was a critical center of his business. A crisis had arisen that needed his attention, but he did not want to leave anything unfinished with Estelle. He had to ask for her hand now, before he left.

Soon he was before the Cœurfroid's front door. He brought the knocker down and it was opened by Thomas, who towered over Xavier, who was considered tall.

"*Bonjour*, Monsieur," he offered.

"*Bonjour*, Thomas. I apologize for being unannounced but I must speak with Mademoiselle Guerrier."

"She is not presently here. Please come in, Monsieur."

Xavier entered. Thomas spoke again, "She is with Mademoiselle, Monsieur."

"Yes, of course. And what was their destination?"

Thomas looked flustered, "Feydeau Island, Monsieur."

It was a popular stop for local sightseers. Men had been trying to build on the deep, wet mud of the Loire island for centuries, only to see anything more substantial than a hut crash into the muck. Strong mercantile ties with the Netherlands had brought back knowledge of building on poor soil. Now exquisite manors were being built on Feydeau. They were almost boats, having a foundation of buoyant wood rather than stone or bedrock. The city was smitten with the progress of the modern work.

Thomas spoke again, "If you go now to find her, I must tell you something, Monsieur."

"Please, Thomas."

"Mademoiselle tells us she goes to a certain place, then when she must be found, she is not there. Mademoiselle Guerrier is not complicit in this."

"Of course not."

"It is quite simple. Mademoiselle provides incorrect information to vex Madame. I do not wish to send you on a false errand, Monsieur."

"Thank you. If I do not find them, I shall return."

"Very good, Monsieur."

The coach clattered south toward the island, and the massive docks and buildings abutting the Loire.

There were many onlookers observing the construction. Some enterprising townsfolk had set up wooden bleachers and rented seats. Local cafes and taverns served drinks.

Xavier decided to start north and work his way south and west.

The girls were not at the Quay Mellier, the most northern observation point. The Castle of the Archdukes was next and probably had the best view. The guards, who knew Xavier well, had not seen either girl. Nor were his quarry present at the Quay de la Polerne, Quay de Brancao, the Port Au Vin, the Hôtel de la Bourle or its gardens, la Hollande. He did not suppose that the girls were in any other building, most of which catered to sailors. Jeannine was headstrong, but Estelle did not budge on subjects of moral turpitude.

Time moved slowly. The emergency had activated something inside of Xavier. He had not felt like this for quite some time.

There was only one thing for it then.

Xavier returned to the Cœurfroid townhome in Centre-Ville.

Thomas again welcomed him, "I'm sorry, Monsieur. They have not yet returned home."

Xavier felt foolish.

The schooner was being readied for a transatlantic voyage. One did not simply traipse into the open sea for a month-long journey. It would be unheard of for a ship from the Americas to spend less than five days at port while it was resupplied and repaired. Deschenes and L'Oublié, not to mention the Americans, were entirely impressed with Xavier's need for haste and had probably hired every hand in the city to ready the ship as quickly as possible. Sails and ropes were being replaced from Traversier stores, charts updated, temporary repairs made permanent. They would most likely leave in the hours of the early morning as long as the clouds did not obscure the moon, which would be more than quarter-full. The ship would have to be drydocked for extensive repairs after the marathon, but Xavier didn't care.

Estelle being gone, he had two choices. He could postpone the voyage until tomorrow evening, which was still an incredibly hasty departure, and leave a note for Estelle saying he would call tomorrow morning. Then, on the morrow, he would ask for her hand. He would spend the rest of the day with her and then leave in the evening, counting on the current moving them to the wide estuary of the Loire before dark.

No.

Xavier found that in his present state of mind, he simply could not wait that long.

He turned to Thomas, "If I could leave a note?"

"Yes, of course." Thomas moved to the parlor and Xavier followed.

"Is Madame or Monsieur at home?"

"No, I am afraid not, Monsieur."

"Very well."

"Here you are, Monsieur," Thomas said as he pulled stationery from a drawer and placed it atop a writing table.

"Thank you, Thomas. I will show myself out," said Xavier as he sat.

"Very good, Monsieur." Thomas bowed and left the room.

Xavier looked over the blank paper. After a moment, a quick note appeared below his quill.

> *Dearest Estelle,*
>
> *An emergency forces me to leave for the Americas this very night. If I spend only one day in Boston, I will still be gone for the better part of two months.*
>
> *I deeply regret being separated from you.*
>
> *Please hold me in your heart as I hold you in mine.*
>
> *I would have dearly appreciated the opportunity to see you in person before I left, and regret this cannot be.*
>
> *Regretfully and always yours,*
>
> *Xavier*

Xavier cursed as he sealed the letter. He strode from the room and exited the townhome, carefully shutting the door behind him.

By the next morning, the schooner was in the estuary.

Madame Traversier found out where he had gone almost a week later, and by accident. She did not feel slighted.

Men do what they must do.

Currency during the time of Louis XVI

Experiments in paper money had been disastrous, and were abandoned. The currency was based on the LIVRE TOURNOIS, a pound of silver. There was no coin worth exactly one livre. The variety of copper, billon (a copper/silver alloy), silver, and gold coins were worth their weight as precious metals. Different mintings of the same coin, however, had different weight. Foreign coins were also used – and sometimes proved more popular than domestic coins.

VALUES
(not coins)

3 denier = 1 liard
1 liard = 1/2 double
12 denier = 1 sol
4 liards = 1 sol
1 sol = 1 sou
10 sols = 1 testons
14 1/3 sol = 1 livres
2 testons = 1 livre
1 livre + 4 deniers = 1 franc
86 sols = 1 écu
1 écu = 6 livres
4 écu = 1 louis d'or
1 louis d'or = 20 livres

2 denier
copper

1 liard
copper

4 denier
copper

6 denier
copper

1/2 sol
copper

1 sol
copper

15 denier
billon

16 denier
billon

2 sol
billon

1 écu
silver

1/2 louis d'or
gold

1 louis d'or
gold

2 louis d'or
gold

30 denier
billon

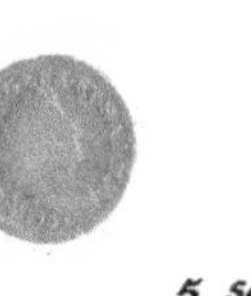

5 sols
silver

6 sols
silver

10 sols
silver

12 sols
silver

15 sols
silver

20 sols
silver

24 sols
silver

30 sols
silver

33 sols
silver

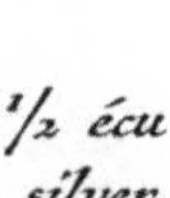

1/2 écu
silver

Chapter Fifteen

November, 1788

A Letter to Guillaume

Dearest Guillaume,

I weep at your wretched circumstances. Please just come home. Between the empires of my friends and my employers, there must be some kind of gainful employment suitable for you.

I don't understand what you are doing or why. This path is not natural, Guillaume. One should not have impossible dreams. The process to achieve them will leave your life a desert. Even if you achieve your goals, you will leave people by the wayside - and be the storm that turns their lives into shipwrecks.

The point of our existence is love, Guillaume. It isn't fame, success, or wealth. Those three things only bear fruit if they enable love - and they give one less than nothing if they do not. A life's meaning is determined by the people around you: your family, friends, and community.

If we do not love each other, and find reason and purpose amongst each other, we cannot hope to love or find God. If one has no family, no friends, no church, and no community, there is no purpose. One begins to think as you do, that such things as money, fame, and fortune will create happiness and quietude of spirit.

This is false, Guillaume. It is a product of the devil's intervention. You pursue a hollow life. You are a wraith on the land, and you will only bring unhappiness to those around you if you continue in this manner.

I fully realize we have nothing. We actually have no home, no village, no family, few friends and, in your case, not even God.

Home is now Nantes. I claim this city for us. Come home.

I do not mean to vex you. It is probably my mood. Oh Guillaume, I am a fright. I am bursting with love and lovelorn emptiness. In attempting to explain, I realize now that I have made a tremendous mistake. In my letters, I have used aliases for everyone in my life because I considered their fixture to be temporary - and I wished to say abominable things about them without poisoning their reputations or revealing their secrets. Ah! I am a Guerrier, always thinking the next move to another place is around the corner. Unfortunately, it now seems that these people-fixtures might very well be permanent – walls and not moveable lamps! Am I making any sense? I fear I am not.

The crux of the matter is this: my courtship with Monsieur Cerf, as we call him, has progressed. We are not engaged, but I believe we both share a deep and abiding love for each other. On the surface, he is a poor match. He is a heathen. He is a hard man, a man who has done what needs to be done. His soul aches from it. Yet he is honorable to the core. He is like a Spring bud on a branch. I reached out and touched it, and even this simple gesture opened him halfway to a beautiful and intriguing flower. I wish to caress it now and have it bloom en toto. We thirst for the healing of the other. We both long for companionship, having both experienced loneliness and alienation.

You might wonder how a man of his means could be possessed of such needs. I would answer by saying although he has tremendous and unimaginable wealth, he does not have God. Gold does not gleam in darkness, it seems. It probably seems strange to you that I would love such a man, but I do. I quite hopelessly do. I can only wish that my example may someday change his heart. No, I do not hope. I know for a certainty that this will happen.

I have nothing, yet I cannot help but to feel that between the two of us, I am more in charge of my spiritual destiny. He has the power to force his own soul into a box and lock it. But such a thing does not bring the serene inner peace of Christ; it is rather the turning of a man into a fierce animal in order to face equally-fierce lions out in the world. In any case, we were together at every opportunity. My feelings grew to the point where it took all my strength not to burst into tears and run into his embrace when I saw him.

And that is the problem, dear brother. He is gone from me. He was called to the Americas on urgent business. It takes every ounce of willpower for me to be a civil and gregarious person. It is some form of dark serendipity that Femme, as I have called her, is only now recovering from her sickness. Her level of physical energy seems to match my depleted level of emotional energy, at least for the nonce. Let us hope my dear Monsieur Cerf returns before Jeannine recovers to full strength, or else she will be taking care of me as I fail.

Femme has been acting strangely as well. She has been strategically cultivating friendships with certain people who attended the last ball. There is something very odd about it. Often, she sends me on errands so I cannot be a part of what she is doing. Since she is in good company, she is able to do this without raising the ire of her mother. I tried to talk about the manner of her actions with her – in a roundabout way, of course. She implied that something very important was happening, she could not tell me of it, but wished my support and assured me that although I could not know what was going on, it was wholly honorable. What a little mystery, this Femme. What is she up to I wonder? Always full of secrets, from the very beginning, this one.

But I digress. Dear Guillaume, I am so worried about you. I do not want you to starve and I do not want you to ever lack funds to return here. I have enclosed money in the form of actions au porteur. Use the money to fund your ventures, secure lodging and a good decent diet. But for me, always leave enough money to return here twice. The first time you return will hopefully be for my wedding, although I am foolish to even think such a thing is possible. The second return will hopefully see you stay forever.

I love you, I miss you.

Estelle

Dearest Estelle,

I am pleased that Monsieur Cerf is blind. I always knew that you would marry a man who could not look upon you, being the off-green goblin that you are. It is unfortunate that he is not deaf as well, for you are a ranting lunatic of rare uniqueness.

I can't believe you sent me money. I am returning it. You are an idiot.

Guillaume

PS – Mon dieu, I miss you. Be well. Still your heart. Everything will turn out fine.

Stock Characters of the Commedia dell'Arte

Les Zannis

Servants of the common people.

ARLEQUIN

Joyous, greedy, stupid, hungry, gullible, lazy. Clever only to achieve ridiculous goals.

SCARAMOUCHE

The wicked side of Arlequin. Spiteful, mean, clever and full of himself. A braggart.

BRIGUELLE

A man who undertakes any employment for money. Urban, insolent with women. Vain and arrogant.

PAILLASSE

Beaten and taunted by all. Dupe of every other character. Excessively awkward.

It is said these forms, especially Arlequin, are beyond ancient. They were old when pagan Gaels took them to Rome.

SCAPIN

A malicious trickster. Out for revenge. Rather than thwart, he corrects his master.

POLICHINELLE

A fat, unsightly peasant. Greedy, rude, simple, but cunning and witty.

Les Vieillards

The most extreme sort of townspeople.

PANTALON

A miserly, meticulous libertine. Old, selfish… but gullible.

LE DOCTEUR

Deeply ignorant, he sacrifices all to appear learned. Selfish and immo

Les Soldats

Swaggering… when not timid.

COVIELLE

Musical, fat, enamored with common sense to the point of insensibility.

LE CAPITAINE

Boastful, exploits his exploits. Will do anything for glory – even run.

Les Amoureux

Ingenuous, but also ingenious… to deceive the old men.

COLUMBINE

A good servant, the only character who uses intellect. Tricky, and fond of disguise.

THE LOVERS

Attractive, elegant, well mannered. Likeable and cheerful with a hint of com

“Introduction to Lavoisier”
Part One of Three

Parts Two & Three to be performed later in the SAME SHOW

w/b
Beau-Brave

Seven Minutes Total
Short Farce
(carried under license)

CAST

- MoC -
Master of Ceremonies

- LAVOISIER -
comedian-acrobat in costume to resemble real man

- ARLEQUIN -
usual cast member

IMPORTANTLY, an open balcony will be part of the show. Prop list separate, already submitted to Monsieur C.

UPSTAGE CURTAIN OPEN EXPOSING DOWNSTAGE CURTAIN

DAMPER LIGHTS STAGE-RIGHT, STAGE-LEFT

SPOTLIGHT STAGE-CENTER

...illuminates MoC, of very humble and serious demeanor.

MoC

Messieurs et Mesdames, we have amongst our audience a very special guest. Although he is a Farmer-General tax man...

(anticipate negative crowd reaction)

Please, please, my good people. He is not just a Farmer-General but a chemist and biologist of world renown. Many of you already know about whom I am speaking. He discovered oxygen and hydrogen. His work led directly to the Montgolfier balloon. Yes, I am speaking of none other than Antoine Lavoisier!

MoC DIRECTS WITH HANDS.

SPOTLIGHT SHIFTS TO OPEN BALCONY

...and the character of LAVOISIER. He waves awkwardly and bows.

MoC

Monsieur Antoine Lavoisier!

As applause renews, Lavoisier waves and bows even more awkwardly. He is a social misfit, completely unsure of himself.

MoC

(even stronger)

Monsieur Antoine Lavoisier !

As applause and laughter intensify, Lavoisier understands he is beckoned. He searches for a way to come over the balcony.

MoC

(impatient too!)

Monsieur... Antoine... Lavoisier!

Lavoisier clumsily begins to climb over the balcony.

MoC

Ahh… could someone please help Monsieur? Fine people of the Danseurs, please help Monsieur. Ah, yes, there we are.

Lavoisier is either (awkwardly as possible) helped to the ground by the audience or takes a violent fall. Either way:

MoC

Messieurs et Mesdames, I present Monsieur Lavoisier!

Lavoisier walks to the orchestra pit, turns, bows and waves.

MoC

(suggesting action)

Monsieur Antoine Lavoisier.

Lavoisier looks panicked, he bows and waves frantically.

MoC

(angry)

Monsieur… Antoine… Lavoisier!

Lavoisier doesn't know what to do. He moves forward and backwards, side to side.

MoC

(screaming)

MONSIEUR ANTOINE LAVOISIER !

Lavoisier attempts to jump the orchestra pit and ends with his hands on the stage, his body hanging in midair and toes on the orchestra parapet.

MoC

(content)

Monsieur Antoine Lavoisier, mesdames et messieurs.

The MoC claps, suggestive looks indicate the audience should do the same. After a round of applause, Lavoisier screams in helplessness.

MoC

Perhaps if the cello player…

The cello player attempts to help Lavoisier.

MoC

Uh, indeed. If we could have the pair of clarinets as well.

The clarinets stand and push Lavoisier as the MoC squats next to him.

MoC

Toward me, Messieurs. More, more.

Lavoisier is manipulated toward the MoC in the most awkward way possible, with one hand of the musicians pushing on his crotch. Lavoisier moans in pain. Finally, the MoC is able to grab the belt of Monsieur and pulls him to roll upon the stage. The MoC immediately straightens and points to Lavoisier's crumpled form.

MoC

(triumphantly)

Monsieur Antoine Lavoisier!

In this moment, the character of ARLEQUIN pokes his head through the downstage curtain and looks around mischievously, his slapstick seen poking out over his head. He is unnoticed by Lavoisier and the MoC.

Lavoisier manages to stand, although he is still traumatized.

MoC

Monsieur Lavoisier, we are honored by your presence. In spite of your primary occupation being the rape of our fair city, we are more than compensated by the education you provide regarding your fantastic discoveries.

LAVOISIER

The what? Who's what? I'm where?

Arlequin tiptoes toward the pair.

MoC

More than anything, Monsieur, we would ever be so appreciative of a demonstration of science. Would we not?

(suggests the audience applaud)

LAVOISIER

Well, harrumph! I am a tax farmer, Monsieur! Not a scientist.

MoC

Oh, no no no. You are both a tax farmer *and* a scientist, one fueling the other. We cannot decide which one for you to be to suit our fancy *and* the crowd, can we? No, no, no!

(suggests crowd reaction)

Arlequin should be right behind them at this point, still unnoticed.

LAVOISIER

Be that as it may, or may be, or not be, or it may be that....

MoC

Yes....

LAVOISIER

I am unable to perform scientific experimentation without my equipment!

MoC

Mon dieu! A problem of insurmountable proportions!

Arlequin whacks the stage with his slapstick, scaring both men, who are unsure of where the sound originated.

A ROLLING TABLE suddenly wheels toward them from SL, holding a profusion of BEAKERS AND SCIENTIFIC EQUIPMENT.

It stops directly in front of Lavoisier, who is smitten. He becomes utterly consumed with his check of the equipment.

MoC

(after a long moment)

Monsieur Lavoisier?

LAVOISIER

(distracted)

Hmm…

MoC

(louder)

Monsieur Lavoisier?

LAVOISIER

(distracted)

I-

(less distracted)

I-

(conversational, strong)

I-

(back to completely distracted)

Hmm…

MoC

(disgusted)

Monsieur Lavoisier!

Arlequin, holding his slapstick sideways and behind his back, begins spanking Lavoisier. At first the action and tempo are gentle. Although the MoC is oblivious to Arlequin, he subconsciously understands what is going on. His speech somehow mimics the rising tempo of the spanking.

MoC

Monsieur Lavoisier?

LAVOISIER

Hmm…

MoC

Monsieur Lavoisier?

LAVOISIER

Hmm…

MoC

Monsieur Lavoisier?

The spanking reaches a fever pitch.

LAVOISIER

Hmm. Hmm. Hmm. HMM ! HMM ! Ouch ouch ouch! Yes yes YES!

The spanking ends. Arlequin wears his mischievous face.

MoC

Since we now have the necessary equipment for a study, let us begin.

LAVOISIER

But Monsieur-

MoC

Hmm?

LAVOISIER

But Monsieur-

MoC

Hmm?

LAVOISIER

We have no subject!

MoC

You are right of course. We have come to a fatal impasse.

Arlequin slaps the stage. A platform rises SR, holding a pile of horse droppings. This immediately has the attention of Lavoisier and the MoC.

LAVOISIER

Mon dieu, what on earth could it be?

MoC

Are you quite serious, Monsieur?

LAVOISIER

I very much would like to study that sample of molecules. But, alas, I have no assistant.

Arlequin slaps the stage. Lavoisier notices him.

LAVOISIER

My good man.

MoC

Him? Oh dear, oh dear. Uh, Monsieur, that is- I-I don't think he's a very proper choice, Monsieur.

Arlequin slaps the stage.

MoC

(very enthusiastic)

Of course, he is! Who could be better?

LAVOISIER

Come, fair assistant!

Arlequin and Lavoisier wheel the cart over to the pile of horse droppings, which is actually a bowl with droppings piled around it. The bowl holds biscuits that resemble horse droppings. The audience cannot see the bowl, and the biscuits are indistinguishable from the real droppings.

MoC exits SL when the audience's attention is diverted.

LAVOISIER

Take a sample, good assistant!

Each of them quickly but carefully picks up biscuits, carefully considering and choosing the right ones.

LAVOISIER

To the alchemical reactors!

They both run behind the cart and place the droppings in beakers. The beakers are quickly emptied into other beakers, placed under flame, et cetera. Smoke will billow, mist will rise from cups, sparks fly, from whatever effects and props we have on hand.

LAVOISIER

We must combine the phosphates of the oxygen with the molecules of the hydrogen! Electricity and steam power will effuse the diluvium and color the elemental proboscis! There! There! We have it!

Lavoisier raises the beaker. Arlequin and Lavoisier carefully look over the contents.

LAVOISIER

Could this be? Could this possibly have occurred? I ask you, have we made possible the unimaginable? Have we now touched the furthest stars, however metaphorically?

Arlequin shakes his head yes and no to the questions, as confused as we are. Finally, they turn and face each other for the revelation.

LAVOISIER

I believe the results of this experiment will affect the lives of the common people of our nation every bit as much as my discoveries of hydrogen and oxygen. For, in my inestimable opinion, based on true and observable fact, I have discovered…

(drum roll)

MERDE… FROM A HORSE!

Arlequin is suitably impressed… then thinks upon it further...

LAVOISIER

But we cannot be sure. No! We must engage in further testing! Come, fair assistant!

Both run from the cart to the droppings. Both men pull huge magnifying glasses from their clothes and study the pile. Alternatively, they could use glasses with a giant eye painted on the side facing the audience if suitable glass is too expensive.

LAVOISIER

Study the texture! See its unique qualities.

Both men pick up biscuits and hold them in front of their glasses.

LAVOISIER

Fascinating! No time to waste! Smell!

Both men smell the biscuits and make faces.

LAVOISIER

Taste!

Both men lick the biscuits and make even worse faces.

LAVOISIER

My fair and good assistant, this is definitely merde.

Arlequin nods sagely.

LAVOISIER

We must place a flag upon it, warning all!

A "No Quarter" flag is produced from the cart and sunk into the pile. Arlequin studies the droppings with an inscrutable expression as Lavoisier gets behind the cart and wheels it offstage.

LAVOISIER

Come, glorious and purulent assistant! There are more hazards to find, more molecules to test, and – more importantly – good people to ravage for coin and gratification. Good people who need salt. Lots and lots of salt. Come my parturiency! Come my enflamed glandular conquest! Onward and upward, my assistant!

Lavoisier leaves the stage.

Arlequin looks right, looks left, then reaches down and picks up a biscuit.

He shoves it in his mouth entire, his expression looking as if it tasted of mana from heaven as he chews.

LAVOISIER

(from backstage)

Onward and upward, my assistant!

Arlequin waves to the audience, then slapsticks the next change of set before exiting SL.

END

***

Beau-Brave finally met Nicolet. He shook his hand in the green room during the performance. "Welcome to our family, young man. This theater is now your home, and all of us your merry cousins," he said. He was an older man, spry and still good-looking, gentle, slow of speech, and yet energetic. Beau-Brave liked him. He was with a young actress, a pretty, pale, light brunette. She was buxom and had rounded curves. Beau-Brave thought such a person had to ride everywhere in a carriage and eat rich foods to maintain such a figure. She didn't look at him and they were not introduced. To her, he did not exist. He therefore despised her, and unwillingly remembered her and her slight of him for a long time.

There were two other Lavoisier skits he wrote in the performance and the audience enjoyed them as much as the first. Although farcical, they were charged with subversive lightning – political, critical and pointed.

Lavoisier was an interesting man. The tax men were hated, as all tax men have been hated since the invention of taxes. There were very few tax men, however, who were as wealthy and high-status as a Royal French Farmer-General. But Lavoisier was also celebrated as a great mind who had advanced the frontiers of science – and not just in chemistry. He was intensely interested in the welfare of his countrymen and had involved himself in everything from providing street lighting to inventing a universal system of measurement, called the metric system. He was seemingly above reproach – and yet here he was, finally mocked. What then was Beau-Brave saying?

It was as simple as it was subversive: the man's charitable actions were not enough. He was who he was and deserved to be ridiculed. He wore the uniform of the wealthy and the medals of the tax man. He was an enemy soldier – and that was that.

This did not go unnoticed. People talked.

Beau-Brave watched the show from backstage, shaking hands every few seconds with congratulatory fellow artists. The man who played Arlequin, who went by Le Gilles, stood before him, grinned, and shook his hand, "As it should always be. A good mix and a good education."

Beau-Brave understood and smiled back, "Thank you, *mon ami*. And well done in turn. And without words - *mon dieu*! I understood everything without a word being spoken."

The performers were always kind to the writers. They did not compete and relied desperately on each other for success. They never mixed outside of the theater itself, unless the writer was a director or fellow actor. In those cases, the writer would never again associate with his fellow writers and would jump ship to the more illustrious and celebrated crowd of actors.

Writers were akin to the Rousseauian idea of God - every atom existed from moment to moment due to their talents, but they were never seen and no one cared – and everyone had better things to do than associate with them.

Writers did not excite.

That night, or early morning to be accurate, a good crowd of playwrights walked to the Eldorado du Dimanche: Braban, Dorvigny, Renout, Beaunoir, Ribié, Pompigny, Villaneuve, and even Saint-Paul – who was both actor and director, and was certainly condescending. Between these men was written nearly every word and action performed at the Danseurs. Luckily, the owner of the Théâtres Associés was coincidentally in attendance and he funded the evening. Why not? The quality of the writing at the Danseurs was higher. No one in the business was above poaching. It was an investment. Who knows what the future brings if initiated with friendship and brotherhood?

And wine.

Beau-Brave drank enough to turn his skin green. He saw the world in flipping double-images, unsure of what was going on around him or what he was doing. When the prostitutes began arriving, several of the heftiest varietals were employed as temporary palanquin slaves. Beau-Brave found himself in a dress, wig and makeup, lofted overhead by the courtesan heifers like a Roman charioteer and certainly cheered as lustily.

Suddenly, he was standing on a table with Saint-Paul.

"We welcome a new whore into the harem!" he said and there were more cheers. "A speech from the new harlot!" "A speech!"

Beau-Brave raised his glass and, in that moment, realized he had none. There was more laughter but he had no idea why people were laughing, for then he saw that indeed he did have a glass, or rather a wooden mug of interesting and sublime color. "Has this fascinating entity always been mine?" he asked, and there was more laughter. Pompigny could not stand and fell to the ground in paroxysms of hilarity.

"Speech!" "Speech!" they clamored.

Beau-Brave nearly teared, "I am a common whore!"

Cheers.

"May God bless Dorvigny, for he said it all."

"Dorvigny!" they screamed.

Beau-Brave waved them off, unsure of why they hailed Dorvigny. "I used to shovel *merde* on the streets of Paris, but now I shovel it onto the stage, where it belongs!"

"Here, here!" "Wisdom!"

"It is much cooler here than in Saint-Domingue."

Braban raised his glass, "Your thought flows naturally and logically from your argument, fair advocate." Laughter.

Why are they laughing? "I also wish to thank Saint-Paul."

Everyone looked at Saint-Paul, who missed not a beat of the composition. "We have spoken once, briefly. What can I say, Messieurs? I am impactful."

"Shh! Enough! Saint-Paul, when I saw your play *The Child of Nature*, I had a revelation."

"Flesh-colored burlap with leaves around the crotch does not a costume make," said a voice.

"A revelation. A real one," Beau-Brave insisted.

"Speak of this at once!" "Speech!" "Less words, more speech!"

"My friends, I will tell you nothing more in this moment."

A cacophony of displeasure arose from his companions.

"I will only say this. My three skits are three steps, three steps only, from the desert to Galilee, where my ministry will begin."

"Less ministry, more whores!" "Better speech!"

"Quiet. I will say one thing, and one thing only. We are not whores, Messieurs. We are destined for something more. I have realized that art is spiritual. More succinctly, art lies within the spiritual realm. We are priests, *mes amis*. We are priests of a new era and a new religion. That is our destiny. And we do not approach our destiny, Messieurs. It rather rushes at us, full blast, like a fired ball from a cannon."

For some reason, this quieted his companions.

Beau-Brave continued, "I see the future, Messieurs, as clear as the peeling bells of the tocsin. And we are the Caesars of the future, and the world is our Gaul."

"Here, here," was said in the silence, and all drank.

Amongst the faces, especially those in the tent who were listening, but not part of the festivities, were those of grim visage – not written with anger, but with determined and inspired vision.

They understood.

Beau-Brave, out of drunkenness and the desire for secrecy, had spoken his words in a confusing and jumbled manner, but, like a spymaster to his sources, his code was understood. Beau-Brave had identified himself as surely as he had waved a flag. Indeed, he announced himself as flag-bearer, and the moment would not be forgotten.

Beau-Brave then turned, threw up, and fell off the table, straight into his own vomit.

He awoke in Quinze-Vingts, which was nowhere near the Eldorado, nor even his closet in the Germain.

His arm was around an enormous sow. He was in a little clapboard swine house, the floor covered in rotted blankets, with hogs and piglets aplenty. All had an odd shine in their eyes as they stared at him.

We liked you last night, but now you are different. Out of respect for the man we knew, we do not attack. But you must leave now.

Beau-Brave gingerly made his way out of the little house, trying to keep away from the piglets. A few dire grunts accompanied him on his short journey, but nothing more aggressive. He found his way to the frozen mud, then climbed the short wooden fence to get to the street.

A lone sow, the one he embraced while sleeping, stared at him from the entrance of the swine hut. Beau-Brave tipped his hat, "I thank you,

Mademoiselle. Were it not for you and your fine sisters, I surely would have frozen to death."

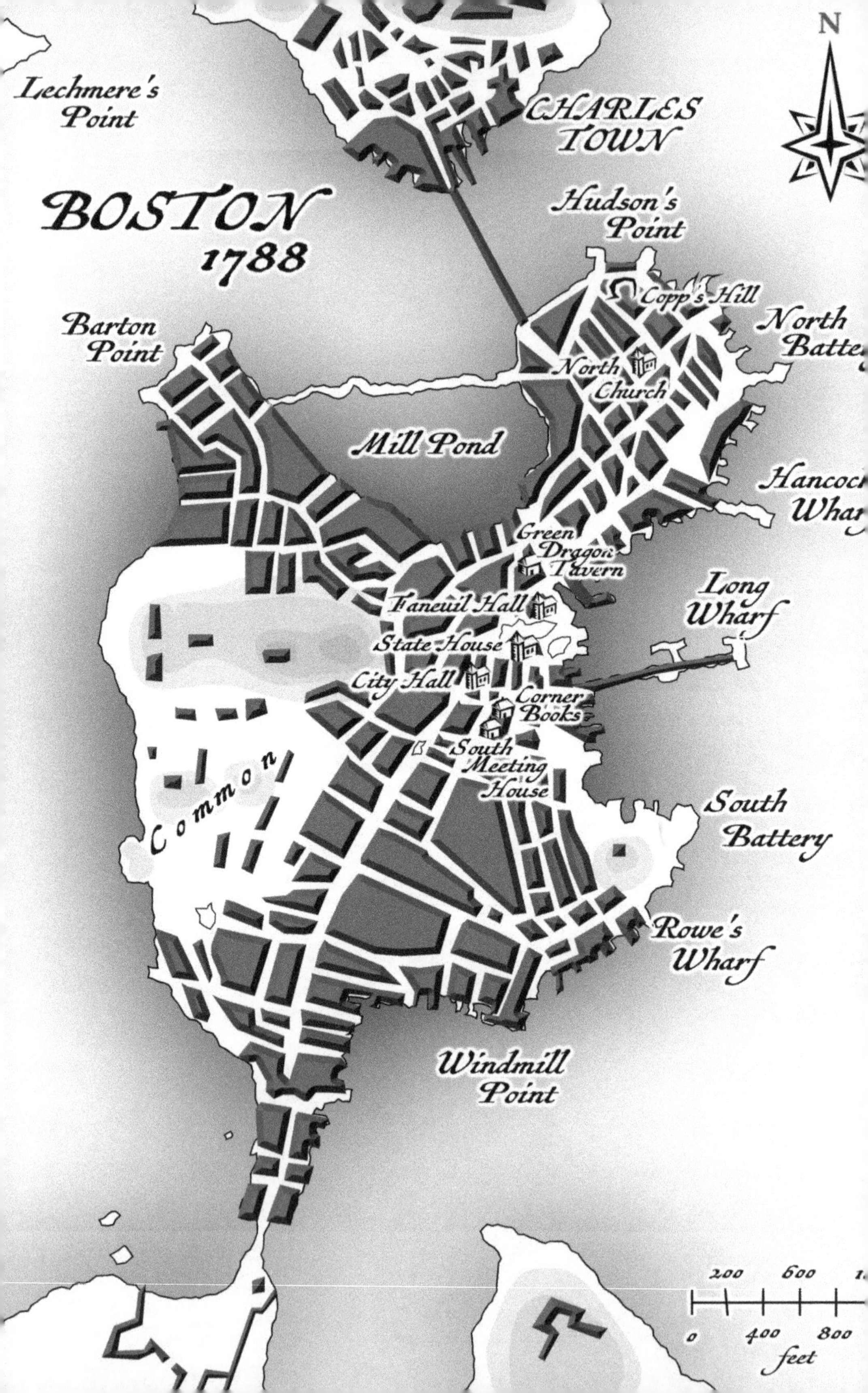

BOSTON
1788

Lechmere's Point

CHARLES TOWN

N

Hudson's Point

Barton Point

Copp's Hill

North Batte

North Church

Mill Pond

Hancoc Whar

Green Dragon Tavern

Faneuil Hall

Long Wharf

State House

City Hall

Corner Books

South Meeting House

Common

South Battery

Rowe's Wharf

Windmill Point

200 600
0 400 800
feet

Chapter Seventeen

November, 1788

Xavier

Boston was not an impressive city, but it was clean, and its lines were elegant if unadorned. It was cold, the kind of cold that found every chink in the armor of Winter clothes and bit the skin like icy fangs. There was not a leaf on a branch, it was grey as Maine granite, and snow was only occasionally seen clinging for dear life on roof corners, for rain came down nearly every day.

The architecture was quaintly businesslike in the Protestant fashion. It had perhaps twenty-thousand inhabitants. In comparison, Nantes had nearly eighty – and was only the sixth largest city in France. But if one scratched the surface, Boston became quite remarkable. For such a small town, it generated a tremendous amount of trade and commerce. It was also a hotbed of Enlightenment thought and intellectualism, and said to be a rising center of art, literature, and learning. To a Frenchman, this sentiment was hard to see with the naked eye. Culturally, the Americans of New England seemed hopelessly backwards, albeit hard-working. They were clean and simply dressed. They drank beer and rum and ate more than their fair share of potatoes, corn and shellfish. Their menu alone was significant evidence of savagery. Mostly Boston loved money, and in that they were in complete accord with Nantes.

The schooner sailed into harbor and was met by a tow cutter who told them to heave to and anchor, for the docks were full. As Deschenes gave the orders to execute a four-bower anchor, Xavier had their own cutter lowered, and he was then rowed into port.

He was met by a grim squad of Rag's men, a bunch of tough, battled-hardened bastards for the most part.

Xavier did not turn, "L'Oublié?"

L'Oublié did not reply. That meant they were in no danger.

The cutter was tied off, and Xavier, L'Oublié, Deschenes and the Americans climbed up onto the docks. A well-muscled, well-freckled blond named Billy walked up to Xavier and offered his hand. Xavier shook it with strength, as was the custom here.

Billy spoke, "I'll take you to him, Mister Xavier."

So, Rag was back.

Foutre-merde.

***

Rag was a huge presence. In the past, he sat behind his desk, his simple Quaker chair made Saturn's throne, the front legs off the floor, his crotch nearly hanging off the seat. His arms were outstretched, his grin dominating, his conversation loud, his presence overwhelming - the pattern weave of Iroquois torture scars intimidating.

Today, he sat slumped in his chair, his eyes downcast, his mien pensive. Rag's historical extroversion was so pronounced, his present demeanor was akin to his skull being inside-out.

When Xavier entered with Billy and his men, Rag looked up, his eyes burning. "Talk alone," was all he said.

Xavier had never talked to Rag alone.

Xavier turned, "Messieurs." Both his men and Rag's backed out of the room, hat in hand, saying their greetings and farewells at the same time.

The door shut.

Rag spoke, "Blanket. Door."

Salope!

Xavier looked around and saw a wadded-up, dusty blanket near the wall. He kicked it straight and maneuvered it to block the air under the door. "*Voilà.*"

"Yep, that'll do."

Xavier sat, "*Bordel de merde*, Rag."

Rag's eyes flashed up once again, "I told you not to come, you dumb bastard."

"And then you left me no choice," Xavier returned calmly.

"Damnit man, I asked you to trust me. I told you not to come."

"Why are you angry? Are you not glad to see me? Perhaps now we eat oysters and drink porter, yes?"

"You weren't meant to come here. It should not have mattered to you. After reading my note you should have tongue-slapped all three of those boys and sent them packing to get back to where they belonged. They woulda come back to see me returned, to get my orders for the next step."

"Next step?"

Rag eyes went downward. "I'm not telling you nothing more."

Xavier did not reply.

Rag spoke again, "I'm retiring."

Xavier again said nothing. He was better at this sort of awkwardness than Rag and was patient.

"I'm giving you my business. All of it."

Xavier stared at the top of the desk, nodded.

"I only want a percentage. A small one. Of the business and however much it grows." Rag fidgeted and spoke again, "Ten percent. Non-negotiable."

"*Putain!* I should say ten, then you say seventy-five, then I say fifty and you say sixty non-negotiable! What in the *foutre-merde* is wrong with you?" asked Xavier, quite calmly.

"I don't want to tell you."

"I am not one of your savage scalpers from Six Nation Country, Rag. I am a Frenchman. I do not mistake good manners or polite conversation for weakness. It is not my intention to pounce upon the sick and the old, like some African hyena. We are *amis*, *oui*? I am here to help."

Rag rubbed his forehead. Xavier waited.

"Everything used to make sense. I thought I had it all figured out. Overnight, I went from everything making sense to nothing making sense."

Xavier said nothing.

Rag scratched his head. "Well, I guess there's nothing for it."

Xavier did not reply.

Rag's eyes darted, his body began to shake. Xavier could not fathom what had rattled the man.

Xavier found himself deeply uncomfortable. There is something unnerving about the strongest of men suddenly becoming weak. Xavier spoke softly, "If you wish to speak of whatever ails you, I am a welcome listener. If you do not wish to speak of it, by all means keep your secrets."

"That's just it. It ain't meant to be a secret."

"Then you can tell me in confidence, I assure you. Whatever it is, it is not my story to… *disséminer*, only yours."

"All right, then."

Rag told him everything.

Rag's subsequent words became a great mystery to Xavier – one he would only unravel decades later. He never saw the man again but they did correspond. Rag would one day do him one last great favor, however, that would not be for many years.

For now, the upshot of everything was that Rag was retiring.

Xavier had to somehow put in place an effective new management in Boston that he could control from Nantes.

He had effectively doubled his business.

There was only one constraint upon his new enterprises, given to him by Rag: None of Rag's former ships, buildings or personnel could be used in the slave trade. Xavier agreed and did not go back on his word. In fact, he used Rag's conditions as a pretext to stop engaging in the trade within the whole of the Traversier enterprise, and issued the orders to all his subsidiaries from Boston. He felt as if a weight was lifted from his shoulders.

He was ready to return to Nantes and worthy to marry Estelle.

He was clean.

American trade was so robust there weren't enough ships to haul all of it to Europe. American lust for European luxuries was equally voracious. The burgeoning cotton mills of Nantes took all of the white fluff Xavier could pour into them, at any price, and grain was nearly as precious.

His ranking amongst the wealthiest in France did fall, however. His decreased income was overtaken mostly by relatives of the king and the richest financiers. He was still the most successful man in Nantes and his lifestyle was completely unaffected. Slavery had allowed him to build a base that could easily weather his decision.

Doubling his resources did not hurt the process either.

Jardins de la cour du Palais-Royal, 1788

Chapter Eighteen

November, 1788

Beau-Brave

There were a few steps taken on the way to Galilee, for now Beau-Brave was on a mission.

First was the creation of the written work. It was not quite original, for he had stolen the idea and the gist from Shakespeare, who was little known in France. The work was completed and sleeping, waiting for the time when it could explode from hiding and light the world on fire.

Second, there was a move.

The closet in the Germaine was vacated with good riddance. Beau-Brave never gave it another thought. The Germaine was for bourgeoisie, journalists and lawyers, blowing hot air and politics at the Café Procope because Diderot, Voltaire and Rousseau did so, little realizing that with the great men gone they all were little more than tourists. Beau-Brave moved into a one-bedroom flat in the Faubourg du Temple, just outside the Farmer-General tax wall. He was a bow-shot from the Eldorado and a short walk to the theater.

He spent a lot more time at the Eldorado getting drunk than he did at the theater, although his work was now frequently utilized. He had come to the point where he could not stand to see his work performed. It was the worst sort of drivel, made to amuse the lowest kind of people. It hurt him – literally, for he had come to have physical pains in his chest upon its witness. It was best to avoid a show.

He drank with other writers from the Danseurs. His feelings regarding them had not changed: he was still full of contempt and judgement – sometimes envy. Despite their frivolity he now knew that they all despised themselves and the world. They were, however, undoubtedly connected at the hip. Outside their own company they were alienated men, being who they were; if people were a complex form of ant, the human queen laid few eggs of the caste. Their souls were few in number and, however much they disliked each other, they were alone unless together.

So, there they were. Beau-Brave, Dorvigny, Renout, Beaunoir, Ribié, Pompigny, and Villaneuve. Some were missing, having better things to do.

They were talking politics.

"D'Epremesnil is an idiot. After all he has done and stood for, to fold like a poor hand and announce no changes to the Estates-General - as if 1789 has anything to do with 1614," said Beau-Brave.

"You are an owl, Beau-Brave. You resemble something noble and wise, but in reality, you are as stupid and crass as a feathered vulture," said Renout.

D'Epremesnil was the august President of the Parlement of Paris, the grandest noble circuit of judges who formed a base of power against the king.

Beau-Brave rolled his eyes, "You've never seen an owl in your life."

Pompigny took a kind tone, "You live in a sewer, Renout. You must understand that your wife is a *grume en merde* and you do not realize it."

Renout threw up his hands, "The calling of the Estates-General is a monumental thing. D'Epremesnil has always stood for this, and now he is an object of ridicule? What do you want from the man?"

Beau-Brave leaned forward. "Let us start with doubling the membership of the Third-Estate. Even so, its lack of representation - compared to what it represents - would be an insult to statistics."

Dorvigny interjected, "Especially if they have the same number of votes as before."

Pompigny nodded sagely, "If my powers of mathematical contusion are correct, that would cut the weight of our voice by seventy-nine thirty-fifths."

Beaunoir, "Well, not all of our voices."

Beaunoir was properly *de* Beaunoir. The theater, for some strange reason, was rife with nobles. Beau-Brave learned that, as a general rule, anyone who had *de* in front of their name was of noble blood. None of them were particularly conservative, sometimes they were radical Socialists. They were invariably spectacular drunks and philanderers.

Ribié shook his head, "D'Epremesnil advocated the calling of the Estates-General before it was fashionable. When they came to arrest him, he was only saved when every single one of the members of Parlement stood and proclaimed themselves to be him."

Dorvigny burped. "Precious good it did him. He still found himself imprisoned."

"Well, he's out now," said Beaunoir, "A toast! To freedom, Messieurs!" Beaunoir did not wait for anyone to raise their glass. It was good that he did so, for he was ignored.

Villaneuve spoke, "Beau-Brave is right. D'Epremesnil walked out of prison a hero, now he is a laughing stock – outmaneuvered by the Throne."

Villaneuve was actually *de* Villaneuve. Another noble.

Dorvigny put on a mournful face, "To be outmaneuvered by the Throne – a piece of stationary furniture! An unbelievable feat of bipedal incompetence."

Villaneuve smiled, "To be honest, there might be larger mistakes in the making."

Beau-Brave sat back, "Go on."

"Some are trying to change the nature of the Third Estate delegation."

"In what way?"

"They say that the Third Estate has the power to elect anyone they desire to represent them. In other words, a peasant can elect a cardinal or his local lord as representative, even though their elected Third Estate delegate would then not be a member of the Third Estate at all."

Renout rolled his eyes, "Why on earth would they do that? Not even peasants are that stupid."

Villaneuve shrugged, "Half the nobles and clergy identify more with bourgeois politics than that of the King, maybe more - no, it's worse than that. Bourgeois politics were invented and propagated by the nobles and the clergy. They are more Socialist than the farmers."

Beau-Brave snorted, "*Salope!* The farmers are Royalists. They stand with the King as his abused but loving children."

"Careful, Beau-Brave," said Beaunoir, "One never knows who is listening. The police and their informants are everywhere."

Beau-Brave rubbed his temples. "If the Third Estate can elect anyone they want, the more radical elements in the First and Second Estates might forego their membership in their ancestral estate to represent the Third."

"What will that effect?" asked Ribié.

"It will polarize the gathering even further," said Beau-Brave, as his mind was flooded with memories of Grenoble.

There was something honest about a riot. When the brilliant colors of the world were conveniently turned to black and white, it made for a less complicated world - and the rare comfort of self-righteousness.

His reverie was interrupted.

A man had come to their table and stood before them.

He was pale and wore a fine powdered wig. His eyes were blindingly blue under black eyebrows and his head was far too wide for its height. He was short and unlovely but dressed in fine blue satin and impeccably cobbled shoes. He spoke, and his mannerisms were odd and his voice unusually timbred. There was something off in his meat, so to speak, but only if there was nothing particularly unpleasant in the rottenness of it. "*Pardonne-moi, s'il vous plait*," he said, "My name is Théophile Gautier-Proust Hocquenghem."

The table burst out laughing. "It taunts us with the alphabet!' screamed Dorvigny.

The man blinked, unsure of what transpired.

"What does it want?" "Will it speak again?"

The man spoke again, "I am involved in the foundry business, which my family has pursued for several generations. Specifically, we create metal parts for steam engines and other large machines."

"It bores us with its poison!"

"It is terrible to behold!"

"It must reverse its nocturnalism and find its warren!"

The strange man continued, unsure of any other course, "I have always loved the theater and now I wish to be a theater owner and put on plays."

"Write us letters when it does."

He continued, "A fairly large space has opened on the second level of the Palais-Royal."

Beau-Brave shook himself from a thought, "Second floor? Isn't that where the prostitutes rent their flats?"

The table choked with laughter.

"I-I'm not sure," the poor man answered, "To continue, a fairly large space has opened and I have become inspired to rent it and perform plays there."

"Yes, on the second story where there are no venues or businesses of any kind."

"But prostitutes!"

"Indeed! The rhythmic sound of wood against plaster beating a steady tempo for your performers."

"Multiple instruments! Each performer can choose their own pounded rhythm!"

The man's voice was hollow but he forced himself to continue, "Obviously, the first step is money. I am not rich, but I have enough, and the space has been secured. The second step is material. A script for a play."

Villaneuve suddenly spoke with a clear and forceful voice: "Leave." The tone was ice and steel.

The mood changed as fast as Spring weather on Mont Blanc. The writers pretended as if the man wasn't there - saying nothing, expressionless except for impatience and contempt. Beau-Brave had no idea why this was so but took their cue.

The man stood there for a moment, then turned and left. The mood and sonority of the table returned just as quickly.

Beau-Brave did not understand, "He would have paid for our drinks."

No one paused their conversation to answer.

He spoke again, "He might have bought someone's play."

Still no answer.

Beau-Brave realized he wished to hear what this man had to offer. If he had a space for plays and he was just starting out, perhaps he would do something different – perhaps he would take a chance on a new writer. Even better, allow himself to be brow-beaten into performing the writer's vision, rather than the writer caving to the owner's ridiculous demands to pander to the gutter.

Stranger things have happened.

Beau-Brave stood.

Dorvigny grasped his hand, "No."

"Why not?"

"You couldn't tell?"

"Tell what?"

Dorvigny beckoned Beau-Brave closer. He moved his lips to Beau-Brave's ear and whispered, "He is a man of… sophisticated tastes, yes?"

Beau-Brave then realized what he meant. "What does it matter?"

"Think about it. Do not trust such a man unless you are like-minded."

"Well, I'm not – and half of Grenoble would attest to it. I have no fear of being manipulated into doing anything uncharacteristic."

Dorvigny shrugged, "Just be wary."

"Have no fear. I don't trust anyone," said Beau-Brave, as he walked out of the tent to find the man.

He spotted him some distance from the entrance, walking toward the Barrière. "Monsieur!"

The man turned, frightened. He saw Beau-Brave and looked even more apprehensive.

"*Bon soir*, Monsieur. I am Beau-Brave of Grenoble."

The man said nothing but looked very fearful. A moment passed before he finally spoke, "I am Théophile Gau-," he managed before being interrupted.

"*Mon dieu! Arrêt!* You are now Monsieur Théo, from this moment until the end of time."

"You are one of the writers of the Danseurs?"

"I am."

"How can I help you, Monsieur?"

"I want to speak with you regarding your theatrical endeavors, in my professional capacity as a playwright."

The man calmed, but looked somewhat disappointed. He faintly smiled, "Of course, Monsieur."

"Have you purchased a license from the Royals?"

"A license?"

Mon dieu!

Beau-Brave shook his head, "You are Moses, Monsieur Théo."

"Well, thank you, I suppose."

"I should have been more specific. You are the *infant* Moses. You are in a little boat of reeds, floating down the river. You will either drown or be plucked from the water – by villains, pharaohs or others, you know not."

"And which one are you, Monsieur?"

Beau-Brave was taken aback. He thought about it, "What I am currently writing is ridiculous and absurd. I have a new understanding of art, especially the theater, but I am powerless to create under this new sun unless I find another venue, a new patron."

"Or another planet. You should not be so critical of what puts food on your plate."

"I honestly do not care if I am eating or not. I have no family and my needs are few."

"I have no immediate family. But my needs are legion. I suppose I was raised amongst too much finery," he said, downcast.

"What I should say to you is that I have much to impart before you can even begin to think about performing anything. I should say you now need to take me to dinner at Le Grand Véfour, in the Palais Royal, so we can speak."

"I suppose."

"Have you been there?"

"I confess I have not."

"A dinner for two is easily one-hundred livres."

"I-I suppose that, uh-," he stuttered.

"Fear not. A *bâtard* tricked me into such a dinner when I was in far worse straights than you. I shall not return the favor."

"Where do you wish to go then?"

"Well, to the *putain* space you have on the second story, Monsieur Théo. We will buy some bread, cheese and coffee somewhere in the courtyard – or rather you will buy it. It is a long walk. From here to there, I will tell you how the Court ties your hands behind your back and what it will cost you to free them. When we get to the Palais-Royal, I will tell you what I have done so far, as I have thought long and hard about how to get around the monopoly to achieve my goals."

"The Palais-Royal must be four miles from here."

"No, not that far. It can't be. Perhaps three."

"Do we have to walk, Monsieur?"

"Well, what do you propose to do, Monsieur Théo? Fly? Oh – I suppose you're talking about renting a cabriolet or something?"

"I have a german."

Beau-Brave chuckled. "Of course, you do. Where is it?"

"They have seen me walking and now approach."

Soon they were inside and away.

It was the second time Beau-Brave had ever been in a coach.

***

Beau-Brave patiently explained the pitfalls of the modern theater to Monsieur Théo, who he ended up liking very much. Monsieur Théo was not a weak man; he was simply not a physical one. Beau-Braved sensed that he was well-intentioned and had no desire to cause harm to anyone. Beau-Brave always appreciated such people, for his mother and father were the opposite. In addition,

Théo was creative and intelligent and did indeed have a true love for the stage. He struck Beau-Brave as someone who did exactly what he said he would do, and would wonder, befuddled, if told there were others who were not that way.

He was also political – a Socialist.

"I feel alone," he said, "Completely alienated, as it were. My family loves me, as I do them, but they are utterly ignorant of me so, oddly, it does not feel genuine. I feel as if I am a fraudulent person, while doing nothing more than walking down the street. Yet, I am honorable and should not feel that way. Why does the modern world create an environment that produces such noxious feelings?"

"You sound like Rousseau, Monsieur Théo."

"Oh, I could not trim his hangnails, but I thank you for the sentiment. Rousseau inspires me, Beau-Brave. Perhaps someday we will have a world filled with men unafraid of their natural state. Perhaps these men will be unafraid of other's natural states as well. Perhaps tolerance will be a common virtue, and all men will feel accepted and understood."

Beau-Brave felt Théo was overly optimistic, but said nothing. His words had come straight from his heart. He felt for the man. There was a wholesomeness to Théo, despite everything. Beau-Brave felt that if he could erase one line, the aberrant line, written on Monsieur Théo's interior chalkboard and replace it with another of proper grammar, he would be living an entirely different life. Perhaps he would have been running his family's business, the patriarch of a happy bourgeois family. He certainly wouldn't have been anywhere near the theater, for the happy reality of his life would have surpassed any theatrical fantasy. Perhaps if Beau-Brave was born into a better family, he would not be either.

When they spoke of business, Théo was disheartened by the news of the monopoly license that he would need, and the poor taxes imposed by the police for the hospitals – but not undaunted.

They arrived at the Palais Royal before either knew it. Théo was intimidated by the villainous nocturnal crowd, but Beau-Brave reassured him. Soon they found themselves on the second level and inside a large apartment.

Both held candles as Théo led them through his new space. It was composed of only three rooms. The first was large, perhaps the exact size of the floor of the Danseurs minus the stage, with the ceiling being much lower. The front door to the outside balustrade walk was set midway in the east wall; the west was composed of floor to ceiling windows. Two doors were set in the north wall, leading to a good-sized toilette and a boudoir.

"What on earth was this used for?" asked Beau-Brave.

"I have no idea. The space doesn't seem to suit anything."

"It's huge. The rent must be extraordinary."

"It is. I want to get started on something right away. Which is why your words regarding the monopoly have affected me. It seems I have much to do."

"You do indeed, Monsieur Théo."

"I wanted to stage theatrical plays. But now I understand I cannot stage plays at all – except for the very basest of melodramas and farces."

"If you are lucky."

"You are saying if I am lucky enough to get a license at all."

"Which you will not, because the amount of theaters is tightly controlled and static."

"It seems so… futile… to limit the dynamism of the human spirit in this way."

Beau-Brave nodded.

"So, what am I to do? I will not sacrifice my family business for this. I am only using my own personal funds, nothing more."

"You must invent a totally unique form of diversion, Monsieur Théo. Then you can apply to the monopolies and secure a license for your previously non-existent entertainment. Then not only are you in business, but you will indeed have a Royal monopoly upon a unique venture; you will be protected by the police if anyone wishes to duplicate your success."

"Yes, but all of that is easier said than done, *mon ami*. I am a businessman and, in this case, a financier. I am not a creative soul able to invent a unique form of entertainment with as much facility as one draws a handkerchief from a pocket."

"But I am that soul," said Beau-Brave softly.

"Can you? Create such a unique idea?"

"Can I? I have done so."

"You probably do not trust me enough to tell me of it."

"I have employed an advocate to secure the sanctity of my work through license of copyright."

"So, your work is then protected from theft."

"Yes."

"Then do not keep me in such cruel suspense!"

"My idea is quite simple but requires some explanation."

"I am listening."

Beau-Brave smiled and made a wide gesture. "Necromancy."

"Necromancy?"

"Yes."

"Could you define such a term?"

"Certainly. Necromancy is magic over the dead. In Saint-Domingue such things are actually practiced. Possession by spirits, the raising of the undead – soulless and enslaved to the magician. African magic of the darkest and most evil sort. Our necromancy, of course, will be theater and entertainment. Our audience will be half-aware that it is staged – and perhaps half-not."

"My first instinct is that such a thing would not work. I thank you, but no. Séances and possessions, horoscopy, tarot cards and such – yes, they are popular with the upper class but I could not see such a thing working on this scale, the scale of the stage and theater. In addition, such a thing offends the Christian.

People have been known to lose their lives making public such arcane practices. Well, to be frank, my consideration of their beliefs, although I do not share them, is of more importance and validity than my fear of retribution. We do live in the modern age, after all."

"Well, Monsieur Théo, I would say this: your space locates itself in the Palais-Royal. Necromancy is bread dipped in milk compared to the perversions I have seen here. You can do whatever you wish and no one can do anything to stop you."

"True. But I desire the entire world to eventually share my beliefs. I do not believe I can convert Christians by disrespecting their values."

"Paris believes in nothing. They have no values. There is not a single splinter of the cross between the six-hundred-fifty-thousand of them."

Théo could not understand why Beau-Brave entertained such a thought. Paris was a very Catholic city – well, Jansenist Catholic to be precise. To Monsieur Théo, it seemed the Church's gentle order dominated all facets of life, more comforting than stifling - usually. Théo especially loved the bells of the churches. He could easily identify the particular church from its song of warm notes, and it soothed him wherever he was. He only wished the church had different ideas regarding *him*.

"The common people are still religious," he said.

"The common *Parisian*? Surely you jest. Rather than pray for each other, they hang each other - *à la lanterne*. Paris is chockablock with gigantic churches, each holding one grandmother each, clutching her beads and praying for her pagan progeniture."

"You exaggerate for effect. There are many, many faithful people in Paris, Monsieur. The churches are notoriously packed."

"The typical Parisian cares for nothing. They *covet*. They desire coin, they crave status, and they lust for diversion. And all of them are willing to swim through streets of *merde* to get it. A production involving necromancy would titillate, nothing more. Bishops would attend – in disguise to give service to their position, but poor disguise so they could be seen in attendance. Any worthy priest who actually believes his host transfigured would never dream of protest, fearing that same bishop would exile him to Guyana. And this show would deliver diversion, Monsieur. Especially the show I wish to put on, which will be political, cutting edge and, more importantly, Socialist. For I have seen the future, Monsieur."

"I see. Are you mad, or perhaps the Witch of Endor, come back from the dead?"

"Well, I am mad, of course," Beau-Brave said with a grin.

"At least you are honest."

"I understand the new meaning of art."

"Which is?"

"Someday I will tell you. Not now."

A moment of silence.

Monsieur Théo shrugged. "If not that now, then what now, Beau-Brave?"

"I give you my script. You read it."

"Most assuredly, I will read it."

"You will have to approach your license carefully. You must think akin to an advocate. You cannot simply say 'necromancy' to the Court."

"I agree. The court supports a Christian monarch – they will have none of it."

"You must say, 'educational, historic theater regarding the religious practices of the heathen of Saint-Domingue.' Something to that effect."

"You are correct: you are no Witch of Endor, Monsieur. You are Machiavelli."

"Procure the license. Purchase my material, put on my play. Bring me to Galilee."

Théo smiled. "Perhaps I will not like your script."

"If such a thing could happen, the devil would not exist, Monsieur. And we both know that is false."

"What a thing to say."

"The world has rejected us, Monsieur. For that, they must pay. Their hate put something inside us. A tumor, a growing disease. NO! I am *their* tumor. We are a tumor to them. What they put inside of us was… a fetus. This thing has grown and developed and now the creature, full-born, has opened its eyes. It screams, Monsieur. It screams at the sheep, who are tired of being led. It can free them, Monsieur. The creature hungers to free them."

Monsieur Théo was at a loss.

He loved Paris. There was an order, everyone had their place. Even the basest of occupations had organizations giving a voice to its members, and ensuring justice and rights. Those of his own persuasion had a huge and thriving community here, although it was far too debauched and cynical for his own tastes. It was undoubtedly a city of extremes and extreme opinions. One could turn onto tony Rue Saint-Honoré and observe men squatting against the trunk of every yew tree bordering the Tuileries gardens, performing their dirty business. One could turn a corner on a far more ordinary street and witness a songster standing on a barrel, singing like a seraph to Glory, captivating a crowd in a magical moment. Sometimes the horrific smells were unbearable, but there were wondrous smells that surprised and delighted as well – baking bread, steaming coffee, the breweries, the perfumeries. Despite conditions, crime was low – albeit rising, concerning to all. No one lacked for purpose, except the refugees. Even those who had no family had the community of guilds, parish and neighborhood – and Paris did have true community in all three. Watching the rhythm of ordered life in the city, ebbing and flowing like the tide, was a wonder and – to Théo - every bit as magical as the sea. To think in such a way as Beau-Brave, and be immune to the truth provided by the senses, one must hate or be in tremendous pain. Théo was neither. He was confused. What did Beau-Brave say? The creature hungers to free them? From who? "To free the sheep from the shepherd?"

"Humanity is a pristine marble statue, carved by a master – for man in his natural state is perfect. But this statue is covered in flesh - rotting, maggot-covered flesh, for society is corrupt and oppressive. To rid the statue of corruption slowly, the maggots must be allowed to do their work - but one is left with stench and horror day after day, week after week. To clean the statue quickly, one needs to burn the flesh away. Verily, I bring the flames to burn the statue clean; for, from birth, I was trained to be the Vandal. And when the statue is engulfed, I will laugh, for the sight of fire pleases me."

There was a moment of silence, then Beau-Brave finally gave a good-natured chuckle. Théo shook his head. "What an interesting man you are. Your words are dire, poetry infected with lycanthrope. Yet, I sense no danger from you whatsoever, as if these dire words emanate from scars that do not penetrate any further than the skin."

"Someday I will share my revelation with you, and you will understand."

Théo looked forlorn. Beau-Brave was taken aback. He genuinely liked the man and, despite his words, was concerned he had affected his mood somehow.

He had indeed, but not in the way he thought. Théo was well-aware of the effect Beau-Brave had on him and was resigned to the sadness and pain to come.

Théo realized, quite simply, that he would die to make Beau-Brave's dreams come true – but what he truly desired from Beau-Brave he would never have.

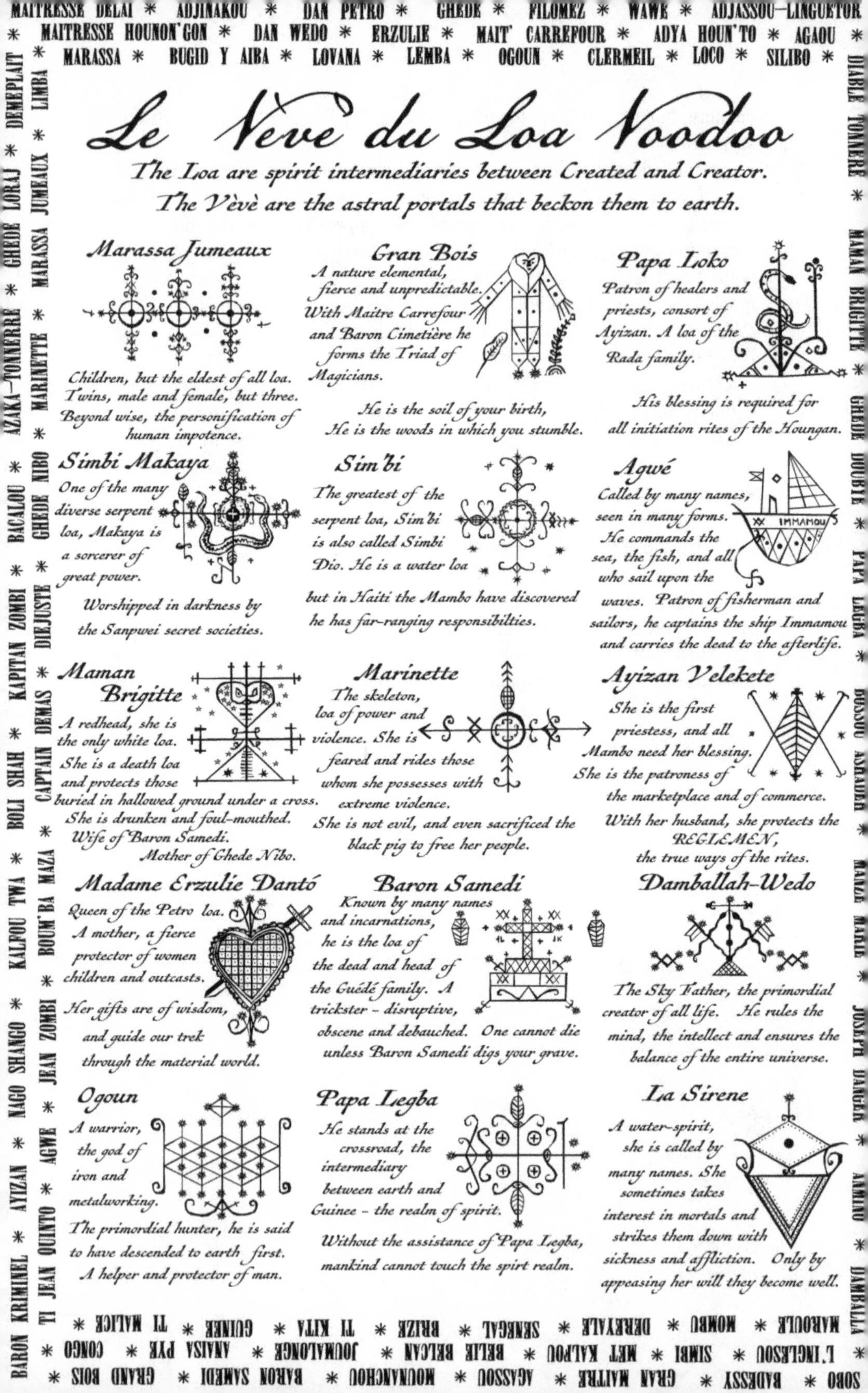
MAITRESSE DELAI * ADJINAKOU * DAN PETRO * GHEDE * FILOMEZ * WAWE * ADJASSOU-LINGUETOR
* MAITRESSE HOUNON'GON * DAN WEDO * ERZULIE * MAIT' CARREFOUR * ADYA HOUN'TO * AGAOU
* MARASSA * BUGID Y AIBA * LOVANA * LEMBA * OGOUN * CLERMEIL * LOCO * SILIBO *
Le Vèvè du Loa Voodoo
The Loa are spirit intermediaries between Created and Creator.
The Vèvè are the astral portals that beckon them to earth.
Marassa Jumeaux
Children, but the eldest of all loa. Twins, male and female, but three. Beyond wise, the personification of human impotence.
Gran Bois
A nature elemental, fierce and unpredictable. With Maitre Carrefour and Baron Cimetière he forms the Triad of Magicians.
He is the soil of your birth, He is the woods in which you stumble.
Papa Loko
Patron of healers and priests, consort of Ayizan. A loa of the Rada family.
His blessing is required for all initiation rites of the Houngan.
Simbi Makaya
One of the many diverse serpent loa, Makaya is a sorcerer of great power.
Worshipped in darkness by the Sanpwei secret societies.
Sim'bi
The greatest of the serpent loa, Sim'bi is also called Simbi Dio. He is a water loa but in Haiti the Mambo have discovered he has far-ranging responsibilties.
Agwé
Called by many names, seen in many forms. He commands the sea, the fish, and all who sail upon the waves. Patron of fisherman and sailors, he captains the ship Immamou and carries the dead to the afterlife.
IMMAMOU
Maman Brigitte
A redhead, she is the only white loa. She is a death loa and protects those buried in hallowed ground under a cross. She is drunken and foul-mouthed. Wife of Baron Samedi. Mother of Ghede Nibo.
Marinette
The skeleton, loa of power and violence. She is feared and rides those whom she possesses with extreme violence. She is not evil, and even sacrificed the black pig to free her people.
Ayizan Velekete
She is the first priestess, and all Mambo need her blessing. She is the patroness of the marketplace and of commerce. With her husband, she protects the REGLEMEN, the true ways of the rites.
Madame Erzulie Dantó
Queen of the Petro loa. A mother, a fierce protector of women children and outcasts. Her gifts are of wisdom, and guide our trek through the material world.
Baron Samedi
Known by many names and incarnations, he is the loa of the dead and head of the Guédé family. A trickster - disruptive, obscene and debauched. One cannot die unless Baron Samedi digs your grave.
Damballah-Wedo
The Sky Father, the primordial creator of all life. He rules the mind, the intellect and ensures the balance of the entire universe.
Ogoun
A warrior, the god of iron and metalworking. The primordial hunter, he is said to have descended to earth first. A helper and protector of man.
Papa Legba
He stands at the crossroad, the intermediary between earth and Guinee - the realm of spirit. Without the assistance of Papa Legba, mankind cannot touch the spirt realm.
La Sirene
A water-spirit, she is called by many names. She sometimes takes interest in mortals and strikes them down with sickness and affliction. Only by appeasing her will they become well.
BARON KRIMINEL * AYIZAN * NAGO SHANGO * KALFOU TWA * BOLI SHAH * KAPITAN ZOMBI * BACALOU * AZAKA-TONNERRE * GHEDE LORAJ * DEMEPLAIT
TI JEAN QUINTO * AGWE * JEAN ZOMBI * BOUM'BA MAZA * CAPTAIN DEMAS * DIEJUSTE * GHEDE NIBO * MARINETTE * MARASSA JUMEAUX * LIMBA *
DIABLE TONNERE * MAMAN BRIGITTE * GHEDE DOUBLE * PAPA LEGBA * BOSSOU ASHADEH * MANZE MARIE * JOSEPH DANGER * ARMINO * DAMBALLA
MAROULE * MOMBU * DERRYALE * SENEGAL * BRIZE * TI KITA * GUINEE * TI MALICE *
L'INGLESOU * SIMBI * MET KALFOU * BELIE BELCAN * JOUMALONGE * ANAISA PYE * CONGO *
SOBO * BADESSY * GRAN MAITRE * AGASSOU * MOUNANCHOU * BARON SAMEDI * GRAND BOIS *

Chapter Nineteen

The Detectives

1832

Jake

Out past Rue Ventnèf, the most northern of the north-south avenues, was a series of breath-taking elevations overlooking the bay. Newer mansions dotted these hills and escarpments, for le Cap was a city the rich now wished to escape, although once it belonged to them. The Dubuclet château crowned one of these hills and was quite impressively sited. It was encircled with verandas, surrounded by outbuildings, protected by walls, and shaded by palm fronds and leaves of Cuban mahogany.

Jake was settled in a suite and halfway through his bath when his chests arrived from the inn at the harbor. After a change of clothes, he was ushered to dinner by a valet.

Somehow Jake had found himself in civilization.

The well-dressed guests, all *Grand Couleur*, were seated at a table every bit as fine as that of the Meilleur. Along with the Dubuclets and himself, there were four other guests. Basile Barès was an ebony black, middle-aged, tall, fine-featured man. Andrus and Anaïs Espree were brother and sister, slightly older than Jake, both light-skinned, and quite good-looking. The last guest was Saint-Denis Snaër, who had the cynical, heavy-lidded attitude sometimes seen amongst the wealthy. It had been Jake's experience at Louis-le-Grand that such types were mostly harmless - except for their sarcasm - but could never really be trusted. The conversation was oddly superficial, as if all wished to speak of opinions they could not politely reveal in front of Jake - who was confident that it was only a matter of time before the topic emerged.

Monsieur Snaër broached the subject first, not surprising Jake in the slightest, "What do you think of our fine President-for-Life, Monsieur Jean-Pierre Boyer?"

Snaër was the kind of man who used words like *fine* when he meant precisely the opposite.

Jake chose his words carefully, "I know two things about him, and two things only. I know he put old soldiers out of work by unifying the island. I know he employs young, terrifying policeman with foreboding nicknames. In all other matters, I must profess ignorance."

Young Monsieur Espree smiled, "You must forgive Monsieur Snaër. President Boyer is actually our favorite topic of conversation."

Monsieur Barès spoke, "Give him more credit. He knows this already."

Jake thought Barès was possibly the smartest man at the table. He didn't care to hide his cards, however, which made him much safer than he might have been otherwise.

Pretty Mademoiselle Espree raised her eyes to Jake, "Does he?"

That meant for him to speak.

Jake cleared his throat, "There is something quite interesting in this dish. There are spices I have never tasted before, but there is something more. A unique taste and tenderness imparted to the meat." Everyone was staring at him, waiting patiently. His efforts to politely change the subject had been politely ignored. Jake had no choice but to hoist colors. "I am a man of the Enlightenment, of the Religion of Sensibility, which has fallen out of vogue in France, I am sorry to relate. I was part of the June Rebellion. I was captured and briefly imprisoned. I am on a specific mission as a condition of parole. My mission is not political in nature and I have not particularly educated myself as to the politics and culture of your nation. Quite honestly, I know far more regarding your mangoes than I do about your ministers."

Mademoiselle nodded. "You are paroled, then?"

"Yes, Mademoiselle."

"What was your sentence?"

"Death, I'm afraid. I was sentenced to be publicly executed by guillotine."

Snaër let out a loud, "HA!" and clapped his hands together once.

Mademoiselle gave him a humorous but piercing stare, then smiled at Jake, "The taste comes from a unique cooking process invented here in Haïti. It is called *barbeque*. It is a specific way of slow-cooking with old coals and without flame. It tenderizes and imparts the flavor of aromatic smoke."

"Thank you," replied Jake.

"We believe in slavery," said Snaër in an even voice.

"I see."

"You have no idea whether I am being serious or sarcastic, do you?"

Andrus exhaled, "Denis…"

Snaër shrugged at Andrus, then turned back to Jake, "Do you?"

"I do not."

"I am quite serious."

"I see."

"And what do you think of this revelation?"

Jake let his temper determine his words but did not raise his voice, "I wonder if you would then sell yourself into slavery, Monsieur. Most American slavery happens to be extraordinarily bigoted in terms of race, and certainly not in your favor."

The table appeared mirthful at his words. Snaër laughed, "Actually, the only race exempted from New World slavery is the Asian varietal, one assumes they are too far away for the honor." He turned to the rest of the table. "Do you see? It is always about race with them! That is always the problem. They cannot escape it."

Jake still seethed, "What do you mean by *with them*, Monsieur?"

"White people, of course! *Mon dieu*, what did you think I meant? All of us, the *Grand Couleur*, all we wanted was to be recognized, to have the same status as the *Grand Blancs*. But we scared you, didn't we? There were too many of us and not enough of you. You had to be better, you could not grant us the same status - and you lost your ally to keep your way of life."

As he put it down, Jake's fork made a loud sound against the side of his plate. "My way of life? I protest, Monsieur! You place guilt on a man who is neither French nor Haïtien, nor even alive at the time of these events. I am a Rousseauian, and Massachusetts born to boot. We have no truck with bigotry and certainly not with slavery. I will not be painted with such a wide brush. However ashamed I am to be associated with great violence, I have been shot at defending the rights of man, Monsieur!"

Snaër threw his hands up in mock surrender, "I have done it now. I've tripped into a duel with an angry Yankee and I am surely dead. My life of pale witticisms and debauchery has come to an appropriate and deserving end."

Madame Dubuclet spoke, "Denis! It is not wise to be humorous around such a subject. Our guest does not know you as we do."

Jake held up a hand. He had allowed this buffoon to affect his mood and his manners. It had to stop now. He turned to his hostess, "Madame, I beg your forgiveness. You and your husband quite literally rescued me this afternoon, and provided me with genteel hospitality and a fine meal. I could not be more grateful. I am the height of coarseness. I apologize without reservation."

Andrus held up a glass, "Hear, hear! Well said, Monsieur! And to be quite honest, all was the fault of your company for indulging such a crass subject at dinner."

Snaër's face fell into a mournful, thoughtful seriousness, "I apologize as well, Monsieur Loring. You have professed ignorance of our politics and culture. Does this apply to our history as well?" His personality had seemed to change completely on a coin flip. He was perhaps not so much of a fool as Jake originally thought.

"I'm afraid so, Monsieur. I know Haïti is the result of one of the few successful slave revolts in history, if not the only one. It is rumored that all of the French on the island were butchered. I have also heard all of the whites. I seem to recall that France officially recognized Haïti. I suppose that opens the door for all nations to do likewise."

They all shared looks. Jake surmised he had somehow misspoken.

Jake decided to patch a hole he could not see. "That is what I have heard, not precisely what I know to be true."

Monsieur Barès raised his glass, as Andrus did earlier. "Hear, hear," he said softly.

He doesn't miss much, that one.

Snaër spoke again, quietly but with intense interest, "You were in the city?"

"Yes, I was."

"What was your impression?"

"That it was once very grand indeed. And perhaps a great event leveled part of it."

"Arson, during the war." Snaër said nothing for a moment, then spoke quietly, "The French colony of Saint-Domingue was only one small part of this island, perhaps a quarter, and it fed the world. One quarter of this island, the whole of which we now control. Sugar, molasses, rum, coffee - even such things as cotton, sisal hemp and essential oils for perfumes – were not only grown here but supplied the world. The world, Monsieur."

"There was a tremendous price paid for this success. One too high for my sensibilities," Jake replied.

Barès disagreed, "The African would have paid the price regardless. Whether here or on his native soil."

Monsieur Dubuclet shrugged, "That is not quite true, Basile. I doubt there is an occupation in Africa deadlier than being a cane slave."

"I assure you, Laurent, that warfare is infinitely deadlier than sugarcane, and that was the unending lot of the African."

Jake nearly interrupted. "But is that really the point, Monsieur? We are discussing human beings, are we not? Is it not our duty to treat our fellow man according to civilized principles?"

"It would be foolish to do so in some cases," replied Barès, "Are not men the greatest threat to other men - through competition, war, crime, greed? And have we not always been at the mercy of greed? And when not of greed, certainly of economics?"

"I do not argue such a basic point, Monsieur. But at what point do we steer a more ideological course and assert justice, and a return to our better nature?"

"When we can afford to, Monsieur. Then and only then."

"But are we not comfortable now, Monsieur? The men and women around this table?"

Barès angrily stabbed a piece of meat on his plate and began eating again, but spoke evenly as he chewed, "I will tell you something else about my country.

Something you do not know. Saint-Domingue was sailing with a strong wind in a very certain direction, one that was plain to see: the *Couleur* were inheriting this island. Understand, there were plenty of *Grand Blancs*, our success took nothing away from them. We were their children, their grandchildren, their great-grandchildren. We did not take, we inherited. We were every bit as French as they were. But they feared us and perceived us as different. We were different only in color. We were plantation owners. We were Frenchmen."

"I see." Jake had lost his appetite. The reason was quite clear - he might as well have been having dinner at a plantation mansion in Vicksburg, Mississippi. The company would have been similarly aristocratic - and equivalently barbaric and self-righteous. The only difference was how the colors of their equally-fine fabrics would have matched their skin tones.

Ironically, Barès was therefore correct.

Snaër continued when Barès paused, "Then the Revolution happened."

How helpful these people are to educate me, thought Jake with rising anger and bile. He made a conscious effort to calm himself.

Even Monsieur Dubuclet joined in the lecture. "The African wanted freedom, the whites desired independence, but the *gen de couleur* simply wished for the equality promised the free man under the *Code Noir*. The *Grand Blancs* formed an independent government without us, therefore we supported France. Within the chaos of that war, the African saw an opportunity to revolt. Making everything worse, the revolutionary government in Paris saw fit to emancipate the slaves. When the Revolution ended, and Napoleon wished them to be slaves once more, it was more or less impossible. How does one enslave free men in a place that will kill three-quarters of your soldiers by disease alone? So, you see, if the whites of Saint-Domingue had simply acknowledged us as equals, history would have been quite different. Perhaps the *Grand Blancs* might have avoided their own slaughter at the hands of the African."

Jake tried to think of something neutral to say. "You see a slave society as being more agreeable than the current system, hence your problems with Jean-Pierre Boyer."

Andrus nodded, "Exactly, Monsieur."

Jake calmed. He would be polite out of gratitude and be on his way in the morning. "So, how would you describe your nation today?"

Monsieur Dubuclet shook his head, "It is the African, Monsieur. The African is a problem."

Jake rolled his eyes, "Does anyone in the world sympathize with the African, I wonder?"

Snaër snorted, "Uh… no, Monsieur. No one, I assure you."

"At the time of the Revolution, most of the slaves in Saint-Domingue were African born, for various reasons," said Barès.

For various reasons? It is because the attrition rate for these poor fellows was so high that they always needed fresh wood for the human pyre. It was a slaughter, a legendary horror that will resonate through the ages.

Dubuclet continued, "The African, you see, is lazy, Monsieur. Left to his own devices, he only performs the bare minimum of effort in order to survive – and here, with the richest soil in the world, that effort is minimal. Ending slavery would not be so odious if the African actually performed work for money, but he has no desire to work, Monsieur, none whatsoever. Even offering generous salary for employment, the African lets the crops wither in the field. When was the last time you ate sugar Haïtien, Monsieur Loring? Or sipped coffee Haïtien?"

"In all honesty, I must say never, Monsieur."

"Never. Of course, the answer is never because it is 1832. We control this entire island, and the island produces next to nothing. When France controlled one-quarter of it, we fed the world."

"At a high price, Monsieur," said Jake politely, to his credit as a gentleman.

"And what is our price now?" Barès asked.

"I'm not sure what you are referring to, Monsieur."

"Our dear President-for-Life Boyer has instituted the feudal system from Medieval Europe," said Snaër.

Jake chuckled.

Barès interrupted his mirth. "Oh, no, Monsieur Loring, he is quite serious."

Jake didn't know how to reply.

"France recognized Haïti in return for one-hundred-fifty million francs and a fifty-percent discount on our trade goods until lost French interests were compensated. To give Boyer credit for cowardice as well as stellar business sense, the deal was struck with French warships filling our harbors."

"One-hundred-fifty million francs?"

Dubuclet shrugged. "At the time, it was a reasonable thirty-year debt. Had we been able to sustain our prior levels of output, it would have been a pittance – indeed, paid already. Now, we fund this debt with more debt. One does not need a Genevan education to realize the dangers of such a thing."

Andrus looked up. "The majority no longer speak French, rather a gutter patois infused with African grammar. We are no longer even Catholic, the very church and its sacraments sullied with African superstition."

"The feudal system, Messiers," prompted Jake.

Snaër made a face. "Yes. The land is taken from people like us, divided between families and clans of Africans with quotas of crops to fill."

"Is it working?"

"No, of course not. The African excels only at failure, unless he has a whip at his back. In order for the feudal system to work, we would need fifty times the police that we have. The quotas are not met, the crops are not produced, and the economy shrinks every year. We were the crown jewel of France. Now we are slowly devolving into Guinea - and Guinea produces nothing. We have managed to create the first African nation in the Americas."

"And you believe slavery is more agreeable?"

Barès spoke, "Agreeable, Monsieur? No. Slavery is simply what was. None of us created it, we were born into its reality. It was fact. Now its legacy is fact."

"And perhaps you were born into a moral obligation regarding it."

"There is no perhaps. As are all human beings, we are responsible for progress."

"Then I am confused."

The table went quiet. Barès collected his thoughts, then began. "With slavery, we were a successful, but immoral, society. Now we are utterly unsuccessful without it, and not precisely a paragon of virtue, either. What we did not need was revolutionary change brought about by violence. What we needed was systematic, slow, well-thought progress from who we were, into what we could be. A successful slave economy turned slowly into a successful *free* society. Rapid, violent change prevented this from happening. With desperate necessity we had to turn our African population into a nation of Caribe. Instantly, we had to convert savages into workers. We did not. And now we reap a bitter harvest."

Jake's head buzzed with a strong feeling of déjà vu. He had heard nearly the exact words before. It was a different subject, but the same turn of phrase.

Lafayette.

He had used the phrase *rapid, violent change* at the Place de la Bastille, exclaiming that the Revolution did no favors for France, arguing in vain for cool heads. If Jake had listened to him then, things would have been very different indeed.

Jake left his thoughts and spoke. "And your answer is a return to some form of slavery?"

Mademoiselle leaned forward and looked into Jake's eyes with an earnest expression, "Perhaps not slavery, let us say something akin to it but more civilized. Do we now have a choice, Monsieur? We cannot afford to have your pure idealism if we wish a prosperous future for our children and our nation."

Gentlemen find it difficult to argue with beautiful women. Jake didn't try. "Perhaps there is a lesson here for my own country. We are half-slave, and slavery has always been a contentious issue."

Barès nodded, "Make sure war does not solve your problems. No good will come of it. All good *cuisiniers* know meat requires *barbeque*, a slow and patient heat, for the best results."

"In any case," said Dubuclet, "Monsieur *le Président Pour la Vie* serves at the whim of the powerful, whom he is greatly vexing. If he does not change something rather quickly to create economic progress, his days are numbered."

Jake chuckled.

"What is so humorous?" asked Barès.

"I meant no offense. I laughed because it has been said that one cause of the French Revolution was due to tension and conflict between the king and the nobles – and the poverty of the feudal system. You are a revolutionary nation, yet have found yourself in the exact same situation, simply with a few different titles."

They nodded with resignation and grim acceptance, for it was true.

Jake continued, "I believe in hope. I believe in the power of positive change. I believe human beings can evolve through the efforts of idealistic and selfless people, united in brotherhood."

"All noble thoughts," said Madame with a smile.

"I also confess that, occasionally, I feel very foolish for believing in such things," said Jake softly.

The meal was resumed in silence, at least for a moment or two. The banter returned, but thankfully there was no more talk of politics.

Une cour du Palais-Royal.
1788

Chapter Twenty

The Time of the Heirlooms

December, 1788

Talma

Talma was, unsurprisingly, tall and muscular. His face was angular, chiseled like tan marble. He was an incomparable presence: brooding, pensive. He was twenty-five years old, a man, but still possessed of the handsome vigor of youth.

In the Winter of 1788, he was a minor share-holding actor in the Comédie-Française and money was certainly a concern – especially after leaving a promising career in dentistry. He played supporting roles, albeit very well, and he was known and respected throughout Paris. He was a half-decent man, certainly thoughtful and intelligent. He was ambitious, but would never consider another person simply as an obstacle to his success. He was extraordinarily thoughtful regarding his craft. Ironically, being heavily interested in politics, he was not overly scheming in his interpersonal dealings. He was not without his flaws and peccadillos. He was an actor and an artist, both in temperament and morals.

Actors were not known for either.

The Catholic church performed no sacraments for actors; they weren't even buried in holy ground.

Talma currently was not where he wanted to be.

He desired three things: to take his craft to the next level, to make it impactful, and to play larger parts. He wanted to bring his beliefs into his performances and somehow share them with his audience, but really had no idea how to proceed.

The French theater was stifling, although the actors were certainly trained in their craft like cut and polished diamonds. In other ways, however, the diamond was in the rough. Actors wore stylish contemporary garb for period pieces. Dialog had to be musical and poetic before it had to emulate reality. Theater was spectacle, it was hyper-reality, it was a show. It was not… how it could be.

Talma knew his craft held deeper mysteries. He just didn't know what they were. There was another level, somewhere.

He was with one of his good friends, the forty-year-old painter Jacque-Louis David – the greatest, most-impactful painter in the world - and a mysterious woman named Mademoiselle Louise Desgarcins, who always wore a veil on her doctor's advice. Such a flimsy thing, however, could not hide her raven-haired beauty.

Talma did not lack for female consorts. He also, however, cultivated true friendships with women with as much ardor as he pursued lovers. Mademoiselle was his friend, and friend only, and he appreciated her as such.

It had been an interesting day for these three and for Paris.

Necker, the Swiss genius, finally back in control of the government as the King's Director-General of Finance, had put his foot down. The Estates-General would have twice as many members of the Third Estate as it did in 1614. Anyone – *id est* nobles and clergy – could represent a Third Estate commoner constituency as long as they were elected by them. The Third Estate would have the same power and vote as before. The decision was made over the hysterical opposition of the nobles. It was not a complete victory, but it was the winning of an important battle.

Paris celebrated.

Talma, Mademoiselle and David had been out and about all day, sometimes incognito and sometimes not. They went from salon to diversion, to salon again. They visited Joseph Chénier, Georges Danton and Camille Desmoulins in the Germaine, getting drunk in Le Procope, as was the want of the professed, affected revolutionary. There were others about – publishers and journalists, mostly – but the three men were, by far, the most compelling voices amongst them. They were, respectively, the greatest playwright in Paris – Chénier – although Paris did not know it yet because he had been utterly stymied by the Royal censors; the ballistic, self-confident lawyer – Danton - and last, one of the underemployed - Desmoulins - an intelligent man who had not yet found his talent. Subsisting on Danton's table scraps, ugly, scrawny, well-spoken, hot-blooded, and educated, no one had any fears in regard to his destiny or perpetual bachelorhood. It would all happen someday, probably.

Chénier was not precisely grouped with the other two, but all were united by their politics. They were professed Republicans, believers in liberty, equality and brotherhood… Socialists - radicals. Frothing at the mouth, they were ready to cross the Delaware river and assault the Hessians of modern France with table implements. Constitutional Monarchy was the covenant of the rebel, the Estates General was its ark.

Radicals are interesting and amusing company. Their violent dreams and poetic speeches were inspiring, entertaining and mostly harmless. One never disagreed with them, as one never pokes a dog in the eye when playing fetch.

Today, the radicals were amusing but too drunk to be interesting.

Talma and his companions decided to divert themselves at the Palais-Royal. They made their way to the right bank, and soon the coach was halted by the riotous celebration. David and Talma leaned out of the coach and waved. They were both immediately recognized. "Talma!' they shouted. "David! David *le grand*!" they screamed. On this day, David was the greater hero, his work encapsulating the essence of the values behind the celebration. Talma believed as David did, but he was only a supporting actor, and his politics were largely unknown to the masses.

The coach began moving again as the respectful crowd gave way. David grinned, "Der cheert lerder for me danu, Mesr Talma."

"Well, from my window, where you could not hear, they cheered louder for me, *mon ami*." David shared a private grin with Louise.

"Ouise, whatrutink?"

Mademoiselle shook her head, "Monsieur David, the cheering was obviously so much louder for you, it is beyond dispute."

"Itsowitoodbe. Painin isamur noble perfeson."

"Oh, I agree, Monsieur David," she said slyly.

David chuckled, "Ur viry kinda indulge me, Mamasel."

"I think I am beginning to like you, Monsieur David. What is your current status?"

"Mtaken, unfertnally, Mamasel."

Such jests could be made, for David was a loyal husband to his wife, Marguerite. She was unadventurous, and therefore not present, but did not resent her husband's many social obligations.

The Palais-Royal neared.

"And who are we to be this time, *mon amours*," asked Louise, "Ourselves? *La famille* Martin? Lords of the American frontier? Perhaps one of us a masked Huron?"

Talma nodded. "We must definitely go incognito. In terms of the disguise, the two of you must decide. I only ask that our costumes keep us warm, for the temperature is falling"

Louise ached an eyebrow at David and he smiled, "Phatms obda ball!"

"Excellent choice, Monsieur."

***

The coach pulled up to the Palais-Royal gate on Rue Richelieu. Three figures emerged, dressed in black, hooded cloaks and wearing masks. To their surprise, and perhaps disappointment, they attracted no attention as they quickly made their way into the courtyard – and were shocked to find a good number of people dressed exactly as they were, standing in small groups under the arcade.

A man crossed to them, rubbing his mittens for warmth. “Do you have tickets?”

After the briefest heartbeat of silence, the tallest of the three spoke for the group. “No, we do not.”

The man nodded, “Forty-five sous.”

The tall masked man gracefully manipulated his purse under his robes and handed him the coins.

The man pinned an odd corsage on each of them. “Do not take this off. It serves both as your ticket and as spiritual protection. The mambo will not perform unless all wear this.”

“We understand.”

“If it pleases you, stand with the larger group to the north. You will be escorted to the second story when there are enough.”

“Very well.”

The man moved away. Louise turned to Talma, “*Mon dieu!* This is so exciting! How did we luck into such a thing.”

“I have no idea.”

“Derrisno tamta wais! Wemusgo!”

“Indeed!”

The three joined the larger group. All light had been extinguished near them and the expectant crowd stood in darkness. All were fidgety, nervous - too loud or too quiet. The three new arrivals did not speak at all, but rather traded looks and communicated through subtle gestures.

“*Bon soir*!” said the deepest voice any had ever heard.

All looked around – but could not find the source. Where did it come from?

Then two eyes and a toothy grin appeared in mid-air. A man with skin as black as his clothes was standing near the wall, completely unseen in the darkness until he opened his eyes and smiled. To have such complete effect, his buttons and buckles must have been covered.

His smile vanished into a grim, expressionless stare, “I trust none of you have removed your protection, for if you have, this is where your journey ends.”

No one spoke. The man was a bit frightening, truth be told.

“Good. Very good. What is being attempted tonight will not be safe. Someone may die. Hope it is not you.”

No one gainsaid him. His eyes slowly scanned the crowd.

“Come!” issued from the man with such strength the startled crowd jumped. He turned and moved away. The crowd twittered with nervous laughter as they followed him.

They entered a staircase enclosed with a high arch of black canvass tenting and were plunged into utter darkness. They moved up the stairs, stumbling as it leveled onto the second story. The tented arches continued down the balustrade and the crowd did so as well. Ahead, the arches curved hard right into an open doorway. There was light in the room behind it, but a dim light, and the doorway glowed black rather than with the inviting orange of flame.

They warily entered the room. The tenting hugged the interior wall to their left, before finally opening into an expansive room.

There was no more nervous laughter.

Forty feet away, bolts of black fabric covered the opposite wall. There were windows to the left, but all were completely dampened with velvet curtains. The room was full of other masked and cloaked figures. From the ceiling dangled incense thuribles and braziers of cheap wrought-iron. From the thuribles came a fragrant, flowery smell, like steamed violets. From the braziers came a woody, herbal scent, akin to burning rope. The smoky air was medicinal, almost narcotic. Almost immediately upon entering, everyone in the room felt to one side of their normal senses.

There was a wide, raised stage where sat twelve dirty, barefoot men dressed in tattered rags. All were in irons, shackled to each other. A French Guard in uniform stood to one side. The shackled men were criminal and low-born, too stupid to be interested in their odd surroundings.

One more group of hooded figures entered, filling the room to capacity, and then the door was shut with a resounding thud, sending a wave of pressure through the crowd.

The pounding of African drums began.

The drummers must have been hidden behind the curtains, five of them at least. They each beat a different rhythm, some a different tempo. It was mesmerizing, especially after the effects of the fog of incense, or whatever it was.

Suddenly - BOOM - a blast of fire and smoke. Appearing out of it, shrieking and laughing, a lithe black woman wearing nothing but crow feathers tucked in leather bands.

"You are mine!" she shrieked and threw dust from both hands at the prisoners. The dust reacted with the candles and burst into flame – WHOOSH – smoke and fire and sparks were raining over them. The convicts convulsed, guttural sounds issuing from their throats.

The crowd panicked and some bolted for the door. They were led by the French Guardsman, who dropped his musket on the floor in his attempt to flee. They made it halfway to the opening when the black man with the basso voice stepped in front of them, "HOLD FAST!" he commanded, his voice heard through the floorboards. "GO BACK!"

The crowd could only turn back to the stage.

"Rise!" came a sorceress voice from the ebony crow-woman.

The prisoners jerked to their feet, gibbering, their eyes completely white. Some in the crowd screamed.

Talma was utterly transfixed.

This was not presented as spectacle: it was truth and reality, it was happening, it was present and now.

"You are mine!" she screamed.

"We are yours," repeated a dozen unholy voices, as if the prisoners were possessed by dark spirits.

Crow-Woman turned. "Release them from their irons."

The man in black stepped to the stage, keyed the shackles from the twelve prisoners, and threw their chains on the guardsman's discarded musket.

"I command the spirits!" she shrieked, "I demand the souls from an ancient time when men plotted against tyranny, where kings and despots feared their people."

Talma inhaled deeply, for he understood.

The twelve stopped shaking, instead they looked around, scared, in wonderment.

"No!" she commanded, "You will not see our time, only nature and constructs of your own – and how they were."

The men calmed to normal. There was nothing – less than nothing – of the convict in any of them. They had been transformed. They spoke amongst themselves… in Latin.

"No, no," came the sibilant commands from the Mambo. "You will speak in French."

One of them, possessed by some commanding spirit, stepped forward, "Who is it in the press who calls on me? I hear a tongue, shriller than all the music, Cry 'Caesar!' Speak; Caesar is turned to hear."

If one but blew a breath upon Talma, he would have fallen board-like to the floor. He knew the next line.

"Beware the ides of March," cried a hunched convict.

"What man is that?" asked the one who called himself Caesar. Talma's silent lips moved as he mouthed the next words.

"A soothsayer bids you beware the ides of March."

"Set him before me; let me see his face."

"Fellow, come from the throng; look upon Caesar."

"What say'st thou to me now? Speak once again."

"Beware the ides of March."

"He is a dreamer; let us leave him: pass."

Talma suppressed the urge to laugh with joy and wonderment. He had lived half his life in London. He spoke perfect, unaccented English. The British theater, far advanced beyond anything in the world, was his northern star - and Shakespeare his patron saint. And here he was, in the backward venues of Paris, smack in the Palais-Royal, listening to Shakespeare, to *Julius Caesar* no less.

Yet, in Paris, and in 1788, the play meant more than it did in London at the time of its first performance. Not only did it regard the assassination of a despot, the Socialists had taken the Roman philosophers as their guides - anything that smacked of Roman Nationalism or Republicanism was, somehow, now a raised flag for Rousseau.

Somehow a genius had found a way to circumvent the monopoly and put on a tragic play, a masterpiece that only the Royals themselves would deign to perform, in the guise of this silly séance, this voodoo play.

Master subversive!

Talma looked around. The crowd was utterly spellbound. As the play continued, the Mambo would interject, interact with the actors, move them from scene to scene. "Take me a day later into your machinations!" she would scream. The possessed convicts would stiffen, then naturally launch into their dialog in a new place and time.

The murder scene was a masterpiece. Caesar was stabbed with the Guardsman's bayonet and blood went everywhere. It actually smelled of blood, it had to be animal of some sort, but it was definitely real.

The man in black screamed before anyone else could, "They are convicts, sentenced to death! Do not be afraid! No one else could be used for such a thing as this!"

The man in black and the guard pulled the murdered convict off the stage and attempted to bind his wounds. It was too late - he was dead, murdered by the spirit of Brutus.

It was brilliant.

No - it was *blindingly* brilliant.

The writer had carefully tuned the ancient play to a French audience, meticulously added detail to make the comparison between ancient Rome and modern Paris unmistakable. It was completely updated, now something entirely new. It was frequently plagiaristic, sometimes pastiche, always homage and cutting-edge revolutionary modernity, all at the same time – while still being a platonic simulacrum, as real in its imitation of reality as it could be, being a play on a stage.

It utterly humbled Talma, for this magnificence represented everything he wished to be but was not. Talma knew that his international perspective and attendance of wildly differing schools of acting gave him an edge, made him better. He could not have had a more ideal physicality for the stage. He worked as hard as he could, meticulously preparing for each role.

But none of that was enough.

Something itched deep in the back of his mind. It was almost as if everything he knew was filtered through a limited spectrum simply by living in his time and place. He could only elevate himself after dispelling this world view - perform his craft under a completely different umbrella of being. Talma realized whoever constructed this séance of Shakespeare had somehow broken through to the other side. He was executing his art under the light of a different sun.

Talma had to know him, her, whomever it was. It was an imperative, every bit as important as his friendships with the artistic revolutionaries David and Chénier.

After the performance, the crowd was ushered to the other side of the door and down the opposite hall they had come in. The light of the stars and a few flickering lamps shone to them as broad daylight after the smoky darkness of the interior.

When he arrived in the courtyard, Talma cornered one of the ticketing agents.

He raised his mask and showed him his face, “Do you know who I am?”

The stunned man jerked his head up and down. “Y-you were quite amazing in *La Jeune Épouse*.”

“It is then my honor to have performed a part of it. I wish to know where the cast of this séance is having their drinks tonight.” A coin of fifteen denier was palmed.

“All will be at the Eldorado, Monsieur.”

“The Boulevard’s guinguette? Outside the Temple Barrière?”

“The very same.”

“*Homme bon. Je vous remercie*.”

***

It was a raucous crowd at the Eldorado.

First, there were the actors. There were twenty-two, and all of them were there.

Twelve were needed on stage playing the roles of the shackled convicts and the subsequent roles provided by Roman spirits. Every fifth day, a different one played Caesar, the idea being that if someone returned to see the show in a week, they would not see a dead man playing the role and at least part of the illusion would be preserved. Caesar, after his bloody death, would become the French Guard - unrecognizably clean-shaven, bewigged, uniformed and powdered. The Guard, switching out with the incoming Caesar, would become one of the four ticket takers, one switching out every five days to become a musician - all of the actors able to play the African drums like Bantu war chiefs. While fulfilling the position hidden from the audience, the actor could again become wretched and unshaved in preparation for a convict role, where the cycle all started again.

Toinette and Bea played the mambo, as it pleased them. Sometimes they would alternate days, other times one of them would play the role for two weeks. No one knew anything about them. They were always a powder keg on stage, never drunk, always on time and universally good-natured. Both were there.

The man who played the host, Shaka-Chef, was another story. Unfortunately, no one could be found to replicate his performance; he had to be there for every show. He was a towering presence; his voice alone was worth the price of admission. Shaka-Chef was, however, a man of many vices. After his disastrous behavior in the first week, someone was always assigned to find him before the night’s first show. One day, Shaka-Chef would be found dead in his bed, in a dark ally, or be executed by the state, depending on the improbity.

Before that happened, an understudy - or two - had to be found. He did, however, make the show infinitely better. For all of Shaka-Chef's flaws, he could be prostrate from drink - or worse - and then, miraculously, perform flawlessly once he was found and retrieved.

Shaka-Chef was there, sitting glassy-eyed and giggling with his monstrous basso, holding a gourd filled with a black liquid. Only the devil himself knew what was in it, for the devil himself may have poured it.

Tonight, Loïc was the drummer behind the entranceway curtains. He counted everyone who entered the room and his count had to match the receipts taken by the four ticket takers. Now he sat with Monsieur Théo and they added up the receipts together. The ticket takers had to produce as many unsold ticket-corsages as matched the count. Once the books matched, all would be paid. There were never any discrepancies.

Most evenings - but not yet tonight - the mysterious, smoldering playwright would arrive, the one called Beau-Brave. He would write all day, going out of his mind with loneliness and creative drive, as if using his sanity for fuel. The actors always wanted to talk about the little victories and the deeply-regretted flaws of their performances. He, in turn, always wished to listen, and his replies were always heartfelt and constructive. The distance between the writer and the actors was enough to make their few interactions pleasant and positive.

The original stage blocking director, Marie-Rémy, never came to the Eldorado gatherings. His relationship with the actors had been explosive to the point of actual violence.

The Eldorado was a huge, nearly twenty-by-twenty-yard canvass tent. Five other smaller tents opened up into this area and were semi-private. The far-right tent from the entrance was the nightly haunt of the Necromancers. What was glaring about this space, at least when it was occupied, was its intensity of human vibration. Modern urban living was alienating and oppressive. Having the odd soul of an artist, especially with the strange forms of petty madness that came with such a distinction, made it even more so. When these alienated madmen found their place, and the project that bound them together, they transformed from depressed lunatics into vibrant demigods, thunderstrokes of personality. They glowed like golden idols with a satisfaction of spirit, a confidence of purpose that was extraordinary, as opposite an energy as one could find from when they were not working, not bound, not found, depressed, lowly, anxious.

Three cloaked and masked figures entered the Eldorado and sat at a table near the entrance to the necromancer's temple. They were quiet and kept to themselves. They ordered wine and olives and started the night by giving a huge *pourboire*. After that, the Eldorado staff would have let them burn the place to the ground if they so wished.

The three seemed interested in the goings-on inside the tent of the Palais-Royal performers but not overly so. The reason was simple: Talma knew the scene and understood who was who and where all the pieces fit. He knew the person he wished to see had not yet arrived.

But soon he did. The writer, Beau-Brave, entered.

Talma was surprised. First, he was young, younger even than himself. Talma, of course, had the look and presence of an exceptional star. This man was every bit as magnetic and even better looking. Part of it was his exoticism. He was almost Spanish Gaelic or Persian Jew – olive-skinned, green-eyed - but not in build, which was a Norman's thin, broad-shouldered frame, albeit covered in soft muscles, akin to a fit West African. His features were inscrutable, but handsome and sharp. His hair was amazing in its waves and curls - a painter could not have invented such perfection. He was wild-eyed and febrile, animated as if drunk, his delirium brought on by the presence of human beings after the self-imposed exile of the writing desk.

Talma gestured and a waiter of the Eldorado appeared. "*Oui*, Monsieur."

"The man who just joined the party behind us."

"*Oui*, Monsieur."

"I would like you to give him a note."

"*Oui*, Monsieur. *Bien entendu*."

The note was palmed with a quarter écu coin worth over a livre. It ensured that the note would be delivered with enthusiasm.

> *Monsieur,*
>
> *My name is Talma, I am a share-holding actor at the Comédie-Française. I am here at the Eldorado with the actress Mademoiselle Louise Desgarcins, and the famed painter Jacque-Louis David.*
>
> *I believe you are the author of the séance-play I watched at the Palais-Royal tonight.*
>
> *We would very much appreciate the honor of speaking with you in regard to the artistic process behind your masterful work - at your pleasure and convenience, of course.*
>
> *Bravo, Monsieur!*
>
> *Talma*

From their perspective, the three could see the missive delivered. The man took the note, carefully observed from where it came, then read it. As he did so, a smile deepened on his face. Afterwards, he sat next to the well-dressed... Producer? Financier?

The man gave the note to – was it the patron? - who, after reading it, was far less reserved. He looked around, nonplussed, excited. The handsome man, amused, patted him and spoke. The patron calmed after a moment, then both of them walked out of the private tent into the main room.

Talma stood and the rest of his table followed. Before the writer and the other arrived, he spoke in a voice that only carried to his companions. "Allow me to corner the writer."

"That might be more difficult than you expect. I am forced to cruelly use Monsieur David in my quest," replied Louise.

"Obedear!" said David.

As the two men approached, Mademoiselle stepped forward in front of the well-dressed man. "I know who you are," she said with a breathless whisper. "You are the one responsible for the play I saw this evening, are you not?"

"Well, I, uh," sputtered Monsieur Théo.

"No - without you there would be nothing. For you are the one who saw the potential of the material and the space, envisioned the success of the endeavor, and made it all possible, are you not? Are you not that man?"

"I suppose I am!" replied Théo, immune to some of her charms, but certainly not all.

"Will you not sit with myself and Monsieur David, the celebrated painter? Do you not know his work?" she said, not giving a crack between verbal bricks for reply, "Have you not seen *The Oath of the Horatii* at the Louvre salon? A man such as yourself? The strength and virility of the masculine figures, the musculature reflected in their steel will and strength of purpose, realistically rendered exactly as they appeared in life?"

Monsieur Théo's eyes seemed to wander to the cloth roof somewhere.

"Monsieur! Will you not sit next to us?"

"Pardon me, Mademoiselle. Of course, certainly, I am at your disposal and that of Monsieur David."

"Oh, wonderful!" she said and took him by the arm.

Et voilà, they were gone. Talma and Beau-Brave stood facing each other. Talma tipped his head to indicate direction and both sat. They admired each other's art, but knew nothing else of the man they faced.

Talma spoke first, "I must have your name, Monsieur."

"I am Beau-Brave of Grenoble, Shoveler of *Merde*, Whore of the Danseurs, and High Necromancer of the Palais-Royal."

Quel ego!

Talma smiled, hiding the fact that Beau-brave had not impressed. "I have heard of you, Monsieur! At least in your political endeavors. What you achieved at Vizille will resonate throughout history."

"My sister knows your friend David."

Talma was intrigued. "Who is your sister?"

"Estelle Guerrier. They met in Nantes. I understand he is painting her."

Talma had been to David's studio more than once. "Does she wear a necklace in the painting?"

"If it is a necklace of red gems, then yes."

"What a coincidence! Well, maybe not. Perhaps serendipity smiles. We must keep this a secret for now, for if we do not, David will wish to speak of it. I must monopolize you, although that word is as distasteful to me as I suppose it is to you."

"It is said you are the greatest living actor."

Talma searched for something to say for one heartbeat too long.

"I say that not to shove flowers up *ton cul*, but as a true statement of fact."

"I am not, though. Not yet. I suppose I could be."

"Go on."

Go on?!

It was all Talma thought about it when he allowed himself to be alone. How does one condense such a monologue? Talma spoke carefully, "Archeologists have found the ruins of Pompeii. We have unearthed ancient statues and frescoes from Egypt to Kashmir. We know exactly how the ancients looked – how they dressed, how they armed themselves. Yet, at the Comédie-Française, the onstage court of Caesar is dressed akin to that of Versailles, complete to the point of Caesar's baton bearing the fleur-de-lis. How can we justify such ignorance in the face of modern knowledge?"

Beau-Brave nodded. "The paintings of David are spellbindingly accurate. The public, the Throne, the court, all thirst for his work. One cannot say a more modern approach does not work or lacks an audience."

Beau-brave was growing on him, Talma admitted to himself. "Some call David's work Neoclassicism, but they are missing the point entirely, are they not?"

"Indeed."

Beau-brave was lost in thought but eager to listen. Talma continued. "For the play *Orphelin de la Chine*, I used my entire salary to purchase properties and costume items appropriate for the time and place of the story. I found that without the focus of the rest of the production, it was simply not enough to impact the play as a whole. I felt small for my efforts." Talma shook his head. "The Comédie-Française! No one in the entire company speaks of an attempt to be modern or cutting edge. They are cast in their role by seniority, paid with shares, and their only responsibility is to not embarrass the court. Now I prepare for yet another miniscule role, that of Proculus in Voltaire's *Brutus*."

"Speak of the devil. Well, different Brutus."

"Indeed. To be honest, if this upcoming production was shown in London to Bellamy, Macklin, and Kemble, they would laugh hysterically at its pompous absurdity. I swear, French theater is three-hundred years behind London. Here we know forty ways to wiggle our nose and have spent months learning to breath properly. Yet, we achieve nothing real. We have an abundance of craft and zero art, Monsieur."

"Define art."

Interesting question. Talma had never been asked, not so directly. He thought about it before replying. "Art is the creation of spiritual communication.

A certain kind of truth found deep within a man, subtly and indirectly told to others, bypassing conscious defenses and directly impacting the soul of an audience."

"I accept this. Go on."

Talma shook his head. "I do not mean to rant, Monsieur. No one has heard such words from me. I keep my own council, and a *stiff upper lip*, as they said in London. I see you as someone I can speak to with frankness."

Talma's words intimidated Beau-Brave. He did not like being emotionally frank. Yet now, in the face of Talma's courage, he had to be as well.

Talma continued. "I fear we French have reached our highest point already, Monsieur. Perhaps with Diderot."

"Beaumarchais!"

"*Mon dieu*, Beaumarchais! Yes! But it is all over now. I feel as if there was some sort of unspoken agreement amongst the courtiers, 'Oh, that is enough change, enough modernity. Let us sink back into the depths. Tut-tut, everything as it was."

"It must all be lit on fire."

"I would be content to find a pathway to change only myself. I am on a personal quest."

Beau-brave's thoughts turned. Perhaps this was the time for honesty, even for revelation. "There is a new meaning of art. With modern thought comes a new role for the artist."

"Yes. But what could it be?"

Beau-Brave gathered his thoughts.

Talma understood. "You have found the secret, Monsieur."

"I have told no one, but I will tell you. I suppose there is a chance you might think I am mad. You will, of course, be quite wrong in your estimation. I have simply seen…" Beau-Brave paused, searching for the right words.

Talma helped him. "You see our age under the color of a different sun."

It took everything for Beau-Brave to remain calm. His heart was beating out of his chest. "You repeat my own thoughts using my very words. Yes. I do. Now I do."

"I need to know, Beau-Brave of Grenoble. I need to elevate what I am doing to the next… level of existence, so to speak, if I am to be whom I am meant to be."

Beau-Brave felt the mad desire to test Talma, to see if he was who he desperately wished him to be. "Level of existence and not performance? A specific turn of phrase, Talma. I will infer from it that you would be the world's *tirthankaras* of your cosmic age." *There. Let us see what he does with that.*

Talma smiled. "I knew we were destined to meet, Monsieur. I had no idea of its pressing importance." Talma leaned forward and continued, "I need to know your revelation. I need to know it now. If you do not give it to me, well, I will continue in our Jainist metaphor; you will affect our *dharma* – you will change our true nature, for we were meant to meet."

Can this really be happening?

Beau-Brave felt this moment was scripted by destiny, and he could do nothing else but perform his part. "Very well, Talma. It is done." Beau-Brave turned to Théo. "Monsieur Théo!"

Théo turned, somewhat irritated, for he had been utterly captivated by his company.

"What is my mystery?" asked Beau-Brave.

Théo did not miss a beat, "That you have discovered the true nature of art in the modern age, what it is meant to fulfill vis-à-vis Socialist politics, and what it is to replace in our present culture."

"And how would you know such a thing?"

"Despite ourselves, all who know you are infernally curious in regard to your revelation and speak of it frequently."

"I will tell it."

"When?"

"Now, Monsieur. Now."

"Right now?"

"To all, in the other tent."

Beau-Brave stood. Théo lurched out of his chair. The cloaked figures rose as well. Louise twittered and put a hand on Théo's shoulders. *Do not be embarrassed*, she seemed to say, *We are all equally excited.*

Beau-Brave walked into the tent of the Necromancers and stood at the entrance. The whole room quieted, especially when Théo practically ran to a seat, and the three cloaked figures who had been spying on them entered and sat as well.

Shaka-Chef spoke with his earthquake of a voice, "He is going to tell us now."

Beau-Brave half-chuckled, somewhat shocked at his accurate prophecy.

Now realizing this, everyone else was enthralled.

A heartbeat.

A heartbeat.

Beau-Brave stepped forward, "Man is naturally good."

The tent's occupants became part of the performance. With finger taps, verbal clicks, hisses and catlike mewling, a musical ruckus rose up that somehow scored his words with sense and purpose. They were performers, Beau-Brave was performing, they could not help it.

Beau-Brave's hands moved in a circle, "Take away oppression and slavery, man reverts to his natural state. Man becomes naturally good. Utopia is ours. Heaven on earth is not only possible, it is the goal. It is all we have, it is our only heaven, for death is the great sleep."

The score rose, somehow a tambourine appeared and beat a fast, tinny heartbeat.

One of Beau-Brave's arms rose into the air, then suddenly came down and pointed at David. "Do you believe this, Monsieur?"

"Res!" David replied, spellbound.

"You do, do you?"

"Res, wiball my hirt."

Beau-Brave's eyes hardened, his pointing finger suddenly accusatory rather than anointing. "Prove it!"

Now there was no score, no music, no tambourine.

"Wab?"

"Prove that man is naturally good."

"Ibdohnerstan."

"Do you not speak French, Monsieur? I said prove it! Prove it now!"

"Aru net unabus, Monsieur?"

"Am I not one of you? Am I not one of what?" asked Beau-Brave, quite mysteriously.

"Dobu not belieb?

"Do I not believe? What an interesting thing to say." Beau-Brave walked in a circle, looking at every man and woman, scaring them, intimidating them, making them hope he did not call upon them. "Do I not believe?" "Am I not one of you?" he muttered and whispered over and over, fast and low, as he returned to the center of the tent. He stopped. Quickly, he stepped forward, straight and proud, "I am the Devil's Advocate. I do not say that as a turn of phrase. I say it accurately."

"He does," said Shaka-Chef.

"Science! The testing of hypothesis! Only the recognition of what has been observed through testing, observations that may change based on more testing, *n'est-ce pas*? Rationality! Empiricism! We do not concern ourselves with truth, rather we acknowledge what is *real*."

The riotous score returned. Shaka-Chef laughed. He was so jovial he brought others into his laughter.

"So, if we believe mankind is naturally good, why then could not such a simple idea be proven? And easily at that!"

The music died again.

Shaka-Chef kept laughing.

"Man is naturally good. This must have been observed through testing, *n'est-ce pas*? We must have arrived at this through science, through rational, empirical testing, for we are intelligent, well-educated and good. And yet, when asked such a simple question, David, the good scientist, fails. Why? Not only that, my intentions are examined for even asking the question. *Are you not one of us? Do you not believe?*"

Suddenly Beau-Brave screamed and crouched, clawed the air. He was absurd, everyone burst out laughing. His voice was beast-like, "The Enlightenment as human science? Ha! *Merde* on science! *Merde* on rationality and empiricism! Do you know what this is? Do you?" Now he screamed, in earnest and loud, "DO YOU?"

There was no more mirth.

Calmly, he spoke again, "Well, it is simple. This is not science - it is *religion*. When I ask for Monsieur to prove that man is naturally good, I am not a good scientist – I am a blasphemer, for I am questioning *dogma*. I must not be indulged with proof of the experiment, I must be burned at the stake. *Am I not one of you? Do I not believe?*"

Silence.

"There are commandments for our faith, carved into stone by the Nature God and handed to Rousseau. Do you wish to hear them?"

Shaka-Chef was loud. "Yes!" he screamed.

Beau-Brave spoke, "I do not like any of you, so I will only give you the first five:

> *"ONE! You will define religion as ancient man's primitive attempt at science. Your faith, therefore, is defined as scientific, because you are modern.*
>
> *"TWO! Thou shalt label thyself a leader, an independent thinker, every belief you hold a product of education, high intelligence and good-intention.*
>
> *"THREE! Thou shalt follow the tenants of your faith without question and with blind obedience.*
>
> *"FOUR! Thou shalt believe that anyone who objects to your faith is a religious, ignorant, poorly-intentioned fanatic.*
>
> *"FIVE! Thou shalt believe your faith is the sole vessel of anything good and moral; therefore, any who believe differently must be, by definition, evil.*

"So, does that not explain my interaction with Monsieur?"

No reply, only silence.

Beau-Brave closed his eyes, "Let the master necromancer take you back into the darkest past. To the very dawn of the Chalcolithic age, to the first city, before Egypt, before Sumer, to dark Uruk we go. High walls of mud and brick. Olive-skinned warriors with oiled hair and skin standing on the ramparts, armed with weapons of copper and wooden bows. Are you with me? Are you there?"

The music returned. Ancient competing melodies – an eerie sound.

Talma, Louise, and David shared looks: this was better than the séance.

Beau-Brave moved back and forth, almost akin to a possessed man himself. "Deep inside these walls, there is a hall of mud and stone - a palace - and in that palace is a man of power. He is called *Lugal* – Big Man - because the words king and pharaoh did not exist. He could order anyone to do as he pleased, and they would obey. Near that palace is another, even more impressive structure. Layer upon layer of whitewashed stone – stairs, levels, courtyards, and halls. This is the ziggurat – for the word temple did not exist. There is another man of power here in this ziggurat. He is called the *En*."

"How do you know all this?" said a voice.

"SILENCE!" screamed Shaka-Chef.

Beau-Brave waved a hand. "The En owned more land than he could see all at once. His temple was a city within a city. He could have been the Lugal, if he wished, but he did not. The Lugal's duties were many and they were difficult. The En had few responsibilities and they were easy. The Lugal held power with the sword. The En held power with fear and expectation, created by something far more diabolical than a weapon. He was the mediator between the people and the gods. Oh! What that meant! He came between them and the life to come. The En could doom his flock to an afterlife of suffering – or grant them a trip to paradise. Not only was he the arbiter of death, but of life, for the pleasure of the gods determined the harvest, floods, and sandstorms, did they not? Therefore, the Lugal served at the whim of the En, and was powerless against him."

Bea, one of the mambos, spoke, "But where are *we*, Beau-Brave? Where is Bea in this place? Why do we listen now?"

"You are there, Bea," answered Beau-Brave with quiet seriousness.

"Then I trust and listen."

"The En was the one who told the people what was happening in the world: all the events they could not see for themselves, whether of man or gods. The En was then a journalist, was he not? Perhaps that and more. The En was the parish priest, who read the news to the people after mass. He was even more then. The En helped the people worship through ceremony, spectacles involving blood, dancers, music. Therefore, the En was entertainment. All celebrated things started with ways to thank the gods and were therefore the purview of the En. The temple was the Comédie-Française, pantomime, *opéras comiques*; it was the fairs, the cathedral, the sacraments; it was all diversions – and the vendors, merchants and performers packing the ziggurat attested to this. Art comes from, and impacts, the soul, therefore it is spiritual. They invented us, *mes amis*. We are not fools and clowns – we come from them! We are fallen Ens. Our present state unhappily stems from when the people converted to other faiths, had new Ens, and the former men of the ziggurat had to find other ceremonies of diversion to coin their basket. We are the lost Ens, but we trace our line to an ancient priesthood!"

"We are lost no more!" said Shaka-Chef.

"We have been found. Now away from Uruk - to France, to now! The Enlightenment posed as thought and progress, but that was not its purpose. It was a magic spell. Lo! It was cast - and spent itself building a ziggurat. Behold! There was then another faith. It can be called nothing else, for I have proven its nature as religious simply and without effort. But the magic ziggurat is empty, *mes amis*. It now clamors for its Ens. It desires from its first laid stone to have its courtyards filled. I will say this: it will be filled, and by two types of men. There will be those who arrive, compelled by a force beyond their understanding, and they will play their part without truly knowing its purpose. But a far smaller group will come as well. These few say to themselves, 'I am an En. I am a priest of the faith that cannot be called a religion. I am here to function as an En. I am here to gain the power of an En. I am here to lead the people in spectacle and worship, through being faithful to a faith that will not call itself a faith. I call my sacraments diversions and spectacles. I know my place. I know what I stand for. I know why I am here. And the Lugal will serve at my whim. Or I will become him, as I wish."

All were spellbound into silence.

Shaka-Chef spoke, "All other Ens must therefore perish or make way."

Talma spoke quietly in the silence, "Who then is the god of the new Ens? What does the new faith worship in the ziggurat of the Enlightenment?"

Beau-Brave spoke softly in return, "We do not surrender our souls to God, rather to the General Will. We worship the enlightened Rousseauian state, composed of natural men freed from all shackles of oppression. These men are incapable of oppressing their brothers, being who they are. The state, composed of the new man, is our god. All progress will come from a virtuous people supporting an enlightened state, dedicated to the welfare of the people. That is what we believe. This is what *I* believe." He turned to David. "Being who I am and believing what I know to be true and real."

David nodded, understanding.

Shaka-Chef, too, nodded sagaciously. "You are not destined to be mine forever, *enfant de boucanier*. But while I have you as my own, you are my serpent, my most loyal servant."

Everyone looked at Shaka-Chef with blank faces, wondering if his words meant anything or were solely the product of drink, drugs, or madness.

As they watched, he slumped to one side, slid slowly off his bench, and collapsed bonelessly to the straw-covered floor.

"Ibelhab whatees habbing," said David.

L'abbaye de Saint-Florent-le-Vieil,
au sommet du mont Glonne.
1789

Chapter Twenty-One

January, 1789
Jonathan

Father Jonathan was the confessor for the Marquis de Bonchamps. What was said between them required no barriers of faux secrecy or anonymity, for Bonchamps was nothing if not fearless and thoughtful. Therefore, they did not use the confessional. Rather, they spoke as they walked the grounds and gardens outside the abbey of Saint-Florent-le-Vieil, a few acres of parkland at the top of the hill, specked and dabbed with people here and there, mostly playing children.

There was snow on the ground and the roofs, filling the space between the barren branches of trees like thin fingers holding clouds. From their height atop Mount Glonne, they could see the half-frozen Loire below them and the white fields of Anjou to the north. It was a crisp, sunny day and the view was stunning and clear. Both men were bundled up warm, pleasant, and comfortable.

Sometimes just a beautiful day moves one closer to God. Jonathan was glad of it. He had been praying for a sign. Perhaps today he would receive it.

Bonchamps was an interesting man, and Father Jonathan was grateful that they were acquainted. He wished he had more souls like the young Marquis in his circle, especially as peers, for it would have lessened the pain of his alienation and loneliness.

Jonathan had already given him absolution. Bonchamps was now speaking of his engagement as an officer in the Throne's army.

"Some of the reforms were inspired and long overdue. Commissions were purchased. Our military schools were little more than finishing schools for *les seigneurs*. Now, in this age of reform, we are, by far, the most modern and well-led army in the world. In everything from independence of command, artillery tactics, supply – even our use of skirmishers and irregulars, learned from the Americans. In terms of élan, technology, training, tactics, grand strategy, administration and recruiting, we are the paragon of martial excellence. We have even surpassed the Prussians, our former role model. We are a far cry from perfect – but we are the greatest military on earth."

Jonathan gazed away, somewhat bored, unfortunately toward the northwest. He was immediately reminded of the most shameful episode of his life. In a fit of selfish pique, he had thrust his responsibilities on his superior, then went to his room. He had been intent on getting a good night's sleep, then walking to Nantes. That was as far as his plans went. When he woke up, he was deeply regretful.

He had caught up with Brother David at breakfast.

"I beg your forgiveness, Brother David. If you are amenable, I would return to my duties."

Brother David did not look up from his porridge. "All men desert their duties at night to sleep, and take them up again in the morning – even in the case of Christ, when he deigned to become man. It seems you are no different, Father Jonathan."

Jonathan would have liked to have been post-whipped, then told he was absolved. Brother David's nonchalance left him still feeling guilty. He made a full confession later that day to the Abbot, Father Vincent. He spoke of secrets he thought he would keep forever, summed up in one word: Estelle. He was glad of it. No one, least of all priests, should keep any secrets. Sins were like wounds: sunlight and air prevented infection. Once an act was forgiven through the sacrament of Reconciliation, it was as if it had never happened, as long as the confessor was truly contrite. Clinging to shame and guilt was an insult to God's grace and forgiveness. In spite of himself, Jonathan did feel deeply ashamed. He had cast aside his oaths, duties and responsibilities. It was only for three hours – but it was truly and willfully done. He was ashamed that Brother David was aware of his cowardice. Out of all the things he did, he was most regretful at having communicated his state to his superior, exactly at his lowest point.

He then, of course, was ashamed that he was ashamed.

Bonchamps was staring at him, waiting patiently for a reply.

"I suppose that is good, *n'est-ce pas*?" said Jonathan, hoping his words lined up correctly with Bonchamps last utterance.

"I am a citizen of the greatest nation on earth and a faithful subject of her King. I believe in our institutions and laws. I am an officer, sworn to uphold and protect."

One had to listen very hard to sense the hard emotion behind his words.

"You sound convincing, Monsieur. But it also sounds as if you are about to say 'however."

"Armies, even ancient armies, have always been organized according to strict laws of discipline. Depending on the time and age, the rules might be different, but there have always been rules governing the behavior of the soldier, even in regard to enemy combatants and civilians. When there is no discipline, the result is disaster, as when Rome was sacked in 1527 by unpaid mercenaries."

Truth be told, spiritually, Jonathan was holding on by his fingernails. He was going about his day in total darkness. He was doing the right thing, moment to moment, only through having faith in doing the right thing. He desperately wished and prayed for a sign. He wished to know he was forgiven, that the universe would return to the way it was before.

"Go on," he said to Bonchamps.

"I had an interesting conversation with my commanding officer, the Comte de Chastenay, the commander of the Régiment d'Aquitaine, in regard to the brilliant men behind most of these reforms, in particular the Comte de Guibert."

Father Jonathan saw a uniformed horseman, the courier, making his way up the hill to the abbey. Both the rider and the horse blew great lungfuls of steam. Most likely, he carried the news that Father Jonathan would tell the congregation after mass on Sunday. "Guibert."

"Yes, quite an interesting man. A man of the Enlightenment, well-versed in science, art, and literature. A man of the salons. A writer."

"Your commander knows this man?"

"Yes. Guibert has been politically out-maneuvered, perhaps because he is the vanguard of the new, and now has little to do with anything, at least personally. His ideas, however, lead the charge at the very forefront of all reform."

"His ideas." The courier disappeared inside the huge gates of the abbey, to the right of the chapel.

Jonathan had an unbidden thought.

God please have this courier be your messenger. Please have him deliver the sign, the one I have prayed for.

Bonchamps continued. Jonathan hoped he was oblivious of his listener's difficulties. "In their conversations, Guibert told Chastenay that his reforms were a direct result of applying the beliefs of the Enlightenment to the martial sphere."

Jonathan nodded. "It is quite interesting how the fundamental tenets of a society color everything, from fashion to war. The lesson is that we must be cautious when we consider what to believe. Our beliefs create our actions. Actions create consequences."

"Exactly, Father."

Jonathan finally realized Bonchamps was troubled. "And what does Guibert believe?"

"His talk was philosophical at first, from what Chastenay understood. The practice of war should not be held back or oppressed by archaic ideas or religion."

"I see."

"Everything must be stripped down to its basic essence, to understand the very chemical make-up of war – preparation, process and outcome - what is truly at stake in its execution, and rebuild the military anew and adamantine."

"And how does this affect you specifically?"

"Guibert has arrived at a new concept, what he calls *total war*."

Jonathan felt something in the back of his mind, as if he smelled the faintest essence of smoke from a faraway conflagration.

Bonchamps continued, "Wars are not fought by two armies, clashing in one or two battles that decide the conflict and give minor gain or loss. War is now fought across the globe, using extraordinarily expensive weapon systems such as ships of the line. Defeat is utterly catastrophic, crippling a society's ability to feed itself, overwhelming a nation with debt. Wars will soon be fought by millions of men, modern industry pumping out the tools necessary to equip, clothe and feed an army of overwhelming size. Due to this sea change, the laws and rules must be sanguine and singular: victory at all costs. Defeat cannot be contemplated; the stakes are simply too high for too many. It is not a king that loses a region, the region yawning and mostly unaware and unaffected by the change, except for the raising of a different flag. Now it is a nation that loses its future, the fate of tens of millions hanging in the balance."

"This sounds quite dire, Monsieur." Jonathan saw the courier exit the abbey, look around and spot them. He led his horse in their direction.

Jonathan had three thoughts at all once.

This new type of war is coming. May God help us.

The courier must bring me a sign.

Strange how he comes near. He has heretofore left the news with one of the brothers when I am not here.

Bonchamps sighed. "It becomes even worse. It occurred to Guibert that the skilled labor and industry of the opponent is an army that must be defeated, every bit as dangerous and fell as the soldiers, without which the enemy cannot make war. Imagine huge armies, able to maneuver as quickly and freely as Mongol touman, spread completely throughout an enemy land, burning towns, factories, farms, and harbors - stealing all the food they can carry and destroying the rest. In the face of the enemy army they concentrate without effort, coming together quickly and efficiently in order to face a threat. Utterly destroying an enemy nation in pursuit of absolute victory, enabled by a state dedicated to war."

"I think the reference to Mongols is wholly shocking."

"That is ultimately my point. We are throwing off a Christian form of war for an Enlightened interpretation of war, which has a dangerous resemblance to a modernized Roman version. What is now being contemplated is utterly unthinkable. How does a Christian soldier proceed in such times?"

I must answer that question well, if I am truly a man of God and Bonchamps is my friend and of my flock.

The courier arrived. "Good day, Messieurs."

Father Jonathan squinted at him. "Good day. I have seen you before. Your name is Orville, yes?"

"Yes, Father."

"Why did you not leave the news with one of the brothers? You could be sitting down to a hot drink by now?"

"I must give this to you personally, Father. And you must sign for it."

That had never happened before.

"Goodness, is that so? Do you have ink and quill? Where is the nearest surface?"

Bonchamps nodded a direction, "A stone table there, Father."

"Thank you." All three men ambled forward.

For over fifteen-hundred years, Catholic jurors had been formulating the right Christian response to every human circumstance. It was an extraordinary well of knowledge. Father Jonathan searched his memory for the catechism regarding war.

"Evil should produce righteous anger in good men. Sometimes the result of righteous anger is war. Righteous anger, and the acts which flow from it, intend to correct the injuries of evil - both for the good of the individual and the common good, to restore order and justice, and to stop further evil. Righteous anger should never produce *less* justice and *less* peace. But fallen human nature is inclined to sin, and prone to respond to provocation with excess."

Bonchamps nodded. "Excess, yes."

"Thus, even virtue and a well-formed conscience can fail to produce the desired result. Therefore, restraint must be shown in the use of violence. All citizens and governments must work for peace. Sadly, it sometimes becomes necessary to use force to obtain justice."

They arrived at the stone table. The courier placed ink, a quill and a leather blotter on the table and the return document to be signed. Father Jonathan obliged. "Do you have wax, Orville?"

"Uh, yes, Father."

"If you help me by lighting it, I will place my seal on the document."

"Of course, Father." Orville took out his tinderbox kit, expertly chipped a fire into existence and soon had a stick burning merrily. He produced a red wax plug and lit it on fire, dripping a blot of vermillion onto the document.

Jonathan signed and sealed as he continued. "As with all moral acts, the use of force to obtain justice must comply with three conditions to be morally good. First, the act must be good in itself. Luckily, the use of force to obtain justice is morally licit in itself, so there we are. Second, it must be done with good intention, which must be to correct vice – the fruits of evil - to restore justice or to restrain evil, and not to inflict evil for its own sake. Thirdly, it must be appropriate to the circumstances. An act which may otherwise be good and well-motivated can be sinful by reason of imprudent judgment and execution."

"Excess again. Severity, perhaps. Yes, I understand."

"There must be four conditions for the legitimate exercise of force, all of which must be met: the damage inflicted by the aggressor must be lasting, grave, and certain; all other means of putting an end to it must have been shown to be impractical or ineffective; and there must be serious prospects of success. Finally, the use of arms must not produce evils and disorders graver than the evil to be eliminated."

Father Jonathan finished, blew on the wax of his final seal.

Orville shook his head. "You don't have to do that, Father. I am interrupting. Please take these documents and I will be on my way."

"You are never a bother, neither you nor your compatriots, Orville."

"Thank you, Father."

Orville went his way. Father Jonathan picked up the documents, noticed Bonchamps was hanging on his next words, and put them down again. "The Church greatly respects those who have dedicated their lives to the defense of their nation. If they carry out their duty honorably, they contribute to the common good of the nation and the maintenance of peace."

"Are there specific rules regarding conduct during war itself? During combat?"

"Yes, not everything is licit in war and conduct must be as Christian as it can be under the circumstances. There are actions which are forbidden, and which constitute morally unlawful orders that must not be followed."

"Such as?"

Father Jonathan searched his memory. "Attacks against, and mistreatment of, non-combatants, wounded soldiers, and prisoners; the destruction of an entire enemy people or group; and indiscriminate destruction of whole cities or vast areas with their inhabitants."

"Therefore, as a Catholic, I cannot engage in total war."

"I would say that, in order to do so, the evil you are fighting would have to be gravely malevolent indeed, in order to justify such a thing. But even then, every action would have to be weighed according to circumstance in order to be godly."

"Thank you, Father." Bonchamps looked off into the distance.

Excellent! His attention is elsewhere.

"You are quite welcome." Father Jonathan could wait no longer. He opened the missive and read. A moment later, unbidden, his jaw dropped.

"Father, what on earth does it contain?"

"I am stunned."

"What happened?"

"I'm not reading the news, which is some paper behind all of this. Rather the King's orders."

"The King's orders… for us? What does he wish?"

"As a prelude to calling the Estates-General, we are – all three estates – ordered to come together in democratic fashion to elect our representatives and compile a list of grievances, the *Cahiers de Doléances* - first-hand descriptions of problems and flaws in our society at every level. I read directly, 'the content of these cahiers will be considered when addressing the needs of the state, the reform of abuses, and the establishment of a permanent and lasting order for the general prosperity of the kingdom."

Father Jonathan felt overwhelmed. A King, an absolute monarch, had asked his subjects – from the humblest to the most powerful – for their feelings, thoughts and concerns.

Every single one of them.

Bonchamps was equally impressed. "*Mon dieu.* Is there any kind of precedent for this?"

"Something similar happened at the Estates-Generals in the past, but nothing on this scale. This *Cahiers de Doléances* involves ten times as many people as a national election in the United States. This is the greatest exercise of democracy that the world has ever seen."

"God bless our King."

"Indeed, may God bless him. What a great man! What an inspired thing this is!"

"Did anyone ask for this? Force it into being?"

"No," Father Jonathan beamed, "No. The king did this because he is our Father-King, and he cares, and he wants things to be better for us. And he has given us – all of us - a voice. We can now be heard. We can be heard, Monsieur!"

Bonchamps beamed, "*Vive le Roi!*"

Then suddenly the smile left Father Jonathan's face.

This was not a sign. God would have given me more. I would be shouting glory to God, not glory to Louis. He did not give me a sign.

Revered French Saints in the time of Louis XVI

Joan of Arc
1412 – 1431
Ordered by God to save France, she did so.

Martin of Tours
316 – 397
A former Roman soldier, he became the third Bishop of Tours and was responsible for great promulgation of the faith.

Francis Xavier
1506 – 1552
Co-founder of the Societ of Jesus, he performed extensive missionary wor throughout Asia.

Rémy
437 – 533
Baptizer of Clovis, Bishop of Rheims, Lord Chancellor of France

Louis de Montfort
1673 – 1716
A well-known writer, missionary, and confessor, he was also a strong proponent of Marian devotion and the rosary.

Margaret Mary Alaco
1643 – 1690
A mystic, she promoted devotion to th Sacred Heart of Jesus.

Geneviève
419 – 502
Patron Saint of Paris. She is credited with saving Paris from the Huns.

Vincent de Paul
1581 – 1660
A great healer and dedicated servant of the poor and downtrodden, he was also taken as a slave by the Muslims of Barbary.

Clotilde
475 – 545
Princess of Burgundy, Qu of Franks, she is responsible converting King Clovis, and ther creating what would become the state of Fran

Denis
Died 270
Patron Saint of France. The Bishop of Paris, he was beheaded by the Romans on the hill that was named for the act: Montmartre. He is one of the Fourteen Holy Helpers.

Louis IX
1214 – 1270
A great king and a better man. Patron Saint o architecture, he led an exemplary life of charit good works and deeds. A strong and just king, his legacy resonates through the ages.

Chapter Twenty-Two

February, 1789

Estelle, Xavier, and Jeannine

Thomas opened the door on an interesting character. He was short, fat, well-muscled and ugly. His teeth were crooked, his features large and misshapen, his hair an unkempt mess of clotted brownish-red locks. He was a *sans-culotte* caricature, probably a stevedore, and smelled of the docks and of himself, the former odor being the less offensive. In spite of being habitually well-mannered, Thomas wrinkled his face. "Can I help you, Monsieur?"

"I must see Mademoiselle."

"Are you mad?"

"No, Monsieur. I am in Mademoiselle's employ and it is imperative that I speak to her at once."

"I find that highly unlikely."

"Please, Monsieur. Simply tell her that Capybara is here."

"Capybara? For God's sake, man!"

"Please Monsieur, I am in a fell hurry."

Thomas shut the door and heard Mademoiselle's footsteps coming down the stairs. "Who? Who? Who?" she said.

"Uh... Capybara, Mademoiselle."

"Open the door."

Thomas did so. Jeannine faced the peculiar man. She spoke before he could, "Yes? Yes?" She did not say it to question his presence, rather as confirmation of an answer she sought.

"Yes, yes!" was his reply. She was then confirmed.

Jeannine turned to Thomas, "Pay him."

"Mademoiselle?"

"Five livres," croaked the curious Capybara.

"Five livres?" asked the incredulous Thomas of Jeannine.

"Yes! Yes!" she said and turned once more to Capybara. Jeannine spoke to him as if he were a trusted spymaster for a Queen, "Then fly, quickly! You know where to go!"

"Yes, Mademoiselle!"

And Jeannine was up the stairs. She caught Estelle in the hall leading to the landing. She had followed Jeannine at a more languid pace. "Estelle!"

"Yes, *mon chérie*?"

"Estelle, I must send you on an errand."

"Of course."

Jeannine regarded her, "It is quite important."

"I understand. You are positively febrile. What has happened?"

"I must send you on an errand to deliver a letter."

"Very well. Where am I going?"

"To Rennes."

"To Rennes? Why, that is nearly seventy miles away! Will I freeze to death?"

Jeannine simply looked at her with a desperate expression. It was an honest expression, which was rare for Jeannine. She was desperate.

Estelle nodded, "Of course. To Rennes."

"Good!" said Jeannine as she made her way into the parlor. She sat at a writing table and placed stationery on the leather pad and began to write. "Please do not try to see what I am writing."

Estelle half-chuckled, but there was no mirth in it. "You are acting quite strangely. How do you suppose I will get to Rennes?"

"You will take the second coach."

"But how will Madame get about town? Or yourself for that matter?"

"*Mon dieu*, Estelle. We have legs, do we not? Do not worry yourself." Jeannine finished the letter and handed it to Estelle. Estelle glanced at it. It was addressed to one *Monsieur de Glisser, 14 Rue de Brouillard, Centre-Ville Rennes*.

Jeannine moved to the door, "You must leave at once."

"Have you asked permission of Madame?"

"No."

"Will the servants do your bidding in regard to this?"

"Do you now jest? They will not thwart me. Pack your things, Estelle. You are leaving as soon as the coach is readied."

***

Xavier had been on many long voyages, some lasting nearly a year. But this particular voyage, lasting exactly twenty-five days, was definitely the longest. Bells were called on deck every ten years as the centuries passed.

Time dragged for Xavier. He had no one to talk to. When Xavier told L'Oublié the mystery behind Rag's disappearance, L'Oublié decided to stay behind in Boston, presumably to speak to Rag.

L'Oublié would take a musket ball meant for Xavier without much thought, of that Xavier had no doubt. In one case out of a thousand, L'Oublié went his own way without explanation. Xavier never questioned him regarding his rare errant choices.

Nantes loomed ahead as the Loire estuary narrowed. Seconds passed like hours. They cleared the tip of Au Duc Island where docks were seen. Xavier commanded the ship to make land nearer the castle. As soon as the ship slowed for the tugs, Xavier ordered the cutter lowered into the water.

Minutes later, he climbed upon the small cutter dock and bounded up the stone stairs to the quay. He looked around for cabriolets to hire; there were none. It didn't matter. It was less than a half-mile to Centre-Ville – more like a quarter of a mile. He began to walk, quickly. The walk turned into a trot. His hands swam through the crowd, "Pardon, Monsieur. Pardon, Madame!" His long strides ate the distance in minutes. Soon he stood before the Cœurfroid townhome. His hand touched the knocker.

He stopped.

He stepped back several feet, then quickly went around the corner. He found himself tearing. He had felt nothing for so long that the sudden rush of emotion devastated him; he found himself nearly unable to control it. He took deep breaths. He walked back to the door and raised the knocker three times.

Thomas answered the door. He was uncharacteristically dour. "Good afternoon, Monsieur."

Despite himself, Xavier felt rising anxiety, "Is everything all right, Thomas?"

Thomas looked at him with an expression similar to pity, "*Oui*, Monsieur. Please come in."

Xavier entered, "I'm sure my reason for… I am calling for Estelle, Thomas."

Thomas said nothing for a moment too long, "One moment, Monsieur."

Thomas made to move away. Xavier reached out and stopped him. He looked the man in the eyes, "Thomas – is everything all right?"

Thomas smiled, touched by Xavier's concern, "*Oui*, Monsieur. Everything is fine. Please."

Xavier nodded and released him. Thomas disappeared.

Not a moment later, a woman appeared from the opening into the main parlor. Xavier turned to face her and was immediately impressed by her grace and bearing, as she had somehow framed herself perfectly in the opening. Less than a heartbeat later, like a second taste of a fine wine, he was struck by her beauty. Her body's curves easily outmaneuvered her dresses' ability to discipline them. Her skin struck him as being pleasant to smell, even though he was not close enough to do so. Her face suggested not only patrician elegance but sensuality – she was a magnet of raw, physical attraction. As he stared, she became even lovelier, more interesting. She was literally stunning, for Xavier was struck dumb.

"Good day, Monsieur Traversier," she said in a familiar lilt - although it could not be familiar, could it? He had never seen her before. "Will you not greet me?"

Xavier realized he had not replied, "Good day, Mademoiselle. Forgive me."

"Do you not recognize me?" she said in a husky voice. It lingered on him, like a cat's tail that swished around his neck. She knew him. He had to know her.

He was being foolish - he was in the Cœurfroid townhome; she was Mademoiselle. This was somehow Jeannine. She had even slipped into the same gown she had worn for the ball, although it now fit her like a lambskin glove. Her green eyes glowed in the dark. He had never seen such beautiful and expressive eyes. "J-Jeannine?"

"Only if I may call you Xavier, Monsieur."

"Of course."

"You look upon me as if you still do not recognize me?" She blinked slowly, and seemed to say more with her eyes than her words. "Am I quite different?"

Estelle could not possibly walk in on them speaking in this fashion. "Forgive me, Mademoiselle. Is Estelle at home?"

"She has run off on an errand."

"When will she return?"

"Most likely tomorrow."

"I see."

"Monsieur, may I invite you for *déjeuner*?"

"Regretfully, I cannot." He could, but he chose not to.

"Then I must insist that you return tomorrow. You will call at ten o'clock and stay through *déjeuner*. Estelle will return at some point, and when she does, she will join us. Is this not agreeable to you?"

There was something about the way she spoke, an undefinable undercurrent. He bowed to her, "Of course, Mademoiselle. I shall return at ten."

"I am very pleased, Xavier." She smiled. Again, he felt subtext. She was a model of appropriate manners, but her inner feelings escaped through her pores.

"I will return tomorrow."

"Excellent, Xavier."

Thomas opened the door and Xavier exited, "Thank you."

"You are quite welcome, Monsieur," Thomas said with sincerity - and a twinge of sadness.

Xavier left, pondering why.

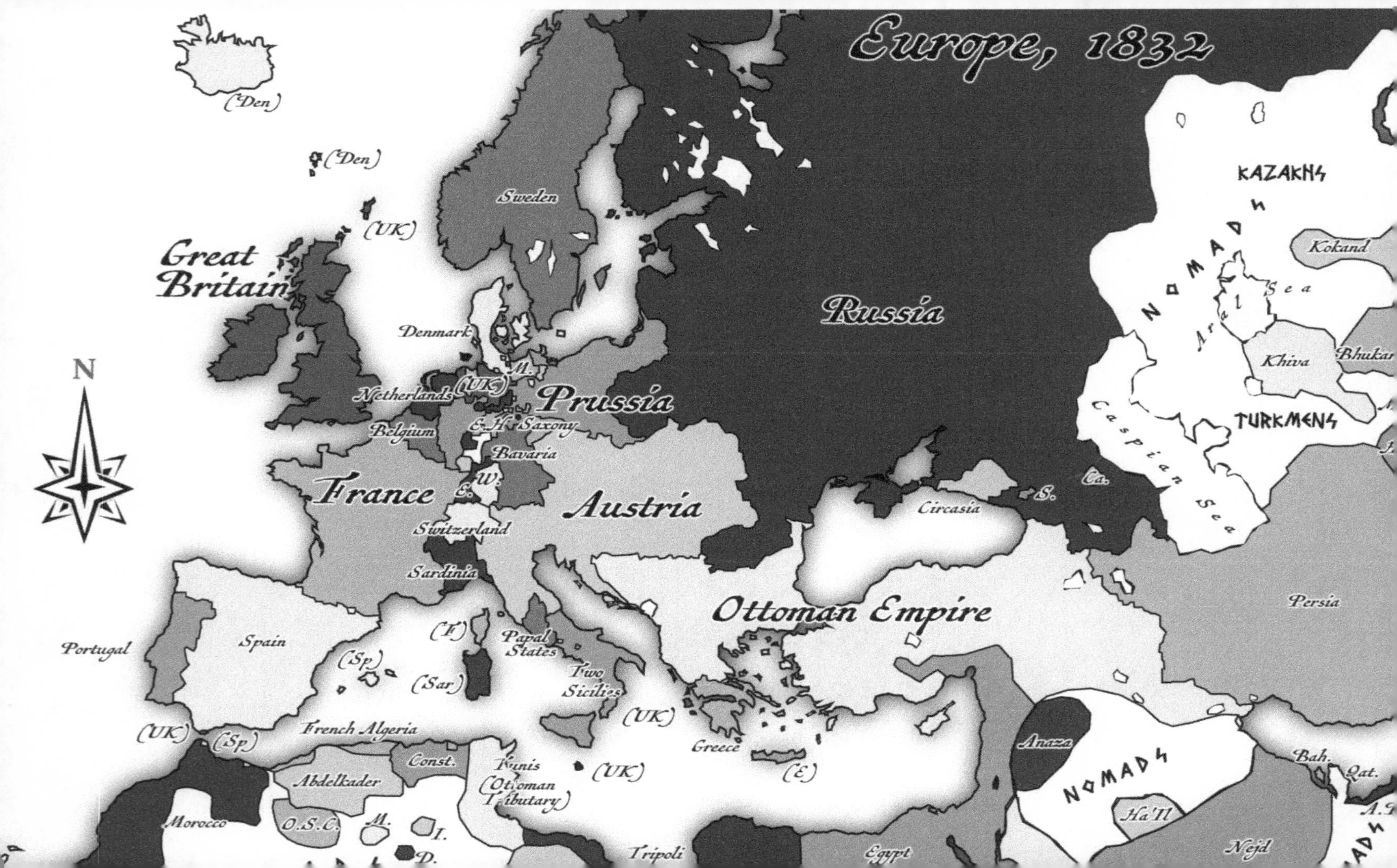
Europe, 1832
(Den)
(Den)
(UK)
Great Britain
Sweden
Denmark
Netherlands
(UK)
M.
Prussia
Belgium
E.H.
Saxony
Bavaria
W.
France
B.
Switzerland
Austria
Russia
KAZAKHS
NOMADS
Kokand
Aral Sea
Khiva
Bhukar
TURKMENS
Caspian Sea
Ca.
S.
Circasia
Sardinia
Ottoman Empire
Persia
Portugal
Spain
(F)
Papal States
(Sp)
(Sar)
Two Sicilies
(UK)
(UK)
(Sp)
French Algeria
Greece
Const.
Tunis (Ottoman Tributary)
(UK)
(E)
Abdelkader
Anaza
NOMADS
Bah.
Qat.
Morocco
O.S.C.
M.
I.
D.
Ha'Il
Tripoli
Egypt
Nejd

Chapter Twenty-Three

1832

Jake

The next morning, after goodbyes and expressing his indebtedness, Jake was relieved to climb alone into the Dubuclet coach. As it moved down the hill, he slid across the cushions and stared out the window, heedless of the hot, rising sun beating on his face. The view was magnificent, a seagull's perspective of le Cap and its harbor.

It was a truly beautiful place, but he felt dirty, covered in filth generated by the ideas of his prior company. His memory brought him to his own errors, as they always did.

It was the death of his friend, Franck. It was a moral stumbling block.

No, it was more than that. It was a moral wall. It did not trip, it utterly halted. It was a complete wrong, an event devoid of any redeeming quality or outcome. At the time, Jake's heart was truly in the cause. He felt that he was doing the right thing, with no reservations whatsoever. How can a man move past such a thing without completely reassessing every aspect of his life? Where had his heart failed him? How did his actions, stemming true from his deepest beliefs, lead to such tragedy?

What makes a man truly moral?

For the sake of this exercise, God exists.

God places me on an island and I must stay there forever. He tells me I can populate this island with whomever I wish.

There is only one condition.

I must tell God one word, one adjective to describe the inhabitants - and one adjective only. The island will immediately be populated with people who fit my one and only descriptor, and there will be no one who does not.

Choose your one word, Jake.

Enlightened? I would not choose it. I might be on an island full of secretive members of The Society.

Neither would I choose Royalist or Rebel. I was a rebel. My best friend is now dead as a result of my actions.

I would not choose white or black, or any other race for that matter, for all races have their share of villains. I might choose interesting, hard-working, or intelligent if I had two words to spare, but not if I only had one.

If I had to choose one word, I would choose kind.

That is my island. My island is kind.

Jake realized he had just taken an important spiritual step – he had come to a conclusion that had ended one path and created another, an intellectual point from which he could not reverse course.

Interesting.

Looking out, Jake could see the *Temps Nouveaux* anchored in deep water. He longed to be onboard and headed home. Instead, he had been ordered by *The Society* to somehow fake his death and meet them in Cuba. Jake did have such plans – but not just to fool Monsieur Tyran. Jake had enough of both of them: Tyran and *The Society*. He would leave them both thinking he was in a coffin, then head home to Boston and forget this entire sorry business. He would have to say goodbye to France forever, on pain of death. He would have to forget his quest. The Heirlooms would remain a mystery to him for the rest of his life.

Jake was torn. In that moment he would not have minded going back to France, back to Monsieur Tyran and the quest. He would deal with the ire of *The Society* later. He would never travel without a knife and a pistol – and he would never travel without Brightly, who would be armed as well. He would simply put Brightly on the ship and worry about his paperwork later. Tyran's finances were a magic wand, he would wave it and money would appear and solve any riddle of French bureaucracy. Brightly had already proven he would rather accompany Jake on his travels than haul cargo and chests on the docks of le Cap. In a way, they were both in the same boat – stranded Americans, homesick transplants; ironically, for neither truly had a home.

The coach entered le Cap by the northernmost gate. Inside and protected by armed men, Jake felt above the dangers of the city. He vowed to remember the lesson.

Near the docks, the coach came to a stop. A casual barricade had been set up by stevedores. Soldiers came up and spoke with the driver in *Kreyòl*. Jake leaned out and the driver soon turned to him, "A new ship has pulled into harbor. This entire street will soon be filled with carts. We can go no further. If you wish, you may walk to the docks from here and the soldiers will find men to help with your chests."

"Certainly, Monsieur, thank you. I will walk." Jake exited the coach without help. His chests were taken down and handed to the soldiers, who placed them on dry ground. Jake looked back at the driver one last time, "Once again, please express my thanks to Monsieur Dubuclet."

"Of course, Monsieur. Safe journey." The coach turned and headed back toward the hills.

A moment later, Jake noticed his chests were still on the ground. He addressed the nearby uniformed police, "Pardon me, do any of you speak French?"

One of the officers replied in a strange accent, "One moment, Monsieur. Your pardon. Here wait, if it please you. One minute only."

"Certainly, Officer." Jake's skin and eyes burned from the sun. He pulled his hat down further, wishing instead he could take it off entirely. It was devilishly hot. Perhaps there was a local variety made of straw or light cotton, hopefully with a much wider brim.

A one-horse, completely-enclosed cabriolet pulled up with a policeman for a driver. The seal on the door indicated a government vehicle of some kind. One of the soldiers opened it. A dark-skinned, well-dressed man peered out and smiled. "Monsieur Loring! I was looking for you. It is a fortuitous happenstance to find you here."

Jake now remembered seeing only the same two ships in harbor on the way down, the same two as when he arrived. He sighed, realizing the roadblock was a sham. He wished he had more of a cautious manner. Such glaring clues would then jump into his conscious mind and aid him at some point, one would hope. "Good day, Monsieur. Why do you look for me? How may I help you?"

"I have been sent by my superior *Inspecteur* Skelèt. He wishes to speak with you."

So, this man and his superior, presumably, are detectives in plain clothes. Tonton Macoute.

Jake smiled, "Of course. Do you wish me to go with you now, Detective?"

The man made a gesture, "If it is at all possible, Monsieur." He smiled broadly.

"Of course." Jake stepped into the cab. The door was immediately closed and the horse switched to a trot.

The man turned forward in the close, hot space. His smile vanished and his face turned completely expressionless.

Jake sighed and looked out the window.

***

The cabriolet took Jake inside the gates of the old colonial prison in *Vieux Quartiers*. The walls were hopelessly high, made of painted, plastered brick. The cellblocks and buildings stood alone; the hallways and corridors were open air with mostly grass underfoot.

The door was opened by police and the stairs deployed. Jake stepped down and the door was shut once again. The coach quickly left the prison and the gate was closed behind it.

A nearby officer indicated a direction, "This way, Monsieur."

Jake followed him inside an airy, plastered-brick building. His eyes could not adjust to the dark interior. He heard a door open, then he was ushered into a room with large open windows, where his eyes could then not adjust to the light. He was sat onto a chair.

As the room took shape, Jake found himself in front of a table, which was covered with papers, a quill and ink set, and several stamps and seals. Sitting across from him was a thin, semi-formally-dressed man of average height, caught in the act of lighting a corn husk cigarette from a long twig. If he was *Couleur*, he was a dark mix. He waved the stick until the fire disappeared into a trail of smoke. His eyes locked on Jake. He smiled, "*Bonjou. Ki jan ou ye, mesye?*"

Jake replied in French, "My apologies, I'm afraid I can only half understand. I do not speak *Kreyòl*."

His brow furrowed as he picked up Jake's papers, "You are not an American?" he said in perfect French.

"I am, Monsieur. I have been many years in Paris, and I spoke French quite well before I left."

"Hmm."

He said nothing for a long while, and just stared at Jake's visa. Jake, in turn, studied him. He was an unassuming presence - a clerk. Amongst the slim, muscular Haitians, Jake sometimes felt like a Bichon Frisé amongst Greyhounds. This man was shorter than Jake and thinner, not handsome, not ugly. He seemed intelligent enough for his duties.

Ordinary.

And then Jake realized why the man created an artificial silence.

Heard through several walls and doors was a distant scream of pure agony.

The sound was so muted, Jake could not have been sure that this man, the presumed Monsieur Skelèt, had even heard it. Jake knew, however, that his position had been situated in order for *him* to hear it. To his humiliation, it had the desired effect. Jake was scared and felt entirely vulnerable. He had no idea what kind of power this man wielded in his own prison. Most likely, Jake was safe, but he did not feel so.

For this well-dressed clerk was indeed *Tonton Macoute*, the headless horseman, the boogeyman. Literally, *Uncle Big-Sack*, the bad man who kidnapped children in the middle of the night.

He finally spoke, "I am Monsieur Skelèt."

"Monsieur," said Jake.

Skelèt smiled with two perfect rows of good teeth, "You will tell me everything, Monsieur Loring. From the beginning."

Angrily, Jake responded, "I am no coward, Monsieur, and I have no reason to be anything but honest with you. I was accosted by thieves in the streets of le

Cap. If your men had done their job, I would not be here. I was instead rescued by Monsieur Dubuclet. That evening I met his other guests at dinner. The company was well-mannered but I found it distasteful nonetheless, for I disagreed with them on a number of social issues and moral principles. I will say this regarding our interaction and nothing else: if having negative opinions regarding the President and his policies is a crime, then they are all surely guilty. If being labeled a criminal in Haïti requires more, such as plotting or executing an action, then they are innocent for all I know of them. I have just now imparted everything pertinent in regard to my dinner companions."

"What makes you think you are here for them?"

Jake was momentarily taken aback. Did this man know about the Cross of Nantes?

Jake cursed himself for a fool - of course, he didn't. Skelèt was bluffing, like a card player, trying to gauge a reaction, which Jake had surely given to him. This was all a well-designed panorama designed to unnerve him – and it had. Jake found himself even angrier, "I have committed no crimes here, Monsieur. I am here legally, I am a guest of this nation."

"You are from the United States?"

"I am from Massachusetts, Monsieur. Near Boston."

"I have never been there. To Massachusetts." Skelèt smoked his little cigar, studied the burn, and tapped the ashes. Jake heard the distant screams again. They were absolutely unnerving. "Who was at the dinner last night?" he said.

"What?"

"The dinner."

"Pardon?"

"Who was at the dinner?"

"Laurent and Ines Dubuclet. Basile Barès. Andrus and Anaïs Espree. Saint-Denis Snaër."

"What was discussed?"

"I did not lie to you. They were all unhappy with the present political situation."

In that moment, something occurred to Jake.

Monsieur Tyran and *The Society* were also *Tonton Macoute.*

They had more in common with this man than they did not. Jake's original plan was the sound one – he had to escape all of these men. He had to go home. Just like that, his mind was changed again.

"In what way?" offered Skelèt.

"I'm sorry?"

"Come now, Monsieur. In what way were they unhappy."

Jake quickly came up with a plan. He initiated part one.

Jake told Skelèt everything. He left out absolutely nothing.

Skelèt was a polite and patient listener, especially once he realized Jake was fully cooperating. He asked questions only to clarify a point or to motivate Jake to elaborate on a certain issue. Once satisfied, he spoke, "I appreciate your honesty, Monsieur."

"Thank you."

"I will reciprocate. There is a question you have been asking, ever since you landed."

"And what is that, Monsieur?"

"Whether it was all the French or all the whites who were butchered during the wars."

Jake remained silent.

Skelèt spoke, "It was all of the French, those who were not smart enough to leave."

Jake did not respond.

"Monsieur le Président is the very essence of a *gen de couleur*. Educated in Paris, switching sides three or four times during the wars, mostly allying with France. He believes his enemy to be other *gens de couleur* who demand and impose on him. Actually, they are both cogs inside the same clock. The true enemy of Monsieur le Président is his *nation*. His people are not part of his machine – no, not the same at all. Mark my words, Monsieur Loring, next into the stewpot will be the *Grand Couleur*, and they will be as surprised as the French for finding themselves there. And they will die. All of them. To our eyes, they are picked out of a crowd as easily as yourself."

The man's words struck Jake as prophetic. There would be another round of cold butchery in Haïti; he had no doubt Monsieur Skelèt would be at the center of the mayhem. "Why would you do such a thing?" Jake asked, "For all of their faults, it is obvious they are the unique tabernacle for Haitian culture, education, and business."

"We are a revolutionary nation. Revolution is a great bag of hot air, Monsieur Loring. It means only one thing: the devious have new words to convince the ignorant - that their lot as sheep is due to machinations of the shepherd, who must die so they may be set free. While the sheep grow fangs and bite, the devious become the new secret shepherd, unseen and unanticipated. And once the sheep develop a taste for blood, they can be used again, by the new shepherd or some other who has found the flock. Someone will feed the *couleur* to these bloodthirsty sheep and win the title of shepherd for his troubles. It is too easy; the opportunity will not be missed."

"And what of the sheep?"

"What of them? Their lot will never change – they exist for wool and for meat, for the old shepherds and for the new. Why *would* that ever change? For what other use can sheep be used? Peasants and government ministers are not interchangeable - it is only easy to convince sheep this is so, to gain their allegiance and have them do your bidding. Sheep become better sheep when they think they are not sheep at all. That, Monsieur Loring, is revolution. And that is Haiti."

Jake was pensive. In Paris, Jake had thought of himself as a leader. He realized, in that very moment, he had been nothing but a sheep himself, who was patted on the back and called a leader by those who really ran the farm. He had been trimmed for wool by *The Society*… and his best friend used for meat.

God, what a horrible thought.

"Does it surprise you? To hear such lofty thoughts coming from a black mouth, *Mesye Neg Blan*?" Skelèt said with a big smile and pure hate, which was apropos of nothing Jake had done or said. The smiled vanished. "You will get on your ship and never come back. Tell no one of my existence."

Jake leaned back in his chair and smiled, "No."

To Jake's endless satisfaction, Skelèt was speechless.

Jake continued, "I have a deal for you, Monsieur. A proposition that will not overly tax your resources."

"Do tell."

"As far as the world knows, thieves left me for dead on the streets of le Cap the night before last. What if I told you I wished the world to keep believing this?"

Skelèt's eyes fixed on Jake.

Jake continued. "I will pay you with everything I possess, except the clothes I currently wear and one other outfit, one map and my compass. All else - my chests, clothing, every coin I possess - is yours. Perhaps a value of two-hundred francs, all told."

That was half a year's salary for a working Frenchman.

"I am a government official, Monsieur Loring. I must be careful and shy away from impropriety. I must know for what service you are offering this."

Jake nodded. "I wish to be taken outside the city – as far to the south as possible, in secrecy and at night - and left to my own devices. I also wish that your men do not speak of seeing me at all."

"My men are discreet. Where do you then go, after this secret ride?"

"To Port-au-Prince."

"You will walk, penniless, to Port-au-Prince?"

"Yes, Monsieur."

"It is nearly eighty miles away from here, over considerable hills and mountains."

"Yes. Besides some poisonous spiders and centipedes, however, there is nothing that can kill on this island, as far as I know. Not even the snakes are dangerous. Only one of your lakes has alligators, everywhere else there are only little caimans."

He shrugged, "You will still die, most assuredly, *neg blan*. You have no chance of making this trek, being who you are, and you will find yourself bedeviled every inch of it. The island itself will kill you. I myself might not survive this ordeal you wish to undertake."

Jake shrugged, "I am unable to sweeten the pot any further. Do we have an agreement?"

"Once I say yes, it is done, Monsieur. There is no going back. You will find yourself on the road to Milot with little more than two pairs of clothes, and I will return to the city alone - even if you run after my carriage pleading for mercy, which you most assuredly will."

"I will not run after your coach, Monsieur. I will be grateful that you have fulfilled your promise to me."

"I will have you searched to ensure you hide nothing from me. This will not be a pleasant experience for you."

Skelèt smoked quietly.

Jake heard the screams again.

"Yes, we have a deal," he finally said.

"I would like to take a nap before tonight. Somewhere cool, silent and comfortable - but where I will not be seen."

"Of course."

"Thank you."

"*De rien*, Monsieur."

Skelèt chuckled, knowing Jake wasn't telling him everything. Perhaps another carriage would clatter up to the rendezvous a few minutes after his own coach left.

He was wrong.

Jake was as ludicrously short-sighted and ill-advised as he appeared.

1832

Chapter Twenty-Four

February, 1789

Estelle, Jeannine, and Xavier

Dearest Jeannine,

I am mortified, sister, that I must report my total failure.

With the aid of wonderful Monsieur Amble, the coach driver, we have scoured the whole of Centre-Ville Rennes, which is nowhere near the size of Nantes. As far as we can tell, there is no Rue de Brouillard. We inquired directly – but discreetly – into the identity of Monsieur de Glisser and no one has heard of this man.

I begin to know now why you sent me on this errand. Obviously, this quest took intelligence and discretion and you assumed I would have both. I have found that I have neither and regret to say that if secrecy was important, there is now but little. Whatever riddle I had to solve in order to fulfill this quest was simply beyond my ability. Please forgive me, gentle sister! I know what this meant to you, only I do not know why! Should I even ask?

I am staying at the coach inn just outside of town, for we do not have the funds to sleep elsewhere. During the day we reenter Rennes and continue our quest. Please send a post with more information as soon as possible, for we have exhausted every avenue of discovery.

Address your letter to me at Auberge de Thabor-Paris, 43 Rue de Paris, Quartier Thabor - Saint-Hélier, Rennes. I am fairly sure your letter will get to me if addressed in this fashion.

We will stay as long as we have coin!

Fumbling but most sincerely yours!

Estelle

Dear Estelle,

Do not worry. Although I sent you away, I truly did not know your destination until minutes ago when I received another missive. Please do not be angry with me!

Here is what you must do: every day at noon you must be in front of Cathedral Saint-Pierre de Rennes, holding a white sash and a bouquet of blue Hortensias. A man will come up to you and ask if where you are standing is 14 Rue de Brouillard. You will reply that it is not fourteen, but rather twenty-three. He will then introduce himself as Monsieur de Glisser, and you will deliver the letter to him. He will, in turn, present you with a gift, wrapped in white crêpe paper and tied with a red ribbon. Do not open it. Return instead to your lodging and open it there away from prying eyes.

Inside the gift, you will find a box filled with coins wrapped in cloth to muffle any sound made in transit. The coin is for you to pay your expenses, for you must stay an additional night. Leave for Nantes in the morning to not attract suspicion.

Please do this for me, sister. I cannot tell you why, only that my intrigue is honorable and for the greater good.

Forever in your debt,

Jeannine.

***

Jeannine had to be doing this for Monsieur. It was the only thing that made sense. What did not make sense was that Monsieur did not have a better agent than his teen daughter and her companion.

The man Estelle met yesterday was short and stocky, wearing a large coat and a Breton *chapeau rond* hat. He looked quite villainous to Estelle. When he spoke, his accent was coarse, urban Nantes.

"Rue de Brouillard," he said.

But that was not quite right. He was supposed to ask her if this was fourteen Rue de Brouillard. "Excuse me?" replied Estelle.

"Rue de Brouillard!" he said louder, frustrated.

"Monsieur!" admonished Estelle.

His face twisted, "Fourteen! Fourteen Rue de Brouillard!"

"This is not fourteen, Monsieur. It is rather twenty-three."

They both stared at each other.

"Well?" he asked.

Estelle said nothing.

"Do you-," he began, but trailed off. "Monsieur de Glasser."

"De Glisser," Estelle said evenly.

"Yes, yes!"

Estelle handed him the letter and it disappeared into his jacket. He pulled the gift from his coat pocket and handed it to her. The paper was torn in places and the ribbon dirty. He then walked off without another word.

The wrapped gift was indeed filled with coins wrapped in cloth. There wasn't much, but there was enough to pay the innkeeper their arrears, an additional night's lodging and provide a small breakfast the next morning. Afterwards, Estelle boarded the carriage and Monsieur Amble drove them home. The icy roads made the journey quite perilous, but, in spite of it, they made excellent time.

Two evenings hence, the coach deposited Estelle, exhausted and confused, at the Cœurfroid doorstep then made for the garages behind the building. She raised the knocker twice and stepped back. The door cracked open on Thomas's face.

"*Bon soir*, Thomas."

"*Bon soir*, Mademoiselle. Please wait here." And the door was softly shut.

That was odd.

Estelle waited.

The door opened on Jeannine, who looked wonderful, as usual. She stepped outside and shut the door behind her. Estelle was not surprised at this point. She only wanted to eat and crawl into bed.

Jeannine spoke, "Estelle, for your own good, your employment must be terminated."

Estelle was stunned.

"Your things have all been packed in trunks. When Monsieur Amble arrives at the carriage house, the coach will be loaded and he will return here to get you."

"Are you quite serious, sister?"

"Estelle, I cannot explain. Not right now, perhaps not ever."

"Jeannine, I'm afraid I have lost patience. Please tell me what on earth is going on."

"I cannot. Your severance pay lies in a note that is being placed on the seat of your carriage as we speak."

Jeannine turned to reenter the house. Estelle felt rising panic, anger, shame. "Jeannine!" she nearly shouted. Jeannine turned. "I-I believe I am in the employ of Madame. She was the one who hired me. I should speak to her."

Jeannine nodded, "You may call upon her tomorrow morning. Early. Eight o'clock. And you cannot stay long."

And with that, Jeannine reentered the house and shut the door.

Estelle brought her hands to her face and burst into tears.

Her tears stopped when she reasoned that nothing was writ in stone until Madame made her decision. She could very well roll her eyes and command her daughter to accept her as companion again.

Her destiny had not yet been decided.

***

Estelle found herself sitting before two nuns and a sister of Saint-Clément in the small, stone visitors' parlor.

Mother Superior, the abbess, was older but had bright, sharp eyes. Within the walls of Saint-Clément, she could order an Archbishop to mop the floor. Next to her was the Reverend Mother, a canoness, who was equally old and sharp, but with more of a scholar's mind than that of a politician. Lastly was middle-aged Sister Marie, who was an oblate of the Third Order. She wasn't a nun, rather like a friar, and lived just outside the convent to help the nuns deal with the outside world. She had a very stern expression.

Estelle told them everything. She was surprised that they were not more welcoming. She had nowhere to go and did not anticipate her frosty reception.

Sister Marie crossed her arms, "Describe your relationship with Monsieur."

"With Monsieur?" Estelle wondered how that pertained to anything, but she answered, "Cordial, of course. Monsieur is a good and decent man. He is rarely at home."

The Revered Mother shook her head, "I don't think that is an issue." She didn't seem to be addressing Estelle, which confused her even more.

Mother Superior regarded Estelle, "You received your pay?"

"Yes, Mother."

"Why then did you not sleep at an inn?"

Estelle reddened.

Mother Superior read her mind, "It did not occur to you?"

"No. Frankly speaking, it did not, Mother. Forgive me."

"Perhaps you were in distress. This was your first home in Nantes, for a time. You came here for comfort."

"Yes, Mother. I'm so happy you understand. I am in such distress and in such need of guidance. To be quite honest, a shoulder to cry on would be appreciated at this point."

"You've grown soft. This is not the Estelle I remember." Mother Superior looked off to the side for a moment, then spoke, "You can stay here as long as you wish."

"Thank you, Mother."

"You will reside outside the walls in the visitor dormitory for one month. If you are here longer, you must move inside the walls to be a postulant, a woman who desires to be a nun undergoing a testing period. No oaths are taken, you are free from any obligation whatsoever."

"Thank you, Mother."

"If you are here longer than six months, you can stay – but only as a novitiate. You will take no vows but live voluntarily as a sister and performed the Liturgy of the Hours, a rigorous recipe of prayer and ceremony that will take up a great deal of your time."

"Very well, Mother," replied Estelle, somewhat confused.

Mother continued, "You may stay as long as any other novitiate – twelve months. Afterwards you must take temporary vows, meaning you are precisely a nun – but only temporarily, three or six years. After your temporary vows expire, you must petition for your perpetual position and take permanent vows in order to stay. Until you take vows, whether temporary or permanent, you are free to leave as you wish."

"Well, thank you, Mother," said Estelle, perplexed. "I only plan on being here until the man I am courting returns from Boston. I would like to pay my way, as well."

She nodded. "When and if you leave, make a donation."

"Of course! An appropriate one. Rent, as it were."

Mother nodded again, "As you wish, Daughter." Mother Superior stood. Estelle curtsied. "Good night."

"Good night, Mother. Thank you." The two elderly nuns left the room.

Sister Marie spoke, "Have you eaten?"

Estelle suddenly became very hungry, "Not since morning."

"Come with me. We will get you some food and I will show you to your quarters. At least those you will use for the month."

"I hope I am not here quite that long."

"One never knows. We may have to bury you tomorrow. It is all God's will."

"Well, let us hope not. I don't feel quite done here amongst the living. Tomorrow seems a bit abrupt," Estelle chided.

"God's will, young Estelle."

"Yes, Sister. God's will. Put the shovel by the door then."

"Do not jest about such things. You have been too long in the city."

The city was within walking distance. "I apologize, Sister."

The meal was bread, butter and hot chocolate. Exhaustion elevated the straw-filled mattress to that of down feather.

***

At eight o'clock precisely, Estelle knocked on the door. It was opened immediately by Thomas. He did not greet her right away. He looked around outside, right and left, then spoke, "Come in, hurry."

Estelle entered, "Good morning, Thomas."

He spoke without looking at her, "Right this way, please. Quickly."

She followed him to the morning parlor. Madame sat in her robes by the open doors into the courtyard, holding her coffee to her nostrils. Estelle curtsied, "Good morning, Madame."

Madame barely stirred. She finally looked in Estelle's direction, nothing more.

Estelle forced herself to remember the time when Madame was kind to her. She smiled, "I'm afraid I was dismissed from service yesterday by your daughter, Madame."

"Were you?"

"I was indeed. It was not seemly to disagree at the time. Out of manners and respect, I did her bidding. It was not Mademoiselle's decision to hire me, however; I believe it was yours. I have returned to respectfully ask from my true employer whether I am retained or dismissed."

"Did you receive your severance pay?"

"I did indeed."

"Where did you stay last night?"

"At Saint-Clément. It is where I resided before coming here."

"Is your lodging secure?"

"Yes, for now. To be honest, for the foreseeable future."

Madame looked off, an intense expression on her face - thinking upon, churning about a great and awesome equation of life, perhaps even changing a belief she had cherished. She finally stood and embraced Estelle, warmly no less. Estelle had never seen her perform such a gesture on anyone. "Estelle, you must listen to me."

Estelle was transfixed. She had never seen Madame like this. She was warm, she was a person who cared.

Madame continued, "You must leave our service, my child."

"I-I understand, Madame."

"When Monsieur Traversier returns, the very first place he will come is here. He will come looking for you." Estelle teared and could not reply. "When he does, we will send Monsieur Amble to find you. You will come back and meet

Monsieur here. Any letter Monsieur Traversier sends will be forwarded to you forthwith. We will be your allies in this, Estelle. Let your honorable admiration for Monsieur Traversier allow you to weather this sudden change."

"I will. I am overwhelmed by your kindness."

Estelle did not have to walk back to Saint-Clément. Monsieur Amble drove her back in the coach, courtesy of Madame. She smiled the entire way.

***

Xavier straightened his neckerchief in the mirror. He had always preferred to dress himself, which was uncommon for a man of his income. At one point, he had dismissed all of the valets due to financial pressures. By the time things had improved, Xavier had been about the world, on ship and land, for a decade. Having another man help him with his hose seemed ridiculous.

But he was now debating whether this was the best practice. He was dressing more fashionably of late, if *of late* could transpire within the last four days. He could use a valet, someone who knew color matching and modern trends, who could help him finish dressing once sartorial decisions were made. Time was precious after all, and fashion was still quite ornate this Winter, although moving in a simpler direction.

He had returned from Boston on Monday and it was now Thursday. His problem with time had not abated; the last four days seemed a lifetime, but an altogether pleasant lifetime, completely the opposite experience of his anxious odyssey on the returning schooner. He had paid formal call to the Cœurfroid home every day. It had become routine.

On Monday, he had come to Centre-Ville and knocked on the Cœurfroid door at exactly ten o'clock. He was ushered in by Thomas and escorted to the salon. He expected to see Jeannine and perhaps Madame. Instead he was greeted by an army of swishing skirts as a cool half-dozen lovely, young women floated from their chairs and approached him.

It was a moment Xavier would always remember. Every young woman in this room was from a wealthy family, *le plus grand bourgeoisie*, and was trained from the cradle in social graces. Xavier was overwhelmed by nothing more than their animated expressions. It was as if he was a returning hero, to all of them, and every one of them had passionately studied, for their whole lives, how to joyfully greet a man such as him. They absolutely radiated this positive and overpowering delight, and there was no discernable sign of negative or false emotion or subtext.

All of them spoke at once, greeting him, and then one-by-one introduced themselves. First there was Mademoiselle Graslin, the daughter of the Farmer-General and developer. She was a gorgeous pale brunette, wore red, and was sharply-featured like her father. Next was the alluring Mademoiselle Olivier, the daughter of the mercantilist. She was raven-haired and Roman dark, and wore yellow. A fair, cherubically plump, beauty in braids wore green – she was

Mademoiselle Duplessix, the daughter of the King's Prosecutor of Brittany. Blonde Mademoiselle Wegelin was the distant relative of the original Wegelin of Swiss banking fame. She was presumably a Protestant; her father was the Wegelin Bank representative for Brittany, a man Xavier knew well. France was controlled by perhaps twelve financial institutions. They were, in essence, a fourth estate – the Phantom Estate. They had more power than they admitted and moved behind the scenes. Next was Mademoiselle Lowell, a thin, tall redhead. Her father came from England – or perhaps from Britain to the United States to… here? - and owned one of the new cotton mills in Nantes. Cotton came naturally to a slave-trading town like Nantes. Her father and those like him were serious competitors with Xavier's linen enterprises. Lastly, there was a plain, but intelligent, exquisitely well-dressed brunette by the name of Mademoiselle De Saint-Philbert-de-Grand-Lieu, who was thankfully addressed as Lulu. Her father owned wineries and vineyards, all planted with a varietal called Melon de Bourgogne. Their wines were altogether complex and interesting, due in no small measure to a fermentation process called *sur la lie*. Xavier was sure he would find out exactly what that meant at some point.

He was wholly spellbound and completely distracted, all at once. He could have listened to any one of them speak for hours, for all the young women were charming, intelligent and well-educated.

After the ladies had approached but before they had introduced themselves, two more women gracefully stood from their chairs – Madame and Mademoiselle Cœurfroid. Madame took two steps forward, a pleasant and likeable expression on her face, and then stood with her arms by her sides as the women introduced themselves.

Mademoiselle, Jeannine, kept moving forward. She moved slowly but with exquisite grace, like a lithe, stalking cheetah. When she reached the outer circle of fine dresses, their eyes met. She smiled at him but did not speak. Rather, she seemed to bestow on him the freedom to enjoy the company of the others, as if they both knew the circle of beauties was but flitting distraction.

She allowed a perfect amount of time to lapse and interrupted no one. "Monsieur Traversier," she said, "Please come and sit down."

He did and the ladies laid siege to his position, their artillery of intense interest and admiration expertly placed and accurate. Jeannine relieved the siege one lady at a time, as if such a thing was a skill gained with time - like a cosmopolitan Madrileño peeling an orange with a knife and fork.

It was the stalking of cats by a lioness.

"I wonder what kind of wine goes well with theater. Is there one flavor for comedy and another for drama?" Jeannine asked Mademoiselle Graslin. The question was designed not to entrance Mademoiselle Graslin but rather Lulu, creating a dialog between the two of them, instead of the two young ladies and Xavier. This was not prompting but rather suggestion. Everything happened naturally. There was only six of them. Three times Jeannine did this, and Xavier found himself speaking to Jeannine alone.

Smalltalk, then talk not so small.

"I could not be more excited to live in this time, Xavier - if only to see what comes next."

"No one could argue. Just in the last twenty years the world has been turned upside down."

"For the better."

"Undoubtedly, Mademoiselle."

"But there is a difference between us, Monsieur."

"More than one, I should hope."

She giggled. Xavier wished he could remember the sound and the expressions on her face forever. *Mon dieu*, she was quite extraordinarily beautiful. Her eyes came up and locked upon his, "One important difference, Monsieur."

She had eyes like emeralds. *How can eyes be so different from each other?* "And what is that difference?"

"You will not witness change. Rather, you will drive it forward at a charge, like a cuirassier on a battle-trained stallion."

"How so?"

"Ah! If you do not know, then truly we were meant to have this conversation."

"Meant? By whom? Are you religious or superstitious?"

"No one is religious any more, Monsieur. But one must admit to serendipity."

Exactly! He nodded, "We must and I do."

"Monsieur, please think upon your circumstances. I cannot hope to know much about you, but my observations cannot be wrong. Have you not placed yourself in the perfect position to be a leader in this brave new world in which we find ourselves?"

"A beautiful turn of phrase, Mademoiselle."

"No, I must object! I am not some placid British milk cow. I am a Frenchwoman in her own salon, and you must consider these thoughts and answer wittily and accurately."

He chuckled, "Very well." *Mon dieu*, she was beautiful. "I am in political and cultural circles of some note."

"Yes, so am I, although I cannot speak of them."

Very well! "I have contacts with a variety of successful people across a wide spectrum of society."

"Indeed, you do."

"I have access to a rare amount of resources."

"Monsieur, you are a leader. Do you not see?"

"I suppose the potential is clear."

"No, forgive me, Monsieur. France needs leaders, there can be no equivocation. In this moment, we Republicans face Caesar, do we not?"

She was the Aphrodite of Freemasonry. "We do."

"Rousseau is dead, Monsieur. Diderot, Voltaire. They have passed. They are gone, but like Cicero, their words haunt us, Monsieur."

"Yes."

"It is up to us to understand that the world now needs leaders - to rise up, to stand upon the speaking platform with their arms waving, proclaiming bold words to the ears of the crowd. To tell people there is another way, the way of Rousseau, who has shown us our world through a different optic. Mankind requires freedom. With freedom our needs are met, with freedom the yoke of oppression leaves us, evil becomes a thing of the past. Who will lead France into this glorious time? Who will organize the people? Who will lead the fight against oppression? It is you, Monsieur!"

He found it hard to focus on her words. She was attractive in the most basic sense of the word. She was so interesting, on so many levels, that her presence was magnetic - she was *attracting* him. He found himself enjoying a passionate interest in her. Rarely was beauty combined with such charisma – and to see both attributes, like paired chariot horses whipped to full speed, was like seeing the universe explode into being.

Lunch was amazing. The main course was shellfish *galettes* with a wondrous sauce made of creamy Pont-l'Évêque cheese and *beurre aux algues* garnished with cauliflower, artichoke hearts and *Coco de Paimpol* beans. Lulu brought the wine, and paired it with each course with the talent of a master sommelier.

Xavier was grateful for Jeannine's gesture. She knew waiting for Estelle would be difficult and her hospitality eased his anxiety. Xavier had always felt rejected by Nantes *société*, at least a part of it. Now he was its center.

Société was a strange word. It was polysemous and evolving. It meant a person's circle of company, any circle of company, really. It could be a meeting of a circle. It could indicate a level of class or culture, or one particular color of a spectrum of such circles. It was a word that only made sense to a Frenchman, who intuitively understood a specific definition within its varied meanings in context. So, to be precise, Xavier had always felt rejected by the *société* of wealthy young women of marriageable age in Nantes.

But here he was, sitting and eating a glorious *déjeuner* with the cream of the milkmaid's vase. He was not only accepted, he was the *sine qua non* of the salon.

That afternoon he commissioned several tailors. He had always dressed well, expensively yet modestly in the Protestant fashion of the respectable *haute bourgeois*. He now wished a more elegant look. He would dress the part of a stylish, wealthy Catholic bourgeois, a wealthy bachelor unafraid to spread his peacock feathers. Why not?

Wednesday at the Cœurfroid residence was amazing. There were different guests, there was music. Everyone who touched an instrument or sang seemed almost apologetic for doing so - they had spent time learning how to do such things whilst Xavier had bettered himself in more important ways. All of them expressed a deference to him, a holistic respect for his life and choices. They were but lesser – albeit lesser who played their instruments as Michelangelo carved stone, who sang like nightingales.

Xavier had no conversations with Jeannine, at least none involving speech. Their eyes met frequently. She had the most expressive face, communicating a continual commentary on every aspect of the *société*: ridiculing, admiring, understanding, being surprised by a sentiment – all by expression. They were apart and together the entire time, but he left with a longing for her conversation.

Thursday. Today was Thursday. What laid in store for him today?

Thomas ushered him inside, escorted him to the salon, bowed and promptly left.

The salon was nearly dark, which was strange for it was meant to be sunlit. The curtains were drawn and the room was enveloped in shadow.

"Will you not bow in greeting?" came a sultry voice. Xavier's eyes adjusted to the light and found Jeannine's silhouette. She was sitting on a gold leaf canapé sofa in white champagne velour set against the far wall.

It was custom for her to stand, but she did not.

Xavier bowed.

"Come," she said.

Xavier moved forward. He could see her now. She was dressed once again in green satin. One elbow rested against the tight back of the sofa, her head coming to nest in her palm. Her legs were crossed, her body slightly angled.

Her eyes flicked a direction. "Sit."

He sat down in a bergère fronting the far end of her sofa. He felt calm, but his heart was beating quickly. The temperature was perfect but he felt a warm, thrilling heat.

They began to talk.

Their conversation regarded nothing as substantial as air.

She tilted her head. "Is Summer better than Spring? Everyone thinks so. Have you ever thought about it, though?"

"I suppose not."

And so it went. There was never a conversation so shallow and yet so interesting. How could that be so? Why did he hang on every syllable? Why did every word hit him like a shot of *eau de vie*? Were they simply continuing their conversation from yesterday, the one without words – now simply talking under it?

Lunch.

They laughed, they joked, they pranked. Soon both had a dot of *chou-fleur à la crème* on the tip of their nose, an adornment neither would have wiped off for the gold of an Egyptian tomb.

She saw him to the door. She said her goodbyes. Her words and her inflection were that of a trusted friend.

A trusted friend.

He rode back to the Meilleur upon the deep cushions of his coach.

A trusted friend.

It almost hurt him, this sentiment. When she had said goodbye, his soul ached for the warmth of their earlier exchanges. He did not want her friendship.

He realized he wanted *her* – and more than he could express. He was entranced by every part of Jeannine Cœurfroid. Even when their conversation was at its most banal, he was utterly spellbound. If they were married, she would become his in every way. The thought made his temples pound.

He had never wanted anything as much as he wanted Jeannine Cœurfroid.

He was inside the Meilleur without realizing he had left the coach.

Out of habit he wandered into the main parlor.

Madame stood above a high, narrow drum table in the center of the room. She appeared locked in a moment of time. One hand rested on the tabletop holding a semi-crushed letter. Her head was cocked in an odd fashion, with her chin halfway to her chest and frozen there.

"Madame?"

She did not reply.

"Madame? Are you unwell?"

"Oh, Xavier," she said in a faraway whisper. However soft, those two words undoubtedly carried an undercurrent of disappointment, of anger certainly.

Wary now, Xavier did not reply.

In the same whisper, "Where have you been going?"

"I have been calling at the Cœurfroids, Madame. As I told you."

"For what purpose?"

He had to think. "To wait. For Estelle to return."

"Where did you think she had gone?"

"I don't know."

"Undoubtedly you asked."

Thinking upon it, he realized his queries regarding her had been almost nonexistent.

Madame brought up the crumpled letter and handed it to him.

> *Madame Traversier,*
>
> *First, I wish to once again thank you for your hospitality and kind ministrations. My time at the Meilleur is one of my fondest and most cherished memories.*
>
> *Secondly, I would like to state that my time as companion for Jeannine Cœurfroid has unfortunately come to an end. I am currently lodged with the kind sisters of Saint-Clément until I am able to find another position or a change in my status.*
>
> *If I could but ask, when Monsieur returns from his business trip, could you please inform him of my new address?*

The Cœurfroids have assured me they will tell Monsieur where I am the moment he appears on their doorstep. In my anxiety and longing for Monsieur's good company, I find myself writing this letter to inform you as well. I am sure that we both pray fervently for his prompt and safe return.

Yours truly and gratefully,

Estelle Guerrier

Reading the letter, Xavier experienced an odd feeling, as if the letter was ancient, written years ago during an altogether different episode of his life - one long over - and that he had seen and read the letter many times since then, until it had no emotional impact on him whatsoever.

She spoke softly, slowly, "You are going to Saint-Clément this very minute, I suppose. Hopping back on your coach with wild eyes and laughter, eager to be off."

Xavier thought for a moment. "No, I do not think so."

She shook her head. "In business, you are so clever. You perceive the subtlest machinations as if they were juggling street performers. I never thought to warn you. It never occurred to me."

"Warn me?"

"Part of me wishes to launch across the room and slap your face."

"I see."

"But then I think, what right have I? You were not instructed properly when it came to the most important things in life. You had no proper examples of behavior to observe. No one to learn from. You were on your own. You were always on your own. You did so well, it was hard to see where you were weak or ignorant."

Xavier took a deep breath, wishing this moment would end.

"Are you going to send a letter to Estelle?"

"What manner of letter?"

"Describing your intentions."

"We were honorably courting. There was no obligation."

"Surely you know she would die for you. Throw herself from a cliff for you."

Xavier said nothing.

"My ring, please."

Xavier crossed to the table and placed her ring upon it.

"I wonder what doom you have now placed upon yourself. If it will be greater or lesser than the last." She shuddered. Her body snapped erect and she quickly strode from the room.

Her ring remained on the table, as if it held no value whatsoever.

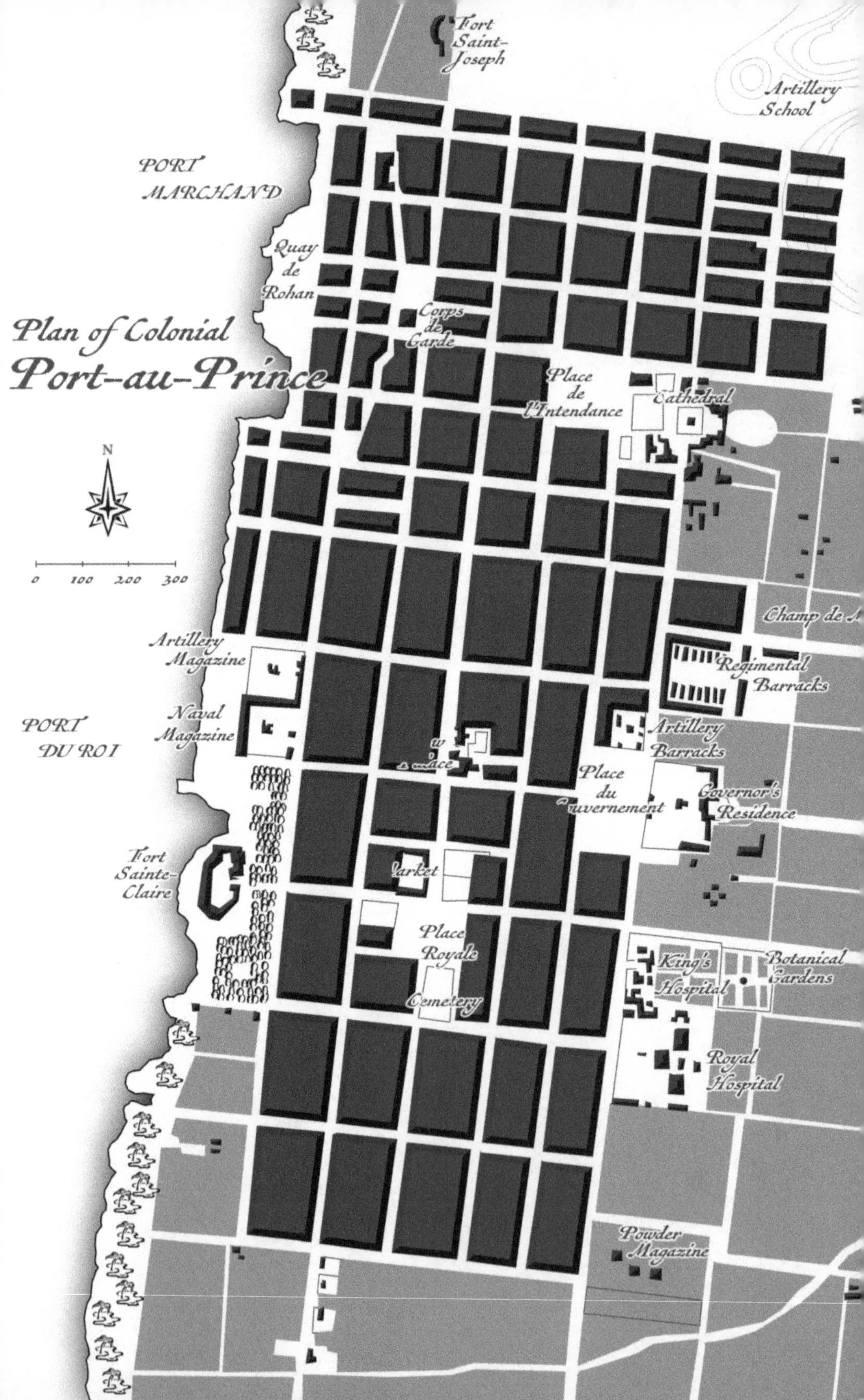

Plan of Colonial
Port-au-Prince
Fort Saint-Joseph
Artillery School
PORT MARCHAND
Quay de Rohan
Corps de Garde
Place de l'Intendance
Cathedral
N
0 100 200 300
Champ de
Artillery Magazine
Regimental Barracks
Naval Magazine
PORT DU ROI
Artillery Barracks
Place du
Governor's Residence
Fort Sainte-Claire
Place Royale
Cemetery
King's Hospital
Botanical Gardens
Royal Hospital
Powder Magazine

Chapter Twenty-Five

1832

Jake

Jake cursed himself. He cursed himself out loud, at a whisper and sometimes at a scream. He had covered every inch of his exposed skin with mud. It seemed to work for a moment, then the hordes of insects would descend once again. He had no idea so many flies and mosquitoes existed in the world. They blocked his vision, what little he had in the cloudy darkness. When he closed his eyes, his lashes would entangle them. They would descend on his eyelids and bite them until he opened his eyes, then they would try to sting his eyes. His ears buzzed with them and when they came close, the sound was unbearable - a high-pitched, wretched whine. He could not wave them away fast enough from his eyes to save his ears. His hands were covered with them, and their blood and guts covered the back of his hands where he had killed them. Once he was so bedeviled that he threw himself into a growth of windmill grass, tossing and turning to get them off, to do *something.*

That was when Jake discovered creatures he called the *angry lice.*

He didn't know what they really were. He knew they were very small, scarlet colored, did not fly, and bit him painfully. Afterwards the bite would itch. Jake would periodically lose his mind, running as fast as he could up the elevation of the Massif du Nord mountain range, mindless of dark, unseen obstacles in the road, screaming at the top of his lungs. He would stop, gasping for air, choking as the insects entered his throat. He began crying, pleading with the insects, as if some sadistic, communal intelligence determined the target of their vicious attacks. His cheeks felt like the surface of rotted cork bark. He knew he was a mass of pox and swelling.

He had lost his mind and regained it a thousand times before dawn finally came. As soon as the sun broke over the mountains, there were less of them. Jake laughed and danced up the hill. When the sun's disc was finally seen entire, they vanished, for the most part. It was then hot, humid, and getting warmer.

Jake took in his surroundings. He was high up in the hills. From his vantage he could see the plains and fields below him to the north, ending at the sparkling, emerald sea perhaps ten miles away, maybe a little more. He had not traveled far.

If Jake had somehow come into his present capacity from a more mundane environment, he would have considered himself to be in a tortured state. His entire body was a painful irritation, so severe he probably would have not been able to think upon anything else. Jake, however, had not suddenly come into his state, rather he had endured a wretched night of constant attack. Because of this, he felt as if he had walked out of hell. A few hours later it was steamy hot; the sun was brutal. Jake was thirsty and hungry, and itched everywhere. He carried some light items in a burlap sack. It now felt as heavy as a sandbag.

He heard a cart clattering down the road. He quickly moved into the jungle, which was, at this altitude, more properly a forest. In some of the darker, cooler copses under the leaves, Jake heard the buzzing of insects. With a whine issuing unbidden from his own lips, he stumbled away in fear.

He soon found a cool stream, which he spent too much time wallowing in. He also found an East Indian cherry bush in full fruit. He ate all he could then walked back to the road. It was obvious, even from a distance, that the road was well-used and now busy with traffic. He decided to parallel the road until it turned sharply to the east. He would continue north, bypass Milot to the west, continue over the highest points of the mountains to the slopes of the south, and emerge onto the high central plateau starting near Saint-Michel-de-l'Attalaye. He would have to sleep during the accursed heat of the day and walk in the brutal doom of darkness, hounded by the malicious insects. The thought of it almost made him sick.

Jake was exhausted. Off the winding curves and switch-backs of the road, the elevations were daunting. Jake would pause, breathing with difficulty with every step. The only force that drove him was the hope that the insects would not be as plentiful at high elevations.

He collapsed at noon. He laid in the dirt, unmindful of the insect bites. It was so hot, the sun so intense, he could not possibly be on earth. He was in some chamber of the *Diyu*, Chinese purgatory, the Hell of Heat and Insects.

At one point, he found himself covered in tarantulas. At first, he was appalled, then realized it was the only time he was not stung and bedeviled by other kinds of insects. He gave them his blessing but they did not stay long. When the tarantulas left, the pests came back, along with other kinds of spiders that were not so kind.

One cruel new spider bit him on his bicep and it stung fiercely. It was not, however, enough to get Jake back on his feet. Finally, a centipede crawled into his mouth and bit him below the tongue. Jake howled and vainly attempted to get it out of his mouth. He jumped to his feet and pulled it out with his hands. He was in more pain than he thought possible. He cursed the land, its people and its horrible, vicious pests.

He had to keep moving.

He came upon a tiny spring on a nearly vertical rock face. He drank as much as he could, even though the water stung the bite inside his mouth. He fell asleep. It wasn't a good sleep, more like a half-sleep where he drifted in and out of consciousness… until something quite odd happened.

Jake felt a malevolent presence approaching him – something so utterly evil there was no chance of facing it. It was as if the spirit's contempt was so pure, it could disintegrate him. He closed his eyes, knowing that he could not bear the sight of whatever it was.

It came with its army, an impenetrably thick air of dark spirits encircling him from all sides. The evilness and spite, the sadistic darkness of the presence was so overwhelming that Jake was unhinged with terror and panic. He knew if this thing got hold of him, he was utterly doomed; his fate would be unimaginably bad; there was nothing so terrible in life that could provide a clue to the fate he would endure at the hands of this approaching creature.

No, not a creature.

Presence.

Jake kept his eyes screwed shut, again knowing somehow that if he did not see the thing, it could not hurt him. He could feel its thoughts, it was clever and devious. It wanted him; he felt its fierce consuming desire to find a way to penetrate through his clenched eyelids and devour him. Jake begged the universe, *Please, let me sleep so I cannot feel its hideous contempt, let me sleep with my eyes closed so it cannot get me.*

Later in the day, Jake awakened, still terrified, hoping it was a nightmare. He knew he would never forget this encounter and dreaded that it would happen again.

As Jake explored the world over the years, sometimes describing the moment to others, he discovered that what happened to him at the spring was uncommon, but not particularly rare.

But, at that moment, he was high in the Massif du Nord near Milot, and it was late afternoon.

Late afternoon.

After late afternoon comes night.

Jake began to cry.

"Please, no," he heard croak out of his mouth.

On the road, below him to his left and far away, he saw a driver stop his cart and brake. The driver lit torches on all four corners of the cart, then climbed up on the driver's bench and cracked his whip. Jake intuited that the torches were used to ward off insects, not just illuminate. He wished he could light a fire and bathe in smoke as well, but that would announce his presence and defeat the entire point of his tortuous marathon. He had nothing with which to light a fire, in any case. He hadn't worried about food, thinking the fertile soil of the island would provide. So far it had, but only barely. He had not lacked for water, which was providential, for if not the heat would have surely killed him already.

He began to walk again, in the dwindling sunlight. He fell asleep, woke up and realized he was walking asleep. It was a blessing. He kept walking and slept again. Maybe it wasn't sleep at all, but some sort of deathly state brought on by fatigue and heat. Soon it would be night. Night would wake him, surely as a devil's pitchfork calls a sinner to his torture.

In any case, Jake was soon to realize that he was dead. He was dead because he woke up in heaven. He had missed the night somehow and it was morning – that alone was evidence of angels.

He was pleasantly cool and wet. There were no insects, although it was still dawn and they should have been out in force. He was covered in something goopy that had a pleasant earthy smell. The inside of his mouth was swollen but he did not itch at all, even though he must have been covered in hundreds of bites. As he slowly moved further into consciousness, he found himself in a sanctuary.

He heard the sound of water and of birds. Looking around in the gathering light, he realized he was in a small hollow on top of a ridge. He was sprawled on the banks of a deep, clear pool set in volcanic bedrock. At the far end of the pool, perhaps fifty feet away, was a rock face with a natural spring flowing down between its cracks and elevations. It was enough water to provide a beautiful sight, but not enough for the sound to overwhelm the senses. Under the water of the pool a rock formation was plainly seen, coming up from the bottom but not quite breaking its surface. There was a ceiling of tree branches from the evenly-spaced white cedars forming a nearly perfect circle around the pond. The pool itself was not circular, and the canopy enveloped Jake's bank opposite the waterfall. A shallow stream was behind him, draining the surface water into a stream running down the hill. It took the detritus of the cedars with it, keeping the water pristine.

There were no insects.

Jake had the overwhelming urge to jump into the deep pool, and he indulged it. The water was nearly cold – it was divine. He could see clearly underwater, even in the early morning darkness. Unconcerned with his presence, some small, harmless fish swam in the eddies and a few plants grew at the bottom. The most interesting feature was the rock jutting from the bottom. It dominated the pool like a lonely mountain and its features were covered with plants and growths. Jake swam for its base, determined to unearth its secrets.

At the bottom of the pool, resting against the rock, was a human skull, partly hidden by a thin layer of sand. Behind the skull and beneath it rested the entirety of the person's bones.

One would think such a sight - plainly viewed underwater and in dim light - would be terrifying, especially considering Jake's former state of mind. In fact, the opposite was true. Jake's calmness and inner peace became deeper attributes. Seeing the skull made his welcome complete. But it was more than a welcome: this place reveled in him, it celebrated him. He was not only welcome, he was home – and missed like a prodigal son. He reached out on instinct and touched the skull, almost like a caress. Strangely, he thought it must belong to Seonaidh Ó Brollachain, and that this place was hers, the sacred pool of the water witch. Of course, it could not be. He now knew Seonaidh had died in the city, unable to use her magic in hot le Cap. Even logic did not alter his conclusion, so he determined to believe it hers.

Minutes later, he finally emerged from the pool and explored the hollow. Mint of all kinds grew in profusion. Catnip and catmint, sea lavender, bee balm, basil, and lemon thyme were overgrown from neglected ordered rows. Jake found several ancient, stone mortars and pestles along with small, rusted, iron cauldrons. Tucked in a crude manmade shelf in the rock, an ancient hardwood tinderbox held flint and steel for making fires. To the north, outside of the shade of the cedars near the ridgeline, grew lalwa aloe. Some of the long, succulent leaves were broken off and laying on the ground nearby, squeezed of their sap and moisture. It was precisely what Jake was coated with when he awoke. There were no footprints but his own in this place, so he must have put it on himself in a daze before he fell to the ground asleep. He had no idea how he discovered the stuff would alleviate his suffering. Jake gave himself another liberal coating of the plants' juices before moving on.

On the south side of the hollow outside the cedar circle grew rows of unharvested avocado trees, dripping with soft fruit. Insects buzzed amongst them, but now Jake was more curious than afraid. Although there were no pests near the pool, the avocado grove was certainly wholly their demesne. Jake took great armfuls of avocadoes and brought them back to the pool. He ate them all and was content.

This place was obviously very carefully nurtured and then abandoned.

Jake felt no need to leave his sanctuary. He would recover here and, if his instincts were right, come away with tools to make his journey much easier.

Jake was not completely right. He had two major problems. The spider bite on his bicep was now the size of his fist. It was red as a sunburn except for its center, which was grey as concrete. The centipede bite inside his mouth felt equally as large. Jake had to cut both open and let them drain before the wounds festered and killed him. He risked a small fire. While he gathered his courage, he sharpened a small rock fragment, then heated it. With tentative movements, he managed to make several cuts to his arm. The grey area didn't hurt at all; the red, however, was all bright-white agony. Horrible-smelling pus came from the wound in astounding quantities. He decided to clean out all of the grey flesh, drain the infection entirely, then stuff the wound with aloe. The bite inside his mouth was considerably more difficult to cut and drain, and was even more astonishingly painful, but he managed to do it by nightfall. He was nearly unconscious from his suffering and exhausted by the effort.

That night, the insects did not come – but he heard them in every direction. That meant the pests were stopped from entering the hollow by some unknown dynamic. Jake laughed and cheered, giddy with happiness. He slept well, woke, bathed, and feasted on avocadoes.

The next morning, nearly on instinct, Jake took one of the mint varietals and ground it in the stone mortar with the club-like pestle. Separating the juice and allowing it to thicken, he produced a substance that was closer to an oil than a liquid. That night he smoothed the aromatic oil on his skin and ventured outside the ring of cedars. The insects glittered in the moonlight in the avocado grove but none came near. Jake realized the hollow was designed as a sanctuary against the evils of the island, and the oils taken from its plants could shield him from insects.

Over the next few days, he tested each and every plant within the cedar circle to see if their essence was a ward against the insects. With varying effectiveness, each one was indeed a repellant. The best was catnip. Jake focused his efforts on that particular plant until he had quite a quantity of oil.

Jake placed dry leaf pulp in bowl-shaped avocado skins and carefully poured his catnip oil onto it. The pulp absorbed the oil like a sponge, protecting it from spillage. He closed his makeshift containers with the other half of the avocado skin and carefully tied it together with homemade string made from some sisal hemp growing nearby. He took one of the rusted iron cauldrons that had a working bail handle and filled it with the avocado-skin vials. The supply would have to last for the rest of his trip – just under sixty miles. Freshly-picked avocadoes were carefully cleaned and placed in the sack with his change of clothes and the wooden tinderbox. The sack itself was upgraded with backstraps of fiber rope.

Before he left the sanctuary, he swam down to Seonaidh, or whoever it was, and placed a small bouquet of lavender flowers beneath her skull and secured them with a small basalt rock. He silently thanked her, or whoever it was. Chances were this random person died by violence and was thrown inside the pool, but everything was so tranquil and idyllic that Jake could not bring himself to believe it. In his mind, then and forever more, this was Seonaidh, the water-witch, the first character he had encountered in the narrative of the Heirlooms. He also believed she now knew him and blessed his quest. This place enjoyed meeting him as much as he enjoyed being here.

Soon Jake was headed down the ridgeline. The view was incredible, a vast panoply of amazing clouds, wide plains and distant mountains. All around him were regular rows of overgrown coffee trees surrounded by weeds and shrubs and even other types of trees that had managed to grow between them. Jake was confident, healthy, and renewed. It was a beautiful day, and not quite as warm as it was in the lowlands.

Jake marveled at his own ingenuity, and thought how remarkable it was that his suffering had forced action and elevated his creativity. Jake remarked that his thought was very Catholic: his suffering had purpose.

Below the mountains was a huge, heavily forested plain. All of the trees were nearly the same age – and Jake recognized it as overgrown agricultural land. As Jake continued south, he now encountered more and more evidence of people, usually living in forest clearings in hovels. They were easy to avoid. They had no reason to be stealthy; their animals and raucous conversation always a clue to their presence. He walked easily during the day, encountering no one as long as he was nowhere near a road. Water was everywhere. Jake had his fill from rainwater collected in oddly shaped leaves and tree hollows.

He ate well. Bananas, avocados, West Indian cherry bushes and cherry trees, super-sweet grenadines, passion fruit, star apples, oranges, grapes, cashew apples, pomegranates, Asian melons, tomatoes, and guava grew in profusion – there was really no need for Jake to carry food at all. There were plenty of rats and insects to eat the fruit, but they could not eat with abandon as Jake did, having as many creatures out to eat them. Jake especially loved a mango varietal that grew small, bite-sized fruit that he could simply pop into his mouth and eat whole. Several times he came upon almond trees. He braved a fire, ate the fruity outside of the nut and placed the seeds on the rocks surrounding the flames to roast them. They were magnificent. He spent entire days doing nothing but eating almond fruit and roasting nuts. There were cocoa trees as well, hanging with ochre fruit. Jake found his first as dusk settled and gorged himself on the flesh of the fruit, the seeds being too bitter to eat. He felt as if he had drunk too much coffee. He had to walk far into the night to feel tired and was sore the next day. He prudently avoided cocoa fruit in the afternoons after that. He saw signs of wild boar but only heard them at night. He slept high in the shoulders of trees, covered in catnip oil, and slept well from his daily exertions, even with the sound of insects and the scuffles of the nightly duel between the snakes and rats below. Saved from mosquitoes and flies, Jake was having an adventure. He began to look forward to walking every day. His only problem was his rapidly deteriorating shoes and clothes, but he could not afford to ruin his second set on the journey. It wasn't ever cold, even at night, and the midday sun was thwarted by the profusion of shade.

Jake had to cross rivers several times. He wasn't a strong swimmer and feared becoming exhausted midway and sinking below the currents. Feeling confident from prior victories, he thought of a solution. He dragged a deadfall log to the river, straddled it and used his arms to propel himself across. He ended up far downriver but otherwise crossed without incident – and with a dry sack to boot.

One day he heard music.

It was dissimilar to anything he had heard before, as different as coffee was to wine.

Jake was accustomed to music dominated by chords and melody. A harmonious ocean, as one wave crashed, another had formed behind it, a subtle influence on mood and emotion. The bow was the ultimate European instrument, the wand of forever, the wand of the waves.

This was different.

It was drums, drums, drums. A multitude, each at separate tempo, separate rhythm. It all came together to form a song, just drums upon drums in time, each somehow perfectly fitting with the next, as if the chaos of differentiation was a purposeful illusion. It was machine-like, the sound of gears in a mill clicking at a host of measured paces, determined by the size of each toothed wheel spinning. But it was altogether organic, earthy. Each drum had a true note to it, like the overtones and undertones of a well-tuned piano forte. There were a host of voices raised in song, but the trained intonations of the European were not in evidence. It was rather a host of wails, somehow harmonic, however anarchic. A chorus of female voices, wailing together, almost as an accompaniment to the rhythm of the multitude of drums and not the other way around.

Jake determined to find out what was going on. He followed the sound from his fields and forests to where the brush of man had left its mark. He crept forward but kept his distance, determined to remain well-hidden.

He came to a crossroads.

The main road traveled northwest to Saint-Michel-de-l'Attalaye and southeast to Maissade. The much smaller road ran northeast to Roberta and southwest to Fort d'Piquant. There were small, painted buildings at all corners. Curiously, every structure was missing one wall – the very one facing the crossroads - and was open to the weather. There stood a high, narrow stave made from a small tree trunk, perfectly straight, set in the center where the two roads met. An ornate design, made in flour upon the dirt, encircled this stick. There was a crowd of Haitians, dozens, scores, all dressed in white, forming another wider circle around the thin, wooden monolith. They moved separately in dance, but somehow perfectly together, like the beats of the multiple drums. There were several men and women closer to the center, dancing with chickens, swords and flags. They spun the heads from the bodies of the birds and waved them over the shapes on the ground. Blood was everywhere, plainly seen on their uniformly white clothing. These men and women thrust out their chests and breasts, bent their knees and thrust out their hips and buttocks – perfectly in time with the advanced and incomprehensible rhythms. It struck Jake as obscene and reverent at the same time. Across the sea, the dances of the noble and bourgeois were validations of elegance, class, and perfection, a physical symbol of order and etiquette. The dance of the peasants was carefree and exuberant, a celebration of leisure and community. This crossroads dancing bore no resemblance. It was something else, Jake thought, a celebration of man as animal, a throwing-off of all custom and convention, and this bestial wildness was pleasing to the gods.

The crossroads.

All symbolism of the crossroads had been lost to the European. Now, it was nothing more than a metaphor for life-changing decisions, but it had not always been so. At Louis-le-Grand, Jake had learned a poem from an ancient, darker time, and he now remembered it.

Sum man eac wæs gehaten Mercurius on life,
se wæs swyðe facenfull
And, ðeah full snotorwyrde,
swicol on dædum and on leasbregdum.
Đone macedon þa hæðenan be heora getæle
eac heom to mæran gode
and æt wega gelætum him lac offrodon oft
and gelome þurh deofles lare and to heagum beorgum
him brohton oft mistlice loflac

There was him called Mercury,
devious and crafty,
deceitful in deed and trickeries,
though his speech rang true.
The heathens took him as their greatest god;
at crossroads they would sacrifice to him,
their offerings brought to hilltops,
as the devil taught them to.
This false god, honored among the heathens in that day,
was too called Odin in the Danish way.

The crossroads had another meaning, another power, that was not yet forgotten by the African. The crossroads was where two worlds met: ours of material, and that of the spirit and void. It was at the crossroads where man met the older, darker gods.

One of the dancers suddenly broke from the subtle order of the entropic dance. A look came over his face, as if the man's body was nothing more exotic than a coach, and two drivers had suddenly switched. Now an infant drove the carriage, an infant unsure of how to move his own arms and legs, but reveling in the sudden, inherited strength and vigor of an adult body. His face was ecstatic and infantile. He bumped into the other dancers and they paid him no mind. He ground into a female dancer - obscenely, suggestively - but she only turned and gave him a mild push. He stumbled away from her, still smiling, as if all of this was as natural and mundane as a line of factory workers on their looms.

And then the man-infant locked eyes with Jake.

It was impossible.

There was absolutely no way he could have seen him – yet there he was, now laughing and pointing at him. The other dancers paid this no mind, as if it was a common sight for a man to suddenly become someone else and see things in the bush. The man-infant's expression was beyond puckish, it was darker, more menacing: Loki, Entropy, Kali. He seemed to say *Jake, Jake, I know you! What are you doing in this place! We were not to meet here; you have surprised me!*

Jake ran away as fast as he could.

It was only his imagination.

He was too far to see much of anything. A distant face does not speak, distant eyes cannot see what is hidden. The drums and dancers together were hypnotic; it left him open to suggestion – that was all.

He came to the second mountain range on his journey, the Montagnes Noires, and began the climb. He was in far better shape, not to mention spirits, and the climb was easier. After he passed a certain elevation, coffee trees and the remnants of orchards were ubiquitous. The fruit was picked over by insects and the trees were in sorry shape. Jake realized that if these trees had been harvested instead of being left to rot, the beans would have filled a fleet of ships – indeed, he was hiking in the midst of a legendary fortune.

He crossed the mountains in less than a day and found himself on the river plains near Boucan-Carré. From there, it was only fifteen miles to where he planned to cross the last mountains of his journey, the Chaîne des Matheux. Jake tarried because his favorite mangoes grew in profusion in the hot, wet plain - and he ate them pounds at a time.

He started climbing the Chaîne des Matheux in the morning and by noon he had made the summit. Below him to the right and west was the blue ocean, and before him the plains of Port-au-Prince. By nightfall he had cleared the mountains entirely. He knew that the next day, even if he tarried – which he would – he would find himself on city streets once again. He was saddened but, truth be told, he had grown lonely. As soon as he spent less time thinking about surviving, he had found himself greatly missing company.

The next day he made a club of sorts, a walking stick with a good weight of stone at the tip, tied tight with hemp fiber. He resolved to soundly thrash anyone who would accost him. He bathed in the cleanest stream he could find, which was difficult on the silty river plains, then changed into his second set of clothes. Just like that, he was Monsieur once again, his time as a *boucanier* sadly over.

He made his way to the road and began his short trek to the city. He passed a few people on the road and a few carts. Jake made it a point to make eye contact with every single man on the road, grasping his stick with both hands and making ready to knock anyone unconscious who had ill-intentions. Oddly, the reaction he received for such threatening gestures was not the one he expected. Everyone smiled and gave him a cheery, "*Bonjou mesye!*"

Jake was surprised. When he walked about normally in Le Cap, he feared for his life. Now that he was a crazy person with a club, the world wanted to be his friend. Jake thought it was sad when people mistook civility for weakness and one had to act like a savage to be treated with respect.

Port-au-Prince was not le Cap, not now - and probably not ever.

It was a city on a wide bay surrounded by hills and distant mountains, a dot of urban thickness bulged near the center of the bay and became thinner further along the crescent of the harbor. It was the capitol of Haïti, a port and an industrial hub – nothing more. It had been leveled over and over again – by nature and by man. Nothing much was old, very little was refined or beautiful, although the streets were well-planned and regular as they had been in le Cap. Jake's first steps into the city were grim. There was vomit and bodily waste in the muddy streets. Sick people laid outside the buildings in the sun – and there were dead amongst them.

Cholera.

It was in Paris, it was in Ireland – and now it ravaged Port-au-Prince.

Jake stiffened his pace and made a direct route to the docks. There was a group of men sitting on the steps of the customs building, doing much of nothing. One of them made eye-contact with Jake. Jake grasped his club with both hands and nearly screamed, "*Qu'est-ce que tu veux? Pourquoi me regardes-tu? Voulez-vous un coup?!*" The man scoffed, looked away and made a dismissive gesture. Jake kept walking. He marveled at his ferocity - it was genuine and ill-intentioned. He would have surely beaten the man to death had he raised himself from the steps.

The harbor was every bit as large and impressive as le Cap, and in much better repair, which he did not expect. He yelled out at the ships, asking for their destinations. The first was Canadian and was headed back to Saint John. The next four were French and Jake avoided them. The fifth was Yankee and headed to New York, or Philadelphia if the Delaware was open. Jake told the Captain he would get back to him. The last was a slim Yankee merchant corvette with good lines, a speedy yar at any tack, four masted and painted white, named *Allie Lucy*. Jake called out his query in English and received the reply of Boston Harbor, spoken in good Charleston brogue from a sailor securing lines on the bow.

"I'd like to speak to your captain, if I may."

"Come around to the gangplank and wait there."

Jake went to the gangplank, avoiding the endless line of near-naked Haitian stevedores bringing sugar and molasses onto the ship. He waited to one side until a grizzled, burly man appeared at the taffrail. "Who wants to speak to the captain?"

"I do, sir. I need but a moment of your time. But I must speak to you alone."

"Come aboard then."

Jake maneuvered into line with the stevedores coming up the gangplank, then left the line to the aft to face the captain.

"Follow me," he said, then crossed and moved up the stairs to the wheelhouse. He turned and looked over the activity onboard, not at Jake, "How can I help you?"

"I need to get to Boston, sir."

"You can call me Captain on my own ship, son."

Jake took a breath. He could not afford any blunder here. "Captain, I need to get to Boston."

He nodded. "Twenty-four dollars you're with the sailors. Seventy-five I'll clean out a cabin and you don't have to cook your own food."

Twenty-four dollars was fair. Seventy-five dollars was steep - perhaps four-hundred francs. It was a luxury price and the service on board would need to be extraordinary in order to justify it. "I understand and I thank you, Captain. I do need your forbearance for a moment."

"Uh-huh."

"I come from a very good family."

"Which one would that be?"

"The Lorings of Wellesley, Massachusetts."

"I'm not familiar."

"What I say next you cannot impart to anyone, Captain."

The Captain turned and fixed Jake in his gaze. Jake stared him square in the eye.

Jake continued, "You are a New Englander and your word is sufficient for me. I'm afraid I do need it, however, in order to proceed... Captain."

The Captain continued staring at him, then finally held out his hand, "I will tell no one what you are about to tell me. That, and that only, I do promise."

Jake shook his hand, "I became involved in politics in another country. Seditious politics. If you understand me."

"And?"

"I found myself in desperate legal straights. In order to avoid serious punishment, I agreed to fulfill a mission which took me to Haiti. Plainly speaking, I now wish to renege on my promise and return home."

"Why did I need to know all this?"

"Because I am penniless, Captain. But my family will readily pay you not only seventy-five dollars for a cabin home, but another seventy-five so you do not turn me in to foreign authorities for a possible reward."

"So, what if your family doesn't want to pay or, better yet, you are some kind of tat-monger and you've made this up from whole cloth?"

"Perhaps a written contract is best. Then, if I cannot pay, you can simply bind me to the ship legally until I can repay my debt to you."

"So you can run off on your word again?"

"If you are not comfortable having me work off my debt, turn me over to the Boston authorities and show them our contract. I am sure they will give me short shrift."

"Hundred-fifty dollars is a year's pay for a sailor."

"That is absurd. No one could live for a year on one-hundred and fifty dollars."

"Think so, huh? Well, either you are a real right dandy or a good actor."

Jake gritted his teeth.

The Captain chuckled, "We'll get your contract going." He moved down the stairs, "Way things are going, we'll leave in three days."

"And what is your name, Captain?"

"Captain's fine. What's yours?"

Jake controlled his temper, "Passenger."

He chuckled, "So be it."

1832

Brittany
LA MANCHE
(English Channel)
ATLANTIC OCEAN
FRANCE
LÉON
TRÉGOR
CORNOUAILLE
PAYS DE ST-MALO
PAYS DE DOL
PAYS RENNAIS
VANNETAIS
PAYS NANTAIS
Ouessant
Pays Pagan
Bas-Léon
Haut-Léon
Brest
Plougastel
Kernevodez
Crozon
Cap Sizun
Penn Sardin
Pays Bigouden
Glazig
Rouzig
Bidar
Poher
Dardoup
Calanhol
Fisel
Fanch
Kost-ar-C'hoet
Chtou
Pourlet
Aven
Quimper
Concarneau
Bas-Vannetais
Lorient
Groix
Bas-Trégor
Grand-Trégor
Petit-Trégor
Goëlo
Saint-Brieuc
Penthièvre
Pays de Loudéac
Pays de Pontivy
Pays de Baud
Mené
Josselin
Haut-Vannetais
Vannes
Vannetais Gallo
Rhuys
Belle-Île
Porhoët
Poudouvre
Saint-Malo
Clos Poulet
Clos Ratel
Dolois
Coglais
Fougères
Rennes
Pays de Rennes
Vendelais
Guerchais
Pays de Redon
La Mée
Mitaud
Guérande
Pays de Nantes
Pays d'Ancenis
Nantes
Vignoble
Pays de Retz
N
0
25
50

Chapter Twenty-Six

March, 1789

Estelle

The sisters came at a run.

The screams were agonizing; they gripped a good soul by the throat as only the horror of true pain was capable. Not only that, these horrible sounds came from Estelle – placid, patient, unflappable Estelle – from her upstairs apartment just outside the convent.

They opened her door. She was in her room, collapsed to her knees, and screaming at the top of her lungs with her eyes to the sky. Her hands were gnarled thorn branches, crooked and curved from the exertion of releasing her pain. Her face was sopping wet but, truly, she was beyond tears.

The sisters and lay women were fanned out in a crescent just outside the door, afraid to go any further. Sister Marie appeared, gave them a disappointed look, and entered the room. Estelle was unaware, perhaps uncaring of another presence as her screams continued to bounce off the walls.

Sister Marie saw a note on the floor. She picked it up.

Dear Estelle,

Unfortunately, my son has decided to discontinue his courtship.

Please know that I have a deep and abiding respect and love for you. I pray that circumstances change, but you must know that this sentiment is mine alone.

In Most Sincere Empathy,

Mme Traversier

"*Mon dieu*," the Sister whispered.

Reverend Mother appeared in the doorway. She turned to Sister Marie for explanation.

Sister Marie shook her head, "She didn't know he had returned. He does not write, only his mother, to say his intentions have changed."

Reverend Mother nodded. "See her calmed. Bring her to Mother Superior."

It was not soon, but later Estelle faced the three women again – Sister Marie, Mother Superior and Reverend Mother – but not in the visitors' parlor. She was in Mother Superior's lovely office. It was spartan, but stone lattice windows took up an entire wall and there were potted flowers nearly everywhere, with some of them in early bloom.

Estelle's face and hair was a matted, wet mess, even after the Sister's ministrations. She looked calm, too calm, as she sat facing the three women. She did not look at them, rather somewhere off toward the ceiling.

"That was rather an extreme display, Estelle," said Revered Mother.

"I suppose," replied Estelle, far away in her thoughts.

"How could such a thing come to be, being who you are?"

Estelle's face swiveled and her eyes locked upon Reverend Mother's face. For a moment, the three women were actually scared. But Estelle spoke calmly, "Whatever do you mean?"

Reverend Mother softened. "I would have thought you had developed a habit. One of turning to God in moments of darkness."

Sister Marie reached out and rubbed Estelle's back. "She simply forgot herself, Mother. That is all."

Estelle fidgeted away from her hand. "No, no. Please." Sister Marie withdrew. "Forgive me, I know you are only trying to be kind." Estelle rubbed her face, "I allowed myself to believe that I was to be the wife of Monsieur Traversier. My love for him eclipsed anything I have ever felt. I longed for him. I felt the blood ran in my veins only because of love. I have never been so happy. If there was a word that meant the opposite of alone and unhappy, that was how I felt. Now I am a china vase thrown on the floor to shatter."

Mother Superior carefully considered her words, "In your state, there is little that can be said that would not appear as barren platitudes."

"I allowed myself to believe the impossible. With my whole heart. There was no reason for Monsieur to love me. I aspired beyond my station."

Mother Superior spoke as if Estelle had not. "In spite of this, I will tell you the truth: Only God can help you."

Estelle laughed. It was a sardonic, mocking laugh that brought tears to her eyes. In the Mother's words, Estelle did not find answers, only the suggestion of hopelessness.

"You laugh but you listen also, Mademoiselle. You will turn to Him now or you will turn to Him... later. Until you do so, you will continue in this state. Your only hope will be diminishment of pain, not healing – no, not a shred of it. If you turn to God now, your healing begins. If you turn to him later, you will be broken until you do so. Those are your choices, Estelle. And you must choose, for making no decision is indeed one of your choices."

Estelle had returned to her faraway stare, "Such hard words for me, Mother."

"Yes, hard words. If you were about to step on a viper, I would pull you back with the strength of Samson. My fondest wish would be to throw you like forked hay, and thereby save your life."

"I think the vipers have stepped on me, Mother."

"This is a dangerous moment for you, child. If I could help you through suffering of my own, I would do so. But I can only help you by telling you what you must do – which is something you do not wish to do, in your current state."

"Which... is?"

"Only the love of God can save you. Throw yourself at the foot of the cross, and feel His hand come down to stroke your face. Believe in the comfort of true, overwhelming love, and separate yourself from the imperfections of the world."

"Your words are hollow, Mother. I can only think upon my pain."

"This earth is not your home. There are no northern stars amongst the promises of this life. To believe in earthly happiness is folly. We enjoy the good moments as they come, but all our trust must be in God. You are overwhelmed, and you have forgotten."

"In this moment, I want nothing of God nor heaven. I just want Xavier to knock on my door and tell me he loves me."

"And God forgives you for it. Think hard on your choices, Estelle."

"I cannot think of anything right now, Mother."

"You will not sleep alone until I tell you otherwise. Revered Mother will take you to your new quarters inside the convent."

Estelle vaguely noticed all three women were standing. She stood and, several moments later, realized she was walking down a hall.

It was strange.

The dormitories proved to be insufferable.

The other sister in her room, Sister Catherine, was a novitiate. For some reason, she was excited that Estelle was now staying in the dormitories. Estelle had no idea why. Estelle truly did not wish to talk but tried to be civil.

"Estelle, I will use your own words against you. Just imagine if you were a cane slave, and you will feel much better, knowing how blessed you truly are."

"That is the crux of the matter, Sister Catherine. If I was a cane slave and married to the man I love, I would be much happier than I am now."

Sister Catherine spoke far less to her after that.

Estelle had no idea how to spend her time. She began taking fast, strong walks. Exhaustion was her only escape from the pain.

One day, midmorning, she found herself near Rue de Nicolas. It was a colorful part of town. It was west of Centre-Ville and further downriver, near the Port au Vin and the confluence of the Loire and Erdre. It was busy with its harbor business and all manner of other wholesome concerns, but it was also where the prostitutes congregated. They fascinated Estelle as exotic animals, but she did not see any of them today. Mostly working people walked on the street; coaches, cabs and carriages clattered merrily on the stones.

And then, nearly lost amongst other wheeled traffic, Xavier's coach passed the gate and headed east, further into the city. It was shocking how mundane it was. Xavier's coach passed the gate like any other coach, unaware of its passenger, unaware of the titanic feelings and emotions that swirled around and about him.

Estelle willed herself to continue walking. She took two steps, then, unbidden, her eyes darkened and she fell. Her vision returned and she found herself on a wide stack of canvass sacks of sugar and surrounded by people. She was unhurt and was on her way less than five minutes later. Everyone who helped her was very kind, but she simply wanted to be alone and on her way.

Where was he going, I wonder?

She tried to outrun the thought, but it stayed with her – doggedly. She couldn't sleep that night until very late. The morning prayers were torture. She was certainly not allowed to nap so there was no escape, except for her walking.

She felt better and certainly more awake. In the back of her mind, she had a plan. She didn't know what it was, only that it propelled her. She found herself on Rue des Carunes, on the intersection of Carunes and Rue Grande. She waited and did not know why.

Soon Xavier's black german passed her on the street. She watched it move up Rue Grande and disappear around the corner.

Her breathing came in ragged knots, as if a hand were around her lungs and squeezing the air from them. She ran down the middle of the wide street after the coach. It was perhaps the most dangerous thing she had ever done. If any of the horses in the street struck her, she would be thrown in front of another carriage, run over and killed. She could hear the bells and shouts of the drivers as they yelled for her to make way. She didn't care.

She reached the intersection of Rue Grande and Haute Grande Rue and looked northeast.

The black german only presently pulled away from the curb, having disgorged its passenger, who presumably had already entered his destination.

The coach had stopped in front of the Cœurfroid residence.

A different coach pulled up in front of her and stopped. Estelle looked up at the calm driver. She had two vague thoughts. The first was that she had been standing in the middle of the street for longer than she realized. The second was that the driver was quite kind to be so patient. But he was not patient out of kindness.

A policeman in a blue uniform, gold sash and black tricornered hat pulled in front of her on a bay Norman Cob. "Please get out of the street, Mademoiselle."

Estelle crossed to the edge of the street, the policeman following her the entire way. After nearly slipping and falling in her nervousness, they both arrived without incident. It took some doing to convince the officer she was not mad or drunk. When he finally left, she walked back to the convent, devoid of any thoughts whatsoever.

Until they came unbidden.

Xavier was visiting Monsieur Cœurfroid. They are friends and business partners.

But Monsieur is never home.

Nonetheless, that was why Xavier was there.

But how often did he visit Monsieur at home? If he visited him at all, you would have met Xavier long before your rendezvous with his german's lead right gelding, n'est-ce pas?

Then what is he doing there?

Why indeed, stupid girl.

Estelle felt like a madwoman who could not stop her thoughts.

What was the nature of my mission in Rennes?

The man she met in Rennes was from Nantes. His accent was unmistakable. Nantes was a cosmopolitan, international city. Rennes was deep in Brittany and isolated in comparison. Their speech reminded one of when French was not spoken in Brittany at all – and not too long ago at that.

Xavier's return was implied by Madame Traversier's letter. Therefore, he returned to Nantes before it was written.

Neither Jeannine nor Madame Cœurfroid had bothered to tell her he had returned.

But it was highly presumptive – almost comically presumptive - to think Jeannine came up with this ornate plan simply to remove her from Nantes. And for what purpose? So she could seduce Xavier? That was ludicrous, wasn't it? She knew Estelle and Xavier were in a courtship. She knew they both felt very strongly for the other. Why would anyone go to such lengths to commit such perfidy on a friend?

Oh, but I am being quite naïve, aren't I?

I would love Xavier if he were a peasant. I would be floored and honored to have his attention if he slept on a dirt floor. But not many people think as I do. In Saint-Domingue, there is no amount of suffering that can dissuade men from generating wealth from the horror of the cane fields. Perhaps Xavier's wealth and status are temptations to other young women, as corrupting as any other.

Mankind steals, rapes, murders, enslaves. Why wouldn't a young woman invent a laughable scheme of letter-delivering espionage to dispatch a rival, if the prize was truly valuable?

Jeannine had hatched a preposterous scheme to remove Estelle from Nantes in order to steal Xavier's affections. He was now in this moment going to visit his new paramour, who was Jeannine Cœurfroid.

Without Jeannine really knowing Xavier's character at all, and motivated by greed, status envy, and ego, Jeannine – who was fond of Estelle, who called her sister – had utterly destroyed her life through premediated and devious means.

Estelle experienced something she had never felt: rage. It was absolutely pitiless - an early morning frost killing vagrants sleeping in a ditch - and cleared her mind of anything else.

She was her father's daughter in a way she never realized before. Her father had a soldier's heart, one meant for danger and violence, the greater the stakes, the cooler his blood. When this kind of blood froze, there remained only an exultant feeling, as if there was no more wondrous place than being subject to mortal danger.

Estelle, for most of her life, followed God and had worried and fretted over serving His will. She realized there was no shred of her former intentions left.

Unwittingly, she had given herself over to her love for Xavier, completely and utterly, as only a heart like hers could do. His absence destroyed her.

Estelle was gone. There was no one left to hold on to God. Estelle was gone and God was gone. She was incapable of any of the actions the Sisters had so fervently advocated.

Estelle made a very serious resolution in that moment.

Estelle was going to murder Jeannine Cœurfroid. If she was incapable of the act, she would instead kill herself on the Cœurfroid doorstep.

France, 1788

PARIS pop. 650,000 Second largest city in Europe, fifth largest in the world.

LYON pop. 120,000 Fifteenth largest city in Europe.

MARSEILLES pop. 115,000 Seventeenth largest city in Europe.

BORDEAUX pop. 105,000 Twentieth largest city in Europe.

ROUEN pop. 90,000 Twenty-Seventh largest city in Europe.

NANTES pop. 80,000 Twenty-Eighth largest city in Europe.

Chapter Twenty-Seven

March, 1789

Féroce

Féroce Guerrier did not have any friends. He had no one with whom he regularly talked or spent time with, apart from Potato – and Potato did not count.

The alienation of Féroce stemmed from his own qualities and subconscious desires. Féroce was arrogant and bullying, and most found this unpleasant. Féroce did not commit any sort of crime – he was the opposite sort – but it was evident to all that he had a temper and could be violent if pressed or thwarted. He was also deeply ashamed of nothing more than being himself - and would never put anyone in a position to find out exactly who that was. Arrogance and bullying were convenient attributes to ensure this.

He was unmarried for most of his life for another reason as well: he was seven-eighths white, a group called *Métis* in Saint-Domingue, although the word meant something different off its shores. To any dark mix of woman, he was a catch – but he would have none of it. Being *Métis* meant that if he married a white woman, his children would be legally white. This had been the impossible goal of the Guerrier family for generations.

In Saint-Domingue, white women who married black mixes were not unknown. They were usually Irish, imported to the Caribbean as slaves by the British. They had dribbled into Saint-Domingue ever since, usually when they were freed from British ships. The Irish immigrants had made an impression on the island completely out of proportion to their number. The Irish and West African were similar in only a few ways, but both were witchy, spiritual people to be sure. In fact, there was now a voodoo loa who was white – a redhead, in fact. Her name was Maman Brigitte - a more Irish name could not be found - and her ire was never to be roused.

Féroce bided his time. He developed contacts, he made good impressions. He knew all of the French military captains. He gained stature as an honorable man: a policeman, a hunter of escaped slaves. In January of 1763, it all paid off. A young Irish woman was delivered into his care by a French captain, with instructions that she be treated honorably. She was strikingly beautiful, dark, and green-eyed. She was mad as a fumed hatter, spoke no French, or even English - only a secret language of spells and curses that had always remained a mystery to him. She was also with child from her former master.

Féroce stepped gingerly. He courted her as if she was a china cup, treating her better than he had his own mother. They were soon wed. Her options were few, and he had made it easy. It was the original intent of the captain.

This beauty, Seonaidh, was moon-kissed at the best of times. In the worst, she was cruel, violent and angry. After the death of her third child, she began to drink as well. Féroce was cruel in return, but never laid a hand on her.

She soon found the words that hurt him the most. He saw their children as the fulfilment of generations of dreams. She called them *merdique nègres*. If she knew how much that hurt him, he believed that she would never have said it.

His reasoning was questionable.

But all of that was distant past. Seonaidh was long dead. Féroce had remained unmarried, but that was not due to his lack of trying. Féroce, in fact, felt somewhat lost without a wife, although when she was alive, he had been gone from her for long stretches of time. He did not realize it until she passed, but she was the rock upon which everything rested. She was cruel to him, but, for some reason, as long as he had her, he had a base of strength to do what he needed to do.

It was no matter now. He wanted another wife but was unsuccessful so far.

Father Jonathan had been little help, "Monsieur Guerrier, I think that you need an appropriate companion. You do not need someone to advance your social status. Your standards are impossibly high."

"I'm a Sergeant in the French Guard. I'm fit as a stallion, and I can read."

"Yes, but you also wish a woman who is beautiful, who comes from wealth, who is younger than you, above your status, and possessed of class and manners."

"You say that as if I can't get such a woman."

"I don't know, perhaps you can. But then you are not looking to secure a wife or companion; you are on a mission, are you not?"

"I suppose I am."

Father Jonathan, or Songbird, or Twinkletongue, or whatever other name Féroce called him behind his back, had not helped. Féroce would keep looking. He was nothing if not persistent.

So, here he was in his little house with Potato, who cooked and cleaned – poorly on both accounts. She was old and round and short.

"Why don't my children write me?" he asked.

"They don't answer your letters?"

"That's not what I said."

"What did you say?"

"I said my children don't write me."

"Do you write them?"

"What does that have to do with anything?"

"You don't write them? I don't understand. If I could write, I would write everyone all the time."

"I'm their father. They should write me and visit when appropriate. I shouldn't have to write them. That's not my position. That's not how it should be. It's disrespectful when they don't write."

"But you don't write them either."

"You're missing the point. I shouldn't have to write. They should write me."

"You are an odd man, Monsieur Guerrier. Sent to vex the earth."

"Perhaps. But no one calls me Potato behind my back, either."

"Monsieur Guerrier, only you call me such a thing behind my back."

Luckily, Potato was mostly immune to Féroce's charm. Being a great-great-grandmother gives one perspective.

There was a knock on the door. Féroce picked up his pistol from the table. "Who knocks?"

"Corporal Travers, Monsieur."

"Enter."

The Corporal entered, seemed a bit concerned with the pistol in Féroce's hand, and saluted.

"Don't salute indoors, Corporal."

"Apologies, Sergeant." He knew that and wondered why he had.

"What's your report?"

"Have the troubles reached here?"

"What troubles?"

"The peasants, Monsieur."

"What about them?"

"Then they haven't. Monsieur, there has been a peasant uprising that is consuming our countryside. It is both spontaneous and nationwide."

"It's those *damné Cahiers*. Everyone believes they have a right to an opinion." It was strange, though. Saint-Florent-le-Vieil could not be quieter. The man seemed to be reporting from Siam.

"I have been ordered to bring you back to the right bank if you are not consumed with the troubles here. We are in dire need of help."

Féroce stood. "Let's go."

***

Varades was just across the Loire from Saint-Florent-le-Vieil but could have been a different nation. It was not part of the unique land between the Loire and the Vendée that had no name, it was simply part of Western Anjou. It was quite poor as well, and neither the nobles nor priests had such good reputations as they did on the left bank.

Varades was small, just a tumble of buildings. The first thing Féroce noticed was that some sort of celebration was in order. Peasants were everywhere in the streets, dancing and singing, all holding staves and implements with a profusion of dead hares hanging from them. A group of them approached and drunkenly hailed them. Féroce grinned and waved, as if he was the star of a parade.

The Corporal stiffened in his saddle. A few too many of the peasants held muskets for his liking.

"What's wrong with you, Corporal? Choke on some spit?"

"Can you not see, Monsieur?"

"Can I not see what, exactly?"

"The hunting of rabbits is strictly forbidden."

"Even in the Spring?"

"Especially in the Spring, Monsieur. The peasants want to hunt the rabbits because they eat the shoots in their field."

"So… *les seigneurs* wish the shoots eaten? Don't they make their coin from the crops?"

"Yes, Monsieur. But they also wish to hunt the rabbits themselves."

Up ahead was a gigantic pile of broken… dollhouses? Féroce squinted his eyes. Whatever could they be? It didn't matter. Within a moment, the pile became engulfed in flame.

Travers was horrified, "*Mon dieu*."

"Why are the peasants burning toys? What celebration is this?"

"They are not toys, Monsieur. They are dovecotes."

"What is a dovecote?"

"It is a little house for doves."

"So, if they burn them, they won't have any doves to eat?"

"No, Monsieur. The nobles keep the doves."

"They are burning the lord's food, then."

"The lords do not eat the doves."

"Why then do they have these dovecotes?"

"They like doves."

"They don't like them too much if they keep them in little houses."

"The doves are allowed to fly away whenever they wish, the dovecote is their nest, their sanctuary."

"But then the doves can eat the seeds that are planted in the fields, can't they?"

"I suppose. But the lords love their doves, Monsieur."

Shortly they came upon a sight that did not sit so well with Féroce. Three dead men were piled a few feet in front of a stag cooking on a spit.

"We should leave, Sergeant."

"Hold on to your manhood, Corporal." Féroce kicked his horse to a trot and the Corporal followed. He pulled his horse sharply in front of the three dead men. His actions were designed to get him noticed, and they succeeded. A crowd gathered around them. They did not look friendly and they were all armed.

Féroce did not need to think about the right tone to strike with the crowd. He spoke in a loud voice, devoid of any emotion save total confidence. "Who's in charge of this fête?"

No one spoke. There were a few cries of *Vive le Roi!*

Féroce put a fist in the air, "*Vive le Roi!*" With that battle cry, he could have pushed a battalion out of a trench into cannon fire.

There was a feral, hoarse cry that answered him from all mouths – *Vive le Roi!*

"Very good," said Féroce, "Now that we have formalities taken care of, would someone mind telling me what goes here?"

A thick, bearded peasant stepped forward, "The King is our father!"

"God willing, *bon fermier*. What is your name?"

"I am Laurent, Monsieur."

"*Bonjour*, Laurent. I am Sergeant Guerrier."

"*Bonjour*, Monsieur."

Féroce pointed at the three dead men. "Who are these unfortunates, Laurent? Placed in front of a fire and spit. Do you cook them after the stag?"

The man did not answer. Other voices from the crowd did, "Gamekeepers!"

"Do we now strike down gamekeepers in Royal Anjou?"

Laurent spoke, "The King loves his people! *Vive le Roi!*"

Féroce cheered his King as loud as the crowd, until their voices died down. "As some of you know, I am from Saint-Florent-le-Vieil. We do not have such strict hunting laws in most holdings, rather lenient ones, in fact. Peasants hunt the doves and rabbits and even the stags bold enough to eat from their fields. I am therefore unsure of what goes on here, but I wish to know, if one of you would tell me."

Laurent spoke, "The King loves his people. We are his children."

"Yes, he is our great Father. We are his children."

"The King has ordered that we defend ourselves against the predations of *les seigneurs*, of knighthood and mitre, in regard to our fields. The King no longer wishes us to starve."

There were no such orders. If there were, men like Féroce and Corporal Travers would have been the first to know.

This was mass hysteria.

Féroce turned to Travers, "This is happening throughout the entire country?"

"Yes, Monsieur. Everywhere."

Féroce turned back to Laurent and motioned toward the dead, "And these three men?"

Laurent hesitated, then spoke, "They would thwart the orders of the King."

"Well, you aren't going to cook them, are you?"

"No, no Monsieur."

"Well, why are they piled about your spit?"

"I-I honestly don't know, Monsieur. I don't know. I was not here."

"Well, give these poor lads to their families and priests, eh?"

"Yes, Monsieur." Laurent and the crowd looked a bit ashamed.

Féroce grunted. "No one else gets hurt. Belt them with your fist, nothing more, or there will be trouble. The King loves all his subjects, Laurent. Not just you. Even the gamekeepers, yes?"

"Yes, Monsieur."

"All right. Carry on then."

Cheers. The celebration continued. The songs started up and the streets were filled with dancers once again.

Corporal Travers was horrified. "What have you done? There are three murdered men here! Their blood cries out from the very stones!"

"Do you bring them back to life with a different choice of action?"

"What?"

"Corporal, listen very carefully. We have two choices. We can attempt to stop this."

"Respectfully, Sergeant, we should do just that." The Corporal was losing his composure.

Féroce answered calmly, "You said this disturbance, whatever odd phenomenon of man caused it, is nationwide. So much so that there are all of two French Guard police to contain the entire town of Varades, the inhabitants of which have all clearly lost their minds. If we tried to stop this, we would end up lifeless and heaped atop the three gamekeepers. Not only that, it would be obvious to anyone save a simpleton that the French Guard, and ultimately the King, has lost control of the countryside. That would lead to greater harm than three murdered men, I assure you."

The Corporal said nothing.

"Our second choice is to let this fire expend its fuel in the hearth. We make sure no one else gets hurt. This madness winds down in a month or two. We figure out who the ringleaders are and we find a reason to hang them. Order is preserved."

"Yes, Monsieur. I see your point now. You are right."

"Of course, I'm right. That's why I'm the Sergeant."

"*Oui*, Monsieur."

"You need to move *ton cul* back to Angers, post-haste, stopping at every sentry and sheriff, and tell them exactly what I just told you - and end at the Commissar's desk with the same speech. If you fail to convince them as I have convinced you, there will be the devil to pay."

"Are you staying here, Monsieur?"

"I'm going to eat some rabbit and dove while I wait for the stag to cook. When it does, I'll have a slice of that. Then I'll set up shop here in Varades for the nonce and head home when things die down a bit. *Vive le Roi*."

"*Vive le Roi*, Monsieur. I will not fail."

The Corporal turned his gelding and rode off.

***

The madness – the burning of dovecotes; the wholesale killing of deer, rabbit, and dove; the murder of the occasional gamekeeper – gripped, quite literally, the entire country all at once, as if on an actor's cue. It was some kind of mad communal decision, the kind of mob event that thwarts even the most brilliant men to make sense of or explain. It was the first time, but not the last time, one of these inexplicable events gripped modern France.

Throughout the country, the King's men rode the unique wave of insanity without giving into it in kind, letting things play out as they would, and therefore preserved what order they could.

It would be the last time they won so readily against the hysteria of the mob.

Oath of the Horatii
(Le Serment des Horaces)
Jacques-Louis David, 1784

Chapter Twenty-Eight

March, 1789

Beau-Brave

Monsieur Théo was awakened in the middle of the night by a great pounding on his door. His ancient housekeeper, Madame Lent, stood in the foyer quivering with fear. "Monsieur, it is the Guard! We are undone!"

"Madame, please sit down at once before your heart gives out."

A voice beyond the door – "By order of the Throne and the Parlement of Paris, we command you to open this door or we shall break it down."

Madame Lent sat heavily in a chair and crossed herself.

"There is no need for that, Messieurs!" said Théo as he quickly unlocked the door. French Guards entered his home and, moving past him, began searching his apartment, the temperature of which immediately went from cold to glacial. A shivering young officer entered last with two men who stood on either side of Théo. "Why do your men ransack my house, Officer?"

"They look for names and the residences of your accomplices, Monsieur."

"Accomplices?"

"Your name is Théophile Gautier-Proust Hocquenghem, I presume?"

"Yes, Officer."

"I am afraid you are under arrest by order of the Throne and the Parlement of Paris."

"Upon what charge, pray tell?"

"You are under arrest for Perjury to the Royal Court, Blasphemy, and Threats Against the Public Welfare, Monsieur."

"Perjury to the Royal Court? In regard to what?"

He snapped his heels, "*Pardonnez-moi*, Monsieur. Perjury to the Royal Court in Regard to Theatrical Pursuits. The Court has revoked your license to produce educational theater in regard to African necromancy."

The last few months had been heaven on earth for Monsieur Théo. He had found his family in the lunatic cast and crew of his play. He loved them all, he loved the magic of the stage and the atmosphere of the theater. Everyone was interesting, personalities bursting from their skin like sun rays, and they loved him, in their own misshapen, misfit ways. He could not imagine being a part of any other world.

He burst out crying. His arrest was one thing - the closing of the show was another matter entirely. "Why? For what reasons?"

The Officer held out a polite hand, then produced an official warrant from his pocket and read. "The performance is not educational in nature, it is contrary to Catholic beliefs and insulting to the Throne, it attempts to usurp the monopoly by the production of full-length tragedy, and opium and sativa burned as incense during the performance is injurious to the health of the performers and audience members alike."

"*Mon dieu*, what are we to do?"

"What are we to do? Monsieur, you had best look to yourself. These charges are quite serious."

"Am I the only one indicted?"

"No, Monsieur. All of your performers are charged with lesser crimes."

"And Beau-Brave?"

"Beau-Brave is charged with the same crimes as yourself."

"You say the charges are serious."

"Your guilt or innocence is beyond my purview, Monsieur, but if you are judged the former, you could be hung in the Place de Grève."

Madame Lent feinted right off with a squeak.

Nearly suffering the same reaction, Monsieur Théo stared at the officer with an open mouth. When the officer realized he had nothing more to ask, he made a quick motion to his men. Monsieur Théo was escorted outside to a waiting coach and was whisked away to a cell in the Conciergerie to await trial.

***

Talma sat in a dark corner of Le Procope with his back to the rest of the café. Rounding out the table were a pair of his friends, Desmoulins and Danton. These two could not have been more different. Desmoulin was emaciated in body, subtle and feeling in spirit – a terrible but energetic poet. Danton was husky bordering on obese, with a thick tuberous head. His face bore scars from smallpox and fights with animals as a child. He was eloquent and intelligent, but without subtlety, and aggressive as a hussar in pursuit. Danton and Desmoulins were good friends, brothers, and no one knew why unless they knew them well.

Talma did, and knew that if politics were vegetables the two would be alike as two peas in a pod.

Desmoulin pouted. "We are all talk. Now I ask you to put your gold where your tongue wags and you balk."

"No," said Danton, loud and peevishly, "You are asking me to give money to some lawyer in Arras in order to finance a campaign that I myself might engage in."

Desmoulin cleared his throat – "HA-hrumph" – which meant that he had lost his temper. He then stuttered, which was another sign, "D-D-Danton loves his wife and he loves his practice. He does not love t-taking risks or performing work for free. Yet you have no chance of getting elected in Paris. You will not go within five leagues of the Estates-General and we both know it."

"Yet you yourself are running – in Paris. Perhaps I will. It's my money. I can do with it as I please. Even pay *you.*"

"Talma, help me." There was no reply. "Talma - he travels to ancient Rome in his profligate imagination, leaving us mortals behind."

Talma stirred, "I apologize, *mon ami.* The premier of *Brutus* is tonight. It is difficult to focus on much of anything else. Tell me more about your friend, Francine."

"Francine?" said Desmoulins, quite irritated. "HA-hrumph. N-no, *Maxime.* My friend is Maxime."

"And what of him, *mon ami*?"

"He plans to run for the Estates-General, for the Third Estate, for Arras."

"I see."

"No! You do not see. He is like us. Better even!"

Danton snorted.

"I have known him for years. We went to school together at Louis-le-Grand."

"Precious good that education has done for you," grunted Danton.

Desmoulin, in spite of being the occasional butt of jokes, despised being mocked. He closed his eyes to control his temper, greatly amusing Danton, then continued in an even voice.

"He is the most honorable of men. He's a Freemason, a die-hard Republican Socialist. Rousseau to him is… a guiding light. He has no ambition but to better mankind. There is no part of him that does not speak of integrity and values."

A pouch was dropped on their table, and it clunked heavily with the sound of coin.

"Then give him this, with the blessings of Beau-Brave of Grenoble."

The three men looked up. Beau-Brave was cloaked and hooded, wearing a cocked hat of black wool. "Do not look up or greet me, Talma," he said cryptically in a soft voice.

"What is this?" asked Danton.

"I will sit and tell you. Do not regard me." Beau-Brave sat next to them at another table, almost back to back but not quite.

Talma spoke quietly, “This is Beau-Brave of Grenoble, the writer of the séance I described. All of you were destined to meet, I have spoken of you both to him. I do not understand the subterfuge he now requires.”

“Then I will explain,” Beau-Brave whispered so only they could hear, “Monsieur Théo has been arrested. Several others in the cast as well, although on lesser charges. There is a warrant for my arrest. Capital offenses, I am afraid. The police are vexed, for there are no address records for half the cast and most use pseudonyms.”

“*Noms de guerre!*” hissed Danton.

“I am destroyed. My reason for being has evaporated. My greatest friend and benefactor in the world is now imprisoned. I mourn for him, for he is a gentle soul. He is stronger than most would think, but the gaol is an enduring trial, even for the strong.”

“*Mon dieu,*” whispered Talma.

“In any case, they look for anyone to interrogate or arrest. It is best that I am not connected with anyone, especially those involved in the cause.”

Danton smiled, “With the enmity of the Throne comes nothing but honor, Beau-Brave. And, in your case, not for the first time. I am an advocate, if you did not know. I will peruse the evidence they have against you and lobby for the charges to be reduced or dropped.”

“Thank you. It is strange. I find myself possessed of great anxiety. I have faced muskets with greater courage.”

Danton nodded, “There are advocates who vomit before a trial but, when the president bangs his gavel, are cold as stone and as hard to crack.”

“Then surely I possess that manner of heart.”

Talma shook his head, “You place a pouch on the table in such straights.”

“I have almost five-hundred livres without it. I have survived on far less.”

Desmoulin spoke, “Hand him back his pouch.”

“No!” blurted Beau-Brave. “I have been listening to you as I determined when it was safe to make myself known. If Maxime is half the man you have described in the last half-hour, I would have you give it to him. Perhaps my time is over and his time is only yet beginning. Who knows what the future brings? I would only have him know my name, and in what straights I found myself when possessed of this generosity.”

“Of course, Beau-Brave,” whispered Desmoulin.

“My next words are for Talma: *Mon ami*, there are so few of us in the arts. Even less now. David holds the torch for the salon, you must do so for the stage. You must stand like Horatio at the bridge for our ideals, holding our enemies at bay and advancing the cause until we gain the ground of the Estates-General.”

“I will. What are you going to do now?”

“Apart from seeing *Brutus* tonight? I do not know,” said Beau-Brave with a grin.

"Don't be a fool. Police swarm the Comédie-Française. It's far too dangerous. Get out of Paris. Return to Grenoble. There, you will be safe as the Queen's diamonds."

"I will be killed at once by jealous husbands."

Danton snorted.

Talma rubbed his temples, "We will not laugh with such abandon if we have to witness your death in the Place de Grève."

"I would think not. I will leave you now." Beau-Brave stood, and placed a hand on Desmoulins's shoulder. "Question Talma in regard to the *Ens* of Uruk. Then tell your friend Maxime of this – and make sure he quotes me and not either of you."

"As you wish, *nouveau frère*."

And then Beau-Brave was gone.

***

Brutus, by Voltaire, at the Comédie-Française – left bank, in the Germaine, *tonight.*

It had debuted long ago, in 1730, the work of a harsh critic of the current order. The play was quickly dust-binned by the Court and forgotten. Voltaire went underground in Brittany and wisely made himself scarce for the nonce. Then, forty-eight-years later, something happened that changed everything.

Voltaire died.

He was beatified, enshrined as a secular saint, one of the nation's greatest minds. As Hannibal's disrespect for the Roman order was forgotten, so too was Voltaire's contempt for the Throne and Altar. His sainthood led to a resurrection of his work, his incendiary politics overlooked.

It was an accident of fate, a boulder braining a passer-by. The play was now staged at a far more delicate time, as if a saboteur's explosives were accidentally moved from the rails of a bridge to its very foundations - by the structure's own architect, no less.

Brutus, then.

First off, the play had nothing to do with the death of Caesar.

This Brutus was an earlier man, but one as well known to the French in their adoration of antiquity. Voltaire's Lucius Iunius Brutus was the legendary first Consul of Rome who lived four centuries before the prophetic Ides of March. Brutus's son Titus – again, a less-famous Titus – fell in love with an Etruscan princess, the Etruscans being the enemies of Rome.

The act was treasonous.

Because Brutus was who he was, the Senate washed their hands of the ordeal and returned Titus to him unharmed. As his father, Brutus forgave Titus, and then, as his Consul, ordered his execution. The laws of the Republic had to be observed, even by - and perhaps especially by - the First Consul, to preserve the state and the people of Rome.

The truth was somewhat less romantic than the play – Titus simply plotted with his brothers against the Republic to bring back a Royal Rome, a Rome with a King and not a Senate. It was irony to the level of good story-telling that four centuries later a different Brutus committed treason by assassinating Caesar in an attempt to prevent Republican Rome from becoming Imperial Rome.

The reason for the Throne's displeasure with the play was simple. The King was an absolute monarch, ruling by divine right, at least according to a convenient lie invented by the agents of the Throne long ago. The King was not a Roman Republican, who considered himself a citizen with a command responsibility and nothing more, with the state being of far more importance than himself.

L'etat c'est moi was a quote widely attributed to the Sun King. He never actually said such a thing but it did clearly explain a sentiment: The King of France *was* the state, not subservient to it. The state served the King, who was the father of the people.

Socialists were modernized Roman Republicans. They believed the state was paramount, of far larger significance than any individual citizen at any level. Republicans therefore believed in *virtue*, *sacrifice* and *devotion.*

Virtue was the sum of morals and ethics to which citizens had committed themselves in order to make a greater state, each citizen contributed as much as they could to the collective as a whole.

Sacrifice was the ability to place the value of the state above oneself. If, by your death or the death of your son, you could preserve the state, you did so – as Brutus did, as Horatio on the bridge, as the Horatii brothers.

Devotion to the state was simply a higher loyalty for the collective than the individual, and it enabled virtue and sacrifice. The state, and what it represented, were the true deities of the Romans. It was said that Rome was tolerant of the gods of its conquered people – but it was only because they did not consider them to be gods at all. Rome demanded absolute unswerving obeisance to her true gods, which were loyalty and devotion to the state, and simply did not care about the pantheons of fancy led by Jupiter or anyone else.

Rousseau felt the same way. A state with all religions had none – except the one that truly mattered, which was the goddess Devotion, and her consort, Reason. Rousseau added a non-Roman footnote: citizens are devoted to the state because the state protects individuality.

Therefore, virtue, sacrifice, devotion and individuality somehow coexisted peacefully in the minds of the Socialist.

The Enlightenment had changed axis. These Roman ideals, along with Rousseau's writing, had produced something totally unique. Even in America, there was no example: states had more power than the national government. The rights of individual communities to enforce their standards and values had trumped those of individuals. France had moved past America to something completely new and European – the belief that individuality could be protected by a strong, central state, and the power of provinces, churches and communities therefore lessened or reduced to ash.

Brutus had his son executed in an act of devotion, sacrifice and virtue. He was the Socialist Isaac. Therefore, interest in this man was not confined to Voltaire. For the last two years, on a canvass of more than twelve square feet, David had been painting the *The Lictors Bring to Brutus the Bodies of His Sons*. Talma, spellbound, had slowly watched the painting come together. It was a marvel of historical accuracy. Staring at it was akin to being in the room as Brutus, barely visible in the shadows, broods as his dead sons are carried into his villa by stretcher, his wife and daughters hysterical with grief. David had researched every aspect of the painting. Everything – down to furniture, clothing, even the wall partitions – was shown as it would have been during the very moment.

So, here was the play, *Brutus*.

There were nine major roles. In importance, Proculus, the role of Talma, was perhaps eighth. Most of the cast had no idea of the current, electrical nature of their production. They were Royal players, the absolute top of their profession and would remain so if they understood their position – which was to serve and honor the Court.

In the Comédie-Française, there was a green room, a lounge for actors waiting to go on stage. No one knew why it was called a green room, but it had been called such a thing for centuries. The green room here was sumptuous, and energized by the glittering actors. They dressed as formally as possible in the style of their time, for anything else would have been an insult to the Throne. They would not have been out of place in Versailles – indeed, some of their costumes were even given to them by courtiers. There was a sense of anticipation, energy and good humor in the green room. All actors had to pass through it on the way from their dressing rooms to the stage. It was always full and never loud, but rather buzzed with subdued conversation and muted laughter. All contract actors of the theater and their entourage could lounge here, and often did, even when not performing in the current play. It was their elegant sanctuary.

Talma entered the green room from his dressing room.

He was dressed from head to toe as a Roman tribune. He wore no wig and his hair was cut in the Roman fashion, short and combed forward. He wore sandals. He carried a scroll.

The green room went completely silent.

"*Bon soir*," said Talma with a confident smile.

There had never been a moment such as this in the green room.

Talma had talent, a currency in this room that had true weight and value. He was also doing something extraordinarily dangerous and avant-garde. Therefore, he had to be confronted - but by whom? Spiderwebs of thought regarding politics, tradition, manners, and etiquette wove their way through all who witnessed.

There were three types of players at the Comédie-Française: the *pensionnaire*, the *sociétaire* and the *une partie entiere*. They were ranks of shareholders. An *une partie entiere* should not confront Talma, that would elevate him. A *pensionnaire* should not question him, for the moment required more import.

Voilà – it had to be a *sociétaire*.

It could not be a man, for that might lead to an argument or a duel.

Voilà – it had to be a woman.

It could not be someone older than Talma, for that might imply that his breach was the product of modernity - and that would never do. It could not be someone younger, for that might imply Talma's conduct was based in more clever wisdom.

It had to be a *sociétaire* ingénue of precise age. There were not many. To be young and also a respected *sociétaire* was rare indeed.

Louise Contat came to the same conclusion as she sat with her considerable entourage. She did not have a part in *Brutus* and was simply diverting at the premiere. She was only twenty-eight, but also the Queen's favorite actress; she had originated the part of Suzanne in Beaumarchais's *The Marriage of Figaro* - truly nothing more needed to be said.

She scanned the room as Talma stood stock still in the silence. It was up to her to confront him, and she knew. She turned to Talma with a smile and a gay laugh, "Look at Talma! How ugly he is! He looks just like one of those old statues!"

Now he had been confronted, and the moment progressed to the next stage. The room twittered in laughter, carefully matching the tone of Mademoiselle Contat.

Then Talma smiled, for he knew this moment was coming and had prepared for it. He half-opened the scroll. "Do you want to see something amazing?"

She grinned, admiring his savoir-faire, "Of course! Do not keep me in suspense!"

He crossed to her and opened the scroll on the Ormolu mahogany and onyx center table. The scroll was full of drawings of the very costume he wore.

Contat was transfixed, "*Mon dieu*, Talma, who has drawn these wonderful pictures?"

"My good friend, the painter Jacque-Louise David. For two years he has been working on a canvass, dealing with the very subject matter of our play. The painting will be shown in the Louvre salon this year."

Now everyone crowded the table as the conversation continued.

Talma had won the green room.

There were a few other places he had to win as well. Next was the parterre – the area around the seats and below the balcony, where the real people of Paris stood to watch the show.

His time in the green room ended.

He walked out to customary encouragements, moved the lengths of the dim halls, and found himself backstage, waiting to go on.

It was a very long, and a very short, moment. Talma, as Proculus, finally took his seat onstage with the actors portraying Brutus, Titus and Valerius.

The audience could not believe their eyes. Here was a ghost of ancient Rome, sitting alongside the Versailles peacocks in their wigs and powder. There was an explosion of murmured whispers and exclamations. The actors did not lead the crowd's emotions, all were rather in character, seemingly oblivious to them.

But there was one man in the audience - standing in the parterre to the far left - who, in past times, had taken command and imposed his anarchic order during far more dangerous moments. There was great risk here for the man, for if he were recognized he would be arrested; he did not care.

He saluted and shouted a slogan.

The gesture was called the Roman salute. The arm shot out, straight and slightly upward; the hand flattened palm-down and pointed. No Roman had ever saluted in such a fashion; it was an invention of Jacque-Louis David, from a painting called *The Oath of the Horatii* - but this man, and the world, believed the Romans saluted in this way.

His war-cry was more accurate, "*Senātus Populusque Rōmānus!*" he screamed. This phrase, and its initialism *SPQR*, were on Roman shields, coins and banners. It meant *The Senate and People of Rome.*

Everyone knew what this meant. They knew what it signified when Talma wore the true garb of the tribune. They understood the themes of the play itself. They knew what it signified when Beau-Brave, the foolhardy hero, saluted and screamed his fealty to Republicanism.

They were also well-aware of what it signified when the parterre went berserk with applause and cheers. Almost simultaneously, those better-heeled in the seats and balconies wisely followed suit, whether they shared the sentiment or not.

Inside the Comédie-Française – left bank, in the Germaine, *tonight* - there was *Aum*, *Shabda-Brahman*, another existence, a universe, exploded into being.

There were few moments in the theater akin to this, even fewer happening in such delicate times in history. It resonated throughout Paris, the rest of France and Europe. Even in Cap Français, in faraway America, did they know of this moment. It changed theater in most of the world forever.

Talma held up his hand, as if the unruly Roman crowd in the courtroom had gone too far. The energetic Parisian crowd quieted immediately – except for Beau-Brave, who was running from the police – and the performance continued.

1422 AD - France is no more. A few staunch lords defy the English king and remain loyal to the dauphin and memory of their once great kingdom...
England
London
Dover
Antwerp
Calais
Flanders
Crecy
Cherbourg
Picardy
Amiens
Bayeux
Elbeuf
Caen
Verdun
Normandy
Poissy
Paris
Chalons
Brittany
Orléans
Anjou
Nantes
Tours
Burgundy
Dauphin
Poitiers
Poitou
N
Lyon
Bordeaux
Guienne
Gascony
Languedoc
Toulouse
Spain

Chapter Twenty-Nine

March, 1789

Estelle

Mother Superior had just threatened Estelle: she had to follow at least part of the sister's regimen of prayer or leave the convent.

"I don't care what happens to me."

"I did not ask you if you did. Will you obey me or not?"

"I need to take my walks."

"We are not discussing walks."

"I do not want to be a nun. I don't want this life. I want what I cannot have. I want to be married to Xavier Traversier. If I am not, I do not care what happens to me," Estelle said evenly.

"And how happy are we to place our trust in the world instead of God?"

"What?"

"We are not discussing your future occupation."

Estelle forced herself to look the Mother in the eyes, "What… what were we discussing again?"

"You must follow at least part of our daily regimen or leave the convent."

"What part, Mother?"

"Well, all of it, in God's world. But I demand a part."

"Which part?"

Mother Superior gave her an empathetic look, "You will wake, breakfast, pray with us and do chores, until noon."

"Very well."

Mother Superior rubbed her eyes. Estelle watched her, devoid of thought. Eventually, through her haze, she noticed Mother was tearing. "Are you well?"

Mother snorted with irony, "*I* am fine, Estelle."

Estelle was not thinking properly but she did as she was told.

She was tired all her waking hours, exhausted, all she could think of was sleep. When she laid her head on her pillow, she became wide awake and all she could do was think. She escaped the convent every day at one half-hour past noon. She always walked directly to Centre-Ville, to Haute Gran Rue. She spied on the townhouse from every possible angle.

There was never anything to see, not really. Jeannine rarely left. Occasionally, Xavier's black german would turn the corner and come to the main entry from the carriage garage in back. Estelle would then flee from sight, knowing Xavier would exit the townhouse soon after.

She didn't want him to see her. Whatever was inside of her that attracted him, she was sure it was gone now, along with everything else. Any meeting would only reinforce his indifference to her. She could only be seen by him when she was ready, on her terms. He would be in a state after Jeannine was killed. She would wait until then.

Thinking of murdering Jeannine gave her comfort and no rest, a stress and tension that somehow also alleviated her suffering. It was akin to cutting a hand to divert the mind's attention from a broken leg.

She found herself lying on her cot in the dormitories. It was night. She didn't remember how she got there or when.

Wearing her night gown, Sister Catherine sat on her bed. Catherine was a plain girl. She had a round face, brown hair, and big brown eyes that stuck out from her head. Her body was thick and thin in all the wrong places. "Estelle," she said in a normal voice.

"What?"

"How do you think of me?"

"What do you mean?"

"Do you hate me? Do you love me? Do you respect me? Do you care about the feelings of my heart?"

Estelle couldn't tell anything from Catherine's even tone - she had no idea where these strange questions were leading. Estelle found she couldn't answer them, either. "Sister, my heart is nothing but a carcass. It does not function. I have no idea what I think or feel regarding anything."

"Would you poison my gruel?"

An odd question. "No."

"If I fell in front of you, what would you do?"

"I think I would help you to your feet and ensure you were hale and whole."

"If I was hungry and had nothing, and you had just enough for yourself, would you share your food with me?"

"Yes, of course."

"In your estimation then, I have value."

"Yes."

"Then I would ask you for a favor. It is far less burdensome than sharing food from a meager plate. Will you grant me this favor?"

"What does it entail?"

"Words."

"Words?"

"Yes."

"I don't understand."

"I want you to say words."

"Is that all?"

"Yes."

"How many?"

"Not many. It will take but a moment. I will ask you a question. You will answer it honestly, then you will repeat one sentence after me. After you speak those few words, I will no longer trouble you."

"Very well."

"No, you must promise beforehand, you must swear."

"Why do you trouble me, Sister Catherine?"

"Because I would not poison your gruel either. I would help you if you fell, and share food from a meager plate with you. Is that not enough?"

"What do you wish?"

"I want you to swear that you will speak the words I need to hear. You must have faith in me. But you must swear beforehand, not knowing what I wish, only knowing that in my estimation you have value and thereby trusting in that sentiment."

"Very well."

"Swear."

"I swear to speak the words you require."

"Then we will begin. You will now answer my first and only question."

Estelle waited.

"Who has wronged you to put you in this state?"

Estelle took a deep, ragged breath. "Jeannine Cœurfroid." As the sound of that accursed name floated through the room, she realized she needed to add one more. "Xavier Traversier."

Catherine nodded. "You will now speak the words I require."

Estelle waited.

"I, Estelle Guerrier, forgive Jeannine Cœurfroid and Xavier Traversier."

In Estelle's heart, in that moment, there was no hate or anger. There was nothing, nothing at all. She duly repeated the words, in a sleepy monotone, "I, Estelle Guerrier, forgive Jeannine Cœurfroid and Xavier Traversier."

A loud *CRACK* echoed against the walls. Sister Catherine had clapped her hands together with as much force and strength as she could muster. The sound was so intrusive, Estelle found herself wide awake and sitting up. Catherine jumped from the bed as if Estelle was going to attack her. As they locked eyes,

Catherine's posture was nearly a fighting crouch. "It is done. You cannot ever take back those words. God has heard."

Estelle felt only numbness. "I do not believe I meant those words, Sister Catherine. I believe I only repeated them."

"No. You don't understand. You spoke out of faith and love – my questioning determined it - and God has heard what you have said. Your faith is a mustard seed, but God in his mercy moves mountains. His will is done. You have set things in motion you cannot undue."

Could that be true? Could such beautiful magic exist? Part of her wished it could be, that God could indeed overcome the death of her soul and bring her back to life. It seemed an impossible task, even for Him.

"I suppose there is a part of me that wishes that could be true," Estelle ventured to say.

Sister Catherine had none of it. She pointed, "Go to sleep."

Estelle sighed and turned over in her bed to face the wall. She heard Sister Catherine move under the sheets of her own cot.

What a strange moment.

For whatever reason, it was also a calming moment. Estelle slept well.

She woke mid-morning. She was surprised. Ordinarily, it was the Sisters' urgent mission to make sure she was out of bed in the early morning hours. In fact, it was their mission to harass her into performing her duties at all times whatever and whenever they were.

Yet, here she was.

She dressed and readied herself for the day. As the minutes passed in solitude, she began to worry. Perhaps the sisters had finally lost hope in her and she was going to be expelled. This was her last day, and allowing her more sleep was a final act of kindness.

Estelle left her room and went into the hall. She heard singing from far away. Sunshine gently bathed the cloister. For a moment, there was no instinct within her as she listened to the singing and watched the dust play in the sunlight.

"Estelle?"

Estelle turned and saw Sister Marie. "Could you come with me to Mother Superior's receiving chamber?"

"Yes, of course."

Sister Marie took her arm and clung to it, quite tightly. As they walked, slowly but surely, Estelle felt like a prisoner being led to her execution. "Is everything all right?"

Sister Marie said nothing for a moment. "Everything will be revealed shortly."

Inside the receiving chamber sat Mother Superior, who was expressionless. Reverend Mother stood in front of an empty chair, alert, eyes darting. Sister Marie sat Estelle in the chair, then stood behind her and placed a hand on her shoulder. It was a bit too much pressure. "I'm fine, Sister Marie."

Sister Marie did not move her hand. Reverend Mother took a slight step forward toward Estelle.

What on earth is going on?

Mother Superior spoke, "I need to know if you have lied to us regarding your circumstances."

"W-what?"

"You have one opportunity to tell us the absolute truth."

"I assure you, I have spoken nothing but the truth to you." *One lie. One thing not revealed. My desire to commit the mortal sin of murder.*

"Were you actually courting Xavier Traversier?"

Estelle was irritated, "Mother, it was printed in *Les Annonces*."

All three nuns shared looks. Estelle resisted the urge to rub her face. She was lost enough without the convent leadership blundering in the dark. Mother Superior suddenly spoke in a loud, upbeat voice, "You have received a letter. Last night. Late afternoon to be exact."

Estelle said nothing.

"It is from Jeannine Cœurfroid."

Oh, what lies do you tell of me, devious sister? Now everything makes sense.

Estelle controlled her voice, "I surmise that you have opened this communication."

"I have."

"It was addressed to me, however. I demand to know its contents."

"Of course!" said Mother Superior in her cheerful, but oddly emotionless, voice. She placed spectacles on the tip of her nose and opened the letter. "Dear Sweet Sister, I have missed you so much! I hope that you have pined for me as well, for it would break my heart to find that you do not miss me as much as I miss you. Oh, sister Estelle, I have some wonderful news. I am to be married."

"Oh Jeannine, tell me you have not written this letter to me," Estelle whispered.

The hand came down on her shoulder with more pressure. Revered Mother slid a foot a few more inches toward her.

Mother Superior continued, "Monsieur Traversier has asked for my hand and I have accepted! Can you believe my good fortune, sister? I am spinning while standing still. I am so happy I think I could burst. You must now be a part of my happiness, Estelle. I want you to be my *témoin*."

Estelle cleared her throat. "What is a *témoin*?"

"A great honor," replied Mother Superior with no expression, "You are the chosen witness of the oaths of marriage on behalf of the bride. There can be a maximum of two *témoins* for the bride and two for the groom, but usually there is only one for each."

"I see." Estelle felt numb again - no anger, no humiliation, simply nothing.

Mother Superior lowered her gaze to the letter. "Hideous L'Oublié will be the groom's *témoin* and I simply cannot abide him. My Xavier indulges me in all things but in this decision, he is unassailable. He is most wrathful and cruel to me on my special day! So, you must and will be by my side for everything. First, you must come to the *fiançailles*, on April the first."

"*Fiançailles*?"

"An engagement party where the man presents the woman with her ring. It is where the families come together as one. There is a meal, then a special mass."

"Special mass?"

"You know nothing of wedding traditions?"

"I have been to one wedding. But it was a country wedding, across the Loire in Anjou. The families knew each other already. They had seen each other at least once a week for their entire lives. There was a wedding mass and a celebration, but in all honesty every mass had a celebration afterwards, at the lord's château. Community was celebrated continually; the wedding was simply another excuse."

Mother Superior looked down at the letter, "Our wedding will take place on May the fifteenth. *Le Vin D'honneur…*" Mother Superior looked up at Estelle, "A reception for all well-wishers," then back at the letter, "…will be at eleven in Centre-Ville. We will parade to the Cathédrale Saint-Pierre-et-Saint-Paul for the wedding mass. Afterward, I will kiss my husband for the first time on the steps of the church for all the world to see. You will parade back with us to Centre-Ville for the *Repas de Noces'* – that would be the wedding dinner, which is quite smaller and far grander than *Le Vin D'honneur*. It is quite an honor to be invited to the *Repas*, although as *témoin* you are as honored as you possibly can be. I continue: 'We will eat, drink and be merry until the morning hours, where we will have a breakfast of onion soup. I cannot wait to see you again and to share this moment of my life with you. Yours, forever and ever – Jeannine."

Mother Superior let the note drop to the desk and took the spectacles from her nose. The hand on Estelle's shoulder seemed less heavy. Reverend Mother actually sat back on the desk from a stand and crossed her arms.

Mother Superior spoke again, "Why is she inviting you to her wedding?"

Estelle calmly considered the question. "I think it could be for several reasons. The first is that she has no friends that I know of, only acquaintances she has cultivated for various reasons. I believe I was the closest person to Jeannine in her entire history, and I was not truly close to her at all. The second reason is that she wishes to erase any resentment I could have toward her. I realize that makes no sense at all. You would simply have to know Jeannine. She is, at all times, the simplest and the most manipulative person when it comes to the human heart. The third reason, of course, is to salt my wounds, to twist the dagger she has plunged into my very bosom, to cause as much additional hurt and damage as she possibly can. Now that I think upon it, I suppose it is all three reasons together, in various measure, which is quite vexing to understand. I do not think that Xavier would have wanted me there at all. I do not know what I am going to say to him, or that I could even retain my composure in his presence."

Reverend Mother rubbed her chin, "Do you believe that we have your best interests in mind?"

Estelle's numbness instantly turned to blind rage. She barely controlled her voice. "I am quite tired of nuns asking me obtuse questions regarding my thoughts and emotions. If you wish to say something to me, then say it. If you wish to ask something of me, do so directly."

All three sisters looked frozen in time. One does not speak to a Mother Superior in her own convent in such a way – not even a Cardinal. Mother Superior finally spoke, "Very well, Estelle. Here is what I wish to say to you: you have been asked to be *témoin* and you will do so, comporting yourself with conscientiousness and honor."

"You are ordering me to attend this wedding?"

"No. I am ordering you to attend this wedding appropriately and with all due diligence and attention as *témoin*."

"And if I do not?"

"You will be punished."

"What will my punishment entail?"

"Three days of solitude and prayer."

"Are you jesting?"

"I am not."

"So, my choice is between attending the wedding of the man I love and the sister who betrayed me, or three days of solitude and prayer?"

Reverend Mother spoke quickly, "Forgive me, solitude, prayer and *fasting*."

Estelle nodded, "Three days of solitude, prayer… and fasting."

Mother Superior spoke softly, "Understand that I am quite serious. It is not my wish that you do this, it is my order. My *order*. *Comprenez-vous*?"

"No, I understand nothing. And your punishment does not seem overly severe for avoiding such a torturous event."

"If you do not understand my process of thought, then I urge you to think upon this until you do, for there is a definite and well-thought method."

"Life has cursed me of late with a proclivity for churning thoughts to make butter when I am trying my very best to fall asleep. I am sure I will be tormented by your words soon enough."

"Very well. You may go. Here is your letter."

Estelle took the letter and left the room.

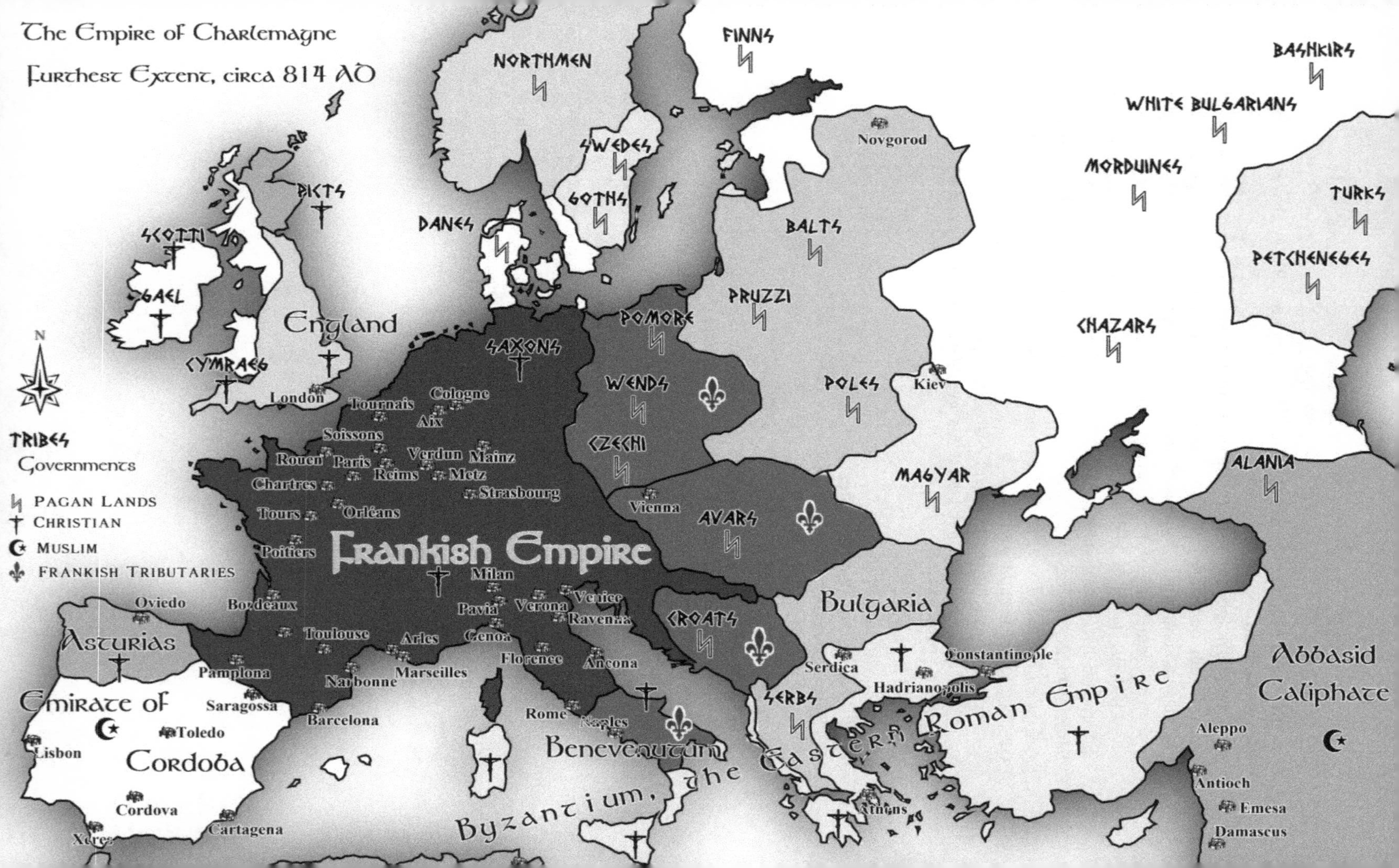
The Empire of Charlemagne
Furthest Extent, circa 814 AD
N
TRIBES
Governments
PAGAN LANDS
CHRISTIAN
MUSLIM
FRANKISH TRIBUTARIES
NORTHMEN
FINNS
BASHKIRS
WHITE BULGARIANS
Novgorod
SWEDES
GOTHS
DANES
PICTS
SCOTTI
GAEL
CYMRAEG
England
London
MORDUINES
TURKS
BALTS
PETCHENEGES
PRUZZI
POMORE
SAXONS
CHAZARS
WENDS
POLES
Kiev
CZECHI
MAGYAR
ALANIA
Tournais
Cologne
Aix
Soissons
Verdun
Mainz
Rouen
Paris
Reims
Metz
Chartres
Strasbourg
Tours
Orléans
Vienna
AVARS
Poitiers
Frankish Empire
Milan
Oviedo
Bordeaux
Pavia
Verona
Venice
Ravenna
CROATS
Bulgaria
Asturias
Toulouse
Arles
Genoa
Pamplona
Florence
Ancona
Serdica
Constantinople
Abbasid Caliphate
Marseilles
Narbonne
Hadrianopolis
Emirate of Cordoba
Saragossa
SERBS
Barcelona
Rome
Naples
Toledo
Lisbon
Beneventum
Byzantium, the Eastern Roman Empire
Aleppo
Antioch
Cordova
Athens
Emesa
Cartagena
Damascus
Xeres

Chapter Thirty

March, 1789

Xavier

Xavier had not attended a meeting of the Freemasons for months. He had naught but a mild interest in coming this night, but thought he must, having no excuse not to. He dreamed only of being in the presence of his fiancée, Jeannine. He had kissed her several times, far less times than he wished. Each time the experience was searing. He burned as he imagined her in his arms.

At the meeting, he expected to be greeted warmly, and he was, but there was an odd reserve. He was a valued member of a body but was now treated as somewhat of a foreign entity. In the past, he had taken long trips away from the Freemasons and this had not happened. As he thought on the situation, he remembered something from his father's writings.

> *Such things happen when a group of men find themselves in a sort of crucible, where they rely on each other and form a strong team. A sailor rejoining a ship will never quite fit in with his old crew if they have saved their own selves from sinking, unless he survives an encounter of equal severity with them as a working part of their collective salvation. Life and death is a struggle that unites men in greater fashion than any other type of conflict. This seems like common sense, and perhaps is, but it is sometimes easy to forget the invisible bonds that unite men and how they affect the context of interactions.*

So, in what crucible have the Freemasons in Nantes been forged that they would now look on him as half an outsider?

The answer was not long in coming. After the meeting, there was a meal. Everyone was strangely quiet, even expectant. Then, without ceremony, Thierry-Alain Bedos stood. Xavier had history with the man, whom he considered a buffoon, but now he looked very serious and full of purpose, his half-baked scheming and jostling for social position forgotten.

He held notes in his hands. "Brethren, as you know I have been tasked by the Masters to be liaison with other lodges and individuals friendly to our cause in regard to developing intelligence on the nature of the *Cahiers de Doléances* for all three estates. I have a good amount of information to impart to you and the Masters have asked me to do so during this dinner, if it pleases you."

There was pounding on the table. Xavier joined in, once he ascertained there was no harm or statement in doing so.

"*Merci, merci.* First, some hard numbers and facts that you may or may not know. The First Estate, the clergy, comprises ten thousand people, give or take, and owns five to ten percent of the land, which is, of course, the highest per capita of any estate. The First Estate is tax-exempt. Some of the funds generated by their holdings are dedicated to caring for the poor. And… some are not."

Laughter.

"The Second Estate comprises the nobility, perhaps four-hundred-thousand souls, the wealthiest and most powerful twenty-thousand amongst them living in Versailles and Paris. This group has enjoyed a renaissance of sorts, since their castration at the hands of the Sun King seventy-odd years ago. The nobles, nearly exclusively, control the paid positions of the central government, the higher church offices and the public honors. The Second Estate is tax-exempt.

"The Third Estate comprises twenty-five million people, and now includes everyone outside of the First and Second Estates, be they bourgeoise, peasants, artists or whomever. The more powerful of the Third Estate have found ways to be tax-exempt, so the burdens of state have fallen on the poorest amongst them: the peasants, working poor and farmers.

"The modern state, not to mention the greatest nation on earth, requires a budget that must be supported by other means, bringing us, of course, to our current financial crisis.

"We begin. Please keep in mind, there are twenty-five thousand *Cahiers* in all. What I present here can only be called a summation. Even so, herculean efforts have been expended in order to provide this information to the Brethren of France, and more detail will be available as needed."

Once again, the table was pounded. *Hear, hear*.

"The *Cahiers* of the First Estate are dominated by the concerns of the parish clergy, in spite of the leadership's attempts to muzzle them. They have called for an end to bishops holding more than one diocese, which is understandable, for the practice stems simply from some noble wishing more than one paycheck. This dovetails with a demand for those who are not noble to be able to become bishops. They care nothing for the tax-exempt status of the church and have expressed a willingness to trade their status for their demands. They are adamant regarding the Catholic church being the official religion of France and there is a considerable anti-Protestant bias.

"The Cahiers of the Second Estate were somewhat surprising, unless one has spent time within those circles. Ninety percent of the nobles are willing to give up their tax-exempt status."

Shouts and pounding erupted, *Bravo! Bravo!*

"Messiers! Messiers!" brought quiet and he continued, "Overwhelmingly, they stated that academic merit, rather than birth, should be the requirement for holding any position, whether military, administrative or otherwise. They viciously attacked the government for being out of date and tyrannical. One can only assume that the nobles have purposefully thwarted the King in his current troubles, not out of greed but in an attempt to bring about the present situation we find ourselves – that of the Estates-General and, potentially, tremendous change and reform. I will remind the Nantes Brethren that Freemasonry was brought to us by them and not the other way around. May God bless the Second Estate. Without them, we would have nothing."

Cheers, as fists thudded against the table top. A few of the noble brothers stood and bowed with exaggerated grace. There were laughs and a few napkins were thrown.

"The *Cahiers* of the Third Estate were quite colorful, if not comic, and usually varied depending on location. These are local concerns mostly. The peasants wish the deer and rabbits off the fields, the dovecotes destroyed, and the pigeons removed. They are livid at having to bear the burdens of state, which is understandable, and they wish equal representation with the First and Second Estate at the Estates-General, which is not going to happen. Generally, they wish a turning back of the clock, not a turn forward: a return of gleaning rights, abolishment of the theater and cafes…"

Chortling laughter.

"…and a return to a nice, normal conservative Catholic kingdom where no one makes waves in the puddle. Not just deregulation, freedom, and mobility of labor but demands for laws against mechanization, unscrupulous hawkers, and cheap goods, especially from other countries, especially from Britain. The Third Estate, may God bless us, is now proved to be backwards, ignorant and hopelessly monarchical."

Hisses.

"I will sum up our findings with a witticism: The commoners desire a strong Father-King to protect their interests against progress, the First and Second Estate wish to go out drinking with Rousseau. That is all."

He sat back down to cheers and applause.

Interesting.

Xavier realized, at this point, that the Freemasons had more information regarding the *Cahiers* than the King. The question was *why*. Why was all of this espionage necessary? They would have had all of this information soon enough. Why did they need early awareness? It was too much effort not to be propelled by some sort of grand scheme or purpose.

Scheme and purpose.

The dinner ended soon enough, Xavier thinking more of green eyes and honied laughter than the taste of any dish.

As they stood from the meal, Cœurfroid caught up to him and touched his arm, "Come," he said.

Xavier followed him out of the temple and into one of the townhome parlors. They did not tarry in the slightest and yet already there waited the elder Bouteiller; the lawyer, de la Chapelle; and the banker and Grand Master of Nantes, Monsieur Wegelin, the banker.

"Messieurs," said Xavier as he bowed.

"Come, sit," said Wegelin.

Xavier did so.

Wegelin continued, as if answering a question that Xavier had not posed. "The Estates-General is a far more complex and varied creature than it is made out to be. As such, there are a host of legal problems that must be determined beforehand."

Xavier tried not to roll his eyes: preamble, to men such as these, was little more than ambush preparation. "Such as, Monsieur?"

"Such as the colonies. How many delegates do they send? Can they vote?"

"I understand." It was nothing but introduction. Soon the conversation would segue.

De la Chapelle spoke from the liquor service, "As you know, the nobles of Brittany are not exactly akin to those described at dinner." He handed Xavier a snifter of *eau de vie de vin*. "They call themselves the *Epées de Fer*. They have refused to participate in the Estates-General at all, due to the decision to double the delegates of the Third Estate."

The shift from Wegelin to Chapelle was purposeful. *Interesting. Do we now begin?*

Xavier spoke, "Brittany will have less representation then. Less but perhaps one with greater impact, considering who will *not* be coming. Who then will represent Nantes?"

Chapelle spoke quickly, "Eight members of the Third Estate. Six substitutes. Three members of the clergy, five substitutes."

"I see."

Eventually they will get to it.

Wegelin spoke, "We have attempted to secure control of the entire lot. Ensure that at least all eight of the primary elected members of the Third Estate are Freemasons, under Freemason control or, at the very least, Freemason friendly."

"Is this drive nationwide or only in Nantes?"

"Let us say partially nationwide. Obviously, France is not a corrupt nation, our laws and rules are respected. This election will be conducted legitimately. Even if we wished to hijack the proceedings, we could not. Obviously, we do not. We do not take ridiculous chances - especially when we can achieve our goals through focus and application of resources."

"So, we are attempting to legitimately gain as much power as possible through adroit diplomacy and financial pressure."

"Yes."

Ahh, they want money.

"We do not need money," said Wegelin. "Although we will take it, if offered."

"I will match the highest donor and then give ten percent more."

"Very generous, Xavier. But I'm afraid that in our present needs, we will not be derailed so easily."

Xavier said nothing.

Cœurfroid spoke, interrupting no one. "This will be a national gathering, composed of the most astute political minds in France, having survived the culling of an electoral process - as well as having been tempered by it. In an educated, politically-active nation, only the brightest and most knowledgeable will be there - but also the craftiest, most devious, and ambitious."

"I agree."

"We cannot afford to send anyone but the *crème de la crème* from amongst our ranks," said Wegelin.

Ahh, they want me to run.

"I wish I had time for such an endeavor," Xavier deflected.

I want to marry Jeannine and spend every waking minute with her. That is all I want.

Chapelle then spoke, which surprised Xavier. He assumed all of this was scripted, and expected a different actor, "I understand completely," he said, "Would you be willing then to give your name as a substitute? It would involve no time, energy or funds on your part, unless someone dropped out and you then had to go to Versailles. In which case, it would then demand all of your talents and resources, obviously."

Why did Chapelle offer this instead of Wegelin? What are they planning?

"Uh, certainly, Monsieur. I will allow my hat to be thrown in the circle of substitutes."

Wegelin stood, "Excellent. We are then finished." Everyone stood and promptly moved to the door, everyone except Cœurfroid.

I have been outmaneuvered somehow. I'm not sure what just happened.

Cœurfroid placed a hand on Xavier's arm once again. "Could we stay behind and talk, my old friend?"

"Of course."

With a grin, Cœurfroid sat down and produced two cigars from his breast pocket. "Ironically, we partake of the leaf in the Spanish way, considering the patriotic nature of our conversation."

Xavier took a cigar. "I would have it no other way, my friend."

"Your romantic endeavors have forced you to miss a great deal of history in the making."

"Are you then not glad of it?"

Cœurfroid looked thoughtful. "Are you sure this is what you want?"

"Monsieur, I am engaged to your daughter. We are to be family. Why would I not want this?"

"I love my daughter. As all fathers, I wish I could have spent more time with her – but probably could not have, considering who I am. She is who she is. I know this, but do you?"

"I think I know her fairly intimately."

"Do you?" He was pointed but otherwise opaque.

He sounds like Madame.

"I believe so. I will tell you this. If she called off our engagement – which she would not, being wholly honorable – I think I would have nothing left to live for. She owns my heart and my very reason for being, Monsieur."

"What has Madame said in regard to this?"

"I would not pull her curtains open, Monsieur, if she does not want the light."

"We are brothers here, Xavier."

Xavier nodded. If his friend asked twice, he would not be gainsaid. "I think she wishes I was marrying another."

"Estelle Guerrier."

"Yes."

"Why aren't you?"

"I was meant to marry your daughter, Monsieur. Every ounce of me desires to be her husband. I once thought I loved Estelle, until I met Jeannine. Then I realized love burns like oil and tinder – fast, intense, consuming. It is unmistakable, and undeniable."

"That is one type of love. Is it the most lasting, fulfilling kind? I do not wish to be crass, but in marriage you are filling a permanent position. One must consider aptitude for long-term companionship, motherhood. Certain attributes are far more temporary than you might think, and should be given less value."

Xavier found himself angry. Cœurfroid was slighting Jeannine. He was speaking of his own daughter.

Cœurfroid spoke again, "My marriage started as yours. Now, it proceeds in the way it happens to be. Young men look for all the wrong things in women; their future happiness is therefore a product of luck and not design. Take my words as you may."

"The type of wife I am pursuing is summed up in a name: Jeannine."

Cœurfroid smiled and his bearing changed in an instant. "Then you must pursue your present course."

"Yes, I must."

"On to politics?"

"Is there more to discuss, Monsieur?"

"Yes. Are you familiar with de Villiers, Mercier, or Linguet?"

"They are writers, I believe. Pamphlets and such."

"They are, indeed. Do you know their politics?"

"I do not. I have not been myself of late. I have allowed the weeds to grow in the garden, as it were."

Cœurfroid sat back in his chair. His expression changed.

"Something troubles you," Xavier offered.

"Yes. A division within our ranks."

"I am listening."

"The three writers I mentioned have developed another definition of the Socialist Revolutionary state."

"Go on."

"As you know, Rousseau wrote that it is the primary function of government to protect the individual. The individual, as natural man, doing as he wishes, and a strong central government protecting him from himself and others."

Xavier said nothing.

"You do not believe this?"

"No. The Americans are correct: Government ultimately might be the greatest threat to the individual. I think that Rousseau was not bright enough to think past Monarchy, his mind could not transcend his own environment. His perfect system was a group of enlightened individuals ruling with the power of a king. A utopian Monarchy, supporting a different religion, if you will."

"What if individuals are starving? Does not the government have a responsibility?"

"With enlightened fiscal policy, only the idiot, the mad, or the lazy will starve – and, even then, only if they have no family. If they do, their care is best left to local communities, not the central government."

"What if someone decides not to take that sentiment on faith alone?"

"Meaning?"

"Disbelief in the idea of local communities being able to elevate its citizens. If the individual is starving, or lacking in some important way such as clothing or shelter - and the government's task is to protect the individual - does the state take on the burden of feeding and caring for the individual?"

"I need not remind you, but that is precisely our current system. It is called strong central government, or absolute monarchy, if you please, and it doesn't work. The British economic system works, we have seen it in action. They have every bit as much debt as we do, yet are nowhere near the dire straits in which we find ourselves. The American and Dutch economic systems seem to work as well, if you pardon the staggering understatement."

"*Laissez faire.*" Cœurfroid closed his eyes and remembered the quote. "Let go, which should be the motto of all public power, since the world was civilized. Instead, they are motivated by the detestable principle of enlarging themselves by the abasement of our neighbors. There is but the wicked and the malignant hearts satisfied by this principle and its interest is opposed. Let go, alas, let go."

"*Mon dieu*, that annoys me! French ideas and words to describe the economic system of the British and Americans. We invent, others act, then we languish. That, Monsieur, is the French way!"

"Alas, our lancers charge tangents. A return, my friend, to De Villiers, Mercier and Linguet." Cœurfroid smiled.

"Yes, the three writers."

"Their ideas boil down to these bones: the wealthy should be taxed to care for the poor. All wealthy individuals, whether bourgeoise or noble, are responsible for the collective. It is as much Jansenist as Rousseauian."

"Regardless, they envision only a better version of our current system. Again, a utopian Monarchy. No. I care far more for the poor by employing them. Why would government disempower one such as myself from expanding my business in order to employ, and thereby feed, those who are not working? It seems a downward slide. No – it does not *seem* to be that way, it has been proven by the King *to be* that way."

"This new group labels all wealth – whether bourgeoise or noble – as oppressive."

Oppression was a very charged word to Rousseau. It meant evil. Worse, the wellspring of all evil. "Oppressive in a Rousseauian sense?"

"Indeed. Not only is Feudalism and Monarchy oppressive, but Capitalism as well - the entire Laissez Faire-Adam Smith economic model. Both systems lead to inequality and injustice."

That did not bode well at all. "Life will never be fair because people are different from each other."

"Rousseau teaches us that all human beings are the same."

"Hogwash and nonsense. At school, the students came from the same background and standing, yet there was a vast difference in their performance, even with equal effort. Even in such a homogeneous environment, there was inequality of result. Yet, there is far more variance in a larger group. There will never be a time when a stupid, lazy individual experiences the same outcome as an intelligent, industrious one. It will simply never happen, not in any system."

"There are many stupid, lazy aristocrats who are wealthy."

"Stupid, lazy aristocrats become poor and destitute every day, equaled in number only to the amount of intelligent, hard-working bourgeoise who become rich."

"And the peasants?"

"I am sure they are divided as well, by their own efforts and abilities. We seek a system where the opportunity for difference of outcome is only more prevalent."

"You believe fairness is impossible to achieve."

"I know that it is. And there is another pitfall, based in human nature, which may arise if these critiques become policy. If the industrious are taxed to the point where it makes no sense to be industrious, men like us will simply forgo industry in favor of government, for that will be the only true place to garner wealth and power. The very people society relies on to create industry will not do so, rather they will join the government and become leaches upon the industry of lesser men."

"Again, you devolve Rousseau's vision to an Aristocracy."

"And is that not my point? Are we not at the stage of development where we transcend these things and force a better system in order to advance all of mankind?"

"Yes, that is the point, Xavier."

Xavier leaned back in his chair and rubbed his chin. "This new take on Rousseau almost has the flavor of the peasants' idea of the idealized Father-King, protecting them not just from the nobles and clergy, but the bourgeois. If the King realizes this, and taxes the rich to make life better for the poor majority, he could win over this new group and recreate himself as Caesar, a tyrant of absolute power with his base in the mob. And life would be far worse for everyone, and our nation would be weaker for it."

Cœurfroid refilled their drinks. "The current Austrian model, in other words. Perhaps true, except this new group hates Kings."

"They want a new King, one that is simply not called a king, in a vain hope that their problems will be solved by a charming prince from a fairy tale. They are afraid of being responsible for themselves."

"Not quite. They think that a segment of the population *is* totally unable to care for themselves, and those who are infinitely capable should be responsible for them."

"They are spellbound and do not see the loopholes in their magical thinking. They are only turning the unable, as you call them, into a lever to gain power for the unscrupulous. Truthfully, if the unable are casualties in the battle for freedom, I am a general who would pay that price."

"Does the government owe nothing to its less-fortunate citizens?"

Xavier wasn't sure if Cœurfroid was being Socratic or disagreeing. "You use the word government as if it were not a group of men, but rather some sort of elevated creature. The government is but a group of men, nothing more and nothing less, and their deepest motivation is for the gathering and continuance of power. The unscrupulous amongst them will immediately see any opening or advantage of law or custom and exploit it."

"Is government so hopeless?" said Cœurfroid wistfully.

"Yes. It has been proven to be a necessary evil. Anyone who thinks otherwise is deeply naïve, and doomed to be betrayed."

"You are not a Rousseauian, are you?"

A loaded question nowadays, even asked by an old friend.

Xavier answered honestly. “I don’t think so. Montesquieuian, perhaps, if such a sentiment can be spoken only between us.”

“These new writers are in earnest, they are influential, this philosophy exists. Be cautious. Your innermost thoughts are safe with me, as they always have been. I only give you knowledge of another predator in the jungle, one of which you must be wary, for he aims to devour you.”

It was a continuing trend.

People were becoming fanatics regarding subjects that, to Xavier, very obviously required nothing more exotic than unbiased, well-educated intellectualism. Fanaticism made no sense to Xavier.

Why is this dynamic occurring? What aspect of the human character am I failing to comprehend? It disturbs me that I cannot perceive the wellspring of this trend.

Xavier forced a smile. “Of course, old friend. I hear and appreciate your words. They are only disheartening because their ideas seem at counter-purpose to our cause.”

“Our cause is being redefined hour by hour, and not by the likes of Franklin, Adams, and Jefferson.”

“They are not overly talented, this new crop?”

“De Villiers, Mercier and Linguet are not without a soupçon of talent but they are ultimately forgettable. Their ideas? Perhaps not. People love their fairytales and fantasies of rescue.”

“It is one thing to be a villain. It is another to be so talentless, and yet so influential, that the perfidy of ideas remains while the originator himself is forgotten - and therefore cannot be reviled.”

Cœurfroid laughed. “You are naïve, Xavier. If the ideas remain, someone will take credit for them - or rewrite them anew. I seem to remember you telling me something about new looms and programs.”

“You’re right. Of course, they will.”

“Heed my words. I do not tell you of all this to convince you to believe in new prophets. I tell you because I believe we are headed into a storm, and you need to know the direction of the wind.”

“As always, your words are appreciated and valued. I will heed them.”

“We cannot take any side right now. The power behind all three estates, everyone who considers themselves to be Socialist or Rousseauian, are united against the current system. When we have a Constitutional Monarchy as a result of the Estates-General, it would behoove us to appear mysterious in our motivations, especially to the factions that will certainly emerge. Let us play things close to the vest, for the safety of ourselves and our business.”

“And the Freemasons, presumably?”

“What I am speaking of transcends Freemasonry, Xavier. I am speaking of your personal survival and the survival of your family and business. Silence is your greatest weapon in this fight. There is no need to fight the storm or look for allies – not yet. You do not seek acclaim or fame and never have – and there is no reason to start now. Hide like a hunter and take only safe, sure shots. Let others show their colors, while you move only behind the scenes and never on stage."

Xavier pondered for a moment. "All of you are going to find a way to get me to go to this *damné* thing, aren't you?"

"It is already done. Monsieur Bouteiller will be elected. He will withdraw, citing age and business concerns. You will go in his place."

"Yes, but how will I make the substitute list if I am not running?"

"All of the candidates will cry out they wish you as their substitute. All of their votes will be a vote for you as well. It has already happened."

Xavier sipped from his glass.

Foutre-merde.

Wilmington
Reading
South
Readi
Bedford
Burlington
Concord
Woburn
Stoneham
Winchester
Melr
Lexington
Lincoln
MIDDLES
Medford
Mala
Cambridge
Waltham
Somerville
Che
Watertown
Cambridge
Char
Tow
Weston
Brighton
BOSTO
Newton
Brookline
Roxbury
Wellesley
NORFOLK
Needham
West Roxbury
Elm Bank
Dorchester
Dover
Dedham
Milton
0 4
Scale in Miles
Medfield
Canton
Qui

Chapter Thirty-One

1832

Jake

Jake was treated with respect and his needs were diligently met. The cabin was not as luxurious as the price suggested, but the food was above-average.

Once they were at sea, the Captain initiated conversation. Jake was not immediately aware of any motive behind this cordiality and reacted naturally. Looking back, Jake realized the Captain was testing him to determine whether his story was true. Perhaps if it was false, the Captain would have rolled Jake off the side of the ship. The Captain was popular with his sailors and might have gotten away with it. Jake was who he was, however, and had no reason to fear penetrating conversation.

The only lie he told was one he was not responsible for originating: he said he was from Wellesley, Massachusetts. In actuality, there was no such place. In fact, explaining the location of his home was hilariously complicated.

The Loring estate was called Elm Bank, on the south side of the Charles river and therefore Dover - technically. It was actually closer to the hamlet of West Needham on the north bank than to anything larger on the south. Some of the West Needham inhabitants had begun calling their hometown Wellesley because the West Needham Wellesleys were wealthy and well-known. By doing this, they elevated themselves to gentry, at least in their own minds. Because Elm Bank did more shopping in West Needham than Dover, they began calling themselves Wellesleyians as well.

Image and status were important in New England.

Jake only knew that when he addressed his letters home to Wellesley, they arrived. Wellesley was, however, West Needham, until West Needham seceded, and then the town could change its name to whatever it wanted – hopefully to Wellesley and hopefully including Elm Bank, but perhaps not, the Charles being an excellent natural border.

Jake discovered that the Captain's name was Mister Paul Banks, who in turn found his passenger's name to be Mister Jacob Loring, Jake to his friends. Captain Banks was not an ill-intentioned man, he was simply cautious, judging men by their actions and not their words. As he began to know Jake, he treated him according to his character. For his part, Jake found Captain Banks to be a fair, even-tempered man. They grew to like and respect each other.

It was really very cold.

The mercury fell near Maryland and continued to do so. Luckily, Jake was given additional clothing at no charge. By the time they sailed passed Philadelphia, which lay beyond the horizon and unseen to the west, there was ice and frost on all ship fixtures exposed to the elements come morning. By the time they reached Cape Cod, water froze into ice in the middle of the day. Jake had forgotten the serious nature of New England weather. Here there were two seasons: Winter and Summer. There was a Fall and Spring, but these were weak things, where days were usually chilly and grey and pointing toward Winter - or hanging on to Winter and refusing to acknowledge change. Perhaps two months out of the year there was an uneasy, equal truce between Winter and Summer, where the weather was undeniably pleasant. At all other times, it was either bone-chillingly cold or miserably hot and humid. When it was Winter, warmth was unimaginable. When Summer, a defeat of the buzzing, verdant, growing aliveness was equally unthinkable. It was a land of extremes, filled with people of extremes, who endured extreme hardship to survive. There were no Europeans in heart and soul here – no, sir. The ancestors of these good folk fought with tomahawks under the leaves of the dark forest, fought and died hacking and coughing their guts out under rough wool blankets in unending, bleak Januaries. In this hard-hearted group of Protestant Elect, there was something of a killer's instinct, a confident courage of optimism, a single-minded drive to self-sufficiency. It was sometimes well-hidden by manners and good will – and sometimes not. However good-natured and smiling the Americans happened to be, a good scratch and they bled a color savage and martial, ruthless and hungry. Americans were independent tigers who, in a heartbeat, could come together as linked army ants.

Jake's professors at Louis-le-Grand said the future very obviously belonged to the United States and to Russia, by fortunes of geography alone. Jake thought Russia had best practice their jab.

To Jake, this was a foreign land – as foreign as the highlands of Haiti. It was also, oddly, home.

As he stood on the bow, which was his wont, he heard a voice from behind him, "Where did your family bank again? Union Bank, was it?"

Jake slightly turned his head, "I didn't say. Bank of Massachusetts, Captain. And we are actually part owners."

Something shocking occurred to Jake.

There are two commercial banks in Boston. Combined, their total authorized capital would only just cover the full purchase price of the Cross of Nantes, which would be slightly over one million United States dollars.

The Captain shuffled his feet. "Bank of Mass - that's William Phillips bank."

"Yes, he was one of the founding partners. So was my grandfather, Elijah Loring. How on earth did you know that?"

The Captain chuckled, "And I thought being at sea kept me from the news. Have you even heard of the Bank War?"

"Bank War? No."

"The President, who is Andrew Jackson if you didn't know-"

"I do indeed, thank you very much!"

"-declared war on the national bank. Not only vetoed the charter, basically dumped the whole affair into the outhouse - destroyed it, as it were. All the banks' drawers and underwear were poured over the newspapers like paint on a harlot."

"Interesting."

"What did he do?" asked the Captain.

"Who?"

"Elijah Loring. What did he do besides invest in banks?"

"In terms of his occupation? To be honest, I don't know."

The Captain smiled. "He was a criminal."

Jake chuckled. "What makes you say that?"

"If he was anything but a criminal, you'd know sure as sunrise what that man-jack did, you'd know it forwards and backwards until you were sick of hearing about it."

"He was a good and honorable man. A religious man. A Puritan. He served in the war."

"Which war?"

"Which one?"

"Think there's only one, do you?"

"What are my choices?"

"Well, we fought twenty-four Indian tribes, seven German states and the British in '75, we tried to finish up the limey-loving Cherokee in'83 – didn't, Chickasaw and Choctaw in '85, Shay's Rebellion in '86, Whiskey Rebellion in '91, French in '98…"

The French?

"…Barbary Pirates in oh-one, Tecumseh's Shawnee and a passel of Seneca, Fox, Winnebago, Miami and God knows what else in '11, British and Tecumseh plus the Spanish, Choctaw, Cherokee and Creek again in '12. The Creeks for a damn third time in '13. Muslim Pirates again in '15. Seminoles in '17, Comanche in '20, Arikara in '23, Greek Pirates in '25, Winnebago in '27. Hell, right this minute we're fighting Sumatran Pirates, plus the Black Hawks and their damn British advisors. Take your pick."

"The United States fought a war against France?"

"Yep. They went after our merchantmen 'til we started fighting back."

Jake had no idea. He was a bit shocked. Why wouldn't he know this? "So many wars."

"Mostly injuns. Fighting the French made us enemies of all the tribes allied with France. Fighting the English left us with no red friends at all. The rest of the world tests us like the new boy on the farm, thinking we're weak. We're proving them wrong one damn pirate, one damn tribe at a time. Don't tread on us. They'll learn. We'll take 'em all, one by one."

"My grandfather fought in the War of Independence."

"Was he an officer or a soldier?"

"A soldier, I believe."

"If he was anybody of note, he would have been an officer. If he was a soldier, that meant he weren't nothing in '83. William Phillips put that bank together in '84. Hard to go from cannon-fodder to bank partner in a year. Lessen you're a criminal."

Jake didn't reply.

The Captain paused and shuffled his feet. "I guess he could have invested any old time after that. I don't mean nothing by nothing. I'm just shaking your chain. I'm sure he was a right old sort."

Captain Banks walked off, probably as a gesture of reconciliation – but he was actually correct in his estimations.

Something in Jake's family history didn't smell right, but Jake knew that already.

***

Boston harbor was large; the city of rolling hills barely covered the winding lengths of shores dotted with docks and wharves. The tides left silty mud and sand exposed to the air in many places. Boston, accustomed to stronger displays of Mother Nature, took this as a sign of weakness, deciding to claim all of that land as their own. A project was underway to turn tideland into land-land, and would take years. Even so, the tidelands were full of carts and people the moment the waters receded. Most of the ships in harbor were the smaller sloop and schooner merchantmen favored by the New Englander, although some behemoth brigantines fresh in from transoceanic ports were docked as well. The city was mostly brick and timber, farms out of place next to warehouses, trade and government buildings. It was a very American city: charming, small, bustling and Protestant. It had a few growth spurts over the years, marked by multiple buildings similar in architecture, but was now back to a fairly hard-working, but understated, existence.

The sleek *Allie Lucy*, flying her stars and bars, was towed to the Central Wharf and had her lines secured by mid-morning. Jake stayed in his cabin for several hours as the Captain took care of his business at customs. Jake was quizzed for some time by the Port Authority in regard to his lack of papers. He was only allowed to enter Boston under the care of Captain Banks. His father would have to send verification of his citizenship as soon as possible.

All is well at the bell.

Mid-afternoon, Captain Banks, Jake, and two burly sailors entered the city and walked to the magnificent Neoclassical building holding the Bank of Massachusetts at the corner of Hanover and Blackstone Street. The bank took a wedge of land smack in the center of the intersection, surrounded by wide avenues on three sides. The bank manager was Mister Bernstein, who had spectacles perched on the tip of his nose and long, thick whiskers running from his temples to his jaw. He was polite and businesslike and listened attentively to Jake and the Captain. He read the contract and assured them that he would immediately contact the Lorings in regard to their position. He had Jake write a short note describing his situation which would be given to his father, who would presumably know his own son's handwriting.

Jake spent the night onboard the *Allie Lucy*.

The next day, Mister Bernstein came to the wharf in a private black cab. He paid Captain Banks one-hundred and fifty dollars in United States paper money. Jake and the Captain said their farewells and then Jake boarded the cab and covered himself in blankets for the long, cold ride.

Mister Bernstein was excellent company. As the cab steered west, he seemed to know the perfect time for small talk and also when to let Jake look out upon the scenery. Outside the cab, all and sundry had a perfect patina of white snow, making the denuded branches far more winsome than they would have been otherwise. There were quaint little homes and snow-covered fields, surrounded by copses of bare hardwood stems covered in white. Small bridges stretched over every icy stream, and laughing skaters swirled over frozen ponds. Jake thought it was actually quite beautiful.

"This is now West Needham, Mister Loring. We are almost there."

It was a charming town. Everything appeared well-built and fairly new, simple but somehow not austere. New England was beginning to win him over. Perhaps it would have been different had Jake not been quite so snug under his blankets.

The cab turned sharply south. Mister Bernstein smiled, "This is Washington Street. I'm sure everything looks quite familiar now."

"No. I'm afraid nothing looks familiar."

"How old were you when you left?"

"I was ten, I believe."

"Well, that explains everything. The life of a ten-year-old is quite local, is it not?"

"In my memories I traveled over hell and half of Georgia."

"Most likely you never went more than a mile from your home."

"I suppose."

"On your right is Lake Waban."

The lake was triangular and the road paralleled one side of it. There were both fisherman and skaters sharing the ice. Did he go there as a child, before the dark times? He couldn't remember. He had forgotten, until that very moment, his itching desire to leave this place. When his mother died, everything changed. There was no more warmth in Wellesley, even in the height of verdant Summer. The Lorings were ghosts.

The lair of these ghosts was more than two-hundred acres of land in a lazy bend of the Charles River, which had created a patch of river-silt in the shape of a wolf howling at the moon - and contained some of the most fertile soil in Massachusetts. In addition to farmland, there were also stands of timber, gardens, animal pens and barns, stables and even some wild forest. The Loring home was built solid by Colonel John Jones of the Third Massachusetts Militia, who saw service in the French and Indian Wars but died before the Revolution. He married a Simpson, which was almost as good as marrying a Wellesley. He planted elms in a regular line on the curvy banks of his two-hundred acres, and very soon his estate became known as Elm Bank. After the Colonel's death, the Lorings were the first to purchase Elm Bank from the Simpsons. The Simpsons had too much land anyway. It was said the entire town of nearby Ashland was carved from only a small part of their holdings.

Just as dusk approached, Jake saw it. The Charles River appeared on his left, with Winter-bare, tall elms covered in snow on the far bank. A laugh escaped his lips. Just as quickly he felt his throat tighten with emotion.

Mister Bernstein smiled, "Ah, you are now home."

The cab pulled left onto Loring Street and clattered over the bridge. Now Jake recognized everything – but all was different, bigger, smaller, broken, fixed. The stout two-story residence was aglow with fires and candles. A young boy stood with a lantern on the porch, dressed in a bundle of warm clothes. As the cab approached, he began to jump from one leg to the other.

The cab stopped and the boy jumped right up onto it, "Are you my brother Jacob?"

"Why, I am indeed!"

"My name is Harris and I am eight years old and I am so excited to have a real big brother!"

It took everything Jake had not to tear.

1832

Nantes

Chapter Thirty-Two

March, 1789

Estelle

Estelle looked over the knives. No two were alike.

All were different for they were designed for different functions. Even so, all were either far too heavy and large, or too flimsy. The closest one to her purpose fit well in her hand and had a thin-but-sturdy blade that wasn't too long. There was, however, no guard to protect her hand from sliding over it.

"I need something different, Monsieur."

The smith was burly and pale. He wore little more than his trousers and a leather splash apron. His hair was cropped short but he had an abundance over his shoulders, chest and back. "Different can be anything, Mademoiselle. How different? What different?"

"I need a blade like this."

"A *couteau marin Breton*."

"Yes, but with a guard."

"A guard? Why do you need a guard?"

"I need the knife not only for cutting but for… punching through leather. I do not wish to cut my hand. But the guard must be flat with the blade."

"Do you need a fisherman's knife or a Parma stiletto?" said the smith with rough humor.

"Do you always quarrel with your customers?"

He threw up his hands, "I do not wish lying lovers stabbed with my knives, Mademoiselle!"

"I am not using it to stab a lover." Technically, she wasn't.

The smith shrugged, "Come back tomorrow. I will have your knife."

The next day, the knife, now hilted, looked quite deadly. One could as readily slit a throat as stab a heart with it. He gave it to her with a leather sheath sewn with a belt strap and a sharpening stone. Estelle paid for it, pocketed the knife, and returned to the convent.

She opened her chests, holding all of the elegant clothes that Jeannine had purchased for her.

All of the formal dresses hid voluminous thigh pockets, but a woman would have to excuse herself in order to access them. It would not do to carry any sort of bag or purse, such was not the fashion. Luckily, the dresses were so full-bodied, one's pockets could hold mason's tools and an observer would be hard pressed to notice. The knife and sheath fit handily in the pockets of all of her sartorial choices.

She would excuse herself, remove the knife from her thigh pocket, hide the blade, then cross to Jeannine and plunge it into her heart.

But how to hide the knife?

Estelle experimented. She walked with her hands clasped with the blade neatly tucked between her forearms. It was easy to grip the handle from the position of her hands. It worked.

A calm came upon her. The days passed easily. All of her problems, her anxiety, her wrath, shame, and pain would all disappear the very moment the blade disappeared into the heart of Jeannine Cœurfroid. There was a plan, and it quieted her soul. Estelle had felt tormented for so long that she had forgotten what it felt like not to feel constant pain. She marveled at the agony she had endured.

Her pacific interlude ended the very day of the *fiançailles*. Within minutes of wakefulness, her heart hammered in her chest. She felt sick, as if she would die. The morning dragged and dragged. She was ready hours before she had to begin walking – and this day she was taking a hired cabriolet. Mother Superior stopped by her room.

"It appears that you are going."

"I am."

"Is there anything you wish to say to me?"

"No, Mother."

Mother Superior nodded and left - and that was that.

In a daze, Estelle allowed Sister Marie and Sister Catherine to give her some last ministrations and drag her to the visitor buildings. She was vaguely aware of them talking, sometimes to her. She wasn't sure whether she answered. She was in a cab. The driver was middle-aged, *couleur*, probably a *Griffe*, well-dressed and polite.

The ride was cold. It began to rain and the driver stopped to put up the top.

They arrived.

Early.

Very, very early.

Estelle tried to open the door of the cab but did not succeed. The driver opened it for her and she walked quickly to the townhome entrance. At just that moment, Thomas swung open the doors and braced them.

Estelle suddenly felt a total loss of control. She turned and sprinted back to the cab. The driver's eyes widened as he ran back to quickly open the door for her. Estelle hid behind the canvass of the lowered top. The driver appeared on the bench. "Go! Go!" she hissed.

The driver complied and shook the reins. He traveled the length of Haute Grand Rue and headed south, turning sharply east on Rue du Château. He stopped after two blocks and turned to look at her. Estelle's whole body was shaking uncontrollably. The driver paled, "*Mon dieu*, you are in a state! What do I do now?"

"I'm fine, Monsieur. I assure you."

"You need a doctor."

"No, I will be fine. It is nerves, only nerves."

"Mademoiselle, are you quite sure? You look quite wretched."

"Yes, I am quite sure. Please, let me shake in peace. I am sure I will calm soon."

A half an hour later she handed the driver a coin but did not speak. He shook his head as if he wasn't going to take it, but finally did. Another half an hour passed and she slipped him another coin. He took it without speaking. The shakes became intermittent soon after.

A policeman rode up, "What is going on here?"

The driver threw up his hands and almost started to cry, "Monsieur, I do not know!"

Estelle did not want to talk to the policeman, she only wanted to calm herself. Her voice was plainly filled with irritation, "Officer, I have a terrible case of nerves stemming from an awkward social situation. The driver has been kind enough to wait until I calm. We are quite all right, I assure you."

The driver was beside himself. He shook his head at the officer, "Monsieur! Monsieur!" he said, over and over.

The policeman looked them over, "Take her to a doctor if she doesn't improve."

Estelle snapped back, "I have already improved, thank you very much."

The policeman gave her a penetrating look, then turned and rode off. Estelle found that the confrontation had somehow eased her trembling. "I think I am better, Monsieur. Thank you for your patience."

"If you had perished, I would have found myself taking you back to the sisters at Saint-Clément, and I would surely go straight to hell."

"I assure you it is no mortal sin to simply witness a natural passing, Monsieur," Estelle said between clenched teeth.

"You have given me quite a fright nonetheless."

"I assure you I was in greater discomfort, Monsieur!"

"Can you assure me? Have you experienced the passing-on of a fare in your cab, Mademoiselle?"

"Monsieur, I am fine as Spring flowers. Please take a moment and calm yourself, then take me back to my destination." She was an hour late. It might be a very noticeable entrance. "No – take me to the servant's entrance across from Saint-Vincent." It would be a far quieter entry.

"*Oui*, Mademoiselle," said the driver, comforted with the return to form.

Estelle suddenly angered, "Besides, you have been hired for the night, have you not?"

He said nothing.

"You have been compensated for your troubles. You drive for coin and more coin has been provided to ease the burden of unusual circumstances, is that not so?"

"Your pardon, Mademoiselle. I was simply flustered."

Suddenly the anger left. Estelle found herself back in her own mind and body, if only for a moment. She leaned forward and patted the driver on the back, "No, Monsieur. I beg your pardon. Forgive my sharp words."

He nodded. "*C'est la vie*, Mademoiselle. It is not an easy life."

"No indeed, Monsieur."

***

Her decision was brilliant.

The staff welcomed her with warmth and Christian spirit. All of them knew that Xavier courted Estelle but was now engaged to Jeannine. Jeannine was not unpopular with the staff, but was not loved as much as Estelle. They said nothing of the circumstance, nor did they comment on how hard it had to be for her to return. They only embraced her, called her "Angel!" or "Poor Child," and proclaimed how much they had missed her.

After Estelle made her rounds, she spoke, "If it isn't too much trouble, could I be led to my seat? I could not bear it if I had to blunder through so many strangers to my place."

Of course, of course! And off she was led by Darcy the maid. The townhome was full, every floor, every room it seemed, and even the very staircases. She did not recognize anyone and the looks and stares she received were frightful.

Darcy led her to a seat in the main dining room, now filled with tables, chairs and people. It was brilliantly lit and almost unrecognizable as the room where she had learned to dance. It seemed like a million years ago.

She was not seated three seconds when arms encircled her and Jeannine's wonderful scent filled her nostrils as she was embraced from behind. "Thank you. Thank you, dear sister," said Jeannine and suddenly the arms were gone, but the scent still lingered. Estelle could only think of one thing. She should have had the knife ready, then she could have turned and murdered her.

Estelle got up from her seat and moved to the hall. The Cœurfroid townhome had s-trap flushing toilets designed in Scotland. They were contained in separate rooms called *toilettes*. She entered the room and shut the door. She hiked up her skirt and quickly took the knife and its sheath from her thigh pocket. She was strangely calm as she slid the array into her sleeve. It would be an easy thing to take out the knife and quickly use it – Jeannine was as good as dead. She folded her arms in front of her, the bulge of the knife against her stomach.

She left the room and went back into the hall.

L'Oublié - Monsieur Souvenu - stood stock still in the center of it, as if he waited for her.

Estelle curtsied. He did not bow. She turned to move around him but he moved in front of her once again.

"Excuse me, Monsieur," she said politely.

"Estelle," he said.

She looked into his eyes. There was nothing there.

"You saw the best part of me, being who you are."

"Thank you, Monsieur."

"I suppose we are connected somehow, for I now see something inside of you. I suppose it would be more accurate to say, I see what is no longer inside of you. Your abyss calls out to mine."

Estelle said nothing. She found herself deeply afraid and ashamed.

"Do not become what I am," he said softly.

"I do not know what you mean, Monsieur."

"Listen to me carefully: Do not decide to be who I am. Do not become me."

"I am sure I have no idea what you are talking about."

Estelle suddenly felt the world spin. She had to take two steps in order to avoid lurching onto the inlaid wood floor. The knife skittered somewhere out of her eyesight.

L'Oublié had slapped her, so quickly and so hard that she did not see his hand move. Her cheek and jaw were flooded with pain. She had not been struck in the face since she was a child. Shocked, her eyes bubbled with tears.

L'Oublié looked as if he had not moved at all. "Do not become me, Estelle. You are unworthy of it."

Estelle stumbled forward and he turned and let her pass. She went directly to the servant's door and entered the service passage. Running, she blew past the startled valets and maids and descended to the ground floor. She avoided the kitchen and ran down the hall to the main service entrance.

She blew into the street. Everyone was staring at her and she did not know why. How could they know what just transpired?

Then she realized that she was sobbing.

By some miracle, her cabriolet was parked across the street. She could see the leather soles of the driver's shoes propped on the door as he presumably slept under a mountain of blankets in the cold back seat.

Estelle ran to the cab, unmindful of the carriage bells and shouts from coach drivers. She tried to open the door, sobbing and crying. Her driver's wide eyes appeared in the darkness, He opened the door for her and she lurched into the cab. He sprung from the other side and jumped on the bench. Estelle could not speak she was crying so hard. It consumed her, she could not think.

She felt the cab move. Nothing more.

The sisters took her from the cab to her bed.

They took off her dress and petticoats, and put her in her bedclothes.

She was tucked into bed.

When she was aware of it, she felt a hand gently stroking her hair throughout the night. She didn't know who it was.

In the morning, she felt rested and calm but otherwise the same. All of her things were put away.

Estelle felt frozen in time. She laid in bed for an hour, for days, for years.

Then, suddenly, Estelle understood the beautiful truth.

This was all a test, a wondrous and mysterious test from God – and she had passed. It was over now. Somehow the sisters had known what was in store for her.

Xavier was always meant to marry her.

She jumped out of bed with the thought. Any day now, Xavier would break off the engagement with Jeannine. He would kneel before her and beg forgiveness. He would explain how his actions had been wholly honorable and he was free to marry her. Oh, how she would do her very best to appear wroth at him! She could not make it easy!

Estelle spun about the room and laughed. Of course! Of course! How could she be so stupid? Who needs to ask? *I am Estelle Guerrier, the most foolish girl in the whole world – who somehow passed the ultimate test and is waiting for her love to return!*

Sister Catherine stopped in the doorway, "Estelle?"

Estelle took her by the hands and danced with her. "Sister Catherine, my love, my Xavier will soon be knocking on Sister Marie's door, holding flowers and gifts and begging for my hand."

Sister Catherine could not but smile at Estelle, who positively glowed when she was happy, but her eyes betrayed her, "But how can this be?"

"I know it! And I know all of you believe it as well. God is in his heaven!"

"He is indeed!"

"Everything will be fine, Sister! Don't you understand?"

"I know the plan of our Lord is mysterious and someday I will die."

"Mysterious and glorious, Sister Catherine! Mysterious and glorious!"

Sister Catherine tried to keep smiling but could not. She curtsied and quickly exited the room.

Estelle floated on air. She had kind words and a smile for all of the sisters. Her chores and prayers seemed to take no time at all, for she was locked in daydreams; her body moved in the real world alone.

Cordeliers, Paris

Chapter Thirty-Three

April, 1789

A Letter from Guillaume

Dear Freckle-Face,

My life is an open sewer of horror. I am miserable.

I am currently staying in an attic room accessed through a hidden staircase in the apartment of one Monsieur Moyen in the Cordeliers district, which is in-between the Germain and the Latin Quarter but isn't quite north enough to be Quatre-Nations. Oh, why do you care? You do not know Paris. It's named after a run-down refectory of the same name, the top stories of which I can see from my window. It once was a center of learning and had purpose, and now it has none, except to host events and meetings for guilds and such. I have been reassured that the Cordeliers is the most radical part of Paris and I am quite safe here. Well, at least the citizenry will not turn me in.

I am a local hero. I keep my door locked always, wishing to avoid trouble, and am awakened in the night by knocks and the trying of the latch. I suppose you didn't need to know that. In any case, I never open my door before breakfast.

First – poor Monsieur Théo. Actually, things are looking up for him. I have been reassured that his quarters are quite comfortable at the Conciergerie, although a bit pricey. Monsieur Théo would not care or be affected by the price, so I suppose it doesn't matter. But but but! Most importantly, his most serious charges, that of blasphemy, have been moved to the Catholic Courts! I have been told that the Catholic Courts are lenient in an attempt to change perceptions fostered by prior abuses. He will most likely be found innocent. If he had been charged with blasphemy in a normal court, he certainly would have been executed. Thank goodness torture has been abolished or his fate could be even worse. So, good news! All of his other charges only merit fines and prison time. Monsieur Théo lives to fight another day!

Talma has forever changed the way French theater operates, but they have punished him as much as they are able, he being who he is. Magnificent Talma has been relegated to minor parts in comedies, although he is still a Royal and is occasionally originating roles in new material. He throws himself into his work and his popularity soars. What a talented man he is! I don't know how he does it. He is worthy of Hamlet yet he must be satisfied with these small, ridiculous parts. I would be miserable. He is not only content but motivated. His ambition somehow does not vex him and is accompanied with seemingly infinite patience and an appreciation of the present. I wish I had his attitude but I do not. If I am not where I want to be, I am in tortured agony.

Talma is convinced that his salvation lies in société. Noble Parisians, the famous and respected, the rich, spend their days going from house to house to house all day and night. I know this sounds strange but it's true. So-and-So will have a dinner every Tuesday for glitterati who like to discuss brass buckles. Her-and-Her will have a late supper for people who like redheaded writers. Him-and-Her will have late drinks to celebrate science and progress. Boom, in the coach, stop by so-and-so's, no time, no time! Only sign the guest book – which is good enough – then off to this supper, then off to this parlor, then off to sign another guest book so you can make so-and-so's parlor debates, then off to late supper, then to drinks, whatever. If you can get into the right salons, you know everyone. If you are someone like Talma, with celebrity and social skills, I suppose with the right entrée you can easily rectify your situation. It hasn't happened yet. I suppose he needs to move his société to Versailles, but that is the only société that won't have him.

I would go insane with the schedule. I must, absolutely must, have time to myself to think and for reflection. Without it, I slowly fade into boredom, until finally I explode. Talma revels in people far more than I do, although he loves ideas as well.

David visits me only very occasionally and always wishes to know how you are doing, even though he knows you cannot write me. Honestly, I cannot stand to hear him talk. I have nightmares about him opening his mouth and that wretched, garbled beef Tartar spewing out of his mouth. It is like eating an entire meal, only after every dish has been cut up and mixed with every other. It is a disgusting mess and you spend your time trying to pick out an edible bite. But David is David. He is a good sort. He's frothing at the mouth due to his anger at the Academy, although I hate to use any kind of metaphor involving his mouth. They denied entrance to one of his proteges. I gather David teaches half of French paintery, if that is a word, and the fellow was one of his favorite students. He is convinced that revolution cannot happen fast enough to right the wrongs of the artistic establishment. His revolution involves only the ascendance of those he believes are talented. His revolution increases his standing and control of the artistic community. Strange, odd, whatever.

I suppose revolution means something different to everyone, which is thought-provoking. When and if it happens, whose revolution will it be? I suppose that is a good problem to have. I'm not quite sure what my revolution looks like. Perhaps, after the revolution, my soul will find quietude. I don't know why I believe a revolution could achieve such an aim, but when I truly analyze my motivations, I find no other drive. Maybe we are all equally foolish. I hope we all find our happiness in the ashes after we light everything on fire. I can hear your voice in my head admonishing me for such thoughts. Sometimes I wish I could be like you.

Danton does not visit, he is not the sort, unless he is dragged by Desmoulins. Danton has tremendous drive and energy and is frustrated by his lack of ability to do anything. He is trying to organize the community, which is easier than you might think. Parisians love to go to meetings, to shout and scream, vent their anger like human steam engines, churning pistons that generate energy for no task or movement. Even Monsieur Moyen, who repairs books, attends the Bookbinders Guild meetings religiously, where the politics and issues are life and death matters... where Madame's interest in what people are wearing or buying for their houses are life and death matters...

Desmoulins, I like. We are similar in some ways. He is the butt of jokes, because he is so miserably unsuccessful. I suppose people like to have that sort of person around - an even less successful someone sitting next to you. You are better than him at least, despite the best efforts of an oppressive world to grind us all into equal gravel. A few quick jabs in Desmoulins's direction and one feels better being small. It is supremely easy to get a rise from him, and the effect makes one feel marvelous. Not to discredit him, though. He is indeed whip-smart, with tremendous political acumen. He pines for a young lady whose father thinks him vermin. So hysterically funny, in a way. It is so very Desmoulins, this situation.

I have met another man named Jean-Paul Marat, who swims in my circles here in the Cordeliers. He visits me in my little prison quite often and most days beats me handily in chess. He is a doctor and a scientist, although retired from both pursuits to pursue politics. I suppose that makes him a journalist. I have read his writings and cannot square the style of his quill with the man I have met. Marat is intelligent, well-spoken, empathetic, and perhaps also a die-hard narcissist desperately wishing to be famous and admired. His writing style is very belligerent, to the point of being in the genre of violent literature. It is pornography for people who wish to fuel their anger through politics. If you don't disagree with him or profess to be an expert on anything he wishes to be the sole expert upon, he is good and engaging company. He really hates Talma, which vexes me because I admire the man so much. There are rumors that Marat was embarrassed and discredited in some scientific endeavor and his anger should be excused, for the incident wounded him deeply. Whatever. Talma is an artistic titan, a promethean bringing fire to man. Everyone in our circle should know this and admire him.

Which brings me to Marie-Joseph Chénier, whom I despise. He is a fellow playwright and I suspect everyone thinks he is a better writer than I am. He has had two plays performed at the Comédie-Française - and both of them sunk like lead anchors. I have had a successful, serious, political smash hit of a theater play that was literally shut down by the police on orders of the Court. Is this opinion of him a product of the weight of importance placed on employees of the Royal theaters? Why should that matter, especially in this day and age? Do revolutionaries scramble for the favor of the Court? Also, he is handsome but not as good-looking as me, but, somehow, I get the impression that he believes that fact makes him more serious, especially as a writer. He served in the dragoons and that has given him physical self-confidence. It is different than what I have, which is just foolhardy anger, and his confidence generates more respect. He also has that odd lack of madness that he shares with Talma. He is very sane, which I find extraordinarily maddening. I think that people sense this about him and they value and trust him more because of it. I wish he would step out of line with me and I could call him out and run him through and watch him bleed out and die with a choking red foam coming from his mouth - but he is too smart for that. The man might have a tremendous ego but he has no temper and never quite says anything disrespectful, although he is smart enough to walk the line between civility and contempt with ease. Mon dieu, I hate him. I wish him dead, I wish him to die of gangrene, in unimaginable agony, from a sword thrust through his intestines as his half-digested food is allowed to run through his bloodstream.

Ha-ha! I know what you are saying to yourself right now!

Something just occurred to me this very instant. If he was in the Dragoons, he is the recipient of extensive sword and pistol training. I have had none. Perhaps I should be more circumspect in my desire for a duel. No, that is cowardly. If it comes down to it, I will take my chances.

In any case, I must relax my attitudes, especially in front of Talma. If he knew what a loose shipboard cannon I am in some respects, he would never speak to me again. I would like to attend some of his salons as well, just so I know who to hate. He will never take me if he thinks I would embarrass him. So far, he holds me in high esteem. I must keep it that way. Perhaps I will not come up with a pretext for killing his friend Chénier, but, if I compromise in this, I do the world no favors. Sometimes we must be selfish.

So, I am trapped. I'm not writing. I am stuck in this little secret place, advised not to look out the window in case the Guard passes. I feel like I am shoveling again but do not have the fire in my soul to see me through. I get drunk a lot. I can drink a prodigious amount of wine before I sprawl comatose. I have been chided by Monsieur Moyen for my habits.

I have decided in this very moment that enough is enough. I am leaving. I will leave and not come back, for a return here would endanger Monsieur Moyen. I swear, dear sister, I have slept in pigsties and in ditches on the sides of roads. I have no fear of not having a bed. It is finally getting a bit warmer. I will live on the streets, between the Cordelier and the Temple, and no one will betray me. I am a free bird, my sister. Beau-Brave was not meant for self-imposed prison, except when he writes.

Lo! I refer to myself in the third person! Am I then the Gutter King? Ha-ha! I will add that to my titles.

I resolve to leave this place this very hour. I am sorry you cannot write me back, I always love to hear from you and I think of you often, dearest sister.

I dearly love you, and rarely tell anyone how ugly you are. I always lie about how you dress - for your own good.

Your Devoted Brother,

Guillaume

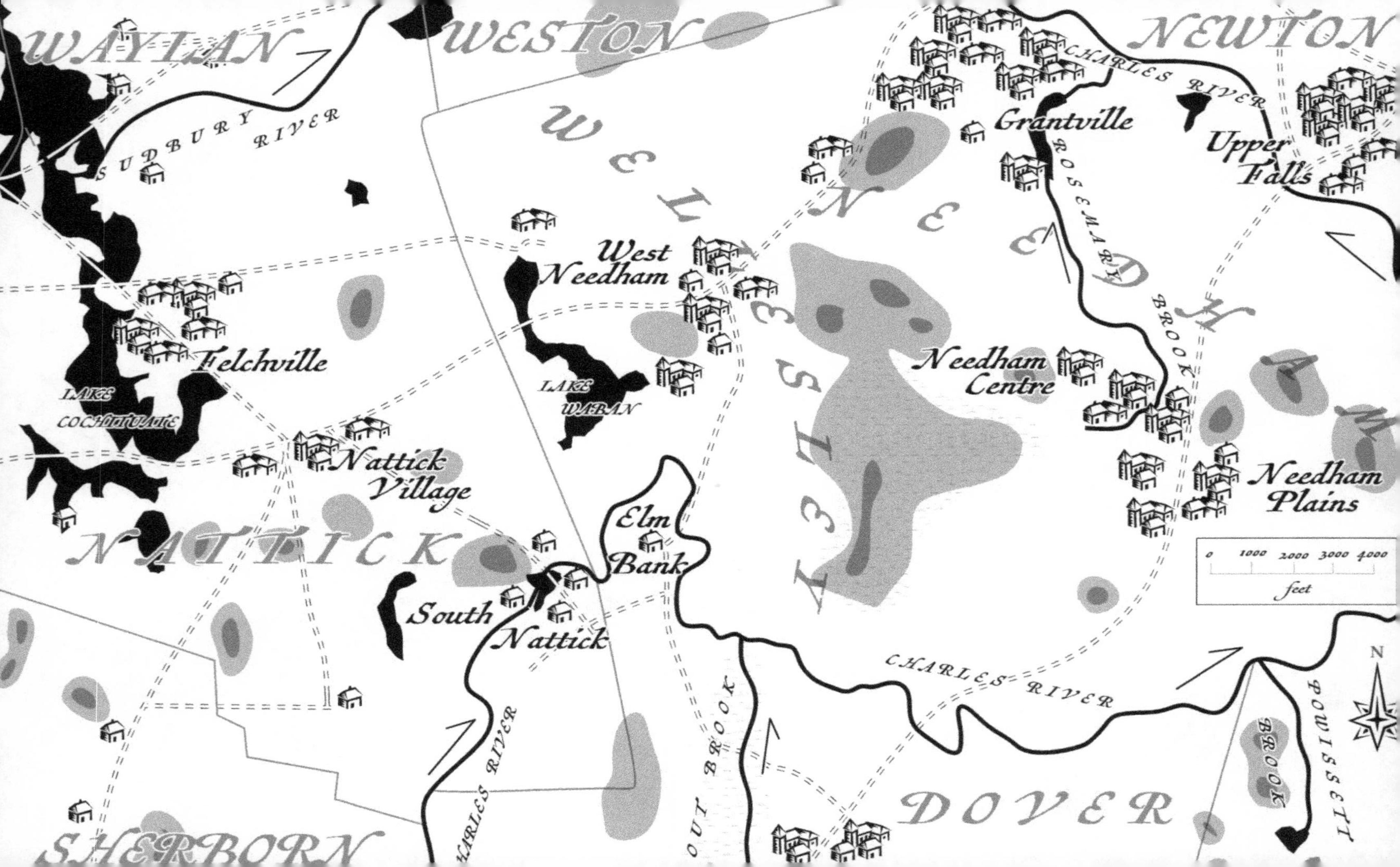

WAYLAN
WESTON
NEWTON
SUDBURY RIVER
CHARLES RIVER
Grantville
Upper Falls
WELLESLEY
NEEDHAM
ROSEMARY BROOK
West Needham
Felchville
LAKE WABAN
LAKE COCHITUATE
Needham Centre
Nattick Village
Needham Plains
NATTICK
Elm Bank
South Nattick
0 1000 2000 3000 4000
feet
N
CHARLES RIVER
POWISSETT BROOK
OUT BROOK
DOVER
SHERBORN

Chapter Thirty-Four

1832

Jake

It was a whirlwind.

The Loring home was ablaze with a million and one candles, each reflected by a thousand mirrors. It was filled chockablock with family and well-wishers. Easton Loring, Jake's father, was positively aglow. Jake could not place this new man in any of his memories. Along with Harris, Jake found he had five other siblings: Joan, Sterling, Cuthbert, Will and Erica, all of whom were under the age of seven. Little Joan waddled around the house yelling, "*Yayka Yayka Yayka!*" which presumably meant Jacob.

Jake's new stepmother was Sophia. Attractive, tall and thin, roughly ten years older than Jake, she was cream pale with straight dark-brown hair and matching eyes that danced with intelligence, wit, and spirit. He liked her immediately, and she was thankfully old enough to dispel any awkwardness between them.

And then there were the extended family and well-wishers. He had two uncles and five aunts and innumerable cousins. He was introduced to friends and acquaintances from childhood - and could not recognize a soul.

Neither could he recognize one young woman who sat straight in a chair reading a book by the fire. He was immediately drawn to her. Her hair was a dishwater somewhere between blonde and brunette. She was so pale that one could not tell she was covered in freckles until right upon her, for every one of them was yellow or cream rather than brown. She had a lively and engaging face, made more so by her grey eyes and small, arching eyebrows. She was short and extremely thin, with almost a boyish build. She interacted warmly with the children and adults who found their way to her, she being always present and smiling, but was then equally focused on her book when they departed.

Once, their eyes met.

She smiled and gave him a knowing look, as if they shared a joke the world could never understand. He smiled back, and had a hard time focusing on anyone else for the rest of the night. He tried his best, wanting to make a good impression on these good people. In any case, it was more or less impossible to speak with her, as he regaled the crowd with vastly-truncated stories of his travels, usually with Harris on his shoulders asking when they could go ice fishing together. All he was able to discover was what she was reading - *Modern Chivalry: Containing the Adventures of Captain John Farrago and Teague O'Regan, his Servant* by Hugh Henry Brackenridge; Jake had neither heard of work nor author – and her name, which was Grace Elizabeth Otis. Unlike the author, he vaguely remembered her from school. She was quiet and attentive, and sat behind him and to the right. He remembered her getting in trouble but causing none, which made no sense at all.

Drink flowed, food was in abundance. Roast turkey in butter, venison pies, porter and cider, squash in molasses and butter, vegetables in cream, cheesecake, cornbread, spinach pottage, and sausages, roasts, and pies of every meat imaginable – bear, racoon, capon, squirrel, and pigeon. Oddly, there was no music. In France, there would have been a quartet at least.

Even more people came, if only to stay for a few hours. It was a proper welcome; Jake felt honored by his family and town.

Why did I leave this place?

He left primarily because of his father's mournful state, his own feelings regarding his mother's death, and to escape the small town that his father had never left. Jake had been years in Paris, across France, a guest in grand châteaux, to Ireland, to Haiti, across oceans, rivers and time. Coming home, he realized that this place wasn't so odious. In fact, it was quite charming - all of it. The people were friendly, his family warm and welcoming. There was little provinciality about them, apart from their lack of guile and sarcasm. They appeared fairly well-educated and even decently well-read, especially when it came to theology. They were all good Reformed Protestants, like his grandfather Elijah, and teased his father Easton mercilessly but good-naturedly regarding his Catholic faith.

Interestingly, the nearest Catholic church – the only Catholic church in the whole region, really - was the Cathedral of the Holy Cross in the Boston neighborhood of South End, nearly ten miles away. A priest or deacon would take the long ride out to Wellesley at least once a week to deliver the host, give absolution and pray with Easton. Most of the ribbing derived from the imagined generosity that Easton would have had to display toward the church to receive such generous treatment. Easton countered that it had always been thus, even when he was a child.

The whole experience, quite simply, was how home feels, when home felt good. Jake felt this way as a child, but not for a long time before he left. But in the back of Jake's mind was a faint, distant feeling of impending doom, as if this could not be true, could not last. He determined to let the warmth of the gathering dispel such a feeling.

Late in the evening the guests began to leave, heaped with leftovers, blankets and generous mugs of hot buttered rum. Jake finally met young Grace as she made the rounds to leave. She held out her hand and he shook it and bowed, for he was not in Paris or Boston, but deep in Massachusetts. "Mister Loring," she said, "I'm sorry we have not spoken until now."

"You were quite involved with your book."

She turned pink. "I wanted to welcome you home but, as an acquaintance, I didn't want to distract you away from your family."

"You would not have, I assure you."

She narrowed her eyes. Jake groaned inwardly. *What did that mean?* He tried to recover. "I hope I have the opportunity of getting to know you better."

"Oh yes, of course." She smiled.

"What would be a good time for me to call?"

"To call?" She looked a bit shocked.

"Tomorrow perhaps?"

"I suppose tomorrow would be fine. At the schoolhouse at four then," she said, almost resentfully, although that made no sense at all.

"Very well." Jake smiled.

"Good night." She smiled again as she left, and all was right in the world, at least for a little while.

Soon the other guests left. Sophia put the children to bed and did not return. Servants had been cleaning and serving all night, and now they cleaned what was left. Jake found himself alone with his father Easton in the expansive main parlor just off the mudroom and entry. Both sat on Chippendale easy chairs. The chair was only just comfortable, as if a cautious Yankee had measured the padding to make sure it was no more and no less than was necessary.

Jake broke the comfortable silence first. "How did Grandfather Elijah make his fortune, father?"

"Shipping and finance. He was a self-made man."

"He found his fortunes after the war?"

"Yes." His father said nothing for a moment. "I am sorry, Jake."

"Why?"

"I know how things must have been for you. Before you left."

Jake looked down and did not speak.

"To a child, a month is forever, a year a lifetime. As an adult, the years begin to fly." There was a moment when only the pops and cracks of the fire were heard. "I was inconsolable for two years before you left. It must have been a dark and lonely time for you, losing your mother and then, after a fashion, losing your father as well."

Jake nodded. "I have only just begun to confront my memories of her. I think her passing affected me in greater fashion than I was willing to accept."

"Of course, it did. And there was nowhere for you to turn. No one to speak to regarding your troubles, no consoling words. And because of our odd circumstance, no community or solace of the church either."

Jake nodded.

"As you can see, now this home glows with love and family."

"It does indeed."

"You lost yourself in Paris. You had an adventure. I am only happy that you are here."

"You will have to help me become a good United States American again."

"America..." he began, then changed tack, "We call the United States of America simply *America*. Does that confuse you?"

"No, it's quite acceptable."

"Then I continue: things have changed in America."

"In what way?"

"We elected our first president who is neither from Virginia nor Massachusetts, and I am not sure that it is a good thing. The world seems full of enemies, our savage neighbors on land, distant predators at sea. There has been a nationwide revival of faith and spirituality, quite a strong one at that. It is as if the Enlightenment never happened. Rousseau and Montesquieu have been quite forgotten. Instead, we fiercely define ourselves as something altogether new and unique: who we are, what we believe, and we reject what has originated elsewhere. Perhaps these trends were observed before you left, but they have accelerated, and continue to do so. To me, this is wonderful. I am a man of faith and a proud American, but I'm afraid this will be quite onerous to you."

"Revival to what faith? Reformed Protestantism?"

Easton gave a wry look. "Well, as the good Danish prince would say, *there's the rub*. It is all certainly Christian, or at least quasi-Christian, and all established denominations have benefitted. A century ago, before the Great Awakening gave way to the Enlightenment, we were a very religious people, a quilt of faiths and beliefs. I suppose we are returning to that age, a Second Great Awakening, if you will. In my mind these awakenings are times of strongly-observed spiritual anarchy, the worst-case scenarios of Martin Luther's rebellion gone awry. There are some truly bizarre beliefs surfacing in some places, I will tell you. There is a church in New York that believes their founder was led by angels to a buried book of gold with God's new revelations engraved upon its pages, and some of these revelations are strange indeed. Catholicism has its flaws, as I'm sure you would point out to me, but we've managed to maintain a semblance of ideological purity when all else has splintered, I will say that."

Jake found it odd that his father believed he would criticize him - then he remembered that, not so long ago, he was once an opinionated firebrand. It seemed like centuries in the past. He had seen too much cruelty, and even death, since then. Men who held hatred in hearts and muskets in hands were dangerous.

How Jake could have criticized those who pursued a spiritual path was now a mystery to him.

"I am no longer such a foe of religion," Jake admitted.

"I am shocked. Your letters were full of vitriol."

Jake was pensive. "Yes. I suppose because I found another type of religion, in the guise of a cause, and it was a jealous faith. It seemed to ease my burdens of soul and provide me with purpose and self-righteousness. But it was a false cause, a bloody and murderous one, and, even had its goals been achieved, it would have given me nothing. I'm afraid by my indirect action, my best friend, who was the most honorable of men, was killed in battle. My only saving grace is that I did not kill anyone directly, though this was not for lack of trying, I assure you."

"I am shocked again. Where did these battles take place?"

"In Paris. It does not surprise me that you have not heard of these troubles. They were minor things to anyone but the participants. Our rebellious efforts were easily quashed. So easily, in fact, that I wonder if such deadly intent was justified at all. We purchased nothing at a precious cost, very precious indeed. Blood is more valuable than gold - a truth I found hard to believe until I saw it spilled on the ground."

"I am so sorry, Jake."

Jake half-expected a lecture, or berating discourse – disappointment – but not empathy. "I suppose my point is that I have learned to value people who do not shoot at each other to achieve some end, and help me if I need help, as a natural action, expecting nothing in return."

"Those are certainly Christian values." Easton nodded and smiled. They had another moment of silence. "Are you in great trouble, son?"

"I don't think so. Not now, not here, anyway. I was."

"If you wish to talk, I would be honored to listen."

"I would like to tell you everything."

"Then do so, as it suits you."

And Jake did. He told him every gory detail regarding Monsieur Bouche, the June Rebellion, the imprisonment, of his lawyer Isaäc Crémieux, the story of his own little pewter cross coming up at trial, Monsieur Tyran and the mad quest for the Heirlooms, the masked leadership of *The Society*, Nantes, the Meilleur, Ireland, Haiti, and home.

His father listened attentively.

Jake finished.

His father kept the same posture for a moment, then began to breath raggedly. His eyes opened wide and he grabbed the arms of his chair with a fierce grip. Jake thought he was going to die on the spot. "Father! Dear Lord, what have I done?"

"Nothing. I am well. I am truly fine. Give me a moment."

"How long have you had these problems?"

"This has never happened to me before."

"I have caused you great distress."

"You have caused me nothing but great joy. It is my own memories that haunt me."

Jake narrowed his eyes. What in Jake's story could have jogged the memories of someone who had never left his place of birth? "What memories?"

Easton calmed. "Things of which I am not allowed to speak."

Neither did this make sense.

Jake realized his father spoke of secrets, the presence of which he would have never revealed had he not been in such straits.

Something hidden had been inadvertently exposed.

Jake sat back in his chair. "I fear many secrets have been kept from me, Father. It would distress me greatly if some of them were hidden by you."

"Rest assured, my son, that if I kept anything from you, it would only be out of love."

Jake nodded, and understood. He realized the mystery of the Heirlooms was partly born in Wellesley, Massachusetts – but he had no idea how that could possibly be. "I thought I would be safe here. That is why I came home."

"You are safe, son, most assuredly. And you are most welcome."

Jake sat back in his chair. "Father?"

"Yes, son."

"Is there nothing you would like to tell me?"

"In regard to your current circumstance? Perhaps. But I am patient. I will tell you when you are ready to hear."

Fair enough. It is enough that you love me and are my father.

"Then there is only one more thing of import to discuss."

"Please."

"Should I now try to find these Heirlooms for my own sake, or should I forget this quest and go about my life?"

"There is no need for a hasty decision. We will talk in regard to this again. In fact, as many times as we need to. If we decide to chase after these ghosts, I will help you."

Jake nodded. This time, it was he who let the silence play. "It is good to be home," he finally said.

His father smiled and patted his hand, and both were content, secrets or no.

Laveuses et un pêcheur de Paris

Chapter Thirty-Five

The First Day

April 25th, 1789

Réveillon

Like Claude Perier of Vizille, Jean-Baptiste Réveillon was a symbol of modern France in that he was a self-made businessman – a success story told more and more often by 1789.

Beau-Brave, on the other hand, was a symbol of an emerging France not yet born, in ways unforeseen by the present.

These symbols were to meet on the twenty-eighth of April, and the outcome would not be beneficial to either man, which was perhaps the most important lesson of all – a lesson, of course, misunderstood, and therefore heeded by none.

A common Parisian, Réveillon started with no advantages. He was an apprentice in a guild, first as a tradesman, then haberdasher and, finally and most importantly, a stationer. In the tightly guild-controlled paper business he caught whiff of an emerging trend: wallpaper. Wallpaper was a cheap, economical way for the emerging middle class to decorate their homes. He hung the textured, British flock-style in dozens of houses, realizing that he had stumbled into a goldmine.

After marrying a woman with a considerable dowry, he changed tack and started his own business - free of guild and Royal control. In the right place and at the right time, he was smart enough to take advantage of it. He began making his own paper, controlling every step of the entire manufacturing process. He was also a scientist, inventing an entirely new way to produce vellum.

He was already wealthy when the nobility began to patronize his business. Soon after, the Queen herself employed Réveillon and he could finally style himself *Manufacture Royale*. By 1789, he owned a papermill, a luxury boutique near the Tuileries, and, most importantly, a storied hôtel in Faubourg Saint-Antoine named La Folie Titon. The former residence of famous writers and scheming financiers, it was complete with extensive gardens and its own theater. The entire first floor was devoted to his business. He lived with his family on the upper floors with plenty of room to spare. It was filled with masterpieces of furniture from previous rich and famous owners, stocked with libraries of books, and the entire basement was a devoted wine cellar, reported to be the largest and most extensive in the world. It might not have been, at nearly three-thousand bottles, but perception trumps reality. Rumors like this always swirled around the house; it was unavoidable, being on the intersection of Rue de Montreuil and Rue de Faubourg Saint-Antoine. To enter central Paris, everyone in the neighborhood had to pass the mansion and its extensive grounds.

Réveillon had begun his career by installing British wallpaper, then he made his own, then - achieving the ultimate victory for a French businessman - exported his wares to England, selling to Britain what they had introduced to France. He employed over four-hundred people and paid them well. The average salary of his workers was fifty-sous per day – and none made less than thirty-five. He even paid them when Winter made work impossible, and made allowances for sickness and emergencies.

It was unheard of.

On the forefront of science, Réveillon associated with others in this rarified air, including Montgolfier, the inventor. The first man-made object to ride the air, a hydrogen balloon, was launched from his own gardens at La Folie Titon. The second balloon, launched from Versailles, was named after him: *Le Réveillon*. The first two human beings to fly through the air were Réveillon's employees.

Réveillon made life better for hundreds of people - if not ultimately thousands - and his advancements and inventions elevated mankind. He was simply that sort of man.

Réveillon was a Republican and a forward thinker, especially in terms of economics, a subject in which he was a world-class expert. He believed that economic freedom would create a better world for all – but his was no whimsical, utopian set of dogmatic axioms. He did not believe or have faith, rather he identified what was put into practice and actually worked – in the Netherlands, Great Britain and the new United States of America, not to mention his own business.

Knowing this, it would surprise no one that Réveillon wished to be a delegate for the Third Estate in the elections of the Estates-General and, on April twenty-fifth, sat in a pew of the chapel of the abbey of the Cistercian nuns of Saint-Antoine des Champs, who had graciously allowed the Third Estate to use the space for their debates and elections.

The sixty voting districts for the Parisian Third Estate had, more or less immediately, formed a parallel city government, completely independent of the

King, nobility and church. In other words, the commoners of the city now had power, representation and organization. More importantly, they had an alternative to the current system and a different perspective to judge it. This should have scared the Throne witless, for it boded ill if the rest of the country followed suit, but the Throne remained placidly indifferent - if not thinking they authored and benefitted from the change.

Réveillon was called to speak.

He stood, crossed to the stairs, ascended, and placed his notes on the lectern. He allowed himself a heartbeat of silence, scanned the packed crowd, then began in a clear, steady voice. "Fellow citizens of Saint-Antoine, you know who I am. You know what I have done, what I have achieved in my life. I think I employ half of the people here, and my good friend and, now, competitor, Monsieur Henriot, employs the other half."

Henriot smiled from his seat, half-stood, and waved at the crowd. Henriot's business was saltpeter. They were friends, they had similar ideas. They would probably both go to Versailles.

Réveillon continued, "It is very simple. Government is like a strong spice - a little goes a very long way, and too much ruins the dish. We need a minimum of government to flavor our national palette. In fact, government should only be empowered when an absolute necessity is found for its intervention. This idea sounds foreign and strange, *mes amis*, but our success, at every level, will be a product of similar counter-intuitive thinking. What do I mean by such a thing? I will explain. The King, in his benevolent wisdom, has decided that in order to help his subjects, it is best to tightly and rigidly control every aspect of French culture and business. He ensures the price of bread does not go up. He ensures that wages do not go down. He makes sure that every subject has employment and a place in society, or attempts to do so. When nature and God have their way and we are tried through poor harvests and such, it is the King who provides flour and succor to the poor. Some call this tyranny, and perhaps that is how it started, but out of respect for our benevolent, forward-thinking King, I do not. I think rather that we are hung by the rope of good intentions. Our way of life is dominated by strong, central leadership, a Father-King who provides for his people and protects them from all enemies. This sounds intuitively correct. It rings true, as if this is how things should be, as long as our King shares our belief in the responsibilities of his station, as our good King does. But if this is so, why then are we in the straights we find ourselves?" Réveillon paused and looked around. He was a good speaker, the audience was rapt.

"There is only one conclusion to be drawn – our present way does not work. If we cast our eyes to other lands and other places, we find systems that do work. America, the very daughter of France, the product of the will of our King and Nation, can only be described as an economic miracle… although I would not drink their wine, if they even grow the vine at all, nor would I readily partake of any of their savage creations of art, decoration or function." Réveillon smiled, waiting for the laughter to subside. "That being said, our best suits are made from

American wool from Vermont. Our best quality wheat comes from the ports of New York and Philadelphia, the best ships from Boston, and so on. Neither can we doubt or question the industry of Great Britain, for it has overtaken our own. Considering that the French subject is not locked within the class system, and is more numerous than that of Britain, we must wonder how this happened at all." Réveillon allowed himself a dramatic pause. "I wonder no more, *mes amis*, for I know. It is our system, our system of absolute monarchy and strong centralized control that has handicapped natural human dynamism and stifled our ability to advance in science, industry and business. We can do better."

A shout, "How?"

"Very simply," Réveillon replied, "By deregulation."

Another voice, more frantic, "Of bread?"

A well-dressed man stood and held his hat, as all lesser men did before their betters. "Monsieur, respectfully, they have already tried to deregulate bread and... and... the price went into the sky like a Chinese rocket."

Rumbles from the crowd. "And then exploded," said another, wryly.

"Yes, that is true. Bread was deregulated and the price skyrocketed. But if the King had not caved on the issue, and allowed deregulation to continue, the country would have been flooded with grain from Pennsylvania to Poland and the price would have eventually gone down and stayed down, and we would never have to worry about our people starving ever again. Listen, *mon amis*, I will illustrate how this works. No one like me, no one of industry and acumen, would ever come near the endeavor of supplying bread to Paris. Why? Because it is so tightly controlled. Even with a mountain of work, an honest man gains very little. Regulation ensures bread prices remain constant, even when the harvest is poor. It also ensures that when the harvest is poor that we will have no bread – for there is no reason for anyone to sell it to us. I ask you this: how important is the price of bread when there isn't any?"

He had them.

"The cornerstone of the French economy is still bread, like it or not. Therefore, the trade bears study. I believe that if you completely deregulated the entire industry, the price would momentarily rise – yes. Thereafter, it would go up and down – yes. But there would *always* be bread. No one would ever starve. People like myself would then be in the industry, making money by ensuring there was enough product in the country, because if there wasn't, we would be missing out on profits. You would always have bread, under every circumstance. The price would be higher during bad harvests - but you wouldn't be burying your children. Since bread is the foundation of our national economy, its distribution should be deregulated, permitting lower prices. That in turn would allow lower wage costs, lower manufacturing prices and brisk consumption. I have written an essay on the subject. It is available for free at the door. Please read it. Forward-thinking is what our nation needs, and, I assure you, I am entirely invested in progress. Man took to the sky for the first time in my very garden. Send me to Versailles and I will send the nation skyward as well."

A thunderous, standing ovation.

"Thank you," said Réveillon with a studied humility. He descended the stairs and sat. The applause continued.

Now there was only one problem.

Henriot.

The moderator took the lectern. "Monsieur Henriot, you have five minutes, starting at your first word, please."

Henriot waited until the moderator left the stairs, then bounded quickly to the lectern. It was a nice touch. He began to speak.

Réveillon hung on Henriot's every word. Halfway through, he realized he needn't bother. Henriot's speech was a rehash of everything he had just said, simply spoken with less eloquence, less finesse, if only slightly more energy.

Réveillon smiled.

It was done.

Barring unforeseen circumstances, this was the beginning of a new chapter for Réveillon and perhaps for France.

He was indeed right – but there was an old proverb that needed heeding:

Be careful what you wish for.

Palais des Tuileries

le dix-septième siècle

Chapter Thirty-Six

The Third Day

April 27th, 1789

Beau-Brave

It had not been a good year for faubourg Saint-Marcel.

It was poor, urban, working class – a hotbed of radical politics. It was an industrial neighborhood, filled with tanneries, breweries and chemical factories. The smells of the faubourg were varied indeed, depending on the whims of the Anemoi. The wind gods, however, had been asleep all Winter. The Bièvre river had frozen, like most rivers nationwide. The majority of industries in Saint-Marcel depended on it, that was why they were there; all had shut down. Most of its industrialist owners were nowhere near as generous as Monsieur Réveillon and the neighborhood had starved for lack of work.

Regardless, Saint-Marcel found itself charitably inclined toward the outlaw hero Beau-Brave. He was staying in an extra room in a flat off Rue Poliveau, the rented quarters of the Trumeau family, who were desperately poor and politically reliable – at least according to Desmoulin, who avidly vouched for them. They appreciated the rent and were proud to have him. Beau-Brave no longer relied on secrecy, only the politics of the community where he resided, and he never stayed in one place for long. Once rumors of his presence leaked outside of his street, he was no longer safe.

It all had to do with what Beau-Brave had learned about the little Paris neighborhoods and how they worked. He had been largely ignorant until very recently, which was telling considering how long he had lived in Paris.

The neighborhoods were little villages in and of themselves; some had even been separate villages until the city crept up on them. Relatives and kin lived in proximity, but also a good number of people from outlying areas. Gossip was rife in the thin-walled, crowded, extroverted streets. People looked out for each other and for the children. Credit was freely given to neighbors. None passed another who did not stop for talk and news. The police had an extraordinarily difficult time arresting anyone unless his neighbors agreed with the charges. They were their own best friends, defenses, enemies and burdens. They were a chaotic tribe, for better or worse.

Beau-Brave was discerning regarding his quarters, but not in any way that made sense in regard to secrecy or comfort. He always brought a wooden wedge everywhere he stayed, hammering the wood under the door with a rock. His benefactors would cluck, thinking this had something to do with paranoia regarding a nightly visit from the Guard, but their thoughts were incorrect: his motivation regarded nightly visitors of an entirely different sort.

In spite of Beau-Brave's efforts, once, while staying in Quinze-Vingts, his door gave way with a tremendous sound. He jumped out of bed and was soon met by the entire family, who were startled awake as well. Madame felt the need to explain, over-explain, for the next hour or so, how she was so frightened that she managed to be up and out of eyesight of her husband at the hearing of the sound.

Evidently, she was very quick.

Beau-Brave thought his quarters in the Marcel were quite safe. Although his benefactors were Neolithic, they were regarded as universally honorable and were very active in Socialist circles. He was therefore surprised to find himself woken at eleven in the morning by a pounding on the door. "Yes?"

The voice of Marie-Jeanne Trumeau, the forty-year-old pregnant wife of his benefactor, a day laborer, squeaked back at him, "Beau-Brave, you must rouse yourself at once."

"I am roused. What goes, Madame?"

"Please! Please, Monsieur! It is… it is quite an emergency."

Beau-Brave attempted to move the wedge from under the portal but had difficulty. He opened the door as far as he could and saw a sliver of Madame's face, which was so worn she looked to be sixty, and now showed obvious distress. She held an infant that she was wet-nursing for coin and two of her own younger children clung to her skirts, who both looked to be wearing dirt and measles pox for makeup. Madame's distress quickly turned to indignant judgement when she looked down at the wedge.

"How now, Monsieur?"

"How can I help you, Madame?"

"What have you done to the door?"

"Only braced it shut. How can I help you?"

"Why do you brace your door?"

"Madame, you said there was an emergency?"

She shook off her perplexity like a dog after a swim. "Yes! Yes, indeed, Monsieur."

The wedge suddenly gave and Beau-Brave's hand scraped painfully across the floor. He stood and fully opened the door. "I am listening, Madame."

"There is a man named Monsieur Réveillon, across the river in Saint-Antoine. He is an industrialist."

"I see."

"He is a hateful man, the worst of the worst."

"The worst of the worst of industrialists?"

"*Oui*, Monsieur."

"That is bold sentiment indeed."

"Once you are done hearing this miserable tale, you will kin the darkness of this blackheart."

"I am listening."

"This *fils de pute* wishes to represent his district in the Estates-General - as a member of the Third Estate! Make me laugh, make me cry! The man's as rich as Croesus. He might very well succeed, being glib-tongued and forceful."

"And rich."

"Aye!"

"The public must be educated to his perfidy, I suppose."

"No, I told you. It is an emergency."

"Go on."

"Réveillon spoke yesterday at Saint-Antoine des Champs, along with Henriot-,"

"Who is Henriot?"

"Another swine, Monsieur! A friend of the cursed Réveillon, an industrialist, a chemical manufacturer."

"I understand."

"These men said…" she paused, emotional and in pain. "He said, without shame, that he was going to cut his workers' wages to fifteen sous a day."

"That is absurd. Fifteen sous? Are you sure?"

"Henriot agreed with him."

"And they think they will be elected!"

"They employ thousands between them, Monsieur. This could impoverish all of Saint-Antoine. And what can these workers do? They must vote for him, he employs them. These two demons will represent Saint-Antoine. Saint-Antoine! Of all places! Something must be done right now."

Beau-Brave said nothing.

"Do you not understand? Saint-Antoine is… how things *should be*. Every family has a trade, a craft. They pass down their skills from generation to generation. They live upstairs and work downstairs. They do not ask for riches, but for purpose. The industrialists put them in plaster caves, hundreds at a time, and have them each perform the actions of a simpleton for criminal wages. This man is an insult to the natural order of Paris, Monsieur!"

Beau-Brave shook his head, but did not reply.

"It was your destiny to be here, now, and during this misbegotten time. You must do something!" She was crying now. "Go outside. The streets are abuzz. Everyone knows. They know yet no one does anything! This evil has brought only laziness, Monsieur! These industrialists put everyone out of business. Here in the Marcel, we have no hope, we are little more than rats - but in Saint-Antoine there are thousands of families crafting goods from their very homes. These accursed men like Réveillon, they think they can get away with murder. They can put everyone out of work. Send fathers, mothers and children out of their homes to work in factories. Destroy the guilds, turn every neighborhood into wretched Saint-Marcel! I do not wish anyone to live as we do. This man must be stopped!"

Beau-Brave said nothing.

"Monsieur, I am originally from Saint-Antoine, my eldest two daughters live in Saint-Antoine. I thank God no one in my family works for these two *bougres vérolée*, but they *chient* on the ones I love. Please, Monsieur. I must beg you to help these people."

Beau-Brave nodded. "That is not necessary, Madame. For your hospitality alone, I must investigate. I will go outside."

"Thank you, *bon homme*. Thank you, hero of France."

Soon after, he went into the street.

The avenues of the Marcel were more like narrow, filthy alleys, with hopelessly tall buildings blocking the air and sun on both sides. Beau-Brave walked briskly in the direction of the church of Saint-Marcel across the Bièvre. It was as she said. The streets were noisy with conversation of the perfidious Réveillon. Those who knew Beau-Brave on sight hailed and acknowledged him, asking, "Have you heard?"

Beau-Brave would only reply, "Yes. Follow me."

And most of them did.

By the time Beau-Brave arrived at Saint-Marcel, he had a good dozen followers. It was enough. There were many more people here at the church and its surrounding streets. He jumped on the stone foundation of a wrought iron fence, then to the top of a pillar. He shouted at the top of his lungs in a practiced voice – it was loud but resembled speech more than scream. "Well now! What do we have here at Saint-Marcel? I see brewers, dock workers, bargemen, log floaters, tanners – all empty pockets, all growling stomachs, hands unemployed by the cold, thick ice of Winter!"

Beau-Brave said his words with purposeful disgust. Challenged, everyone in hearing distance was coming his way. He waited until they arrived. "It isn't enough that the price of a four-pound loaf is fifteen sous and we trade our clothing for bread. Oh, no. No, indeed, Saint-Marcel. You have even read the *Cahier of the Poor*, advocating for a minimum wage and guaranteed sustenance for all citizens. You have read the *Cahier of the Fourth Order*, urging a tax on the rich to support and feed the poor. De Villiers wrote that society has trod down the working man, creating a world where men are treated as if they are disposable. Abbé Sieyès said everything that needed be said in *What is the Third Estate?* You know his answer: *The Third Estate is everything. What has it been hitherto in the political order? Nothing. What does it desire to be? To become something*... only not in Saint-Marcel. For you have read all of this, heard these criticisms and alternatives from brilliant men who would help you raise your station if you would but support their ideas. Yet here you are, stumbling aimlessly, as if you were cattle grazing on mud and *merde* in these narrow, sunless alleys. The fact that the daily wage of half of Saint-Antoine will now be the price of a loaf of bread means nothing to you. You wait for your masters to do the same to you if they haven't already, you starving sheep of Saint-Marcel. Tell me, what better things do you have to do today than fight for justice and equality?"

A thick working woman yelled up at him, "Who are you to speak to us like this?"

The crowd chastised her and she looked around in fear.

"You do not know me? Everywhere I go in the faubourgs of the working man, hats are tipped. But I will tell you who I am nonetheless. Do you listen now, woman? Do you?"

One could hear the carts on Rue Moffetard rumbling toward the Barrière, the crowd was so quiet.

Beau-Brave spoke, "I am the Pretend General of Saint-Domingue, mover of wooden cannon and lead musketeers." Beau-Brave grinned, inviting reply.

"Try again," said a voice above the laughter.

Now Beau-Brave shouted with an intensity that could not be gainsaid. "Behold the Gutter King. Shoveler of *merde* on streets and stage. *Enfant de Boucanier*, a murderer before I was a man. I am the Whore of the Danseurs, Necromancer of the Palais-Royal, the Loyal Serpent Servant. When Talma came upon the stage in Roman garb, it was I who stood and saluted first, though I am a fugitive of the law."

The crowd was spellbound.

"I am Beau-Brave of Grenoble. I have come to burn what rots – and all maggots garbed in silk culotte fear me to their very bones, as well they should."

There was naught but silence - until one voice asked the question all wished answered. "What would you have us do, Beau-Brave?"

"To the Place de Grève," he replied, "We gather more soldiers for our battalion. Then, on to Saint-Antoine. We hang Réveillon and Henriot, sack their castles, burn their furniture, and drink their wine."

A chorus of savage cheers went up. The crowd began moving north. Beau-Brave hopped down from the pillar. He recognized someone in the crowd and tipped his chin, "Do we know where they live?"

"Who?"

"Why, Réveillon and Henriot, of course."

The man laughed.

***

The Place de Grève was no stranger to crowds or even to bloodshed. It was the place where public executions, and, in the past, the most heinous forms of torture, had taken place for centuries. Usually the crowds were cowed by the activity taking place there, which happened on the orders of the officials of the bordering Hôtel de Ville. Today, however, the Mayor and his staff were locked tight inside the town hall, not about to gainsay the will of the hundreds upon hundreds of *sans-culottes* flocking to the square.

But there was another city government now, kindly housed at the Archbishopric at nearby Notre Dame. The quickly-coalescing Paris voting districts for the Third Estate claimed the city now. In their minds, this disorder was happening on their watch. Bravely, they sent three men on a mission to investigate the disturbance.

Rumor had it that the crowd was after the blood of Jean-Baptiste Réveillon, but that made no sense. Réveillon's credentials as a friend of the people were nearly impeccable. He was a rising star in Republican politics and a beloved fixture of Saint-Antoine. Just in case, his home was surrounded by a platoon of the French Guard with strong orders to protect his property at all costs.

Monsieur Charton, a textile manufacturer himself, was in charge of the three brave men of the delegation. They made their way to the Place de Grève by coach but were forced to walk before they had even reached the bridge. To be fair, the bridges were always problematic for coach traffic in the best of times. This day the crowd – the mob – was purposefully shutting down traffic on all neighboring streets.

Hearts pounding in their chests, they made their way on foot across the bridge and toward the square. The crowd was animated, loud – all carrying staves or other implements that could be used as weapons.

A woman cackled at them,

"Oh, look at these culotte,
Now they come to us.
We need no rope to hang,
Perhaps they'll do the truss!"

Laughter.

Charton kept moving. "Say nothing, acknowledge nothing," he whispered to his companions.

They did so, and crossed the bridge and made it to the square. Up ahead, where there appeared to be a nexus of people, rested sinister mock gallows of a man hanged in effigy. A sign read, *Edict of the Third Estate Which Judges and Condemns the Above Réveillon and Henriot to be Hanged and Burned in the Public Square.*

"Who here hangs Réveillon in effigy?" asked Charton.

"I do, Monsieur!" said a thin, animated man wearing spectacles.

"And who are you?"

"I am Siméon-Prosper Hardy, Monsieur! Who are you?"

Hardy was a writer, the creator of a very detailed journal of Paris life that was popular in some quarters, mostly outside of Paris. He was a minor celebrity.

"I am Charton, Monsieur Hardy. I have been sent by the true government of Paris, the sixty voting districts of the Third Estate. I represent the common people of Paris. Are you in charge here?"

Hardy looked momentarily lost. "Uh, no Monsieur. I-I brought the gallows though."

"*Mon bon homme*, who is in charge of this venture."

"I'm not sure. I don't think anyone is in charge. I know who started it. I think he's over there." Hardy pointed toward the northwest corner of the square where it met Rue Saint-Martin. "We should escort you." Hardy looked around, "These men need to be escorted! They are from the government!"

Charton silently cursed. *The government* could mean anything. He was soon surrounded by men brandishing weapons, "Come with us, Monsieur *Culotte*," said one.

That did not bode well, either.

Charton and his two companions were pushed and goaded further into the square. There was no escape in any direction.

They soon found themselves near the center. A man of devastating handsomeness and powerful command stood out in a pack of grinning, ugly, dirty, savage day workers: Lucifer amongst his imps.

Beau-Brave, for his part, saw three rich bourgeoises being brought to him by angry men. He said nothing but casually looked them over.

"I am Charton. I have been sent by the true government of Paris, the sixty voting districts of the Third Estate."

"*Bonjour*," said Beau-Brave. It was echoed by the others around him in a taunt.

"I understand you wish to hang Réveillon, Monsieur."

"And?"

"We are all quite shocked. We have no idea how this has come to pass."

A man in the crowd spoke, "Who are you and why do you wish to stop us from hanging Réveillon?"

Charton knew his next words would determine much. "As an employer, I am the provider for many of you. As a citizen, I am the brother of all of you."

"Well then, if you are our brother, embrace us!" Beau-Brave nodded a direction – toward a disreputable man next to him. The man smiled, showing a mushy yellow bar where caked-over plaque had formed one bony ridge over his teeth.

The crowd hooted and hollered. Charton held up his hands, "Willingly, if you put down your weapons and show brotherhood to me first."

Beau-Brave gave a subtle nod. The men surrounding Charton shrugged and placed their implements on the ground. Charton crossed to the decrepit man, kissed him on both cheeks then threw his arms about him. The crowd cheered, Beau-Brave smiled. "All right, leave us be." The crowd dispersed.

Charton stood before Beau-Brave, "Monsieur, I am Charton."

"And I am Beau-Brave of Grenoble."

Charton had heard of him. He had even been warned of him. "Why do you wish to hang Réveillon, Beau-Brave?"

"He is reducing the wages of his workers to fifteen sous a day, the very price of a loaf of bread."

"Are you certain?"

"Quite. Everyone knows this to be true. He said it himself yesterday at the abbey of Saint-Antoine. He also published an essay in which he wrote his excremental sentiment to be preserved for all ages."

"I am glad you have told me of this, for it creates an easier situation."

"Why is that?"

"Why, very simply, you have been misinformed. Réveillon did speak at the abbey, but it was the day before yesterday, and, additionally, he said no such thing, whether from his mouth or printed in pamphlet. He is the most honorable of men, absolutely committed to the cause. I would be shocked if his scullery maids were paid less than thirty-five a day. I assure you if there was indeed such a man who wished to reduce wages to fifteen sous, Monsieur Réveillon himself would be at your side in this square, angry and homicidal as any other. In fact, we are so sure of Réveillon's standing and honor that, on our orders, a full platoon of French Guards has been posted in front of his home and factory."

Beau-Brave looked around at the unruly crowd and threw up his hands – *what can I do?*

Charton took a step forward, "Please, Monsieur. We are on your side. Réveillon is on your side. We are here now brother-fighting-brother for no good cause. Tell me you will disperse the crowd."

"I will tell you we will not hang Réveillon, that is for certain."

Charton took a deep breath. "I will take you at your word, Beau-Brave."

Beau-Brave made a cross in the air. "Go in peace, Monsieur Charton." Beau-Brave motioned to a nearby man, who nodded.

Charton bowed and made a quick exit. Beau-Brave's man followed as his protector.

Beau-Brave waited until he was sure Charton was half-way across the bridge.

He turned to the crowd, "*Mes amis*! Citizens of Paris! Listen!"

His words were repeated across the square. All went quiet.

Beau-Brave screamed, "We have been lied to! Réveillon is one of us! The true culprit is Henriot! He is the one! To the home of Henriot! To kill, to burn, to avenge!"

A savage cheer greeted his announcement. They all moved as one.

April 27th, 1789

***

Henriot had the foresight to vacate Paris for Chantilly with his family and household servants. His factory workers were dismissed with pay for the entire week.

This was highly auspicious.

Three thousand angry people descended on his home and utterly destroyed it from top to bottom. The broken pieces were thrown into a bonfire in the street.

All of the miscreants responsible for the devastation had travelled to be there. Amongst the three-thousand were only a handful of citizens from Saint-Antoine, and no one whom Henriot employed.

Although everything that could be guzzled was certainly drunk, nothing was stolen. These Furies were honorable working people who considered themselves to be above such things. They came to Saint-Antoine because it was the right thing to do. They came in righteousness - and committed no act they deemed criminal.

They did not come to steal, they came to destroy.

The Americas
1832
N
0
500
miles
Newfoundland
Canada (UK)
New Britain
Nova Scotia
Lower Canada
Upper Canada
ALGONQUIN
IROQUOIS
BLACKFOOT
NEZ PERCE
YAKIMA
LAKOTA
SIOUX
DJIBWA
FOX
KIKAPOO
CROW
CHEYENNE
SHOSHONI
PAIUTE
UTE
NAVAJO
PAWNEE
APACHE
KIOWA
COMANCHE
APACHE
(Zamorano)
(Echeandia)
UNITED STATES OF AMERICA
SEMINOLE
SANTA ANNA
MEXICO
PACIFIC OCEAN
ATLANTIC OCEAN
Bermuda (UK)
Bahamas (UK)
Turks & Caicos (UK)
Cuba (Sp)
Cayman (UK)
HAITI
Puerto Rico (Sp)
Guadalupe (Fr)
Martinique (Fr)
Jamaica (UK)
Belize (UK)
CENTRAL AMERICA
Mosquito Kingdom (UK)
British Guiana (UK)

Chapter Thirty-Seven

1833

Jake

Harris was playing sick, or Jake would have walked him to the schoolhouse to refresh his memory of its location. Luckily, that afternoon, the schoolhouse was exactly where Jake remembered it to be. He arrived as the students trudged into the snow on their way home. One of them had thoughtlessly left the door open; Jake ducked inside and quietly shut it.

The interior was fairly bright, owing to a row of windows - purposely built high, so it was impossible for seated students to be distracted by the freedom of nature. The hearth fire was middle-aged and the embers glowed comfortably warm. It was, oddly, positioned on the wall to the left of the door rather than opposite. Jake remembered being banished to the right side of the room as punishment one cold, misbehaving Winter day by one Mister Perry, educator. The desks were empty but Grace stood at the front of the class talking with a young boy.

"Miss Otis, when will Mister Blake return to teaching?" he asked.

"On the fifteenth of January."

"I think you are a much better teacher than Mister Blake. Is there any way you can stay?"

"Well, I have never been taught by Mister Blake, so I cannot comment. But Mister Blake has a wife and two daughters to support and he must therefore return on the fifteenth."

And with that the child turned and filed out of the classroom, heaving with deep, dramatic breaths and looking downward. When he left and the door shut, Jake and Grace laughed.

"Jacob Esau Loring."

"Grace Elizabeth Otis."

"Will you help me with my coats and my books?"

"By all means."

After putting on her outerwear, Grace loaded him with books, papers, and charts like a Moghul's coolie. She regarded him, then placed a box of chalk atop it all. "Shall we?" she said.

They walked out into a light snow. The temperature was falling quickly. Jake carried such a load he could not see his feet.

"How far away do you live, Miss Otis?"

"Oh, call me Grace."

"Then call me Jake."

"Less than a mile. Near where Worcester and Washington meet."

"Excellent. I shall know everything about you by then."

"No. I think I should rather like to know everything about you, Jake."

"What do you wish to know?"

"You have returned from France."

"I have."

"Having spoken over twenty-five words to each other, I feel entitled to asking you a barrage of rude, personal questions."

He smiled, "I am at your disposal." She spoke quickly, albeit clearly. He was glad he had the time on the ship to brush up on his English.

"France is not thought of as a particularly moral place."

"It is an ancient and complex culture. Mostly, I spent my time studying. My education was world-class. I was very lucky to attend such a prestigious school."

"Ancient and complex," she goaded.

"Uh, yes. The pendulum swings back and forth. The French, in the majority, wish a return to the way things were, but even that sentiment becomes complicated. France has been many things in the last few decades. Catholic and Royal, revolutionary, Imperial, Constitutional, moral, immoral, as you say, and everything in between. The nation suffers from anarchy and cholera. Socially and politically, it has yet to recover from chaos. The rest of Europe has punished her like a misbehaving child. It is pushed and pulled as different forces vie for control."

"Chaos?"

"Yes, of every sort. Spiritual, political, cultural. And that left by war, of course."

"Did you have a girlfriend?"

Quite a change of subject. "No."

"None at all? Dancers, stray actresses?"

Am I in New England?! "I did not involve myself with such people. Are you envious of French liberalism?"

"In America, usually both bride and groom are pure on their wedding day." Her tone was cryptic.

"I think some Frenchman would be horrified at such a thought. I myself am a romantic. I desire a loving wife and nothing more."

"What did you find appealing during your stay abroad?"

"I enjoyed my school, obviously. My… friends. The cuisine, the art, and – God forbid, at one point – the politics."

"Where do your sensibilities lie now?"

"My sensibilities have spun like a windmill in the past year."

"Where are they this very second?"

"I don't know, Grace."

"Are you a Christian Theist?"

"No, I am more of a recovering Rousseauian Deist."

"What an interesting conversation we are having. I think most young men of West Needham would be running for the hills had they partaken of it."

"Perhaps the young women as well."

"I think I am the same, Jake."

"The same? You wish to run for the hills?"

"No! I mean to say I am a recovering Rousseauian Deist. You probably don't remember, but I was quite scandalous when I was younger."

"I remember something. I don't remember what or why."

"I would frequent church with less frequency than a young lady should, and I was therefore the scourge of the town. Had I been born two-hundred years earlier, I would have surely been pressed to death for heresy."

"Goodness, what a grim thought!"

"Religion never made enough sense for me to be faithful."

"Yes. Religion is mostly incomprehensible to me as well."

"That opinion is unique in Wellesley. At one point, I felt as if the entire town was drunk on God, and I was sober. When one is alienated, one becomes resentful. I found myself being fairly hateful, to my shame. Hence my rebellion."

"I found my rebellion behind a barricade, being shot at by government troops."

She gave him a piercing stare. "I might have been standing by your side, had this melee occurred during my bleakest moments. I have since changed my perspective, as you have."

"How so?"

"I have come to realize that I am a fish living in a tree."

Jake chuckled.

She continued, "At first, I looked at all the other fish – obviously, to a fin, swimming in the lake - and I was completely perplexed, not to mention resentful at being alone. I liked living in my tree; I didn't understand why all the other fish swam around in the darkness. Then it came to me, like a lightning bolt: they were precisely where they should be, doing exactly what they should be doing according to their purpose. Simply because I myself live in a tree does not indicate that the other fish should change their habitat."

"In fact, if they did, they would perish."

"Indeed! So, if I love my fellow trout and perch, and wish to interact with them, I must stop being judgmental. I need to climb down and jump into the lake and swim, at least every once in a while, and be kind and generous with my aquatic brothers and sisters. And certainly not find myself resentful when they do not follow me back into my branches."

"So how does this metaphor translate into the realities of your life?"

"I remained the same inside but changed my actions. I go to church every Sunday, I participate in all religious events and celebrations, and do everything as I should. As a result, I am a respected member of my community and happier for it. No one needs to know I do not believe in a Puritan God."

We have only just become reacquainted. Why the airing of such secrets?

Jake did not speak his thoughts. "I sensed something of that in you."

"Then you are an intelligent and thoughtful observer. Of me, no less."

"You are different but you do not hate. You delight in humanity and have a deeper understanding of your role in society. You are a kinder, more understanding Voltaire."

"Flattery! There is something else, but I hesitate to tell you, for it will certainly influence your opinion of me." She said it lightly - perhaps in jest, perhaps not.

Jake decided to answer seriously. "I would only ask to have a true opinion of you, and you of me, and, to be honest, there is much to tell you of my life and the constraints upon it."

"Are you married, profligate, or inclined to deviancy?"

"No, no, indeed." *Mon dieu!*

"Then I will go first. Being who I am, I sought out those who were like me. Those who did not believe, the quiet rebels. Do you understand?"

"Yes, I do."

"I have found them to be unreliable miscreants, in the majority. Relationships of hard alloy cannot be forged within my group. Thus, I gained a new respect for my Puritans of Wellesley. I know their faults, but I have come to respect their integrity and their sense of honor and responsibility, none of which I found amongst those whom I would consider my peers. A Rousseauian man sees women as an interesting new dish of food. They partake of it until they become bored, then they find another dish. Do you fully understand what I am saying?"

Is she saying what I think she is saying? If so, she is bold indeed. Where did this woman come from? Who is this Yankee Eleanor of Aquitaine?

Jake came from Paris, from the best education in the world amongst the world's elite, to this small town outside a small city in a sparsely populated, remote land… only to find this erudite, utterly fearless creature before him. Was it the unique properties of these strange people that could produce such a person? Were there many? *Mon dieu! And to think I was once one of them!*

Jake realized she was staring at him with patient eyes. He quickly answered. "I believe I do fully understand. Thank you for your trust in my discretion."

"I believe humanity needs moral uniformity, not only in their families, but in their communities. I think it is a necessity. We are very obviously social creatures. It is common sense that a tribe must be in moral agreement to provide foundation and stability. Only weathered adults can survive in moral anarchy, and only just so at that."

"The tree-dwelling fish now respects the pond dwellers. You came to understand how unethical it would be to convince others of the righteousness of your path, especially considering how loathsome the other tree-dwellers have shown themselves to be. Instead, you gracefully swim with your brethren, in a gesture of love and respect for who they are, hiding your true nature not out of cowardice, but out of love and compassion."

Her look changed. On her face was a look of… loss? No, something different, but then it was gone, and Jake had to focus on her words once more.

"I am beginning to tire of my own fish-tree metaphor, but yes. To be self-righteous and critical, knowing what I know, such a thing could only stem from vanity – or perhaps even of contempt."

"I myself have been a fish in a tree, although with far less wisdom and compassion."

"Well, it does sound as if you are finally ready for the compassion tree, fellow *Piscis Arboreum*." They smiled at each other and kept walking. "I think they deserve us and our compassion, our little Wellesley. It is quite amazing, this community."

"How so?"

"Your grandfather was Reformed but your father was Catholic."

"Yes."

"Do you know much regarding the Reformed faith?"

"I confess I do not."

"They believe man is hopelessly fallen, but God places the gift of faith within those who will achieve grace."

Jake searched his memory, "The Elect."

"Exactly, those lucky few would be God's Elect. Now, how does one tell if someone is of the Elect?"

"I'm not sure."

"Shame on you! The gift of grace leads to faith. And faith leads to…?"

"I'm afraid my ignorance lingers."

"Good works!"

Jake struggled to redeem himself. "So, faith is wholly a gift from God, but others can tell if you have this gift by your good works."

"Precisely. And we all know, all observers of the human condition, that perception trumps reality, what others think is always more important than what is true and real. And, now knowing this, fellow *Piscis Arboreum*, what is it like living in a community of Reformed protestants, the doughty Puritans of New England?"

"Everyone is performing good works as fast, as often, and as publicly, as they possibly can to convince others they are of The Elect."

She laughed gaily, "Yes. And what an absolute wonder it is. There is no such thing as peeling paint within a hundred miles. I would say we are hard-working, if hard-working meant doing nothing but work as fast and as intensely as one could from before dawn until well after dusk. Responsibility and integrity are commonplace values and can be counted on. Everything is just about perfect. Well, not quite – but as perfect as humanity is liable to get, I must say, if one does not count worrying about appearances as a fault. If it wasn't for a bit of occasional snippety judgment, I would say I am quite honored and lucky to live here."

"You are also capable of sharing their values."

"Yes, I can fit in. But what odd birds we are. Talking about this place as if it were wholly separate from us, rather than our home."

"Fish living in trees are the very definition of odd birds, are they not?

"Indeed."

They walked contentedly. A memory came to Jake. "Modern Chivalry."

"My book! In one way utterly plagiaristic and in another wholly original."

"Plagiaristic?"

"It is Don Quixote, to the very bones of the story."

"And original?"

"It is a criticism of America's stanchless desire to move west. An insightful look into our nation and culture."

"Cervantes's tale seems to haunt me."

She stopped and turned. They were evidently at their destination, a very nice-looking farmhouse. Nearly everyone in West Needham was a farmer, he had learned at the party. "How so?" she said.

"I must leave you in suspense."

"Until when?"

"I would like to see you again."

She looked away and mirth left her visage, "Is what follows now between us of France… or New England, Jake." She looked into his eyes with a piercing intensity. Suddenly, he realized everything he thought, up until this very second, was dead wrong. What came before, however odd and intellectual, was indeed courtship, and she thought the same way about him as he did about her. "And please," she continued, "do not embarrass me by asking what that means."

Jake swallowed and took a breath. "New England, Grace. Most assuredly, New England."

She smiled and met his eyes, "Can you come for dinner tomorrow? My parents die of worry for me and my impending spinsterhood."

"I would be honored."

"Very well. Hand me my books." She smiled mischievously, "I gave you five pounds more luggage than was necessary. I don't know why. I think I was testing you."

He smiled and laughed. "Careful now. They say turnabout is fair play."

"Don't tease."

"Who says I am teasing?"

With her books, she turned and walked to the door. "Goodbye, Jake."

"Goodbye, Grace."

Grace heard Jake turn and go.

Her heart began to beat faster, but not in a good way, not from excitement or anticipation. It began to beat anxiously, in a fearful panic. She opened the door and heard her family's greetings. She did not respond but kept walking. She heard her mother and her sister follow her. She continued out the back door… and vomited in the snow.

She might have made a tremendous error in judgement.

She had been quite positive in her descriptions of the Puritans of Wellesley. She wasn't being completely honest with Jake.

At their darkest, the Puritans were pitch.

Grace's behavior and attitudes could devastate her. More importantly, they could hurt her family. If her past actions became public, it could drastically change the fortunes of everyone she loved.

She had been discreet.

So, why had she done this? It was absolutely guileless. Was she now, after her last failure, so lonely and desperate that she had revealed her cards before the first bet? He appeared a kindred spirit, but other kindred spirits had not lived up to her expectations.

Her mother and sister were talking to her but she could not focus on their words.

Grace suddenly had an idea, and it made her feel better almost instantly.

If her worst fears materialized, she would simply hang herself in the barn.

Jake, for his part, walked back to Elm Bank, deep in thought.

When he was with Grace, he was entranced by her very presence. Everything was right and good in the world. Everything that passed between them was delightful. Now that he was separated from her, the words they shared appeared on paper in his mind, as if he was proofing an essay for school.

What did she mean to imply?

Was she a fallen woman polluted by the modern age, sick of soul, a barren field where nothing could grow? Perhaps she was the victim of the age, making regrettable mistakes brought about by alienation and false truths. Jake had made the same mistakes for the same reasons, although the consequences of his actions had been far direr. Regardless of what she had done, he was assured there was no blood on Grace's hands, as there was on his.

They were both complex people, finding themselves in a simple place that demanded much and was unforgiving. Could his actions hurt his father – a precarious Catholic surrounded by Puritans? Easton Loring was accepted because a better man could not be found – and he was the richest man in

Wellesley. But good men have good sons, as good works issue from the true faith of The Elect.

The conflict gnawed on Jake's peace of mind.

***

The mystery wasn't really much of a mystery.

Grace had met a young man who worked in Boston as an apprentice silversmith. He was seemingly a kindred spirit, a man of the Enlightenment. They enjoyed each other's company, and their relationship naturally progressed on a physical level as she fell hopelessly in love with him.

Their relationship continued, then stopped for a reason she could not explain. Ten months after the last time she saw him, he married another.

Grace felt as if she had fallen into a cesspool, and somehow the filth had found its way inside of her and not just on her skin. She was hopelessly saddened and traumatized.

She did everything right, according to what she believed. When it felt right, she did it. She had been her natural self and so had he, so why, then, was her soul so utterly rent? The experience was something that she thought she could never recover from.

Her values, not to mention love, had failed her.

April 28, 1789
Conciergerie
Place de Grève
Hôtel de Ville
Notre Dame
Road-Block
Bastille
Arsenal
Faubourg Saint Antoine
Bassin de l'Arsenal
Folie-Titon
Hôpital Saint-Antoine de Quinze-Vingts (for the blind)
Luxembourg
Faubourg Saint Michel
Faubourg Saint Jacques
Faubourg Saint Victor
Seine
Bièvre
Salpêtrière Hospital
N
0
1000
2000
feet

Chapter Thirty-Eight

The Fourth Day

April 28th, 1789

Beau-Brave

Beau-Brave was awakened by a serious pounding on his door at eleven in the morning. "Yes," he said.

"It is Trumeau, Monsieur."

Beau-Brave stared at his door and realized he was so drunk last night that he forgot to hammer in the wedge. "Come in."

Monsieur Trumeau entered. He was all dirt, sinew, sweat, and hair. In fact, every part of him not clothed abounded in hair. It came out of his nose and blended seamlessly with his moustache. One could have braided the hair on his knuckles and fingers. His beard started nearly at his eyes and his hairline came to his eyebrows. "It is an emergency, Monsieur."

"Yes, what goes, Trumeau?"

"Madame is gone."

Ah. "She comes and goes throughout the day. She runs your household and has many responsibilities."

"You misunderstand, Monsieur. I had the good fortune to secure work helping a roofer this fortnight. From my perch, I saw Madame."

Beau-Brave sat up. "I see."

"There is no other way to say this, Monsieur."

"She was with someone?"

"She was with many people, Monsieur. Many, many people."

"I don't understand."

"Neither did I, Monsieur. I begged my employer for his patience and off I went. It seems that my wife and another man, a writer, have somehow raised an army and now march on Saint-Antoine."

"A writer? What writer?"

"Pierre-Jean Mary."

"Pierre-Jean Mary? What? Who? A writer? I have never heard of this man. Wait – where are they going?"

"To Faubourg Saint-Antoine. They mean to hang Réveillon."

"I spoke to the Paris electorate yesterday. The accusations against him are smoke and nonsense. He pays his scullery maids more than I made shoveling."

"They march, Monsieur. I assure you."

"How many?"

"There are perhaps ten-thousand, held up by a roadblock of the Guard just outside Titonville."

Beau-Brave shook his head. "That cannot possibly be true. We only had three-thousand yesterday."

"And only twenty-five hundred left Saint-Marcel this morning. But I assure you, Monsieur, there are ten-thousand or more at the roadblock."

"You are telling me that a forty-year-old pregnant woman and some imbecile of an unknown writer are leading an army of ten-thousand on Saint-Antoine?"

"More or less exactly, Monsieur."

"Are they fighting with the Guard?"

"No, no Monsieur, they have no problem with the Guard, only with Réveillon."

"That is good, if the situation remains unchanged. Wait – who is looking after your good children, Monsieur?"

"My eldest living at home, Aubrianne. She is nearly thirteen and more than capable. But there is a problem, Monsieur. I must return to work. Please tell me you will find my poor wife and bring her home from this madness. She is with child, Monsieur, and she is not seventeen anymore – not by a stretch."

"I will do everything I can."

"Thank you, Monsieur."

The door closed and Beau-Brave was left alone.

He realized he had just committed to finding one woman in an angry crowd of ten-thousand. That was the easier part. The hard part would be changing the woman's mind to lead her home.

.

***

It was even worse than Beau-Brave imagined.

Coincidentally, it was racing day at Vincennes. Everyone of status in the city was attending.

Vincennes was to the east, on the right bank. Unless attendees undertook an extraordinarily inconvenient detour, they had to go through Saint-Antoine. The barrière gates at Arsenal in the Place de la Bastille, however, were closed to stop the rioters from reaching La Folie Titon. Between the mob and the parade of carriages trying to get through the gates, it was absolute chaos.

As Beau-Brave fought his way through the crowd, he saw a fine coach and a beautiful young noblewoman inside. The crowd yelled out, "Third Estate! Third Estate!"

The woman leaned out the window, flourished her hat and yelled with a toothy smile, "May God bless and keep the members of the Third Estate!"

She was cheered hoarsely and the crowd moved to make way. A woman next to Beau-Brave was overcome, "She is so lovely. Like an angel."

Beau-Brave scanned the crowd. He had no idea what Madame was wearing, and he had never seen her companion before, this idiot who styled himself as a fellow writer. It was pointless. He turned to the nearest man, "Where is Madame Trumeau?"

"Who?"

"Madame Trumeau. She led this army from the left bank, starting in Saint-Marcel."

"Oh. I do not know, Monsieur. I joined at the river. I am a *flotteur*." He shrugged.

Beau-Brave moved on.

Another coach approached.

Another noblewoman was seen through the coach windows. She was as equally beautiful, but younger - in her teens. She looked terrified. The crowd yelled at the coach, "Third Estate! Third Estate!" The young lady only became more frightened and – worse – looked neither right nor left.

It was the worst thing she could have done. It is better to be insulted than to be ignored.

The crowd jeered the coach and slung mud from the street across its boards and its liveried attendants. The young woman screamed in fear and the drivers sped the horses on, heedless of those in their path.

Beau-Brave moved east. He came to a bolt of women hunched over another who was prostrate. He silently swore as he came upon them and looked down.

It was not Madame. One of her helpers looked up at Beau-Brave, "She was overcome, Monsieur. I think she needs water."

Beau-Brave palmed her a coin, "One of the nearby taverns will sell you a mug of watered-down wine."

"Bless your heart, Monsieur."

"Do you know Madame Trumeau?"

"No, Monsieur."

"She leads this crowd."

"No, Monsieur."

"Third Estate! Third Estate!" screamed the crowd. Beau-Brave turned and saw a magnificent coach. The door swung open and an older nobleman emerged and held his hat high in the air. He had a smile on his face and a twinkle in his eyes. The crowd cheered with abandon.

Beau-Brave turned to a man waving his hat. "Who is that?"

"Do you not know the Duc d'Orléans?"

The King's brother, the owner of the Palais-Royal.

Beau-Brave smiled. "Phillippe!"

Phillippe held up his hand and the crowd quieted, "*Mes amis*! *Mes frères et sœurs*! Where do you go? What is the purpose behind this gathering of the good people of Paris?"

A chorus answered him.

"Why, Réveillon you say? What has he done?"

Another chorus.

"Fifteen sous! Why, that is outrageous! That cannot be true, *mes amis*! No, indeed."

Shouts, frantic voices attempting to be heard.

Phillippe shook his head, "Oh, you do not mean what you say."

We do! We do! they shouted back.

"You must go home. Why do you vex this man? Go home, good people."

Urgent shouts answered him. *Oh, no no* he pantomimed, but to no avail. More shouts – *see it our way* – more pantomime *oh, no no.*

Phillippe shrugged, then leaned back into the coach. He appeared again with a fat coin purse. He took handfuls of the contents and tossed them over the crowd. Cheers, laughter, as the coins were caught. Another thick handful went into the air, another – then another. Two more and the purse was empty. He disappeared – then reappeared with another purse! Handful after handful went into the crowd. Finally, Phillippe waved, blew kisses, waved again, blew more kisses and then finally disappeared into the coach. As it moved forward, the crowd cheered until hoarse.

Beau-Brave used the opportunity to move forward. He reached the gates of the barrière, manned by dozens of men. Most of them maintained control of the east gate, with a few on the other side dealing with westbound traffic. The crowd was easily controlled because of the foresight of the Guard, despite their disparity in numbers.

Beau-Brave noticed an old, tough-looking sergeant determined whether the gate leading east was opened. The Guard and the crowd were jovial toward each other, all smiles.

"I have to see my lover in Saint-Antoine!" shouted someone in the crowd.

"You and all your friends, eh?" shouted back the Sergeant.

"Exactly!"

"She is very generous, this girl. Give me a note and I'll make sure she gets it."

Laughter.

Beau-Brave felt better. This was going nowhere. If the Guard continued their yeoman work, everyone was going home with their teeth and fingers. Madame Trumeau did nothing more than take a long walk with ten-thousand friends. She would be clocked in the eye by her husband and that would be the end of it, unless she clocked him back. In the meantime, he'd try to find her.

An hour passed. He did not find her.

Another hour passed – once again fruitlessly.

Beau-Brave, hungry, made his way out of the crowd to an intersection. A thick, florid man was selling skewers of meat. Beau-Brave bought one. The meat was old and dry, and reminiscent of dog, which he had eaten in Saint-Domingue. "What is this?"

"Chicken, Monsieur."

"What? I've a better tongue than that."

"Are you calling me a liar, *jean-foutre*!" The seller became indignant, arguing and gesturing with practiced anger.

Beau-Brave poked him hard in the chest, enough to hurt. "Eh!" Beau-Brave shouted.

The man quickly backed down and whispered, "It's cat, Monsieur. Please don't tell the Guard."

"Give me another for half-price. Not because I will tell the Guard – they have better things to do - but because of your lie."

"I am sorry, Monsieur. Take one for free."

"No, half-price, as I said. That is fair."

Beau-Brave ate the second for half-price, then had two more at full price. He was about to buy another when he smelled vomit from the crowd. If it was normal-smelling it would not have dissuaded him, but it was instead sublimely acrid, as if someone had not eaten for days then drank too much wine and then eaten some cat himself.

Beau-Brave found another vendor and drank a mug-full of watered wine. He wandered back to the crowd – which had not moved. How could ten-thousand people have so little to do? They talked with each other, some sang and danced, others joked – an occasional fight was broken up. It seemed an interminable activity. Many looked drunk.

How can so many afford to drink when they can't afford to eat?

Where was Madame? Had she gone home? The mob did not seem to have a center, it took no orders.

"Have you seen Madame Trumeau or the idiot Mary?" *No* they said – usually.

Once they cheered, "Madame Trumeau! She is Madame Franklin! Madame Washington!"

"Where is she?"

"With Mary the writer!"

"Where is Mary?"

"Who knows?"

"Why does everyone call him a writer? What has he written?"

They don't know, they say.

"Well, don't call him a writer then."

"What are we to call him?"

"An *idiot, imbécile, crétin, sot, bête*. Anything but a writer, *mes amis*."

"Should we tell him you said so?"

"If he has a problem with my appellations, tell him they came from Beau-Brave of Grenoble. If he's lucky, I'll meet him with fists. If not, then anything else, the *bâtard*."

Hoots, laughter – but no help.

Beau-Brave decided to continue his search starting back at the roadblock again to make his way forward. Approaching, he noticed the older sergeant stood near an eastbound coach, talking and joking with the passengers. Commanding the westbound gate was a younger, junior sergeant. As Beau-Brave completed his observations, an ornately decorated coach pulled up moving westbound. The young sergeant was annoyed, "Vincennes traffic has been redirected. No one is to come this way."

The driver spoke defiantly, "I have been ordered home by the most direct route, and no one has gainsaid our direction until now."

"You will turn at once."

"I will not, Sergeant."

"You will indeed, Monsieur, upon my order."

"I will not, and if you continue to assert yourself upon our direction, I will be forced to ask for the intervention of my passenger."

"Who is?"

"Can you not see the seal upon our livery, Monsieur? I bear the Duchess of Orléans!"

Philippe's wife. The King's sister-in-law. The richest woman in France.

The young sergeant turned to the men at the pole, "Open the gate."

Beau-Brave, however, caught sight of the older sergeant, still absorbed in his conversation with the coach passengers, gesturing for his men to open the eastbound gate.

Both halves of the gate were now swiveling at the same time, opening up the entire street. The crowd took notice. For a moment, all were silent: it looked for all intents that the Guard opened the gates for them.

With a hoarse roar, ten-thousand people poured through the roadblock. The younger sergeant, nonplussed, looked to the older - who simply shook his head *no*. There was nothing they could do apart from firing into the crowd, composed of men, women and children of Paris. The good soldiers of the French Guard would never contemplate such a thing on their own.

It was a stupid mistake, almost an accident, but there would now be blood. Beau-Brave followed the crowd.

It was what it was.

April 28th, 1789

***

There were no police or troops anywhere near La Folie Titon, Réveillon's residence and factory, and the devil's work began immediately.

The only constraint upon the crowd's appetite for destruction was the immense size of the place. Connected buildings formed a wall to one side of the gardens, which itself formed a gigantic square – so large the center of it would safely be out of range of musketeers standing on the border. Ten-thousand people evaporated into the space as ten-thousand ants would disappear into a Versailles dining room. The gardens looked scattered with people, nothing more, and the interior of the hôtel did not look crowded through the windows. Beau-Brave arrived late to the party, at a stroll rather than a run.

A bonfire had already been started and was roaring. Beau-Brave had no idea how such a large fire was started so quickly – until someone threw a jar of paper-gum on it. The jar shattered and the flammable gum nearly exploded. Furniture was being thrown from the second and third story windows to crash and break on the stones. Books flew like chickens, their pages fluttering like wings of white feathers. Some rioters stumbled out of the buildings drinking from wine bottles that were, in all likelihood, older than they were.

The furniture lying on the pavement was made of wood and stone, the wood shattered, the revealed innards starkly white and in direct contrast with the stains of caramel, onyx and maroon of the inlaid surfaces - the alabaster legs of ravished unfortunates revealed from ripped dresses. And it was a rape, a horror of senseless destruction. Looking around, Beau-Brave could not help but be struck by the beauty, art and craftsmanship of the once-wondrous items, all now broken and waiting for the fire. In a time of beautiful things, this home had been renowned for the splendor of its furnishings. Antique masterpieces rained down from the windows, all accompanied not with dirge but with insane laughter and cheers, like caged howling macaques throwing piles of their excrement at passerby's. Even the books were leather-bound, hand-sewn works of art. Those who rushed inside the building paused to pick them up and throw them into the fires behind them.

Beau-Brave picked up a volume, gently smoothed the pages, closed the cover then opened it again, as if resanctifying the work and christening its value anew.

It was *Candide*, by Voltaire.

He turned the pages as if they were locks of hair over the face of a lover. Words caught his eye.

All is for the best in the best of all possible worlds.

One could draw many lessons from *Candide*. Some said the most obvious was that the world was an insane king-rat of a mess - and an individual was best served tending to his own garden. Beau-Brave certainly stood in a wondrous garden, albeit sacked by imps, but it was not his own.

Drums.

The book snapped shut.

Beau-Brave turned. Across the gardens on the street, soldiers advanced. French Guard held the right; the Guet, the City Watch, held the left. In the center were regular army and three six-pounder cannons. There were hundreds of troops in all.

The emboldened mob began moving toward the soldiers, ignorant of their profound change in status: they were now perpetrators of serious crimes, not innocents who simply might do such things. They were in mortal danger.

Beau-Brave hoped that the soldiers would fire while the crowd was still out of range. A huge volley might scare the disorganized mob into submission or flight. The cannons, however, had to remain silent. Even if they fired grapeshot, the people in the rearmost rooms of the hôtel would not be out of danger.

The officers screamed commands and the soldiers stopped advancing. The crowd, however, still moved toward them. More commands were issued and the soldiers readied their bayonets and angled their muskets.

Beau-Brave had a terrible feeling in the pit of his stomach.

He noticed that to his left stood a filthy ten-year-old boy wearing nothing but ratty trousers. Beau-Brave gave him a nod. "Get down or hide behind something."

The boy just shrugged. Beau-Brave backhanded him across the face, "I said get down, boy."

The boy ran off. Beau-Brave hoped he didn't stop.

Suddenly, there was an indescribable sound. The first line of muskets and three six-pound cannons fired at once. Beau-Brave saw hundreds of people fall to the ground. The rest of the crowd ran from the soldiers at a full, heedless sprint – the very worst thing they could have done. Between the crowd and the soldiers was a huge, rising grey cloud of smoke completely obscuring one side from the other. The soldiers could not see the devastating effects of their volley, could not see the total lack of necessity for a second. A moment later, another volley of muskets fired. Fewer people were cut down, but fewer was still many. A third volley claimed its share, thickening the carpet of dead and wounded obscuring the ground. Soon after there was a fourth volley, and then the cannons roared again.

Beau-Brave was spun to the ground. His shoulder, hip and knee stung hopelessly from the impact with the stone. Soon after his side burned, as if touched by searing metal. The pain was so great he could not scream. Finally, it subsided just enough for him to look down.

His shirt and jacket had been completely rent, as if by an attacking tiger. The skin of his flesh had been torn open, and part of it twirled upward from the wound like a white ribbon. He could see a layer of raw, white fat above muscle that had been badly scored, and then a sliver of exposed rib. The wound suddenly filled with blood, spilling out and over his skin, shockingly crimson in color and effect. The pain came again and a horrible, startled grunt sputtered from his lips.

He heard a chorus of moans and screams from distant wounded. His own pain was unbearable. It would render him unconscious, then he would wake and the pain would come again. Time passed.

At one point, he looked up and saw the hairy face of Monsieur Trumeau. Beau-Brave spoke, not sure if he was real or a dream. "I could not find Madame. I looked everywhere."

"She is unhurt." Monsieur Trumeau lifted him from the ground without effort "She has been arrested by the police." Beau-Brave noticed *Candide* was clinging to him, glued by dried gore. The book was ruined, a stained mess of red, brown and black blood in various stages of coagulation. Monsieur noticed as well and gently rocked Beau-Brave until the book fell to the bloody stones.

Trumeau began to walk. It was horribly painful. "Where do you take me?"

"To the hospital."

"Is it far?"

He shrugged. "I will not take you to the Hôtel-Dieu. Salpêtrière is better and closer to home. We will be there in less than an hour." Beau-Brave supposed carrying his weight for an hour was beneath Trumeau's consideration.

The pealing of several large hand-bells was heard approaching from different directions. It was the sound of priests coming to give last rites. Even if the King himself heard such bells, he would take to his knees on the floor of his coach to pray for the dying. Today, for all hale men, there was too much to do for such a luxury.

Beau-Brave turned to look over the carnage and saw blind men leaning over the wounded, fumbling with bandages, trying to feel the location of wounds. The panorama of blind, fumbling medics was a shocking image to Beau-Brave, almost hellish – as punishment, the wounded sinners' only succor was in the form of blind doctors. Some of the wounded howled in terror and recoiled from their touch. "The blind. Why are they here?"

"They are from the sanitorium, Monsieur. Saint-Antoine de Quinze-Vingts."

"It is surreal. It must mean something."

"What must?"

"This image, the blind fumbling to help the dying. It is symbolic."

"It means they have no eyes, but still a heart and soul."

"How many?"

"Of the blind, Monsieur? I don't know."

"How many were hurt?"

"They say eighteen-hundred, but it looks a lesser number to my eyes. I would say fifteen-hundred, although many may have been moved already."

They passed a bolt of soldiers. They stared at Beau-Brave with the most forlorn expressions he had ever seen - as if they had accidentally run over their own children with a cart. Their faces were so hopeless and blank that Beau-Brave had to look away. They were broken men, every bit as broken as the furniture and people lying on the stones.

***

Drenched in guilt and gore, never again would the army or police be so ready to fire on their own people. No one knew it yet, or of its paramount significance, but the preservation of order through violence was no longer an option in Paris. This happened at the exact same time that violence became known as an effective instrument for political change. Indeed, the Estates-General was a product of the violence in Grenoble, as Beau-Brave well knew.

The massacre had gutted the will of those who were armed and honorable, and made them unfit to face those who were neither.

Réveillon and Henriot were not elected.

Cathédrale de Nantes

Chapter Thirty-Nine

May, 1789

Estelle

Estelle stood in the Cœurfroid ballroom near the wall. She said nothing and did not stir. Even if she wished to move, it would have been difficult - the crowd was gigantic and the press of people was a swirling school of color and perfume.

She wished her former feelings would return - the elation, the hope - but she felt nothing but the stares in her direction. It was the necklace, the Cross of Nantes, nothing more. Why did she wear it? Why did it now seem so inappropriate? She had worn it for years, every day; it was a part of her body.

Not now.

Xavier appeared across the room. He was soon surrounded by well-wishers. Estelle knew that their eyes would soon meet. He would move across the dance floor, parting the crowd like the Red Sea. She felt his arm encircle her waist, as if it was real. Her breath left her lungs, she leaned against the wall to prevent falling.

He was still across the room, however. What would happen to her when he began his move in her direction? She would burst into tears, that is what she would do. But she didn't care.

He never noticed her.

Jeannine also came into the room. She did notice Estelle but her eyes flicked immediately from Estelle's face to the necklace, and a strange look passed over her, but then her eyes travelled elsewhere.

Estelle tried to remember the look on Jeannine's face when she gazed upon her for that flickering moment. It was no use, though. Jeannine was inscrutable.

Madame Cœurfroid, too, entered and spied her. Her eyes registered Estelle but moved past her, as if they had never met.

Years passed for Estelle, as she leaned against the wall. She was ancient ruins, watching as the moss crept further up her stone blocks, as least what was left of them. The rain came, then snow, then Spring. There was the illusion of change, but the change was the same, so nothing really changed at all. Why did she even exist? What was the purpose of the ruins? Why did no one come down the roads anymore?

But the centuries ended and soon, with much diversion, the guests filed out of the house and into the street. A light rain had just ended and the streets were wet, but, thankfully, all was stone from the townhouse to the church.

Estelle remembered that she had additional responsibilities. At the cathedral, there was an earnest young priest by the door. He noticed her, looked away to the guests, realized she had not moved. "Bride or groom, Mademoiselle?"

"I am the bride's *témoin.*"

"You are with the bride's *témoin?*"

"No, I am the bride's *témoin.*"

"I met the bride's *témoin* at rehearsal. Her name is Mademoiselle Wegelin. Are you the second? I wasn't told. What is your name?"

Estelle was not particularly surprised. She replied without emotion, "I am the bride's prior *témoin*."

"Are you Jewish?"

"W-what?"

"You do not know where to sit?"

"No, I suppose I do not."

"In a Christian wedding, the bride's family and friends are on the left."

"Thank you."

Estelle entered the church and sat down. A fat man with a terrible cough and sniffles sat next to her, stinking of wine and *eau de vie*. On the other side of her was a young teen girl who whispered to an identical girl to her right. Every time she looked upon Estelle, she suppressed giggles, then immediately turned to her friend and whispered. Estelle found this even more maddening than the ill gentleman. She imagined the girl knew her deepest, darkest secrets and found them all risible and ridiculous.

Estelle ordinarily loved mass, and felt as if she was an intimate part of its proceedings. When this mass started, she felt as if she had come in late. It was as if it was someone else's mass, from a different religion.

No – worse.

She was a ghost haunting the proceedings, powerless and ineffective in the daylight. The service was spoken in a language she couldn't understand.

The bride and groom spent most of the mass kneeling, facing away from the congregation. At one point, Jeannine and Xavier faced each other and showed their profiles to the guests. At that very moment, a glimmer of crimson fractal light played across Jeannine's face. She suddenly turned and looked directly at Estelle, without any prior search, and a look of pure hatred came over her face.

She immediately turned back to Xavier, beaming with happiness.

She was quite far away. The vitriol was Estelle's imagination. But Jeannine had turned to look at her, quickly and accurately, and that was not imagined.

More ceremony. More, more, infinitely more, infernally more. Every movement, every gesture chained Xavier and Jeannine together.

How can this be happening?

When would it stop? When would Xavier suddenly come to his senses and run to her and they would both escape from all of this madness?

Never.

Xavier and Jeannine were getting married.

It was such a simple, obvious truth.

Estelle almost came apart. It took every bit of control she possessed not to wail and scream. Her heart beat in her throat, constricting her breathing. She was going to die.

The wedding ended, everyone filed out, jubilant and loud, expectant. Soon the bride and groom exited the church.

Jeannine and Xavier shared their first kiss as husband and wife as all cheered.

They were married. It was done.

Estelle had been invited to the *Repas de Noces*, but intuited her invitation might not be as secure as she thought. She would avoid further humiliation. She walked to a cab.

"Do you need a ride, Madame?"

"Mademoiselle Guerrier, if you please. I need to be taken to Varades."

"Why, that is fifteen miles away, Mademoiselle!"

"Will you take me or not?"

"You should hire a coach."

Estelle lost her temper, which she had never done before in her life, and yelled at the man as if he had committed grievous harm to her honor. In the end, he had his fill of her and left.

Estelle walked to the Rue de Ports, shaking with anger, shame and woe, and bought a coach ticket to Varades.

***

The sleeping inhabitants of the Meilleur were soon roused in their entirety.

The howls came from a woman.

The shrieks were loud and constant but not quite from a tortured soul. There was an added ingredient to these screams – rage.

The epicenter of volume proved to be the Carrera Room.

Young Madame Traversier was a few steps down the right staircase with her hands on the balustrade. Monsieur Traversier stood on the opposite stairs, an equal number of steps downward. It was Jeannine Traversier who shrieked, and words from both husband and wife were soon differentiated and understood.

The elder Madame soon appeared with her servants. "What is the meaning of this?"

"I have been assaulted!" screamed Jeannine, "I have been purposely assaulted by your son in the most base and prurient manner. I am physically injured and bleeding profusely. I require the police and a doctor!"

Madame looked to her son, who was red-faced and humiliated. He looked as if he wished to speak, holding up a hand. The hand balled into a fist and he said nothing. Madame, looking at all of these serious faces and observing the emotion, was suddenly filled with mirth.

She knew she could not possibly show it.

She turned back to Jeannine. "I do not think the police are necessary, Madame."

"You take his side?"

"I simply said-."

"I will tell you this – you will fetch the police or, so help me God, I will throw myself to the marble floor of this very room." She turned to Xavier and spoke with pure vile, "How dare you! How dare you, Monsieur! My father will hear of this. Do you not know who I am? I will see you hung, you disgusting creature! I will never forgive you for this! Never! Even when you think this moment has passed, know that revenge lurks in my heart forever!"

And then she proceeded to scream at the top of her lungs.

The Elder Madame turned to Monsieur Fidèle. "Please contact the Police. Specifically, Commissar Monsieur Berlière, if you please."

"Are you quite certain, Madame?"

"Do you wish to be discharged, Monsieur? Fetch the police, fetch the very Commissar of Nantes this very minute!"

"*Oui*, Madame, at once."

***

Commissar Berlière showed up much earlier than expected, but looking as if he had spent hours getting dressed. He was with a full squad of French Guard in similar display. He brought along two coaches.

He patiently listened to the litany of offenses that young Madame Traversier brought against her new husband, as the elder Madame stood nearby nodding her head in agreement. Monsieur Traversier stood near the door, humiliated and rubbing his face. "Indeed, Madame," said Berlière, "Your husband should certainly be arrested at once."

"Yes! Yes! Yes!"

Monsieur Traversier looked about to die but Berlière was stone-faced. "Place Monsieur in irons."

The Guards, with very, very serious expressions on their faces, immediately but gently placed Monsieur in handcuffs.

Young Madame gloated. "You are not so high and mighty now, are you Monsieur? I will see you hung for this!"

Berlière replied instead. "That is not for you to decide, Madame, rather the Parlement court. I bid you adieu."

And, with that, the police left with Monsieur.

Elder Madame turned to the servants, "Go back to bed."

The room emptied. Madame turned to Jeannine. "Now that this unpleasantness is behind us, we should speak, Madame."

"I will hear no defense of your son!"

"No, indeed, but I cannot possibly leave you alone in this state. You need comforting."

Jeannine looked as if she was going to cry, "Perhaps I do. Madame, you have no idea what that man has done to me. I have been desecrated."

"I am sure. Come to me, child. Everything is better over chocolate."

***

Xavier had never felt so humiliated in all his life. The coach ride was agonizing. There were soldiers to his left and right and Berlière sat across from him.

"This is more common than you would think, Monsieur."

Xavier sighed. He could not bring himself to speak.

"Since we have dealt with this situation so often, we know the right course of action to take, especially with elder Madame being present in the house."

Xavier sighed again. He imagined himself speaking but nothing came from his mouth.

"Farm girls do not have this problem, Monsieur, having… examples. They have nearly the opposite problem. City girls, the daughters of the bourgeois, they are - shall we say? - another story. Young Madame's mother is a Protestant, yes?" He shrugged. "If their mothers do not explain, well..." Berlière threw up his hands.

Xavier finally croaked, "What now, Monsieur?"

"We get drunk at the station, of course. In the morning, you return home. Elder Madame will talk to Young Madame and she will be quite contrite. This situation will not arise again. This night, well, human anatomy works against us, Monsieur."

"I think I need a drink before our destination."

Berlière produced a pewter flask and offered it. "To your health, Monsieur."

Xavier took the flask.

***

It was a rosy-pink morning, damp and cold, when the police dropped Xavier at his home. He walked to his door, not expecting the servants to be awake to open it.

The door opened.

He looked up and saw his wife, dressed as if for the court in her green dress, holding the portal open for him. Her expression was demure and submissive. "*Bonjour*, Monsieur. May I take your hat and coat?"

Xavier had no idea what was happening, half-believing that his wife would become a ghastly terror once again any minute. He took off his hat and coat and gave them to her without a word.

She took them and spoke softly, "*Merci*, Monsieur."

She placed them on a nearby divan, then crossed back to him and wrapped an arm around his waist.

"You must be very tired, Monsieur."

"I am indeed."

"Please allow me to take you to bed."

"Thank you, Madame."

"Come."

Xavier allowed himself to be taken to his bedroom. She helped him into his nightclothes and tucked him under his covers. She herself laid next to him and held him. Xavier allowed himself to sleep.

It was not the perfect ending to the night, but was much better than he expected it to be several hours earlier.

It was nothing like, at one point, he dreamed it would be. He should have known, looking back. Nothing in his life had really turned out the way he thought it would.

Jeanine, for her part, eventually came to enjoy her wifely duties - indeed, perhaps too much.

Elm Bank, 1832

Chapter Forty

1833

Jake

It was an unusual sort of dinner.

Miss Athaliah Otis, one of Grace's sisters, was two years younger. She stared intently at Jake, "You are extraordinarily handsome."

Jake thought the Otis family would surely die.

Athaliah noticed as well but shrugged it off, "I express my sentiment in a purely objective way. As a beautiful pond surrounded by trees is winsome and evidence of God's glory and attracts us to sit on its banks to read or picnic." She turned back to Jake, "You are good-looking in a way that is transcendental and invites conversation."

Grace would have no more of it. "And if he were ugly, would you then say he was objectively so, as a pile of refuse outside a tavern, and therefore transcendentally repulsive, so as no one would ever wish to enter the establishment? It is better not to comment on such things. You are being rude, Athaliah."

"I meant nothing. It is just that… he is so extraordinary-looking. It seemed to be appropriate to speak of it without the assumption of prurience."

Missus Otis, one Mariana, lost her temper and whispered with a clenched jaw. "That is quite enough, Athaliah."

The rest of the dinner was spent in silence. Jake looked at Grace, hoping they would lock eyes and share a private joke over the moment but she seemed to take this breech of etiquette with hopeless seriousness as well.

Jake thought on the moment, for in the silence he had nothing else to do. Athaliah was quite matter-of-fact. Jake had never thought upon his appearance one way or the other. He knew he wasn't bad-looking, and that was enough.

After dinner, they all went for a walk. The fading light necessitated a short circle of a walk around the house, mostly through deep snow, but it was taken at a pleasant amble. Jake was amused. There was probably nowhere on earth, save Siberia, where an after-dinner walk would have taken place under such circumstances. Grace and Jake were allowed to walk ahead and out of earshot.

"I apologize for my sister's comments. She will be punished, I assure you." Grace had to practically raise her knees to her chin to move through the snow, but she did so with such capability that the moment was painted with hilarity.

"Truly not necessary." And then another lengthy moment of silence, which did not play out pleasantly.

"Yesterday, we spoke of many things."

"We did."

"I feel perhaps that I said too much, considering the state of our familiarity."

"What is your fear?"

A palpable wave of anger flowed from her, like an explosion under water, although she said nothing.

"I have no ill-intentions toward you, Grace. If you regret speaking to me in such a revealing matter, I am not an appropriate target for your anger or fear. I wish nothing but peace and happiness for us both."

Jake was taken aback by his words - they were mature and thoughtful. Not long ago, he did not consider himself to be either.

Grace nodded, "At some level, I perceive you are correct."

"We are an odd pair."

"Yes, we have established that *ad nauseum*."

"I did not find our conversation annoying or tiresome."

She did not speak.

"Grace, I have no battle plan. I have come to value life, and there is no reason why I would not value yours. I feel drawn to you, as men who wish families are drawn to women. But at this point, it would be unsuitable for me to draw any conclusion regarding you. It is better to discover truth than to invent it. I am a gentleman, who has referred to himself far too often as Citizen or Comrade. You need not fear me in any way, neither my discretion, my actions, or my trust. Whatever shall be, shall be. You are now someone I know more intimately than most and I am better for it. I am happy to be here, walking with you, and quite content being compared to forest ponds by your sister."

She snorted. "Could you imagine something for me?"

"Certainly."

"I want you to imagine me taking you by the arm as we walk and resting my head upon your shoulder, in an expression of fondness and relief."

Jake realized the moment in his mind perfectly, giving his imagined Grace a great deal more height in order to do so. He smiled contentedly at her, gratified that she had the same expression.

"It is amazing," she said, "what happens when people can step back, see past themselves, and just consider others for a moment."

After the walk, Jake stayed quite late, sitting with Grace, apart from the rest of the Otis family in the parlor.

He enjoyed talking with her. There seemed to be more emotional and intellectual architecture behind every door. He was fascinated by her perspective. She had never travelled, yet she had developed her own ideas, seemingly immune to the constraints of culture that had been imposed upon her. But she was neither immoral nor mad; in Jake's estimation, in fact, she seemed wholly good. He judged her petrified to gain the bad opinion of her family, and sometimes this fact forced speech that was out of character. She hinted at one of her flaws – placing trust in those who did not deserve it. She did not speak overly of what she had been through – mostly in riddles and parables. By her demeanor, she did not seem resentful, although she certainly had a right to be, if Jake's suspicions were correct. He was captivated by her wisdom and objectivity, which seemed to emanate from nowhere, like a spring.

She spoke softly with a subtle melody. She was a medium tenor and her words played on her face, especially in her eyes, as if they were a keyboard for the music of emotion, wit and humor. She was well-read and intelligent, thoughtful and even-tempered.

Harris liked her. She was a *much* better teacher than the horrid Mister Blake, who seemed to have no admirers at all.

The next day was Sunday.

His step-mother Sophia was attending church – more properly called the Congregational Meeting House. Ordinarily, she attended with only his brother Harris, the rest of the brood being too young. There was no question of the children being anything other than Protestant. Catholicism was seemingly his father's cross to bear and no one else's.

Jake decided to attend with her, knowing Grace would be there with her family.

Harris's reaction was, unsurprisingly, kinetic and positive. His father's reaction was the opposite. He teared and patted Jake on the back and quickly left the room. Jake had no idea his father had such emotions regarding his faith.

It bothered him somewhat, as he walked to the chapel. On the way, and in between interacting with Sophia and Harris, he wandered in his thoughts.

Jake did not believe in God. He might exist - who knew? - but there was no real evidence, at least none that Jake could see or accept. The emotions that people seemed to feel in regard to religion were completely incomprehensible to him. Grace felt the same way but attended church anyway, as a celebration of her family and community – and to avoid the judgement of her neighbors.

So, here was Jake.

Was he betraying himself? Was it sufficient that he was going to church solely to be with Grace? Was he a hypocrite? Was he betraying himself and his own ideals? Jake, for the second time, decided to have a conversation with thin air.

If you are there, creator of the universe, and desire anything from me, I must tell you true: I cannot see you. I cannot see evidence of you. Some say the fact of creation itself is enough, but I cannot. I understand the imperfection of my senses – and that of my own intelligence used to sift the evidence with which they provide me. I could be wrong. I have been wrong and right in regard to a great number of different things. Yet, I am a slave to my senses and how I interpret them. With supreme arrogance, I say to you, maker of stars, if you wish to have a relationship with me, it is wholly up to you. I must have evidence of you.

I see no purpose in blind faith. If you created me, you gave me my senses and my wits. I see only unanswered questions in regard to you. I can only promise, in my supreme arrogance, to you, maker of stars, that I will not have faith in the fact that you do not exist, that I will pursue a righteous course through your universe, whether you appear to me or not.

A feeling of peace descended on Jake. He was not a hypocrite; he was a man trying his best to navigate a righteous course through his life with his eyes open. For now, that was enough.

He entered the chapel minutes before the service started and sat next to Grace and her family. "Good morning!"

The Otis family looked extremely pleased with him and returned greetings of their own. Grace's expression was far subtler and more complex, but also pleased and warmed by his appearance.

Jake could not pay attention to the singing or sermon. Grace's presence was overwhelming. Every time she moved, it meant something, every expression of hers was a page of literature. He tried to communicate with her as well, assured that what was unsaid was clear and discernable.

After the service, he spoke with the Otis family. Was Jake spending time with his family now? "Well, we are having a family dinner. But before dinner I am taking my brother Harris, who is a precocious eight, ice fishing upon Lake Waban."

They all spoke affirmations at once. Grace added, "Faith is eight as well."

"Has she ever been ice fishing?"

"No, I don't believe she has."

"Well, if your family obligations do not start right away, perhaps you both could come."

Jake had no idea at the time, but he had just found the secret to spending as much time as he wanted with Grace. They could go anywhere and do anything - as long as Harris and Faith came along.

Eventually, as they spent more time together, Jake told Grace about his trials and adventures. She looked around to see where Harris and Faith were off to, then gently caressed his shoulder, "So much loss," she said.

Jake nodded.

"How did you survive the trek I wonder? In Haiti, that is. Nearly everyone in your whole story warned you of the dangers of that place. There was a substantial amount of time when you were exposed wholesale to every hazard. Yet you did not become sick in the slightest."

"Yes, that is true." Jake hadn't really thought about it. Who dwells upon being well?

"I envy you your adventures."

He could sense the longing in her voice, and replied gently. "Well, if you ever wish to replicate them, I'll tell you which ones to avoid."

"I am glad that you are here with me. I feel safe with you, Jake. Very comfortable and very safe."

Jake was glad she said such a thing. He needed to hear it, after other things that she had said. "I am usually only very cold with you, Grace, for we are always outdoors."

"Itching for a snowball, are we?"

Jake smiled, "I feel that all is right in the world when we are together. And in a very comfortable way, as you said. I feel as if I have known you my whole life."

She closed her eyes, "I hope you stay here. I really do."

"What would make me leave?"

"I don't know." She looked down, but then met his eyes.

"I want to kiss you." The words came from his lips nearly unbidden. He was mortally embarrassed for a heartbeat, but then forced his eyes to engage hers.

"There is a lot to do if you wish to kiss me. We are basically engaged if the children see us."

"What must I do?"

"Your father should meet with mine to discuss the match. Then you should meet with my father. Then you ask to marry me. Then we tell my mother and father."

They were discussing marriage.

For some reason, Jake wasn't intimidated. In fact, he felt as he did before he left for France for the first time. There was nothing but excitement, not a single look back or impulse toward reflection. "So much to do," he said with a smile.

"We haven't known each other very long."

She didn't fool him. "What would happen if I left Wellesley within the hour?"

"I would curl up into a ball and die."

"As would I."

It was then that Harris and Faith's well-placed snowballs hit them both in the face. Such a boldfaced attack required their immediate attention, and both children were immediately in retreat, shrieking and laughing at the top of their lungs.

Flags of the Royal Provinces

Provence

Anjou

Poitou

Gascony

Touraine

Lyonais

Foix

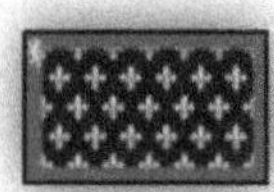

Maine

Brittany

Hainaut

Auvergne

Alsace

Franche-Comté

Roussillon

Artois

Normandy

Saintonge

Picardy

Île-de-France

Aunis

Flanders

Béarn

Angoumois

Nivernais

Languedoc

Dauphiné

Bourbonais

Limousin

Berry

Burgundy

Guyenne

Champagne

Marche

Lorraine

Corsica

Orléanais

Chapter Forty-One

May, 1789

Beau-Brave

Beau-Brave opened his eyes on Jean-Paul Marat, standing at his bedside, looking over him with a clinical eye. It was day, but he couldn't tell the time.

It was how things were now.

He had been more alert when he first arrived, he had no choice for the pain was extreme. He had many visitors at first, but they had dribbled off as the weeks and days burned down like a thick candle. He was aware that his condition had worsened. He woke once to see Talma wiping tears from his eyes, but drifted off without speaking to him. He began to stink of infection and pus, and it was foul indeed. A man must throw off a mighty stench to offend himself.

When and if he began to smell of rot, his goose was cooked.

Once he awoke to see a middle-aged doctor staring at him as if he was a cobra in a glass cage. The doctor had a Roman look. He wore no wig and his black hair was pulled back into a pony-tail. He was of medium build, with dark stubble showing on his face.

"Yes, doctor?"

The doctor looked away, then faced him again, "I'm afraid any question I would ask of you in this moment would be inappropriate, considering my station."

"Fire away, with permission, Monsieur. I am mightily bored."

"You have only just awoken."

"Even so."

The doctor said nothing for a moment.

Then he spoke suddenly and with emotion. “Why? Why all of this violence?”

“You do not see the necessity for change?”

“They do not equate, yet more and more they are associated. Things can always change, everything can be made better. Why must we force change with violence?”

“The oppressors will not give up their privilege so easily.”

“But they have already. Change happens so fast in this day and age, it boggles the mind. I am living in an entirely different country than that of my youth.”

“I did not lead the riot against Réveillon.”

“Even so, they say you are famous for your ideas and actions.”

“Things must happen fast when you are starving.”

“Again, Monsieur, change does not equate with food, yet more and more often they are associated. Do you think the King wants his people to starve?”

There are few people who can hear the same lies day in and day out, then analyze and identify what is false. Beau-Brave was this sort, and so, evidently, was the doctor. Beau-Brave knew the doctor’s words were reasoned, but Beau-Brave didn’t like to lose. When logic fails, good platitudes would have to do.

“I know that the King himself does not starve, and others do, and perhaps that is enough.”

The doctor stared at him, and finally whispered, “How many lives does a four-pound loaf cost, Monsieur? For scores upon scores have died, and it did not purchase a single one.”

Beau-Brave paused. He cleared his throat. “They will think twice about starving us now though.”

The doctor’s head twitched. He was not convinced, only civilized and well-mannered. “I apologize, Monsieur. I must resume my duties. Thank you for your indulgence.”

“It was only now getting good.” Beau-Brave smiled, trying to encourage the good doctor to continue their tête-à-tête.

But the doctor swiftly left.

More days passed, maybe even more weeks, when Beau-Brave opened his eyes on Marat.

He always thought Marat had an odd look. He wasn’t ugly so much as completely strange-looking – although, admittedly, he was probably ugly as well. He didn’t look French, although he was, and what race he could be was a mystery. His skin was corpse-pale and his hair was two shades off pure black, a dull, listless dark brown. He was quite thin but dressed nicely. He was not the type to be married: he was focused and intellectual, not of the earth but of the swirling vapors above it. “Marat!” said Beau-Brave. He was astounded hearing the weakness of his own voice.

"Beau-Brave," said Marat, "I do not know how you sleep at night. This room is no larger than a village church and holds over two-hundred patients, all of them foregoing the ability to be silent in their trials."

"When I first arrived, it was quite problematic. I think this place is some kind of asylum for the mad as well. The women's ward must be nearby, for I hear their howling at night. Well, not anymore. It is all I can do to remain awake." Beau-Brave was suddenly consumed by a spasm of white-hot agony. His hand shot up and was brought short by the manacle and chain on his wrist.

"It does indeed contain such an asylum." Marat looked around, said nothing more.

"You are very clinical today, *mon ami.*"

"Forgive me." Marat procured a nearby stool and sat beside him. He took a folded note from his jacket and opened it. "I have a letter."

"Read it to me."

> *Dear Beau-Brave,*
>
> *I wished to write in order to thank you personally for the donation you have made to my efforts to secure election to the Estates-General. I wish to assure you that I will attend as a dedicated Ens, eschewing all earthly pleasures, committed to self-denial, in order to gain energy and focus in order to advance our cause.*

"Do you know what that means? The word *Ens*? I do not and wonder if I read his words correctly."

"You read his words correctly, *mon ami*. Read on."

> *I understand you completely, Beau-Brave. I myself have thought of this new way, although in my internal conversations I used different terms and ideas to express similar ideas, admittedly far less succinct compared to yours.*
>
> *Beau-Brave, the essence of our ideology is this: we are able to eliminate human suffering through our action and will, and we must. There is nothing more. Slavery and oppression must end. Those responsible must be purged from positions of power.*
>
> *I am utterly humbled by the fact that I have greatly suffered but meet, every single day, those whose suffering eclipses my own. I do what I do for a child who lived long ago in great pain and suffering - and for the children of the future who will live without such torments through our efforts. It is the duty of the new citizen to create a world where the child grows to adulthood without terror, without soul-deep pain, and with abundant love.*

I will never forget you, nor your generosity. Your gift fills me not only with the spirit of gratitude but with that of responsibility as well. I must force myself with great discipline to forgo the trappings of ego, greed and desire and dedicate myself completely to the cause.

Any man who loves humanity must be of equal mind now.

Please understand, I am your most loyal servant.

Maxime

Beau-Brave shook his head. "What an amazing missive."

"Indeed."

"Is there more news of the trials?"

"Madame Trumeau has been pardoned and released."

"I am shocked and pleased."

"It was only through direct intervention of Réveillon himself. Monsieur Mary, however, has been executed, along with several others…"

Beau-Brave suppressed the urge to smile.

"…a handful have gone to the galleys. Mary was a great man. He was forever on the street talking with the common workers, always active, always teaching and raising more soldiers for the cause."

"I did not know him. How many more will perish, do you think?"

"I believe it is over. The excremental King had to show resolve, there had to be a token exercise of strength and firmness." Marat said nothing for a moment. "Monsieur Hocquenghem's trial has ended."

"Monsieur Théo!"

"He has been found guilty of all Parlement charges and innocent of all those Catholic. He has been fined five-thousand livres and given a sentence of five years. He was transferred to the Bastille."

Mon dieu! He is ruined.

"What of myself?"

"It has been ruled that if you survive, you are pardoned by the will of God."

"What does that mean?"

"Simply that. If you survive your wounds, you are free."

"That is good news," Beau-Brave said as he coughed.

"No, it is not."

"What do you mean?"

"It means the doctors have told the court that you will not survive your wounds."

Beau-Brave chuckled. "Well, yes, there is that. But I come from hardy stock, Monsieur."

"You do. You have been holding on for weeks."

"But I will eventually succumb?"

Marat said nothing for a moment, then spoke. "Yes."

Beau-Brave took a breath. "The letter I sent to my sister?"

"Has been returned."

"When?"

"Recently, after our last visit. I have withheld nothing from you."

"This vexes me greatly. Can you tell Monsieur David of this? That I am still bedridden and chained, and my sister needs to be located immediately."

"He is David, Beau-Brave. I am only Marat. I do not have your celebrity. Not yet."

"Can you tell him I asked you? Or just send him a letter. Even if it is intercepted by underlings, he will eventually know of my request."

"Very well."

Beau-Brave rested his head against the pillow. "Deep in my heart of hearts, I desire something so trivial and ridiculous it would astound you."

"I would hear of it."

"I want to find a woman who loves me. No – that isn't true. Rather this - I want to find a woman who makes me feel loved, who excites in me a desire to love her in return. That is quite a different animal. It does not matter if someone loves you if you do not feel it."

"Yes, perhaps we all long for such a thing, but believe the very world must change before such a wonder even becomes possible."

"That is exactly how I feel. I mourn for my unloved heart."

Perhaps from his expression, so did Marat.

Beau-Brave spoke quietly, "I worry for my poor sister."

"You need to worry about yourself right now, *mon ami*." Marat cleared his throat, "I am a doctor."

"Yes, I believe I knew that."

"I will tell you this, Beau-Brave: I am a better doctor than all attending you – more talented and experienced than any at this hospital. I was physician to the household of the Comte d'Artois, the King's youngest brother. I was paid two-thousand livres a year plus allowances. I conducted experiments on electricity, fire, heat and light. Were it not for Lavoisier and the other dull minds of the Academy, I would have been Descartes, forever remembered and celebrated. It was fate that intervened and redirected the course of my life. Had not my true purpose been to change the world, I would be a doctor still."

Lavoisier! Ha! No wonder he likes me!

"Have you cured such wounds as mine?"

"Let me phrase it differently: before I even attended medical school, I cured a friend of gleets."

"Are they related? Gleets and the rot of wounds?"

"I believe that they are."

"Well, nothing that these idiots have performed accomplished anything."

"I will put you under my care. I warn you, the treatment will be painful."

"Everything is painful now, *docteur*."

"Very well."

"What does the treatment entail, out of curiosity only?"

"The scraping away of the pus and infection, which will be torture, then the application of poultices made from brie crust, and a diet solely of brie crust until you are well."

"Your cure is… cheese?"

"No, *mon ami*. My cure is brie crust. The crust only."

"You are curing me with mold then."

"I am indeed."

"You are no doctor. You are a witch. My mother was a witch. Every sprig of grass and weed held hidden secrets. I drank wretched concoctions of black hazel for every ill."

"Black hazel has many medicinal properties, but that is not the subject of this discourse. You must trust me and I will tell you why: the world never moves by the action of the majority, rather a small minority, leaders and dedicated soldiers are the ones who change history. You are special, Beau-Brave. You have a revolutionary destiny that cannot end here, in this gloomy mausoleum of the dying. I will save you, for my cause demands it. And you will obey me without question. Do you understand, my new patient?"

"I do and I obey," said Beau-Brave as he tried to salute, but the chain stopped him once again. "You have good turn of phrase, Marat. You should use it in your writing more often."

Saint-Florent-le-Vieil

Chapter Forty-Two

May, 1789
Jonathan

Father Jonathan stepped out of the confessional, his gentle parishioners pelting him with their cotton balls of venial sins all morning.

The darkest secrets of the confessional were certainly as dire as other places, but mostly they were acts of thought, not performance, and they were rare. Saint-Florent-le-Vieil was a good place. They lost many children and sometimes mothers, as humans are wont to do, but they weathered these sad episodes and kept strong. There were several ways, not just the church and confessional, where the folly of the citizenry was ironed out, where socialization and community aided them in returning to God.

France was roiling like the North Sea, but this land was utterly placid.

It had taken a while for Father Jonathan, a product of this environment, to realize his home was rare earth indeed. He wished to know what made the clock tick in this unique land stretching from the Loire to the Vendée.

Why were the people content? Why were they so fulfilled? Why was there no crime, no madness, no social disorder? Even chronic drunkenness was more or less unknown, and wine readily available.

It was telling that when Father Jonathan described his parish to outsiders, some thought he was exaggerating, or inventing some kind of utopian lie. In reality, if anything, he was understating. Catholic village life in Western Anjou was simply an ideal human habitat. In most places, things had devolved beyond the realm of being even barely suitable. People had forgotten how human beings should actually live, and how to properly care for them. Outsiders grew rice in the desert, thinking the plant was sickly, brown, barren, and always close to death. They laughed at Jonathan, thinking him a liar when he described terraces of verdant abundance.

Father Jonathan was now part of a network of communicating priests throughout the region and even the country – a network of his own creation. Through his letters, he knew there were perhaps a handful of places in the country that were similar to this land in their social functionality, but mostly France was a nation composed of places that did not work, rice in the desert, environments that had somehow devolved out of being good human habitat.

Father Jonathan could describe his home – but he had no map to get there. He had no idea how to lead other, less functional communities to become like his. Without this insight, Father Jonathan felt quite useless to help. Here, he had the answers – but no proofs, no equations to lead anyone to understand how those numbers were derived.

No one was starving here. But was that a product of the environment, or a product of the relationship between nobles and peasants, where both were partners in the land?

There was a true sense of community; no one was alone. If a man was sick, his neighbors tended his fields. Families were strong and large, and felt as responsible for each other as they did their own. Everyone in the village saw each other at least once a week, at church and at the celebrations at the lord's manor afterwards. Individuals found themselves within smaller groups more often than that, and everyone talked openly, working through their problems with one another – or with Jonathan, or both. People were never left alone in their distress - no one, even in the darkest recesses of their own hearts. People with candles would venture in, bring light, and help clean. It was what they did for each other, in nearly every aspect of their lives. No one's roof was repaired alone, figuratively or literally.

The tradition of the church was strong, and it was ancient - wise men and women had determined much regarding what action was godly in nearly every situation. Everyone thought and believed in the same value system, everyone shared the same sense of right and wrong. The priests were not personalities forced on the people, but members elevated and chosen by their communities. The priests were social mediators, neutral and knowledgeable, to be consulted in regard to how life should be lived to enter heaven.

And, of course, the peasants tended to have a relationship with a personal God, where all felt as though they walked with their creator, were known to Him in all their actions, and were as responsible to Him as they were to anyone else, perhaps more so, and on a level where subterfuge was impossible.

How does one create all of this in another place, one where human corruption has unraveled community in every way that it can be?

Where the nobles are oppressive and greedy.

Where the church is not trusted, or has been taken over by predators, or the unscrupulous?

Where the harvests are poor and taxes high.

Where drunkenness has taken hold.

Where families are broken or corrupted.

Where children are neglected or abused.

Where crime or the abuse of power has left ugly scars.

It was the job of people like Father Jonathan, with God's help, to make eggs from omelets - to take what was mixed, scrambled, and cooked and make it whole again.

Unfortunately, this knot became tighter with unraveling. Human complexity was daunting, solutions to its problems nearly outside the intellectual range of the species, truth be told.

Fortunately, all of these ideas had once again consumed him. He was smart enough not to think on it overmuch, for if he did, he would realize he was grateful to not think of Estelle, and then he would be thinking of her once again.

Perhaps that is why, when he left the confessional, he did not recognize who waited for him. He saw a woman, who somehow drew his entire attention. As he walked toward her, it finally registered that it was Estelle Guerrier who stood before him, but a different person had been placed in her body. She was dressed like a princess. She seemed older but was not really that much older at all. Mostly the change was in her eyes, for they were wholly separate from the woman he knew. Jonathan was disquieted. Estelle could be gone forever, with only this new person in her place. He hoped beyond hope that such a thing was not true.

"Father Johann," she said. It was her old nickname for him.

Her expressionless, monotone voice was even more disconcerting than her looks. "Mademoiselle Guerrier, how nice to see you again."

Something is very, very wrong.

"Do you still have time at this hour for parish concerns?"

"I do indeed."

"Could you take a walk with me?"

"Where do we go?"

"In the same direction we always did."

No emotion.

"Certainly, Estelle."

They walked.

Jonathan thought it was perhaps the most bizarre conversation that two reunited soulmates could have ever had.

Many of the townspeople recognized her. They would stop, open their mouths to greet her - and suddenly be struck dumb. Then Jonathan and Estelle would pass the open-mouthed statue in silence. Estelle's appearance and demeanor were so different no one said a word - the entire way down the hill. Had the town known she was coming, the entire parish would have celebrated her return. She was now so different, in such an intimidating way, that she could walk the length of Grande Rue without being hailed.

He tried small talk with her. She was barely responsive. By the time they reached the bottom of the slope, he was disconcerted, yawning bored, and still nonplussed, all at once.

They walked south, a path leading off into the fields.

"It is not much longer," she said.

"We have a specific destination? We are not on a walk then?"

She did not reply.

They left the fields behind and entered the woods. Off the road they followed what was little more than a deer path. Jonathan assumed she still knew these woods well; he had no idea where they were going.

Father Jonathan was being led astray by a stranger. He felt he should stop, turn and walk back to the abbey without another word. For some reason, he did not. He continued to follow her, a mark being led into the forest by a trickster-thief, who would turn at any minute, stab him and take his coin.

They entered a clearing. Father Jonathan could hear nothing of man, nor of his animals. Blankets had been spread on the ground.

What on earth is going on?

Estelle began to undue her bodice.

"Estelle, what are you doing?"

"You will not lie to me. You dream of me. You dream of me as a man dreams of a woman. You want me. You know I feel this way as well. We have always wanted each other."

Father Jonathan said nothing.

"You will make love to me," she said.

"No," he answered.

"Don't lie to me," she snarled.

Jonathan found himself strangely calm. "No, I won't. I am not. Everything you say is true. Everything."

"Good," she said calmly, and began unlacing herself once again.

"I cannot do as you wish."

Her eyes burned at him, hatred, fury. She moved across the clearing and her arms reached out to him. He easily stopped the movement - but her head then came closer and she kissed him. They were hot, inexperienced, angry, furious kisses. For a moment, he was quite overcome, but the emotion was quickly replaced with shame. He moved her arms down and between them.

"What happened that you would bring me here, Estelle? Will you not talk to me?"

"Kiss me."

"No."

"If you do not, I will kill myself. I will tell your name to the devil."

"No."

"Yes. Kiss me."

He shook her suddenly and violently, in an attempt to snap her from her madness. "See yourself with my eyes. What do you see?"

"No."

"See yourself. Tell me what you see."

She jerked out of his grasp. "I see an insect. Something beyond loathing. A disease, invisible dust. Beneath consideration, beneath even contempt."

"Why would you think such things?"

"I only ask that you make me a woman. Is that such a difficult task? Show me that I am worthy of being touched."

"Can you not see yourself as I do?"

"I answered your question."

"I love you, Estelle."

She answered quietly, "Then why do you not do as I ask?"

Jonathan closed his eyes and spoke, "Very simply, because I love you. I love you as much as my heart is able. I would sacrifice anything for you."

"Lies."

"No. In this moment, you are asking for my contempt, not my love."

"If you do not help me, I will die. You are my only hope."

"I love you, Estelle. Do you believe me?"

She only stared off.

Father Jonathan brought up every beautiful memory of her that he could. He tried to feel what she had created in him. He knew that if he truly did love Estelle, he desperately needed two things in this moment: absolutely sincerity and total self-control, although the latter was easier, for she was clearly out of her mind. After he had gained these things, and his heart was bursting, he said only three more words, "I love you."

Estelle slowly turned and walked away from him. Her first three steps were normal, but then she began to falter. After two more steps, almost at an infant's wobble, her knees buckled and she slumped to the ground and began to cry.

"I have betrayed us. I have destroyed the only beautiful memory of my life," she sobbed.

He now saw before him Estelle. He was so relieved his hands were shaking. He sat down as well. "Thank God. I was so worried, Estelle. I thought you were lost forever."

She looked at him with total lack of comprehension.

"Estelle, the light of God shrines through you. Everyone has seen it, everyone knows it. It befuddles me that you cannot sense how others have felt about you. You are so incredibly beautiful in so many ways."

She nearly snarled. Whatever he just said had not sat well.

He quickly spoke, "You have always been my greatest temptation. My only temptation, really. I love you. I love you poorly, for my love for you should only be that of a priest and father, and I have betrayed you with a more complicated love. But I tell you this, Estelle. My love for you is so abundant that I would never dream of hurting you with it. I think I would rather die. There is nothing on earth more precious to me than you." To his surprise, he felt tears well up in his eyes.

Estelle saw him tear and closed her eyes. "I am so sorry, Father. If you only knew how I feel about you as well."

"I am happy you came to me."

"In order for our mutual humiliation to be complete? So that we could never look at each other again without feeling ashamed?"

"No, because I know you, who you really are. And I realize how much pain you must now be feeling. In your words, I heard only 'help me.' And I am glad I could. Regardless of my own failings, I see you first as God sees you. Please do not be ashamed. I think perhaps this honesty between us is long overdue. I am blessed to help you."

"Can I ever see you again without dying of shame?"

"I always thought the Parable of the Prodigal Son was amazing and beautiful. A fellow priest told me something that elevated it in my mind even further. He said that all people are the prodigal son, a thousand times a day. A thousand times a day we betray our Lord, and a thousand times a day he celebrates our return. Estelle, I celebrate your return, as the Lord celebrates when I return, a thousand times each day."

She did not reply.

"What happened, Estelle?"

"I cannot dream of speaking of it. It threatens my life and sanity when I bring memories to my conscious mind. Every aspect of my existence is now thrown into dangerous waters. I don't know what to say. The confusion of my soul is total."

"If you are falling in darkness, you cannot help but scream – but it must be only one word, which is the name of the Lord."

"My brother told me that the first thing one should do when drowning is calm yourself and think clearly upon your immediate salvation. How can solutions be so simple and yet so impossible at the same time? How does one calm when drowning?"

"Estelle, you need to come home."

"Home is Nantes."

"It is better here."

"Thoroughly, Father. This land is so abundantly blessed in so many ways. If I could but fit here in some way, I would never leave. But I have always been a filly in a pigpen in Anjou. I know this is not where I belong. However wonderful it is here, it is not my home. I do not have a home. I have never had a home, really. But Nantes is as close as it has ever felt."

"Cities always seem warmer to strangers, but it is deceiving, for there is only one temperature for all and forever, and it is only lukewarm."

"Perhaps. Do you know where my father is?"

"The rumor is he was called away on urgent business across the Loire. It seems troubles have broken out throughout the country, although not here."

"No. Nothing bad ever happens here. I wish I was stupid and beautiful and patient, and some farmer's son wanted to be my husband and I could live here, happy and free, forever."

"You do not give yourself enough credit, Estelle," said Father Jonathan with a gentle smile.

Estelle smiled back, then was downcast. "I will never forgive myself for this moment. You are a beautiful man, Father. And you have always been kind to me."

"God forgives. To not believe in forgiveness is to not believe in the power of God."

"Yes, Father."

The answer was perfunctory. Although Estelle was pacified, Jonathan intuited that nothing had truly changed or healed inside of her. "No, I'm afraid that is not good enough," he said gently.

"What do you wish of me?"

"I wish you to say 'I know I am forgiven' three times."

"You are as strange as the nuns of Saint-Clément."

"Do so now, please."

She did.

"I know that I am forgiven
I know that I am forgiven
I know that I am forgiven."

"It is done." Father Jonathan smiled. "Do you feel better?"

"I feel terrible. But I feel more of myself." Estelle suddenly exhaled and brought her hands to her mouth. "I had a knife crafted for murder. I was going to kill someone, Father."

"Are you sure you will not stay?"

"I am sure."

"How will I know you are all right?"

"You are now fairly worried about me, aren't you?"

"Yes."

"I will write. Often. Every day."

"And I will write you."

"You are properly a great man, Father."

"I have fooled them all."

They both smiled, then almost on cue, looked downward and downcast.

Father Jonathan spoke again, "You are in my life for a reason, I am convinced of that. God has brought us together for a specific purpose. We are in God's plan somehow. Together."

"For this moment."

"No, something of greatness."

"There is nothing great in me."

"I think you are destined for sainthood."

She looked at him with utter contempt, and he was scared again, "Sainthood?"

He could only nod.

"Saints lead lives of suffering and die horribly, all the while thanking God. Is this what you wish for me?"

Such pain behind her words. This grieves me beyond measure.

"If you could but see the joy of paradise, you would understand," he offered. It sounded so hollow – but it was true. It was true! Why did his words fail him now?

"It is too hard. It asks too much of the living who suffer. To see what cannot be seen."

Perhaps now she is ready. I must try. She deserves the very best of me. "Everyone suffers, none are exempt. There is only one difference: do you suffer for a purpose, or for no reason at all? Your only recourse is God, Estelle. It is the only recourse any of us have, if what we truly desire is a tranquil soul."

Suddenly, Estelle crawled over to him and kissed him, gently and fervently.

She was so normal, but a moment ago, that Jonathan was completely taken by surprise. There was nothing in her in the seconds before it happened that even hinted at the action. He was so surprised that he was unable to stop her.

As soon as her lips touched his, something strange happened. Jonathan was separated from his body. He felt akin to a pure spirit, in some ethereal womb. His spirit only reacted to hers. He loved her completely, purely, and unselfishly. When the moment passed, he found he was kissing her back.

He pulled away.

Mon dieu, what have I done? What have I done to her?

Jonathan stood.

"Stay," she said.

"No." He cursed himself. He cursed himself that he could no longer call her daughter, could no longer be an example of how things should be. He had betrayed her.

She teared, "Please do not reject me."

"Never. I would never reject you. If I said yes now, I would betray you."

"Come to me, please."

"No." Father Jonathan walked away. It was all he could think of doing in the moment, for better or worse.

So, now, not only do my words mean nothing, not only do I not represent God, but in embracing her as I have done, I must now reject her as a man rejects a woman, not just as her friend and her priest. What have I done? What have I done, dear God?

He could hear Estelle sobbing with abandon, as if she had nothing left in the world. "I will become a prostitute," she said. He heard the hopelessness in her voice. He shut his eyes and kept walking.

"At least someone will touch me."

He kept walking.
She did not stop crying; her sobs only faded with distance.

Lake Waban, Massachusetts
in Winter

Chapter Forty-Three

1833

Jake

As Jake and Harris walked home, Jake realized he had never been happier. For a moment, he wished this very second could last forever. Just as quickly he realized he actually did not, for one day he would marry Grace, in another he would take his own son ice fishing. In another, he would attend Harris's wedding. There was a series of beautiful events stretching into the future, surrounded by his family and community. All was right, all was as it should be. Time was free to pass. Time only increased wonder and joy when all was right in the world. Future tragedy could be born, it was a cheap price to pay for all of the wondrous magic of passing time.

They jumped hard on the bridge over the river, as was their custom. It made an incredible racket, which delighted Harris to no end.

Sophia was waiting for them. Two carriages, both coaches, were parked outside and waited fully-staffed for journey. One was incredibly large and must have been from Boston. The other was much smaller and could have been hired locally. Sophia waved, standing by the smaller one, "Harris, do you want to ride in a coach?"

Harris ran two steps then stopped, "Can Jake come?"

"No, he has to speak with father. We'll be back soon."

Harris turned, downcast, "Bye Jake."

"Bye Harris." Jake smiled but the feeling of impending doom returned threefold. He silently admonished himself. He walked to the house, tipping his hat at the coachmen, "Good morning, gentlemen."

"Good morning, sir," came the accented replies.

They were most definitely from Boston.

Jake entered the house and secured his boots and Winter clothing in the mudroom. By the time he put on his shoes to enter the house he felt much better.

In the main room sat his father and Monsieur Tyran.

The sight was nightmarish incongruity, akin to walking into a house where livestock and people had changed places to the point of wardrobe and speech. Jake's knees crumbled under him, only a hand against the wall prevented his fall. He was about to pass out.

He smelled something wondrous. Jake, with his extraordinary hyperosmia, made petitgrain, cardamom, lemon, orange and fir. Then, just under, was a hint of jasmine, rosemary, rose, and lily-of-the-valley; all placed on a base of vetiver, musk, oakmoss, and rosewood.

It was Monsieur Tyran's scent, of course. His colognes were custom-made and unparalleled, a unique treat for the senses.

Tyran smiled up at him, but his grin never carried goodwill or mirth. His father sat back in his Chippendale, resting his chin on a hand and looking out, as if Jake was not there at all.

Tyran.

The sharp-dressed, sharp-tongued, diamond-sporting, divinely-smelling, foul, ugly, middle-aged, commanding, in-control, madman-killer of a *Touton Macoute* had suddenly appeared in his family's parlor, like an evil anti-Saint-Nicholas dressed in a black, virgin Vermont Merino, Parisian-tailored suit.

Jake felt a wave of repulsion, as if he had seen a cockroach. "What are you doing here?"

"*Bonjour*, Monsieur Loring."

Jake was consumed with anger. "Speak English, sir!"

"I have found to my delight that *ton père parle*, as was stated at your trial. All three of us speak fluent French, so why then should we not?"

"What are you doing here?"

"I have come to fetch my dog," he said pleasantly.

Jake spoke through clenched teeth, "I will run you through and bury your body in a field."

Jake was surprised to see Tyran's face fall into an expression of loss and sadness – utterly uncharacteristic, as much as if he had waved his arms and flew. "No," he said softly.

"No?" Jake yelled.

"Please do not kill me," he said evenly, as if possessed by a more rational man.

Jake snarled, "Do not play with me, Monsieur."

"I know you have heard but little from my mouth that was not commanding and confident. I assure you, however, that I am not playing with you. I am, in actuality, begging you not to kill me, or even to entertain the thought – at least for now."

"Coward!" Jake spat.

"No, not exactly. I do not fear death. *No* – that is not true. I fear dying before I complete my one task remaining in life – which is helping you find the Heirlooms."

Helping me? I thought I was helping you!

He shook his head, "No, I do not wish to die before they are found. And, above all, I cannot die at your hands while we are looking for them. Once they are found, you may do with me as you please." He smiled again, "Is a short stay of execution so much to ask, Monsieur?"

Something just occurred to Jake. "You know where they are, don't you?"

Tyran thought for a moment, then spoke, "Unfortunately, I think there is a good chance we will not find them."

He wasn't lying.

Easton finally spoke, "Please sit, Jake. I'm afraid that you must listen to this man."

"Has anything he said contradicted what I have told you?"

"No. Nothing at all. Please, Jake."

Jake sat. He felt nauseated.

Tyran stood and looked around. "Monsieur Loring *père*, do you have anything substantial besides corn whiskey, cider, or rum?"

"No, Monsieur," answered Easton.

"*Mon dieu!* Monsieur Loring *fils*, my apologies," he said, as he handed Jake a glass. Jake quickly swallowed it. It was rum.

In the back of his mind, he realized the choice might mean something.

"Don't insult my father," Jake said between clenched teeth.

Tyran sat back down. "Feeling better?" he asked.

Jake did not answer.

Tyran shrugged. "I left Nantes before you."

Jake did not reply.

"I did not say where I was going. I will tell you now. I went to the new United States capitol, Washington, in the District of Columbia - with French coin, which bought American lawyers. The Kingdom of France has attempted to seal the rift with the United States caused by the revolutionaries, the rift only partially healed by Napoleon. France has made progress and my task was not so onerous as it could have been."

"Washington, you say?"

"Yes, Washington."

"Why?"

"Because I knew that you would flee, Monsieur Loring. I knew that you would attempt to come home, believing you were then safe from me."

Tyran had anticipated his final destination while Jake was still in Nantes. Perhaps before that. But it didn't matter. This was Massachusetts. Jake had nothing to fear.

His confidence returned. "Am I not?"

"No. You are very much in my clutches, Monsieur Loring."

"How on earth can that be? I am no longer in France. You have no power over me in Wellesley and no ability to force me to leave my home."

"Are you familiar with the word *extradition*?"

"It is a legal term. To extradite is to remand a criminal from one nation to another to face charges. It does not relate to me in the slightest."

"The concept is ancient. Hittites and Egyptians had formal extradition treaties. In the modern era, France has such treaties with several neighboring European states. No one has extradition treaties with the United States, for if a criminal left for America, well… good riddance."

Tyran took a sheaf of papers from his jacket. He peeled off the first and tossed it to the coffee table. "This is a formal American acknowledgment that you could have already been executed for your crimes in France but were not, having instead been given the far-lesser sentence of finding the Crimson Heirlooms." Another paper descended, missing the table and falling to the floor. "That is a document making this decision legal in America, giving me five years of your life in return for you receiving the rest of it." Another paper lazily floated to the table, landing on the edge. "This is a federal writ authorizing your recapture and extradition." Another flitted to the table. "This is a writ from the Commonwealth of Massachusetts authorizing your recapture and extradition."

Jake leaned down and grabbed them.

"They are all copies, Monsieur. Tear them, burn them. It will not matter."

Jake frantically perused them. It could not be.

But it was.

Easton spoke, "You will have to serve the rest of your sentence, Jake."

"I would rather die."

Tyran smiled, "Oh, ye of little faith."

Jake's eyes snapped up and fixed on Tyran.

Tyran quoted himself from long ago, only now with a smile, "Do I appear casual in my pursuit, Monsieur? Do I seem poorly-funded?"

Jake did not reply.

"There are four good constables in the coach outside. If you thwart them, well, one supposes the ire of the Commonwealth would then be drawn in its entirety."

"I must say good-bye to someone."

"*Ta gueule*!"

"I beg you."

Tyran stood, "Enough!"

"You made a request of me, Monsieur. I only ask for the same respect in return."

"Listen closely, *tête carrée*," Tyran said in a hissed venom, "I required an additional ninety seconds of time in order to explain that you are just as beholden to me here as you were in France. If you were to lay a hand on me here, you would now hang as assuredly as your head would leave your shoulders in France.

For I am known to be here, and I would be missed and searched for. Do you understand?"

This viper was then the old Monsieur Tyran, and Jake was ashamed to find himself petrified.

Easton spoke, "Go now, Jake. I will speak to Grace. I will tell everyone who needs to know."

"Tell her I love her. Tell her to wait for me."

Easton could only nod.

Tyran grabbed Jake by the collar and, with ease, pulled him out of his chair and pushed him toward the mud room. "Don't bother getting your coat. Everything you left on the *Temps Nouveaux* is on a ship waiting in Boston harbor."

In shock, Jake put one foot in front of the other. He soon found himself outside, then in the humid cabin of the large coach, staring at four burly constables in uniform. Tyran joined them. Jake burst out crying. He did not care how he appeared. He was inconsolable.

Tyran tapped the roof panel with his cane and they were away.

Tyran spoke casually, "There is actually a way that you could leave this coach. Right now."

"How?"

"Do you still have your necklace?"

Jake pulled his flat, pewter necklace from his shirt.

Tyran stared at it with something approaching fear. He was, once again, the odd man who begged for his life, "Would you give it to me? Destroy it, perhaps? Or hand it to another?"

"Is that how I leave this coach?"

Tyran jerked his head up and down – yes - his eyes wide and transfixed on the cross, as if it were the Cross of Nantes.

But Jake's cross was only a flimsy, flat pewter thing of no account. Its only real value was its stamping: L-L-L-G-10-17-05-4, which now held no value whatsoever. It was also printed with a design, a representation of Elaine of Astolat, dead in her floating bier, the river current taking her to Camelot. It was a mystery, one that Jake was convinced Tyran had already unraveled. As far as Jake knew, the imprinted mystery had no value either, apart from its curiosity.

Tyran spoke in a hoarse whisper, "If you give that away of your own free will, or destroy it, you are free of me. But I beg you not to do it. Please. If ever there was a spark of goodness in your heart, do not do it. Just help me."

Tyran was mad as a rabid dog. That, of course, was no surprise.

Jake wiped his face, then put his little, flat, worthless cross back inside his shirt. "*Vas te faire foutre!*"

Tyran calmed immediately, back to the old silver-tongued viper. His eyes turned hard and they bored into Jake.

"Don't do this again," he said.

Une rue de Paris

Chapter Forty-Four

1789

Four Letters

Dear, Dear Brother Guillaume,

This will be a short missive, for I have no desire to tell you of my pathetic struggles.

I simply need you to trust me. A situation has arisen. I'm afraid that I have somewhat lost control of my destiny and at least one part of my life is in danger. Fortunately, this part is material, a simple possession.

To be clear, if things continue, I will no longer be able to safeguard our family heirloom, which I now know to be the Cross of Nantes.

I have enclosed the necklace, which I wish you to safeguard for now. What I am telling you is no ploy; there are forces arrayed against me. This sounds ridiculous to you, I know, but you have not seen me for quite some time and have no idea how dire and complicated my life has become. I am in danger with this thing and I am in no danger without it. Please understand and keep it safe. If it makes you feel better, simply believe you hold it in safekeeping for me.

I love you, I miss you, I hope that we do not see each other for the foreseeable future, for I do not want you to see me in such a state.

With Love and Adoration,

Estelle

1789

Dear Estelle,

Cave troll!

We both know that necklace is quite valuable. I have received it, but upon reflection I think it was unwise to send via post. We really shouldn't do that again. I received it, but what if I didn't? You are a hippopotamus, Estelle. Really.

Your letter was quite bizarre and uncharacteristic. Do you need help? Can you be slightly more specific about your troubles? Mon dieu, Estelle, I am your twin. If you cannot trust me, who can you trust?

I had forgotten how beautiful that necklace is. It is truly a wonder. I can stare at it for hours. I wear it under my shirt to keep it safe. Anywhere else I think it would be in danger of being stolen.

If I cannot help you, I hope you feel better.

Anyway!

I have the most amazing news. I am in love. I am so impossibly in love. It consumes me, it devours me, it occupies my every moment.

Allow me to explain how this came about.

Since I left the hospital, I have been cultivating my friendship with Talma, which is now possible since I have been pardoned. Dr. Marat is a wonder, although our relationship is a bit strained now because he hates Talma. Everyone in my circle is very Rousseauian, possessed of huge emotion and energy, drive and passion. Sometimes it makes things very difficult indeed.

Talma has thrown himself into salon life, more so than most actors who prefer the company of their own. I have been tagging along, on my very best behavior. Luckily the salons are usually divided along political lines and we really never find ourselves in places where our strong political opinions are unwanted.

Probably the most respected, haute société salon we attend would be that of Louise-Julie Careau on Rue Chantereine in Chaussée d'Antin. You don't know where that is. Shall we say south of Montmartre, north of the Louvre, west and north of the Marais? It's quite nice, two of the three Royal theaters are there. I would not say that Mademoiselle Julie is the most respected of the salonnières, that honor would probably go to Madame Geoffrin, Mademoiselle de Lespinasse, and Madame Necker. That being said, I have as much chance of being invited to their salons as I do of sprouting wings and flying, so I content myself with more Rousseauian, less aristocratic gatherings.

Mademoiselle Julie - what an interesting lady! She is beautiful, with a wide face and big eyes – perhaps too thin. She was abandoned when she was quite young and grew up on the streets. One of the king's advisors rescued her and raised her as his own. She was part of the Opera's ballet corps and was quite skilled. Using this entrée, she became a professional mistress to powerful men. Her story does not end there though - no, indeed! She began speculating in real estate and soon made a fortune. She owns the home she lives in and welcomes all devotees of the arts and sciences, along with the rich and powerful who desire to be in their company. Lavoisier comes, it is only a matter of time before he finds out I am the one who slaughtered him in effigy at the Danseurs. My mortal enemy Chénier attends as well, the dark and handsome bitte. It would take me all day to list the luminaries at these gatherings. Mademoiselle Julie is quite possibly the most charming and witty person I have ever run across. I am stunned that her history did not leave her with more scars. Knowing her, you would never suspect her past.

I suppose she will strike you as being immoral. It's strange. Amongst the rich and powerful, so many compromises are made for money and position that all is overlooked as long as appearances are kept. Not a particularly moral age we live in. At least it's interesting.

You cannot believe the conversation at these gatherings. Everyone is a wit - educated and intelligent. The level of discussion is such that letters are sent from attendees to people around the city, indeed the country and the world, spreading our words as if we are ancient philosophers on Mars Hill, albeit infused with scientists, painters, actors, engineers, and scions of business and government. I will but use a real incident as example. One of the salons in Paris – Madame Necker's? – is renowned for its cuisine. The chef de cuisine is very well known as well – my God what is his name? You will come to Paris and talk of the chef de cuisine at Madame Necker's gatherings and people will look at you cross-eyed because you have all the names wrong. Whatever, names are beside the point. The chef de cuisine was taken to another gathering and ate a dish. He pulled it apart with his fork, tasted every part of it, then proceeded to tell listeners precisely how it was cooked and every ingredient – and he was exactly right! He told the reasons why the specific ingredients worked together and the theme of the dish – what it was trying to accomplish, as if it were a theatrical play. It ends up that food has been an art and object of serious study for more than a hundred years, at least since the publication of Le Cuisinier François. This particular chef de cuisine then was blindfolded and took sips of different wines, thereafter telling the gathering exactly where the vines were grown and in what year. It was said he was seldom wrong and even when he was, his guess was very close to the real answer. Imagine, sister! I tell you this because everything is the same way. We are tearing apart everything with intellectual forks, seeking knowledge and method of every human endeavor. It is not enough to live a life without contemplation. Everything is taken apart, examined and rebuilt, reengineered and discussed, from art to politics to religion to philosophy. You simply can't understand unless you'd been here. I have found the secret headwaters of the Enlightenment.

Everyone says the société of Versailles, although composed of luminaries and aristocrats, has devolved under the new King. He is simply too boring and concerned with respectability. It is said he has the personality of an engineer. From the engineers I have met, this does not bode well.

But I digress!

I am not in love with Mademoiselle Julie. She is too clever, too steely, too sane and calculated. Talma might be. In fact, I think he is. I am in love with a woman whose name I do not know, for I have yet to tell anyone of my feelings and we have yet to be introduced.

Yes, dear sister, it is my pleasure to be afflicted with a coup de foudre, love at first sight! It is the single most sublime thing to have ever happened to me!

You will think me mad but I tell you, when I first saw this woman, I was indeed struck by lightning. I had the most profound experience. It was as if all of my ancestors were standing with me, and in that moment, I could see and feel them. All of them stood with their hands on my shoulder whispering, "She's the one! She's the one!" Do you think me mad? Perhaps I am. Perhaps I have always been mad, and my glorious madness has waited for this wondrous moment to come out and envelope me with rapture!

But let me tell you about this! She came to the salon with a man, I believe them both to be haute bourgeoise, but I tell you no princess has ever had the grace and manner of this woman. She is probably married to the man with whom she came, but I do not care. She was never meant to be with him, but with myself only. The very stars in the sky aligned to bring her to me. I know you think I am foolish, being in love with a woman I have never spoken with who might be taken, but I know her, Estelle. I know everything about her. The very moment I saw her, I knew everything about her as if I had spent my life with her. I know her expressions, her mannerisms, her innermost thoughts.

She is, without exaggeration, the most beautiful woman I have ever seen. All I think and dream about is her. I remember every detail of her, even though I saw my future love but short moments.

The problem is, I am unworthy of her. I am not who I once was. Talking to her would be a shepherd asking for the hand of Aphrodite. I must regain my standing, regain my fame and my salary and truly be someone important once again. Perhaps I need even be more than I was in order for this woman to be mine, as she was destined to be.

I only hope that Talma does not bore of me, so that I can attend salons and meet my angel once again. I fear that such a sentiment is a reality. Already, Talma spends more time with Chénier than myself. It is hard to hold his interest. Being only ashes of what I once was, this affects me more than it should. Perhaps I am trying too hard.

The woman! How can I now digress, speaking of her as I was? I will find out who she is, where she goes, who she knows. At the same time, I will become a god of Paris theater and politics, heaping honor on myself as a Horatii of the muses. When the time is right, I will bring about our meeting, with everything I am and everything I learn being for only one purpose, which is to shine at that very meeting to win her. I long to tell her I love her, for I do. The very moment I set eyes upon her, I loved her. My life is worth nothing except for the pursuit of her.

Please do not call me mad.

Miss you.

Guillaume.

Dear Monsieur Traversier,

Please accept my humble apology for taking so long to write!

What an honor, what a wonderful gift, to be a guest of yours in your wondrous abode. Meilleur! Meilleur indeed! Your staff, my room, Madame's hospitality! I felt like a king, yet humbled by the honor I was shown. I was equally humbled to become part of a certain organization that must remain unwritten in this missive, and I have already contacted the brothers in Paris, to whom you have already graciously written, to accept me as one of their own.

For France, for the Nation, and for progress!

I wish to talk to you of another matter as well, although your hospitality was such that it deserves a letter entire to do it justice. I must speak to you of a young lady named Mademoiselle Estelle Guerrier.

I must ask you to be protective of her in my absence. I was so impressed with the spirit of this girl. She is humble, faithful, kind, gracious and good. She does somewhat lack refinement, but I found her to be so utterly charming that to turn her away from conversation and toward learning the piano forte seemed a disservice to myself.

She inspired me, Monsieur, every bit as much as the light in that bedroom. The bedroom! Why is it there, I wonder? I have never heard of a bedroom so close to the main entry of a great hall. Was it once a guard room, I wonder? Deep in the age of religious war or banditry, a great room for quartered guards to respond to the booming sound of a ram against the main door! That would be an impressive painting, Monsieur! If ever you wish to commission it, my only condition would be that we find a true event that happened in the past on which to base our panorama. But I digress. The light puts Vermeer to shame - and his pathetic bedroom he painted on little more than postage stamps - and the angelic daughter, whose energy must be harvested to imbue the canvass with spirit and character; to compete with the formidable Vigée Le Brun, were both present to catapult the ensuing work into platonic perfection. Let us not have a royal monopoly on emanating character, whether Baroque or Neoclassical! Let us challenge the royalists and the artists they patron! Our art defines our virtue!

Ah, but it cannot be! This masterpiece I have finished cannot be seen, not yet. But it is finished. Should it languor in my studio, wrapped in brown paper and twine? I do not know. Perhaps I should destroy it. I do not know. In any case, if I did sell it, I would only do so to a party of discretion, who could appreciate it, and afford the immense costs of such a work. It would surely be worth at least five-thousand livres. We shall see.

I am calling this work The Mystery of Nantes. I can think of no other title, given the fact that Estelle is a humble colonial of the petite bourgeoise - and she wears the Cross of Nantes upon her neck. The Cross beguiled me. I would write more about it, except the light and girl were more of a wonder – to a humble painter at least. If the light and subject were of lesser quality, the cross would have had my full attention – of that I have no doubt!

Thank you again, my friend and comrade.

Forever in your debt,

David

1789

Monsieur David,

I'm afraid I must insist on buying the painting.

When you read this letter, L'Oublié will be standing before you. He has six-thousand livres in gold Louis that he will presently deliver into your possession. Please, in turn, provide him with "The Mystery of Nantes," and instruct him in its preservation for the return journey.

Please know you are most welcome, brother – at any time, under any circumstance, announced or not.

Your Humble Admirer,

Xavier

To Father Jonathan Courgeon
Abbey of Saint-Florent-le-Vieil
Anjou, le France

From the Office of the Keeper of Seals
Versailles, Royal Court of France

Transcribed by V.M. Poyet, Clerk of the Office of Jérôme Champion de Cicé, Keeper of Seals

OFFICIAL MISSIVE

Father Courgeon,

Unforeseen circumstances have greatly delayed the delivery of this summons. The servants of the Throne of France apologize and take full responsibility for any inconvenience this will cause.

Given the order from King Louis XVI, the Chancellor of France, René Nicolas de Maupeou, has been tasked to gather the Estates-General of France, to assemble at Versailles, Palace of the King, on May 5, 1789.

You have been elected to represent the First Estate for the Seneschal of Angers, Generality of Tours.

By order of the King, you will report to Versailles and the Estates-General as soon as possible. We understand that your tardiness is entirely the fault of this office and your peers will be informed of such.

Keeper of the Seals Jérôme Champion de Cicé

To Be Continued

Les États-Généraux, 1789

Appendix:

Pronunciation and Definition Guide

For the sake of easing the process of alphabetical search, *ce*, *le*, *la*, *d'* and *de* will be ignored, except for quoted passages, or if part of a title. All words are French unless otherwise noted. This appendix will include entries from all previous books.

French *zh* is meant to be the "z" sound in "azure," but is actually even more pronounced and exotic. *R* is a mild trill, akin to Spanish but to a politer degree.

There are three very distinct Irish dialects. With apologies to the south, all Irish herein is in the Ulster dialect for obvious reasons. Unfortunately, Irish spelling does a drunk bee twirl through the ages, and not all words are in Modern Gaeilge.

"Historical Figure" denotes a character in the book who actually lived. This does not include historical figures only mentioned in passing. I fear I have missed labeling some of them.

A generous thank you to Microsoft Word. Your helpful correction of punctuation from my typed English to the entirely different French was always helpful. Many writers frequently switch global grammar and punctuation rules from line to line in the same document, and have mourned the lack of programs that did not automatically perform such things without asking. Huzzah!

***

A Coruña – (ah CORE-OON-ya) Spanish.
abbé – (ah-BEY) "abbot," the second lowest rank of priest in France.
Abruti – (AH-broo-tee) "fool."
absagen – (AHB-sahgen) German, "cancel."
Académie Royale de Danse – (AH-CAH-day-mie ROY-ahl duh dahnz)
Académie Royale de Musique – (AH-CAH-day-mie ROY-ahl doo MOO-zeek)
actions au porteur – (AK-zion OH POR-tair) Royal France was behind on the paper money train. Actions au porteur was as close as it came. They were more like bearer bonds or travelers' checks.
Adela – (AH-del-lah)
Adèle – (AH-del)
Adelgunde – (AH-DEL-gun-DEH) German, fantastical.

adieu – (AHD-dyu) “goodbye,” literally “with God.”

Affranchis Commandeur – (AH-fronchee COM-mon-dare) “freed commander.”

Agesilaus c. 444 – c. 360 BC (ah-JESSE-lay-os) Greek. He was a great king of Sparta, some would say the ideal king, and a brave and competent warrior. Ironically, he was lame from birth, and the Spartans were deeply prejudiced against the handicapped - even after his reign.

Agwé – (ahg-WAY) Haitian Creole.

aides – (AY-duh) “succor,” “assistance,” “help.”

Alban – (AL-ahbahn) Irish, “Scots”

Albanach – (ah-la-bah-nah) Irish, “Scottish.”

Allou, Gilles – (AHL-loo, Zheel) Historical figure.

Almo – (AHL-MO)

Ambigu-Comique – (AHM-bee-goo COHM-eek)

Amble – (AHM-bleh)

Anemoi – (AHN-NEM-moy) Greek.

Angers – (OHN-zher)

Anjou – (OHN-zhoo)

ansagen – (on-ZAW-gen) German, “declare.”

Aquinas, Thomas – (ah-KWAI-nas or ah-KEY-nahs) but he was actually Tommaso d'Aquino (toh-MAH-so dah-KEY-no), 1225 – 1274, an Italian Dominican friar, priest, and juror. He was an immensely influential philosopher, theologian, and jurist in the tradition of scholasticism. His impact, in the Catholic church at least, is still omnipresent. If one wished to pursue a moral path in any pursuit, Aquinas codified a route. It is odd to think modern man is philosophically primitive compared to man in 1274, but I assure you, this is indeed the case. Our downward slide started in the Renaissance. Modern man is intellectually savage and primitive in many key respects - albeit relaxed, entertained and well-fed.

arachide – (ARA-sheed) “peanuts.”

Arachne – (AH-ROCK-NAY) Greek. In a strange way, this character fits with the themes of the story. Don’t know who she is? Lose a point, turn off one screen.

Araguani – (AHR-ah-GWAH-nee) Spanish or Portuguese. A highly-sought-after, Venezuelan cocoa bean.

Arakawa – (AH-RAH-KAH-wa) Arakawa, uhm…

arrêt – (AH-ray) “stop”.

Aristobelus – (AH-ris-to-BEL-us) German, fantastical.

Aristobolus – (AH-ris-to-BOH -lus) German, fantastical.

Arlequin – (AHRL-leh-cahn)

Arnauld – (AHR-no)

Arouet, Daumard and François-Marie (AH-rooay, DOO-mar, fran-swah mah-ree) François-Marie Arouet was Voltaire’s real name. Daumard was the maiden name of Voltaire’s mother. These are very Republican aliases.

Arquebus – we say AR-kwib-is, most Europeans say AR-kay-boos. This is a catch-all term for a heavy, one-man firearm mounted on a forked stick, utilizing some kind of pre-flintlock firing mechanism. They were not regular in parts or caliber, and were created by a variety of craftsmen - or sometimes even the shooters themselves.

arrondissements – (AHR-on-deese-mon) "districts."

Arthaud, Éric – (AHR-too, AIR-eek)

D'Artois, Comte –(COM DAHR-twah)

Artus, Charles-Melchior, Marquis de Bonchamps – please see "Bonchamps."

aspirans – (as-PEE-ran) "midshipmen"

Astley's Anglais – (AST-lees ON-glay)

Athena – (AH-THEEN-ah) This entry is a test of the Western Civilization Educational System. It is only a test.

Auberge de Thabor-Paris, 43 Rue de Paris, Quartier Thabor - Saint-Hélier, Rennes – (OW-bearzh doo TAH-bore PAH-ree CARE-on-twa ROO doo PAH-ree KAHR-tee TAH-boar SANTEE-yee REN)

d'Aubeterre – (DOOB-tear)

Aubrianne – (OO-bree-ahn)

Audibet – (OO-dee-bay)

Au Duc – (OO-dook)

d'Auray, Marquis – (MAR-key DOO-ray)

Aurélien – (AH-rel-yah)

Aurelius, Marcus – (MAHRK-oos AHW-RAY-lee-oos) Latin. Last of the Five Good Emperors, last emperor of the Pax Romana. A stoic, as well as a philosopher-king and warrior-poet. Good example for people who want to be hellified studs.

Austerlitz – (OUSE-ter-litz) German, a small town currently in the Czech Republic, and site of one of the greatest battles of all time – Napoleon's crushing, brilliant victory over the Austrians, assorted Germans and Russians at the battle of the same name in 1805.

Autolycus- (AU-TUL-ih-cus) Greek. In Greek mythology, the son of Hermes and the grandfather of Odysseus.

Avenir, Marc Marie-Florent – (AF-neer, MAH-rkh MAH-ree FLU-rahw)

avocat – (AV-oh-cah) "lawyer."

baise, baisée – (BEHS) (BEHS-ay) f---king, f—ked.

baise la taxe – (BEES la tax) "F—k the tax."

barbeque – (BAR-er-beck) Betcha didn't know THIS was Haitian. Taken to America by French colonials fleeing the Haitian revolution.

Barnave, Antoine – (BAR-nev, ON-twon) Historical figure.

Barrière d'Enfer – (bah-REE-air DON-fair) "Hellsgate."

Barès, Basile – (BAHR-es BAS-eel)

bâtard, ce – (SOO bah-tar) "this bastard."

Béarla – (BYUR-lah) Irish, "English."

Beau-Brave – (BOO brahv) "Beautiful Brave One."

Beauchamp – (BOO-shom)
Beaujolais – (BOO-zhou-lay)
Beaumarchais – (BOO-marsh-ay)
Beaunoir – (BOO-nwah)
Beccaria – (BEY-cah-REE-ah) Italian.
Bedos, Thierry Alain – (BED-ohs, cherry AL-ahn)
Benyovszky, Comte de – (BEN-yov-skee, COMPT duh)
Bergères – (BEAR-zhair) – An enclosed, completely upholstered French armchair.
Berlière, Jacques – (BEAR-lee-air, ZHACK)
Bernard – (BEHR-nar)
Bernier – (BEAR-nee-ay)
beurre aux algues – (BEHR-roos-alg-eh) "Seaweed butter."
Bhiorog Ó Baoighill – (BEA-wok OH-BOY-ill) Irish.
Bichon Frisé – (BEE-shon FREE-say)
bien entendu. – (BYON ON-ten-doo) "Of course."
Bièvre – (BEE-ehv-rh) Even phonetic English just doesn't do this one justice.
bitte – (BEET) "Penis."
blan - (BLEN) Haitian Creole.
Blin, Francois-Pierre – (BLAH, FRAN-swa PEE-air) Historical figure.
Bò – (BOH) West African, perhaps Fon.
Boissière-sur-Èvre – (BWA-sair-sur-EHV)
Bò madichon – (BOH MAD-ee-shon)
Bonchamps, Charles-Melchior Artus, Marquis de – (BOHN-shamp, SHARL-MEL-key-or AHR-tus, MAR-key duh) Historical figure. One of the greatest unsung heroes of France. George Washington meets Dietrich Bonhoeffer. He was truly a model for the ages, in every way.
bon fermier – (BOON FER-me-ay) "Good farmer."
Bonjou. ki jan ou ye, mesye? – (BOO-zhou kee-ZHON oo-YAY MEZ-yay) Haitian Creole. "Good day. How are you, sir?"
bonjour – (BON-zhoor) "good day."
Bon sang ne saurait mentir – (bohn sohn na-SUR-ray MON-tier) "Good blood cannot lie."
bonsoir – (BON-swah) "good evening."
Bordeaux – (BOAR-doo)
bordel – (BOAR-del) "whorehouse."
bordel de merde – (BOR-del doo MER-deh) "whorehouse of crap." A big mess.
Borgia – (BOAR-hee-ah) Spanish.
bossale – (BOO-sal) Spanish or Portuguese. A bossale is a person who is ignorant of any European tongue. Used throughout the Americas.
Botz-en-Mauges – (BOOTS-uhn-moozh)
Boucan-Carré – (BOO-con CAH-ray)
Boucanier – (BOO-can-yay)
bouche – (BOOSH) "mouth."

Bouchon – (BOO-shawn)

Boufflers, Stanislas de – (BOO-flay, STAN-is-slaws dey) Historical figure.

bougre – (BOOG-r) "buggerer."

bougre de vérolée – (BOO-grah duh VEY-roh-LAY) "sodomizer of the syphilitic."

Boulevard du Crime – (BULL-vard du CREAM) "Boulevard of Crime," actually Boulevard du Temple, but called such because of all the theaters on the street and their salacious dramas.

Bourbon-Penthièvre, Louise Marie Adélaïde de – (doo BUHR-bon-PAR-tiev, LOO-ease-MARIA-de-laid)

Bourdaloue – (BUHR-dah-loo) a woman's chamber pot.

bourgeois – (BOOR-zhwa) Spelling is different based on whether its for a woman and men, groups of women and men, mixed groups. Thank the might of the Roman legion.

Bouteiller, Guillaume – (BOO-tay-yay, GHEE-yohm)

Bouvillon – (BOO-vee-yohn) Jérémie D'Uts (ZHER-eh-mee DOOT), Sitis (SIT-tees), Jemima (ZHEM-mima), Ketsia (KET-zia) and Kéren (CAIR-ren)

Boyer, Jean-Pierre – (BOO-yay ZHON PYAIR) Historical figure.

Boyve, Abraham – (BOY-vee, AY-bra-HAM) Europeanized Hebrew.

De Braban, Destival – (DO BRA-bon DES-tee-val) Historical figure.

Brelan – (BRU-lon) – Resembles poker.

Bressuire – (BRES-soo-eer)

Brevet – (BREV-ae)

Brienne, Cardinal Étienne Charles de Loménie de – (BREE-en, CAR-dee-nahl ET-tee-en SHARL duh LOH-men-ee duh) Historical figure.

brocóg – (BRAH-COG) Irish, "smudgy-faced girl."

Le Brun, Élisabeth Vigée – (LAY BRON AY-lees-ah-bet VEE-zhay) Historical figure.

Brutus, Lucius Iunius – (BROO-toos LOO-choos EE-OON-yoos) Latin. Love him or hate him, this dude was tough.

Bue-Bue – (BOO-BOO)

Cachemarée, Aleaume – (CASH-ew-MAW-RAY AH-loom)

ça ira – (SAY-rah) "it'll be fine."

café – (KAHF-fay) "coffee." A drink made from the sacred bean.

Café Procope – (CAF-ay PRO-cup) Building still there, mojo long gone. Sometimes called Le Procope.

Cahiers de Doléances – (CAH-yay doo DOLE-ee-ahntz)

Caïn le Laboureur – (KAH-ahn le LAH-boo-rare) Cain the Farmer, from the Bible. He didn't have much luck with his offerings either.

Caisteal Dhuni – (CAIS-til DOO-nie) Scottish, "Castle Dhuni", the battle cry of the Frasier clan.

Calais – (KEL-lay)

Cale, Jacques Bonhomme – (CAL, ZHACK BON-uhm)

Calonne – (CAL-uhn)

Camembert – (CAH-mohm-BARE) A cheese from Normandy.

Candes – (COND)

Candide – (CON-deed) My dad made me read this when I was twelve.

Cap Français – (CAP FRON-say)

Cap-Haïtien – (CAP HEY-ee-si-ohn)

Capitaine – (CAP-ee-tan)

cardo – (CARR-do) Latin. Has several meanings, in this context, "an important hinge point."

Careau, Louise-Julie – (CAR-oh LOO-eese ZHOU-lee) Historical figure.

Carême, Marie-Antoine – (CAH-rem, MAH-ree-ON-twon)

Caribe – (CAH-ree-bay)

Carrara – (CAH-rar-RAH) Italian.

Cathédrale Saint-Pierre-et-Saint-Paul – (CAT-eh-drahl SAN-PEE-aire-ee-SAN-pohl)

Cavalla – (CA-vuh-lah) Portuguese. A river that meanders through Côte d'Ivoire, Guinea and Liberia. Also called the Youbou and the Diougou.

céalmhaine – (KAYL-woon) Irish, a classification of "oracle" "augury," or "omen." There are not enough words regarding magic and the supernatural in English to properly translate this. It is an omen, but one that does not deal with death or battle.

Centre-Ville – (SON-tra-VEEL) "downtown."

Cerf – (SER) "hart."

Chaîne des Matheux – (SHANE doo MAT-oo)

Chambarde, Pierre de la Ville de – (SHAM-bard, PEE-air-duh-leh-veel-duh) Historical figure.

chamois – (SHAM-wah)

Champ-Élevé (SHAWM-EL-vey) "High Fields."

Chantilly – (SHON-tee-ee)

chapeau rond - (SHAP-oo ron)

de la Chapelle – (DOO-la SHAP-el)

Chapelle-Saint-Florent - (SHAW-pell-SAN-FLOR-on)

Charentais – (SHAW-ron-TAY)

Charlemagne – (SHARL-lo-MAN-yeh) The greatest king of all time, ever. Charlemagne plus King David = the model for King Arthur.

Charles – (SHAR-leh)

Charleville - (SHAR-le-veel) A town with an important armory for the manufacture of muskets which were called by the same name. There was a bewildering variety of Charleville models and upgrades. The Charleville was the official arm of the French infantry from 1717 to 1840.

Charton – (SHART-on)

Chartres – (SHART)

Chasseurs-Volontaires de Saint-Domingue – (SHASH-air-VO-LOON-taire duh SAN-DOM-ang) "Volunteer Light Infantry." This unit existed historically and performed well.

De Chastenay, Comte – (DOO SHASS-ten-ay, COMBT)

Château de la Baronnière – (SHA-toh duh la BAR-roh-NEY-air) Historical place.

Château de Vizille – (SHA-to doo VEE-zile)

Château des Ducs de Bretagne – (SHA-toh de DOO du BRE-tain) "Castle of the Dukes of Brittany." Five stars from Hunter. Go there.

Château Meilleur – (SHA-toh ME-yair) "Best Manor"

châteaux – (SHA-toh) "castles" "manors"

chatte – (SHAT) "twat."

chattes pourries – (SHAT POO-ree) "rotten twats."

Chaussée d'Antin – (SHASH-ay DON-TON)

De Chauvirey, Maurice Roland – (doo SHOW-ver-eh, MOH-reese ROH-lon)

Chef de Bataillon – (CHEF duh BA-tai-yon) "Battalion Leader"

chefs de cuisine – (CHEF duh COO-zine) "cooking chiefs," "cooking heads."

Chénier, Joseph – (SHEN-yay ZHOU-sef) historical figure.

chèvre – (CHEV) "goat"

Chevrolet – (CHEV-re-lay) Name meaning is "Place of Goats." In English, you say "Harrington." As in, Megan Harrington, a woman who will not read my books.

chient – (SHEEN) the verb "crap," i.e. "to crap."

chinoiserie – (SHIN-wahz-ree)

Cholet – (SHOO-lay)

Chouette – (SCHWET)

chou-fleur à la crème – (SHOO-floor ah la CREM) "cauliflower cream."

Ciarraighe – (KIA-ray-HE) Irish, an ancient tribe who gave their name to County Kerry.

de Cicé, Jérôme Champion – (duh SEE-say, ZHER-ohm ZHOM-pyon)

Cicero – (KEY-KAY-roh) Latin.

Ciel – (SEE-el)

cinniúint – (KEN-you-went) Irish, "fate," "destiny," "chance." Another word with no true English equivalent, English being a language of muggles.

Clamart – (CLAH-mar)

Clarent – (CLARE)

Cléonte – (KLEE-ont)

Cloître Saint-Merri – (CLOY-ahtr SAN-MARE-ree) If you have been to the obnoxious Centre Pompidou and its grounds, most likely you have walked on the footsteps of rebels and troops from 1832.

Coco de Paimpol – (COCO de PAM-pol)

Code Noir – (KOOD NWAH) "Black Code." Kicked the Jews out of the colonies for fear of Dutch influence, made the Catholic conversion of slaves nearly mandatory, gave some rudimentary laws for the treatment of slaves… and enabled freed slaves to become almost normal citizens. Although French slavery was brutal and efficient, its end result was quite different from other nations.

Cœurfroid – (KER-fwah) Maurice Adam (MO-rees AH-dom) Jeannine (ZHA-neen) Caroline Lacroix (CAR-oh-leen la-kwah)

Colle – (CULL)

Colonne – (CO-LOAN)

Columbine – (COLE-um-bine)

comédie-ballet – (COHM-ed-ee BAL-ay)

Comédie-Française – (COHM-ed-ee FRAN-sez)

Commedia dell'arte – (COHM-ed-ya DEL-art-tay) Italian.

Commis de Bureau – (COM-ee doo BOO-row) “office clerk.”

Commissionaire – (COM-eesh-on-air) Most of the policing in Paris was done by underemployed locals, one per neighborhood, who mostly relied on his neighbors to help make an arrest.

comportement – (COM-por-tee-mon) “behavior.”

Comprenez-vous? – (COM-pron-ay VOO) “Do you understand?”

comte – (COHMT) “count”, the noble title.

comtesse – (KUHM-tess) “countess.”

Conciergerie - (COHN-serg-zher-ree)

Contat, Louise – (CON-tah LOO-eez) historical figure.

conversatio morum – (CON-ver-ZAH-tio MOR-um) Latin, “changing behavior.” An oath to lead a good and godly life.

corail – (COR-rai-yeh) “coral.”

Cordeliers – (COHR-do-LEE-ay)

Corneille – (CORN-ay-eh)

corvée – (CO-er-vey) literally “drudgery”

coup de foudre – (COO-duh-FOOD-re)

Cour d’Assises Spéciale (COOR-da-ZEEZ-SPESS-al) “Special Assessment Court” would be a somewhat close translation.

Courbet, Marcel – (COOR-bey, MAR-sell)

Courgeon, Father Jonathan (COOR-zhon, ZHON-a-tohn) Historical figure.

Cousin, Jean Younger Elder – (COO-za, ZHON)

couteau marin Breton – (COO-toh Mahr-on BRE-tohn)

Cowan – English, actually, for a sneak or eavesdropper.

Coypel, Charles-Antoine – (KWUO-pel, CHARL-ON-twon)

Creeslough – (KREES-low) English.

crémas – (CRAY-ma)

crème de la crème – (KREM doo lah KREM) “Cream of the cream.”

Crémieux, Adolphe – (KREM-you, AH-dolf) Historical figure.

Croesus – (KRI-zuss) A Greek King who had the distinction of being very wealthy… and having his ass very kicked by the Persians.

croissants au beurre – (KWAH-son-au-bear)

croix pattée – (KWA PAH-tee) Think the Iron Cross or what's on the side of the Red Baron's Fokker.

Le Cuisinier François – (LAY COO-zine-ay FRAN-swah) "The French Cook."

cuisiniers – (COO-zine-ay) "cooks."

culotte, Sans-Culotte – (SAN-COOL-loht), "leggings," "without-leggings."

cum laude – (KOOM-louday) Latin, "with honors."

Cyril – (SEE-reel)

Cyrille – (SEE-reel)

de Damas, Duc – (day DAH-mas, DOO)

damné – (DAM-nee) "damned."

Darcy – (DAR-see) Yes, Mr. Darcy is of French extraction, or at least Norman.

Dauphin Royal – (DOO-fohn ROY-ahl) "royal dolphin." Dauphin was the nickname for the heir apparent to the throne of France.

daus – (DOWS) German, "deuce."

David, Jacque-Louis - (DAH-veed, ZHACK-LOO-ee) Historical figure.

décolletage – (DEE-cohl-tazh) "a low neckline, or that area thereof."

Déguig – (DAY-geeg)

déjeuner - (DAY-zhun-ae) "lunch."

Délassements-Comiques – (DAY-las-mon COHM-eek)

demi coupé – (DEM-ee COO-pay)

Denis – (DUN-nee)

département – (DAY-part-em-on)

de rien – (DOO REE-on) literally, "of nothing." We would say, "you're welcome." At least seventeen million ways to say thank you in French, for any possible circumstance.

Descartes – (DAY-cart)

Deschenes – (DUH-shen)

Desgarcins, Louise – (DAY-gar-son LOO-eez) Historical figure.

Desmoulin – (DAY-moo-lon) Historical figure.

Despres, Franck – (DES-preh, FROHNK)

Dessein, Onfroi – (DEE-sahn, ON-fwa)

détective – (DEE-take-tiv) surprisingly, "detective."

Deux Frères – (DOO FRARE)

Deux-Sèvres – (DOO SEV)

Diarmuid and Gráinne – (DEER-mut and GRON-ya) Irish. These two created a love triangle with Fionn Mac Cumhaill, who was a terrific badass. This is never a good idea, and flight precipitated.

Diderot – (DEED-roh)

Dijonnais – (DEE-zhon-ae)

dîme – (DEEM) "dime."

dîner – (DEEN-ae) "dinner."

Dionysus – (DEE-oon-EE-zuss) Greek. Eventually became "Denis."

disséminer – (DEE-sem-in-ay)

dis tout – (DEE-too) best translation is "crap!"

Diyu – (DEE-yeh) Chinese.
dlo sòsyè – (DAY-LOW SO-see-ay) Haitian Creole.
docteur – (DOC-tear)
Donegal – (DONNY-gol) English? Corrupted Gaeilge?
doppelkopf – (DOP-el-KOPF) German, "double heads."
Dorvigny – (DHOR-vin-yee) historical figure.
draíochta – (DREE-oc-tah) Irish, "magic."
drochthuar – (DROCK-oo-er) Irish, "bad omen, evil foreboding."
droits féodaux – (DWAH FEO-do) "feudal rights."
DuBois – (DO-bwa)
Dubuclet – (DO-BOO-clay)
duc – (DOO) "duke".
Dumas – (DYU-mah) see *gens de couleur* libre for more information.
Dumort (DYU-more)
Duplessix – (DOO-play-see)
Durain – (DUHR-ah)
Durante – (DHUR-ont)
eau de Cologne – (OO doo COL-own-yeh) "Water of Cologne." Giovanni Maria Farina, an Italian, made the first mass-produced men's scent with a consistent smell in the German city of Cologne in 1709. It became such a sensation that the city's name became synonymous with men's perfume, probably to the irritation of Italians ever since.
eau de vie – (OO-doo-vee) "water of life." In France, a general term for strong fruit spirits of various types, which may be differentiated further, i.e. eau-de-vie de vin – "water of life of wine," which would be brandy.
écu – (EH-coo) "crown."
Écureuil – (EE-coo-ray)
"Ego sum umbra, olim magnus. Lignum in umbra mortis - nisi illud occidit scutum lux" – (EH-go some OOHM-bra, OH-lim MAN-yus. LEEN-yum in UM-bra MOR-tis. NEESY ill-ood OCH-chid-it SCOOT-em LUKES-ah) Poor Latin.
Éirinn go brách – (AYE-rin GOBROCK) Irish, "Ireland forever."
Eldorado du Dimanche – (EL-dur-ado doo DEE-monsh)
élégant – (EE-LEE-gah) "elegant."
Eliphas – (EL-lee-fah)
Emile – (EM-eel)
enchanté – (ON-shon-tay) "Nice to meet you." Literally, "enchanted."
en enfer – (ONON-fair) "in hell," but a better translation would be "to hell."
enfant de boucanier – (ON-font doo BOO-can-yay) Child of, not infant of.
en masse – (ON-MAHS) "in mass."
en vogue – (ON VUG-uh) "fashionable."
encule toi – (ON-cool TWA) "f—k you."
En – (EN) Old Sumerian.
Enns – (ENCE)

entré – (ON-TRAY) "entry"

Eoin, Athair Mac Giolla – (Owen, Uh-hair MUCK Gihl-lah) Irish. Athair means "father."

Epées de Fer – (AY-pee doo FAIR) "Iron Swords."

D'Epremesnil – (DAY-prom-en-eel) historical figure.

Erdre – (AIR-dreh)

Ériu – (AIR-ru) Irish, ancient name for the island of Ireland.

Espree, Andrus, Anaïs - (ES-prey ON-droos AN-ah-ees)

esprit de corps – (ES-pree doo core) "spirit of the body," body used in the sense of group or unit.

D'Estaing, Comte - (COMPT-DES-tohn) Historical figure.

"Être foutu tout les messieurs!" – (ET-tra FOO-two TWO lay MAZE-uhr) "F--k all gentlemen!"

Eugène – (OO-zhen)

Évry – (EV-ree)

D'Évreux, Pierre – (DEEV-roh, PEE-yair)

Fabre, Captain Henri-Marie Jacques, Comte l'Aigle – (ON-ree-MAR-ree ZHACK FARB, COMPT-laig-leh)

faim de plus – (FAM doo PLOOS) "hungry for more."

fais ce que voudras – (FACE-say-kay VOO-dra) "do whatever you want."

fait niquer la gueule – (FAN-eek-ah-lah-GEHL) "completely f—ked."

Falaise – (FAL-laze)

famille – (FAHM-ee-ya) "family."

Fantom An Asasen – (FAN-tome ON AHZ-az-ohn) Haitian Creole. "Ghost Killer."

fasces – (FASH-shehs) Latin.

fatiguer – (FAH-tee-gay) "tired."

fauteuil néoclassique – (FAT-ool NEO-class-eek) a simple, Roman-style armchair.

faubourg – (FWAH-boor) "suburb." Keep in mind, a suburb for walkers is a lot different than a driver's. In the 18th Century, being less than a mile from the city center usually put you in a faubourg.

Femme – (FAM) "woman." Usually not capitalized.

Feydeau – (FAY-doo) Not an island any more, but one can easily tell it was since what used to be docks and river is now a big park. Nantes is cool. Go there. They have a real thirty-foot steampunk elephant that walks around the city… that you can ride. Jules Verne was from there, you see – but he is a little too modern for our tale.

fiançailles – (FEE-on-say-yeh) "engagement"

Fidèle – (FEE-del)

fils de pute – (FEES duh POOT) "son of a whore."

fils de salope – (FEES duh SAL-ohp) "son of a whore."

De Flaine, Marquis – (FLANE, MAR-key duh)

fleur-de-lis – (FLOOR-doo-lee) sometimes fleur-de-lys, "Lily Flower." The three petals of the stylized lily had a legion of symbolic meanings and representations. It represents the Trinity, the French monarchy, and the three estates, amongst other things. No one knows for sure, but most likely (i.e. in my opinion) the symbol was brought to France by the Umayyad Muslim invaders in 719 AD. The Umayyad used the emblem as a symbol of warrior prowess.

Fleury – (FLU-ree)

flotteur – (FLO-tehr)

foie gras – (FWA-GRAH)

förbaskad – (fer-BAS-kad) Swedish, "damn."

fouetté – (FWIT-tay) "whipped. "

foutre – (FOOT-reh) "f—k."

Foutre la merde! Foutre-merde – (FOO-treh la MER-deh FOO-treh MER-deh) "f—king sh-t. "

foutu – (FOO-chew) "f—king."

franc – (FRON) First used as the name of the one livre coin, it became the name of the entire French currency in 1795, and remained so until the adoption of the Euro which took place between 1999 and 2002.

Française – (FRON-says) "French. "

Franche-Comté – (FRANSH-a-COMP-TAY)

frappante – (FRA-pont) "striking."

fricassée – (FREE-cah-say)

gabelle – (GAHB-el)

Gabin – (GAHB-on)

Gaeilge – (GAY-lick) Irish, "Irish." The Irish are Celts… but a celt is actually a tool, a kind of implement - archeologists named a people after something they dug up from ruins. The Celts call themselves Gaels, the origin of words such as Gaul, what the Romans called Celtic France.

Gagneux – (GAN-yew)

Gamelin – (GAM-eh-LOH)

Gap – (GAP)

garance – (GAH-ronce) "madder," the plant, not the emotion.

gavotte – (GAV-ot) Yes, this is the dance mentioned in "You're So Vain." Kind of impressed with Carly Simon. This would have been extraordinarily esoteric knowledge in the 1970's.

gens de couleur libre – (ZHON DAY COO-lore LEEB) "free people of color." One of my favorite authors was an aristocratic gen de couleur libre. His name was Alexandre Dumas, père ("father," his son of the same name was also a writer) and he lived from 1802-1870. He wrote The Three Musketeers, The Man in the Iron Mask, and The Count of Monte Cristo. He was also responsible for most of our modern Robin Hood stories, and our mythology regarding werewolves and vampires. Jake saw one of his plays!

Gerard – (ZHER-ahr)

Geoffrin – (ZHOH-frah)

Giambolgna – (ZHAM-bol-on-ya) Looking this up? Really? Go to the Uffizi. Right now.

Gigant – (ZHI-gant)

ginguet – (ZHAN-gay)

de Glisser (Glasser) - (DUH GLEE-say, GLAHZ-air)

Glonne – (GLUN)

Gobelins – (GOOB- lah)

Godavari – (GO-dahv-ree) Hindi. A river in India.

gomme arabique – (GAHM AH-ra-beek) "gum arabic," acacia sap, used in makeup, paints, wine production, and food as a stabilizer and sweetener. It is also an edible glue. We use it on postage stamps.

gourde Haïtienne – (GOOR-dray-see-en)

Grand Blancs – (GRAN-BLANHK)

Grand Danseurs du Roi – (GRAN DAN-sehr doo RWA)

grande cuisine – (GRAN COO-zine) "grand cooking." Fine dining.

Graslin, Jean-Joseph-Louis – (GRAH-lah ZHAN ZHOO-sef LOO-ee) historical figure.

Greffier, Antoine Thibault – (GREF-yay, ON-twon TEE-bolt)

Griffe – (GREEF)

Grimpeurs – (GRAN-pear)

grume en merde – (GRUM on MER-duh) "log of sh-t. "

guède – (GEHD) "wode." Remember the blue face paint in Braveheart? That was made from wode. I think "Getcher wode on!" needs to become an expression… immediately.

Guerande – (GAHR-ond) Part of Brittany.

Guerrier – (GEH-ree-ay), Féroce (FAIR-rus), Seonaidh (SHIN-aid), Estelle (ES-tell), Guillaume (GHEE-yome).

Guet – (GET) "Watch. "

De Guibert, Comte – (DAY GEE-behr COMT)

Guigou, Solange – (GIE-goo, SO-lahnzh)

Guillaume Tell – (GIE-yome Tehl) "William Tell."

Guillere – (GILE-ray)

Guinguette – (GAHN-get)

Gutek – (GOO-teck) Polish.

Haïti – (AE-ee-tee)

Halle – (ALL-eh) "halls."

haluciner – (ALU-seen-ay)

Hamann, Johann Georg – (HAH-man, YO-hahn GAY-org) German.

Hardy, Siméon-Prosper – (AR-dee SEE-mohn PROS-pehr) Historical figure.

haute bourgeois – (OOT BUHR-zhwa) "high bourgeois."

Henri – (ON-ree)

Henriot – (ON-rio)

Haute Grande Rue – (OOT GRAN ROO) "High Street," more or less. Now Rue Saint-Pierre.

haute société – (OOT SO-see-eh-tay) "high society."

Hegemone – (HEDGE-mon-ee) Greek.

Hervé – (AIR-vay)

De Heulee – (doo OO-lee)

Hocquenghem, Théophile Gautier-Proust - (HOCK-en-gehm THEO-feel GAU-tee-ay PROOST)

la Hollande – (la OH-lond)

Homme bon. Je vous remercie. – (UHM-bun. ZHEY-voo RAY-mahr-say) "Good man. Thank you."

honnêteté – (ON-net-ah-tee) "honesty, integrity, trueness."

Horatii – (ORE-ah-tee) Latin.

Horatius One-Eye – (HOR-ah-tee-us) Latin. The Romans, early in their career, were routed in battle nearly at the gates of Rome. A junior officer, Horatius Cocles (COCK-lees, One-Eye – having lost one in battle previously), waited until the Roman forces were across the Tiber, then he held the Sublicius (SOO-blee-choos) bridge himself - and ordered the Romans to destroy it… while he was still fighting on it. He fought the entire enemy army until the bridge was gone, then uttered a prayer to the Gods, jumped into the river, and managed to swim to safety. He single-handedly saved Rome. I'll hold your beer – your turn.

hors d'âge – (ORE dazh) "past age"

hôtel – (OH-tell) This word means "manor," or "great house," more than "fancy inn." Although a fancy inn can certainly be in a manor…

Hôtel de la Bourle – OO-tel doo la BOOR-leh)

Hôtel de la Première Présidence – (OH-tell doo la PREM-ear PRES-ee-dahns) "Manor of the Presiding Premier."

Huguenot – (OO-gen-oh)

id est – (EED est) Latin. "that is."

Île de Gorée – (ILL doo GO-RAY) Historical Place.

Île de la Cité – (ILL doo la SEE-tay)

imbécile – (AHM-bay-seal)

indiennes – (ON-dee-en)

instinct de survie – (ON-stant day SUHR-vee) "survival instinct. "

Íosa Críost – (EE-sa CHREEST) Irish. "Jesus Christ."

Isaäc – (EE-zak)

Jacmel – (ZHAC-mel)

Jansenius – (YAN-sen-ee-oos) Latin.

jardinière – (ZHAR-deen-yair) "planter, vase."

je ne sais quoi – (ZHU-neh-say-kwah) "I don't know what."

Jean – (ZHON)

jean-foutre – (ZHON-FOOT-reh) An American would say "motherf—ker."

Jean le Cinquième le Sage – (ZHON leh SEN-kem leh SAZH) "John the Fifth the Wise." Ruler of Brittany, when it was independent.

Jeziorkowski, August "Gutek" – (YEZH-er-KOF-ski, AU-gust "GOO-tek") Polish.

joie de vivre – (ZHWAH doo VEEV) "joy of life." It is a philosophy of finding joy in the moment, especially through the elevation of small and routine tasks. Sitting down and enjoying your coffee, rather than getting a paper to-go cup. To an American, in regard to caffeine, this is more like torture. Bring good instant coffee to France. You are warned.

Joliefille – (ZHO-lay-fie) "Pretty Girl."

Jourdain – (ZHOR-dah)

Journée des Tuiles – (ZHOR-nay day TWILE) "Day of Tiles."

Jozef – (YO-zef) Central European

juju – (ZHU-ZHU) Haitian Creole.

keine – (KINE-ah) German, "Negative."

Ki moun? – (KEY moan) Haitian Creole. "What man?"

Ki sa nou genyen isit la? – (KEY-sah new ZHEN EE-seet lah) Haitian Creole. "What do we have here?"

Ki sa ou vle? – (KEY-saw OO-vey ah LEW) Haitian Creole. "What do you want?"

Kreyòl Ayisyen - (CRAY-ohl AH-yee-yen) Haitian Creole for… Haitian Creole.

kontra – (CONE-tra) German, "counter," as in something that is contraindicative.

Lady Pè koupe lang ou? – LAY-dee PAY COOP-long-oo) Haitian Creole. Best translation, although not perfect, is, "Cat got your tongue?"

La Folie Titon – (la FOH-lee TEE-tohn)

La Jeune Épouse – (la ZHUN EE-pooz) "The Young Wife."

Lamarque – (LA-mark)

de Landerneau, Marquis – (doo LON-der-no, MAR-kee)

lanterne – (LON-tern)

Laurent – (LOU-rahn)

de Lavoisier, Antoine-Laurent – (DAY LAV-wah-see-ay ON-twon LOU-rahn) Historical figure.

Le Bourgeois Gentilhomme – (la BOOR-zwah ZHEN-tee-em) "The Bourgeois Gentleman."

Lefaucheux, Casimir – (LOO-foo-shoe, KAS-ee-meer)) Brilliant weapon smith, easily forty years ahead of his time. He invented the first metal cartridge. Most of his weapons were categorized by his last name and a number or date.

Lefleaur – (LEF-fluer)

Le Grand Véfour – (lay GRAN VAY-four)

Le Menu du Duc Mort – (LUH MEN-oo doo DOOK MORE) "The Menu of the Dead Duke."

Lent – (LOHN)

le plus grand bourgeoisie – (lay PLOO GRAN BOOR-zwah-see)

Le Procope – (lay PRO-cup) Still there and awaiting those who can return its mojo. Not going to happen, taxes are too high in France.

Le professeur a réussi au moment où son élève devient original – "The teacher has succeeded the moment his pupil becomes original." This is a Lane Cooper quote. He was an American, a polyglot, a Cornell professor, and known around the world – far more than his own nation, being neither Kardashian nor Marvel.

Le Page – (luh PAGH)

le Président Pour la Vie – (luh PRES-ee-don pour la VEE) "the president for life."

Leroux, Pierre – (LOO-roe, PEE-yaire)

Les Amours de Charlot et Toinette – (les-AM-oor de SHAR-loo ay TWIN-et)

Les Annonces – (LAYS-anons)

de Lespinasse – (doo LES-peen-as)

L'etat c'est moi. – (LAY-tah SAY-mwa)

lettre de cachet – (LET-treh doo CASH-ae) "sealed letter." With a signature, the king could arrest anyone. Amongst the drawbacks of this arrangement was the fact that people with royal influence could get the king's signature on a lettre de cachet, and arrest anyone too.

levée – (LOO-vey) "raising."

le Vin D'honneur – (lay VON DOO-nare)

Lille – (LEEL)

Linguet – (LON-gay)

livres – (LEEV-reh) French currency. Established by Charlemagne as a pound of silver, it was divided into 20 sous (or 20 sols), and each sous of 12 denier. It was the model for nearly every other European currency, including the British pound, Italian lira, Spanish dinero and the Portuguese dinheiro. In use from 781 to 1794, discontinued due to the revolutionary slogan of "if it's working, change it."

Loa – (LEW-ah) Haitian Creole.

Loïc – (LOO-eek)

Loire – (LOO-ar)

Loire-Inférieure – (LOO-ar IN-fer-ee-air)

Louis-le-Grand – (LOO-ee-le-GRAHN)

Louis-Philippe – (LOO-ee FEE-leep)

Louvre – (LOOV-reh)

Loys – (LOO-ah)

Lucille – (LOO-seal)

Lugal – (LOO-gal) Ancient Sumerian.

Lully, Jean-Baptiste – (LOO-lee ZHON BAP-teest)

Lundberg – (LUND-bear) German.

Luxembourg – (LOUKS-am-buhr)

Lycée – (LEE-say) "high school."

Lycurgus – (LIE-kur-gus) Greek. Lived during the 9th Century BC. The founder of the Spartan way. Also called "Triple Badass Motherf---er."

Lyon – (LEE-ohn)

Mac Cumhaill, Fionn – (MA-cool, FYUN) Irish. The Hercules of Irish mythology.

Machiavelli – (MA-kia-VELL-ie) Italian. Pray for his soul.

MacInnes, Ivor – (MAC-innis, EYE-vor) Scottish. A character name from "Trinity," a nod to Leon Uris.

Madame – (MAH-dam)

Mademoiselle – (MAH-dem-wa-zell)

Madrileño – (MAH-dree-LAIN-yo) Spanish. 1 - Go to Madrid. 2 - See them peeling oranges with knives and forks. 3 - Marvel.

Maine – (MEHN)

Maine-et-Loire – (MEN-eh-LWAH)

Maissade – (MEE-sad)

maître d'hôtel – (MAY-treh DOH-tel) "Master of the Manor." Head servant, majordomo, butler.

ma jolie sœur – (ma ZHOU-lee sore) "my pretty sister."

Maman – (MAM-oh) "Mom."

mambo asogwe – (MAM-bo AH-sog-way) Creole/African.

Mamelouk – (MAM-loke) "Mamluk". Ancient Muslim warrior-slaves of Christian heritage.

manoir – (MAN-wah) "manor."

Manufacture Royale – (MAN-yu-fac-chuhr ROY-ahl)

marabou – (MAR-ah-boo) an African stork.

Marais – (MAR-ae) literally "swamp."

Marat, Jean-Paul – (MAR-RAH, ZHON POHL)

Marie-Lynn – (MAH-ree LEEN)

Marie- Rémy – (MAH-ree REM-ee)

Marillais – (MAH-ree-yay)

Marmont – (MAHR-mon)

Marquer, Edmée– (MAR-kay, ED-me)

Marquis de Bonchamps – see "Bonchamps"

Marseillaise – (MAR-say-yehs) This genocidal Nazi rant is still the national anthem of France. Read the lyrics carefully, they are horrifying.

Marshalbes – (MAR-shalb)

marshall – (MAR-shall)

Martin – (MAR-tohn)

Massif du Nord – (MAZ-eef du NOR)

Massillon – (MASS-ee-yohn)

de Maupeou, René Nicolas – (day MOO-poo REN-ay NEE-co-lah) historical figure.

Meaux – (MOO)

Melon de Bourgogne – (MEL-on doo BUHR-gon-ya)

merci – (MARE-see) "thank you."
Mercier, Paige – (MER-see-ay PAGE)
merde – (MARED) "shit."
merdique nègre – (MARE-deek NEG) "shitty n----r." Americans would say (or hopefully not say) "f---ing n----r."
mes amis – (MES-ah-me) "my friends."
Mes amis! Mes frères et sœurs! – (MESAM-ee may FRER ay SARE) "My friends ! My brothers and sisters!"
mesdames – (MAY-dam) "ladies."
messieurs – (MISS-yer) "gentlemen."
Mesye Neg Blan – (MEZ-ee NEG BLON) Haitian Creole. "Mister White Man."
Méthode – (MAY-tod)
Meyerbeer – (MY-er-BEER) German.
Miette – (ME-et)
mignonette – (MIN-yahn-et)
Milot – (MEE-low)
minuet – (MIN-you-et)
Minuscieu – (MIN-you-syoo)
Miragoâne – (ME-rah-gwan)
Miroiter – (MIHR-wah-tay)
míthuar – (ME-huar) Irish, "ill omen or foreboding."
mojo – (MOH-zhoh) Haitian Creole.
Molière – (MOH-lee-air) If you have read "Fifty Shades," but don't know who this is, turn off one screen.
Moliniere – (MO-leen-yair)
mon ami – (MON AH-me) "my friend."
mon chéri(e) – (MON share-ee) "honey," "sweetie."
mon dieu – (MON-dyuh) "my God."
Monsieur – (MUH-schur) "gentleman, sir, lord, mister."
Montagnes Noires – (MON-tan-yan NWAH)
Montesquieu – (MON-tes-queue)
Montparnasse – (MON-par-nas)
Montreuil – (MON-tray-ee)
Montrouge – (MON-roozh)
Montserrat – (MON-ser-ah)
Morte d'Arthur, le – (lay MORT de-DAR-tour) "The Death of Arthur." Elaine (EE-lay-neh), Astolat (AZ-do-lah), Lancelot (LON-say-low), Guinevere (GUIN-vair), Arthur (AH-tur), Camelot (CAM-low).
Du Motier, Gilbert, Marquis de Lafayette – (doo MOH-tee-ae, ZHIL-bear, MAR-kee doo LAF-aye-yet) Historical figure.
Mounier, Jean Joseph – (ZHON ZHO-sef MOON-yee)
Moyen – (MOY-yah)
Mulâtre – (MOO-latr) "Mulatto."
De Musset – (doo MOO-say)

Nantais – (NON-tay)

Nantes – (NONT)

Napoleon – (NAH-po-leon) There are only three titans of war: Alexander the Great, Hannibal, and this man – Napoleon. He was brilliant and devious in just about every way in which a person could be. His only mistake was severely underestimating the Russian will, and their absurd, nearly inhuman capacity for self-sacrifice. If not for that, the world was his oyster. In his defense, he was not the only one to ever make that mistake. Russia is God's cure for martial narcissism.

Nattier, Jean-Marc – (NAH-tyae, ZHON MARK) Historical figure.

neg – (NEG-eh)

n'est-ce pas – (NEZ-pah) "is it not?"

ne plus ultra – (NEH ples UHL-TRA) "nothing above," the perfect example of its kind.

Nicole, Pierre – (NEE-cohl PEE-yair)

Nicolet – (NEE-coh-lay) Historical figure.

Nîmes – (NEEM)

Nooit Sterven – (NO-it STAIR-va) Dutch, "never die." We would say, "die hard."

Notre Dame de Paris – (NO-tr DAHM doo PAH-ree) "Our Lady of Paris."

Nou gade pou yon moun. – (NEW gad POO-yoon moon) Haitian Creole. "We're looking for someone."

nouveau frère – (NEW-voh FRARE) "new brother."

nummo – (NEW-mo) Latin. "Single."

Ó Baoighill, Bhiorog – see "Bhiorog Ó Baoighill."

Ó Brollachain – (OH BRAHL-lehk-ahn) Irish. Seonaidh (SHIN-aid), Iníongael (EE-nan-gail), Aodh Dubh (AE DO), Ingen (EHN-ghen), Eigneachan (AE-gah-nakh-an)

Ó Conchubhair – (OH CON-aghk -wer) Irish.

obers – (OO-bahs) German, in cards, the equivalent to a Queen.

octroi – (OOKED-twah) "granting, bestowal."

Olivier, Jérôme Charles – (ZHER-ome SHARL OH-liv-ee-ae)

opéras comiques – (OH-pehr-ah COHM-eek)

orans – (OH-rans) Latin, "praying."

Orinoco – (OH-reen-OH-co) Spanish.

Orléanais – (OR-lay-on-ae)

Orléans – (OR-lay-on)

d'Orléans, Louis Philippe Joseph – (DOOR-leon LOO-ee FEE-leep ZHOH-zef) Historical figure.

Ormolu – (AH-er-mo-loo)

Orphelin de la Chine – (OR-fel-ohn de la SHEEN) "Orphan of China."

Orville – (OH-er-veel)

Oscuro – (OHS-cureh) Spanish, "dark." Alternatively, OHS-coo-ROH.

Ostervald – (OOS-ter-vad) German.

L'Oublié – (LOO-blee-ae) "the forgotten."

oui – (WEE) "yes." You should really know this.

Ou-La – (OO-LA) Haitian Creole.

l'Ouvrinière – (LOOV-rin-yaire)

Palais de la Cité – (PAH-lay doo la SEE-TAY)

Palais Livre – (PAH-lay LEEVR)

Palais-Royal – (PAH-lay ROY-al)

Panthéon – (PAHNT-eon)

Panza, Sancho – (PAHN-zah, SAHN-cho) Spanish. Sancho Panza was the trusted side-kick of Don Quixote in the novel by Miguel Cervantes entitled *El Ingenioso Hidalgo Don Quijote de la Mancha* written in 1605. El Don was a little Cloud Cuckoo Land, and poor Sancho had to follow him everywhere.

Pardonne-moi, s'il vous plait. – (PAR-don MWA see voo play) "Pardon me, please."

pardonnez-moi – (PAR-dohn-ay MWA) "Pardon me. "

Paris – (PAH-ree)

Parisien – (PAH-ray-zee-uhn)

Parisii – (PAH-ris-ee) Latinization of French Gaelic.

parterre – (PAR-taer)

Pascal, Blaise – (PAS-cal BLASE)

pas de bourrée – (PAH de BOOR-ay)

Passage du Saumon – (PASS-azh doo SEE-mon)

Pechegru – (PAY-shay-groo)

Le Peletier – (le PAY-LOW-tyae)

pensionnaire – (PAHN-see-ohn-air)

Pépin, Anne – (PAY-pohn, AHN) Historical figure. She had a bit of a reputation in her day, something between Mata Hari and the Queen of Sheba.

père – (PARE) "Father. "

Périer – (PEHR-ee-ae)

Perier, Claude – (PAY-ree-ay CLOOD) Historical figure.

Petit – (POH-tee)

Petite Princesse de Nantes – (POH-tee PRAN-sess doo NOHNT) "little princess of Nantes."

Petite Rue de Reuilly - (POH-tee ROO doo ROO-lee)

Petit-Goâve – (POH-tee GUAV)

Petit-Pont – (POH-tee pon)

petit roi – (POH-tee RWA)

pianoforte – (PEE-ah-no-FOR-tay) Italian, "piano."

Pierre, Jean-Baptiste Marie – (PEE-air, ZHON BAP-teest MAH-ree)

Pierrot – (PEER-roh)

Pinceau – (PAN-so)

d'Piquant – (PEEK-ahnt)

pisse – (PEES) "piss."

Pistole – (PEES-tohl) A Spanish gold coin in widespread use in France during the Sixteenth and Seventeenth centuries.

Place de Grève – (PLAHS de grave)

Place de la Bastille (PLAHS doo la BAS-tee-yeh)

Place d'Oratoire - (PLAHS DORA-twah)

Place Plumereau – (PLAHS PLOOM-air-roh)

Place Royale – (PLAHS ROY-ahl)

Place Vendôme – (PLAHS VON-doom)

Plantarum Americanarum – (PLAN-tar-oom AH-mare-EE-can-ah-room) "American Plants."

Pluche – (PLOOSH)

Plumier, Charles – (PLU-mee-yay CHARL) Historical figure.

Poissard – (PWESS-arh)

Poitín – (PWAH-teen) Irish. Do not drink this shite. Ever.

Poitou – (PWA-too)

Pompadour, de – (POM-pa-durh, doo)

Pompigny – (POHM-pee-nee)

Pont-l'Évêque – (PON lee VECK)

Le Poney Piquant – (lay PO-nay PEE-cahn) "The Prancing Pony." Hobbits, wizards and rangers are usually not seen in the Paris franchise.

Port au Vin – (PORO-vah)

Port Saint-Nicholas - (POUR-san-NEE-co-lah)

Port-Au-Prince – (PORU-PRANCE)

Port au Vin – (POR la VAHN)

Port-Royal-des-Champs – (POR-ROY-al doo SHAHM)

pourboire – (POOR-bwah) "for beer." We would call it a tip.

pour encourager les autres – (POOR AHN-coor-ah-zher lesoht) "to encourage others," a quote from Voltaire.

Pour le Mérite Militaires – (POOR lay MAY-reet MEE-lee-taire) The vaunted Blue Max, the highest Prussian, then German, military medal. The influence of French thinking and culture was such that it was named and inscribed in French, and not German.

Pour les droits de l'homme, mon ami.- (POOR lay DWAH de-LOME, MOHN AH-mee)

Poyet – (PWA-yay)

Presbytère – (PRES-bee-taire) "presbytery." Priest's quarters.

Président – (PRES-ee-dohn) "president."

Prévost, Augustine – (PRAY-voh, AW-gus-teen)

Proculus – (PRO-koo-loos) Latin.

procureur – (PRO-kyu-aire) "prosecutor."

programme du bal – (PRO-gram doo bahl)

Prospel – (PRO-spell)

prostituée à bas prix (PROS-tit-oo-AE ah-bah PREE) "cheap whore."

Pułaski, Comte – (POO-ahs-kee, COMPT)

putain – (PYOO-tah) "whore."

Quarteron – (CARE-tour-on) "a small number."

Quartier-Morin – (CAT-ee-ae MOHR-uh)

Quatre-Nations – (CAT-treh NAY-shon)

Quay de Brancao – (KAY doo BRON-sow)

Quay de la Polerne – (KAY doo la POH-lern)

Quay Mellier – (KAY MEL-yay)

Que diable se passe-t-il! – (COO DIA-bul say PAS-teel) "What the hell is happening?"

Quel ego! – (KELL egg-oh)

quéquette – (KAY-ket) "pecker," as in the male member.

Questa – (KES-tah)

Qu'est-ce que tu veux? Pourquoi me regardes-tu? Voulez-vous un coup?! – (KES-ca choo veh POR-kwa me RAY-gard too VOO-lay VOO un COO) "What do you want? Why are you looking at me? Do you want to get hit?"

Quinze-Vingts – (KONZ-ah-VAH) "Fifteen Score."

Quod erat demonstrandum – (CODE eh-rat DEM-on-STRAN-dum) Latin. "It can be shown," "it has been shown."

Rabelais – (RAB-lay)

Rabourdin, Daniel – (RAB-or-dohn, DAN-yell) unless he's in America… then its Daniel Rabordin. He needs to be in France, because France needs him. But now he's in Alabama. Go figure.

Racine, Jean – (RAH-seen ZHOHN)

Raphaël – (RAF-ah-el)

Rapide – (RAH-peed) "fast."

Raucourt – (RUE-KUHR)

Le Ray, René, de Fumet - (REN-ae le RAY doo FOO-may)

Raymond – (RAY-mohn)

Redoute Chinois – (RAY-doo SHIN-wah)

Régiment d'Agénois – (REYZH-ee-mon DAZH-en-wah)

Régiment d'Aquitaine – (REGH-ee-mon DAK-ee-tain)

Régiment Royal-La-Marine – (REZH-ee-mohn ROY-ahl la MA-reen)

Régiment Royal-Suédois – (REZH-ee-mohn ROY-ahl SWEE-dwah)

Reims – (RONCE)

Renout – (RUE-new)

Rennes – (REN)

Repas de Noces – (REH-pah de NOHS) "Nupital meal."

République d'Haïti – (RAY-poob-leek DAY-TEE) "Republic of Haiti."

restaurant – (REES-tah-ranh) unbelievably, "restaurant."

Restif de (la) Bretonne – (REH-teef de BREE-tohn) I've seen it both ways.

Réveillon, Jean-Baptiste – (REV-ee-yohn ZHEN BAP-teest) Historical figure.

réverbère – (RAY-ver-BAYR) "street lamp."

Ribié – (RAY-byay)

Richard, Pierre – (REE-shar PYAIR)

robe à la Français – (RO-BELLA-FROHN-say) "French dress." A formal, very beautiful, wide skirted dress of the 18th Century. Sometimes called a "sack-back dress" by the muggles.

Robert le Diable – (ROH-behr lay DIA-bleh) "Robert the Devil."

Robespierre – (ROHB-ess-pee-yaire) one of humanity's many angels of death.

Le Roi Midas – (leh RWAH MEE-das) "The King Midas."

Roitelet, Étienne (ROIT-lay, ET-tyehn)

Roquer – (ROH-kay)

Rosalie – (ROOS-ah-lee)

Rossini – (ROH-see-nee) Italian.

Rousseau, Jean-Jacques – (RUE-so, ZHAHN ZHAHCK)

Roussel, Joseph and Casimir – (RUE-sell, JOE-zeff, KAZ-eh-meer) Historical figures.

Roux, Marie-Pierre Alphonse – (ROH, MA-ree PEE-yair AL-fohns)

rúad – (RA-uht) Irish, "red."

Rubens, Peter Paul – (ROO-bahns, PEE-tear POL)

Yes, I capitalize *Rue*. In French, it is not correct to do so. I also capitalize the seasons, for the very simple reason that it is actually correct to do so. I am utterly unapologetic in both regards.

Rue Cambon – (ROO CAM-bohn)

Rue Chantereine – (ROO SHAT-er-en)

Rue de Brouillard – (ROO doo BREW-yar)

Rue de Castiglione – (ROO de CAS-tee-lyon-ae)

Rue de Charenton – (ROO de CHAR-ohn-tohn)

Rue de Goyon – (ROO de GWEE-yon)

Rue de Nicolas – (ROO doo NEE-coh-la)

Rue de Richelieu – (ROO doo REESH-el-you)

Rue de Rivoli – (ROO de REE-voh-lee)

Rue des Carunes – (ROO de CARH-uhn)

Rue Ef – (ROO-ef) Haitian Creole.

Rue Dizuit – (ROO diz-WEET) Haitian Creole.

Rue du Fer - (ROO doo FAIR)

Rue Grand – (ROO GRAHN)

Rue Moffetard – (ROO MOFF-tar)

Rue Neuve – (ROO-nuhv)

Rue Poliveau – (ROO POH-lee-vo)

Rue Saint-Honoré – (ROO SANT-OHN-or-REE)

Rue Saint-Jacques – (ROO-SAN-ZHACK)

Rue Saint-Nicolas – (ROO-SAN-NEE-coh-lah)

Rue Ventnèf – (ROO VONT-nef) Haitian Creole.

Sabès, Louis – (SAH-bess LOO-ee)

Sacatra – (SAH-CAH-tra) Hindi? Taken from an Indian word for those of mixed race in India.
De Sade, Marquis – (DOO SAD MAR-key)

If you are talking about the actual saint, there is no dash. The saint in any other context has a dash.

Saint-Antoine – (SANT-ON-twon)
Saint-Bernard – (SAN-BER-nar)
Saint-Clément – (SAN-CLAY-moh)
Saint-Denis – (SAN-DON-ee)
Saint-Domingue – (SAN-DO-mang)
Saint Florent le Jeune, le Vieil – (SAN FLOR-en lay ZHUN, lay VEE-ae)
Sainte-Geneviève – (SAN-JUHN-viev)
Sainte-Ursule – (SAN-teh ER-sule)
Saint-Gatien – (SAN-GAS-tyah)
Saint-Germain-des-Prés – (SAN-GER-man-DE-PRAY)
Saint-Jacques – (SAN ZHACK)
Saint-Just – (SAN-YOOST)
Saint-Laurent-du-Mottay – (SAN-LOO-rahn-DOO-MOH-tay)
Saint-Malo – (SAN-MAL-oh)
Saint Martin – (SAN-MAR-tuh)
Saint-Michel-de-l'Attalaye – (SAN MEE-shel doo LAH-tah-lie)
de Saint-Paul, Mayeur - (DOO SAN POLE MAI-er)
de Saint-Philbert-de-Grand-Lieu – doo SAN FEEL-behr doo GRAN LOO)
Saint-Recipas – (SAN-RESS-ee-pah) Made-up, no such dude.
Saint-Sulpice – (SAN-SOOL-piece)
De Saint-Vincent, Gabriel de Bory – (doo SAHN-vahn-sant, GAB-riel doo BORY) Historical figure.
salon – (SAL-ohn) "living room."
salonnières – (SAL-on-yair)
salope – (SAL-up) "slut."
salpêtrière – (SAL-petrie-aire) "saltpeter."
Samana Cays – (SAH-MAH-NA) Lucayan, "Little Forest."
Sanaga – (SAN-AH-GAH) Bastardized German, a river meandering through Cameroon.
Sang du Christ – (SOHN doo CHREEST) Christ's blood.
sang de merde – (SOHN doo MAIRD) "blood of sh-t."
Sangréal – (SOHN-grey-ahl) "real blood." Anything pertaining to the Holy Grail.
Sans-Culotte – (SAN-COOL-oht) "without leggings."
Santa Cruz de Tenerife – (SAN-TAH KROOZ day TEN-air-EE-fay) Spanish.
De Sarra, Jean-Augustin Frétat de – (doo SERA, ZHON-au-GOOSE-than FREY-tah) Historical figure.

Saumur – (SOO-muir)

savoir-faire – (SAV-wa fare) "expertise." Especially social expertise.

De Scépeaux, Marie Renée Marguerite Françoise – (DES-ee-poh, MAH-ree REN-ay MAR-gah-reet FRAN-swaz-eh) Historical figure.

schwars – (SHWARZ) "black suit."

Seigneurs, Les – (les SEN-yehr) "the lords."

Seine – (SEHN)

Senātus Populusque Rōmānus – (SEN-ah-TUS POP-oo-LOOS-KAY ROHM-ah-NOOS) "Senate and Roman People."

Sené bergère – (SOO-yay BAIR-zhair) a type of comfortable upholstered chair.

Senegal – (SOO-nee-gahl)

sensuelle - (SAHN-shoo-el) "sensual."

Sèvis lwa – (SAY-vee LWA) Haitian Creole. "Service to the Law, Spiritual Law or Spirits."

Sèvre – (SEV-reh)

Shaka-Chef – (SHAH-KAH SHEF) African/French. "Boss-Boss."

Shaulis, Svajone Smilte – (SHAO-lis, SVI-oh-nee SMILE-tah) Lithuanian… with a Polish accent…

Sherbro – (SHER-BRO) Sherbro. An island and river in Sierra Leone named after the Sherbro people.

Sitbon – (SEET-bohn)

Skelèt, Inspecteur – (SKEL-et ON-sepc-tehr)

Snaër, Saint-Denis – (SNAIR SON DON-ee)

sociétaire – (SO-see-ah-tair)

soirée – (SWA-ray) "evening," "a party in the evening."

soldat – (SOL-dah) "soldier."

Sorbonne – (SOHR-bun)

sorcière d'eau – (SO-see-air doe) "water witch."

Souck – (SOOK)

sous – (SOO) see livre for definition.

Souvenu – (SOO-ven-oo)

Spiorad Naomh – (SPEE-rad NOY-am) Irish, "Holy Spirit."

Studium Generale – (STOO-dee-uhm GEN-ai-RAHL-ae) Latin, "general studies."

sud-est – (SOO-dest) "south-east."

sur la lie – (SUHR la lee) "on the dregs." Fermenting everything - leaves, stems, et cetera - in order to impart unusual flavors.

Sylphide – (SILL-feed-uh)

Ta gueule! – (TAY gel) A particularly rude way of saying, "shut up."

Taig – (TAYG) Irish, masculine name meaning "Poet." It is alternatively spelled Tadhg. It was such a common name that it became a nickname or slur for Irishmen, i.e. Johnny as a term for American Confederates or Fritz as a term for Germans.

taille – (TIE) "cut."

Taillon – (TIE-yohn) "talion," the law of equal vengeance, an eye for an eye.
Talma – (TAL-ma)
téméraire – (TEM-EHR-rair) "reckless."
témoin – (TEHM-wah)
tête carrée – (TET cah-ray) "square head."
Théâtres Associés – (TEA-trez AH-soh-see-ay)
Théâtre Graslin – (TEE-ah-tre GRAY-lon)
Théâtre-Italien – (TEE-ah-tre TAHL-ee-ohn)
Théâtre des Associés – (TEE-ah-treh des AH-soh-see-ay)
Théâtre des Élèves – (TEE-ah-treh des EL-lev)
Thermopylae – (TER-moh-PIE-lay) Greek.
Thouars – (TWAHR)
Tír Chonaill – (TIER-hahn-ahl)
Titonville – (TEE-tohn-veel) The area around La Folie Titon. Nearly every Paris block had a unique identity and name.
Titus – (TEE-toos) Latin.
ton cul – (tohn cool) "your arse."
ton père parle – (tohn pear PAR-leh) "Your father speaks."
Tonnelier, Quennel – (TOHN-el-yay, KEN-el)
Tonton Macoute – (TOHN-tohn mah-COOT) Haitian Creole.
torchière – (TOR-shee-air)
touché – (TOO-shay) "touch." This is what a fencing gentleman says when an opponent's sword touches him – an acknowledgement that a point has been scored against him in a match.
Toulouse – (TOO-loose)
touman – (TOO-mahn) Mongolian.
Tourcoing – (TOOR-kwah)
De la Tour d'Auvergne, Comtesse – (doo la TOO-da-vern, KUHM-tess)
Tours – (TOOHR)
tout court – (TOO-COOR) Best translation is "And nothing more." This is the "QED" expression of philosophy.
traite – (TRAIT) "treaty."
Travers – (TREE-verhs)
Traversier – (TRA-ver-syae) "ferry." The family started out as ferrymen before their own recorded history, only the name remains as a hint to their origin. Xavier Érinyes (ZAV-ee-yay EAR-en-yee) Philippine (FILLY-peen), Priam Paul (PREE-am POLE), Jules César (ZHULE SAY-zare), Sevan Gédéon (SAY-von ZHEY-dion) Gwenaëlle (GWEN-aile), Athénaïs (AH-ten-ais). Genèse de Gaul (ZHEN-ess day GAOL)
De Trémargat – (doo TREY-mar-gaht)
très bon – (TREY-bohn) "Very good."
très riche – (TREY-reesh)
Tribus Coloribus – (TREE-buhs COH-LOHR-ih-buhs) Latin, "tri-color," "three colors."

trireme – (TREE-reem) Greek.

Trumeau, Marie-Jeanne – (TRUE-moh MAH-ree ZHAN) historical figure.

tuar – (TOOR) Irish, "omen." Again, a hard one for the muggles. Tuar is more like a seer's vague outline of the future, if the future vision is forbidding and dark.

Tuffeau – (TOO-foh)

Tuileries – (TWEEL-ree)

Tu me fatigues! – (TOO-may FAH-teeg) "You annoy me," or, "you tire me."

Turgot – (TOOR-goh)

Tyle (v), Tyler (n) – a guard for a Freemason lodge. More like a bailiff or castellan than a security guard.

tyran - (TYR-ah) "tyrant."

Uí Ceinnsealaigh – (EE KEN-sha-lie) an ancient area of Ireland near present day Leister.

unters – (OON-tahs) "under," or "between."

une partie entiere – (UN PAR-tee-uhn-TAIR) "an entire part."

Uruk – (OO-ROOK) Ancient Sumerian.

va au diable – (VA ah DEE-ab-leh) "go to hell."

Valerius – (VAL-ler-ee-OOS) Latin.

valet de pied – (VAH-lay doo PEE-ay) "footman."

Valiere – (VAL-ee-yair)

Valiere – (VAL-ee-yair)

Vanier, Jean – (VAN-yay, ZHON)

Varades - (VAH-rahd)

Variétés-Amusantes – (VAH-ree-ay-tays AH-moo-zahnt)

Va te faire enculer, fils de pute! – VA tay FAIR OHN-coo-lay feels de POOT) "Go f—k yourself, son of a whore. "

Va(s) te faire foutre! – (VA doo FARE foot) "Go f—k yourself."

Vaucanson – (VOO-cow-sohn) They say that these programmable looms were the first true progenitors of modern computers.

Vaux – (VOO)

Vendeans – (VON-day-ahns) Anglicized French. In French proper the word is Vendéens (VON-day-ohn).

Vendée Militaire – (VON-day MEEL-ee-taire)

Du Verdier – (doo VER-dyay)

verge – (VERZH) "penis. "

Verne, Robert Alain – (VERN, ROH-behr ALAHN)

vérolée – (VEY-roh-LAY) "syphilitic."

Versailles – (VER-sigh)

De Villaneuve – (doo VEEL-nuv)

Vico – (VEE-co) Italian.

Victor – (VEEK-tohr)

Videment, Julien – (VEED-mohn, ZHU-lee-ahn) Historical figure.

Vienne – (VEE-en)

village – (VEE-lazh) "town."
Villiaume, Claude – (VEE-ee-yawm CLOD) Historical figure.
De Villiers – (DOO VEE-yay)
Vincennes – (VAN-sen)
vingtième – (VON-tee-em) "twentieth."
Vionnet – (VEE-oh-nay)
"Vive la France" – (VEEV leh FROHNZ) "Long live France."
"Vive le Roi" – (VEEV leh RWAH) "Long live the King!"
voilà – (VWAH-la) "here." Frequently used in our context of "bingo," or "there we go." Et voilà!
Voltaire – (VOLE-taire)
Von Stedingk, Colonel Comte Curt – (COMPT KURT VOHN STED-ink) German-Swedish. Historical figure.
Voudon, Vodon – (VOO-dohn) Not quite Voodoo. Voodoo is a slice of Voudon plus a mixed bag of other stuff, including a bit of Catholicism, and a lot of Bò.
Wauxhall d'Hiver – (VOCKS-olm DEE-vehr)
Wegelin – (VAY-gah-LEEN) German.
Wete tout rad ou yo, neg blan! – (WEY-tay doo RAD-ah-you NEG BLON) "Take off your clothes, white man!"
Xavier – see Traversier.
Yoruba – (YOUR-oo-bah) A tribe in Nigeria and Benin.
Ypres – (EEP)
zanni – (ZAH-nee) Italian.
Zacharie – (ZAH-cah-ree)
Zara – (ZER-ah)
Zut – (ZOOT) "heck," "crap."
Zwingli, Huldrych – (ZVING-lee HOOL-drech) You cannot pronounce this unless you know German. The "drych" thing has no equivalent in English.

Pronunciation and Definition Guide

In regard to Jonathan and Estelle,
The Parable of the Prodigal Son
Luke 15:11-32

Then he said, “A man had two sons, and the younger son said to his father, ‘Father, give me the share of your estate that should come to me.’ So the father divided the property between them.

After a few days, the younger son collected all his belongings and set off to a distant country where he squandered his inheritance on a life of dissipation.

When he had freely spent everything, a severe famine struck that country, and he found himself in dire need. So he hired himself out to one of the local citizens who sent him to his farm to tend the swine. And he longed to eat his fill of the pods on which the swine fed, but nobody gave him any.

Coming to his senses he thought, ‘How many of my father’s hired workers have more than enough food to eat, but here am I, dying from hunger. I shall get up and go to my father and I shall say to him, “Father, I have sinned against heaven and against you. I no longer deserve to be called your son; treat me as you would treat one of your hired workers.”’

So he got up and went back to his father. While he was still a long way off, his father caught sight of him, and was filled with compassion. He ran to his son, embraced him and kissed him.

His son said to him, ‘Father, I have sinned against heaven and against you; I no longer deserve to be called your son.’

But his father ordered his servants, ‘Quickly bring the finest robe and put it on him; put a ring on his finger and sandals on his feet. Take the fattened calf and slaughter it. Then let us celebrate with a feast, because this son of mine was dead, and has come to life again; he was lost, and has been found.’ Then the celebration began.

Now the older son had been out in the field and, on his way back, as he neared the house, he heard the sound of music and dancing.

He called one of the servants and asked what this might mean.

The servant said to him, ‘Your brother has returned and your father has slaughtered the fattened calf because he has him back safe and sound.’

He became angry, and when he refused to enter the house, his father came out and pleaded with him.

He said to his father in reply, ‘Look, all these years I served you and not once did I disobey your orders; yet you never gave me even a young goat to feast on with my friends. But when your son returns who swallowed up your property with prostitutes, for him you slaughter the fattened calf.’

He said to him, ‘My son, you are here with me always; everything I have is yours. But now we must celebrate and rejoice, because your brother was dead and has come to life again; he was lost and has been found.’”

HUNTER DENNIS has lived in several places in the United States and also in Europe. Since his first script sale to the studios in 1998, he has alternated between writing full-time and working feverishly to sell something written. He has been sane for over a decade, has found himself in Southern California in spite of it, and is the least dangerous member of his family.

Merchandise
https://www.zazzle.com/arb_books

Patreon
https://www.patreon.com/hunter_dennis

Facebook
https://www.facebook.com/hunterdenniswriter

Website
https://www.arb-books.com

Illustration and Photography Credits

All maps and schematics by Hunter Dennis, executed with CC3+, used under license.

All "photoshop" alterations by Hunter Dennis, using paint.net and CC3+, used under license.

Château de Vizille

Courtesy of Shutterstock, photography by Irakite.

Haiti, 1832

Flag image courtesy of Wikipedia.

Le parc au sommet du Mount Glonne, regardant au sud, 1788

Photography by Hunter Dennis.

Engraving of Nantes and the Loire

Photography by Hunter Dennis, courtesy of the Nantes History Museum.

Palais Royal Theater, 1788

Courtesy of Shutterstock, reimagined by Morphart, unknown illustrator.

Foyer

Photography by Hunter Dennis.

Playbill

Photography by Hunter Dennis.

Comédie-Française

Courtesy of Shutterstock, reimagined by Marzolino, Created by Guesdon, published on L'Illustration, Journal Universel, Paris, 1858.

Château des ducs de Bretagne

Courtesy of Shutterstock, Photography by DaLiu.

Ballroom

Courtesy of Shutterstock, photography by Michael Warwick.

Currency during the time of Louis XVI

Photography from cointalk.com.

Stock Characters of the Commedia dell'Arte

Created by Hunter Dennis, images from Wikipédia en Françai.s

Jardins de la cour du Palais-Royal., 1788

Photography by Hunter Dennis.

Le Véve du Loa Voodoo

Layout and images by Hunter Dennis.

Une cour du Palais-Royal, 1788

Courtesy of Shutterstock, photography by marieshh.

L'abbaye de Saint-Florent-le-Vieil, au sommet du mont Glonne, 1789

Courtesy of Shutterstock. A Morphart creation from Magasin Pittoresque 1852.

Revered French Saints in the Time of Louis XVI

Created by Hunter Dennis from images from Wikipedia. Pre-alteration archway illustration from free service, credit unnecessary.

Parlor

Photography by Hunter Dennis.

Oath of the Horatii (Le Serment des Horaces), Jacque-Louis David, 1784

Photography by Hunter Dennis, courtesy of the Louvre.

Nantes (Ramparts and Skyline)

Courtesy of Shutterstock, Photography by Michal Ludwiczak

Cordeliers, Paris

Photography by Hunter Dennis

Laveuses et un pêcheur de Paris

Photography by Hunter Dennis, courtesy of the Musée des égouts de Paris.

Palais des Tuileries, le dix-septième siècle

Photography by Hunter Dennis

Cathédrale de Nantes

Courtesy of Shutterstock, photography by Xavier Pironet.

The Gardens and Main House of Elm Bank, Massachusetts, Summer 1832

Courtesy of the Massachusetts Horticultural Society.

Flags of the Royal Provinces

Images courtesy of Wikipedia.

Saint-Florent-le-Vieil (Countryside)

Photography by Hunter Dennis

Lake Waban, Massachusetts, in Winter

Courtesy of Shutterstock, photography by Igal Shkolnik.

Une rue de Paris, 438

Photography by Hunter Dennis, courtesy of the Musée des égouts de Paris.

Les États Généraux, 1789

Courtesy of Shutterstock.

Antiquarian Scribe and American Scribe by Oldfonts.com used under license.

CPSIA information can be obtained
at www.ICGtesting.com
Printed in the USA
LVHW091720171219
640801LV00005B/64/P

9 780999 493656